Edited by Kerry Carter

DIE LAUGHING: AN ANTHOLOGY OF HUMOROUS MYSTERIES

Published by Mystery Weekly Magazine

Publisher: Chuck Carter
Editor: Kerry Carter
Editorial Assistant: Dee Overduin
Custom Artwork: Robin Grenville Evans

For information contact:
AM Marketing Strategies
Suite 22 - 509 Commissioners Road West
London, ON N6J 1Y5
Canada
info@mysteryweekly.com

CONTENTS

INTRODUCTION

Steve Shrott

Welcome to *Die Laughing: An Anthology Of Humorous Mysteries*, filled to the brim with hilarious short stories. And that's not just my opinion, it's also the publisher's who wants to sell a ton of books.

Seriously, as someone who's been a comedy writer and performer most of his life, I've learned that writing truly amusing shorts is not an easy task. But the writers in this volume have really come through with some fabulous and funny tales.

You'll chuckle, giggle, guffaw, titter and possibly emit other weird noises that may cause some people to suggest therapy, and the rest to run for their lives.

But you'll be having a grand time.

These stories may also improve your health. According to scientists who have a lot of spare time on their hands, humour can strengthen your immune system, fill your body with oxygen-rich blood and improve your mood—even if the last time you smiled was during the Eisenhower Administration.

On the other hand, the mystery section of the stories will give you a mental workout as you ask yourself who committed the crime, what was their motive, and how did the killer's left hand strangle the victim without his right hand knowing about it?

In my opinion, mystery and humour go together like hot dogs and buns, computers and swearing, not to mention blunt objects and people's heads. You have the intrigue of mystery and the fun of humour. What more could you want?

Okay, maybe a beer. (Sorry that's not included.)

The stories do include a cat detective who has a sexy feline for a client, a man who goes to see his dealer in a shady alleyway about buying some Lego bricks, an exterminator who tries to talk some sense into bugs and a writer whose characters force her to complete her unfinished manuscripts.

Of course what would a mystery collection be without a story about the great detective—Locksure Homes, and his loyal associate, Dr. Watsup.

While some of the talented writers contributing to this volume are dedicated short story authors and novelists, others come from uniquely diverse career paths such as professor, film maker, yacht broker, federal agent and even astrophysicist.

I should mention that one of the writers never went down any of these exemplary career paths and has to be satisfied with just being devilishly good-looking. Tremendous humility prevents me from telling you which one that is.

As a final note, the lawyers want me to clarify that while they think you'll love the tales in Die Laughing, they don't want anyone to actually, Die Laughing, as this might seriously limit the number of good reviews.

So sit back in your favorite chair and enjoy these hilarious tales with a beer in your hand. (Again, not included.)

SELFIE OF AN ACTRESS AS A YOUNG WOMAN

Michael Cebula

Her name was Penny Price, but she wasn't cheap. Frank Blunt knew that because she walked right in to his one-man detective agency and declared, "My name is Penny Price but I'm not cheap."

Frank Blunt was an observant man—being a private investigator demanded it—but he was not a particularly descriptive one. If asked, he would have said that Penny Price was female, late twenties, symmetrical face, the expected number of appendages. But if he loved purple prose as much as the rest of us, he might have said that Penny Price was a breathtakingly beautiful woman with bright eyes liked plucked stars, skin soft and white as new snow, and long black hair that fell across her thin shoulders like silk spun by angels.

Both were equally accurate accounts.

"You look like an exceptionally average accountant," Penny Price said. That was true, so Frank Blunt, honest to a fault and not blessed with Penny's movie star looks, said, "That's true."

The details of Frank Blunt's appearance are not important, just know that they are such that it's easy for practically anyone to imagine themselves in Frank's place, doing and saying the things Frank did, winning and losing with Frank along the way. It was very easy to identify with Frank Blunt, is the point.

Frank shifted in his seat. He knew there had been enough talk about appearances, it was time to get things going, to get to the action. "How can I help you, Ms. Price?" he asked.

"I'm being blackmailed," she said. "Don't ask who it is, or what he has over me, because I won't discuss it. I just want to pay him off and have this whole nasty thing disappear."

Frank Blunt considered this. "How much is he demanding?"

"Fifty thousand dollars."

Frank Blunt whistled. "A pretty penny."

"Thank you," said Penny Price, blushing. "But let's focus on the blackmail. I'm supposed to pay him off this evening at six o'clock. I would like you to be there with me, to provide protection. I don't trust him."

"Well, Ms. Price, the problem with blackmail is, once you pay up, it never ends, until you're squeezed dry." Frank Blunt didn't actually know that for sure—he had never handled a blackmail case before—but he had heard fictional characters say it in movies and it seemed to make sense and be the kind of thing he ought to say in real life. Although, on the other hand, presumably there were times where a blackmailer is paid off, and goes away for good, and everyone is happy with the transaction. That means there had to be times when paying blackmail was the *smartest* thing to do, right? You probably just don't hear about those cases because it doesn't make for an interesting story. So, maybe it was dumb advice. Still, Frank thought he had to warn her. "You can contact the police. If they arrest him, he won't bother you again."

"You're not listening," Penny Price said. "I don't want the police involved, I want this handled as quietly as possible. The whole thing is a private matter that is terribly embarrassing. And if you knew what I know, you would realize that he can only blackmail me once."

It was a portentous comment, a mysterious remark, and so to give the words their proper weight, to make sure Penny Price's statement really had a chance to breathe, Frank Blunt didn't respond immediately. Instead, he reached into his jacket pocket and took out a flask. Frank Blunt didn't like to drink, let alone have a drinking problem, but he pretended he did. God knows why, but people expected every cop, detective, gumshoe, flatfoot, private investigator, private eye, and private dick to be a drunk. He supposed it made them seem grittier, more complex. Frank's business nearly went under the first year before he realized he needed to convince people he was a lush. So now he kept a flask in his pocket everywhere he went and drank it at key moments. It was filled with Diet Snapple. He bought it in bulk, once a month, at Costco.

Now[1] Frank took a sip and grimaced. It was cranberry, and he had been expecting Trop-A-Rock. Penny Price observed the drink and nodded, looking pleased. He had her trust.

"This man, this blackmailer, said he will call me thirty minutes before the payoff with the address of where we will meet," she said. "Once he tells me, I will call you, and we can meet there. Whatever you do, don't be late."

Penny Price looked at Frank Blunt expectantly. By far the hardest part of being a private eye was responding with cool one-liners. The constant demand to come up with the perfect, succinct line that conveyed a hard-bitten, world-weary, yet confident charm was exhausting. And Frank Blunt simply wasn't good at it. He thought hard, feeling the seconds ticking by, knowing the moment demanded something special, and blurted: "You got it, Ms. Price!"

Frank Blunt did other stuff for the next several hours. It is not particularly interesting so it will not be described here, though scholars writing about Frank Blunt's place in American Literature can find details of those activities in the accompanying appendix. See Appx. II.B(c)(ii). For the more casual reader, just know that it involved things like writing letters to clients regarding unpaid fees, scheduling a dental appointment, and cleaning the office bathroom. Not particularly heroic, which is why these activities are always left out of mystery stories and were arguably a poor choice to be included here in this rapidly expanding paragraph, but necessary activities nevertheless. Let's not engage in the fiction that Phillipe Marlowe and Sam Spade never picked up a toilet brush.

At 5:30 p.m., Penny Price called. She gave Frank Blunt the address and told him to be there at six o'clock. He hoped she would say "and don't be late," again, because he thought he had the perfect one-liner ready (it was okay, not perfect) but instead she simply hung up. Frank Blunt grimaced again and this time it wasn't because of the Snapple. Life was full of disappointments.

The address Penny Price gave him was a home in a well-to-do section of town, a neighborhood filled with large houses and gigantic lawns. It was not where Frank would have thought a blackmailer would pick but, on the other hand, how often do you look at a place and think, you know, I bet a lot of blackmail goes down there? Not very.

The drive from Frank Blunt's office should have taken about twenty minutes, but along the way he stopped several times. Once it was to joke, chat, and slip ten bucks to a homeless man he knew. Then he helped a random old woman unload groceries from her car. He also played around with a dog for a bit, petted it, tossed it a treat, etc. Several similar events followed, events not related to the plot, but events that humanized Frank Blunt, made it easy to cheer for him. Due to space limitations, the editor cut a really fantastic scene where Frank Blunt did something charming with a child even though Frank himself is childless (protagonists should be good with children, because it is charming, but not actually have children because, obviously, kids are fun to hang around with for like fifteen minutes or so but what kind of madman would actually want to be responsible for them?).[2] So, basically, Frank Blunt is a nice guy, is what these events said.

The problem (or one of the problems) with being a nice guy is that it requires, by definition, doing nice things, which slows you down immensely and makes it impossible to be on time for anything. You ever meet someone who does everyone the courtesy of always being punctual? Trust me, that guy is one of the most selfish jerks on the planet.

So, anyway, Frank Blunt was a few minutes late when he arrived at the address Penny Price had given him. Picture a huge, expensive house in your head, triple it, and that is what the place looked like. Oh, and there was a gardener doing gardener stuff on the front lawn too, absolutely covered in mud. Before Frank could get out of his car, his phone rang.

"Where are you?" Penny Price said.

"I just pulled in."

"You're late. I told you how important it was to be on time."

"Sorry," Frank Blunt said. "I was petting a dog."

The phone was silent for a minute, then Penny Price said, "I won't pretend to know what that means. But I will pretend you never said it. Hurry up, I'm already in his office, it's all the way in the back."

Frank hustled inside and started walking toward the back. He wondered what the blackmail was about. He figured it was selfies, ladies these days really had a courageous if absurdly misguided idea of what kind of selfies it was safe to take. Frank kept walking. You had to be pretty confident to invite your blackmailing victim to your house, he thought. But, on the other hand, who wouldn't be confident, living in a home like this? It was the most beautiful, not to mention largest, home Frank Blunt had ever seen. You could fit his childhood home inside it ten times over, and still have room to spare. Clearly, blackmail paid better than podiatry.[3]

After a series of hallways that were more like runways, one dead-ended at a large oak door. Showing off his deductive skills, Frank said, "This must be the office," and went inside.

Now things began to move very fast. Frank Blunt stepped inside the office and froze. In front of a gigantic oak desk, an old man lay on the ground, covered in blood.

Frank rushed to his side, and saw two gunshot wounds. He felt for a pulse and found nothing. Frank's own heart raced. What a juxtaposition. Still kneeling, Frank reached for his phone in his back pocket and felt a rush of air behind him. Then everything went black.

In that lightless swamp of unconsciousness, Frank Blunt's mind drifted. He thought about cases he had solved, women he had loved, dogs he had petted.

And he thought about Curt and Snippy. Both of Frank's parents were alive and he had a healthy relationship with them, and that caused him no end of regret. He knew he would come across as grittier and more complex if, say, they were dead, or he never knew his father, or his mother had died some mysterious way or one or both of them were abusive alcoholics. But unfortunately, Curt and Snippy Blunt were kind and supportive parents, a fact Frank kept close to the vest, terrified that if that awful secret were known, no one would think he was interesting. It was true, Frank Blunt often thought bitterly, you can't choose your family.

Still, while Frank Blunt was cursed with a well-adjusted, loving family, he was nevertheless haunted by his past, as all good detectives should be. When he was sixteen, he fell in love with a girl named Hope Chase. She was a year older than Frank Blunt and, in compliance with the long-standing rules of high school, Hope treated Frank like he was invisible. For months, Frank Blunt loved Hope from afar, writing love poems about her symmetrical face and satisfactory number of appendages. Finally, one day he worked up the courage to ask her out. In the cafeteria, he boldly walked up to her and said, in front of everyone, "I'm Blank Frunt, would a movie like to see you?"

Sometimes, in the middle of the night, that memory would float through his mind and he would wake up screaming.

Frank Blunt woke up screaming.

"Thinking about some girl from high school?" a man's voice asked.

Frank got his bearings. He was in a hospital bed, staring at a lanky, middle-aged man in a trench coat. "How did you know?" Frank asked.

"I'm Flex Stone, Homicide Detective. It's my job to know. And you," the man said, flipping through Frank's wallet, "are Frank Blunt."

Flex Stone tossed the wallet on to the hospital bed. "Frank and Flex. Flex and Frank. That's going to be a problem."

Frank Blunt's head ached horribly. "What do you mean?"

"Our first names," Flex Stone said. "They both start with 'F.' It will be confusing."

"To who?"

"Anyone who reads about this."

"Who would want to read about this?"

"You'd be surprised."

"Well, how would it be confusing to them? Just because they both start with 'F'?"

"I don't know, it's just what I've been told, and I don't want to appear amateurish. We need to create new names, and they have to sound like real names, not made up."

"But my name really is Frank Blunt!"

"And my name really is Flex Stone. But it will never work, Frank and Flex, I'm telling you it will look like amateur hour, it's the first thing that will get changed. Now, let's think, all we need is a realistic-sounding name. It can't be that hard to come up with one."

Frank (the protagonist) and Flex (the homicide detective) stared into space for twenty minutes. Finally, they gave up.

"Good God, coming up with names that don't sound made up is hard," Flex Stone said. "Okay, here's what we'll do, we'll just stick to last names. I'm Stone, you're Blunt. Got it?"

Frank said, "Fine."

"Good. Now, I'll be frank, Blunt. This looks bad for you. We've got a dead man that you're lying on top of, knocked out cold. There's a gun with your prints on the floor. And, we've got an eyewitness who says she saw you going through the dead man's pockets right before she brained you with a lamp."

Frank Blunt tried to sit up in the hospital bed and a bolt of pain shot through his head. "None of that is remotely true. Wait, am I under arrest?"

"I'll be blunt, Frank: yes. Sorry, strike that. I mean, I'll be blunt, Blunt: yes."

"Look, there's been a terrible mistake."

"Explain it to me then. Was it self-defense? Or maybe the gun went off accidently? We found your flask, we know you're a drinker. What's your story?"

"There's no story here, only the truth. I don't even own a gun, I hate them. I wasn't drunk either. I just went there to help a client with ... a transaction. I walked in the man's office, he was already on the floor, I checked for a pulse, and then someone knocked me silly."

"Silly?" Flex Stone said. "Silly? We are talking about a man's murder, Mr. Blunt. Murder is no laughing matter. Only a psychopath would joke about it. To try to draw a laugh from it is distasteful, the product of a diseased mind—"

"Okay, okay."

Stone cracked a smile. "I'm only kidding. Now listen, what transaction were you helping your client with?"

"Blackmail. She was paying blackmail."

Stone raised his eyebrows. "Selfies?"

"I assumed."

"What's her name?"

"Penny Price."

"*Penny Price?*" Flex Stone said. "Sounds made up."

"It's not, trust me. She came into my office, hired me, told me to meet her there."

"What does she look like, this Penny Price?"

Frank Blunt could sense that a discussion of face symmetry and expected appendages would not be helpful. He reached far back into the sole creative place in his mind and said, "You know the actress —— ——? Penny Price kind of looks like —— —— did before —— —— started getting all that awful plastic surgery."[4]

Flex Stone looked at him strangely. "I think I may know who you are talking about." He went to the door, opened it, and spoke to someone in the hallway. A moment later, a police officer walked in to the hospital room, accompanied by Penny Price.

"Ms. Price!" Frank Blunt exclaimed. "Please, explain to them what happened."

Now everyone looked at Frank strangely.

Flex Stone said, "Blunt, this is Mrs. Prudence Goodwife."

Now Frank Blunt was very still.

Flex Stone turned to her and said, "Mrs. Goodwife, is this the man you found in your husband's office, going through his pockets?"

In a trembling but sure voice she said, "Yes."

"And had you ever seen this man before that moment?"

"No," she said. "Never."

Frank Blunt was in shock. Because he believed every word she had just said.

After the police officer led a sobbing Prudence Goodwife away, Flex Stone said: "She told us what happened. She was on the phone with her friend, Brock Thrustwell. She heard a loud argument coming from her husband's office, so she made her way there, then she heard two shots, and when she ran in, you were going through Mr. Goodwife's pockets, robbing him apparently. That's when she put you to sleep with a lamp."

"Must have been a perfect shot, to knock me out like that," Frank said.

"No, it's remarkably easy. Anyone can knock somebody out with a smack to the back of the head. We try to keep that quiet, but it's true. You ought to try it sometime."

"Well, my head is aching."

"Really? That's surprising. Most people totally recover within minutes." Flex Stone rapped his own head a few times with his knuckles. "The human skull is impenetrable. It's impossible to injure the brain."

"That doesn't sound right."

"It doesn't? Hmm, maybe she injured your ears. You should have someone check that out. You don't want to mess around with ears, they're important. If only God had encased them in a nice thick skull."

Now Frank Blunt's head truly began to swim. Was it possible he had imagined the whole thing? Penny Price walking in, saying she was being blackmailed, and asking for his protection? No, it was not possible. Who would make up such a scenario? It had happened, it was real, he was sure of it. But he couldn't discount the fact that Prudence Goodwife seemed to have spoken with complete honesty.

"Where's my cellphone?" Frank Blunt said. "I need my cellphone."

"Don't ask me, you didn't have one with you."

"What? Of course I did," Frank Blunt said. "Look, it's not what you think. I can't explain it, but I know I never shot anyone."

Flex Stone sighed dramatically. "Sigh," he practically said. Then he literally said, "Blunt, it will be easier if you just tell the truth, if you admit that you're the killer."

"Easier for who?"

"Me, of course. Then I won't have to collect any more evidence. Who cares what's easiest for you?"

"Okay," Frank said, after a moment. "I'll tell it to you straight. But first, can you get me a drink of water, from that sink right behind you?"

When Flex Stone's back was turned, Frank grabbed the clock on the bedside table and smacked him upside the head with it.

Stone had been right. It was remarkably easy to knock someone out.

An hour later, Frank Blunt was driving around downtown, wearing Flex Stone's clothes, and driving Flex Stone's car. He'd worried at first that he wouldn't be able to recognize Stone's vehicle in the hospital parking lot, but it turns out that spotting an unmarked police car is remarkably easy. It also helped that Stone had parked in a no parking zone with a placard on his dash that read "Police Vehicle" so he wouldn't get a ticket.

Frank knew he had to ditch the car soon, but walking would have wasted too much time. His destination was not far from the hospital, but there would have been no end of dogs to pet and old women needing help with their groceries. Hence the old saying: sometimes being a nice guy means you have to steal a police car.

The clock in this particular police car showed 9:00 p.m. It being a normal business day, that meant all government offices had been closed for at least eight hours, probably more. Frank Blunt left the car in an alley, wedged between a dumpster and a wall, and walked two blocks to the City Records Office. Getting into the office took feats of daring and creativity that are difficult to believe and because they are so difficult to believe, that precise sequence of events will be omitted from this narrative, so that the author will not receive emails like, "It wasn't believable how Frank got into the City Records Office" and to which the author would invariably respond, "And yet it happened, pal!"

So, anyway, Frank Blunt was in the City Records Office. First, he looked through the marriage records. Then he looked through the birth records. And his suspicions were confirmed.

"My God," Frank said portentously, looking up from the records dramatically as the camera zoomed in on his shocked face. "Prudence Goodwife is a twin."

Now things were starting to come together and Frank helpfully summarized them in his head just to make sure everyone was all caught up. Prudence's twin had, for some reason, pretended to be a woman called "Penny Price," then killed Prudence's husband, Mr. Goodwife, and framed Frank for murder. And, well, that's what he had so far.

Along with Flex Stone's keys and clothes, Frank Blunt had also nabbed the investigative file, and he looked at it now. It was slim. Notes about Stone's conversation with Prudence Goodwife, recounting exactly what Stone had already told him she said. Notes from an interview with Brock Thrustwell, confirming he was on the phone with Prudence when she heard a fight in her husband's office. Several pictures of Mr. Goodwife, looking rich and dead. There were also notes from a brief interrogation of the gardener, Rhett Helling, who said that he heard two shots, then a moment later a scream, then Prudence Goodwife ran outside, crying bloody murder. The only other thing in the file was a note that the family's housekeeper, Linda Cebula, was in the kitchen baking at the time of the murder, but she apparently had nothing of interest to say.[5]

Could Cebula or Helling have been in on the plot? Frank wasn't sure but he decided they could wait. First, he had to find Mrs. Goodwife's evil twin, "Penny Price." Or, as the birth records showed her true name to be: Constance Cheer.

The short, squat woman who answered Constance Cheer's door laughed happily and exclaimed, "We're *fraternal* twins, not identical! Oh God I wish I looked like Prudence. She looks just like —— ——— did before all that awful plastic surgery."[6]

"You're Constance Cheer? You?" Frank Blunt said. "This is perplexing information. I'm perplexed. I had been so sure ..."

"Daddy always said, Prudence got the movie star looks, I got the moles and morals. Guess which one of us married a rich man and which one of us is still single?"

It was the morning after the murder. Frank Blunt was still in Flex Stone's clothes, still flashing Stone's badge and pretending to be a police detective. So, picture that scene. Oh, and Constance Cheer's house was okay, but not even close to as nice as the Goodwifes' place. A podiatrist could definitely afford it.

"How long have Mr. Goodwife and your sister been married?" Frank asked.

Constance Cheer fairly beamed. “Two years.”

“Were they happy?”

She grinned and said, “Oh, you never can tell with Prudence.”

“How do you mean?”

Now she laughed and said, “Prudence is such a great actress. She could convince anyone of anything. One time she tricked me into thinking that I was allergic to meat. So, I became a vegetarian for the next three years. And I actually *am* allergic to leafy greens, carrots, wheat, tofu, starches and beans! Which I didn’t find out until later. Of course, even being a vegetarian, I still managed to gain weight. The doctors said it was on account of all the inflammation from my vegetable allergies.” Constance laughed again. “Then, another time, she convinced our father that he had lost his job. He went into a massive depression and never really recovered.”

“Sounds awful.”

“Oh, it was,” Constance Cheer said with a smile.

“Why did she do those things?”

“Why does a cow eat grass?”

Frank was stumped. “Because ... she convinced the cow it was allergic to meat?”

“Because it’s the cow’s nature. Just like it’s Prudence’s nature to be conniving. It took me years and years to figure out that the trick was to never, ever look at her when she talks.”

“Nice word choice, conniving,” Frank Blunt said, writing it down.

“She always loved money,” Constance went on, happily. “And always had men wrapped around her finger. I knew she’d marry rich.”

Blunt wrote a note in Flex Stone’s notepad and circled it: *Rich who?*

“Prudence had lots of boyfriends when we were growing up, but most of them were poor, and none of them ever lasted long.” Constance paused for a moment, thinking. “Except one boyfriend she had, in high school, he was always tagging along, even after she broke up with him. Ron or Rick or something like that. He was really in love.”

Frank flipped through Stone’s notes. “Was it Rhett? Rhett Helling?”

“No, that’s not it. Hold on a minute, it will come to me,” she said. Then she snapped her fingers and said, “Wright Mann, that’s his name.”

Frank Blunt was dubious. “Are you sure it isn’t Rhett Helling? I really think it’s Rhett Helling.”

“No, it was definitely Wright Mann. Who could forget a name like that? Wright was so nice and sweet. But Wright made some mistakes after high school and went to prison for a few years for mail fraud. We all figured Prudence was behind it and somehow convinced him to take the blame. She sure can be persuasive if you look at her! And Wright especially would do anything she wanted."

Frank Blunt thought about this for a minute. "When is the last time you saw Prudence?"

"Six months ago, but I remember it like it was yesterday. Daddy was in the hospital, in his last days, and she came around to argue about his will. The doctor was giving Daddy some information about his prognosis and Prudence was on the phone with that friend of hers, Brock. Daddy asked her if the call could wait, so he could hear the doctor, and she stormed out."

Frunk Blunt made a note of this story. He knew full well that anyone with poor cell phone etiquette was a sociopath and more than capable of murder.

"But that's just Prudence," Constance said. "She always said no man would silence her."

Frank Blunt stopped short. "What did you just say?"

"Prudence always said that no man would ever silence her."

"Just that last part."

"Um, silence her?"

The words bounced around Frank's head. Silence her, silence her. "That's fortuitous," he said. "That's very fortuitous that she said that and you told me about it."

Frank smiled brightly at Constance. He thought he knew how Prudence had set him up.

And then just as quickly his smile turned upside down (*i.e.*, he frowned). Because he saw Flex Stone sprinting toward him at full speed, with his gun drawn.

Frank made it to his vehicle before Flex could apprehend him. What followed was one of the coolest, most epic car chases ever.

The amount of traffic was perfect—enough to swerve around, but not so much that it brought the chase to a halt or slowed it down to an uninteresting speed. Awesome weather too, really a good chance to test what his mom's van could do.

That makes this a good time to note that at this point Frank was driving his mother's Honda Odyssey, which she was happy to let him borrow earlier that morning without inquiring why he couldn't use his Camry. The scene where Frank borrowed his mom's van is not very heroic, plus it emphasizes how Frank's parents are loving and supportive, so it was left out (it was never written). But, anyway, that's how Frank Blunt is getting around now, in his mom's van. If you'd rather pretend it's an Aston Martin or a 1968 Ford Mustang 390 GT 2+2 Fastback (which would be much cooler), feel free, but unfortunately in real life it's a Honda Odyssey.

So back to the epic car chase. Frank Blunt in his mom's purple Honda Odyssey, Flex Stone in another unmarked police car (with a Police Vehicle placard on the dash), racing through the city streets. Multiple times they went over hills with all four wheels off the ground. Frank was really amazed at the Honda Odyssey's shocks (Honda *does* make a quality family van). Then, at another point, Frank crossed some railroad tracks in front of an approaching train and Flex Stone juuuust made it across without getting hit (it was close!) All sorts of stuff like this happened.

Finally, Frank ran a red light and, just after he passed through, two bread trucks travelling in opposite directions screeched to a halt in the middle of the intersection, blocking Flex Stone, and allowing Frank Blunt to get away. Fortunately, despite this long and extremely dangerous car chase, nobody was hurt, so it was still easy to cheer for Frank Blunt even though he broke a bunch of traffic laws and was kind of being a reckless idiot.

Frank Blunt, still without his cell phone, spent the next several hours searching for a payphone. When he finally found one, he placed three calls. They will be described below but, to build tension, not every detail of the calls will be revealed immediately, even though up until this point each scene has been described for the reader without leaving anything out.

His first call was to his mother.

"Frank!" Snippy said, when she picked up the phone. "We saw your picture on the television! Was it your DMV photo? You looked so handsome."

"Thanks, Mom, but listen—"

"What is going on? Some silly reporter said you were on the run and wanted for murder? Is that why you needed the Odyssey this morning? Not that I mind, everything we have is yours, you know that."

"I'll explain everything later, Mom," Frank Blunt said. "But right now, can you please go to the City Records Office? I need you to do a little research on a man named Rhett Helling."

Frank's next call was to his buddy in the state crime lab.

"This is Joe Smith," Joe Smith said.[7]

"Joe, this is Frank, I need your help."

"Frank Blunt, you ol' murdering son-of-a-gun. I saw your picture on T.V. You looked *terrible*!"

"Joe—"

"Did they use your DMV photo? You had this sort of vacant, dead-eyed look, and *paunchy*. And, by the way, your hairline is really starting to recede."

"Joe—"

"You should have used a bat instead of a gun. Think of the headline: *Frank's Blunt Object Kills Goodwife*."

"Joe, listen, have you finished the ballistics report?"

"Yep, just sent it to the Chief of Detectives," Joe Smith said. "All the tests confirm that it was your gun that did the deed."

"Not my gun. You know I hate guns."

"Okay, the gun with your fingerprints that was used to kill the guy that you were found on top of. Is that better?"

"Much. Thank you. Now listen, can you tell if the gun was fired with a silencer?" Frank was thinking *silence her, silence her*.

Joe Smith was saying "A *silencer*? A *silencer*?" He chuckled condescendingly. "You mean a suppressor? Because that's the correct term."

Joe Smith is actually a pretty cool guy to hang out with (the apartment complex he lives in has a pool and a hot tub, and he is generous with the snacks), but the one thing about Joe is that he always has to make very clear that he knows way more about guns than anyone else in the world. Frank cursed Prudence Goodwife for not saying that no man would ever suppress her.

"Yes, a suppressor," Frank said. "Was one used?"

"Actually, it was," Joe Smith said. "There were a few marks and plastic particles that indicate you used a homemade suppressor."

"Hey!"

"Fine, I mean that indicate that the killer used a homemade suppressor. Pretty shoddy police work though, they didn't even bring the suppressor to me. It's probably in an evidence bag in the trunk of some detective's car. That's just sloppy."

Sloppy, or the perfect frame job, Frank Blunt thought.

"I hope you beat this case," Joe Smith said. "You ought to come out to my place next weekend, if you're not locked up. Weather is supposed to be perfect."

"Sounds good," Frank Blunt said. "And I really owe you one. But tell me one last thing: how many times was Mr. Goodwife shot?"

Frank's mom dropped off the reports regarding Rhett Helling that she found in the City Records Office, along with a turkey and Swiss sandwich, and a Snapple. The reports said exactly what Frank thought they would. And the sandwich was delicious.

Frank Blunt made one final call, to the housekeeper, Cebula. He disguised his voice to sound like Flex Stone.

"Do you have something in your throat, sir?" Cebula asked, when she answered. "Are you choking? If this is a medical emergency please hang up and dial 911."

Frank switched back to his normal, sort of reedy, accountant-type voice.

"I'm investigating Mr. Goodwife's death," he said. "And I need to ask you a few questions."

"Anything to help Mr. Goodwife, he was a good man."

"Did Mr. and Mrs. Goodwife get along? Did they fight often?"

"Oh, I'd say they fought as much as any other married couple."

"How often is that?"

"Every day, like cats and dogs."

Frank nodded. "And what did you think of Mrs. Goodwife?" he asked.

"She was a floozy," Cebula said emphatically.

"I'm sorry?"

"A hussy. An easy make. Fast."

"Again, I'm not sure I understand—"

"Harlot? Doxy? Slattern? Tramp? Modern-day Jezebel?"

"You lost me."

"She slept around."

Frank nodded and scribbled a few notes on the pad he had taken from Flex Stone. There sure are lots of ways to say whore, he thought. Then he said, "I want you to tell me everything that happened the day of Mr. Goodwife's death. And everything you know about Rhett Helling."

Cebula talked and talked and Frank filled several pages of Stone's notepad with the details. When the call was finished, he sprinted to his mom's van. He had to find Rhett Helling, and he didn't have much time.

Frank Blunt found Rhett Helling in the same place he had last seen him, in the front lawn of the Goodwife house, doing gardener stuff. He was still as muddy as ever.

"Rhett Helling," Frank said. "Or should I say, Wright Mann?"

Helling/Mann's eyes grew wide, but before he could speak, three police cars pulled into the driveway, sirens blaring. This time, Frank didn't run.

Flex Stone jumped out of the lead car, followed by three police officers, their guns drawn. "Put your hands up!" Stone ordered.

Frank and Helling/Mann shot their hands into the air. "Don't shoot!" they said.

Prudence Goodwife came out of the house with a startlingly handsome man Frank Blunt had never seen before. "What's going on?" she said.

"Put your hands down, Blunt," Flex Stone said. "We know you're innocent."

Flex Stone walked past Frank, grabbed Helling/Mann's wrists, and cuffed him.

"Rhett Helling," Stone said. "Or should I say, Wright Mann?"

"I already did that bit," Frank told him.

"Damn, I planned that on the way over," Stone said. "Wait, you knew that Rhett Helling was really Wright Mann? How?"

"My mom discovered his name change at the City Records Office," Frank said.

There was an awkward silence. Then one of the cops sniggered.

"Well, you're lucky to have such a, uh, supportive mother," Flex Stone finally said. He turned to Helling/Mann. "Wright Mann, a.k.a. Rhett Helling, you are charged with the murder of Rich Goodwife. You have the right to remain silent, you have—"

"Wait!" Frank shouted. "You've got the wrong guy! Rhett Helling might be Wright Mann, but that doesn't mean he's guilty."

Flex Stone chuckled. "You and your mom did a solid job, Blunt, but that's no substitute for the work of actual police officers. See, what you don't know is that Wright Mann has been in love with Prudence Goodwife all his life. She had no interest in him, but out of the kindness of her beautiful heart, when he was released from prison she got him a job as a gardener at her husband's estate. He should have been thankful, but he wasn't. No, he was eaten up with jealousy until one day he couldn't stand it any longer and killed Mr. Goodwife."

"You've got it all wrong," Frank Blunt said. "Wright Mann is innocent."

"He's got it totally right," Helling/Wright said. "I'm guilty."

"No, you can't take the blame for her again, not like you did on that mail fraud case."

"Take the blame for who?" Flex Stone said.

"Prudence Goodwife!" Frank Blunt told him. "She's behind it all. You're forgetting what I told you. Prudence is the one who hired me to come here, she's the one who directed me to Mr. Goodwife's office. I never spoke to Wright Mann at all."

"That's the part we couldn't understand," Flex Stone said. "Why were you here, Blunt? Maybe you were blackmailing Rich Goodwife?"

"No, there was no blackmail," Frank said. "Prudence made up a story to get me here so she could pin the murder on me, say it was a robbery gone bad."

"He's lying," Prudence Goodwife said believably.

"I'm guilty," Wright Mann said again. "Prudence had nothing to do with this. She is pure as the driven snow."

"Wright is wrong," Frank Blunt told Stone. "Listen, I talked to the housekeeper, Cebula. She said that on the day of the murder, Wright was repairing a retaining wall and putting new bushes in. He was caked with mud, before and after the murder. But there was no mud in Goodwife's office or anywhere else in the house. So, it couldn't have been him."

"Well, then that brings us back to you as the killer," Flex Stone said.

"Not quite," Frank told him. "Remember, Prudence claims she ran to Rich's office when she heard two shots. But we know the gun that killed Rich Goodwife had a silencer—"

"Uh, the correct term is suppressor," one of the cops said.

"—so how could she have heard the shots that killed Rich Goodwife?

She didn't. And whatever happened to the suppressor anyway?"

They all looked at Prudence Goodwife. She offered them a winning smile.

"Don't look directly at her!" Frank yelled and all the men shielded their eyes.

"I can explain," she said. Then she stopped. "If you just look at me, I can totally explain."

"Officers, arrest Mrs. Goodwife for the murder of her husband," Flex Stone said, still shielding his eyes. An officer grabbed Prudence before she could run, and handcuffed her.

"I didn't kill my husband!" Prudence screamed.

"She's correct, technically," Frank Blunt said. Then he pointed to the handsome stranger standing next to Prudence. "Because the one who pulled the trigger was Brock Thrustwell!"

"Another twist," Flex Stone said appreciatively. "Explain."

"Prudence wanted Rich dead so she could inherit his money, then she was going to shack up with her lover, Brock Thrustwell."

Flex Stone said, "Is it true, Mr. Thrustwell? Were you having an affair with Mrs. Goodwife?"

Thrustwell said nothing but he couldn't stop himself from flashing that huge smile every man gets when other people find out he's hooking up with an extremely hot woman.

"You're sleeping with Thrustwell?" Helling/Mann screamed. "I can't believe you!" Helling/Mann had the same look on his face that kids got when Flex Stone explained that Santa Claus is a lie.

"Prudence hired Wright Mann because she thought she could convince him to murder her husband," Frank Blunt said. He pulled out copies of student participation certificates his mother had found in the City Records Office. "But Prudence didn't realize that during his stay in prison, Wright had completed several classes on non-violent conflict resolution."

"I told her she should just divorce him and forget the pre-nup," Helling/Wright said, sobbing. "Violence is never the answer. And we don't need money to be happy."

Prudence smirked, sneered, and sniggered.

"So, when she couldn't convince Mr. Mann, she turned to her boy-toy, Brock Thrustwell," Frank continued. "That's Prudence's way, she gets others to do the dirty work for her. And Thrustwell was willing to do it, for the girl and the money. Prudence told Brock to sneak into the house, shoot Rich with a suppressor, leave the gun, take the suppressor, and sneak away just before I was scheduled to arrive, then he would call Prudence so they would have alibis. Prudence would use a burner phone to call me, wait for me to come over and find the body, then knock me out, steal my phone, fire two shots out of the window, get my prints on the gun, and pin the blame on me. A great plan, the kind that only an incredibly smart and talented person could conceive. But Prudence made two mistakes. She didn't know that ballistics experts can tell whether a bullet was fired with a suppressor. And she didn't realize that Brock shot Rich in the chest twice but missed once, and Joe Smith found the errant bullet in the wall behind Rich's desk. There were really three shots, not two."

"This whole story is a farce," Brock Thrustwell said.

"Is it?" Frank Blunt said. "Then perhaps you won't mind turning over your phone to the police, so they can see whether you have any recent searches for how to make a homemade suppressor."

Brock Thrustwell chuckled confidently. Then he took out his phone, threw it as far as he could, and started running in the opposite direction.

"Gentleman, you know what to do," Flex Stone said, and two officers took off after Thrustwell.

Frank and Flex watched quietly as the officers tackled Thrustwell, and the remaining officer escorted Prudence to a patrol car.

"Excellent work, Blunt," Stone said, after a moment. "Excellent work. What tipped you off that it was Thrustwell?"

"Well, I finally realized that most of the evidence pointed to Rhett Helling, so that meant it couldn't be him. And no evidence pointed to Brock Thrustwell, so it was probably him."

Stone nodded. "It always seems to work out that way, doesn't it?"

Frank Blunt was proud of solving the case. But he was prouder still that he had thought of a decent one-liner to end on. He turned and looked at Stone with a huge smile on his face, but before Frank could say a word, Stone took a peek at the script and said, "I guess this time, Prudence was a little too rash."

Hey! Frank Blunt thought, *that was supposed to be my line!*

Notes

1 "Now" is perhaps not the best word to use, though it will be used other times throughout this text. "Now" as used herein refers to a particular instant in relation to the narrative, not literally "now" in relation to the reader's existence. Because, in relation to the reader's existence, what is happening now is that the word "now" is being read. And, obviously, by the time the word "now" was written above to describe Frank Blunt's actions, then printed, published, and read by the reader, the moment of "now" as it relates to Frank Blunt's actions had passed. That is to say, the events described herein are not occurring simultaneously with the act of the reader reading about them, though it is the intention of the author to write with such immediacy that it feels like they are. That these events are not occurring simultaneously with the act of reading about them can be proven by re-reading the sentence above that starts "Now Frank took a sip ..." Of course, it can't be "now" now, because it was "now" a few minutes ago when the reader first read that sentence. Lastly, as previously noted, it should be noted that "now" will be used several times in the pages that follow, so those "nows" are in the reader's future, but they refer to the past, though they are intended to make the reader believe it is the present.

2 For completeness, it should be noted that, in addition to humanizing the protagonist, children may also serve as victims or, at key points in the plot, computer genius/hackers who obtain information from well-secured databases that the protagonist needs to solve the case. So, children are not totally useless, for the record. Just mostly useless.

3 Frank's father, Curt Blunt, was a podiatrist and owner of an apparently modest home, in which he raised his children Frank, James, and Emily. Frank's mom, "Snippy" Blunt (née Snippy Short), was a hairdresser, her nickname derived from a lifelong love of cutting people's bangs. Her real first name is lost to history and could be Matilda for all anyone knows, though probably not.

4 ——— is a famous and once beautiful actress who had some unfortunate plastic surgery and now looks like a permanently surprised and completely wrinkle-free frog. For obvious reasons, the publisher refused to print her name. This led to a big debate with the author (who made ponderous arguments about the importance of art, etc.). Eventually, a compromise was reached where "———" would be used and readers, if they wished, could Google around to figure out who Frank meant. Unfortunately, this explanatory footnote takes the reader out of the story—it reminds the reader that this is a fictional account, contrary to the typical goal of fiction, which is to make readers believe, at least while reading, that the account is true (*i.e.*, the characters really exist, the events really happened) because it's better if people care about the characters/events and no sensible person cares about imaginary characters/events. This is like judging a hammer by whether it can convince someone it's a nail, I mean why not just read non-fiction, right? Anyway, this is what you get when you have a nervous publisher and an obnoxious writer.

5 No relation to the author, they just happen to have the same last name. But isn't it sort of surprising this doesn't happen more often in the stuff you read? Like,

Patricia Highsmith—a not uncommon last name—wrote twenty-two books and a million shorts (all of them amazing), that must have included hundreds of people, and not one of them happened to also be called Highsmith? Like, not even some random guy at the apothecary or whatever? Seems odd.

6 Yep, same actress.

7 Extremely common name, right? Both first and last name. In fact, according to the Internet, several thousand people currently living in the United States are named Joe Smith. Yet, it still seems made up, right? Or at least low effort. *Joe Smith*? Flex Stone was right about one thing, names are hard.

THE STRANGE CASE OF THE QUIKEE MART STICK-UPS

William Sattelmeyer

At something like 11-ish pm on Tuesday the 3rd, Ned Lund backed into Rooskie's Quikee Mart where Bobby Briscoll, who nobody really liked, and I were stacking the milk crates midway through our shift. Unusual for Ned, especially on a bowling night, he shuffled in the opposite direction from the beer cooler.

He hung out in front of the Wonder Bread rack, squeezing bags of hamburger buns for another two minutes while Jerry rang up Doc Simms's regular poker night six-pack and Wendy Amundsen's third illegal carton of cigarettes this week. Everyone knew Wendy was underage, but if you called her on it, she was quick to prove she knew how to do things she couldn't possibly have learned about unless she was over 18.

"Unless she's a ho," Bobby said once, but no one pays attention to Bobby, not since his old man fried himself repairing an electrical circuit outside the high school girls' locker room, even if his mom did still work at Micro Center and knew how to get free cable, and Wendy never bought cigarettes from him after that anyway. Besides, we all knew she was stuck on Jerry, and sometimes she was stuck on him back in the milk cooler.

At 11:07:23, according to the security camera recording, Ned sauntered over to the sad piece of industrial carpet in front of the register that was always wet from sopping up the condensation from the stubby freezer with the Good Humor bars, fudge pops, and the Strawberry Scooters that no one older than three wanted. He slid a pack of Juicy Fruit across the counter, followed immediately by pointing the business-end of a chrome-plated .22-caliber barely-even-works-on-a-Saturday night special at Jerry's nametag. In deposition, Jerry said Ned threatened to shoot his nipple off if he didn't give him the money, but the security cam didn't record audio, and the angle of the camera made lip-reading inconclusive.

What I am certain of, because I'd just come up front with a box of frozen hot dogs for the grill, is that at exactly 11:10, Jerry had just opened the till with the No Sale key as Ned suddenly threw his pistol hand into the air like he'd just won the Superbowl or something and slammed his head on the counter three times hard enough to permanently dent the aluminum before sliding to the floor and flopping on the carpet like a carp on a hook.

When he woke up in the hospital, Ned swore he hadn't been near the convenience store since Thursday and could prove it because he was having some of the guys over to watch the pre-season exhibition on Saturday, and they'd started the party not long after work on Friday night. It had gotten real good about dawn, and they'd gone for a sack of breakfast sliders—just ask Ellie—and then decided to go fishing in the river south of town. He figured he must have slipped on a rock and hit his head because he couldn't remember much after that, and could he go now, because he didn't want to miss the game.

Most folks wasn't buying it, though he was pretty convincing, even moping for a full day after Bobby told him we'd lost by six points and Ned owed him five bucks. Actually we'd won by six, but we figured if Ned didn't really know, then it was at least worth a couple of beers. He wasn't going to need the money if he went up-river anyway.

Old Mister Ruskiwicz wanted to make Jerry pay for fixing the counter and was planning on sneaking in the cost for replacing the fluorescent lights that flickered all the time and dimmed whenever the cooler cycled on, but the cops said it was evidence and either he left it like it was, or they'd cut it out and store it until the trial, and being as how Ned's uncle was also his attorney and running against Judge Voss for Mayor, it looked to be a long time before Ned wore anything that wasn't orange.

Of course word soon got around town that Jerry was an easy mark—although not as easy as Wendy—and would empty the register just by threatening one of his body parts, so we weren't surprised much when some fat guy with hair buzzed short like a bad wrestler and eyebrows like old shag carpets fumbled a sawed-off 12-guage from under his coat. Jerry had already tripped the silent alarm, 'cause who wears a coat in August, but since it was the third or fourth time he'd done it in the last week, and seeing as how Ruskiwicz charged full price for day-old donuts no matter what color your uniform shirt was, it wasn't clear how long it might take the call to be shuffled down to some do-gooder rookie.

Fat Guy put a load of buckshot into the camera to show he meant business and probably because he thought it would keep anyone from knowing what he looked like, like maybe buckshot would erase the recording of him doing it, then told Jerry he could choose which ear to lose and that at this close range it might not only be one ear that got shot off.

"Ya g-gotta buy something," Jerry stuttered.

"What the hell you talking about," Fat Guy said. "This is a hold-up. Gimme all your money."

"Ya gotta buy something," Jerry repeated, "or I c-can't open the register."

"Bullshit." He hung his belly over the counter and jammed the muzzle into Jerry's forehead for emphasis, leaving a red sideways eight on his forehead. I thought about backing Jerry up, but the stack of Bud Light that apparently made me invisible might not have also made me bullet-proof, so I thought I'd see where Jerry was going to go with this.

"If I don't ring a sale again," he whined, "I could lose my job."

A big glob of sweat ran off Fat Guy's nose, spattered onto the counter and rolled into Ned's dent. He twitched the shotgun closer to Jerry's nose. "Open the damn drawer or you'll lose more than a frikkin' job."

Jerry blinked about a dozen times, which is what he did when he was thinking, which wasn't all that often, and finally said, "How about some beef jerky, then?" And Jerry quick-drawed a stick of Old LeatherLips Genuine Peppered Chew out from under the counter.

The Fat Guy screamed "I warned ya!" loud enough that the milk in the cooler curdled, and he swung his shotgun for the center of Jerry's right ear. Jerry's eyeballs rolled up in his head as he swatted blindly for the No Sale key, and I was wondering if I was going to be stuck cleaning the walls—and what did you use to get blood out anyway—when the front door snapped open with that stupid little *bong*, and Wendy Amundsen said, "Hey, boys, where can a girl get a BAM."

Actually, I don't think she said BAM, but that's all I heard, as the shotgun cut a two-foot circle in the water-stained ceiling tiles, filling the air with chips of paperboard swirling like milkweed seeds on a windy day in September. Jerry must have found the No Sale key because the cash drawer clacked open unnoticed as Fat Guy bounced once on the floor in front of the rack of gentleman's magazines before the butt of the shotgun pounded his nose across his lip, did a half somersault and clubbed him on the side of the head with the still-hot muzzle.

Wendy looked disappointed.

The cops were waiting for Jerry when we cruised in for our shift the following evening. They had already confiscated two large cups of coffee and a dozen donuts for evidence and asked Jerry politely, with much patting of clubs and holsters and twirling of handcuffs, to come downtown and answer a few questions, since Fat Guy had died without regaining consciousness, and the robbery was now a lively murder investigation.

I told Jerry to go ahead, don't worry about me, I'd be fine, figuring if the cops didn't ask for my assistance I'd be kind of stupid to volunteer that I'd been a witness, and maybe Wendy would need comforting if he didn't come back before dark. I relieved Bobby who promised to hang around back catching up on his *Sports Weekly* in case I needed him, and bought a pack of cigarettes—no filters, extra nicotine—and rolled it up in my t-shirt's sleeve so Wendy might think I was a studly rebel like Jerry. Wendy wasn't amused.

When she lit up a cigarette, it was with one long inhale that left ash an inch long hanging hypnotically in front of lips that matched the cherry slush in her other hand. "Jerry's no murderer," she said. She made a pouty little circle with her lips, inserted the moist end of her smoke and sucked the rest of it lifeless in a single draft.

"Sure. It was self defense," I said. "He didn't know the jerky was loaded."

Wendy replaced the butt with the straw and blew smoke bubbles in the slush that popped and smoked and spat red glops like a frozen volcano. "Don't be an ass," she said, and since it looked like I wasn't going to be getting any, at least not in this life, I volunteered as how we ought to look into hiring Jerry a lawyer or maybe starting a Free Jerry GoFundMe.

Wendy eyed the hot dogs spinning up and down on the rack of hot, greased rollers, and I had a sudden need to recite all the stats for the Indians' 2021 run for the pennant before I flew a pennant of my own when she offered, "You're next, you know." I coughed and swallowed my gum. "Not *that*, Darwin. You're the target behind the counter now. Every jerk-off looking for a rep is going to be gunning for you." She assumed a pose on the lid of the ice cream freezer, arching one deeply tanned leg over the other and tossing her hair in the breeze from the air conditioning. "How's it feel, Sheriff? Think you can handle Johnny Ringo on your own?" She whistled the theme from that Western Clint Eastwood made before he got old while she examined her perfectly shaped toes. "What's the count now? Three?"

"Four," I said, "counting Ned who doesn't remember he did it and the Fat Guy that Jerry didn't kill even though it looked like he did."

"Can it, wiener boy, and toss me another pack of smokes before I go into withdrawal." She fielded my high toss which I made look like I intended to do it that way, slit the cellophane with the edge of a fingernail painted blood red, and tapped the bottom of the soft pack. A single cigarette snapped fully erect, vibrating as she licked the tip before pulling it out with her lips and stoking the end with a single-handed match-lighting trick. Bobby brought out a six-pack of Natty Light from the back, looked from me to Wendy back to me and back to Wendy again. "What?" he said.

"Four," Wendy said, removing a can from its plastic girdle with a groin-lifting twist as she locked eyes with Bobby who flushed and suddenly found something very interesting to look at behind the chip rack. "Four is a lot of till-busters for a dip-shit on-the-edge-of-nowhere market like this, don't you think? And maybe especially high," she added, hopping up onto the dented counter and tugging at the frayed edges of her size-too-small denim cutoffs, "considering how none of them was successful."

She exhaled a plume of smoke that arrowed for where Bobby was pressed up against the ice cream freezer, chugged her beer, and overhanded it into the trash can by the door. "Damn peculiar, don'tcha think?"

"It's the economy," Bobby offered.

"Oh, puh-leeze," Wendy said.

"Maybe it's the heat," I said. "Heat will make people do crazy things."

"Just the heat, Sheriff?" Wendy said as she leaned backwards, legs in the air and toes pointed, her breasts shifting freely under her blouse, just before she rang up a sale with a knuckle and the cash drawer shot out for my belt-line. Both Bobby and the cooler gasped. Wads of dirty-green bills strained at the levers in their steel trays, not a one of them crisp and new and not a few with serial numbers circled from playing dollar poker and one five-dollar-bill marked with a phone number, the words "For a Gd Time" and Lincoln's lips drawn into a fat "O."

I paid for Wendy's cubebs and slammed the drawer closed with a quick glance at where the security camera would have been if Rooskie had bothered to replace it.

"Maybe," Bobby gulped, "maybe it was the devil."

"Oh, eat me," Wendy said. She crossed her ankles, spread her knees wide and bent at the waist to stare at the floor beneath the counter. If I'd have been deaf, I still could have heard Bobby's eyes pop out of his head.

"And they were all standing right here. There something special about this spot?"

"We don't take customers at the other register," I said, thumbing toward the space plugged with a Twizzler jar, a pyramid of beer nut cans, a rack of horoscopes rolled into tiny tubes that hadn't been changed since 1997, and a sign showing the fifteen winning lottery numbers that no one had guessed yet again.

Wendy slid slowly off the dented aluminum that had momentarily cupped her hips, and I wondered if it wasn't now a historical site, and could I find another place for the beer nuts, but then I remembered Jerry and realized he and Wendy had been going at it for long enough for the whole damn store to be a national monument. I momentarily blanked out as Wendy inserted fingers alongside her fly and tugged her shorts back down all of a half inch.

"I said," Wendy said, "do you have a gun back there? Or do I gotta use friggin' sign language, and while you're trying to remember, my eyes are up here."

"Uh, gun, yeah," I said as Wendy planted her elbows on the counter and dared me to even flick my eyes toward the open V of her blouse. "Gun. Yes. Gun. Somewhere. Pretty sure." I rummaged beneath the pork rinds and jerky, wondering, if I found it, if I shouldn't just put myself out of my misery. I heard the door lock click as I came back up with a blue-washed .357 magnum with a two-and-half-inch barrel and pearl handle inserts.

Wendy threw a shoulder against the door which clacked firmly against its latch. She smiled as she stretched across the counter and grasped the gun by the barrel, tugging it out of my hand. "Now we have a locked room mystery," she said as she flipped the gun in a back half-somersault with a twist, cocked it with her thumb and pressed the muzzle to my forehead. "Whyn't you show me what you've got, sweetcakes, before I see what you look like with an extra orifice above your eyebrows."

I had just started unbuckling my belt when she smacked my forehead with the pistol. "The cash register, cowboy, the cash register." She stepped back, hopped up on the ice cream freezer, and gripped the pistol with two hands, probably in case I revealed myself to be a kung-fu master.

"Oh," I said, which sounded like "Nooo-o-o-o-o-o-o," which is what Bobby was screaming as Fritos bags exploded before him in what I assumed was his mad rush to save my life. I hesitated, but just in case he wasn't successful, him having no real hand-to-hand combat genes that I was aware of,

I tapped No Sale and the register opened with a *cha-ching* the same time that Bobby screamed "Yieeee!" as he tripped on the carpet and knocked himself unconscious against the Coke display. It was getting damned musical in here.

I was working on stuffing the few lousy bucks into a plastic bag and trying to decide if I should double-bag it or put the money into two bags to make it look like more, when Bobby's moaning began to really annoy me. He was flattened against the stack of soda pop, elbows out and twitching in a pretty good chicken impression, and head tilted down the better to squeeze his eyes shut.

"Interesting," Wendy said. She pointed the gun at the blinking overheads as Bobby drizzled to the floor. "If they don't stop that, I swear I'm going to shoot them all out. It's like a damned disco in here."

"You want the change, too?" I asked holding up the sack I was filling.

"Put the money back, you moron. I'm not robbing the store. For crying out loud."

"Oh." I slowly closed the till and set the bag of money on the counter while I rummaged for the twenty I had accidentally put in my own pocket. Wendy, hands on her hips, studied Bobby, which looked pretty gangster with the gun in one hand. The lights stopped blinking and the milk cooler kicked in with a thunk and a gasp of freon. She slid off the cooler, stepped over Bobby, and tossed me the pistol.

"There's no bullets in it, you know."

"Uh, no, I think we shot them all off on the Fourth of July."

She studied the sack of cash before tracking her eyes up to my face. "But you still were going to give me the money." She smiled with all her teeth and most of her eyes and ran her fingernails down my chest. "You're so sweet. I think I'll let you get me another pack of cigarettes."

"You're not going to rob the Mart?"

"No, dummy, I'm not," she said, jumping up and settling herself into Ned's dent again, "but zip it up and fasten your pants before I get other ideas." She snatched the pack out of the air and tucked it into her exceptionally fine breast pocket before tapping out a cigarette from the opened pack she'd left on the counter.

"Then, what?" I said, rather cleverly I thought, hoping I could still keep the extra twenty somehow.

"Didn't you notice how Ned and Fatso and all the other midnight marauders, for all I know, threw their hands over their heads and screamed when they oughta be making plans for running for the door?"

"No."

"Well, they did, and I wondered what would make a guy do that and then want to slam his head a couple of times into a counter." She glanced at Bobby wobbling to his feet. "Clearly it's not masculine overcompensation."

I tried to grasp the concept, immediately ruling out Jerry leaning over the counter and checking if size mattered, as I was pretty sure he wasn't fast enough to get away with it and didn't think it would ever have occurred to him to try, at least not since eighth grade. "Who would do that?" I wondered, mostly out loud.

"An invisible super-hero, goofball. How the hell should *I* know? Maybe the store's guardian angel gave them an invisible goose."

"Angels?" I said, slipping the twenty into the bag with the other cash. I hadn't seen any angels and wasn't sure if they actually cared about such things but, then again, if they happened to catch St. Peter's ear just as I was trying to slip through the Pearly Gates ...

"Ghosts?" Wendy pondered, exhaling a thick blue cloud that tornadoed ceilingward. "Maybe they screamed because something scared the crap out of them."

"I didn't see any ghosts either," I said, putting the twenty back into my pocket. I'd decided if you couldn't take it with you, probably nobody cared about a measly twenty bucks on the other side. "Maybe Bobby saw something."

"What about it, babycakes," Wendy said, leaning her elbows on her knees and throwing her charm spotlight across the aisle to where Bobby was holding a Creamsicle against his forehead. "What do *you* think happened?"

"Screw you," he mumbled.

Yes, please, I thought, as Wendy laughed, lightly, like a mockingbird, although I'd never heard a mockingbird, but I was pretty sure it must sound like Wendy laughing lightly. "I'm shocked," she said and then got that quizzical look you get when you miss winning the lottery by one number.

Bobby stuck out his lower lip and turned away. Wendy looked down at her feet, dangling over the carpet in front of the counter. The last half of her slush was sweating on the counter, and she ran it across her forehead just before she tipped it over on the floor. "Oops," she said. "Look what I've done."

She rotated at the hips and blinked her eyelashes at me so hard that I was afraid chips of eyeliner would fly off. "I'm so clumsy and so hot. What would I have to do for you to get me another slush?" She ran the tip of her tongue across her lips. "Oh, but I guess you need to clean up my little mess, first." Her sigh was the essence of sadness.

"Bobby, get the mop," I said with a strong twitching of my eyebrows to let him know I meant now and a tilt of my head to point to Wendy who had hooked her heels into the candy rack below the counter and was leaning backwards on her elbows, eyes closed and knees parted like she was catching a few rays from the fluorescents.

Bobby was back with bucket and mop before I could snap the lid on a fresh new slush and was concentrating on cleaning up Wendy's spilled drink as slowly and carefully as possible, although he wasn't really looking at the floor.

"What do I owe you, baby?" Wendy murmured when I brought the slush over to the counter.

"It's my treat," I managed to say, pretending to search my pockets for change.

"You're the best, sweet cheeks," she said scissoring her legs impossibly high in the air, flipping backwards and landing behind the counter in front of me in a full split. Bobby leaned over the counter in disbelief as Wendy reached up and took the slush. "Go. Fight. Win. I owe you," she said. She looked up and tapped Bobby on the nose. "And you, too," she said. "For letting Jerry take the rap for you. Right?"

"No, don't!" Bobby said pushing off the counter as she swept her hand in an arc over her head to the register and pressed No Sale.

The register spit out the till again with its bass give-me-money clack, the overhead lights dimmed, and the handle of the mop embedded itself in the ceiling. Bobby pogoed up and down like a clog dancer before slipping in the wash water, and belly-flopping into the motor oil display.

Wendy, still stretched out on the floor at my feet, reached up and shut the register drawer. The lights sputtered and resumed their semi-steady illumination, and Bobby's feet stopped kicking the cooler. "Shocking," she said taking a big gulp of her drink, "Simply shocking."

This time the cops took the counter and the rug and the register Bobby had rigged as payback for everyone who had ever poked fun at him as well as the previously hidden wires connecting all of them to the breaker panel. They even took the breaker panel, which the electrician's union said Bobby's dad had installed before his accidental electrocution. Ned's uncle volunteered to represent Bobby on account of he was really a hero for preventing potentially life-threatening burglaries, even if Bobby had almost cooked his nephew in the process, and when Jerry was released from lock-up—he hadn't known that pushing No Sale would trip a relay that would run 240 volts through anyone standing on the wet carpet and touching the counter—my fantasy of me and Wendy spending the summer at the submarine races along the river were over.

Bobby got eight-to-ten which shouldn't be all that long with good behavior, and a home security service offered him a job on his release and was already marketing a do-it-yourself alarm kit with a nice picture of Bobby and Ned on the box.

Jerry moved to South Carolina to be near Wendy after she enlisted in the Marines to pursue a career in the Military Police, and old Ruskiwicz promoted me to night manager for my part in keeping his insurance rates down. It's not a bad gig, especially on Friday nights when the varsity cheerleading squad stops in to see if what Wendy told them about me was really true, and after only a little encouragement, I dutifully retell the whole story and even let them sit on the section of dented counter the cops finally returned, and at exactly 11:10 pm I show them how we locked the door, turned out the lights and discovered what all the moaning and screaming was really about.

A DICK NAMED BROWN

Richard Lau

The name's Brown, and I'm a private dick.

Brown's a good name for someone in my profession. Plain, ordinary, easily fades into the background and instantly forgettable, like an old station wagon that still runs quietly.

I stand behind my desk, stretching out an old shoulder injury from my baseball-playing years. The day has been business as usual at my office, which basically means no business at all. Most days I entertain myself answering calls from debt collectors, telling them some cockamamie bull about a bill-eating tree. They tell me to go fly a kite, and I tell them ... well, I guess that shows my desperation for entertainment.

I don't even open the curtains to my office window anymore, but I can see the crack of light between the drapes growing dimmer. The sun is catching the evening train home, and so must I. It's time to go.

At the hat rack, a baseball cap awaits to greet and comfort me like a warm puppy dog. The cap's two sizes too large, and with the thinning hairs on my balding head, there's not much up there to keep a snug fit.

I put on my yellow trench coat and check my look in the full-length mirror that has been here since the office was originally a tailor shop. The mirror's one of the few things in the office that remains unbroken. I wish I could say the same for myself.

I sigh. I've fastened the black belt crooked again, missing a loop here and there, giving it an odd zigzag pattern. But I'm probably the only one to notice, much less care.

I glance at my watch. I'm going to be late.

Granted I don't seem to do much to justify my existence in this world, but I still try. And that includes bringing food to the old guy who lives next door.

He's a former World War One flying ace, or at least claims to be. He may be a bit off due to either a war injury or senility. I remember the scare I had the first time seeing him sitting on his roof, calmly typing up his memoirs. He says the sky still calls to him, and who am I to argue?

When I arrive, he's at a much more reasonable altitude, waiting on my doorstep, an impatient scowl marring his usually joyful fuzzy mug. At least he's not wearing his food bowl on his head again.

"Where have you been?" he grouses. "I've been kicking at your door for over an hour!"

"I'm not that late," I protest, unlocking the door. "Why can't I have a normal neighbor, like everyone else? Can't your stomach wait?"

"Oh, I've already eaten," the veteran writer explains. "You really shouldn't leave your window open."

My glare clearly states I'm considering punching his big nose, so he quickly adds philosophically, "A dog's gotta do what a dog's gotta do."

"Then wha ..."

"I'm just here to tell you Lucille wants to see you. As soon as possible. She left a message on your answering machine."

My neighbor may be snoopy, but he's also one of the most informed people I know, which always helps in my line of work. I've long stopped asking about his sources and contacts, as he'll usually respond with a cryptic, "A little birdie told me so." Some folks might think he's being facetious, but I know he's not. I've actually seen the bird.

"Anything else?" I ask.

"Yeah, your belt is crooked again."

For someone his age, he's lucky he's able to retreat back to his rooftop so quickly.

I know where to find Lucille.

"Sc ool." The old neon sign hangs off the side of the building like a single Christmas ornament loosely fixed to a twig of a tree. Since the letter "h" burnt out, folks just refer to the joint as " 'S Cool."

"Nice to see you again, Chuck," says the bouncer, a tough biker chick, whose breath always smells like peppermint and vodka.

"Pat," I reply, tipping my cap.

Inside, people shuffle back and forth in some oddly rigid dance moves, like stiffly animated characters grooving to a bouncy jazz score.

In a far back corner room, I find them. Schroed, tinkling the ivories of a long out-of-tune grand piano. He's so good, even the off-notes sound in key.

His eyes never leave the keyboard, not because he needs to see where to place his fingers, but because he's avoiding the adoring gaze of the woman draped across the top of the instrument, hovering low and tight, like the clinging fog over San Francisco Bay.

Lucille performs a much-practiced slide off the piano lid, straightening her blue velvet dress. "About time you got here, Brown. Leaning on that bust of Bert Hoffing was getting painful."

"Beethoven," corrects Schroed, still playing, still looking down.

She blows him a kiss, which he also ignores. "Anyway," she says, turning her attention back to me, "I've got a lead for you."

"A lead?" I ask. "On what?" I hadn't had a client or a case since I helped my sister Sally with her homework long ago. And that paid me peanuts.

"On what you're always working on," Lucille says, extending her lower lip and blowing upwards her thick black bangs in frustration.

I feel an immediate tug in my chest. "Where is she?"

"I don't know, but I know someone who might." She smiles, and after a dramatic pause adds, "And where to find them." Lucille loves showing off her smarts.

With the superior tone of a school marm reciting a particularly grueling assignment, she spills the location of an alley near the baseball park.

Before leaving the club, I call my buddy Linny.

Linny meets me at the subway station just a few blocks from the alley Lucille told me about. He looks relieved to see me.

"This is a bad neighborhood," he says, nervously glancing up and down the empty street bordered by abandoned cars with shattered windows and stripped wheels.

"I know," I reply, "that's why I called you for back-up."

Even though there are two of us and no one else on the dark street, we walk fast, past the shuttered shops, down an uneven, cracked sidewalk strewn with faded wrappers and broken glass.

"This place needs a neighborhood improvement program," I tell Linny, "or at least a block captain, like I am for my neighborhood."

"Not everyone can be a block head, Captain Brown," Linny informs me, using my neighborhood watch title.

We come to the alleyway in the middle of the 700 block, right where Lucille said it would be. The pale orange glow of the dim streetlight we're under somehow makes the shadows in the alley seem even darker.

"You first," I say.

Linny looks shocked. "Me? Why me?"

"You're the one with the weapon," I point out.

"Weapon?" Linny's usual sleepy expression is fully awake in panic mode now. "What weapon?"

"Damn it, Linny!" I curse him, knowing it's no time to play games. "I thought you carried a gun around like a security blanket?"

Linny pulls out a long, ragged piece of cloth from under his jacket. "Good grief, Brown! I keep telling you, it's the other way around! I carry a security blanket like a gun!"

I swallow an anguished "Aaaaarrrgghhh!" suddenly feeling very vulnerable, but I'm not going to let Linny see it. "You, first," I insist.

Linny grinds his teeth. He knows he owes me for that all-night stakeout I did with him in the pumpkin patch that Halloween night. He slowly moves into the alley. I can see that under the terrycloth blanket, Linny has his thumb and index finger posed like a pistol.

The mouth of the alleyway swallows him up, like a lump of stale gum.

It's probably only a few seconds, but it feels like hours.

"Linny?" I call, forcing my feet around a pile of debris at the entrance of the alley, straining my eyes to pick up any trace of my friend. A match gets struck, and I see Linny at the far end of the blind alley, looking at the ground around him.

"This place is as filthy as a ..." Then the match goes out, and I hear what might be a muffled cry.

"Pig pen?" I finish for him.

"Yeah?" comes a gruff voice from behind me. There's a rustle as I choke on dust and a rotten smell before getting clobbered.

I open my eyes. The first thing I notice is Linny. He's slumped over in a wooden chair, his wrists tied to the chair arms, blanket curled at his feet like a hungry cat. His breathing is slow and even.

I whisper silent thanks that he's still unconscious. Being unable to reach his blanket or suck his thumb would probably freak him out.

I look around, and I can't see walls, just stacks of cardboard boxes.

We're in some sort of warehouse. Two lamps are hanging from the unseen ceiling. One over me and Linny. The other over a cloaked figure standing about ten yards away.

I shift, testing the ropes binding my arms behind me. I find, unlike Linny, I'm not tied to the chair I'm sitting on.

My movement catches my captor's notice. The cloaked figure swaggers a little closer.

"Mwoooohh wooowh mahooooo."

"Pardon?" Mrs. Brown raised a polite boy, no matter what the circumstances.

"Waaahwaaah blaaah blaaaaah maaaawwww!"

It is like a car horn honking in my head. I can't make sense of the words, but the threatening tone is definitely clear.

"Huh? What's that? Speak up! Annunciate!" I say, stalling for time.

Exasperated, the cloaked figure points to a device on the floor and states clearly, "Detonator. To blow up the one you seek."

Two things become immediately clear: the garbled attempt at vocal disguise and what the device on the floor is meant to do.

My adversary crouches over the device and starts to twist two wires together.

Without thinking, I leap to my feet and charge, meaning to kick the device out of my opponent's gloved hands.

For the briefest moment, I am triumphant; in my mind, I save her, never to lose her again.

I'm almost there, when the cloaked figure pulls the device away. My feet and hopeful dreams fly uncontrollably into the air, like ducks scattering after a gunshot.

When I regain consciousness, I'm lying at the base of a familiar wooden lemonade stand. The lemons are long gone, but as usual, the advice, wanted or not, will soon be pouring forth freely.

I sit up and see Lucille seated behind the stand, smiling smugly down on me. On the counter where she's resting her arm are a now-familiar cloak and a voice-distorting megaphone.

"It was you," I groan, and then feebly add, "again."

Lucille smiles and points to the sign that says, "The Doctor is In." "Really, Brown," she admonishes, "how many times do we have to go over this? You need to give up your unhealthy obsession about finding her. She's long gone. You need to move on."

I don't like Lucille's five-cent psychotherapy, but I can't afford anything more expensive. Somewhere deep inside, I know Lucille is being a fussbudget to help me, and I appreciate the effort.

Lucille continues. "Good grief! Even Linny knows when it's time to go home, which he did. But you? We do these scenarios to show you how painful this obsession of yours can be," Lucille explains, repeating herself for maybe the hundredth go-around. "Yet you fall for them time after time, again and again. You need to ask yourself why, Brown. Why?"

The only answer I have for her is the coin I toss over my shoulder as I leave.

Back to 'S cool. It seems like I always end up back here. I've decided to leave the office closed for the next few days.

The dance floor is empty. It's so quiet, Schroed's piano tinklings are echoing off the walls like hammering tongs. I restrain myself from saying, "Play it again, Schroed." He claims he's playing different tunes, but all that classical stuff sounds the same to me. Especially in the mood I'm in.

The bartender Spike sort of looks like my neighbor. Perhaps they are related. Perhaps someday I'll care enough to ask.

But today, like many days, I order a stiff drink, another, and then another. Spike leaves me be, as I close my eyes and dream of the little red-haired girl who long ago stole my heart.

WITH FRIENDS LIKE SYKES

Martin Zeigler

I rushed outside and hit the pavement like an FBI agent fleeing a bunch of mobsters in an all-beef restaurant. That's because I *was* an FBI agent, and the restaurant *did* serve all beef. And, yes, mobsters *were* inside.

Even worse, so was Eldon Sykes.

Halfway to the car, I stopped and wondered if I should rescue him. He was, after all, a fellow FBI agent. And he was a friend, depending on how you define it. But he was also the nasally, multi-sweatshirted SOB who had got me into this mess.

The dress code at the Denver field office was fairly lax: *Dress as you would want others to dress.* Basic, easy to follow, and everyone seemed to abide by it, including Eldon. Since he didn't care one iota how others looked, he figured he could go total slob. So, every day, he arrived at the office in wrinkled trousers and layers of sweatshirts, the topmost being a faded treasure from a faded college. The fair-sized holes at its armpits revealed the purple sweatshirt underneath, whose rips and tears, in turn, exposed bits and pieces of the olive drab number three layers deep.

And who knew what lay beneath all that? His daily getup was like a lesson in geology, in which each sweater charted a significant epoch in Eldon Sykes's existence.

Come the deadest cold of winter or the globally warmest summer on record, that was his uniform of choice, and it looked no different the day he popped into my cubicle, bearing what he claimed was good news.

"Jimmy Corliss," he said, "your lifelong dream of working undercover is about to come true."

I responded in the only way that seemed natural. "My lifelong *what*?"

Other than being FBI agents at the Denver field office, Eldon Sykes and

I had little in common. I was *field*, Sykes was *office*. I preferred working outdoors, as far away from my desk as possible. Eldon loved nothing more than to sit inside, surrounded by wires, cords, and cables. That is, until the world went wireless, at which point he loved nothing more than being bombarded by digital signals.

And yet I considered him a friend, probably for the same reason he thought of me as one. We were just two guys with nothing better to do outside of work than watch lousy movies and eat at crummy restaurants. Male bonding, I suppose you'd call it. Except that the term didn't quite take into account Eldon's thousand and one irritating habits.

Take his habit of slumping down in his chair to where the nape of his neck ended up near the bottom of the backrest. This would result in his hips protruding out over the front edge of the seat and his legs splaying out over the floor. This was not a normal way to sit in a chair, especially at an FBI field office, but if he was at your desk fixing your computer, you somehow let it go.

Or take his habit of answering yes or no questions with a nasally "yaaah" or "naaah." If he was for something, but only slightly, it would be an abrupt "yah." If he was adamantly against something, it would be a long, drawn out "naaaaaaaaah." Often, the two sounds would be indistinguishable, so you couldn't tell if he was in favor or opposed. Unless he was at a restaurant and the waitress asked him if he wanted something to drink. In that case, you could tell the difference right off, because it'd be either a "naaah" or a "yaaah, just water."

Or take the way he always responded to the slightest jest or jab with, "That's it. Beat up on old Eldon."

He once asked me to ride up North with him to his favorite eatery. He didn't mention it by name, but he swore I'd love it. His treat, and he'd do the driving. An hour and a half up there. An hour and a half back. And an additional hour or two devoted to actually eating.

By this time I had come to know Eldon Sykes pretty well. I realized that being in his company for any duration longer than your average movie was about as much male bonding as I could take. So, when he invited me on this five-hour odyssey up to the Great North, I politely declined with some variation of, "Eldon, I'd just as soon submit to the Chinese water torture."

I knew what was coming, and sure enough he slumped in his seat and said it. "That's it. Beat up on old Eldon."

And then there was his habit of doling out faint praise. One time, after learning I had helped bust up a major pyramid scheme, he came into my cubicle, slumped in a chair, and said, “It's lucky you had a team leader who gave orders you could follow to the letter. You're good at that.”

“Well, Eldon,” I said, perhaps a little defensively for a field agent, “I *was* allowed to follow my own hunches. And one of them *did* crack the case wide open. You do understand that, don't you?”

He slumped even further down and whined, “Yaaah.”

Or it could have been, “Naaah.”

But his worst habit, the one I dreaded most, the one which kept me up nights fearing what he would do next, was this one: doing me favors. Buffing that scratch off my car. Buying me that digital wristwatch whose numbers kept getting stuck. Lining me up with that woman named Charlotte.

And then there was the favor he was doing for me now, in my cubicle.

“Yaaah, Jimmy,” he said, sitting at my desk as if he worked there and I was the visitor, “I went ahead and talked to your supervisor. I let him know how much you want to work undercover with the mob.”

“Wait a minute,” I said. “You mentioned this to Ned? You didn't think of coming to me first?”

“Naaah. I didn't see any need. You already told me it's what you always dreamed of doing.”

“I never said any such thing.”

“Yaaah, you did, Jimmy. Remember that time, over dinner, when you said how much you admire FBI agents who had the guts to infiltrate the bad guys?”

“Sure. And I also said how much I admire concert pianists. But that doesn't mean I want to be one. I can barely tell a black key from a white one.”

“Yaaah, but going undercover is different.”

“That's right,” I said. “It's where your first wrong note is your goodbye note.”

Eldon must have thought I was making light of him, because the next thing he said was, “That's it. Beat up on old Eldon.”

The fact is, I *was* making light of him, because what he said was ridiculous. So I tried for a more serious tone, because this whole thing was serious. Even more serious than when he “buffed out” the scratch in my car, turning it into a collision-sized dent. “Look,” I said. “I don't even know enough to fake it. The only crime I've ever committed in my life, apparently, was ordering a root beer with ice in it. My date let me know right before she slammed her napkin on the table and stormed out of the restaurant."

"Who would do that?"

"Charlotte. Remember her?"

"That's it. Beat up on old Eldon."

Okay, my seriousness didn't come off as intended. So, while he slid further down in his chair, I gave it another try. "Eldon, listen. I wouldn't fit in. That's what I'm trying to tell you. I don't have what it takes to act like a criminal. Your average mobster would see through me in the first three seconds and put a bullet through me in the fourth."

Eldon sat straight up, seeing his opportunity to do me a further favor by relieving my anxiety about his current one. "Yaaah, but old Eldon is here to help."

Which was another irritating thing he said a lot.

"Nowadays," he went on, "you don't need to act tough to come off as a crook, like actors do in movies. Now you can just be yourself!"

I snickered. "Myself?"

"Yaaah," he said. "Donny Grimes."

"Who's Donny Grimes?"

"You, Jimmy. You're Donny Grimes."

"No I'm not."

"Naaah, not right this second, but you will be soon."

"But I don't want to be, either soon or late. I want to keep doing what I'm doing—tracking down conmen who peacefully cheat people out of their life savings without pulling a gun on them. What I don't want is to belong to a nationwide den of homicidal goons."

"Naaah, you won't," Eldon assured me. "Donny Grimes will belong to a smaller den of homicidal goons, not the nationwide one."

"I feel better already."

"I'm glad. I want to make this transition for you as smooth as possible," Eldon said.

"And how exactly will you pull that off?"

Eldon looked up at me and smiled proudly. "Through the miracle of email."

The way Eldon explained it to me from the bottom of the chair while managing the keyboard on his stomach and still being able to see the monitor up high on my desk—a feat that bordered on the miraculous—was like this.

What he had showing on the monitor was the email account belonging to the boss of the East Coast syndicate. Eldon had hacked into this account and composed an email from this guy to the boss of the West Coast syndicate.

"What's great about my hack," Eldon said, "is that the East Coast boss won't even know this is happening."

He rolled his chair aside to let me peruse his masterpiece, his email from the East Coast boss to the West Coast boss. It read: "Please watch over Donny Grimes until the heat dies down. Set him up with a nice place, plenty of spending money, and a snappy car. And treat him to a nice dinner now and then. And one more thing. Don't even think of emailing me back or calling me up about this, unless you want to be able to roll your eyes back and see your own head on a platter."

Eldon looked up at me. "You like that last part?" he said. "I thought it up myself."

"Oh, yes," I gulped. "This should go smoothly."

"It sure will. The West Coast syndicate will welcome you into their fold and not do a thing to bother you."

Eldon went on to explain that you couldn't have gotten away with this in the old days. But these days, if it was up there on a computer screen, it had to be true. The big boss out West just naturally would assume this email came from the big boss back East, never suspecting that it sprang from the fertile mind of a guy wrapped in a bargain basement's worth of old sweatshirts.

"By the way," Eldon said. "I showed this email to your supervisor."

"Please tell me Ned thinks this is a stupid idea and you shouldn't send it."

"Naaah, I can't. Because he thinks it's a great opportunity for the both of us. You'll be out West working with the mob, and I'll be right here at my desk in the Denver field office prepared to lend you a helping hand whenever you need it."

While I slumped Eldon-like in my chair, the tech guru himself reached up and clicked the send button.

The wheels of fate, powered by the Seattle syndicate of the mob, by Eldon Sykes, and by the US taxpayer, were now in motion.

That's right. Seattle, Washington. From this point on, unless I was told otherwise, I would not only be working with gangsters, but working with them in the pouring rain.

To get the ball rolling, I couldn't just fly from Denver to Seattle, even though that was the shortest route. That's because Donny Grimes didn't live in Denver. Eldon had him living in New York. Which meant that the taxpayer had to pay for my flight from Denver to New York so that the West Coast syndicate could pay Donny Grimes's way from New York to Seattle.

Donny Grimes hated flying as much as I did. But we landed at Sea Tac Airport as one, and from there, carrying an FBI-issued mobster suitcase containing FBI-issued mobster clothing, I stepped outside under a clear blue sky.

Somehow that didn't make me feel any better.

Just then, thanks to an FBI-issued mobster cellphone, I got a call from the Seattle crime boss's secretary. "Hello, Mr. Grimes," she said. "I work for Mr. Big."

I'd never noticed the name in the email Eldon wrote, but I caught it now. "Mr. Big?" I said, unable to suppress a chuckle. "You're kidding. His name is actually Mr. Big?"

"Something funny?" she said.

This. *This* was exactly why I didn't want to work undercover.

"Oops, sorry," I said. And in an effort to smooth things over, I added. "I thought you said Mr. Pig. That's all."

"No, you didn't," she said. "Because you asked me if his name was actually Mr. Big. You didn't ask if it was actually Mr. Pig."

"Yes, well, uh," I began. "You see, what happened was I thought you said Mr. Pig, but when the name came out of my mouth, it came out as Mr. Big."

"So if it came out as Mr. Big, why did you think it was funny?"

"I, well, uh, I guess, even though I said Mr. Big, I was still thinking Mr. Pig. Mr. Pig is funny. Mr. Big isn't so funny. Not anymore. What I mean is, it never was funny. Especially now."

"But how do you know his name isn't Mr. Pig? All I mentioned was the name, and you began laughing. And when I asked you why you were laughing, you said you thought I said Mr. Pig. Well, maybe I did say Mr. Pig. And now you're telling me the name Mr. Pig is funny. So I'd like to know why."

Besides being utterly convinced my goose was cooked, I was marveling at what an asset she would be to the FBI.

"Anyway," she said, "just something to think about when you meet Mr. Big—with a B as in *bat*, not a P as in *pat*—for the first time. Now let's get you situated, shall we?"

After that, she was very cordial, and I was very cold, having wet my FBI-issued mobster trousers.

Following her instructions, I eventually found my way to a completely furnished apartment in West Seattle. It was certainly nicer than my own place in Denver. And at mobster expense, no less.

I unpacked and hung up my FBI-issued mobster clothes, then used the built-in washer and dryer, along with available detergent, to give those soiled mobster trousers a spin.

Things seemed to be moving along well.

But an increasing sense of agitation and indigestion came over me, an ever-mounting dread that, at any moment, someone with a very long, thin, sharp, and shiny, serrated knife would find me out and slit my throat.

It was during one of these bouts of intestinal upset when I heard a rap at the door.

The visitor, without so much as a hello, walked right in and took a seat. He sat back and examined me. "What, Grimes, you going to a funeral?"

It was probably the dark blue trousers I'd wet, washed, dried, and was now wearing, along with the white shirt rolled up at the sleeves, all FBI-issued. Because all this guy had on was a casual pair of shorts and a loose-fitting t-shirt, probably all purchased for a song at the local big box store.

Anything dealing with funerals would've been a guess on my part, so I didn't have an answer. And he didn't wait for one. "Mr. Big wanted you and me to have a little talk, Grimes," he said.

"Sure," I said, taking the other chair. "What's your name?"

"Why?"

"Just to get acquainted," I said. "You know. I tell you my name, you tell me yours?"

"I didn't come here about me," he said. "I came here about you. What'd you do back East to get yourself in a jam?"

"I thought my boss told Mr. Big not to ask him any questions."

"Mr. Big ain't asking your boss questions. I ain't either. I'm asking *you* questions. And it's just one. Why are you in hot water?"

Suddenly I didn't feel so good. When I said, "Look, I need to go to the bathroom. Something I ate doesn't agree with me," it was partially true. I did need to go to the bathroom. Except it wasn't because of what was in my stomach. It was because I was in over my head. I had no clue why Grimes was in hot water.

"Go ahead," the guy said. "Use the crapper. Don't take all day."

I was at the bathroom door when he said, "By the way, what's your nickname?"

"Nickname?"

"Yeah, nickname. Everyone in the mob has a nickname. You don't?"

"Sure, I have a nickname."

"What is it?"

"What's yours?"

"Why do you wanna know?"

"You know. You tell me your nickname, I tell you mine?"

He was about to say something, but whatever it was, I couldn't wait for it. I ducked into the bathroom, grabbed my cellphone, and planted myself on the toilet. Then dialed.

"ELDON SYKES HERE!" came the response. That was another habit. Screaming into the phone.

I quickly wrapped my hand around the speaker, glancing back at the locked door. "Eldon," I whispered, "Will you hush? It's me. I need help."

"That's what old Eldon is here for."

"I need a nickname! And quick!"

"Naaah, you don't need a nickname."

"Yes, I do. Every mobster has one!"

"Yaaah, okay. Let me take a look at BLOTCH."

"What's BLOTCH?"

"It's a database I developed and maintain. It's short for Big List Of Thugs, Crooks, and Hoodlums."

"How will that help?"

"It has the names of everyone in organized crime. First names, last names. And, get this, Jimmy—I mean, Donny—it has nicknames."

I pictured him looking at a screen, because it sounded as if he was reading them off, one nickname after another. "Let's see. We have Fish

Face, Diaper Breath, Whale Meat, Awful Shot, Lucky Shot, Never Miss, Ice Pick, Bungee Cord, Guinea Worm, Yellow Shorts—"

"All right. I get the point. So what about me? If I don't give him a nickname right away, he'll know I'm fake for sure."

"Okay, okay. Let me think." I waited a few seconds, too many seconds. "Got it," he said. "Ten Pins. From now on you'll be Donny (Ten Pins) Grimes."

"What kind of name is Ten Pins?"

"What kind of name is Fish Face, Diaper Breath, Whale—"

"All right. But where'd you get Ten Pins from?"

"That time you and I couldn't agree on a movie or a restaurant. So we went bowling. You'd never bowled before, and you ended up getting that strike."

"Yes, in another person's lane."

"Good enough. Who's asking?"

"He won't give me his name, but I think he's Mr. Big's right-hand man."

"Let's see. Yaaah, that would be Melvin Meadowbrook."

"Gee whiz. I'm sweating bullets over a guy named Melvin Meadowbrook?"

"Melvin (Throat Slitter) Meadowbrook."

Thank God I was already on the toilet with my FBI-issued mobster drawers down.

"What's that noise?" Eldon said.

"Dropped something," I grunted.

"Sounds like it's still dropping."

"Talk to you later, Eldon."

After washing up, I closed the bathroom door behind me and returned to my chair, pushing it back a little to give Throat Slitter and me a little more space. "Okay, I'm here," I said.

"Try to imagine how pleased I am. So what's the story?"

I sat up straight and puffed out my chest, trying to look intimidating. "They call me Ten Pins."

He shook his head. "Oh, right, your nickname. Who cares? I wanna know what's got you on the lam?"

I just realized that this question was why I had to hit the bathroom to begin with. And now I felt my insides gurgling with the urge to go again.

"Sorry," I said, standing up with my hand to my gut. "Food's still giving me grief."

"Where the hell did you eat?"

"Fish joint down the street," I said, hoping there was a fish joint down the street.

"Thanks for the recommendation," Melvin said. "Go."

Back in the john with the door locked and back *on* the john with the seat down, I pressed the speed dial.

"ELDON SYKES HERE!"

"Jesus, Eldon. Quiet!"

"That better? How'd your nickname go over? I thought of a few others."

"I can't keep coming out of the bathroom with a different nickname. How would that look? I'm stuck with Ten Pins."

"Not a bad name. Not a bad name at tall."

That's another thing that bugged me. He could never say, "at all." It always had to be, "at tall."

"Listen, Eldon. That email you wrote to Mr. Big saying I had to lie low because I'd done something. What was it that I supposedly did?"

"I have no idea. That's why I told Mr. Big not to ask."

"Great. Thanks a lot. Now Melvin Meadowbrook is going to run a knife blade across my throat and leave me here to bleed out on the carpet."

"That's it. Beat up on old Eldon."

"I will if you don't come up with something fast."

"Okay, okay. How about you just tell him you smuggled stuff."

"Smuggled what?"

"He won't care."

I remained seated like I did before, but this time I hung up first.

Toilet flushed, hands washed, bathroom door closed behind me, I went back to my living room chair. I tried to look relieved. In a way, I was. In a dozen different ways, I wasn't. Trying to keep my stammering to a minimum, I said, "You asked a fair question. And you deserve a fair answer, since your boss, Mr. Pig—I mean, Mr. Big—was so generous putting me up in such a nice place. The reason I had to pack up and leave the East Coast in such a hurry was that I smuggled stuff."

The Throat Slitter nodded. "Smuggled what?" he said.

I didn't think anything was left, but there was plenty, and when I emerged from the restroom a third time, I said, "Diamonds."

He got up out of his chair and padded across the carpet toward me. I didn't know what scared me more. Him pulling a knife, or him asking me what kind of diamonds.

He did neither. He clapped me on the shoulder and said, "Good enough, Ten Pins. I'll let Mr. Big know you check out."

He pulled open the apartment door, gave me one last look, and left.

That last look was one of supreme disgust, with the squinting eyes and the curled lips. I figured it couldn't have been me, because my head was still attached to my neck. Then I felt my own eyes squint and my own lips curl, and that's when I spotted the bathroom door. I'd forgotten to close it. It stood wide open, releasing unto this apartment a history of my three previous visits.

Alone once again, I lay on the couch and contemplated the meaning of existence. While the world's greatest philosophers through the ages pondered their purpose and place in the universe, all I wanted to know was what in the hell I was doing in West Seattle.

I rang up Eldon again. After reminding him to lower his decibels, I came right out with it. "Eldon," I said, "just answer this one simple question. When will my job here be considered finished so I can come back home?"

"You want to come back home already, after all the work I did writing that fake email and giving you a fake name?"

"You better believe I want to come back home."

"You've been there less than a day. Give it time. I hear the Northwest grows on you."

"Eldon, will you just answer my question? What's my specific mission?"

"Yaaah, well, the way I see it is, you're kind of supposed to go out to dinner and shoot the shit with these guys once in a while and kind of see what you can dig up."

"That's it?"

"Yaaah, pretty much."

Or, as a great philosopher once said, "Yaaah, if I sit around and think about it now and then, maybe I'll find out if I am or not."

As soon as that call ended, another one came through. "Hello, Mr.

Grimes," the voice said.

It was Mr. Big's secretary.

Please, God, I said to myself, whatever you do, don't even mention Mr. Big's name. "Hello," I said. "We've spoken before."

"Yes," she said. "I remember. I just called to let you know Mr. Big's private jet will be leaving Sea Tac Airport tomorrow morning at seven. He's taking eight of his best men along. And he would very much appreciate it if you joined them. So please be on time."

"Thank you," I said. "I'll be there.

Not one word out of my mouth about Mr. Big—or Mr. Pig, for that matter. I was proud of myself.

But I still wet my pants.

I almost wet a fresh pair the following morning. On my way to the airport it suddenly struck me that I was about to fly on a private jet in the company of gangsters. Mr. Big, for starters. Throat Slitter, of course. And then seven others, God only knew what their nicknames were.

Fortunately, as I was about to enter the cabin, the pilot met me at the door and said, "Mr. Grimes? Mr. Big thought it would be fun for you to ride up front with me."

That was the good news. The bad news was that Mr. Big thought it would be fun to ride up front with the pilot.

"You look like you're about to throw up," the pilot said as I took the seat next to him in the cockpit. "I have a whole assortment of barf bags in my emergency supply kit. What color would you like? Yellow, green, orange?"

The colors were enough to make me want to puke, but I took a few deep breaths and smiled. "I'm good," I said, gripping the armrests.

He gave me a nod and taxied out onto the runway, exchanging jargon with the control tower. Within moments we were up in the deep, majestic blue.

Like hell it was majestic.

There were windows to the left, windows to the right. And the unavoidable windows up front. And then I noticed the moonroof. A moonroof in an airplane cockpit!

I felt myself turning green. Or maybe it was yellow or orange.

Whatever hue it was, the pilot was looking at it. "You don't fly very much, do you, Mr. Grimes?"

"I fly a lot." Of course, I didn't tell him it was for the FBI. "But I prefer the aisle seats, away from the windows."

"Well, sad to report, there are no aisles and plenty of windows."

"I—I can see that."

"Want my advice?" he said.

"Sure."

"Whatever you do, don't look down."

"Thanks."

"Anyway, Mr. Grimes, if you need to use the restroom, we have our own private one right in back of us."

"Good to know," I said.

"Only I call it the water closet, like they do in Europe, or simply the closet, because that's about the size of it."

"Closet. Got ya."

"No need to raise your hand and ask permission. Simply get up and go. In the closet, I mean."

"Will do."

"Speaking of which ..."

He unhooked his seatbelt, whipped it aside, and looked over at me. "If you'll kindly take the controls, Mr. Grimes, I might as well hit the closet myself and play bombardier."

I gripped the armrests tighter. "Wait a minute. You want me to do what?"

"I was told you had a pilot's license, and you'd be my second."

I felt my fingers on the armrest leaving a lasting impression. "I don't know a thing about flying," I stammered.

He reached out and gave me a punch in the shoulder. Laughing, he said, "Just messing with you, Mr. Grimes. You gotta learn to relax."

As he buckled back in, I wiped the sweat off my forehead and said, "I think I need to use it. The closet."

"Go right ahead. Just one piece of advice while you're in there on the throne."

"W-what's that?"

"Don't look down."

He started to laugh. He was still laughing when I emerged and sat back down, feeling none too great. While crunched in that tight space, I'd discovered that I'd left my cellphone back at the West Seattle apartment. Which meant there was no getting in touch with Eldon. In a way, I was relieved. In another way, I was doomed.

I tried to avoid the windows but I caught a glimpse of Mount Rainier bulging up from the earth like an enormous white pimple. "Where are we going? Spokane?"

"Spokane? Hell, no. We're bound for Wyoming."

"Wyoming? That's in the middle of the country!"

"Yes, Wyoming," the pilot said. "Home to Mr. Big's favorite restaurant in all the world. Maybe you've heard of it. Uncle Beefy's All-Beef Dinners."

"Never have."

"We'll get there around lunch time, but it'll still be considered a dinner. Because that's the name of the place. Uncle Beefy's All-Beef Dinners."

"I'll try to remember."

"It's all on Mr. Big's dime. He does this once a year for his top performers, in appreciation for all their hard work. Flies them out to Wyoming and treats them to an Uncle Beefy's All-Beef Dinner. And this time he wanted you in the loop."

"Great," I said.

"Speaking of loop, it's about time I go into one."

"A loop?" I quavered, forming a shaky circle with my finger.

"Yeah, one of those. The gang loves it when I do that. The FAA doesn't care too much for it, but then they don't care for a lot of things. Like me not having a copilot. Unless, you want to pretend to be one."

"No, I don't," I said. "And I don't much want to fly in a loop either."

He reached out and punched me again. "Aw, you'll do fine, Mr. Grimes. When we're at the top of the loop, though, just one piece of advice."

"What's that?"

He pointed to the moonroof. "Don't look up."

After stepping off the plane and kissing the ground, I headed toward the restaurant, right across the street from the small airport where we'd landed. It was a long and lasting kiss, so by the time I got there, everyone else had already piled out of the plane, arrived at the restaurant, and been seated.

I took the one empty spot remaining, at the end of the table nearest the entrance. Sitting opposite me, at the far end, had to be Mr. Big, since he took up four seats duct-taped together. Throat Slitter sat at the side, to his right. Everyone else sat around the table like your average guests at a business luncheon.

The guy to my right introduced himself as Stu. Stu (Staple Your Eyelids) Spencer. I told him who I was and said hi. He said hi back. He said he saw me when he got off the plane and wondered why I was on my knees with my lips to the tarmac. I told him the tarmac and I go way back. He nodded as if he understood.

The door at the back, behind where Mr. Big was sitting, swung open, and in marched a waitress who looked as worn out as the restaurant. She laid a hand on Mr. Big's shoulder and said, "Well, honey, the usual for everyone?"

Mr. Big let out a belly laugh that lifted his end of the table and shook everyone's ice waters.

"Why, Claire," he said. "You must be Claire-voyant."

This got everyone else to laughing, except for me. Then I started laughing, because that's what you do when your boss laughs at a business luncheon.

Claire, apparently satisfied with that answer, pushed through the same door and disappeared into the kitchen. I had no idea how she could possibly remember everyone's orders from last year, but she certainly couldn't have known what I wanted, since I didn't even know. I was thinking maybe a French dip sandwich or a bowl of beef stew. So I picked up one of the menus to see what they offered.

The entire menu was blank except for a single line of print along with a photo.

The print read: Uncle Beefy's All-Beef Dinner.

That was the choice. No sandwiches, no soups, no mashed potatoes, no fries.

Just Uncle Beefy's All-Beef Dinner.

No wonder everyone was in hysterics.

Beneath this one choice was either an old, yellowed photo of meat, or a brand-new photo of old, yellowed meat. The meat was cut in thick slices stacked on top of each other in ever decreasing sizes, the largest chunk at the base, the smallest morsel at the summit, so that the entire entrée took on the appearance of a Mayan temple.

Pictured alongside this ancient wonder was a bowl of thick gravy. I was so busy wondering how to pour it over my own Mayan temple so it wouldn't spill over the plate, that I almost jumped when a presence made itself known behind me. A very massive presence in the form of Mr. Big, who was sporting a quadruple-X polo shirt and a super-wide pair of shorts that I doubt one would find in any FBI-issued clothing catalog.

"Glad you could join us here at Uncle Beefy's All-Beef Dinners," he said with a slap of a big beefy hand on my back.

"Glad to be here," I said.

"I try to fly the boys out here once a year. It costs a pretty penny, but it's worth it. And your boss back East—Mr. Gargantuan—kindly suggested I invite you out to eat every now and then. So here you are."

"Thank you."

"Enjoy the ride in the cockpit?"

"Yes. It was—uh—eye opening."

"How about flying the loop?"

"It was memorable."

"Pilot mention Uncle Beefy's All-Beef Dinners at all?"

"Only that it was our destination."

"Uh-huh. He say anything good about it?"

"Not that I can remember."

"Anything bad?"

"No, nothing bad."

"Good. Because if you ever hear anyone—and I mean anyone—bad mouth Uncle Beefy's All-Beef Dinners, you let me know."

"You can count on me."

He slapped my back again. "Good man," he said. "They call you Ten Pins, right?"

"Uh, sure."

"You like bowling, I take it."

"That's why they call me Ten Pins," I said.

"Ha ha. I'll let you in on a secret. They're planning on attaching a bowling alley to this joint. What a draw that would be, eh? Roll the ball down the lane a few times, then cap the night by coming in here for an Uncle Beefy's All-Beef Dinner."

"That would really be something," I said.

"I'm thinking, if everything works out with this remodel, I can get you a regular gig out here showing off your fancy bowling skills. I mean, you had to be named Ten Pins for a reason, right? The crowd'll eat it up. Watching you hit the pins by standing on your hands and bowling with your feet. That's the kind of fancy stuff you do, right?"

"You nailed it, Mr. Big."

"And you'll be safe here. Whoever's hunting you down back East will never think of looking for you in frigging Wyoming."

Mr. Big nudged me with his elbow and added. "This gig will be right up your *alley*, if you get what I mean."

"Right up my alley. That's good, Mr. Big."

"I mean, it'll be a temporary thing until the heat dies down for you."

"Of course," I said.

"And maybe, to provide a little variety, I can work things out so you can bump off a handful of my enemies on a regular basis."

I swallowed hard. "Handful of enemies. Regular basis. That'd be great, Mr. Big."

"Anyway," he said, with a final whack that almost sent my face into the sticky table, "I better get back. Uncle Beefy's All-Beef Dinners ought to be out real soon."

I looked outside the grease-smeared front window, wondering what other happy news would be coming my way. That's when a familiar car pulled into the parking lot and an equally familiar figure climbed out in wrinkled slacks and layers of sweatshirts.

I held my hand to the side of my face like a horse blinder and tried to look invisible. That made Eldon invisible too. I sensed the front door opening. I sensed footsteps approaching along the gravy-stained carpet. I sensed someone coming to a halt behind me, a little to my right.

I sensed a voice whining, "That's it. Beat up on old Eldon."

I peeked across the table. Mr. Big was looking this way. Not at me but just beyond me, a little to my right.

Eldon said, "I drive up here all the time, and I just asked you once. I said let's go up North to my favorite restaurant. I'll buy and I'll drive. But, nooo, you said. It'll be like the Chinese water torture, you said. And now I come in and happen to see you with all your friends."

Seeing no point in hiding anymore, I dropped my hand to my lap. "Hey, Eldon," I said in a tone somewhere between a half-hearted greeting and a desperate plea for him to get the hell away from me.

Then Mr. Big chimed in. "So that's your name? Eldon?"

"Yaaah," Eldon said, with his hands in his wrinkled pockets. "Eldon

Sykes."

Great, I thought. Give them your full name.

"So, Eldon Sykes, did I hear you right? That you like driving all the way out here to Uncle Beefy's All-Beef Dinners?"

"Yaaah, I love it here."

"And you drive out here all the time?"

"Yaaah, at least ten, fifteen times a year."

"Eldon Sykes, you have my full admiration. I thought I was doing good making it out here once a year."

"Yaaah, thanks."

Mr. Big shouted back toward the kitchen, "Yo, Claire! Get your beautiful body out here front and center!"

The kitchen door opened and Claire magically appeared. "What's up, honey?"

"Dish up another plate of Uncle Beefy's All-Beef Dinner for our guest here."

"You got it," she said, and back into the kitchen she went.

Mr. Big hit the table with his fist. "Stu, where are your goddamn manners? Slide over and give Eldon some room. And grab him a chair."

Stu did as he was told, and Eldon sat down between Stu and me.

Mr. Big said, "Eldon, I take it you work with Ten Pins here?"

"Ten Pins?" Eldon said. "Oh, right. Ten Pins. Yes, I get you. Yaaah, I've worked with him for over two years now."

"And he told you it's too far to drive out here to Uncle Beefy's All-Beef Dinners?"

"Yaaah, and I don't know why. It's not that far at tall."

Not only was I not liking where this conversation was headed, but there he went again with the "at tall."

Mr. Big let out another belly laugh, nearly upsetting the ice waters again. "Not that far? Are you nuts? It's halfway across the country. Just like it must be for the two of you working back East for Mr. Gargantuan. I mean before Ten Pins here got into a scrape."

Eldon looked confused. "Come on," he said. "We don't work back East. We work in Denver. That's why it's not that far."

Mr. Big held up his thick hand. "The distance ain't the point. No matter how far it is to Uncle Beefy's All-Beef Dinners, you never bitch about it. If Uncle Beefy's All-Beef Dinners was up on the Moon, you better ride the damn rocket ship up there and not piss and moan about how long it takes. Know what I mean?"

"Yaaah," Eldon said. "But I wasn't pissing and moaning. Jimmy here was."

Uh-oh, I thought to myself. Here it comes.

"*Jimmy?*" Mr. Big said. "Don't you mean Donny? Donny (Ten Pins) Grimes?"

"Naaah, I don't. Come on, you guys. Let's quit the act. We all work at the Denver Field Office. I haven't met any of you, but it's a big place."

"Field office?" Mr. Big said. "What the hell is a field office?"

Throat Slitter, to Mr. Big's right, supplied his employer, as well as everyone else in the room, with the necessary information. "It's where the Feds work. They got offices scattered like zits all over the country."

Eldon sank deeper into his chair and slapped his forehead with the flat of his hand. "Boy, did I screw up."

His eyes gazed upward at the beef-stained tiles in the ceiling. "Oh, God! Did I ever screw up big time."

"Something eating at you, Eldon?" Mr. Big said.

As Eldon sank even lower, his keys dropped out of his pocket, barely making a sound on the gravy-stained carpet. "When I came in here and saw my good friend Jimmy Corliss sitting with all of you, I assumed he quit his undercover assignment in Seattle. Maybe because of the pressure of being around so many lowlife thugs, crooks, and hoodlums. And I naturally concluded he hooked up with some of his old colleagues in the bureau and came up here to Uncle Beefy's All-Beef Dinners. I never stopped to think you guys could be the very same lowlife thugs, crooks, and hoodlums. And when you mentioned his nickname—Ten Pins—I just thought you were kidding around. But you weren't. In other words, old Eldon Sykes has screwed up bad. And I mean baaaaaad."

I glanced around the table at the looks Eldon and I were getting, and two words quickly came to mind. "Oh" and "shit."

Mr. Big's eyes were closed, but they were closed in my direction. "A spy," he said mournfully. "A spy for the Feds. A spy for the Feds who turns up his nose at Uncle Beefy's All-Beef Dinners. That's not a good combination, Ten Pins."

I happened to agree.

I launched myself out of my chair, scooped the keys up off the floor, whispered thanks to Eldon, and flew out of the restaurant. I should've left a tip but didn't. I'm sure Claire deserved it.

Eldon's car was close, thank goodness, and one press of his key fob opened the driver-side door. That's when I asked myself: should I or should I not extricate Eldon from this mess? Eldon Sykes, the nuisance who said yaaah all the time and naaah all the time and who was about to get me killed.

Sure, I should. He was a friend, however you define it.

And deep down, beneath all those sweatshirts, he was a brother FBI agent.

I ran toward the entrance, with the aim of rescuing him, when Eldon came busting out, flailing his arms like a panicked bird, and shouting, "They've got guns!"

I raced back to the car, flung open the driver-side door, and jumped inside. Eldon was at the passenger door. I unlocked it, shut mine, and turned the key in the ignition. He opened his door and whined, "It's my car. I want to drive."

A gunshot sounded, and the door's window shattered to bits, leaving an empty frame. "Look what they did!" he cried.

"Get in!"

He threw himself inside and slammed the door, which slammed so much easier without a window. More shots went off, and there went the right side-view mirror.

But a look in the rearview told me all I needed to know. The entire party was outside now, armed to the teeth. Teeth which would soon be clogged with the shreds from Uncle Beefy's All-Beef Dinners. There was just the little matter of Eldon and Ten Pins to take care of.

They kept firing, and I stepped on it. Sped off toward the parking lot exit. Eldon was sitting straight up. "My car!" he shouted. "They're wrecking my car!"

"Get down, Eldon! Pretend you're sitting in your office chair!"

He understood, and slumped down to safety.

It wasn't an exit, but a chained-up service entrance. I slammed on the brake and threw the car in reverse. And suddenly, at the blown-out window next to Eldon, there appeared the very face of evil—Melvin Meadowbrook, living up to his nickname with a butcher knife, likely from the restaurant kitchen.

Rushing alongside the car, he thrust the knife through the missing window and began swinging it around. Eldon sank down further to avoid it. Just then a bullet came through the rear window and went through the part of the seat where Eldon's head was a second ago.

Lucky break.

But not as lucky as when the bullet ricocheted off the butcher knife, made a beeline right out the empty window, and flew straight into Throat Slitter's right eye.

Letting go the knife, Melvin fell away from the car, got struck by a volley of wild shots by his compatriots, and crashed to the pavement, where the emancipated knife would've clanged harmlessly had Melvin's throat not been there to intercept the blade.

I stopped the car again, shifted it back into forward, turned slightly, and ran him over. First with the front wheels, then with the back, just in case the shattered eyeball and the two dozen bullet wounds and the deep gash in his throat were all superficial.

Eldon, now crumpled up under the dashboard, hollered out, as if from a cellar, "I want to drive! It's my car!"

"Not on your life, Eldon."

I tightened my grip on the steering wheel and did a one-eighty. I memorized the scene in front of me: seven men, three in the front, each on a knee, and four standing behind them, all shooting at the car like a firing squad. Ducking my head, I floored the car in their direction. The blasts got louder, the windshield cracked and shattered, and Eldon cried out, "That windshield was mine!"

After a pretty impressive meeting of grill and tissue, the firing ceased.

Then, to my right, I saw Mr. Big himself in the distance, holding something rectangular in his thick fingers. He was hard to miss. But then I didn't try to miss as I plowed right into him at eighty miles an hour. The thing he'd been holding was a full-sized menu to Uncle Beefy's All-Beef Dinners.

I'd recognized it right off. That's why I hit him.

Miraculously, he went down for good on the first try.

"What did you just hit with my car?" Eldon whined from under the dash.

Off to the side, I glimpsed the pilot reaching inside his flight jacket. Now, it could very well have been for a passenger manifest whose entries he could now easily check off, but I thought it best to mow him down anyway.

After that, because I hated driving long distances, I let Eldon take us home.

By the time we got back to the Denver field office, word had got around. There was much clapping and hooting. Someone shouted, "Nice job, Ten Pins! There were ten of them, and you got them all!"

In my supervisor's office, my boss said to Eldon, "That must have been some sight outside the restaurant. So how do you think our man Jimmy here did?"

Eldon sank down in his chair until his head was positioned where his butt once was. "Yaaah, he did okaaay. But my car pretty much drove itself."

NAPPER

Mistah Pete

Here's where the story starts.

Sorry if that seems obvious, but I've read these stories where stuff happens you think is important and then it turns out it's just character stuff or preamble or something and you've invested all this time only to find out it's got nothing to do with the story.

Not here.

Here's where the story starts, right here.

Taking out the trash.

I'm taking my bag to the can in the alley behind the duplex the clinic rents for me, and I guess I hear the sirens and alarms, but I don't really think about what they mean, and then there's another person in the alley, a man, running.

Running into me.

He's looking over his shoulder at someone behind him and I'm moving too slow to get out of his way, so we hit the ground, cans rattling and banging all around us. He carries a garbage bag, like mine, and between that and the running and the sirens, what I think is, hey, he's stealing someone's garbage, which doesn't make any sense, but it's like that sometimes.

I see his face, there on the pavement in front of me, looking up as if he's been buried in cement up to his chin, only it can't really be his face, all green and scaly and he's a crocodile, or maybe an alligator, can anyone tell those two apart? I can't.

But wait, no, I look again, and it's a mask. Isn't it? Plastic, like a kid wears for Halloween. Yeah, it must be a mask. Funny, I coulda sworn it was his head, just for a second.

He scrambles to his feet real easy and quick, just like I can't, and he snatches up the mask and puts it onto his face, only I don't see the face he puts it on, nothing is there at all, why does he need a mask if he already doesn't have a face?

As he runs away, I watch as the trails of light stream behind him, pretty. Hypnotic. I'm still seeing them after he's gone.

You know what narcolepsy is, right? The sleeping sickness? You can't control when or where you fall asleep.

I'm not a doctor, but I know a few things about this subject. Scientists think it's an autoimmune thing. The hypothalamus releases hypocretin, which stimulates adrenaline, the stuff that keeps you going during moments of stress. It's good to have when you need it.

But in narcos, the body's natural defenses attack those cells, wipe them out, and so the body goes into what they call catalepsis.

Sleep, more or less.

When it's happening, the narco may be aware of it, but often the people around him can't even tell that he's out of it. It's pretty freaky.

Or so I'm told. I've never been on that side.

But, yeah, as you might've gathered, I've got a dose of the stuff. Narcolepsy.

Pretty extreme, from what my doctors say. In fact, I'm kind of a special case. Gonna wind up in medical books, one day. Might even get a disorder named after me. Not sure how I feel about that.

There are more sounds, voices, and I see more runners, men in uniforms, it's hard for me to make them out clearly, and I hear them talking, talking to me, voices fast and loud and urgent, asking if I saw the guy, where did he go, could I identify him, and I'd like to answer but my head drops down onto what feels like the world's puffiest garbage bag, and I'm asleep.

Treatment for narcolepsy.

I bet you can guess. I mean, what do you take to keep awake?

Right. Pep pills. Study buddies. Caffeine. Nicotine. Over-the-counter speed; or under-the-counter, if you know how to get it. Even those energy drinks made from Amazonian berries and ginseng root and baboon glands.

You know. Stimulants.

Might work for you. For me? They've got a little something extra.

Injections. I do it myself, gets delivered to my house weekly. I keep it in the fridge. Enough to wake up a statue, one of my doctors likes to say. Pop an elephant's eyes out, another says. Gotta take it twice a day is all my nurse says about it.

It works, mostly. But I still get my spells now and again. Only, there's wicked hallucinations to go with them.

I wake, blinking and refreshed, in a police interrogation room. Not that I've ever been in one before, but cop shows play a lot on the TVs in doctors' waiting rooms. That and cable news. I don't watch the news. Makes me sleepy.

"Nice nap?"

There's a woman across the table from me. She wears a dark jacket and white shirt buttoned up to her chin, no tie. Her face seems pleasant, radiating an electric blue, eyes painted like a Hindu deity.

"Sorry," I tell her. "I have a condition."

Yeah, she says, she figured that out, and she holds up a bracelet. It's mine, Medic-Alert, tells people things like how I have a condition.

Her face is normal now, or I assume it is. Not blue. She doesn't have the thick black lines around her eyes anymore, either, which is kind of a shame, it was pretty. She looks a little impatient. But I recognize some sympathy in there. I know from sympathetic looks.

"Your doctor's on his way," she says. I wonder which one.

She tosses the bracelet across the table at me and I get my hand up just in time for it to hit me across the chin.

"Oops," she mutters, then, "What did you see in the alley?"

"What alley?"

"The one behind your house," she continues, and I detect a tightening around her eyes. I'm familiar with looks of annoyance, too. "Where we picked you up."

"Uh-oh," I say. "Did I do something wrong?"

She breathes through her nose. "You don't remember?"

"Remember what?"

Thing about the whole narco deal, people underestimate you. Assume everything that happens is related to it, and that you're kind of an invalid who needs help all the time. I resent that, even if it might be true.

Which I guess is why the police feel the need to drive me home, even though one or another of my doctors was right there and, if not willing, at least already paid to do it.

"The perpetrator will think you saw his face," the lady police who wasn't an Indian goddess had told me. "And he's violent."

"He is?"

"Look, I doubt he knows where you live, but since it happened right behind your place, can't hurt to have some protection."

"Okay."

She told me, "We'll be looking out for you." She said, "Don't worry." She said, "No reason for you to lose any slee ... uh, break a sweat over this."

People do that a lot around me, try not to say things they think will offend me. I'm never bothered, but I don't tell them.

I wave at the cop car stationed at my curb as I enter my house, but the officer's busy on his phone and doesn't see me. I don't know how protected I feel.

That hypothalamus business I was talking about? Keeps your motor running in times of stress? Turns out, joy is a stressor, too. That's when it tends to hit me. Times of joy.

Like now. A girl I've been asking out for a while just said okay. That's why I'd been cleaning the house. We were going to meet for coffee, and if there was a chance it might end up at my place, well, you only get one first impression, right?

So when I get inside, I pick up the broom I'd pulled out before I emptied the trash, and I went at the kitchen floor.

I see the answering machine on the counter blink at me.

Landlines are easy to trace. That's why the doctors insist on me having one. If I pass out while dialing 9-1-1, the ambulance can find me.

And since I have that, I don't have a cell. And since I don't have a cell, I do have an answering machine. Because I'm sometimes slow getting to the phone. But no one ever leaves me a message anyway.

Until now.

I click the blinking button and sweep.

beep

"Hey, where are you? I'm at the coffee shop, you gonna show or what? You've been bugging me for weeks, and now you stand me up? Call me."

beep

I keep sweeping. There's more.

"I'm leaving. I'll stop by your place on the way and see if you're there. If you're asleep, I'm kicking your ass."

beep

I bend and scoop the dirt into the pan. I have to move it a few times to get it all, and still there's that little trace line of dust, so frustrating.

"Hello-o? I'm knocking on your door. Right now! You are such an ass.

Y'know, I think this sleep thing is just an excuse for you being rude. Later."

beep

Last one. That hurt.

I open the trashcan, then realize I never got a new bag into it. I reach under the sink for the box, and that's when the phone rings.

I manage to get to it before it stops, and I say, Hello?

The voice on the other end isn't hers.

It says, "I have her."

I step out the back door, the phone conversation still playing in my head.

Where's my stuff?

There's a few bags spilled around the pavement, dented cans overturned from when I fell.

How would I know? I don't have it.

I pick up a bag, look into it. Trash.

You didn't give it to the cops, did you?

I tilt a can upright, drop the bag into it.

Give what to the cops?

I also tip up the can across the alley, old Mrs. Lerma's. She'd never be able to lift it herself, dear thing.

Do you mean to tell me no one found it?

There's another bag over there, I gather it up and toss it into the can. I smell cat litter. I don't open that one.

I still don't know what you're talking about.

Another bag. This one trapped under a scrubby bush growing through the wooden fence. The vertical panels have warped around the stem over time, and I watch for a bit. I like how it looks.

The trash bags. I got yours, you got mine.

I squat, pull the bag gently free of the prickly branches.

You have my trash?

A thorn grabs my finger. Ouch. I put it to my mouth, then remember I'm digging through trash, so I spit.

Well, the bag I have is full of old cantaloupe rinds and coffee filters. Damn, you drink a lot of coffee. You got stock in Folger's?

I lift the bag, ease it open.

And your old prescriptions, with your phone number on it. You should invest in a shredder, they're really invaluable.

I see cash, stacks of bills, hundreds of them with presidential faces I don't entirely recognize, and they start to dance and spin like 1776 hoedown and I can feel it coming on—

Oh, and keep it together, Snoozy!

I close my eyes, close the bag, breathe deep.

You don't show, you can run what's left of your gal pal through your Mr. Coffee. You get me?

I toss an end of the bag over my shoulder and start down the alley. It's the long way to the bus stop, but I figure if I go out the front the cop might look up from his social media long enough to offer me a ride, and the voice on the line had been quite specific about police involvement.

The bus driver pokes me when we get to the stop. I'd shown him my bracelet and explained my issue when I got on, and he was helpful enough to keep an eye out for me. Not so helpful as to be gentle about it, but I can only ask for so much.

I step out at a corner of the park. There are walking paths, and ever since I was a kid I was told you shouldn't be there after dark. Maybe that's just the sort of rumor they spread to keep kids from getting lost, but all the same, I'm glad it's still daytime.

There, on the far side of the empty swing-sets and jungle gym, I see a man with a reptile face. I breathe again and walk toward it. I hope it's a mask.

He walks away from me for a bit, deeper into the trees. I should probably turn and run, but I don't.

A clearing, a picnic table. He's sitting on it when I get there.

"You came on the bus? You don't got a car?"

"For some reason, they won't give me a license," I tell him, and I look around us. "Pretty isolated," I comment.

He tilts his dinosaur nose at my shoulder, the bag still over it. "That my stuff?"

"No one around to see or hear us, huh?"

"My stuff?" He puts out a hand, and I swing him the bag. He catches it and looks inside. He tilts his green head back up and I'd swear his beady eyes blink sideways, just like the big lizards you see on nature documentaries. "Guess you know I have to kill you now?"

"Guess so," I nod. "Would it help if I told you I could never see your face? Even without the mask?" I resist asking if it's really a mask.

"Oh, yeah," he says. "They got you on some heavy drugs, I saw in your trash. You must have some kinda crazy going on, right?"

Some kind, I agreed.

We wait a thoughtful moment, him sitting, me standing, then he says, "No, I still gotta kill you."

"What about her," I ask.

"Her?"

"You said something about my friend?"

"Oh, right. No, I never saw her." He looks again into the bag. "I was in your house waiting for you to come back. I heard her messages when she called."

"You were in my house? Why didn't you get the bag then?"

"Now, if I'd known you were irresponsible enough to leave it in the alley, I would have, wouldn't I?" I can hear the exasperation in his tone. Even in a mask, I read this stuff pretty well. But I get a lot of it.

We pass another moment, then I say, "So, the killing?"

"Right," he says, and hops down off the table. "I must say, you're handling this real well. I'm impressed."

"Oh," I tell him, "that's because I know what's in the bottom of that bag."

He stops, turns his long snout down into the bag, and I bring the syringe out and jab it into the exposed flesh below his ear and push the plunger so everything in it goes into him. I know he's not really a gator because there's no way this needle would've gotten through that hide, right? I mean, they make shoes and luggage out of it.

Still, the eyes bug out and the big mouth drops open as a human hand goes to the spot where I injected him, and he makes some sounds, and then he falls. His body jumps and shakes a few times, real jerky, then he stiffens up for a minute or two, I think, and then he's still, but stuck in that stiff position.

Frothy liquid dribbles out of the mouth and onto the grass. He doesn't get back up.

I hate going off my meds. There'll be no controlling it for a while, I guess. So annoying.

But you don't want to hear my troubles.

I walk back to the bus stop.

Detective Shiva comes to my house a few more times and asks me questions, and I don't really have anything to tell her, and she doesn't really think I do. Like I say, people tend to underestimate you when you got something like this, so before long, she stops coming back.

I'm a little disappointed about that girl, the one I had set up for a date. She's still not talking to me. But that's okay. I can find another girl. Eventually.

I lie down once I'm alone. The bed isn't really lumpy, it just feels sort of like it, now that there's all that money under my mattress. I remember some cartoon about a goofy millionaire who kept all his money under his mattress. He said he wouldn't put it in the banks, because people rob those places. And he was right, they do.

I close my eyes, but hey, what do you know?

I can't get to sleep.

Anyway, here's where the story ends.

A BRUSH WITH DEATH

Stephen J. Levinson

CHAPTER 1: A BRUSH WITH DEATH

The blaring ring jarred Jake Rhine from his daydream. Instead of the dank basement office surrounding him, he liked to imagine himself in a sleek, glass-enclosed escalator. He had almost reached his favorite part, the top, when the disturbance occurred. Damn! He contemplated tearing the phone from its socket and hurling it across the room. Then an even better idea occurred to him—answering it.

"Rhine."

"Morning, Jake. It's Manny." It was his partner's voice alright, only Manny didn't seem like himself. Something told Jake that he was anxious, distressed. Jake asked if he was OK.

"No, Jake," Manny answered. "I just told you, I'm anxious and distressed. It's this headache. I'm probably going to run down to the pharmacy to pick up some aspirin. But maybe I'll just get some rest instead. This headache is killing me."

Who would try to kill Manny? A jealous lover? An overeager bookie? Perhaps a mad scientist, bent on revenge for Manny's tireless work at the Academy? It didn't fit. Manny had no lover, he wasn't a betting man and he certainly had never set foot in any academy. Sure, everyone had enemies and Manny was no exception, but killing a man ... that was a different story. What kind of person would want Manny dead? Jake wondered aloud.

"What the hell are you talking about?" Manny inquired. "Anyway, I gotta go. I'm just calling to say I won't be in this afternoon."

"Fine," Jake responded. "And why don't you take the rest of the day off as well. Get some rest."

"Goodbye, Jake."

Jake put down the phone. Something was not right, something was nagging at him. He could still hear his partner's voice, softly in his head: "... anxious and distressed," "... I gotta go ..." "Jake, hang up the phone. Jake, will you please hang up the phone!"

Jake replaced the handset onto that other part of the phone, I think it's called the base, and walked towards the door, towards trouble. Then he walked out the door, away from trouble. (The door was a lot of trouble). He could deal with the rest of his cases later. Besides, he'd accomplished enough for one week. He had already solved the Case of the Socialite's Missing Spectacles (they were on her face) and the Mystery of the Kidnapped Great Dane (also, on her face) and he had cracked the Case of the Faberge Egg wide open, regrettably destroying the egg in the process. He had yet to locate the jewel-encrusted medallion missing from the governor's mansion, but he felt that a solution was just around the corner.

However none of his recent successes gave him comfort when he contemplated his partner's peril. What the hell was up with him? In all the years they had worked together Manny had never, ever missed a day of work, except a couple of times a year when he was ill.

Jake walked into the nearby parking garage and approached his car, a well-worn '74 Chevy Speedbump. He opened the door, pushed aside a jewel-encrusted medallion that was covering the driver's seat and sat down. That car had lasted longer than two marriages, Jake thought, although not his own. And unlike a woman, a car would never betray you, never break down, never go flat with age, never guzzle up his money. He loved that car. But sometimes he still missed Jill, missed her for the kinds of things that a car could never provide—her gleaming skin and her plush interior, the way she stared at him with her big, headlight eyes and the way she hummed and vibrated when he turned her on. He cleared his thoughts and swerved quickly to miss an oncoming tree. Today wasn't about himself and it certainly wasn't about Jill, it was about saving his partner. That is, unless he was already too late.

CHAPTER 2: ANOTHER BRUSH WITH DEATH

The police had already reached the pharmacy by the time Jake Rhine arrived on the scene. Officer John Tucker was casing out the toiletry section while Fitzpatrick, a basket full of evidence in hand, was interrogating a young woman at the checkout counter.

"Do you accept Diners' Club?" Fitzpatrick grilled her.

"Leave the poor lady alone." Jake cut in. "She can't help you. She doesn't know a thing."

Fitzpatrick apologized to the offended woman, then turned to Jake. "Well, if it isn't Jake Rhine. What brings you back to our lousy precinct?"

"Who wants to know?" asked Jake warily. He'd had enough of the police for one lifetime; seeing them took him back to his own days as a cop. Like so many other things in Jake's life, that job ended badly. After losing one too many men for the commissioner's taste, he was transferred out of Community Relations and given a mindless desk job and a giant one-way ticket to No Futureville. But paperwork just wasn't Jake's style. When he misspelled a word in his resignation letter, he was booted off the force.

"Well, no one actually. Just making conversation," explained Fitzpatrick.

"Why don't you and your 'girlfriend' Tucker stay out of my way," sneered Jake. "Shouldn't you be cleaning up the city?"

"We're off duty. Anyway, nice to see you again."

After missing a beat, Jake shot back. "I hate you. You are stupid and ... you are also ugly."

Defeated, Fitzpatrick gathered his 'girlfriend' Tucker and slouched out of the store. Now that the cops were out of his hair, Jake had some questions of his own for the checkout girl.

"I'm looking for a guy, goes by the name of Manual. About seven feet tall, shoulder-length blond hair, smells terrific, probably wearing an 'I'm with stupid' T-shirt, with an arrow pointing upwards, towards the heavens. He would have been belting out the lyrics to 'New York, New York' in an annoying falsetto, possibly to the tune of 'Sweet Home Alabama.' Oh, yeah, and he has an odd number of arms."

"One or three?"

"That's right. Have you seen him?"

"I don't remember seeing anyone like that, but I can't be certain. We get a lot of customers on Wednesdays," the checkout girl pondered. "But I did see another guy. Short, stocky, balding. I remember him specifically because he was wearing pants. We don't get too many of those types around here."

"That's him, sweetie! Any idea where he was heading?"

"Yeah. He kept shouting, 'I'm going to the diner, I'm going to the diner, I'm going to the diner' just over and over again. When he left he started walking east down Jefferson—towards the beauty salon ... or maybe the diner."

"You're the best, toots." Jake said as he placed a quarter in his hand. Then he waved his clenched fist near the salesperson's ear. He slowly opened his hand and, as if by magic, it still contained the quarter! "You really ought to clean those things more often. Never know what you're going to find in there," he suggested as he pocketed the coin and hurried out the door.

CHAPTER 3: A BRUSH WITH DEATH

The restaurant on the corner of Jefferson and Third was the kind of dive where all the filth in town seemed to congregate for a warm cup of jo served up with a heaping portion of no-questions-asked. There probably wasn't an honest buck being exchanged in the whole joint. The cholesterol content of the grill food was through the goddamn roof.

Jake sat down at the counter, just in time to nip a fight in the bud.

"First I order a small burrito and you give me a soft taco!" shouted the stout, burly man in the next seat. "Then I ask for mild salsa, and you give me medium! Someone is going to die."

"Settle down mister." Jake interrupted, in a voice that said 'I'm gonna punch you in the mouth.'

"You're gonna punch me in the mouth?" laughed the troublemaker. "I'd love to see you try."

Jake said 'I'm gonna punch you in the mouth' again—this time, in sign language.

"Ah, Hell," whimpered the bruised man, "you punched me in the mouth." It was true; Jake had punched him in the mouth.

"That's right. Now you'll eat your taco and you'll like it, and you'll apologize to this nice lady for having to look at your ugly mug." Jake turned away in disgust.

"Thanks," said the waitress. "What'll you have? It's on the house."

"I'll have an egg—hard boiled, like my inner monologue. And how about a cup of coffee to keep it company, gorgeous."

"I've got a name and it ain't 'gorgeous.' It's O'Reily. Babydoll O'Reily. And what's a respectable guy like you doing in this filthy stink-pit?"

"I'm not as respectable as all that, Babydoll. And I'm looking for a few answers. Think I might find them around here." Jake drew a rough sketch of his partner on a napkin and showed it to the waitress. "You recognize him?"

"Sure thing. That's Charlie Brown. He heads up the Peanuts gang. You'll find him at the newsstand every Sunday."

Now she was just toying with him. Sure, she was a looker, but underneath that pretty face was a horrifying skeleton. Jake didn't like skeletons, and he certainly didn't like being insulted by one.

"Here's my number," said Jake, removing his business card from the woman's ear, "give me a call if you think of anything useful."

Jake had hit another dead end. This path was turning up nothing. Nothing except ... free eggs! That was pretty cool, but it wasn't going to save his partner's life. Jake knew what his next move would have to be, and it wasn't going to be pleasant. It was time to pay a visit to Nancy Rinaldi.

CHAPTER 4: A BRUSH FULL OF DEATH

Nancy was once married to Manny, a marriage that had the life expectancy of a hot pizza in Dom DeLuise's kitchen. That is to say, anywhere from one to three days, depending on the appetites of Mr. DeLuise's houseguests. On the way home from their honeymoon, Nancy started hitting the bottle hard. After that, the honeymoon was over. A week later, Nancy pawned her wedding ring for a day at the races. She never even made it to the finish line. By then it was clear that the marriage was history. Two years after the divorce Nancy was living in a plastic doghouse on the wrong side of the tracks—the inside—and had gone more than a little mad. Day and night she was tormented by ghosts, and there wasn't a power pellet for miles around. She still kept tabs on Manny, Jake suspected, and she just might be able to answer a few of his questions ... if she was sober enough to talk.

Jake got out of his Chevy and walked up to Nancy's hovel. She was on the porch reading Hemingway's treatise on amputation, A Farewell to Arms, and sipping homemade bourbon through a straw.

"Well, if it ain't Jake the Jackass!" howled Nancy.

"It's been a long time, Nancy. I've had my name legally changed since then. These days I go by Jake Rhine."

"Hasn't been long enough," said Nancy, as she shot him one of her go thither looks.

"I'd love to stay here and chat all day, Nancy, but I wouldn't enjoy it very much. I'm afraid I'm here about Manny."

At the mention of her former husband's name, Nancy suddenly seemed to sober up. She took a long, deep breath. As she set her glass onto the cold, hard pavement, a single tear trickled down her cheek and fell to her soft white breast.

"Who's Nanny?" she asked.

"No. Not Nanny. Manny. Your ex-husband. My partner. You know ... Manny."

"Oh, Manny! How's the old perv' doing these days?"

"The old perv' might be dead or dying. That's why I'm here." Jake explained. "Try to think, Nancy. Do you know anyone who would want to see him dead?"

"Want to kill him? Well for one I'd like to ... wait a second, what are you going to do to this killer?"

"I'll see he gets what's coming to him. And it ain't gonna to be no birthday cake."

"No cake, eh?" Nancy seemed distraught. "Nope. I can't help you. I got nothin'. Nice to see you again though, Jackass."

"Take care of yourself Nancy." Jake said as he turned to go.

"Wait a second." Nancy called back to him. "Now that I think about it, there was someone who wanted Manny dead. Down at the dock. A sailor, or a dock worker or a pirate or something."

The news made Jake nervous. The dock was on the exact opposite end of town; it couldn't have been farther from Nancy's place. In heavy traffic, the trip could take hours.

"Thanks, Nancy."

"Go. Hurry."

CHAPTER 5: A BRUSH WITH DEATH

The Southside Docks were like a giant aquarium of murder, graft, corruption and fish. Jake arrived late in the afternoon, in no mood for trouble. But trouble was in the mood for Jake, whatever that means.

Jake needed information fast, so he headed straight to Little Mort's. Mort had done it all, and knew it all, and he knew it, too. Name a dirty job and Mort had worked it: racketeer, raconteur, racquetball coach, rocket scientist, rock 'n' roller, he even did a brief stint as a Robocop. A fly didn't croak in his city without Mort knowing about it, and he knew about some other stuff, too. There was just one problem with Little Mort: people who got involved with him had a nasty little habit of dying. Actually, it wasn't much of a habit, since they each only did it once, but still ... dying!

These days Mort was a restaurateur; he owned a trendy theme restaurant near the docks. The theme was drug front. Jake walked in through the kitchen door. Mort was leaning against the meat locker, a cigarette dangling from his rubbery lips.

"Employees only," Mort coughed. "Do you have a reservation?"

"Here's my reservation." Jake raised his hand in the air. A certain finger, I think you know the one I'm talking about, was extended.

Little Mort got straight to the point. "Give me one reason why I shouldn't kill you on the spot," he said.

"Here's one," said Jake as he struck Mort in the face with the butt of his handgun.

By then, Mort had begun to slap Jake in the butt with the face of his hand.

Next, Jake butted his face against Mort's gun hand.

Mort turned to face Jake, but handed him his gun.

"Thanks," said Jake. He pointed the gun at his adversary. "Now, tell me where my partner is."

"How should I know! Who are you?" asked Little Mort.

"I'm the guy who's holding a gun at your face." Jake snapped, "Now where is he?"

"I don't know. Where was the last place you saw him?"

"At his place. I stopped by for a drink last night."

"Well, maybe he's still there. Try looking there, I guess."

Jake leapt into his Chevy and tore down the interstate, back towards Manny's place, cutting and winding his way through the early evening traffic. After an exciting adventure at a rest stop and another at the Big Boy, he arrived.

Jake sped into Manny's driveway. He pounded on his brakes in time to avoid ramming into his partner's vehicle. What was it doing there? Had Manny's killers returned it? Was it a trap? Jake Rhine's head burned with questions.

Jake exited his car and looked up through the hazy night. From Manny's bedroom, he noticed a small, flickering glow. Slowly the agonizing truth crept over him, crept over him like a dark, twisting vine—strangling and suffocating. Manny hadn't returned home.

He had never left.

PHILOSOPHY 101

Martin Hill Ortiz

Pitiable. Pathetic. Dimwit. Dumb jock. Bimbo wannabe. Maybe owns a brain cell. Wouldn't know where to rent one. With the beginning of each new class, Dr. Tivoli tilted his head down and looked over his half-shell glasses, glaring at his students, taking a mental attendance as he happily sorted them into types. He recalled Socrates's warning regarding the decline and delinquency of youth. These students were the end result of 2,400 years of downward spiral. This was truly the Golden Age of Dullness.

He faked a smile that would fool no one and greeted the menagerie, "Welcome to Philosophy 101, An Appreciation of Thought. My name is Dr. Tivoli. Let me write that down." As he spelled his name on the dry erase board, a host of pens began to scurry into action as though it were new information and not in the course directory or on the syllabus. "I realize you are not destined to become philosophers but the key word here is appreciation. Let me write that down."

He wiped his name from the board and began to write "appreciation" when a hand shot up. His heart skipped: *perhaps a thinking mind.* "Yes?"

"I hadn't finished writing your name," the student said. He was bone-skinny, had some sort of helmet-like hairdo that went extinct in the 80s. His eyes were cow-dumb. Maybe the class could have some fun tipping the kid over after the lecture. Tivoli searched his mental notes for the name he had his assigned this beast. *Dimwit.*

"Did you just call me a dimwit?" the student asked.

Tivoli stammered, "I thought, I said. . . I said, dammit." He caught his breath. *All right, I've been under pressure ever since the incident, but Jesus, I don't even know when I'm talking out loud?* "I said, dammit. I just realized I'd locked my keys in my car." He regrouped and rewrote his name in the corner of the board. "Dr. Tivoli. That's my name and what is yours?" *Dimwit.*

"Um."

Um, the mantra of a generation.

"Um, B.V. People call me B.V."

B.V.? Beefy cow. Bo-vine. Tivoli shifted his focus to the student he had tagged with "Bimbo." A pleasant mane of mahogany brown hair, a catty smile, and green eyes so perfect that they could only be colored contacts. "What is your name?" he asked her.

"Lindy," she said. "I'm majoring in police science."

"Ha! The other poly sci," Tivoli said, then let out a self-satisfied chortle. He reassessed her. She was not a bimbo, but someone to watch. "Let me warn you that we will not be dealing with easy questions in this class. We will be dealing with impossible ones." Tivoli sensed their fear. "But don't worry about the exams, because every answer to those questions is correct." This declaration rang the magic dinner bell and the happy puppies began to salivate.

"In philosophy we deal with the eternal questions. Tell me, how many of you have asked yourself, 'Why am I here?' " He gave the question a moment to settle into their minds. Instead of taking root, it blew straight out the other side like a tumbleweed. No response. "None of you. Nobody. Nobody has asked themselves why." Finally, Lindy raised her hand. *Yes*, he thought, *I was right. Someone to watch.* "Why are you here?"

"I need the credit," Lindy answered.

"You need the credit," the professor echoed. "Well, I won't write that one down. How many of you are here because you heard this class makes for an easy A?" Those who already knew looked away as they tried to hide their naked greed. Those who had just heard looked up as though they hit the jackpot.

The professor moved on. He pointed to cow eyes. "B.V., tell me. What is the meaning of life?"

"I haven't read that chapter yet."

"It's not in the textbook."

Doesn't-know-where-to-rent-one raised his hand. "And what is your name?" the professor asked.

"My name? Jules."

"Yes, Jules. What is the meaning of life?"

The student raised up a pocket-sized Webster's.

The professor shook him off. "It's not in the dictionary."

"Life, noun," Jules said. "The state of existence possessed by living organisms."

The professor thought of semester's end. Vacation. Miami. Beautiful women on the beach. He plunged ahead. "All right, philosophy is the exchange of ideas. So, let's have a debate. A classic one. Perhaps you've heard it before, but this is the first day of class so we'll stick to the basics. A tree falls in the wilderness. No one sees it fall and its fall is not recorded in any way. How do we know that tree fell?"

B.V. slammed his hand on his desk, "Boom!"

"I'm not asking what sound the tree made," Tivoli said. "The tree fell, no one recorded its fall, how do we know it fell?"

Jules answered, "I was there."

All that the professor could verbalize from his gaping mouth was, "What?"

Jules embellished. "I had to take a crap, so I pulled the car over and headed out into this forest. The tree practically hit me."

"You were not listening," Tivoli countered. "This is a hypothetical tree."

"Hypothetical, my ass. It nearly creamed me."

Lindy took charge. She rose from her desk, strode to the front of the room, and gave a gentle splay-fingered shove to Dr. Tivoli's chest, saying, "Excuse me, but this sounds suspicious. This tree just fell over? My class in criminal analysis taught me to trust my instincts, and my instincts tell me this tree was pushed." She hitched her shoulders, took the marker to the board, and wrote the word "Pushed."

Tivoli had enough. "There was no tree!"

Lindy turned to face him. "How would you know? Unless you were there?"

Tivoli's hands were beginning to have a life of their own and his fingers bent in a strangling motion. "That's my point, that's the point of the question. No one was there. It's a hypothetical question."

Jules added, "And this was no rotten tree. It had to have been sawn through."

Lindy gave a triumphant "Ah!" which she wrote down. "Just as I suspected! Let's look at the facts so far. We have a healthy tree, cut down in its prime, falling over, and nearly killing this here student." Each member of the class nodded. "We have a professor who swears the tree never even fell and yet claims he was not there. Why the deception? The inescapable conclusion is that Professor Tivoli is the one who cut the tree down just missing this student. But why would the professor do that? Attempted murder!" She erased "Ah!" and wrote down "Murder."

Jules raised his hand, saying, "I hadn't finished writing the word 'ah.' " Lindy put it back on the board.

Tivoli collected himself. "Okay, class. Let's all take our seats. This has gone as far as it can go."

Lindy stood firm. "Not nearly! Why were you trying to kill this innocent student?"

Jules shook a finger at his would-be assassin. "Yeah! I was just trying to take a crap. What do you have against me?"

"Nothing," the professor said. "Nonsense. I wasn't trying to kill him! I never even met him before this class!"

Lindy asked, "Then who were you trying to kill?"

The professor said, "No one."

Lindy walked behind Tivoli. "Where is your wife?" she asked.

This question peeled the scab off a wound in the professor's chest. His breath went for a moment. When it came back, he said, "My wife? What could she possibly have to do with anything?"

Lindy clasped the professor's left hand and before he could shake her off, she raised it so the class could see. "I noticed an untanned line around your ring finger. If you were trying to pick me up in a bar, I would say that you had removed your ring to hide the fact that you're married. However, in your case, I suspect a very different motive." She wrote "motive" on the board.

The professor gawped at Lindy. She wasn't a bimbo, she was a Fury. He wanted to dismiss all of this as nonsense, but the pain in his face would betray any attempt at glibness. He said, "It's personal. Not as if it's any of your business, but she ran out on me."

Lindy leaped on this. "She disappeared. How convenient. I will bet, if we look under that tree, we will find her dead body!"

Jules added, "And then you tried to kill me to cover up the crime!"

"Exactly when did she leave, Dr. Tivoli?" Lindy asked.

"I haven't heard from her," he said, expecting a different question. "I last saw her two weeks ago."

Lindy turned on Jules, "And when did you almost get hit by this tree?"

Jules's eyes widened. "I don't remember exactly. A month ago. It could have been two weeks."

Lindy nodded as if this confirmed her theory. "In criminal justice we call that opportunity." She wrote "opportunity" on the board.

In philosophy, we call it stupidity, the professor thought. The wound in his chest was now accompanied by a pain in his head and such anger. *You silly bimbo. My wife isn't under a tree. I walled her up in my basement.*

"You think I'm a bimbo?" Lindy asked.

And Jules said, "You killed your wife?"

The professor caught himself with his mouth open. "I ... did I just say that?" The class members stared at him with various expressions of shock. He felt his finger for his wedding band, and realized he was reaching for the phantom pain of a lost appendage. He regrouped. "No. I couldn't have. I have an alibi. I was in the forest pushing down trees."

Jules said, "I knew it was you. You nearly killed me!"

The professor continued, "I was mad at you for taking a crap in the forest."

"Sorry, man," Jules said. "I didn't know anybody was looking."

Lindy dry erased the words "murder," "pushed," "motive," and "opportunity" from the board. All that was left were "Dr. Tivoli" and "appreciation." "There you have it!" she said. "Case closed." She sat down, a glint of triumph in her eyes.

Dr. Tivoli looked over the menagerie. They had become oddly quiet, waiting for their zookeeper to signal what was next. He said, "Well, wasn't that exciting? This is an example of how invigorating philosophy can be. For that brilliant discussion, you will all receive extra credit. We will end our class a little early today. Before our next class, read Chapter One. As for me, I have things to do." *I have to move my wife's body out of my basement.*

The class gaped at him in horror.

Did I just say that out loud?

IT MIGHT BE MURDER FOR HIRE

Ricky Sprague

I'm not exactly quick on the uptake, literally so to speak, so when a dude tries to subtly imply that he'd like to hire me to kill his wife I'm unlikely, in the strictest sense, to pick up on this fact right away.

I'd been doing what I guess you'd call unlicensed subcontracting work —cash on the barrel, bypassing all the *withholding* and *reporting* nuisance—for my friend Ry Green. He had more than he could handle and was passing out work to a few of us here and there. To be totally honest I'm not a big fan of "work" as a concept although I do understand its literal necessity and I needed the money.

For seven Thursdays in a row I'd had a regular job at the estate of this bigshot real estate attorney called Benjy Dortch. The night of that seventh Thursday I got back to the apartment that Chris and I share and I ordered our shawarma delivered on Chris's card but I gave Chris a one-hundred-dollar bill to cover it and told him to keep the change and then I added that I would be kicking in the full rent that month, all the utilities, and some of the streaming channels besides.

His eyes goggled out of his head. "Where'd you get that cash?"

"Well, as a matter of fact, it is a down payment on a job that I'm supposed to do next Tuesday. Penciled in, I guess you'd say."

"What job?" he asked warily. "And why is it only *penciled in*, if you got a *down payment?*"

"Well, that's the funny part, really, when you think about it. See, it's just entirely possible that I have been hired to kill this dude's wife."

He started that thing he does when he gets flustered, panting and stammering. I arrested this unpleasant ritual by reminding him, "I'm still *not sure* that's what I was hired to do. Maybe I wasn't."

He finally calmed down enough to command, "Tell me why you think it's possible."

"Well, it so happens that I have been doing some landscaping and maintenance work, freelance, on behalf of my friend Ry Green. You know, Ry, don't you? He's the one who used to work at—"

He waved his hand dramatically, a real prima donna. "Just get to the part where you were hired as a hit man."

"Fine. I wanted to tell the story in my own way but if you insist on editing as I go then I'll defer to you, your majesty." I made sure I said this in a *very* ironic tone, then I proceeded: "So he's had me working for this mousy little Dortch dude, sort of like you except more confident and oily—"

"Is there any way you can tell this story without insulting me?"

"What are you talking about? I just compared you to a very successful lawyer, except I said that you were more compassionate and sincere."

"Hm," he hmmed skeptically. When I could see he was going to keep his trap shut I went on:

"We have been talking off and on for the last few weeks. Kind of friendly like. He offering me drinks and so forth. He's a drinker. Drinks a lot when he's home. He is a bit of an over-sharer in terms of his personal life. I'm not sure why a part-time freelance landscaper needs to hear about his marital woes but I figured he needed a friendly ear and besides I don't really pay very close attention to him anyway, if I'm being honest.

"He makes me a whisky sour. Get this: He makes it with Blanton's, you know, the Single Barrel stuff, about $100 a bottle at least. He uses an egg white in it—a *real egg white*—then he says something about not having a lemon, so he uses that lemon juice stuff, you know, in the little plastic squirt bubble thing? That's sort of the size and shape of a lemon?"

"I know it," he sighed. "I don't know why you're talking about it now, though."

"It's just weird he uses this expensive bourbon, and even puts an egg white in, then he *ruins it* with this cheap lemon squirt stuff. Hey—that might be a clue!"

"A clue to what?"

"That he's, I don't know—that he's sort of careless about some things but a stickler for others, you know?"

I could tell by the look he gave me that he didn't know. Anyway, I went on:

"Let's put a pin in that. So today we were discussing this possum infestation—is it 'possum,' or '*o*-possum'?" I asked for the sake of verisimilitude.

"I think either is acceptable. Or maybe it's a regional thing. I'm not sure, but I know what you're talking about."

"There are lots of them around."

"It is surprising," Chris conceded.

"They're ugly too. When you see one of them racing across the street at three in the morning, their beady little eyes glinting in the headlights ..." I shuddered, mostly for show I admit although there was a lot of literal sincerity behind it.

"Let's get on with the story."

"Fine. I bring it up because Mr. Dortch had a massive infestation of possums and opossums. Not just one family. It was like a colony or a cult or, whatever a group of possums is. A school? A swarm? Anyway, he had a lot of them all over his property. So he invited me into his den for a drink after I was about done for the day and I needed to sort of re-hydrate.

"I go in and he's clearly gotten a head-start on the drinking. He's looking at this photo of himself and his wife Reyna, who is quite a curvy and attractive lady, and is about six inches taller than he is so he must have been standing on an apple crate in that picture because they appear to be the same height. He's got this sort of wistful look on his face, sort of like he wished he was that tall in real life, at least that's how I interpreted it. To be honest, I just wanted a drink. He's got expensive taste. At least when it came to the bourbon, you know? Why he skimped on the lemon juice is beyond me and I admit I had a hard time thinking about anything else."

He sort of nodded vaguely.

"Anyway, to get back to the story. I started telling him about how, you know it's really dry lately and the ground is pretty hard, and there's this separation in the backyard, underneath the patio, and there are all these possums under there. Like, a commune of possums. Then out back of his shed there's like, another one. A nation of possums, basically. I told him that they could do some real damage, they were pests and so on, and he might want to have them exterminated, or words to that effect. Simple advice of course.

"He starts talking about how rough his life is. Something about his wife, coming up on ten years of marriage and how she'll automatically get half of everything if they divorce, and so on. He's a lawyer and it's all law stuff mingled with self-pity and, as I've said, I'm really only there for the drink and to humor the man because he pays relatively well.

"I'm sort of nodding and um-hmming at the pauses in his monologue. Occasionally I'll offer him a sympathetic, 'That's too bad' or something.

Well he's talking about the inconveniences of life, and how it can be a real challenge living with someone. At that point I tell him I can relate to that, so I start telling him about what a pill my roommate can be sometimes—"

At that point I stopped my narrative and gave Chris the once-over. I'd gotten so caught up in the telling of my story that I'd forgotten that Chris was in fact my roommate. I expected him to offer some objection to being categorized as a "pill," but it appeared he was going to go the silent martyr route, which was fine by me I supposed, so I pressed forward:

"But of course this isn't about the specifics of the conversation, most of which I can't remember anyway because, as I previously stated, I was barely paying attention.

"Then I hear him say, 'Well, it might be worth, about, $20,000 if you could get rid of my problem for me.' Well, now I've perked up a bit because it almost sounds like he's offered me $20,000 to do a job for him, so I figure it's probably best if I pay closer attention now that so much money is involved. And I know that $20,000, in retrospect I can appreciate that $20,000 to solve a possum infestation maybe sounds like a lot of money, but you've got to remember as I said, there were a lot of possums. Practically a zoo of possums. So I'm thinking between actually killing the things and disposing of them and so forth, it's going to be a sort of what you might call a logistical nightmare. So $20,000, at that time, didn't seem all that unreasonable."

"And you were both drinking," Chris helpfully pointed out.

I snapped my fingers. "Thank you. While I hadn't had enough to suffer any real effects, *he* had at the very least a good buzz going on. Plus, he's a lawyer so he probably doesn't want to actually come right out and say it explicitly, thinking as he does that I've been paying attention to the conversation and that he's trying to maintain a sort of plausible deniability.

"So I'm taking a drink at the time he says this so I just sort of nod and I couldn't exactly say anything so I made a sort of sympathetic sound, you know, so he knew I was listening and cared even though, to be strictly and literally honest about it, neither of those things was literally true. Then he lets out this sort of relieved sigh and says, 'I'm so glad to know you'll help me with this. Somehow I could tell you were the man for the job.' I'm thinking of course that the possums are a nuisance but he seems *really* relieved that I'll help out with it.

"Then he goes to—oh, get this: he's got an actual *wall safe*, behind a painting, behind the desk in his home office. The painting is on a hinge, you know? You swing it open? I thought they only had those in movies."

I waited, to let Chris appreciate this fact which I realize in retrospect wasn't all that important, in the grand scheme of things. But it had impressed me.

I went on: "Anyway, from the safe he gets $5,000 in cash. Fifty hundred-dollar bills. He says, 'This is a down payment. You get the rest once the job's complete.'

"Once again, in retrospect, I appreciate with hindsight being 20/20 and so on, that you might think maybe this should have aroused in me some suspicion."

"You were probably still reeling from the wall safe thing," Chris snarked.

I let that pass and continued unfazed: "However I was thinking, again, that this is a logistical can of worms and I've got to get supplies and so on. So, I didn't really, not consciously anyway, think anything was amiss.

"He continues onward, saying that he'll be out next Tuesday for a deposition, and can I just do the job then? I say, 'Well, that's awfully short notice and I do have another job lined up for that day.' His eyes kind of popped out and he says, 'Wow, you're really hardcore.' That appealed to my vanity which might have had an effect of lowering my critical thinking skills which, if I'm being perfectly honest, are not honed to the finest of sharp points."

"Can confirm," Chris said with unnecessary relish.

"So then he says, 'How about if I bump it up to $25,000 total? I'll give you $20,000 after you've done the job.' To which I reply, 'Sure. I can probably take care of the other thing in the morning and then get started on your job in the afternoon.' Now at this point, in fairness, *he* probably should have realized that we weren't both talking about the same thing, so it's not all my fault."

"If in fact that's what he was talking about," Chris said.

"Which is still in doubt, I know," I had to admit. "So, to continue with the story: He asked me how I might go about handling the job. He said something like, 'Just in general terms. I don't want any specifics. But how do you plan on ... doing it?' And I didn't want to come across as unprofessional so I said, 'Well, poison is the best.' But even when I said it I thought to myself that actually I might *trap* the little critters and turn them loose in the hills somewhere, because I'm not really that interested in actually *killing* them, but before I could say that he sort of shuddered and said, 'That's probably the cleanest.' I agreed. He said something like, 'What will you do with ... the end results ...' and I just thought he was being squeamish, a real *I'd-never-even-hurt-a-fly* kind of a dude so I, to spare nauseating him, merely said, 'You leave that to old, reliable, trusty Dan.' "

"You wanted to spare the feelings of someone who was trying to hire you to murder his wife?"

"Again I emphatically state I didn't know that's what was happening, and I still don't know for sure it's what *did* happen."

"But you *suspect*. So far, from what you've told me, it could go either way."

"Mm-hm," I said. Then I added, "At that point, old Benjy put his drink down on the desk and he picked up the wad of bills and he said that his wife would be home alone on Tuesday, and that he'd make sure that she had to be home in the afternoon ..."

"Is that when you thought you'd just agreed to a murder-for-hire?"

"Well, no," I had to admit. "At that point I thought maybe I'd been hired to, perhaps, *seduce* his wife. Like, for a divorce thing? He gets pictures of the two of us in bed together, me satisfying her like she's never been—"

"Please try to stick to the story."

"Sorry. But you know what I mean. He could use the photos of us to sue for divorce and get some sympathy from the judge and not have to pay as much alimony or whatever it is before the ten-year deadline thingy. It wasn't until later that I remembered all the poison talk and so forth. I mean, if he wanted to pay me to sleep with his wife, first of all I'd have agreed for a *whole lot less* than $25,000, let me tell you. He definitely married *up*. Then also, again, if he was talking about me seducing his wife and I told him I was going to use *poison* to do that, then, well, he probably would have objected."

"That makes sense," Chris said. He didn't look calm but he was trying to be.

"Unless it's a metaphor, like in the sense that 'love is a form of poison,' or he was 'stuck in a poison marriage,' something along those lines."

"I don't think he'd use a metaphor here. I also think that there is a pretty good chance that your suspicions are correct."

"You do?"

"The artificial lemon juice is a dead giveaway. We should probably go to the police."

While I appreciated his use of the word "we" in that context, I most certainly did *not* appreciate his use of the words "should probably go to the police" immediately following. Ruined the positive effect, if you will, in a very literal way. I said, "Here's why I think that's a bad idea. First, we don't know if I was hired to kill someone. And if I was hired to kill someone, murder is illegal, at least in this context, so I could be tried as an accessory, or something."

"You didn't know. And you have information that might potentially save someone's life—"

"Or might get me into a lot of trouble. Look, I have a plan of my own. I won't do anything. I won't go to the house, or try to get rid of the possums—which I didn't want to do anyway. Now, if he *did* hire me to kill his wife, what's he going to do? He can't do anything—he's not going to go to the police and tell them, 'I hired this man to do a job and he stiffed me ...' There's no hit man regulatory board or anything that he can complain to ... So it's free money—"

"It's blood money," Chris said smugly. "There's a difference."

"Ah-ha—that's only true if it's a down payment on murder. Now, if he *really* hired me to take care of his possum problem, then he'll call me and complain and so on. But even then, you see, we still get to keep the money because he's been paying me under the table anyway and there's no recourse for *that*, either. So in that case, it's *also* free money—"

"It seems to me he could come after you in either case. He's a pretty famous lawyer who clearly has no trouble engaging in illegal activities, even if it's just under-the-table yard work. No, Dan—I don't see any way around it. We need to go to the police." At that point he called his favorite homicide detective, Holly Rose.

Detective Rose scowled at me as she said, "I don't like to jump to conclusions, but it sure sounds like a murder for hire scheme to me."

"Okay, well, go ahead and arrest him."

"I can't do that. It's your word against his, and your word is ... kind of garbled and confused. You yourself don't even know what happened."

"I think what I should do is just return the money. I'll tell him that something came up and I can't *take care of his possum problem*. I'll say it just like that, with emphasis on the 'possum problem' part. That way he'll know he can trust me to keep my mouth shut and so on."

"Don't take this the wrong way, but, if he's willing to hire you to kill his wife, he might not trust you to just keep your mouth shut. He seems a bit desperate and unpredictable."

"In that case, I'd like twenty-four-hour police protection."

She managed not to scoff at me. "That is *very* unlikely."

"You're supposed to protect me," I said. "What am I paying taxes for?"

"Well, according to your own story, you *don't* pay taxes—"

"That's irrelevant in this context. You know what I mean."

"I do know what you mean. And I intend to help you. To start, I'm going to clean up your statement a little bit and then I'm going to see about getting a judge to agree to let us wire you for sound."

"Whoa! I object! I'm not wearing a wire."

"If we can get a recording of him admitting to hiring you to kill his wife, we've got him. Simple as that."

"Just arrest him from my statement," I protested. "If he was poor you would."

"That kind of stings. In part because there's some truth to it. But the fact is that you're what we might call an unreliable witness—"

"Thank you."

"Having a recording of him will remove all doubt. So give me a few hours and I'll see what I can put together."

What Detective Rose was able to "put together" was a massive surveillance setup involving several undercover police officers, a van, some unmarked cars, and a microphone setup for yours truly. All up and down Sunset, in the block or so around his house.

This was Monday night. The night before I was to make the "hit." Maybe. There was some chatter about Benjy's connections and some stuff about legalities and so on that went clear over and around my head, literally, but the plan was largely that I was to go to his home and "verify" that it was "on" for "tomorrow." The hit, I mean, of course. Nobody was happy about it but this was such short notice they wanted me to push things the night before it was to happen.

If I'm being honest, sitting there in the cramped surveillance van with Chris (acting as my attorney, or conscience or something), Detective Rose, and another Detective called Su (who was in charge of the surveillance equipment), it was occurring to me just how literally frightened I was starting to become. Or annoyed at least.

"Since when is it my responsibility to help the police?" I asked yet again. "You people need to compensate me."

"We'll see about that," Detective Rose said vaguely, in such a way that led me to believe that she wouldn't be seeing about anything.

Finally came the announcement from the cops watching Benjy that he was on his way home from his Wilshire office, near Brentwood. So I got out of the van and hoofed it over to my Rio, parked on Edgecliffe Drive. I sat in the car and wondered how long they'd let me keep the temporary parking pass now hanging from my rearview. So far it was the only perk of being a narc. There were a few decent clubs in the area and parking could run as high as $25. The pass would come in handy.

After about half an hour I got a text from Detective Rose saying that Benjy had returned home. I drove around the block and to the front gate. Hit the buzzer.

"Who's there?" Benjy's voice came over the speaker.

"It's me. Dan the Landscapin' Man. Just wanted to talk about the job for tomorrow." Maybe, I thought, I could get him to incriminate himself over the speaker and I wouldn't even have to go to his home?

But the buzzer sounded and the gate started sliding so I pulled on through.

He greeted me at the door with a confused look. A kind of a slight smile, such as he probably literally practiced on juries and such. A *glad-to-see-you-but-I-don't-know-why-you're-here* kind of look. "Dan," he announced in a cheery tone. "It's nice to see you, although I'm not sure why you've made the trip just to talk about the regular landscaping work that you've been doing for me."

"Right," I said knowingly. "The *landscaping* work."

"By the way—I've been meaning to get your social security number and all other relevant information so that I can properly record your services for tax reporting purposes. As I'm sure you know, as a freelancer, you have a responsibility to report any income received from me and anyone else for whom you're doing any freelance work."

This was going very badly right off the bat. The last thing I wanted was that kind of talk on the record. I said, casually as I could, "Let's get to that later. For right now, I thought it would be important to discuss tomorrow's job. There are a few logistical issues I wanted to clear up."

"Okay," he said skeptically. "But I don't understand why there's anything particularly special about tomorrow's job, since it will be exactly the same as all the other work you've done for me over the last few weeks. Just regular maintenance in full compliance with all applicable laws and ordinances, including the recent rules regarding water usage ..."

"Why are you talking like that?"

"What do you mean?" he asked innocently.

"You sound like, well, like a lawyer."

He smiled disarmingly. "I *am* a lawyer."

"I know you're a lawyer. But you really sound like one now."

"I'm not sure I should take that as a compliment. I know that people often have a low opinion of lawyers, but it's important to keep in mind that members of our profession serve a valuable purpose, protecting the rights of citizens and ensuring that the mechanisms of our justice system continue working smoothly."

Before he launched into a dissertation on the finer points of torts or something I had to get him to incriminate himself. I said, "Let's talk about the job you already paid me $5,000 for."

"*$5,000?* What are you talking about? You do some freelance landscaping work, I fully admit that. I also fully admit that I've been paying you in cash for the last few weeks—I've kept meticulous records of the amounts for tax reporting purposes, those records are available for your perusal at any time and I'm sure that they match up fully and completely with the records that *you're* keeping for tax purposes as well—but I've *never* given you $5,000 for *any* job."

Now I was starting to feel a mixture of annoyance at him for being so coy and nervousness over all the dumb stuff he was saying into the listening device which was literally on my person at that time. For the record, I was not being fully meticulous in my recording of the cash payments I'd received and it was just possible that if someone from a tax collecting office were to learn of that fact they might interpret it as a sign that I wasn't going to report the money on my income taxes. Which wasn't the case at all. I kept all the information stored away in my memory, which I was going to use when I did my taxes whenever they were due.

"Let's get back on topic. Specifically, I want to talk about the job we discussed last Thursday."

"The yard work," he said.

"Yes. '*Yard work.*' " I repeated it back in italics to let him know that we were using euphemisms. As far as I was concerned that should be enough for a conviction but I figured with all the legal loopholes and so forth that were available to get criminals with money off I should make sure to be as explicit as possible. "The yard work of removing that little problem that you've got—your *ten year* problem."

"What are you talking about?"

"You know—after ten years that little *yard work* is entitled to half of your property in a divorce ..."

He looked at me dumbfounded for a few seconds. Then he said, "The reason I'm not saying anything is that I'm so startled by what you're saying. I have no idea where this is coming from. It almost sounds like you're trying to entrap me into saying something incriminating, when the fact is I've done nothing wrong."

"You've done nothing wrong, unless you count trying to hire me to kill your wife." I decided that a straightforward approach was probably warranted here.

He poured it on like syrup. "That's not true at all! I would *never* try to hire anyone to—to—I *can't* even *say* it, it's so against my nature and my desires! I love my wife passionately and unconditionally and frankly, you're really starting to scare me with this bizarre crime story fantasy you've apparently concocted in your mind!"

"I suppose I just invented that whole discussion we had, about the possum infestation and how you wanted me to use poison on them, but we were really talking about how you wanted your wife dead?"

"You're delusional."

I wanted to say "Delusional like a *fox*," but I didn't because I wanted to remain casual. Instead I said, "If you didn't hire me to kill your wife, then how do you explain the $5,000 cash you gave me?"

"I didn't give you $5,000—" Here he let out a little gasp and he said, "Wait—are you telling me—did you *steal* $5,000 from me?"

"What? No!"

He rushed to the other side of the room, moved the painting and punched numbers on the keypad. As the safe opened he turned around, without even looking in it, and dramatically announced, "The $5,000 in cash that I keep in my wall safe is *missing!* You must have *stolen* it and invented this *unbelievable* story to cover for yourself! I feel so betrayed!"

"But—that's not—I didn't—"

"I *trusted* you!" he said in a wounded tone.

This was really getting away from me now. I was starting to feel just slightly nervous, sort of like Chris gets when he sees an attractive woman he has to talk to. I decided to try to get things back on a more positive track for myself.

"Do you *want* to hire me?" I asked, casually. "Maybe get her killed before that ten-year rule thing kicks in? I can just take the $5,000 you already gave me, and then the other $20,000 that you already said you'd pay me after I was done—"

"This is really starting to scare me. I think I need to call the police now."

At that point there was a sound from the left as the door to the den creaked open. Standing there was Ry, holding a gun which was pointed sort of toward the middle of the room, as if to quickly point at either of us, should the need arise. He said, "Maybe hold off on that for a few more minutes."

Benjy looked back and forth between me and Ry, a confused look on his face. This was, I noted, the first time since I'd arrived that he looked genuinely confused, in a literal sort of way. "Uh, what's going on?" he asked.

"I dunno," I said.

"This is too perfect," Ry said. "The only thing is, I'm sorry that you had to be here, Dan."

"That's okay," I said. "I can just head on out—"

Now the gun was pointed at me. "No, no, no. See, Reyna and I want to be together. Benjy's money would make that a lot easier. I was gonna make it look like a random break-in but with you here, and now the wall safe open, it's just—it's too good an opportunity to pass up. I can make this look like you broke in, Benjy caught you—"

"Okay!" Benjy shouted into the air. "Now! Come in now! Ry Green is here and he's holding a gun on me so now would be a good time to send the police in!"

"What are you talking about?" Ry asked.

"The police have been listening to this whole conversation and I'm sure *they're on their way into the house right now* because you have a gun pointed at me and you've just threatened to kill me!" Benjy squeaked.

Ry was even more confused. "Nice try. Don't move."

"I'm not bluffing!" Benjy pointed at me. "That dummy is wired up! He came here to try to get me to confess to hiring him to kill my wife—" at that his eyes widened like he realized he'd said something wrong.

Triumphantly I pointed right back at him and shouted, "You did it! You just *confessed!*"

"No! I said you *tried* to get me to confess! I never said I *actually hired* you to do it!"

I appealed to Ry. "Come on, man—he admitted it!"

"No I didn't!"

Ry pointed the gun at me. "It did kinda sound like he confessed," he said. Before he had a chance to squeeze the trigger, however, there was a thunderous crash of breaking glass and splintering wood and he fired in the direction of the noise. The SWAT team that had just crashed through the front door returned fire and Ry's body became messy and fell to the floor in the hallway.

All things considered, it was difficult to hold it against Ry. Reyna was quite a hot little number. Also, Ry was now dead.

Benjy had known all along that I was wired because the cops who were supposed to be "tailing" him told him. Turned out he had a lot of informants on the police force. It was a huge scandal for a couple of days, then something else took over the news cycle. But he spent a long time dealing with it in the courts. He probably would have been better off staying with the whole murder-for-hire thing.

Reyna copped a plea and got about three years for her part in the murder-break-in conspiracy she and Ry put together.

For helping expose the crooked cops, Detective Rose made some friends on the force, and made some enemies too. *Come see, come saw,* as the French say.

Chris really ended up with the short end of things, as I mentioned over shawarma the following week.

"How so?"

"Well, I actually had money to help out with the rent and stuff. And now—*pfft*. And I probably shouldn't do anymore cash only jobs for awhile. Until the heat dies down."

"You could get a regular job ..."

"I think we both know how unlikely that is to happen ..." I shrugged, to convey the existential unfairness of fate's fickle finger. I did let him have the parking pass. It was good for another two weeks.

PANDORA, HAUNTED

(OR, IN WHICH NATALIA HARTLOWE BIDS ON A DELACROIX)

Robert Mangeot

A guy met us outside Customs. Black shirt, slick hair. Didn't hold a *Hartlowe chauffeur* sign, didn't welcome us to De Gaulle. Just appeared and said, "Madame H.," and took Natalia's bag. Natalia didn't break her stride. Perks like premium bag dudes surely happened to the megabucks Natalia Dare Hartlowe, my godmother and boss. I donned these killer cat's eye sunglasses scored on clearance. Natalia had her Lasik-enhanced sights on a major art collection and launching it with a bang. A newly surfaced Delacroix believed a legend: *Pandora, Haunted.* If Natalia wanted to bid live from Paris, show me some bienvenue.

Still, the guy looked like he carjacked limos more than he drove one. He didn't speak English, but I spoke *très bien* French. Boy, he hated me from *bon jour*. Natalia, though, he lugged her bags out to an idling Mercedes. I must've come off like her terrier scampering behind, me jet lagged and rumpled from a transatlantic flight, Natalia somehow belle of the ball sleek.

Weird, how I hadn't found mention of this auction on-line, especially with its Delacroix rumored but never before confirmed. A forerunner to more ambitious subjects, or so Natalia claimed. There should've been beaucoup press, a fancy catalogue. "It's not that sort of auction, Clio dear," Natalia had said.

Hey, what did I know about high-end collecting? Two semesters of art history and Dad's museum pass, that was what. Clio Cathcart, faking it until making it in my knock-off designer sundress as close to Natalia's ripped-from-*Vogue* outfit as an undergrad could swing. I wore flats not to out-height the mover and shaker set to pad my references.

I'd practically leapt through the phone accepting her out-of-the-blue summer job as collection assistant. Research projects, she'd said, and "simple arrangements as required." As required meant as to-be-nailed. I had ambitions myself: international relations, a career in State Department elbow-rubbing. In that spirit, I did my shimmiest Natalia shimmy into the Mercedes. The driver could've been Bag Man's brother. So, two guys. Bag Man wanded us and confiscated our electronics.

"Natalia," I said, "you went a tad overboard on the car service."

"These gentlemen are with our host's firm. Mallorcan, I believe."

Prison ink peeked from Driver Guy's sleeves, a saga in tentacles and knives that was best not decoded.

"Firm," I whispered. "I think you mean 'the family.' "

"I do adore your imagination. That's your mother in you."

The guys drove us into suburban communes, with tinted window views of endless apartment blocks as my sight-seeing. We pulled up at a backstreet dive restaurant. Le Centaure, blazed the red awning. Bag Man shuttled us inside past a cooking spit, past a thirtysomething manager guy with a mop of hair and scowl like he'd pre-branded us philistines, down past gloomy basement seating, past a dusty wine cellar, and into a super-damp tunnel carved through limestone. Next thing, we were ushered into a sealed-off bomb shelter and handed glasses of red wine. Electronica jazz pulsed from a DJ station. Impeccably dressed ladies chatted with tuxedoed and uniformed men of a certain age, everyone sampling hors d'oeuvres. A dozen hi-res posters of paintings and sketches ringed the shelter. Hired muscle hovered, as if to complete the dictionary illustration for hot art sale.

"We can't be here," I hissed to Natalia.

"Have you seen him?"

"Zero clue who you mean. I pretend a heart attack, and we bounce quick."

"Mssr. Volavega, our host."

"You didn't mention any Volavega."

"Well, I'm certain I did," Natalia said. "Let's mingle, shall we? Whoever corners him first, turn on the charm and give a wave. Not too obvious."

"Natalia, auction scrubbed. Interpol raids this place any minute."

"Have your Burgundy, dear. The Delacroix's provenance is beyond reproach. It's Mssr. Volavega's sales tactics that are mildly unusual."

Said in the diesel air of bootlegger central.

Natalia glided over toward a hi-res poster of a hazily painted woman.

I sipped that Burgundy. It was acidic or dry or whatever Burgundy was supposed to be. *Could out-hawk a hawk*, Mom had said about college BFF Natalia. *And would.* No out-hawker flaunted a black market buy. This auction was legit, then. Mostly. Enough that a State Department prospect needn't mention it during background vetting. Or to her father—ever.

Anyway, Natalia had vanished.

All righty, I did not have a boring gig. I shuffled along and studied each painting on offer. A Gaugin, a tropical villa in those thick strokes, and Matisse, a calculating self-portrait. And Delacroix's *Pandora, Haunted.* Smallish canvas, a frankly bland woman of indeterminate age set against an odd cobalt sky, oil globs for an opened box. Pandora frowned vaguely at nothing or no one.

Yikes, but a Delacroix was a Delacroix. Clio freaking Cathcart, helping acquire a headliner. I'd asked Mom once why she'd never jumped in on Natalia, Incorporated. *We're not hawks*, Mom said. Mom, who Natalia swore kept a horse racing book and the apartment vodka flowing. My version had been the cotillion chaperone, the location tracker, the hair chewing patrol.

She should've hawked a little.

A steel hatch rasped open across the shelter. In came a sawed-off man, late fifties, his scant hair bunched as eyebrows or billowing from an open-collar linen shirt. He smoked a cigarette like it'd fallen behind on its payments. Mssr. Volavega, I presumed by his espadrille shoes and sulfurous aura. Volavega trained his gaze my way, snapped a wicked snap, and strode out how he came.

Bag Man crowded in on me. Fine. I went rather than get hauled. Through the hatch was a bricked-off corridor, with that dank tunnel taking it from there until I hit velour curtains. After a prodding through them, I was back in Le Centaure's basement. Natalia rose oh-so-genteel from a café table. Volavega lounged across from her and smoked his storm cloud.

"Clio," Natalia said, "thank heaven. Mssr. Volavega and I are at polite loggerheads. You'll help straighten this out, won't you?"

"Doubt it," I said.

"There is problem," Volavega said.

"That's rather charitable," Natalia said. "Mssr. Volavega claims not to have possession of the Delacroix. I needn't remind him he has it set for auction tomorrow."

"Most embarrassing," Volavega said.

"Mssr. Volavega, this is Ms. Clio Cathcart, of the West Meade Cathcarts. Her mother was a Truxton."

Volavega stubbed out his cigarette. Lit another. "To friends, I am Vole."

"What did I tell you?" Natalia said to me. "Polite. We've agreed to an advance sale of the Delacroix. As our deposit, I've wired two million dollars where and as he instructed. He's a shipper and financier, you understand. The money part is intricate."

"Shipper," I said.

"Precisely. In return, the Delacroix is delivered to me or I to it. Upon authentication, we wire another two million. Yet suddenly the Delacroix has gone missing."

"My idiot nephew," Vole said. "Fantin hides the paintings. I cuff his lazy head, but to do worse means war with my sister."

I sniffed at my hair. Four million, likely also France's prison sentence in years for trafficking.

"Sir?" I said. "May Natalia and I huddle briefly?"

"Watch the freight yards, I tell him. Run the restaurant, keep things greased. Do it, I find him bigger job. No, the idiot takes my profits and buys these paintings. Paintings! Even after I show him, physically I show him, how business works. Low profile, reputation, always liquidity."

"Sir?"

Vole blew a smoke barrage. "Go."

I edged back into the tunnel. Natalia followed at a slink.

"Clever how you handled him," Natalia said. "Very less-is-more."

"I'm like ninety-nine percent sure he confessed to money laundering. The State Department hears word one about this, I'm toast. And did you and he commit wire fraud?"

"Relax, dear. Insurance brokers and museum boards won't touch us without acquisitions so pure they sing hallelujah. How Mssr. Vole moves his funds afterward is his concern."

"Concerns," I said. "I have concerns."

"I agree. This shell game of his. What do you propose?"

Mad dash up the steps and hope like hell that Target sunglasses made me incognito. "Get your money refunded."

Natalia traced a nail extension along the tunnel wall. "Large sums flying back and forth piques interest among our accountants, doesn't it? Certain regulators. Onward and upward."

Not upward in my opinion, but Natalia parted the curtains and announced to Vole, "It's settled. Clio here will see to the Delacroix."

Vole said, "I like it. Idiot listens to pretty buyer."

I've got a brain, I wanted to inform Vole. Mitts off, I wanted to tell Bag Man, but he'd already plunked me out on the boulevard. Here was my welcome to France, a dusk walk with a crime boss and secondhand smoke machine, two bruisers lumbering a couple meters behind.

Somewhere, Mom was conjuring her ashes into zombie form so she could kill me before Vole's guys did.

"Paintings," Vole said, as if art generally was my fault.

"Right. Delacroix. Okay, where was it last? If your nephew is into those pieces, he kept them close. Someplace with proper light and air conditioning."

"There is warehouse in the Neuf Trois. Temperature controlled. Shipping demands this, yes? I tell him to bring the money suck paintings to Le Centaure. Fantin says they are brittle. He must pack and seal them, but he packs only crates with plaster board."

"A switcheroo?"

"Somehow, in this single thing he is not idiot." Vole swiped me a sunflower without protest from the florist. "Advice, pretty buyer. Spain is not what it was for business. I let Spain cool for a time. Maybe I buy a French vineyard house. The Loire."

Mom in my head, her weaponized sigh. "You should."

"The Romans started vineyards here. The Norse come, the English. The Germans build the air raid shelter today I sublease for cheap. Liquidity, pretty buyer. Nothing else keeps me young, strong."

Vole stopped us after a few blocks at a soot-streaked apartment building. "The idiot's flat. Paintings must be hidden here."

"Cool. Cool, cool."

"Explain to him."

"About liquidity?"

"About what happens to nephews who test uncles too far."

I cleared my throat—some. "No offense, but please deliver your own threats."

"Also, what happens to pretty buyers who fail in explaining."

Literally the last thing you wanted to hear when stepping into a cage elevator. My heart still clanked when Vole let us into an apartment with high ceilings and splattered floor cloths. Oil and charcoal pieces cluttered the room, pieces so rough that they must've been practice. The mop-haired manager squeezed against an open window and dabbed at a canvas in the fading light. Fantin, in a gangling painter's smock.

Vole lit a cigarette as if my cue.

My international studies program drilled us in extemporaneous speaking. Surprise topic, stopwatch, land your point. Tonight, I managed, "Sweet apartment."

"Get out," Fantin said. He was painting those blocks toward Le Centaure, but his sidewalk scene came off like spackle run amok, all muddled sapphire and cold beige. For Le Centaure's awning, he'd gone with a lumpy scarlet.

"Intriguing texture," I said. "I'm with the Hartlowe Collection. Your uncle and my boss are in advanced dialogue, and everyone agrees that, given these uncertain times, a family business—a respectable maritime logistics business—benefits from a healthy cash position. Mrs. Hartlowe is, shall we say, cash healthy and interested in *Pandora, Haunted.*"

"I find her as overlooked market junk. Does he tell you this?"

"Come on. Picture yourself at the Louvre, special exhibits, and you're taking in *Pandora, Haunted* where it belongs. On view." Of its mediocrity, but it was Natalia's dime.

"Uncle," Fantin said. "I beg you. Think of this beauty we collect. *La Pandore* invades the soul like no other."

Vole gusted out smoke.

"There we have it," I said. "Where's our *Pandora?*"

"Leave!" Fantin said. "I part with her from my dead clutches."

"Flip to Vole's perspective. He's hosting a swank auction, everybody here for a turnt party and some not-stolen-at-all art. Now, no auction? That's rough on the reputation."

Fantin doubled down on slathering a color palette gone wrong.

"Nice surrealist touch." I twirled my sunflower, gave him the Natalia grin. "Hey, if you need a wistful mademoiselle, I could model for you. I'm told I'm quite beautiful."

"Capitalist wench. I would paint you as a horror."

That was it. Fantin had no eye at all. "Fork over Vole's paintings, poser boy. *Pandora* is headed for the States."

Fantin smoothed his ridiculous smock and stomped from the flat.

There I was, surrounded by twilight gloom and hack art no one could give away.

Vole smoked through what a fair read would've called a murderous silence. It sped me along to search the place. Books on painting technique and famous artists were strewn on the floor amid Fantin's dreck. Fat-fingered sketches of prized works were taped along the walls: Picasso reduced to geometry, Matisse's self-reflection gone distorted, Gauguin's Polynesia as kitschy Hawaiian—Fantin desperately seeking craft and getting nowhere. I scanned around for any hint of a stashing spot. I checked mattresses for slits and closets for false backs. I even looked behind sketches large enough to hide a finished piece.

And came up with diddly squat.

Vole flicked his cigarette out a window. "We drink."

We drank, a red sangria that Bag Man hustled in. Drinking wasn't murdering.

Vole studied me through his ribbons of smoke. "You are, what, Madame H.'s transcription girl? Because you are terrible at this."

Sangria. A gulp of it. I heard Mom's breath winding up for her gotcha special. *Watch what company you keep*, she'd loved repeating. Neither of us would've dreamed she'd meant wine carafes with Spanish crime lords.

"Summer job," I said. "Where else did your guys check besides the flat?"

"Paintings!"

"Let's stay calm. Have yourself a smoke."

Vole smoked. "We search Paris. The rooms of his bohemian friends. My other facilities. But we keep observations on him, yes? Yesterday, he brings me the money suck crates. Idiot stops only here with his idiot supplies. Then, he works until past close and locks himself in this overpriced hole. Idiot sees no one, ships nothing. Paintings must be here."

Another cue. I took my sangria along because why not and again scoped out the flat. Cabinets, closets, nooks, crannies, floorboards that might've wobbled underfoot. Nothing.

I munched my hair steeped in tobacco. Outsmarted by Fantin, a guy who couldn't navigate smock length. And yet give him props. He'd pulled a timeless switcheroo: Hit someone familial with something they wanted to hear and bearing an important whiff of truth. Dangle, say, that you were going to the movies with your squad, and was it really a major lie if it'd been the movies but with an undisclosed boy? Yes, according to Mom whenever the parental intel network or a slip-up busted me. When I didn't slip up, Mom brought out the dreaded *you'll tell me when you're ready*, her master class in head-casing.

I wondered what else I'd gotten wrong about Fantin. That sidewalk painting and his study sketches were the same high-passion, low-talent pileup, but the more I stared at them, the more purpose I saw. Fantin was crashing and burning to apply Matisse's color genius, Gaugin's boldness. Delacroix's expression and romance.

But not as a teaching exercise. Anybody desperate and devious enough to pull a bold switcheroo was desperate and devious enough to keep on pulling switcheroos.

"Vole?" I called. "How large is *Pandora, Haunted*? The measured canvas size."

"What do I know size?" Vole said. "It is painting size."

"We'll get the dimensions. Next question, and please withhold any incriminating response. Do you own a mobile x-ray machine?"

"Come, I neglect my guests."

"Fantin might've painted over your auction slate to conceal them. He went for tricks once, didn't he? Imaging equipment detects if there's a Delacroix or whatever beneath this top mess. I saw a historian do it on cable TV."

Vole gave that a long drag's thought. "The films? Expensive to arrange."

But sounding fantastic to certain ears. "Your stuff is here, right? It's get techie or tear the place up."

Vole drained his sangria. Said, "I like it," and spun on his espadrilles for the cage elevator. Here it came in its death rattle, and me and my clanking heart followed him in.

"Madame H.," Vole said. "What monies does she pay for this painting?"

"Your other two million. Natalia is all aboard."

"I suspect this. Four millions was fair, but now, idiot nephew, this expense of films, much effort and anguish to avoid embarrassment. I honor my word, but since we are friends, Madame H. pays six millions to cover this anguish."

My heart stopped clanking. Stopped altogether for a second. "Six? For that? It's like Delacroix scrawled that poor woman as he was dying."

"I cannot be blamed for uncontrollable difficulties. If Madame H. argues this, I have her two millions and the painting. There is a Greek here, big in tahini. A true aficionado. He pays another four easy. This is six millions. To match this is a bargain for Madame H.'s collection."

Vole should've run negotiation workshops. We reached the boulevard, and Vole said, "We drink, and we dance."

We drank, and then we danced, back in the bomb shelter turned makeshift disco. Everyone was there, the swank ladies and generalissimos, a Greek I took as our main competition, Natalia at a roulette table, Fantin under goon watch. Yes, Mom, I was Miss You Never Learn amid an underworld laser-light rave and shakedown-palooza. Vole put everything he had into his boogie spins, hip swings, a leg split. He kept his cigarette going through it all.

So much for cotillion etiquette. On the other hand, I knew where *Pandora* was.

Ish.

Vole assumed the paintings were squirrelled away at Fantin's apartment, an apartment smothered in proto-copycats and a lone sidewalk scene disaster. One lone non-copycat which happened to feature Le Centaure. Fantin was either tracking the restaurant comers and goers or just leaching guilt onto canvas. I didn't tell Vole that, like I hadn't shared that the x-ray thing was as doomed as my life prospects or that his supposed Delacroix on that auction poster was totally forged.

Strategic flexibility, for extended non-murdering.

Vole started a conga line. On the first lap, I bumped into Fantin at the four beat. I kicked the step his way and shouted, "I know where *Pandora* is. The real her."

It left Fantin twisted inside his smock.

People were cutting in, and I ghosted Vole for a Natalia hunt. Odds were in the last hour she'd been appointed to several foundations of dubious funding. I found her wafting pure posture and sipping dirty martinis with a Japanese man she introduced as chairing an insurance syndicate. "Powder break," I requested after a careful bow exchange.

Natalia moved us to a dark patch of bomb shelter. "That gaming table is clearly magnetized," Natalia said.

"Hello? Me. Your Delacroix."

"Clio, you're perspiring."

"I'm sweaty," I said. "I'm ugly sweaty, my lungs are screwed, and I gnaw hair, okay? *Pandora* is stashed here at the restaurant."

"Of course, the Delacroix is here. Volavega can't afford to be so clumsy a liar. Ergo, the nephew did as accused. That young man would be watched constantly. He drops the Delacroix where no one questions his moving around crates."

"You had that?" I said. "This whole time?"

"The thing is, we've divined Volavega's intentions. Will he sell?"

"As many times as he can. Long story involving a Greek, but Vole upped his price to six million."

"That man is beginning to irritate me."

"Also, Fantin painted a fake *Pandora* as a double switcheroo to fool Uncle. That poster version? Fantin's signature ick sense of color or sharpness."

Natalia appraised me over a martini swizzle. "I'd worried the photo actually did the Delacroix justice."

"Hold it," I said. "Did I suss that out first, or did you?"

"My dear Clio," Natalia said.

Which was all the answer I got. Natalia slipped into the conga line, her drink never summoning the audacity to spill. Fantin's goon nannies were getting their groove on too. I watched him fade off and then scram for the hatch tunnel.

Onward and upward.

It should've been easy spotting a head case in a giant smock. No such luck on my frantic basement sweep, other than the disco song boom-boomed on as an extended dance mix. Fantin had to be in the basement. Privacy, tunnels, decent enough conditions for temporary storage.

And dumb me, there was yet another bootlegger tunnel, behind a wine cellar rack with its dust recently disturbed. Dim light flickered through a break in the limestone. It took wriggling and nudging the rack free, but bam, I slipped into a mildewed corridor set to collapse but for sawdust-fresh lumber supports. Fantin kneeled twenty meters deeper in and shone a lantern on blanket-draped shipping crates.

With drama, I said, "Busted."

Fantin got this wild expression frozen in lantern light, despair or fury or both. I would've better savored getting the drop on him if he hadn't carried a crowbar.

"Go away," Fantin said. "And keep silent of this."

"How's Uncle Vole reacting when he hears about your long con? Nice, a poster shoot of all your real collection but *Pandora*. A little truth spice for when you weepingly surrender the fake."

"I mean this. Say nothing, or I fix you."

I hit him with the cockiness that comes with a head start and beaucoup sangria. Clio Cathcart, outwitter of fiends. Someone patted my shoulder, though, and major spine chills doused my moment.

Natalia drifted in amid bass woofers and disco strings. "Bravo," she said. "Is this my Delacroix?"

"*La Pandore* is mine forever," Fantin said. "And I am hers."

"We were discussing Vole," I said. "How we hip Uncle to the situation."

"Why on earth would we?" Natalia said. "Before us is an experienced restaurateur and intelligent businessman. Let's talk terms."

Fantin drew up his full height. "No terms. Never terms. She owns my soul."

"Really, young man. That Delacroix belongs on tour."

"Tried that," I said. "He's too emo."

"But did Clio mention we have the Dare Hartlowe name behind us? Marketing budget, the full splash. And our rising star Fantin in the program as our salaried Romantics expert. Or choose any period you like."

Fantin deflated by degrees. His face became a conflicted hungry he could never paint.

"Full splash and credit," Natalia said. "Dears, the only reason for having an art collection at all is to make damn sure everyone knows we have it."

Fantin had melted into a mop-puddle. He removed the blanket and unfastened a transport crate beneath. Framed in his lantern popped a flowing-haired woman in glorious focus and vibrant oils, a woman bursting with regret and curiosity, her wayward gaze trained over your shoulder, toward a beyond all her own. *Pandora, Haunted.*

"She's gorgeous," I said.

"It'll do," Natalia said. "I've meant to ask. How are your local contacts regarding helicopter access? Flown low to the ground, I mean."

"No contacts. And what the what?"

"We're leaving with my Delacroix. There's an ex-legionnaire in Rouen who comes highly recommended. Better we pay him a king's ransom than give Volavega another cent."

"Wait, wait. Double-cross Vole, and Vole goes unfriendly."

"No, dear," Natalia said. "Volavega double-crossed us. Let's see how he enjoys bartering without possession."

Hawk, outhawked. More new experiences abounded, like wheeling a crated Delacroix past drunk guards and driving a caterer van steady enough that gendarmes didn't stop our reaching a private heliport a bunch of France away. Natalia let me pick the landing pad. "Spain," I said. Loads of shampoo, direct flights home. I said, "I quit," but Natalia said that sounded rash. Labor Day was ages off, and Pamplona was a brilliant idea. She had a line on a Goya there, captivating in its darkness. I tried focusing on the road and thought about Mom's expression just now and about this sundress I couldn't return.

THERE'S LOTS OF LEG ROOM

Steve Shrott

Marcel adjusted the "We Kill Pests" sign in the window of the small storefront as Edward entered.

He gave Edward a slight nod, then took a seat behind the large oak desk in the otherwise empty office. Edward sat in front combing back his hair like he was one of the Rolling Stones even though he'd been bald since he was twelve.

Marcel pointed toward the front window. "Brilliant idea of mine eh? Making it look like we're exterminators."

"Yes, Brilliant, Marcel. No one would suspect the Tovely Crime Family is situated in this suburban area right under their goody-two-shoes noses."

Marcel rubbed the long scar on the left side of his cheek. "I even make a couple of extra bucks whacking the odd rodent. Keeps me in shape."

"Right, boss." Edward paused a moment, his left hand shaking. "I have news."

"Oh?"

"I uh took out Alfonso."

Marcel's forehead crinkled which meant one of two things. Marcel was happy with what Edward had done or he was about to shoot him in the family jewels. Edward mentally berated himself for not wearing the bullet proof underwear.

"Splendid. The traitor deserves to die. He stole our last shipment of drugs, then sold them to the Rantazo Family. To add to the insult, he joined them. What do the Rantazo's have that we don't?"

"I hear they offer a pretty good dental plan. Full coverage."

"Okay, but with us, you whack a traitor of your choice and get a free weekend at Disneyland with unlimited candy floss."

"I believe all that candy floss is why they need the dental plan."

Marcel picked up a mirror from the table and admired the twelve crooked teeth he had left. Then he leaned toward Edward staring intensely into his blood shot eyes. "Did you bury the body in the usual spot?"

Edward started breathing heavily, worried about telling his boss what had actually transpired. He moved his hands to cover the crotch area of his pants just in case.

Kevin Reynolds wiped the perspiration off his forehead with his right hand as his left hand holding the steering wheel of his 2004 Ford Fiesta dribbled more perspiration onto his pants. He worried he might be the first case of someone drowning in their own sweat.

Every few moments he would steal a glance at the blonde girl sitting beside him.

It was happening.

He was on a first date with the most beautiful girl in his high school—Jenny Denova. With her radiant blue eyes and long blonde hair, Jenny was his dream girl. She wore jeans and a red blouse but to Kevin it didn't matter if she wore a potato sack. Well, it might have mattered as he'd planned on some dancing later and he would have to cut holes for her feet.

So far everything had gone smoothly, well except for a few minor issues. It took Kevin ten minutes to get his car started, the radio dial had fallen off several times, Jenny had accidentally touched some loose wires under the dashboard which gave her a large shock, and she couldn't get the passenger side door to lock. Actually that last one was the biggest problem. When Kevin started driving, the door flew open, and Jenny had to hold onto the seat belt to avoid flying into oncoming traffic.

Except for all that, it had been perfect. Now they were on their way to the restaurant. It was definitely going to work out. Kevin didn't even feel he needed the sixteen lucky charms he wore throughout his body. But he rubbed the four-leaf clover taped to his right nipple just in case.

Suddenly his dream girl spoke.

"Listen, Kevin, you know this is a test date, right?"

"A test date?"

"Yes. We meet for half an hour, drink some coffee and then I see if you're someone I want to go out with on an actual date."

"I thought this was the actual date."

Jenny shook her head so intensely, it seemed as if strong winds were pushing it from side to side.

"The thing is I wasn't really sure about going out with you at all."

"Why?"

"I did some research. Shirley Robertson dated you once last year and said you were weird."

"Weird?"

"You told her there were going to be lots of surprises. Then at the restaurant you got down on your hands and knees and proposed."

"I didn't propose. I had half a beer and got a little drunk. That's all. Then I knocked the rest of the beer onto the ground and slipped on it. Ended up on my hands and knees."

Jenny gave him a wry smile. "That sounds very believable. Didn't you tell her you would love her forever."

"I uh don't remember. You know having the beer and all."

"Look, I don't want any surprises tonight. You can propose to anyone you want, just not me. Got it?"

"Oh, well the thing is ..."

"God, you do have surprises. Maybe I should leave ... slow down. I'll get out over there."

Kevin stopped the car. Jenny put her hand on the door struggling to get out. "Now the door locks?"

"Stay ... please. I ... I ... I really like you. I know I already screwed it up. I go overboard sometimes. But it would mean a lot if you'd stay." Kevin looked into her beautiful blue eyes with his sad pathetic eyes.

Jenny thought a moment.

"Alright, just no surprises, okay?"

Kevin nodded even though he wasn't sure he could go the no surprise route.

"Can you put the heat on, Kevin? It's freezing."

"Sorry, it's uh broken."

Jenny grimaced. "Does anything work in this car?"

Kevin could only shrug.

Jenny turned around and looked at the back seat. "Do you think I could at least wrap that blanket around myself?"

"Blanket?"

Kevin stopped at the light, then looked back and saw the pink blanket on the seat.

"Sure, take it."

Jenny pulled on the blanket and suddenly started screaming.

"What? What happened?"

"There's ... a ... man sleeping in your backseat."

Kevin pulled over to the curb and looked unable to speak for a moment.

"Is that supposed to be funny Kevin? You wanted to see if you could scare me by not telling me your dad was sleeping in the backseat?"

"That's not my dad."

"I can totally see the resemblance."

Kevin looked at the man with the small beady eyes, fat nose and dumbo-sized ears and realized that maybe the lighting wasn't so good and Jenny couldn't see what he felt were his Johnny Depp-like features. On the other hand maybe he really needed to look in a mirror more often. "He's probably some homeless guy who came into the car at night to keep warm. As you know the lock doesn't work so well."

"Yeah, I noticed that when I was one of the Flying Wallendas."

Kevin called out to the man. "Sir, sir, wake up. Wake up." He turned to Jenny. "He's really out of it. Probably drunk."

Jenny pulled the blanket further down the man's body, and screamed again. This time because there were bullet holes in his chest.

Marcel slammed his hand on the desk. "I will ask you one more time, Edward. Did you bury the body in the usual spot?"

"I uh couldn't. There were uniforms all over the freaking forest. They were digging up the ground."

Marcel's face turned the color of a ripe tomato as he stared into Edward's petrified eyes. "So where did you bury him?"

Edward's whole body stiffened. "Well the thing is I had to think fast."

"That's not something you're known for, Edward. It takes you two days to decide if you're going casual or formal when you whack someone."

"I like to go classy, but I want to fit in too."

Marcel rolled his eyes.

"The thing is there were no other forests around. But there was this car."

"Car?"

"It looked abandoned. So I loaded the body in there."

Marcel shook his head. "You put the body in a car? What were you thinking? If the cops find it, they'll make the connection to us. They know we hate the Rantazo Family."

Edward started talking fast. "I guess I wasn't thinking. See, I had to get home. You know I need my beauty sleep, Marcel. I've noticed a few wrinkles lately, and my moisturizer can only do so much." Edward pointed underneath his eyes to emphasize the point.

Marcel stared at him a moment, not believing this. "Didn't you use the Neutrogena I gave you?"

"It itched. Anyhow, the car was old, the paint was peeling, the lock broken. No one in their right mind would drive that thing. We have nothing to worry about."

Kevin stared at the body not knowing what to think. The closest he'd been to something dead was when he dissected that rabbit in science class and threw up on his lab partner, Lily Feinstein. He decided then that maybe it wouldn't be a good idea to ask her to prom. "This guy's not breathing."

Jenny stared at him. "Right here, Kevin. I didn't need the update."

"He's dead."

"Again, I kind of put two and two together with the holes in the middle of his chest and him not saying, 'How-dee-doo.' "

Kevin took the blanket from the back seat and handed it to Jenny. "You still want this?"

She drew in a long breath, then a scowl appeared on her face. "You're giving me a blanket that covered a dead guy. You really know how to treat a lady, Kevin."

"Oh right, sorry." He threw the blanket into the back seat, hoping he hadn't just ruined everything. He rubbed his left nipple with the horseshoe charm taped to it, just in case.

"Do you have some kind of nipple fetish? That's the second time you've done that."

Kevin anxious to change the conversation, sniffed the air. "This guy's starting to smell, I'm going to put him in the trunk."

"Shouldn't we go to the police?"

"Yes, on the way to the restaurant." Kevin shrugged. "The dead guy's not going anywhere."

"Fine."

Kevin got out of the car and looked around. The street was deserted, but he had to do this quickly just in case someone came by. He lifted up the trunk, then went to the back door and opened it. He reached in, trying not to smell the worst odor ever since that time he dissected that snake in biology and ralphed on Tom Dinty, his other lab partner. He really was not good with dead things, lab partners or aiming, for that matter.

He grabbed the shoulders of the man and using all of the strength he had gained from doing Pilates, pulled him out. He breathed in short gasps as he shut the door with his foot and moved the body upright, leaning it against the car. Kevin turned his head to the side to breathe some fresh air, and noticed Jenny standing by the open trunk. She had come to help him. That was nice. But more than that her mouth was puckering up and her eyes had this wild, maybe, erotic look, to them. Did she now want to kiss him? Maybe things weren't as bad as he thought. Maybe his quirky charm had gotten her all roused up. Suddenly, filled with a new vitality, he walked as quickly and seductively as he could toward his dream girl with his arm around the corpse, looking like a ventriloquist with the world's largest dummy. When he reached Jenny, he moved close.

Closer.

Closer still.

He was nose to nose to her now. He was about to lay one on her when—

She screamed again.

"No need to scream, Jenny, I'm a good kisser."

She gave him a look like she needed five bottles of Pepto-Bismol. "What are you doing?"

"It seemed like you wanted me to kiss you. You were all puckered up."

"I see. And what? You thought holding the dead guy would make me hornier?"

Kevin realized he may have misread the situation.

"I wasn't puckering up, I was trying to scream. But I was so shocked I couldn't get it out."

"Why?"

"Because of this." She pointed to the trunk.

That's when Kevin saw the other dead body.

At this point he realized the date was not turning out exactly as he had hoped.

The phone rang and Marcel answered leaning back in his chair. "Shut Your

Mouse Exterminators. We take care of all intruders no matter what the size ... I see ... uh huh .... uh huh ... you killed some mice and now there is another one chewing on your gas lines. It sounds like the mice you took out were part of The Family, if you know what I mean. Before they passed on they probably called in a pro to do a hit on your petrol. I think it's a vendetta type of situation. We specialize in vendettas. I'll be there Tuesday at four and take care of everything.

Marcel hung up and wrote the appointment down in his book. "You know, Edward, I wish our lieutenants were as loyal to The Family as the rodents."

Edward nodded, forming his hands into fists. "Marcel, I uh have something else to tell you. The thing is that while I was loading Alfonso into the car, I got a call. Victor wanted to see me."

Marcel nodded. "One of our most loyal lieutenants."

"Yes. He needed the money I borrowed from him. Unfortunately I'd already spent it on facials and waxing. "Feel this."

Edward lifted up his trouser leg and Marcel rubbed his hand along it. "Smooth."

Edward smiled at the compliment. "The problem is this one." He lifted up the other pant leg and Marcel gasped at the enormous amount of hair.

"This is after the electrolysis, boss."

Marcel covered up his eyes and looked away. "Pull that down now. So what the hell happened with Victor?"

Edward pulled at the trousers, but was having trouble getting the left leg completely down due to all the hair. "Well, I was a little nervous due to Victor's temper so I left the car with the body. Then I got in my jag and drove as fast as I could to his place. When he opened the door, I was shocked—he had the whitest teeth I'd ever seen. And that's when I knew he had joined the Rantazo's too."

"Damn dental plan."

"Yes. So I whacked him, stuffed him in my jag and drove back to the car on the street. Then I dropped Victor into the trunk."

Marcel rubbed his forehead. "So Alfonso was in the backseat and Victor was in the trunk."

Edward's whole body began trembling. "The uh problem is I started celebrating my handiwork and got a little tipsy. Now I don't remember what street the car is on."

Marcel rubbed his hands together which meant he would either give

Edward a raise or break his neck. Edward realized he should have worn the much thicker turtleneck.

“You know Kevin, this may surprise you but the dates I go on don’t usually involve two dead guys. I’m a one dead-guy kind of gal.”

Kevin nodded, still standing in front of the trunk holding the dead body. “I’m sorry. I don’t know what’s going on.”

Jenny examined the trunk. “I never realized there was so much leg room.” She spread her hands. “What are you going to do with stiff number one? Not a question I ask my dates a lot.”

“I’ll just toss him in there.”

“With the other guy?”

“Yeah.”

“You don’t think that’s a little unnatural. I mean you don’t know their uh sexual orientation.”

Kevin rolled his eyes. “What, you think they’re going to have fun in there? They’re dead.”

“Right.”

Kevin moved the second body into the trunk and closed it.

Then both of them went back into the car.

Kevin sat in the driver’s seat looking at his shoes. “Things are so screwed up. I had it all planned—a nice drive, us getting to know one another, a lovely meal at C’est Bon.”

“C’est Bon? How can you afford that?”

“I cashed in a bond my dad gave me. That’s how I bought this car yesterday.”

“Did they charge you extra for the two dead guys?”

“They weren’t there before. The man showed me the trunk and it was empty.”

“So someone loaded the bodies in later?”

“I guess. I parked it on another street ’cause I didn’t want my dad to know I broke the bond.”

“Oh.”

“Listen, Jenny, I’m sure you haven’t noticed but I’m uh not really good at dating. I thought tonight would be different. But it doesn’t seem to be. I sort of figure I’m cursed in that department. Anyway, I’ll take you home and then go to the police station with the bodies. Explain it all.”

He started up the car.

Jenny looked over at Kevin and put her hand on his arm. "You know, I'm kinda hungry. Do you think it would be alright if we went to the restaurant first? Then you can go to the police?"

"You'll go with me?"

Jenny nodded.

An enormous grin appeared on Kevin's face.

As Kevin drove, he looked at his watch. He realized he'd have to speed up if he was going to make the eight o'clock reservation.

They passed stores, farmlands, a zoo and a few supermarkets. They both enjoyed the scenery and laughed about the situation they were in. Everything was going well until they heard the police sirens right behind them.

Kevin pulled over to the side of the road.

"What are you doing?"

"I'm stopping. It's the cops."

"And you think they're going to understand why you have two corpses in your trunk?"

"I was going to the police station anyways, right?"

"It's different when they stop you on the road and find the Bobbsey Twins."

"They're not going to ask me to open the trunk. They'll just give me a speeding ticket and tell me to go."

"Yes, of course that's the way it's going to be when the stars have all lined up to give us the perfect night."

A moment later there was a tap on the window. Kevin rolled it down and a friendly-faced cop appeared. "Sir you were speeding back there." He held a yellow ticket pad in his hands.

"Yes, I know, officer. It's just I have reservations at a restaurant and I'm late."

"License."

Kevin opened his wallet and gave him the license.

Jenny smiled her sweetest smile to the officer. "It's our first date together."

"Oh? How's it going?"

"It's been a magical night so far."

"That's great, miss."

"Only I'm worried we'll be late for the restaurant. So if we could leave now ..." Jenny pretended to wipe her eyes.

The officer looked at them both a moment. "I'm not going to give you guys a ticket. But slow down. I hope you have a wonderful night. You two look great together."

Kevin felt his whole body tingle, delighted.

The officer was about to hand the license back when his phone rang. "One minute.

Kevin looked at Jenny. "See I told you nothing to worry about."

Seconds later, the officer's face appeared back in the window.

"Just one more thing. I just heard there have been some murders in the area and I have to check out your car. The backseat seems fine. I just need to look in your trunk."

Marcel and Edward sped down the road in Marcel's station wagon with the words "Shut your Mouse Exterminators" painted on the side and the three-foot-tall Paper Mache mouse on the hood looking like it was begging for its life.

"I don't understand, Edward. Do you have a rodent-whacking appointment?"

"No. We're going to find that car with the bodies."

"How?"

"I've been worried about Alfonso's loyalty for some time. So the other day I took him out for lasagna, and put a tracking device disguised as a noodle in his food. Now I know exactly where he is."

"You took him out for lasagna. I've been a member of the Tovley Crime Family for five years and never got lasagna."

"Didn't I buy you lots of candy floss when we went to Disneyland?"

Edward thought back, then smiled showing off the seven teeth he still had in his mouth.

Marcel reached into his pocket and pulled out a small phone-like device with a screen. "See the blue dot blinking? That shows that the car is on Ventura and Forsythe."

"You never put one of them tracking thingies in me, did you Marcel?"

Marcel stopped at the light and looked over at Edward. "Oh, uh, no, of course not. I know how loyal you are."

"But why does that red dot seem to be stationary on the street we are now?"

"Oh, that's uh the tracking noodle I ate with my lasagna. Sometimes I uh don't trust myself."

As Marcel continued to drive, he took in a few deep breaths which meant Edward might get another container of Neutrogena, or he could end up at the bottom of Lake Nimrod, a lead pipe attached to his very smooth leg.

Kevin felt like he was going to faint. "My trunk? You want to open my trunk. The trunk in the back of this car?"

"Yes, that one."

"Why is that again?"

"As I said there's been a murder in the area. It's just a formality. Keys, please."

Jenny trembled all over, but put on her cop-pleasing smile again. "Do you really think we've got two dead bodies in there, officer?" She started to laugh like she just inhaled a gallon of laughing gas.

"Pardon, ma'am?"

"Nothing."

"You said two dead bodies."

"Oh, I said that because I uh just had eye drops so I see double. So if there was only one body, I'd see two, and uh you know you have lovely eyes, Officer."

"Thank you miss. The chief says we need to check every vehicle. It'll take a minute, Mr. Sauci."

The officer left and Kevin shook his head. "Oh no."

"What?"

"He called me Sauci."

"Well I'd take it as a compliment. You are kinda saucy in a way."

"No, I gave him the wrong license. I got fake ID in case we wanted to go to a bar later. I just hope he doesn't notice."

"Notice what?"

"The birth date. The creep got it wrong. I'm the only high school senior who's forty-five years old."

"Oh my God. He's gonna think we're like Bonnie and Clyde."

"Sauci and Shufflebottom."

"What?"

Kevin reached into his wallet and took out another license with Jenny's picture on it. "I got you a license too."

Jenny took it from Kevin's hand. "Miranda Shufflebottom?"

"You couldn't get me a better fake name than Shufflebottom?"

"Sorry."

Jenny grimaced. "And the date indicates I'm thirty-five. We're really old."

They didn't say anything for a moment, then burst into laughter.

Jenny looked at Kevin. "Actually, that's kind of sweet. Maybe you aren't a total goofball after all." Jenny moved closer to Kevin about to kiss him. But her pucker disappeared when she looked out Kevin's window and saw the cop now holding a gun in his hand.

"Both of you put your hands on your head and slowly leave the car. You're under arrest for a double murder."

The officer reached for the door when Kevin heard gunshots. A moment later, the cop slid down the window leaving a trail of blood.

Kevin stared at the blood on the window and felt as if a two-hundred-pound electric eel had just shocked him. He looked in his rear view mirror and saw a man walking toward their car. "We got to get out of here."

Kevin tried to turn the car on, but it wouldn't start. He tried again. Then again. Nothing happened.

He looked back and saw the man getting closer.

Kevin gasped for air as he began rubbing both his lucky nipples, the rabbits foot taped onto his left leg and the seven 7's he had magic marker-ed onto his right leg, not to mention the rainbow he had drawn on his ankle.

Jenny looked at him puzzled. "If this is some kind of weird mating dance, Kevin, it's not the time. Get the hell out of here."

Kevin tried the key one more time and it worked, just as Kevin saw the man's face through the blood-stained window.

Kevin slammed down on the accelerator and raced to ... anywhere. As he drove he turned to Jenny. "I just realized something. That wasn't a real cop."

"What?"

"Cops don't wear running shoes."

"He looked like a cop."

"Sometimes there's more to someone than their appearance."

Jennifer stared at him. "Is that about the crack I made about you looking like the dead guy? You don't. You actually look quite nice, and smell ...

slightly better."

"Kevin looked in the rear view mirror. "Oh my God the trunk is still open. Everyone's going to see the bodies and I'm going to go to jail and be around bank robbers, murderers and men who shoplift jockey shorts with Home of the Whopper written on them."

"You have to close up the trunk, Kevin."

"Okay, there's an alley on the next block. I'll stop beside it."

As the sky became overcast, Kevin parked in the alley. It was next to a demolished building. He looked around and saw the streets were empty, then went to the back of the car, about to close the trunk. "Oh my God."

"What's wrong now?" shouted Jenny as she got out of the car and raced over to where Kevin stood, his hands covering his eyes.

Kevin pointed to the trunk. Jenny looked in and put her hand over her mouth when she saw two more dead bodies.

Marcel and Edward sat in their parked mouse-car across from the building staring at the parked Ford Fiesta. Marcel looked at his tracking device. "That's the vehicle that has Alfonso."

Edward pointed at the two figures standing by the car. "But who are they?"

"No idea. But the fake cop who stopped their car was Roberto Lemchuk, a member of the Rantazo Family. If they were after these two, they must be pretty high up."

Marcel pulled a license out of his pocket. "I found this on the ground after I shot the cop. The guy's name is Reginald Sauci. You know I think there was a Sauci in the Russo Family. Bad dude. He didn't just whack, he tortured. They gave him the jobs no one else would take." Marcel nodded toward Edward. "We better be very careful when we talk to him."

"And by talk, you mean 'Whack,' right Marcel?"

Marcel smiled. "You know me so well." Marcel left the car and began walking across the street. Edward stayed a moment looking at the tracking device on the seat. The red button didn't move. "I knew it, I got a tracking pill in my tummy. And I didn't even get the free lasagna."

Jenny looked in the trunk, shaking her head. "How is there two more? I mean I'm not an expert on dead bodies but do they multiply in the dark?"

"I'm thinking the fake cop loaded the bodies in."

"Do you still want to go to the police?"

"I don't know if it's a good idea, Jenny. What do you think the cops will say when we show up with four bodies in the trunk of my car?"

"They'll think we're fantastic serial killers. I mean you gotta admit that's a pretty good haul for one night."

Kevin looked across the road from the alley. "Uh oh."

"What?"

"Over there." Kevin pointed to the black car across the road."

"You mean the station wagon with the giant mouse on top. It's just an exterminator, Kevin. I can't believe after all of this, you're afraid of bugs."

"One of the men leaving the rodent mobile has a scar. So did the man who I saw heading toward our car when the policeman was killed."

As the men walked closer, Kevin had the urge to touch all the lucky spots on his body. But he knew it wouldn't help. He was in another arena now with killers. The rules were different.

"What are we going to do Kevin? They're coming straight toward us."

"I just thought of something. When I was bullied as a kid, my dad used to tell me ..."

"Is this a long story, two killers are coming closer and I don't think they want to give us an award for most bodies crammed into a Fiesta."

"He said, to thwart an enemy, you have to show you're bigger than them."

"Your dad's in the construction business. I don't see him using the word thwart."

"He's been reading the dictionary a lot lately, or as he calls it, the lexicon. What he meant is that when you confront a bully you have to show that you're tougher than they are."

"But they didn't just steal our ball, Kevin, they murder balls, uh, people."

"And we have four bodies in our car. Who knows what we'll do next? We're Sauci and Shuttlebottom. We're crazy."

A moment later, Marcel and Edward approached the alley holding guns.

Marcel looked at Kevin as if he were an insect, a dangerous one. "You guys stay right where you are."

Kevin and Jenny were too nervous to say anything anyways as Marcel examined the open trunk of the Fiesta. He turned to Edward. "They killed

Sisco and Alverez. Those were our two top lieutenants."

Edward nodded. "I remember they received Employee of the Month plaques for most whackings, June and July."

Marcel turned to Kevin. "I guess the Rantazos paid you to take them out because we whacked two of their men eh, Sauci?"

Kevin and Jenny looked at one another, now getting it.

Kevin took a deep breath and tried to appear defiant by moving his legs apart hoping they wouldn't notice they were shaking more than Jell-O during an earthquake. "Yeah, they only told us to take out Sisco, but we were in a fun mood and took out Alverez as well."

Edward grimaced. "I bet you tortured them too. Didn't you, you animal?"

Kevin nodded. "Yes, we uh tied them up. Then we uh got on top of them and uh rode them like horses."

Edward stared at him. "Like horses."

Kevin continued. "Yeah for hours. Made them say, 'nay' a lot too."

Edward didn't quite understand the torturing methods but figured they knew their business.

"And before I torture you guys, any last words?" After Kevin said it, he thought that maybe it might have been overkill as he had no gun and even if he did he would probably end up accidentally shooting off his own toe.

Edward whispered to Marcel. "I don't want to be ridden and made to say, 'nay.' "

Marcel nodded, then moved toward Jenny. "Who the hell are you?"

Jenny was shaking, but she felt courage seeing Kevin's new attitude. "Miranda Shufflebottom. Sauci and I work together. Sometimes he does the hits. Other times I do them."

Marcel pointed his gun at Kevin. "Enough chat, let's get this over with." He was about to shoot when Edward interrupted. "There's just something I need to know before we take you out. It says on your license that you're forty-five years old. You look like a kid. You too, lady. How old are you?"

"Thirty-five."

Edward's eyebrows shot up like rockets. "What the hell kind of skin care regimen are you two using?"

"It's a uh complex chemical compound composed of polypeptides and polysaccharides."

"Poly what?"

"They keep you young."

Edward pointed his gun at Kevin. "Lift up your pant leg."

"What?"

Marcel nodded. "Yes, lift it up."

Kevin's eyebrows crinkled not sure what was going on. But he did as he was told.

Edward viewed the leg from different angles. "Now that's smooth, Marcel." He was going to ask where he got his electrolysis when Marcel noticed something. "What the hell are those seven 7's written on your leg?"

"Oh. It's uh the way I work. I whack people in groups of seven. That's just the victims this month."

"Well sorry, Sauci, this is the end of your rein. You took out two of our men. It's the code that we take you and the lady out." Marcel raised his gun.

Jenny trembling all over grabbed Kevin's sweaty hand and ... kissed him.

As the gangsters looked at them both, Edward whispered to Marcel. "Maybe we're being a little hasty here."

"What do you mean?"

"Don't you think we could use Sauci and Shufflebum on our team? We just lost our two best men. That only leaves us, Horhey. And his complexion is a mess."

"I don't know."

"Think about it. It could be amazing with their knowledge of whacking and skin care."

Marcel thought about that and turned to Kevin and Jenny who were still kissing. "Hey enough with the smooching. We've made a decision. Currently, we're having kind of a membership drive. We could use you two in the Tovely Family."

Kevin thought about that a moment.

"And if we don't accept."

"We'll whack you."

"Then we'd be happy to join. We just have one request."

An hour later, Kevin and Jenny were in C'est Bon eating their fancy meal. Beside them sat Marcel and Edward. Marcel raised his glass. "To Reginald and Miranda. May you have long happy lives and don't get whacked too early."

As he did, his left eyebrow twitched which meant Edward would either have a lovely meal or else there was arsenic in the lentil soup, and he would be bloated and dead. Not his favorite combination.

MOBY, DICK

Jonathan Stone

"Call me, Ishmael."

That's the voicemail I left Ishy. I only use his full name when it's something serious. He gets back to me right away, knows why I'm calling. A new case.

Me, I'm Abdul Hab. (Lebanese, if you're wondering. Last name Americanized from Habib.) Yeah, that's my name on the door: *A. Hab*. Why just my first initial? Come on—no one's hiring a P.I. named Abdul.

Oh, the other name up there? That's my partner, Moby. Private eye too. Phil Moby. He does matrimonial, I do missing persons. But Moby and me, we go way back. You don't really get one of us without the other.

Anyway, this new case. Simple. Locate the Big Finn. Helsinki billionaire, shipping magnate—practically Albino, look at this picture, probably weighs what, 300 pounds?—living large, comes once a year to Vegas, treated to a high-roller suite—and on his last trip he just disappears—out into the vast featureless sea of Nevada subdivision and desert beyond, and not seen since.

So—find the Finn.

My team: Ishy you met.

Starbuck is my point man. He's an informant. (That's actually just my nickname for the guy, don't know his real name, but we always meet at a Starbucks where he passes me info and I pass him cash.) He's the guy got us these pictures and figured out the Finn's point of disappearance.

I steer my American iron out I-15. Thing's a friggin' boat. But to head off into the sand, Starbuck has lined up a Polaris Quad. We take the P-Quad out into the desert.

Rest of the crew: Stubb and Flask. Yeah, he's short, and yeah, he's got a drinking problem. But by the size of the Finn, I figure I might need manpower to pull him in.

My team knows me. They know I'll do whatever it takes to find the Finn.

Seems like we're out there forever, searchin'. Nothin' for days. Then, all of a sudden, who appears out of nowhere, heading straight for us?

But we're ready. First, I try to hook him gently: "Listen, Finn, come nice and quiet, and maybe it'll go easier on you." But when he's about to turn tail, I stick it to him: "Face it Finn, we both know why you're out here. It's all about the oil."

It's always about the oil.

I've got to digress a little here and explain the oil shipping business. Hope this doesn't slow down the story too much.

See, it's all about how and where you store oil at sea. That's how you game the oil market. You buy oil futures low, then keep the oil out at sea for months, a year, until you can pull into port and sell at a much higher price. But see, the Finn went further: he didn't actually *own* any ships, only leased them. So if he could hide out long enough, he could renegotiate lower lease rates, or his "disappearance" could even render the leases void, and lease-wise he'd be off the hook. But the oil contracts were separate, so he'd retain ownership of the oil.

"So let me get this straight," says Ishy. "He's keeping his oil out on the sea, but he doesn't have a ship?"

"Exactly."

"Wow. Talk about profitable."

"No sunk costs," observes Stubb.

Pretty slick operator. Scuttling ships, financially speaking, but keeping his oil cargo intact. The Big Finn was plenty famous in the shipping world, but he was totally about the oil. His only cargo. His lifeblood. What made him tick.

We wrestle him into the back of the P-Quad. The Big Finn in the P-Quad. Talk about a fish out of water.

"Let me go, and I'll give you a big cut," the Finn pleads.

But I've dealt with creatures like this all my life. I knew he was just pulling my leg. First chance he got, he'd cut me off at the knee.

"Stop your blubbering," Ishy says to him, disgusted, as we head the P-Quad back toward civilization.

Greed. Corruption. Obsession. Classic American story, I guess.

But hey, case closed. No need to turn this into some big epic tale, right?

If it's fishy, I go after it and never let up.

And that's how I earn my "A." on the door.

MACMURPHY UNBOUND

Michael Wiley

Larry MacMurphy, age thirty-seven and with a full head of hair, convinced Lisa to act out the fantasy that had played through his imagination since he studied Comparative Literature at the University of Chicago. Early on a summer morning, they drove north to a forest preserve, stripped off their clothes, all but their Nikes, hiked a half-mile trail from the parking lot, and screwed in a field of dewy knee-high grass. No dryads or fauns peeped from the trailside stones as they did in Theocritus's *Bucolics*, but a graying man with a golden retriever watched from beside a tree.

Three days later, when MacMurphy found the deer tick on the inside of his thigh, the rash around it looked like a *Ripley's Believe It or Not* thigh-nipple. Soon he lay in bed with fever, stomach cramps, burning feet and swelling toes, twitching, fatigue, and dizziness. The works.

Meanwhile, Lisa, liberated by their morning in the field, started up with a guy who serviced their Volvo. MacMurphy would have minded less if Lisa hadn't drained their bank account paying for needless car repairs. "The transmission," she said, and she drew lipstick onto her lips. "Catalytic converter," and she spritzed perfume. "Next time we should buy a Buick," and up went the thong.

When she took pictures of the car mechanic lying naked in the forest preserve field and accidentally texted them to MacMurphy instead of her lover, MacMurphy could take no more. His wife and the mechanic were in *his* fantasy field, with not a deer tick in sight.

MacMurphy figured he had three options:

Sell the Volvo.

Kill himself.

Kill Lisa.

Selling the Volvo was out. He'd bought it as a gift to himself when he dropped out of grad school. He and Lisa had driven it more than a hundred and sixty thousand miles—mostly around the city, but once all the way from Chicago to California where they'd slept on the beach.

Killing himself seemed hardly worth the bother. On bad days, when the stomach cramps kept him doubled up in bed and his fever-sweat stained the sheets yellow, he felt mostly dead already.

Killing Lisa? Sure, he loved her. She'd ridden alongside him in the car. They'd slept together on the California beach. She was a wisp of a woman, with blonde hair to her shoulders, little eyes, and thin bones. She'd run two marathons but looked as if she could be a bird or a Virgilian sylph. They'd been through thick and thin, good times and bad, sickness and health—well, not sickness: in his sickness she'd found herself a car mechanic. But still.

Then she told him she was going away for a girls' weekend—a trip with her friend Margaret, who worked at the children's desk in the public library. She dropped a pile of magazines on his bed to keep him company: *Field & Stream*, *National Geographic*, and, Jesus Christ, *Hustler*—he didn't even know they published it anymore. She kissed him on his forehead and trotted out the door. Saturday morning, he crawled from bed and drove to the library. Margaret stood in the science aisle showing a nine-year-old a book on quasars.

"Larry!" she said when she saw him peering at her from the end of the aisle.

"Margaret!" he said.

He went home and started planning. Poisons were good—manageable for a suffering man, a man with little strength—but messy, according to the Internet. Bleeding noses. Vomit. That kind of thing. He could cut the brake line on the Volvo but the mechanic probably would find the problem and charge him double, and if the mechanic missed it and Lisa crashed into a tree, MacMurphy would be out the car.

He called his friend Richard, who taught French Literature at a college in the western suburbs. Richard had finished the Comparative Literature program when MacMurphy dropped out. He'd written his dissertation on *The Discourse of Torture in Provincial France* and liked this kind of thing, so MacMurphy thought he could help.

"Have you considered couples therapy?" Richard asked.

"I'm going to hang up on you," MacMurphy said.

"Don't hang up," Richard said. "I'll help. I will. I'm just trying to think out of the box."

"Stay in the box, Richard," MacMurphy said. "I want to get away with this."

"Understood."

MacMurphy invited Richard over for the afternoon. Richard bought a six-pack of Rolling Rock and sat on a chair next to MacMurphy's bed. He drank his beer and thought. When he grew bored of thinking, he picked up the *Hustler*. MacMurphy watched him and fumed. He considered kicking his friend out of the house, but that would take too much energy. Instead he picked up the *National Geographic*. The lead article explained the problem of orphaned elephants in Kenya. Like MacMurphy gave a damn. The next article included a centerfold aerial picture of a stretch of forest in the Adirondacks. The leaves on the trees were autumn red and orange. The black mountains in the background rose toward the clouds. In the middle of the forest, a lake reflected the clouds back toward the sky. MacMurphy let his mind wander. In his imagination, Lisa ran through the forest, naked except for her Nikes, dropped to all fours by the lake. ... No. He couldn't go there.

He turned the page. An article titled "If We Only Had Wings" told the history of "Personal Flight" and showed pictures of men who'd strapped jetpacks to their backs, or hooked rocket-propelled wings over their shoulders, or pieced together webbed wingsuits that they hoped would enable them to jump off cliffs and glide to the ground like flying squirrels. MacMurphy learned that in medieval England a monk had tied wings to his arms and feet, jumped out of an abbey window, and broken both legs. Later, a German engineer had constructed a double-winged contraption and crashed to his death. An American, "Bird Man" Clem Sohn, had sewn together a pair of canvas panels that looked like albino bat wings and stayed in the air for seventy-five seconds before crashing to his death. In France, Patrick de Gayardon had made a wing suit out of nylon and crashed to his death too.

MacMurphy started laughing. Richard looked at him, concerned.

"These guys"—MacMurphy's eyes teared up he laughed so hard—"nuts."

Richard reluctantly put down *Hustler*. "Huh?"

"Look at this." MacMurphy showed Richard a picture of a man diving off a mountaintop. As far as MacMurphy could tell, the man could go only one direction. He read the caption to Richard: " 'Australian Jim Mitchell leaps off Ottawa Peak on Canada's Baffin Island while wearing a wing suit. He died weeks later when a jump from a nearby mountain went tragically awry.' " MacMurphy burst into laughter again. "These guys—"

"It's not funny," Richard said.

But tears rolled down MacMurphy's face—cleansing, reviving tears. "'*Tragically* awry?'" he said. "When Icarus's wings melted, *that* was tragic. Everyone after him should know better. What do they expect? They load themselves into rockets and light the fuses—"

"I don't get it," Richard said.

MacMurphy stopped laughing. He caught his breath. "This is how I want to do it."

Richard smiled at him. "You're going to convince Lisa to put on wings?"

"Not wings. I want her to fall. Don't you see? It's about pride."

"I thought it was about sex," Richard said.

"You can leave now," MacMurphy said.

"No, no—I'm with you. I'm in," Richard said.

They brainstormed. They drew diagrams. They calculated speed of descent and angle of impact. By dinnertime, they had a plan.

Sunday morning, Richard picked up MacMurphy and drove to Soldier Field where the Bears were playing the Broncos. While the crowd cheered and roared, MacMurphy and Richard roamed through the stadium from the 100 level to the 400 level, gazing over the balconies and buying food at the concessions. Inside the concourses, they watched big television screens as the cameras focused on live action from the field and panned through the crowd. Outside, they watched a bigger screen attached to one end of the club lounge playing the same scenes. When the screen showed a section of the stands behind the 400-level balcony, MacMurphy said, "Perfect." The balcony dropped forty or fifty feet to a 300-level walkway.

"Um. Sixty thousand people will see you," said Richard.

"Plus the television audience."

"This is good?"

"If I do it right," MacMurphy said. "Sixty thousand alibis. Plus everyone watching TV."

"And how do you do it right?"

"That's where you come in," MacMurphy said.

Over the next three weeks, when Lisa went to her law office or the auto body shop, MacMurphy and Richard practiced in MacMurphy's living room. They knotted two blankets together and strung them across the room from a doorknob to a steam radiator. The blankets served as a fake balcony rail. The couch that they shoved up to the blankets stood in for his and Lisa's 400-level seats. Richard propped his phone on a bookshelf and recorded video so they could see what the fan-cams and security cameras would see.

Time after time, MacMurphy and Richard stood up from the couch and cheered imaginary touchdowns. Time after time, MacMurphy shoved Richard over the blankets. Richard landed on the coffee table, breaking one of the wooden legs. He stumbled within inches of the glass door on the curio case. MacMurphy threw his hip into Richard's as he shoved him. He hooked his foot around Richard's ankle. He gave him a simple thrust to his back. Time after time, the video clearly showed MacMurphy tossing Richard over the blankets. No one would be fooled.

"There are martial arts you can use to do this kind of thing," Richard said. "Judo. Hapkido."

"You're pissing me off," MacMurphy said.

By the end of the third week, using a combination hip check and ankle hook, MacMurphy managed to make his own role in Richard's ejection from their imaginary stands nearly invisible to the camera's eye.

"Lisa's much smaller than you are," MacMurphy said. "It'll be easy."

Richard said, "I don't know."

The next Thursday, Lisa came home with a tattoo on her hip. The image could only be described as a carburetor.

MacMurphy said, "I got tickets for this Sunday's Bears game."

"Great," she said, smearing a coat of Bacitracin over the carburetor. "You going with Richard?"

"I thought the two of us could go."

"Oh," she said.

He heard disappointment in her voice, the regret of a woman who had suddenly gained and just as suddenly lost an afternoon of lovemaking. "You don't already have plans, do you?" he asked. "Another weekend with Margaret?"

Lisa looked distracted. "I have no plans."

Three days later, MacMurphy and Lisa found their seats at the southern end of the 400 level. The ticket agent had offered MacMurphy seats in either Section 432 or Section 434, and MacMurphy hadn't hesitated. Now, as the stands filled around him, he kissed Lisa on the cheek and said, "432-1-*blast off*!"

"Huh?" she said.

The game started badly. In four quick passes and a run around the left end, the Vikings scored, while Lisa thumbed text messages into her phone. Before the end of the first quarter, the Vikings scored again. When the Bears kicked a field goal midway through the second quarter, MacMurphy jumped to his feet, beside himself with joy. Although his body had strengthened during his practice sessions with Richard, the sudden movement dizzied him and he toppled forward. He caught the balcony rail and steadied himself. He glanced at Lisa. She remained in her seat, smiling at her phone. She hadn't noticed his near-fall.

He sat beside her and waited, his thoughts calm now. When, less than four minutes later, the Bears kicked another field goal, he stood and yelled with the rest of the crowd. Then he glared at Lisa in her seat and said, "Cheer!"

She looked up from her phone. "What?"

"Don't you want to cheer?" he said. "The Bears scored."

She said, "I don't like football."

He jumped up and down. "This is how you do it."

She frowned and said, "Yay."

"That's more like it," MacMurphy said.

At half time, Lisa left to use the bathroom and get hotdogs. MacMurphy watched the *Frisbee Dog* halftime show—watched and waited. Could he shove Lisa over the rail before the second half started? With her hands full of food, she would have poor balance. No, he decided, he should stick to his plan. He would wait for a moment of such excitement that even Lisa jumped from her seat, and, using Lisa's own momentum, he would lift her off the floor, out of the bleachers, and into the air.

It was just as well. Lisa returned, empty handed, midway through the third quarter.

"The hotdogs?" MacMurphy said.

She looked at her hands as if surprised by them. "Sorry."

The Vikings moved within twenty yards of the Bears' end zone and then, against all odds, missed the field goal, and the Bears drove the ball back up the field and completed a short pass for a touchdown. MacMurphy jumped up and cheered again. Lisa remained in her seat and watched him.

He said, "*Cheer*, dammit!"

"I don't know what's wrong with you," she said.

The score was fourteen-thirteen, Vikings up, going into the fourth quarter. As the minutes passed, MacMurphy anticipated the end: the Bears would lose by one point, and he would drive home with Lisa texting to her lover from the passenger seat. He would climb into bed, and Lisa would head out to get the tires rotated on the Volvo.

But with a minute, thirty-one seconds remaining, the Bears intercepted a pass and returned the ball to the Viking eighteen. MacMurphy leapt to his feet. The crowd around him leapt to their feet. Lisa remained sitting.

MacMurphy sat down next to her. He said without looking at her, "If the Bears score, will you please get up and cheer?"

"You need serious help," she said.

The Bears scored. The quarterback dropped back in the pocket and fired the football cleanly into the hands of his man in the end zone. Everyone in the stadium stood, everyone but Lisa. MacMurphy danced in front of his seat. His grin was real. He slapped hands with the guy standing next to him. He turned to Lisa. She frowned at him. He chanted, "Bears! Bears! Bears!" He reached for her and she drew away. He pulled her to her feet. He chanted, "Bears! Bears! Bears!" She tried to push away, past the man standing on the other side—leaving. MacMurphy held her arm and spun her toward him. For a moment, they stood so close they could kiss. Then he shoved her toward the balcony railing. She stumbled, arms flailing, toes skimming across the balcony floor, light as a sylph. One of her feet caught, and she spun backward, her face looking at his as if to ask, *Why?* and he reached for her—or *half*-reached, as he and Richard had practiced, so that his effort would look good on camera—and she reached for him, and, Christ almighty, she grabbed his sleeve, pulled herself toward him, and pulled him toward her.

He tripped.

He tipped.

He saw the rail as he went over it. He glanced back and saw Lisa tumbling into the safety of her stadium seat. But *he* was flying.

Then he was falling.

How had this happened? For an instant, as the faces in the crowd kaleidoscoped past and the cold wind whistled in his ears, he felt glorious and tragic—he was Icarus plummeting toward the sea, Phaeton falling from his father's Sun-Chariot—and then he slammed into the aluminum roof of a popcorn concession.

When he woke in the hospital two days later, a heavy-set nurse was adjusting his bed covers. Sunlight shined through a window. MacMurphy said, "I thought I was dead."

"We all did, honey." The nurse smiled. Her nametag called her Grace. She tucked the sheet under the mattress as if strapping MacMurphy into a restraint. "Now rest easy. You're one of the blessed." She left the hospital room.

MacMurphy tried moving his hands, his legs. They worked, but pain stabbed through his body. So he lay still and watched dust motes dance in the sunlight until the doctor, a man named Gajani, came in. He said, "You didn't break every bone in your body, though you came close. But we've found no organ damage. I've never seen anything like it. You're a lucky man."

"Is Lisa all right?"

Dr. Gajani grinned. "You saved her life."

"I did?"

"You're a YouTube sensation. She tripped and you pulled her back from the rail. Amazing."

"Is she here?" MacMurphy asked.

The doctor shook his head. "She's been doing radio and TV. Near death experience, tunnel of light, and all that. I'm sure she'll be here soon." He patted MacMurphy's head.

Lisa visited six days later. Though the weather remained cold, she wore a short, sleeveless yellow dress, which would have made MacMurphy's heart pound, except for the thing on her left arm.

"What's that?" MacMurphy said, pointing.

A new ointment-slathered tattoo extended from her elbow to her shoulder. It was an image of their Volvo. "You like it?" she asked.

"No, I don't like it. What are you doing, Lisa?"

"I want you to meet someone."

MacMurphy's belly tightened. Had Dr. Gajani been toying with him? Would the police rush in with handcuffs?

Lisa called into the hall. "Dwayne?"

A man entered wearing an all-white one-piece mechanic's jumpsuit. His tennis shoes gleamed white. His teeth gleamed white. His sleeves, rolled above his elbows, revealed an ointment-slathered tattoo. It matched Lisa's.

MacMurphy lunged for him, ripping away the bedcovers, yanking the IV drip from his arm, but before he touched the floor, pain shot through his body—piercing, flaming. MacMurphy collapsed on the cool tiles. He couldn't breathe. The room went dark.

When his vision cleared, he was staring at Dwayne. Up close. Dwayne had performed mouth-to-mouth on him. Dwayne wiped his lips on the shoulder of his jumpsuit and the nurse and Dr. Gajani moved in.

"What happened?" asked the nurse.

"I fell out of bed," MacMurphy said.

The doctor and Dwayne helped him up. The nurse reconnected the IV. Dr. Gajani said to MacMurphy, "You're lucky they were here."

"Blessed," added the nurse.

Two days later, Richard brought a box of chocolates. He unwrapped the cellophane and offered a piece to MacMurphy.

MacMurphy shook his head. "My teeth hurt. *Everything* hurts."

Richard pulled a chair next to the bed and ate a pecan cluster. "You're just depressed."

"What would I have to be depressed about?" MacMurphy said.

"I watched you on YouTube. For a moment, you looked happy. You were flying."

"Then I fell."

Richard nodded. "Sure did."

MacMurphy said, "I'm going to kill her."

Richard ate another chocolate.

On the winter morning that the hospital released MacMurphy, rolling him to the exit in a wheelchair, the city council member whose district included Soldier Field arrived with two photographers and presented him with a certificate citing his courage for pulling Lisa from the brink. As Richard drove him home, MacMurphy asked him to stop by a Walgreens.

"Pain meds?" Richard asked.

MacMurphy pulled a short shopping list from a pocket and gave it to him. It said,

Liquid-Plumr

Tomcat Rat Bait

Antifreeze

MacMurphy said, "Drāno's fine if they're out of Liquid-Plumr."

"You're going to hurt yourself," Richard said.

"I've been thinking this through."

At seven o'clock that evening, Richard drove MacMurphy back to the hospital after he splashed antifreeze in his eye. The ER doctor flushed the eye with water, told MacMurphy to stay out of direct sunlight, and sent him home again.

Lisa came in at eleven that night. She wore a leather jacket, a little skirt, and stilettos. She carried a motorcycle helmet.

MacMurphy decided not to ask. He limped to the bookshelf and, his eye burning, read aloud from a book, " 'I envy not in any moods the captive void of noble rage.' " He put the book back on the shelf and looked at Lisa.

Lisa raised her eyebrows and said, "Yeah?"

MacMurphy nodded. "Tennyson." He pulled another book from the shelf, paged through it, and read, " 'Ah, love, let us be true to one another! for the world, which seems to lie before us like a land of dreams, so various, so beautiful, so new, hath really neither joy, nor love, nor light.' "

"Hmm," Lisa said.

"Matthew Arnold," MacMurphy said. "Just saying." He limped to their bedroom and climbed into bed.

After a few minutes, Lisa stripped off her clothes and climbed in beside him. She smelled of cigarette smoke and tequila. He turned from her but she put her hand on the small of his back.

For the next week, MacMurphy spoke to her only words that he found in books. He looked at her across the breakfast table. " 'I crave your mouth, your voice, your hair. Silent and starving, I prowl through the streets.' Pablo Neruda."

"Sexy," she said, and drank her coffee.

He watched from bed as she slid her feet into leather boots before taking the Volvo for another servicing. " 'It is not because other people are dead that our affection for them grows faint, it is because we ourselves are dying.' Marcel Proust."

"Pathetic," she said, and jangled the car keys.

When she returned, exhausted, from getting the steering aligned, he gazed at her from the couch. " '*Omnia vincit amor.*' 'Love conquers all.' Virgil."

"More," she said. When he said nothing, she added, "You know, we could work this out."

MacMurphy knew how he wanted to work it out. Richard joined him when he could, but he'd started writing an article on the Figurations of Medieval French-Norman pain, and that was taking most of his free time.

Still they managed to talk each day by phone, and MacMurphy bounced ideas off his friend.

"What do you know about Semtex?" he asked.

Two hours later, he called again. "If I go with carbon monoxide, how do I convince her to stay in the car while I hook up the tube?"

One afternoon, MacMurphy drove to the library and found Lisa's friend Margaret at the children's desk. "Larry!" she said.

"Where do I find books on industrial accidents?" he asked.

"You're looking healthier," she said. "Are you feeling better?"

He realized he was. His bones were healing. He felt more energy than he'd felt since the deer tick fastened to his thigh. "I am," he said. She stared at him as if marveling at how good he looked, so he asked again, "Industrial accidents?"

Margaret said, "Section three sixty-three, next to tsunamis. More in Government Documents." As MacMurphy walked away, she added, " 'Revenge is a dish best served cold.' "

MacMurphy stopped. He said, "A proverb of unknown origins."

Margaret smiled. "But often misattributed to Choderlos de Laclos."

MacMurphy liked this woman. Maybe after he killed Lisa, he would ask her for a date.

Along with books on chemical spills, boiler explosions, and machine-related amputations, MacMurphy found studies of common workplace injuries. The leading causes were slips, falls, and strains. If MacMurphy wanted nothing more than to sprain Lisa's ankle, he could smear the floor of her law firm restroom with Valvoline or saw the heel on a shoe so it would break when she ran for a train.

Next on the list were collisions with vehicles and moving equipment. But Lisa's office stood seven floors above street-level traffic and the elevator was the only moving equipment at that height. An elevator accident might be nice—plunging into the subbasement would have the same benefits as a fall from the fourth-level balcony at Soldier Field—except MacMurphy couldn't assure that Lisa would board alone, and he preferred to avoid general slaughter.

Next was electric shock—a fine option since he could electrocute her either at work or at home. A toaster could fall into the kitchen sink while she washed dishes. A cup of coffee, spilled onto her laptop, could turn her fingers into sparklers. A cross-wired photocopier could jolt her from her feet to her nose.

"Yes," MacMurphy said, so loudly that Margaret smiled at him.

He drove home and disassembled a waffle iron. He threw out the iron griddle plates and unwrapped a span of bare copper wire from inside the housing. He spliced the copper wire onto the ends of the electrical cord, making a loop the size of a small lasso. In the bathroom, he pressed the copper loop into the space where the rim of the toilet bowl hung over the water, so the wire was invisible whether the seat was up or down. He tucked the cord behind the toilet and plugged it in. When Lisa flushed the toilet and water ran over the live wire ... *Zap!*

No one would mistake her death for a common accident. But if MacMurphy disposed of the cord and wire afterward, no one would suspect murder either. Even hardened investigators would be too embarrassed to look into the death closely. A freak lightning strike sent a charge through the plumbing, they might say—or maybe Lisa dragged her socks on the carpet before sitting down. Whatever. No one would want to know.

MacMurphy went to the kitchen, filled a drinking glass at the sink, and returned to the bathroom door. After catching his breath, he tossed the contents of the glass across the bathroom toward the toilet.

He expected a small explosion when the water hit the basin. He expected blue electricity to arc into the air.

Nothing happened.

He inched toward the toilet and peered in. Water from the glass had splashed up the sides of the basin and made contact with the copper loop, but no red-hot glow circled the bowl.

What had MacMurphy misjudged? The copper loop should close the circuit from the two ends of the electrical cord. The splashed water should carry the electrical charge from the loop and jolt anything and anyone nearby. This seemed like basic electronics.

He checked the places where he'd spliced the wire with the electrical cord. He jiggled the plug in the outlet. He tossed another glass of water into the toilet bowl.

Nothing.

Maybe he needed to prime the mix. He went to the garage, brought back a jug of gasoline he used for the lawn mower, and poured a quarter inch into the toilet bowl. The gas would float on the toilet water. The fumes would rise around the copper wire loop.

But the room smelled like gas. What would Lisa think? MacMurphy put an air freshener, scented like Mountain Mist, on the toilet tank.

He filled the drinking glass again. He threw the water into the toilet bowl.

He heard a pop—a little one—and then a fireball engulfed the bathroom. The toilet blew into baseball-sized chunks of white ceramic, breaking the window and mirror, cracking the tile, embedding in the sheetrock. The flames and debris threw MacMurphy out the door, across the hall, and into the living room.

His hair and pants were on fire.

He rolled on the floor. He got up and danced. He tamped down the flames with the couch cushions.

Then, as fire licked across the living room ceiling and wrapped around the window curtains, he ran outside onto the front lawn. When the police, the fire department, and the paramedics arrived, he was sitting cross-legged on the driveway, moaning as flames poked out of the second-story windows.

"What happened?" the police asked.

"Ooooh," he said.

"What happened?" the firemen asked.

"Ooooh."

"What happened?" the paramedics asked.

"The toilet exploded," he said.

"What?"

"Ooooh."

Dr. Gajani and the nurse named Grace came to him at his hospital bed. The doctor checked the bandages that the ER technicians had wrapped around MacMurphy's legs and head. When the doctor saw that the injuries to his legs extended no higher than mid-thigh, he said, "You're a lucky man."

"Blessed," Grace said.

The doctor said, "The investigators figured out what happened"—words MacMurphy had been dreading. The doctor touched his left leg. "Does this hurt?"

"Yes. What do the investigators—"

"And this?"

"Ow."

"And this?"

"Please don't."

Dr. Gajani nodded. "A gas line ruptured under your house. Chances were ten to one against you surviving."

But when Lisa visited, she whispered, "What *really* happened?"

Sweat broke between MacMurphy's legs and on his forehead, needling his burns.

She leaned close. "Did you try to kill yourself?"

"I don't know what you're talking about," he said.

"Because tragic men turn me on," she said. She kissed his bandaged head, and the pressure of her lips shot pain deep into his skull.

When Grace checked on him later, his burns ached, but he turned down her offer of Demerol. Was he tragic? The idea appealed to him. Maybe it was time to stop fantasizing about chasing sylphs across pastoral fields. Could he grow into someone bigger? Someone heroic and broken? He could try.

He lay watching the dust motes in the sunlight. He looked out the window as clouds obscured the sun and a gentle snow began to fall. He regarded the light on the heart monitor as it charted each little earthquake in his chest. The voices of doctors, nurses, and family members visiting other patients filtered into his room from the corridor. The hospital had put him in a ward for stable cases—a mistake, surely, but, for now, he played his part, remaining quiet, untroublesome, even good-humored. Grace spent her work breaks sitting in a chair by his bedside. She said, "It's good luck to stay close to someone who's blessed."

On discharge day, Lisa and Dwayne the mechanic came to watch Dr. Gajani and Grace snip the bandages from MacMurphy's scalp. When the last layer of cotton gauze came off and the doctor washed away the healing salve with a damp cloth, the nurse held a mirror so MacMurphy could see. His smooth, hairless head shined pink, with a wrinkle over his eyebrows where the burn was scarring.

"Like a baby's bottom," Dr. Gajani said.

Dwayne laughed.

Lisa said, "Shut up, Dwayne."

Dwayne looked hurt.

She said, "It looks ... *hot*."

The nurse nodded.

MacMurphy asked, "You think so?"

Lisa said, "I've always fantasized about you bald."

The nurse said to Dwayne, “Time to scram.”

“I’ll drive you home,” Lisa said to MacMurphy with that look in her eyes.

“We don’t have a home,” MacMurphy said. “I burned it.”

Lisa said, “I’ve always fantasized about doing it in the Volvo.”

MacMurphy smiled a tragic smile and pulled Lisa to him. “ ‘Love is blind, and lovers cannot see the pretty follies that themselves commit.’ ”

THE VACUUM GANG

Bev Vincent

Mikey looked more excited than usual when he arrived at Marty's, our regular hangout at the end of Beacon Street in Chelsea. We watched him come in from our table at the back, across from the restrooms, and called out his name in greeting when he was halfway across the pub. He paused to greet Holly, because he knows that gets on my nerves, but I could tell from the look on his face he was up to something.

He slid in next to Vinnie, who was sitting beside Huey. Edgar and I were on the other side of the table. Edgar takes up the same amount of space as any two of us combined.

"You guys heard about this new thing called 'jackpotting'?" he asked.

That sounded like something I should know about, seeing as how I spend so much time at the casinos across the state line in New Hampshire, but I shook my head, as did the others.

"Jackpotting?" Huey asked. "What's that?"

"It's this thing where you hook up a laptop computer to an ATM and convince it to start spitting out money," Mikey said, his falsetto voice even higher than usual.

Holly brought Mikey his PBR draft and graced me with a smile. Everyone else was so caught up by what Mikey had said that no one noticed. Just me, which was perfectly fine.

I could almost see visions of $20 bills flying through the air in everyone's faces. I could certainly picture it myself. I could imagine us driving around Boston in Vinnie's car, going from ATM to ATM, gathering up mounds of cash.

I don't want to give the impression that all we do is sit around, drink beer, and try to come up with new ways to steal stuff. Well, we do spend a lot of time sitting around drinking beer—slowly, making each one lasts as long as we can. And the subject of money does come up a lot, because we don't have any, and we always need some.

Huey, for example, has a couple of kids and he has to pay child support, even though his ex hardly ever lets him see them. They live down in Chatham and he doesn't have a car, so it's hard on the poor guy. It takes over three and a half hours on the bus each way to get there. Vinnie drives him when he can, but he signed up with Uber lately, so he's busy with that a lot.

And Edgar, he's working as a janitor at a department store. A few years ago he decided to file his taxes without anyone's help and he got in a ton of trouble with the IRS over undeclared income and unpaid back taxes. Mikey told him he needed a legitimate source of income to explain where his money was coming from, because every now and then we do hit on a scheme that works out and we're flush for a few weeks.

As for me, I'm always on the hook to someone—sometimes several someones—because I always fall for the sure bet that's really sure to do only one thing: cost me a bunch of money. I'm trying to kick the habit—Holly goes with me to Gamblers Anonymous meetings when she's not working at Marty's—but putting a bunch of gamblers together in a church basement isn't as good an idea as it might sound.

"So how does it work?" Vinnie asked. "Where did you hear about it?"

"They were talking about it on the TV news," Mikey said, "when I was at the gym."

"You go to the gym?" Edgar—whose muscles have muscles—asked.

"I work out," Mikey said. He flexed a pale, skinny arm. We did our best not to laugh.

"Lifting mugs of beer doesn't count," Huey said.

"A buddy lets me use his membership card at his club," Mikey said. "I go a couple of times a week."

"Anyway," Vinnie said. "Jackpotting, right?"

"Yeah, apparently it's been going on overseas for a couple of years, but it started happening in the states recently. These guys dressed up like they were fixing the ATM but they were really installing malware that let them take it over. Then the machine spit out a bill a second until it was empty."

Vinnie pulled out a smart phone and pushed a few buttons. "If they're all twenties, that's $1200 a minute."

We all stared him.

"Where'd you get *that?*" Mikey said, his voice high enough to pierce eardrums. Dogs in the back alley were probably barking their heads off.

Vinnie pretended to look confused. He knows what that looks like, because it's Edgar's normal expression, but Vinnie couldn't quite pull it off.

"What? This?" He glanced at the smart phone.

"Yes. *That*," Mikey said. When he's mad he gets very terse.

"I need it for my job. You can't be an Uber driver without using their app."

"You know they can track you with that, right?"

We all knew who "they" were. Mikey has lectured us countless times about "them," the dark web of agents who spend their time spying on law-abiding citizens. It sounded like a boring job to me. One time Huey told Mikey we didn't need to worry because we weren't law abiding. Mikey didn't appreciate the joke.

We knew better than to take his bait. We were too caught up in this vision of money spewing out of ATMs. Vinnie pushed a few buttons and clicked around until he found an article about jackpotting, which he read to us. The story confirmed what Mikey said. The thieves were targeting older model ATMs that weren't at banks. Like the ones in convenience stores, where there wasn't as much security.

"Does anyone have a laptop?" Huey asked.

We all sat there quietly and stared at our beer.

"And if anyone did have one, does anyone know how to program malware for an ATM?"

More silence. I took a small sip of beer. The bubble had burst, and that cloud of $20 bills floated away. I was glad we hadn't ordered another round on the promise of all that cash. I wasn't flat broke, but the tire was definitely soft.

"Oh well, it was just an idea," Mikey said, although I could tell he was disappointed.

"I hear money zipping past my head every day," Edgar said all a sudden.

Vinnie opened his mouth to respond, but stopped. I knew how he felt. Sometimes Edgar says things that make absolutely no sense. He lives in his own special world, Edgar does, and that's okay because it's a happy place. Edgar, for all his shortcomings, is the happiest guy I've ever met.

If he noticed our confusion, Edgar didn't let on. "Yeah. They have this new automatic system. It looks really old, but cool. Delivers the money from the cash registers straight into the safe."

"It looks old but it's new?" I asked.

"Yeah, Frankie. They call it new automatic. Something like that. Looks like it's been there forever."

"Maybe pneumatic?" Huey said.

Edgar thought for several seconds. "Maybe."

"Tubes in the ceiling that they send money through with air pressure?"

"I guess," Edgar said. "I can hear them whiz past when I get to work and they're closing for the day."

"And these tubes go straight into the safe?" Vinnie asked.

"Yup," Edgar said. He seemed pleased, as if he had suggested something important.

"Hmmm," Vinnie said. "Do you think you could take some pictures?"

Two days later we were back at Marty's. Well, to be honest, I was there the next day too. I go every chance I get because I don't get to see Holly very often otherwise.

Edgar was the last to arrive and he grinned like the happy idiot he is when we all yelled out his name when he came through the door. He was carrying an envelope from CVS and I wondered—not for the first time in all of our years of doing questionable things together—how wise it was to have the pictures we needed to case a joint printed at the local pharmacy. Edgar had probably charged them to a credit card too. Mikey gets worked up over imaginary groups spying on people, but I think it will be a simple goof-up like this that gets us in big trouble one of these days.

Vinnie took the envelope from Edgar, and I wondered if he was thinking the same thing. He shrugged—nothing we could do about it now.

Huey wiped up the water rings from our beer mugs with a napkin. Then Vinnie spread the pictures out on the tabletop for us all to see. Holly knows to leave us alone when we're doing stuff like this. She doesn't approve, but she likes me for who I am, not what I do—or so she's told me whenever the subject comes up.

The department store was fairly new, but they'd made it look old-fashioned, like one of those places in a black and white movie with Santa Claus and all that. The pictures showed a system of pneumatic tubes that relayed the day's take from the cash registers to the safe. They met up at a junction box six feet from the safe, where the little plastic trays holding the envelopes were ejected. A single tube carried the envelopes the rest of the way.

Huey tapped the pipe. "What's it made of?"

"Aluminum, I think," Edgar said.

We stared at the pictures a while longer, as if some new detail might miraculously pop out of them.

"I think it's doable," Mikey said.

So, this is how our thinking went. Air carried the envelopes of cash into the safe, so air should be able to spirit them back out again. Not air, exactly. The envelopes weren't *pushed* into the safe—they were *pulled* in by reduced pressure. Like ...

"Like a vacuum cleaner," I said.

"Exactly," Vinnie said. "Who has one of those?"

We all looked at each other. The chance of any of us owning a vacuum cleaner was about the same as one of us owning a laptop computer.

"Holly might," Mikey said.

"Leave her out of this," I said. "We're not getting her involved."

There was a long pause. I stared at Mikey until he blinked first.

"Fine," he said, but I could tell he wasn't happy.

"I have a Dust Buster," Edgar said. "My sister gave it to me for Christmas a couple of years ago. It picks up any Cheerios I spill real good."

I gave him a second before letting him down. His heart is in the right place even if his head isn't always. "Um, it probably needs to be a little bigger than that. With a hose, you know, to fit in the pipe."

Edgar took it in stride. "Oh, yeah, Frankie. Sure."

We gathered up the pictures and moved our beer mugs back onto the table while we contemplated the problem. "We could always buy one," Huey said, but we hate to spend money on something that might not work.

A few seconds later, Vinnie slapped his forehead. "Guys! Guys! This is a department store. I'll bet they sell vacuum cleaners, right?"

Edgar shrugged. "I dunno. I just mop the floors and sweep and ..."

"Let me guess," Mikey said.

When he didn't go on, Edgar gave him a look. "Go on, Mikey. Guess!"

"You vacuum the floors."

"I do. I do."

"So we're all set," I said. "When's your next shift?"

We decided to go on a night when Edgar wasn't working, which meant a Sunday night. We knew there were probably cameras that Edgar didn't know about, so we took every precaution. We dressed all in black and put on ski masks that Edgar pilfered from the sports department. We only wanted four, we said, which made Edgar put on his confused face.

"Dude," Huey said. "Look at you."

Edgar looked down.

"If they get us on a surveillance video and they figure out we didn't break in, they're going to wonder who has a key and the alarm codes. If a big guy like you shows up on the video, it's game over."

I'm not sure Edgar really understood the problem, but he's smart enough to know when he doesn't know something, so he didn't argue.

"Just tell us where to find your cleaning equipment and we'll do the rest," I said.

Our plan wasn't to empty the safe. That would have been a onetime thing. The store owners would figure out they'd been robbed and take countermeasures. That was Vinnie's word. "It's like taking blood from someone," he said. "Take it all, and the patient dies. Take a little, and he makes more."

If we could get in and out undetected, we could keep going back, he said. It would be like our own personal ATM. We didn't know exactly how much was in the safe at any given time, but it was a pretty big store. Three stories with dozens of departments and two or three cash registers in each. Not only would we have to cut the pipe to tap into the safe, we'd have to replace it when we were done in a way that no one would notice and, ideally, in a way that would let us tap into it more easily in the future.

The first night didn't go as well as we might have hoped, but we had plenty of experience with failure, so that didn't get us down. We had no trouble getting into the store. Edgar's key fit, and he got the alarm code mostly right. We had a bad minute or two when it didn't work at first, but Mikey guessed that Edgar had mixed up two numbers and he figured it out before the alarm went off.

The room where the safe was located was in the basement, to let gravity work with the pneumatic system instead of against it. That door was locked, too, but Edgar's master key opened it. I guess they hadn't done much of a background check before handing him the keys. Either that or they put a lot of faith in the robust safe that held their intake.

It was an impressive safe, I had to admit. I'm not sure we could've gotten into it with a blowtorch and all the time in the world. The pneumatic inlet, though, was a different matter. Although Edgar had guessed it was aluminum, it turned out to be some kind of impact-resistant plastic. That meant most of the tools we'd brought wouldn't work. The problem wasn't cutting the pipe—that was easy peasy. The issue was that we were going to have to reassemble the tube when we were done. It had to be a good enough job so no one would notice, and the seal had to be perfect or the pneumatic system wouldn't work anymore, and someone would investigate. Our ATM would be closed.

So we scavenged around the hardware department to find the things we needed to complete the job. Vinnie wouldn't let us start until we had everything all lined up, which was smart, I guess. We didn't want to get into the project only to discover we were missing that one important tool to finish the job. We couldn't exactly head off to Back Bay Hardware in the middle of the night.

It was frustrating, though. We were all eager to get our hands on the cash. While Vinnie and Mikey worked on the pneumatic tube, Huey and I rounded up Edgar's vacuum cleaner from the janitor's closet and ran an extension cord that reached into the safe room.

It was after 3:00 AM when we were ready to give it a shot. Or, we thought we were ready. It took another ten minutes to figure out the vacuum cleaner. We could turn it on and run it across the floor, but we didn't know how to disconnect the hose so we could run it into the pneumatic tube. Once we solved that problem, we inserted the nozzle into the pipe as far as it would go. Finally we were ready to flip the switch.

"Too bad Edgar isn't here to see this," Huey said. Our oversized friend hadn't been happy about being left behind. He had pooched out his lower lip, looking like one of those sad sack dogs they show on the Internet.

Vinnie slapped his forehead. "We could have called him on Face Time. It's just like being there."

Mikey snorted. "Two problems with that." He stuck up a thumb. "Edgar doesn't have Face Time, and ..."—he glared at Vinnie as he raised his index finger—"... do you really want to broadcast our crime on the Internet so *they* can watch us?"

Vinnie grimaced and for a few seconds we were all quiet, waiting to see if Mikey would launch into one of his tirades.

"Let's do this," he said, and stepped on the foot pedal that started the vacuum cleaner motor.

For several seconds, nothing seemed to happen. The vacuum cleaner whirred and whirred, its pitch rising until it almost matched Mikey's voice. Then we heard a rumble and clunk, a swishing noise and a thunk. The vacuum cleaner started to whine as if it had something stuck in the nozzle, which was the whole point after all.

Mikey gave the vacuum cleaner a kick to turn off. I grabbed the nozzle and slowly pulled it out of the pneumatic tube. The room grew quiet as we held our breath in anticipation. Finally, the nozzle was clear.

Nothing.

I stared into the nozzle, cautiously, as if it might go off like a loaded rifle.

Still nothing.

I shook the nozzle and felt along its soft pliable length. I disconnected it from the base—we knew how to do that now—and looked through it. I could see light at the other end.

"Check the bag," Vinnie said.

"Of course," I said. It took me a few seconds to get the little door open with trembling fingers. I pulled out the bag and was about to tear into it when Vinny stepped in.

"Careful," he said. "We don't want to get dust everywhere." He took the bag from me and squeezed it. A cloud of dust emerged from the opening, covering his ski mask in dirt and lint. If Edgar had been here, he would have guffawed loud enough to set off car alarms three streets away. As it was, the rest of us snickered, but then tried to pretend we hadn't.

Vinnie sputtered and wiped at his face, twisting the mask so that his eyes no longer lined up with the holes. He thrust the bag out and I took it while he got himself sorted out.

I'm no dummy. I learned from Vinnie's experience. I gently squeezed the bag with the opening pointed away from my face. A little more dust came out, but not much. I should have been able to feel envelopes inside, if there were any.

"Gimme a flashlight," Mikey said. He stuck the end into the pneumatic tube and tried to peer around it. "Think I see something. It's in quite a way."

Vinnie slapped his forehead. One of these days he's going to give himself a concussion. "When you turned the vacuum off, it let go," he said. He grabbed the hose and pushed Mikey aside. While he threaded the nozzle back into the tube, I scrambled to reinstall the dirt bag and shut the compartment door. I had just finished when Vinnie stepped on the pedal and the machine roared to life again. A second later, that thunking sound repeated and the vacuum cleaner whined. Vinnie pulled the nozzle out of the tube slowly.

A white envelope was stuck to the end of vacuum cleaner nozzle. Just one, but it was something. While Vinnie opened it, Mikey investigated the pneumatic tube with his flashlight. A few seconds later he shook his head. "I don't see anything else."

Vinnie put the nozzle back in the tube and fired up the cleaner, but nothing happened.

"We need a stronger vacuum, I think," Huey said.

That made sense to the rest of us.

"We'll figure something out for the next time," Vinnie said. "It's getting late. Let's clean everything up and get out of here."

Mikey was looking at the envelope. His brow was furrowed. "Uh, guys."

"What?" Vinnie said.

"It's labeled. STATION G-14. With yesterday's date."

"So?"

"Don't you think someone is supposed to open this envelope and record the amount in a ledger or something?"

Vinnie frowned. "Maybe," he said, stretching the word out.

"So they'll notice if there's no envelope from STATION G—14 for Saturday."

We stood there for a while, four grown men in black clothes, wearing ski masks, one of them coated with dust, and contemplated the problem.

"We can't take all the money," Huey said finally. "We have to put some back and stick the envelope back in the tube. It'll get sucked into the safe when they fire the pneumatics back up again tomorrow."

"How much is in it?" I asked.

Mikey did a quick count. "$327."

"Let's take half," Vinnie said. He calculated the amount on his phone, ignoring Mikey's glare. "One sixty."

Mikey counted out five twenties, five tens and ten ones. "That'll be $32 each. Big haul."

It would buy food and beer for a few days, I thought, but it wouldn't make a dent in what I owed the bookies. Not much child support for Huey's kids or gas for Vinnie's car either.

"Next time we'll do better," Vinnie said as we reassembled the pneumatic tube and cleaned up after ourselves, returning all the equipment we'd borrowed to where we found it.

The first traces of morning light were pushing away the gloom of night when we emerged from the side door, reset the alarm, locked up after ourselves and made our way around the corner to where Vinnie's car was parked.

A ticket was tucked under the windshield wiper. In the middle of the night, if you can believe it. We'd parked too close to a fire hydrant and some bored cop had written the car up.

The fine? A hundred bucks.

Our second visit to what we were calling our department store ATM went a little better. First, we made sure we parked well away from hydrants. Not only could we not afford to pay any more fines, we didn't want to have our movements on record with the police department. That was how they caught the Son of Sam, Mikey told us on the drive to the store.

Edgar had told us where to go to find the shop vacs. We picked the one with the most suction and carried the box down to the room with the safe. Huey and I unboxed it carefully so we could repack it when we were done, while Vinnie and Mikey worked on opening up the pneumatic tube.

"Here goes," Mikey said when he stuck the nozzle into the tube. Or tried to—it wouldn't fit. Huey searched the box and came up with a long attachment that was narrower and another one that was narrower still. Vinnie attached one to the end of the other and connected both to the hose. These fit into the opening and extended our reach well into the tube.

"Second time's the charm," Mikey said. He nodded at me and I flipped the toggle switch on the side of the stubby little shop vac. It made a hell of a racket, but it sounded powerful, and we were rewarded a few seconds later with not one but three solid thunks. Remembering our mistake from last time, Vinnie withdrew the hose attachments while the vacuum was still running.

Lo and behold, three plump envelopes were stuck to the end of the narrower attachment. What's more, when Vinnie reinserted the nozzle, we heard a couple more envelopes attach themselves to the end. We had this down!

Except when Vinnie pulled on the hose to remove our second catch, the narrower of the two attachments came loose and stayed in the tube.

"Crap," Mikey said. That was strong language for him. He hardly ever swore, although he has plenty of words that sound like cusses that he uses in their place.

It took a good half hour to fish the attachment out of the pneumatic tube. We ended up using a bent coat hanger from the men's department, but it took quite a few tries and lots of words stronger than the ones Mikey used. And that only got the attachment. The envelopes were still in there, and we weren't leaving without them. So we taped the two attachments together and went back in to retrieve them.

We carefully removed half the cash from each envelope and stuffed them back in the tube. Huey had the clever idea to reverse the flow on the shop vac and push the envelopes back into the safe, which worked pretty well. We packed the vacuum cleaner in its box, taped it shut and returned it to its place in the hardware department while Vinnie and Mikey reattached the pneumatic tube.

The next afternoon, we met up at Marty's and gave Edgar his share of our ill-gotten gains. Each of us cleared $250, which was nice, but nothing like what we'd imagined. The jackpotters were pulling in $1200 a minute, and it was taking us hours to get that much.

We decided to go for broke next time, so to speak. After only two trips to the department store, we were getting frustrated with the process, so we would do one more job and keep everything we took. No putting half of it back. No worrying about covering our tracks.

We were going to suck that puppy dry.

Edgar told us he had found the perfect solution to our problem in the lawn and garden department. "It's for sucking up leaves off the lawn," he said. "It's really strong." It sounded like a great idea.

We decided to bring Edgar with us this time. He'd been really down about being left behind, and since it was going to be our last time, we thought: why not?

Obviously we should have paid more attention to what Edgar was doing. It was Edgar, after all. But our heads were too filled with visions of armloads of cash. That's always the way, isn't it? At least, that's how it is with me. Somebody tells me about a deal that's too good to be true and I get taken in like the sucker I am.

Mikey and Vinnie went to work on the pneumatic tube. This time, we wouldn't have to worry about putting it back, so they cut into it as close as they could get to the safe. Edgar went off to get his super powerful leaf blower. I've never used one, but I've heard them, generally at some ungodly hour like ten o'clock in the morning when people should still be in bed. I figured anything that made that much noise must put out a lot of power.

Like I said, visions of armloads of cash.

Edgar, bless his soul, had thought ahead. He knew the diameter of the tube and he had rigged up an attachment that went *over* the pneumatic tube. That meant we didn't have to worry about pieces falling off inside. We were all surprised by his ingenuity.

The side of the box said the thing could blow 150 miles per hour, which sounded terrific to me. As I kept reading, envelopes went whizzing down the tube into the leaf blower and then into the bag at the back where, according to the specs on the box, debris was reduced by a factor of eight to one.

It took me too many seconds to work out what that meant.

"Stop!" I yelled. "Turn it off!"

I do believe we sucked the safe dry that evening. We also reduced several thousand dollars—we would never know how much—into confetti, all neatly tucked into the leaf bag attached to the mulcher.

"Effing heck," Mikey said, which pretty much summed things up.

We left everything like it was and headed back to Vinnie's car. No one said a word on the drive home.

"That's me," Edgar said the next evening at Marty's, pointing at the surveillance video of the five crooks who had tried to rob the department store and made such a botch of it. "Dumbest robbers in the state?" the text on the bottom of the screen said.

I felt my face go red. Holly must have noticed, as she showed up a minute later with a round on the house. I've lost track of how many times she's done that for us. I put a $20 bill on her tray as a tip, which was a good chunk of my profits.

"Jackpot!" Huey muttered once the news team got done laughing at us.

"Jack-effing-pot," Mikey agreed.

LLOYD'S LISTS

Steve Beresford

"Dead?"

"Yes, dead." Lloyd Archer seemed almost pleased to be the bearer of such bad news. "How about that, eh?" Said like it was some funny anecdote he'd just read on Twitter.

"Jack's dead?" Donna felt as though someone—well, Lloyd—had punched her in the chest. Her heart thudded. Her lungs were shutting down. She struggled to keep the reactions from reaching her expression. "How?" she managed to say.

"Some sort of random mugging. Head bashed in. Apparently." Her husband waved his phone. "According to Phil." Lloyd had taken the call from Phil—who was a neighbour of Jack's. He put the phone down on the breakfast table, next to the lists and aisle diagrams he was using to plan their next trip to the supermarket, and seemed to be waiting for some response. "Terrible news, don't you agree?"

Donna couldn't decide what was the best way to react. Keep it blank, maybe? Or give it some loud wailing and gnashing of teeth? She obviously had to react in some way. But as she couldn't really decide how she felt—felt inside, in the secret place where these days Lloyd was excluded—reacting outwardly was offering up something of a challenge. Was she sad? Relieved? A mixture of both?

Trouble was, Lloyd was still staring at her, still waiting.

"Oh dear," she said, simply to buy herself some time and come to grips with the news. "What a shame."

Of course—obviously—she was upset. She'd known Jack Wentworth for ages, after all. He and his wife Lucy were major figures in Little Wickham. They lived in the big house on the outskirts of the quiet village, which Donna and Lloyd had visited many times. They had no children—Lucy's internal whatnots weren't up to the job, apparently—but they did have two dogs, Whip and Fedora. Jack was a big Indiana Jones fan. Those two would be devastated. Lucy too. Because Jack was in many ways a really great chap. Always optimistic, full of energy, very handsome. He did have the rugged features of a young Harrison Ford about him. He did a lot for charity too, mostly endurance cycling events. And Lucy baked a lot, selling her creations at village fetes and festivals, which Jack always helped to organise. The village raised a lot of money because of Jack and Lucy.

But Jack Wentworth was also a lying, two-timing adulterer with a definite tendency towards kinky games in the bedroom department.

Which Donna Archer knew because she was the woman he had been two-timing with. She never actually heard Jack do much lying, but reckoned he must have been a very good liar because Lucy—not quite a friend of hers, simply a friendly neighbour—hadn't suspected a thing. As far as Donna could tell anyway. And as for the kinky bedroom stuff, well, Donna still had the bruises from their last encounter.

Donna knew she should have felt more upset than she did about Jack's sudden death. But also bubbling up was a strong sense of relief. Jack had been getting serious. Too serious. Also too kinky, like he wanted to keep pushing the boundaries, when all Donna wanted was a bit of commitment-free passion and occasional excitement. Then Jack recently starting talk of leaving Lucy, getting a divorce, declaring their newfound love to the whole world. Basically, spoiling everything and ruining lives.

And Donna didn't want any of that. What started as a bit of fun, an escape from Lloyd and his lists and his general boringness, was turning into some sort of nightmare.

In fact, she was actively trying to think of a way to end it as amicably as possible, to protect both her and Lucy. She wanted to return to the old days before that first drunken fumble in the dark at the village's New Year party. Jack's grand ideas of a new life together might have suited him, but for Donna the whole affair had been a mistake. A fun and highly exciting mistake—at least in the early days—but a mistake nonetheless.

So news of his death wasn't exactly unwelcome. Horrible, but it did solve a problem.

"Are you all right?" Lloyd said.

"Hhmm?"

"You haven't heard a word, have you?"

Donna snapped back to the present, realising Lloyd was talking, but with no idea what he was saying. "What? No, sorry. It's the shock." Her head was swimming with what-might-have-beens. She had foreseen the utter chaos an announcement from Jack about their affair would have caused—and suddenly that threat was lifted.

"You don't imagine things like this happen in our village," she said. "A mugging, I mean. It's usually so quiet around here."

"Oh, it wasn't round here. It was in town actually." Lloyd cleared his throat. "So I understand anyway."

"It's still a shock."

"Clearly. You've gone as white as a sheet." Lloyd ushered her from the kitchen to the sofa in the lounge and forced her to sit. "I'll make some tea. That's good for shocks. You should drink it hot. I'll put something in it too."

"Poor Lucy," Donna said, trying to imagine what it was like to lose your husband. Then she thought of losing Lloyd. Well, his regular wage would be a loss anyway.

"Yes, poor Lucy." Lloyd returned from the kitchen. "Here, drink this." He forced a mug into her hands, then went to the drinks cabinet and took out the sherry, pouring a slug into the mug. Donna sipped it. It was hot and tasted foul. "Police are round there now, apparently," he said. "With Lucy."

Thinking of Lucy, Donna did now feel really upset. And the tears started to come. She put her tainted tea down and went directly to the sherry instead.

Lucy was a decent woman. They probably could have been really good friends, if circumstances were different. Donna never wanted to hurt her. She certainly wouldn't have wished this on her. Lucy had no doubt been totally in love with Jack and now he was gone. What would she do? How would she recover and carry on? What would she have done if she'd found about her husband's relationship with Donna?

"What a mess, eh?" Lloyd said, as though reading her thoughts. "There's a lot that needs organising now. People to tell, forms to fill in, a funeral to arrange. Crikey, when you think about it, a death really does generate a lot of hoo-ha. A lot of paperwork too. Maybe I should offer my humble services." He sounded rather excited at the prospect. "Least I can do really."

"I'm sure she's got family to do that." Donna couldn't imagine meeting the widow of her lover. Not quite yet. She was scared she would break down and blurt out her secrets when faced with the other woman's grief. A few more sherries might be required first. So she started quickly on the next.

"Yes, I suppose you're probably right." Lloyd sounded disappointed. "Maybe give it a day or two."

Lloyd liked organising. He was one of life's great organisers. If he wasn't making a list of jobs to do, then he was bullet-pointing the major sub-areas of one of those particular jobs. Even shopping trips were planned with frightening efficiency, like some sort of military campaign. And holidays could generate a whole binder full of lists and plans. Route plans for getting there, with alternatives for roadworks and hold-ups. Packing lists for suitcases. Daily itineraries to keep them occupied.

Which was partly why the affair with Jack had been so much fun—to start with. Jack didn't need lists. He was a go-getter. He grabbed opportunities. He grabbed Donna, in all the right places. The only things Lloyd ever grabbed these days were his notepad and pen. He wasn't like that when they married. Well, he was, but not to the same degree. His organisational skills were part of his charm back then. Sort of cute, in a nerdy kind of way. Now: simply brain-meltingly annoying.

The following day—lists at the ready, which included more sherry, added by Donna—Lloyd drove them to the big supermarket at the retail park on the outskirts of Chilfield, the nearest town. But they were hardly three minutes from home when it all started to go peculiar.

As they approached the bridge that marked the boundary of the village, Donna spotted the rather forlorn figure some 20 metres or so from the roadside, half-hidden amidst the trees. She was just standing there, staring into the tumbling river, her long ginger hair flowing down her back, her ankle-length white dress billowing in the breeze. Almost pre-Raphaelite, she looked.

"Lucy." There was the wife of the man she'd been sleeping with.

"She's not going to throw herself in, is she?" Lloyd brought the car to an abrupt halt, making the tyres squeal.

No, Donna didn't think so. Lucy looked more like she'd simply gone for a walk and stopped, as though she was run by clockwork and her internal spring had wound down.

They got out and approached. Lucy didn't even notice them, until Lloyd trod on a twig.

"Oh, hello." Lucy appeared blank and empty, her eyes unfocused as though watching something in the distance that only she could see. "You've heard, I suppose."

"Yes, and we're terribly sorry," Donna said.

"We were going to come round later," Lloyd said. "To offer our condolences."

"We didn't want to intrude. Not yesterday. Not straightaway. We know you'd have a lot to do, to process."

"But anything I can do for you," Lloyd said, "just give me the word. Any arrangements you want me to take over? I know there's a lot to organise."

"Thanks, but my parents have come down. They're taking care of all that."

"Yes, right, of course." Lloyd looked heartbroken, more at the missed opportunity for some solid list-making than anything else.

Lucy's mouth trembled. She was close to tears. In fact, she looked like she'd been crying a lot, which was hardly surprising. She glanced round as though unsure where she was and how she'd got there.

Donna had no idea what to say. She wanted to apologise, but that was impossible. Had Lucy been a close friend, one Donna hadn't betrayed, she might have opted for a silent hug.

"Don't suppose," Lloyd said, "the police have got any leads, have they?" Proving there was always something to say if you were insensitive enough. "Any evidence at all? The murder weapon perhaps?"

Lucy's mouth dropped open, unsure or unable to respond.

"I suppose in a case like this," Lloyd said, "with it being a random mugging, there's virtually no hope they'll catch the man responsible. Not unless he hands himself in and makes a full confession." He was oblivious to Lucy's increasing distress and to Donna's urgent rib-nudging. "Because really they're dependent on witnesses, aren't they? If no one saw anything, then they have nothing to work with. And I don't suppose ..."

"Lloyd!"

"I was only saying ..."

"Well, don't."

"The police wanted to know if he had any enemies," Lucy said. "But it was a ridiculous question. Everyone loved Jack."

"Yes," Lloyd said. "Ridiculous, indeed. Jack was very popular."

Donna wanted to say something about Jack—preferably something nice, although also as bland as possible—but Lucy beat her to it, dropping a bombshell into the already awkward conversation.

"I think Jack was having an affair," she said.

Donna's heart might have actually burst at that moment, such was the odd and painful sensation in her chest. And the woody air was suddenly impossible to breathe. "An ... an affair?"

"Jack?" Lloyd barked out a short, sharp laugh. "Jack would no sooner have an affair than I would."

Lucy shrugged. "It was a couple of weeks ago. I called him at work in the afternoon and he wasn't there. I tried his mobile and it was switched off. Doesn't really mean anything, I know. I asked him that night where he'd been and he said he was meeting a client. Anthony, he said his name was. Anthony something-something. Double-barrelled. Said he switched his phone off because he didn't want to be disturbed. And at the time I believed him. But then the next day I spoke to Sarah ..." Sarah? Donna didn't know any Sarahs. "... and she said she'd seen Jack the previous afternoon going into that hotel in town, the one on Beacon Road. With a woman. I didn't know what to say, so I played along. I told her he was meeting his sister. Made out that it was perfectly normal. Except, of course, it wasn't his sister ..."

No, Donna thought. That was me he was with. In that hotel. They rented rooms by the hour there, for special customers, if you knew how to ask properly. And Jack knew how to ask.

"... and it wasn't perfectly normal," Lucy continued. "Jack wouldn't be meeting any of his clients in a hotel like that. And why did he lie, if it was completely innocent?"

"Doesn't prove anything," Lloyd said.

"No, it doesn't," Donna said. Oh hell, the guilt! What if she'd been recognised?

"There was probably a completely innocent explanation."

Donna could have kissed her husband then, which was an urge she didn't have very often any more.

"But it wasn't just that," Lucy said. "There were other things. Other times. He was different. I could tell. There was another woman."

"Any idea ..." Donna could hardly get the words out. She had to painfully swallow away the lump that lodged in her throat. "... any idea who it was?"

Lucy shook her head. "And now I'll probably never know."

Which was probably for the best. Lucy had enough to cope with. There was no need to add to her burden.

"Are you going to be all right? Do you want a lift back home?"

"No, I'm fine. Really. The walk back will do me good. It's not as though I'm in any rush."

"If you're sure ..."

"I'm sure. Thanks all the same." Lucy set off walking, heading back along the path through the trees towards the village.

Donna and Lloyd watched her go.

"How do you cope with something like that?" Donna said.

"Hhmm, yes." Lloyd was frowning. He seemed troubled. He had become a fairly unemotional man—nothing much seemed to affect his equilibrium at all—but maybe this tragic incident was making him realise that life was for living, not listing.

"Come on," he said. "Let's go shopping."

A detective sergeant appeared on their doorstep later that day.

"Mrs Archer? Detective Sergeant Barnes." He held up identification, then tucked it back in his jacket pocket. "If you could spare ten minutes ..." He was a tall, bulky man with a grizzled expression and a crumpled suit. The village grapevine—well, Phil on the phone again—had already informed them that the police were going house to house.

"Just a few questions about Jack Wentworth," DS Barnes said. "If you don't mind."

"Of course," Lloyd said, appearing at Donna's side. "We've got nothing to hide, sergeant. Have we, Donna?" Making it sound as though they had much to hide.

Donna wondered if Lucy had mentioned her suspicions about Jack's adultery to the police. She hoped not.

They installed the detective sergeant in an armchair, offered him a drink, which he refused, and he took out his notebook. They sat on the sofa, next to each other, like a loving couple. Although other loving couples might have held hands for moral support.

"What would you like to know?" Donna said.

"I understand you might have a list ..."

"Oh yes?" Lloyd sat forward, suddenly eager.

"... of recent events in the village. I was given to believe you were the man to come to."

"Indeed!" Lloyd was overjoyed. "If you'll just wait a moment ..." He nipped out of the room and returned with a bundle of papers. He sat down again, riffled through them and extracted one sheet in particular. A second sheet tried to escape with it, like they were stuck together, but Lloyd hastily snatched that one back and tucked it at the bottom of the pile. "Don't know how that got in there. That's one for the shredder." He chuckled nervously, his face oddly flushed. "This is the one you want, sergeant." He handed over the first sheet. "As you can see—dates and time and attendances of recent village events and meetings. I do like to keep track. Any particular reason you're interested?"

"Just background. We're following a few leads and it appears that the mugging might be connected to people or events in the village. Doesn't seem, you see, like this was any old random mugging. It looks too staged. Too organised."

"Organised?" said Donna.

DS Barnes nodded. "As though someone was trying to make it look like just another mugging, but got the details slightly wrong." He smiled. "So we're checking out Mr Wentworth's background."

"Gosh," said Lloyd, who ran a finger around the inside of his collar, like he was suddenly hot.

Sergeant Barnes copied any relevant information into his notebook, then handed the sheet back. Lloyd tucked it away in his haphazard sheaf. Donna wondered how Lloyd could love his lists so much, but be so untidy about storing them.

"We've also heard," said DS Barnes, "that it's possible Mr Wentworth was having an affair."

And there it was! Lucy had mentioned her suspicions then. Donna tried not to react.

"There's nothing concrete apart from a couple of unexplained absences from the office and a sighting of Jack with a woman two weeks ago."

"Identified the woman yet, sergeant?" Lloyd said.

"All we have is a vague description. It could fit an awful lot of women." DS Barnes looked directly at Donna. "Could even fit you, Mrs Archer."

Donna wanted to shrivel up and vanish.

"Are you accusing her of having an affair with Jack?" Lloyd laughed loudly. Probably too loudly. And for far too long. "Sergeant, my wife is about as likely to have had an affair with Jack as I am to have murdered him." And Lloyd laughed some more.

Donna stared at her husband. And a chill ran through her, raising goose-pimples on her arms. No, it wasn't possible. Was it? She realised the sergeant was looking at her again.

She forced a smile and said, "Jack was nice, but he wasn't really my type." Which, in a sense, was true. That's why she wanted to end the affair.

Sergeant Barnes asked a few more questions and was apparently satisfied with the answers—and the lies—that he was given.

"Thank you, Mrs Archer. Mr Archer. Here's my card if you think of anything else that might be relevant." Then DS Barnes headed off, down the garden path and along the pavement, presumably to put similar questions to their neighbours.

Donna closed the front door and turned to stare at her husband. Lloyd stood in the doorway of the lounge, clutching his batch of papers.

"That went well, I thought," he said. "Shall we have a drink to celebrate?

"What?" But she barged past him, heading straight for the drinks cabinet. Actually, a drink sounded like a brilliant idea. Then maybe another. And another. She threw down DS Barnes's card and poured herself a sherry—a large one—demolishing it in a single swig.

Then she turned on Lloyd, all her thoughts coalescing to form a single horrible truth. "Lloyd, what have you done?"

"Done? In what way?" But he was blinking and his cheery smile was faltering. "I only gave the man a list of ..."

"You killed Jack." Donna was going to frame it as a question, but it came out as a statement of fact.

"Only because you had the affair with him!" Lloyd snapped back.

Donna gasped. Not because of his accusation, but because he admitted the murder so easily.

"Oh yes, don't try to deny it," Lloyd said. "I knew. I've known for a long, long time. Then, one day, I realised all it would take was a little careful planning and organisation." He shook his papers at her, as though they were evidence of his planning.

"But you didn't have to kill him!"

"Well, no, I suppose not. But the more I thought about it, the more it seemed like a good idea. At first I thought that once he was out of the way we'd be able to settle down into the old routine. Just you and me, husband and wife again. No outside interference."

"You killed Jack for that? Why not just tell me you'd found out? Ask me to stop? Tell me you still loved me?"

Lloyd frowned, as though he hadn't considered that option.

"I was going to dump Jack anyway!"

"You were?" He frowned. "Well, it doesn't matter now anyway. Because once I realised I could do it, I also began to see that with Jack out of the way there'd be a vacancy in the village. Jack has always been the go-to guy to organise everything, to arrange the fetes and the fundraisers. But that ought to be me. I'm much more qualified." He rattled his papers again. "I have organisation in my blood. And with Jack out of the way I'd be the obvious next choice."

"You're insane! What's more, you're boring and insane!"

"And then I really began to see things clearly," Lloyd said. "If I, too, were no longer married, because, say, my wife also died, then I'd be free."

"What?" Donna was beginning to feel light-headed. Woozy. Her vision was wavering. "Free? I don't understand."

"You will soon." Lloyd smiled, a smug sort of smile.

"You see, I reckon Jack and Lucy didn't belong together. And I don't reckon you and me belong together. But me and Lucy? Now that could be a match made in heaven!"

"You and ..." Donna had to put a hand on the mantelpiece to steady herself. Her knees were turning to jelly. "... and Lucy?"

"Both grieving for our spouses. Me organising everything that Jack used to organise. We'd be drawn together, me and Lucy."

"But ... But ..."

"Won't be long now, Donna. You see, in a fit of despair and grief at losing your secret lover you succumbed to an overdose of drink and drugs." He nodded at the bottle in the drinks cabinet. "Sherry, to be exact."

Donna could feel something cold and evil creeping up her spine, taking away control of her limbs. Her fingers tightened around the empty sherry glass.

"I knew nothing about your affair," Lloyd said. "Or so I will tell the police. But you told me everything after that detective came and I stormed out and when I returned you'd killed yourself."

"No!" Donna slumped down on to the sofa. What had he put in that sherry bottle? Had he just done it, while she escorted DS Barnes out of the house? Whatever it was, it was acting fast.

"Well, yes, I'm afraid. I have it all planned." Once again, he shook his papers. "Slight mishap when I picked up some of the planning for my murders as well as the records of village events, but there you go. No harm done, as it turns out. I should really start shredding now the endgame has arrived."

Donna was having trouble processing all of this. First the affair with

Jack. She couldn't believe she'd been stupid enough to get involved with a married man. Then he'd been killed. Then her husband revealed himself to be the killer. And now he was apparently killing her. She blinked repeatedly, trying to focus. Tried to gather some strength into her arms and legs.

Lloyd stepped closer and leaned over. "Don't worry. It won't be long now. Just go to sleep and let yourself drift awa—"

With every ounce of power she could summon, Donna slammed her fist into the side of Lloyd's head. The sherry glass, still enclosed in her fingers, exploded in a shower of glass. Lloyd went down instantly, his papers scattering. Donna hauled herself up and stretched towards the sherry bottle, reaching for the card DS Barnes had given her, which still lay where she threw it down in anger. All she needed now was her phone. Luckily it was on the mantelpiece, she stretched and struggled a bit more and got hold of it. Dialled. Waited.

"Barnes here."

"This is ... is Donna." Every word was agony. She could barely stay awake.

"Donna?"

"Donna Archer." She slid to the floor. "Help me!"

Lloyd chose that moment to rouse himself. He slapped the phone from her hand and it skittered away beneath the sofa.

"You're ruining it all!" he whined, briefly touching his temple and looking surprised when his fingers came away blood-stained. "All my beautiful planning!" Then he set about retrieving his scattered papers, maybe thinking he could still get away with everything if only he could destroy the evidence before DS Barnes arrived, galloping to the rescue.

Donna couldn't let him do it. She snatched at some and he tried to snatch them back. There was a tussle, yanking back and forth. One sheet ripped and Donna ended up with just the torn corner clutched in her hand. She slumped back, strength leaving her abruptly, and Lloyd stood up, panting.

"I can still make this work," he said. "I only need to—" But whatever it was he thought he needed to do, Donna never did find out. Because Lloyd was turning as he spoke, but some papers were still on the floor and he slipped on one, his knee buckling awkwardly. He went down like a tree felled by a lumberjack. His head cracked the side of the coffee table. He was still breathing, she could see, but out cold.

Once again his papers fluttered down around him.

She could see some of them. One was the list of village events. Others listed jobs to be done around the house, errands to be run. But then, more importantly, there was a list of places that Jack Wentworth often visited. Another list detailed different murder weapons. There was a plan of some buildings, with a red cross marking a particular location. Another list showed times of day and listed journey lengths. Bullet points and tables. Lists and plans. Even a few diagrams.

It was, in effect, the complete outline of two murders. Lloyd had even detailed where and how he would dispose of both the murder weapon with which he had bashed Jack on the head and the clothes he had worn while doing it.

One more page had a corner missing, roughly ripped off. Donna held that corner in her fist. She reached for the rest of the page as she heard the front door crash open.

"Mrs Archer!" It was DS Barnes, coming to her rescue. "Donna!" He arrived in the lounge like a whirlwind, taking in the chaos. He spoke quickly into his phone. "And an ambulance too. Fast as you can!" He knelt amongst Lloyd's lists. "Are you okay?"

"Drugged," she managed. "Need help."

"Help is coming. Stay with me." He cradled her head and she knew she would be all right. Lloyd hadn't killed her after all. She looked down at the page she was holding and laughed when she read to the bottom. She showed it DS Barnes.

The page comprised a list of vital steps, like a summary. No, more like a checklist, each item listed for further work and elaboration in big handwritten block capitals.

CHOOSE WEAPON.

CHOOSE LOCATION.

BUY DRUGS.

COME UP WITH FIRM ALIBI.

DISPOSE OF WEAPON.

DISPOSE OF CLOTHES.

But that bottom corner was ripped off, removing the first word of the last three-word phrase.

The fragment was still in her hand. It contained one word.

DON'T ...

The two words that came after it were still there for them to read at the bottom of the page. Knowing Lloyd, he'd probably written all three as a humorous coda, a joke to himself. And Donna did laugh when she read them. Because now his accidentally amended checklist would be complete.

Lloyd groaned as he started to come round, possibly in pain, possibly in frustration. Possibly both. He certainly wouldn't be getting up any time soon though, not with two head wounds—especially not with DS Barnes cuffing him, just in case.

And those last two words at the bottom of the page?

... GET CAUGHT.

Oh yes, Lloyd had finished off his list perfectly.

THE 'B' WORD

Bill Kelly

She stood on the edge of the old railroad station, waiting on the Uber.

A cold grey sky did little to flatter the charmless wooden building, all bleached black shingles and peeling green paint. Built a hundred years ago with not much thought behind it and not a single thought since, it was the kind of structure that once Amtrak stopped running would be converted into a failing coffee shop, or a local museum that nobody visits, because really, how many black and white pictures of dead people and rusty farm implements can you look at anyway?

The concrete platform she was standing on was chipped and oil-stained. Blotches of discarded black gum lay spotted around her feet like the pelt of a sick Dalmatian ready to be put down.

If this fucking gum gets on my Gianvito Rossis, she thought, her short fuse growing shorter by the moment. *Someone is going to pay.*

And she meant it.

Hoping to avoid unnecessary dry cleaning, she hiked the cuffs on her chartreuse pant suit, lest they brush against the dirty cement. Not entirely reassured by her efforts, she exhaled an irritated trail of noxious smoke from her long brown cigarette, a thin cigar with penis envy.

The sign in front of her read: *Welcome to Gatlin, Kansas. Population: 11,320.*

A message scrawled in indelible blue Sharpie directly below it read: *SUCK IT!*

Beyond the sign was what was left of downtown, a couple of post-war brick stores with a tired *oh hell, I give up* appearance that mirrored the faces of the few stragglers still patronizing them. You didn't have to see into the future to know that the new river walk three towns over would soon strangle the last breath out of whatever life this sad place had left in it.

This is one shit town, she thought to herself.

And if anyone in this world knew about shit towns, it was her.

How many had she visited over the years? More than her share, that was for certain. In every land, all over the world. From First World capitals to Third World hole-in-the-walls. From major metropolises to one stop cowpie-kicking burgs and everything in-between, she'd seen them all. Most more than once.

She was one busy bitch.

That was, after all, what she was.

It was the first impression that formed in people's minds when they met her, whether they liked it or not. They took one up and down glance at her—emaciated thin with a clown red perm, leathery-tanned skin stretched tight like-a-drum over her skull, penciled arched eyebrows, flared judgmental nostrils and a frosted lipstick scowl—and they couldn't help themselves.

Even if they were a good person, a kind person—the most charitable person you've ever met—the words would arrive fully formed in their head despite themselves.

My God, this woman looks like a total bitch.

And when she opened her mouth, to paraphrase Mr. Clemens, she "erased all doubts." All the political correctness and women's studies classes in the world weren't gonna change that.

She didn't mind the word, took no offense to it, the way so many did these days, pretending as if it didn't exist for a reason. It wasn't just what she was, it was *who* she was. Not as if it was a point of pride, mind you. You couldn't be proud of having brown eyes, could you? You just did.

Except her eyes were black. Black and piercing and soul-less, and if you stared into them too long you risked falling inside and never climbing out again.

The car pulled up along the curb. A red early model Prius. She frowned.

All these guys drove Prii. So careful and prissy—"environmentally friendly." The smugness of the drivers annoyed her, their preening self-righteousness. There was a time not so long ago on the evolutionary clock when "environmentally friendly" meant that the thing you were trying to eat didn't eat you first.

And wasn't it only yesterday that the cars were big and spacious? Hung-over, overpaid union men working the line in Detroit? Churning out giant engines and eye gouging chrome lighters and genuine leather seats as wide as mattresses. There was an uncomplicated exuberance in their gregarious design, a kind of joie de vivre she could almost find pleasure in.

But she wasn't here for fun.

Not that she didn't enjoy her work.

"You can't smoke in here."

Mike had rolled the window down before he even stopped the car. He was leaning over the passenger seat staring up at her. A big man with a large build and round face, he could be described, depending on personal preference, as either fat or husky. She glared back at him through the car window.

"*That's* how you greet your customers?"

"Excuse me?"

But she was not to be placated by throwaway courtesies.

"You can't even be bothered to say 'hello?' 'Good morning?' Some cursory remark that resembles a passable greeting? You just start in lecturing people on how they're not allowed to smoke in your pathetic little excuse for a car?"

Mike stared at her, at a loss. What was this woman's problem? Maybe she was crazy? Like that dementia shit his grandma had died of. He took a breath and consulted his cellphone, propped up on the dashboard.

"Uh, excuse me, but—?"

"Do you really think you can get away with not acknowledging what I said? Or were you born without a learning curve, Mike?"

What the hell? She *was* fucking crazy.

"Look, I don't appreciate the way you're talking to me. The company has rules about this kind of stuff. I don't have to take this ride." There was no way he was going to take a rash of shit from some crazy-ass woman, this fucking ... bitch.

Mike started to put the car in drive, his hand gripping the transmission.

But she was too fast. Hearing a loud click, Mike glanced in the rear view mirror to see she was already sitting in the back seat, her seat belt buckled.

"Hey, wait. I just told you ..."

"Just drive."

Still, Mike didn't move. "I'm going to have to ask you to get out."

"Yeah? You gonna ask them not to repossess this tin can when you fail to make the payment?"

Mike was silent. How the hell did she know that? Was it something in his appearance? It couldn't be his clothes. He dressed far beyond his means—that was part of his problem. Was it something else? His attitude?

The way he talked? Some obvious quality he couldn't see in himself that screamed *I am the abject opposite of prosperous.*

Because she was right.

Despite his bravado, Mike *did* need this ride. This and all the other rides he could scrounge, as many as time allowed so that he could hang on to this car, his apartment, what was left of his life. He needed them all. Badly.

Putting the car into drive, Mike opted for silence. He guessed he could swallow a little shit. After all, her destination was only three blocks away, and then he'd be rid of her. Maybe she'd keep her big mouth shut.

But she didn't. She opened it again immediately.

"And don't be taking some out of the way route just because I don't live here.

'Cause I'm not one of your gullible, dumb girlfriends."

"What the fuck?" Mike thought he'd said it to himself, but he'd actually spoke the words out loud.

"You heard me. How many young women have you made your way through so far? Six? Seven? How many have you put in the hospital?"

"I don't know what you're talking about," Mike responded with genuine surprise and absolutely no conviction.

"Right. You don't know about your predilection for hunting out weak girls you predatory fuck ... culling them from the herd. You sense it, don't you? The ones who grew up with assholes just like you? Their sad idea of what's normal? Even the beautiful ones. And you know that too. You recognize it. The ones who find a warped comfort in having their own worst image of themselves confirmed by flaccid cowardly pukes like you."

Mike had heard enough.

More than enough.

"Okay. This ride is over."

But she wouldn't relent, not an inch. "You think I can't see it? Do you think you can conceal your true nature from me, the way you do with that cloying "nice guy" smile you drag out whenever the cops take you in and you have to convince her to drop the charges?"

Mike took a breath and counted to three, just like they made him do in those court-ordered anger management classes. He was turning off Main now, driving slow past the old courthouse. It was crowded here. That stupid yearly Daisy Festival was in full force on the village square. Everyone from town was out en masse: daisy knick-knack booths and barbecue tents, daisy chain necklaces and daisy bouquets and flavored snow cones for the kids. There were cops there too. Cops who *knew* him. Mike had to be cool. He put the car in park, taking out the keys.

"Okay, I don't know who told you that stuff about me. But it's all lies," Mike said into the rear view mirror. "This ride is over."

"I'm curious, Mike. What is it that animates you? What pushes your buttons? Mommy didn't titty feed you? You compensating for a limp dick, so now all of womanhood has to pay for it?"

What in the hell? She was talking about his dick now? Mike's enforced calm abandoned him as he stepped out of the car and opened up the passenger door.

"I think you better just shut the fuck up and get out."

For an older woman she seemed to move quicker than he did. In the blink of an eye she was out of the car and in his face, invading his personal space, pointing at him with a bony-forefinger, a razor-sharp pink press-on nail in danger of bursting his retina.

"You think I was put on this earth to take instructions from you, you self-loathing little head case?"

Mike caught a glimpse of the festival goers turning their way at this commotion, Moms and Dads glancing up from the snack booths and kiddy face painting. He backed away from her as she moved toward him in a twisted two-step. A trace of Mike's tenuous survival instincts kicked in as he shouted at her. "Look, just leave me alone."

"Or *what*, you sack of shit? You'll break my collarbone like Cindy? Disconnect my cornea like Monica? Fracture my skull like Sheila?"

Mike looked in her eyes and looked away just as quickly. Her accusations were less a question than a statement of fact, as in *I know you're guilty, motherfucker, so don't even—*

Mike felt a panic rising up inside him.

"*Who* the fuck are you?"

"I'm the piper, Mike. You ever hear of him? Or 'her' in my case."

She smiled and Mike was unnerved. She wasn't like all the others. Cindy and Monica and Sheila. All those girls who didn't get it, who pushed him too hard, who didn't give him any choice but to lay into them. How else could he make them understand?

But this one wasn't intimidated by him.

Mike was filled with a sudden alien emotion, a feeling he'd inspired in others with no small regularity since pre-adolescence, but one he hadn't felt himself since he was a kid, and the old man came after him with the belt.

Mike was afraid.

But why? Of what? What did she weigh? Ninety-eight pounds? Maybe?

"The piper?" Mike asked. His voice was trembling.

"The one it's time to pay," she said. And then she laughed at him. A cruel, emasculating cackle.

Mike felt a chill run up his spine. He knew all that stuff about him being a predator was true—sensed that *she* recognized it. After all, it took one to know one. He saw her face and he *knew* she knew. In this moment, she was the predator and he was the prey. He was the dumb insecure bitch. She'd picked him out and had come for him. And what choice had he given her? How else could she make him understand?

And then suddenly, finding an angle perfectly concealed from curious eyes by the open car door, she kicked him hard in the gonads. Her aim was surgical.

Mike fell to the ground, his face red and flush as he gasped.

A smarter man would have stayed down. But Mike Neymar could never have been confused with a Mensa candidate. His thirty-seven years on earth were a testament to the same. If life was a multiple-choice test, Mike could always be counted on to choose D: the stupidest choice possible.

Sucking in air, Mike got up again, struggling to his feet. She had to give him credit. For a gutless serial batterer, he was a fighter.

Mike staggered toward her, his face seething with a burning hateful vitriol, practically spitting out the words.

"You ... bitch."

"Smile when you call me that."

It was done. The dye was cast. No one was going to treat him like this, consequences be damned. Muttering an indecipherable stream of obscenities like a drunken slam poetry contest, Mike swung at her jaw and connected ... hard.

Blood sprayed out of her mouth along with a set of coffee-stained dentures, turning the blouse of her pants suit into a crimson Rorschach test.

Like a swarm of paparazzi at a red-carpet premiere, a phalanx of clicking cell phones captured every moment of Mike's unprovoked assault on this defenseless woman, more than a few recording in high-definition video.

She laughed louder, even as the blood flowed down her chin, her words garbled but still intelligible through her teeth less lips.

"Smile for the cameras, you dumbshit."

Too enraged to notice, Mike pulled his arm back for another rage-fueled punch. He would have landed it too if not for the sudden pile-up of pudgy and polite small-town dads, rabidly tackling him to the grass.

It was a group effort thirty years in the making.

They'd all had their run-ins with that asshole Neymar over the years, that fucking ... bully, always barricading someone in their locker or grabbing them in a head lock, pinning them down and spitting in their mouths. Deathly afraid of him, no one had ever fought back. Instead they'd all tolerated him, turned a blind eye, even as the so-called 'rumors' of his beating on women became common knowledge.

But something in this attack on this innocent older woman had galvanized them into action, had necessitated their taking the situation in hand. Crushing Mike beneath their collective hush puppies and beer bellies, getting in more than a few pay-back punches in the process, many would remember it as the best day of their lives.

Concerned witnesses looked everywhere for the lady Mike had assaulted, willing and wanting to help that poor injured woman, to see that she was safely transported to the hospital over in Gainesville for immediate medical treatment, to express to her, even if only with their eyes, their silent gratitude.

But the woman was nowhere to be found.

She had vanished completely.

Minutes later, off duty County Sheriff Sean Casey cuffed Mike with some plastic ties he kept in his glove compartment. Many was the night he'd gone home late to his wife and girls due to last minute calls to the scene of Mike's latest domestic thumpings, only to have the girl recant, either on the scene, or later, after they'd taken the prick into the station. Knowing that Mike had two strikes against him, that this last act would send him to the Hutchinson Correctional facility for forever and a day, made this arrest an act of both professional and personal pleasure. Slamming Mike's soft fat head onto the top of his Explorer with just the slightest touch of excessive force, Sean leaned in close and whispered in his ear.

"Karma's a bitch, isn't it?"

Mike looked back at Sean Casey, his eyes wide as he suddenly realized—

She is.

HOLLYWOOD DEAD NAKED

Shakurra Amatulla

It's time for me to get naked on TV. Hooray!

I'm not a porn star. I'm an A.C.T.O.R. and among the distinguished and elite union background actors. Or as the Unenlightened People call us: *Extras*. Or as Hollywood sees us: movable furniture. I modestly tell my friends: I'm just there to make DA STARS look as beautiful as their plastic surgeries allow. In truth, we're told to shut up and endure being "placed," i.e., pushed, pulled, shoved, glared and scoffed at while being resented for breathing in the same sanctified air as DA STARS.

I have this plum assignment to play a dead naked body. No, not to portray a young, nubile, fleshy and curvaceous dead body. Wake up, people, they asked me, a *68-year-old actor*! Hollywood needs me to portray an old dead woman's body. Specifically, an *African-American* dead woman at that. I'm game because such a specified role calls for a substantial salary—forgive me—"bump."

Hey, this is a big deal! As an older black woman, I much rather prefer the term "matured" or "seasoned," but Hollywood doesn't have time for such niceties. Instead, Hollywood scoops out your heart with a rusty scalpel, spits into the cavity and bellows: "*You're OLD! Begone!*" Since they can't realistically age-progress their sweet, young cuties, Hollywood must begrudgingly—and sparingly—give the role to a real senior citizen. But I must say, as an aside, that Hollywood's infatuation with using young adults does not extend to young African-American and all people of color actors, as they too, struggle to secure roles. But I digress. ...

For this naked gig, I get a fake arm fitting by a celebrity special effects artist. I'm guessing something is going to happen on set to this arm. But what's going to occur, I'm not worthy to be told in advance. I marvel as the artist expertly sculpts out an appendage that is an uncanny reproduction of mine. By the way, this special fitting represents additional pay for me. *Ka-*

ching!

The day of the shooting, I'm waiting outside a certain sound stage when someone whirrs in front of me in one of those cute little putt-putt karts specifically reserved for DA STARS. He calls out my name and tells me to hop on board. Wow! Not too long ago I was at the same studio and had to walk a mile to set in my heels, dragging a suitcase of wardrobe changes behind me while carrying my own portable chair. (Hollywood doesn't believe in providing chairs unless, you guessed it, you're DA STAR.) That time, about a million of these empty karts whizzed by my over-burdened, teeter-tottering body, only to fart-beep me out of the way because they were on a special mission to pick up ... oh, you know!

So giddy am I to be riding in the kart of the privileged that I can't resist giving out a few Queen Elizabeth demeaning waves to the lowly awestruck pedestrians. (I imagine them jealously wondering: "*Is that Cicely Tyson or a nappy headed Diana Ross?*") When we arrive at the set, lo and behold, I'm given my own private and spacious dressing room with a private bathroom *and* placed under the loving care of a special effects makeup artist. I undress and luxuriously stretch out on the couch as she painstakingly applies body makeup to ensure that my skin shines like a diamond. Yes, she brown-bodies me and I'm loving every minute of it! Just before I go to set, the artist hands me this strange-looking tiny hairy adhesive strip and jerks her head toward the bathroom.

"I don't know how to say this politely, but you need to tape this over your—" and she trains a stern gaze at my lower nether region.

I instinctively clench. "You mean ... my weewee?"

"Exactly. It's mandatory."

So, the law-abiding citizen that I am, I attach this caterpillar-like thing over my you-know-what. I briefly consider how to handle the strip if I have to go to the bathroom, and then I remember that I'm a star now. Stars don't pee.

As I enter the set accompanied by my protective stylist, I nearly bump into a young woman who, like myself, is wearing a dressing gown. I'm told that she just played a scene as a very alive naked woman wriggling in bed with the leading man. Out of professional courtesy, we avoid each other's eyes, but I can't help sticking my nose up in the air because, at this moment, I am the naked woman *du jour*!

On set, everyone knows my name. They can't smile wide enough at me or do enough to make me comfortable. I stretch out on the floor in the middle of a cluttered apartment scene which eerily mimics my own messy abode. My special effects minder fusses over my fake arm placement as I hide my real arm under my body. The fake arm is now liberally splattered with fake blood and chewed out meat chunks.

The series star appearing in the scene with me actually beams down on me like a prideful mother watching her ugly newborn transform into a starlet. I wish this glorious moment never, ever ends; I'm close to grateful tears being treated like a ... a ... STAR!

This is a closed set out of respect for my impending nudity. Normally, there would be about 500 crew members on an open set. On a closed, modesty set, it's respectfully whittled down to about 495 people. Men. The five who get sequestered—the only five female crew members that exist—are told to go shopping and pick themselves up something pretty.

Rehearsal time and I'm still wearing my robe as the animal wrangler introduces her cute little dog who, I realize now, will be chewing at my fake arm on cue. Time to shoot. My minder helps me to disrobe. I think no one told the dog wrangler beforehand that I was going to be buck naked as I hear her gagging from her hideout in the corner. No matter ... I'm a STAR!

Several takes later and I exit the set amidst applause. And then it happens. The smiles disappear and the eyes of all those around me go dead and ignore me. I'm now declassed as an undesirable Extra. A production assistant snarls at me: "Get dressed!" Chaperone-less, but still holding my head high (I *was* a star, you know!), I enter my dressing room.

And I freeze. Miss Young Cutesy Naked Girl from the last scene is stretched out spread-eagled across *my* sofa and taking a nap. I clench my teeth and say, with indignant aloofness: "Hey, this is my dressing room!" No movement from Naked Girl. I stomp over to the couch to give her a superior poke on the arm. "I said 'hey—' " but the words jack-knife in my throat as her arm falls unnaturally by her side. No, it's not a fake arm. She's—

I would scream like a banshee, but because I'm a professional actor, I eject a bloodcurdling shriek, much like Scarlett O'Hara would if Mammy Hattie McDaniel asked Scarlett for a day off to attend a Black Lives Matter rally. Crew members come running, not out of concern, but because my scream interrupted a live shooting and they were out for blood. Eventually, the two LAPD cops assigned to oversee production security rush in from their self-imposed duties of jealously manning the catering table of *hors d'oeuvres*. They immediately zero in on me, their fingers twitching toward their guns. I now realize that I am the only black amidst the honorable hordes of whites. That's it: I'm going down!

I nervously ask for permission to show my SAG-AFTRA card as proof of my actor existence. I stand rock still until I get said permission because I am not a stunt person swathed in Kevlar to repel off any "accidental" bullet releases that may occur from said cops if I make any sudden movements. One of the cops orders me to get dressed and posts himself in front of the bathroom door. I guess it's in case I do a runner, but there's no windows in the bathroom. I checked. When I emerge, a surly plainclothes man identifying himself as Detective Leatherman (*I can't make this up, folks!)* places his rotund body before me to block my sight of the real dead body being inspected by a medical examiner. Detective Leatherman's face contorts into a remarkable imitation of a pissed-off pit bull. I can only guess it's due to his having just arrived on set and discovering his cop buddies had already eaten up all of the free food.

By the way he asks for my contact information, I already surmise that I'm regarded as a prime suspect. But something I saw earlier on the naked girl's dead body—Chloe was her name, rest her soul—nags at me. It needs to be said.

"Sir, may I say something?"

"You wanna confess?"

"Uh, no, sir, but I noticed something strange about the girl—"

"Did you touch her?"

"Only to gently wake her because I first thought she was sleeping." I mentally make the sign of the cross as the good ex-Catholic that I am, as an act of attrition for my white lie. Or is it a black lie now?

"So?"

"She had this awful rash on her, um, genital area—"

The detective's head snaps back and he quickly retrieves it, sneering at me at the same time. "How do you know?"

"Sir, when I opened the door, she was naked and her legs were spread wide open and I could see her, um—"

"Va—"

"Weewee, yes, sir. And it was really red and inflamed from this major rash going on down there."

"You a gynecologist?"

"No, sir." Then, as it was a matter of life and death—*my* life and death—I reluctantly reveal to him the Hollywood secret of the weewee caterpillar strip requirement for nude scenes.

"And that strip was missing when I found her. Sir."

"So what? She could have tossed it into the toilet when she peed."

"She didn't pee, sir."

"What makes you so sure?"

"She's a star, sir."

He gives a brisk referential nod. "Hey, do you have a home phone number?"

"No, sir, just the cell."

He narrows his eyes as if I just committed a felony. He waves me out of his sight.

Several weeks pass, the studio death is a distant memory, and I still hadn't secured anymore acting work since. At 7:30 at night, there's a pounding on my door. Looking out of the peephole, I nearly faint seeing Detective Leatherman impatiently waiting. That's it. I'm getting arrested. I didn't do anything wrong. But does it matter? I just wish I had time to Google whether bail bondsmen accept food stamps.

"Yes, sir, may I help you?"

The detective barges in as is his God-given right from some legal rule book I'll never be privy to.

"Doing any naked acting work lately?"

"No sir, not even non-naked acting work."

"Good."

I try not to take that as an insult, since I need to appear non-combative when he cuffs me.

He sweeps a jaundiced eye over my place, which only takes him three seconds as it's a tiny studio. "Gotta hand it to you. You got good instincts."

"I do?"

"That va—uh, weewee strip was doused in Strychnine. Got right into the poor girl's bloodstream and killed her."

"I didn't do it, sir."

He pauses for a beat. "It was her makeup girl, Bonnie. Turns out Bonnie's husband had a fling with Chloe a while back. Then Chloe dumped him, but he didn't go back to Bonnie and took up with someone else. Been driving Bonnie crazy especially when Chloe got a regular gig on the same show she works on."

"But Strychnine ... how did she get that, sir?"

"Bonnie was a chemist before she got downsized by Dow Chemicals and took up being a makeup girl."

"Wow. Sir."

"Wow is right. She still had the poisoned strip hidden in all her makeup supplies."

The detective and I share a shudder.

"You got quite a brain there. You should get a job working for the police."

"The police, sir?"

"Yeah, like being some lieutenant's secretary. They could use somebody with a noggin like yours."

"Thank you, sir."

He peruses my bookcase for a good while. "A lot of murder mysteries here." He pulls out a couple of books and rifles through them as if searching for a cache of crack cocaine.

"I'm planning on becoming a mystery writer. Sir."

"A writer? You?" He gives me a quick parental-like stink-eye as he snorts. "Don't know about *that*!"

He chuckles as he exits, slamming the door behind him.

"You're probably right, sir," I say to the empty air.

GAME WARDEN SHEARS IS HAVING NONE OF IT

Jeffrey Hunt

It all starts at school, during hall duty, on a regular Monday morning with Gary. "Turkey hunting!" he exclaims.

"I've never gone turkey hunting."

"Me neither," Gary admits. "Which is why we should go."

"And I don't know anything about it."

"Me neither," Gary says again.

The tardy bell goes off. Lockers slam.

"Turkey hunting?" It's such a surprise, but then you remember—you told Gary about your parents shipping a gun over. They were clearing out your things, and though you told your mom to sell it, the firearm in question was a gift from your late grandfather. But why is Gary bringing it up now?

Well the man can apparently read minds. "There's only one spring hunting season in North Carolina," he explains.

You happen to be in North Carolina. And it's spring. So you begin to nod your head.

"Wonderful!" Gary shouts.

"Wonderful?" you repeat.

"Get a hunting license by Saturday!"

"Yeah ... sure."

Gary turns, but before walking away he asks if a 3:00 am pickup is OK. You reply that 3:00 am is *perfect*, because you know that he's joking. But at lunch Gary says the hunting grounds are hours away, and that he wants to set up before daybreak. And he's just so enthusiastic! So later, when you should be prepping for a lesson on *Julius Caesar*, about how the eponymous character gets killed by who you tell the students is his best friend, you watch turkey hunting videos. And you learn there's a lot of conflicting information: is it best to stalk turkeys, or to sit in stands? And are box calls the best, or slate calls, or mouth calls? What ammo? About camo? To slightly misquote the bard, it's all Greek to you, and with a 3:00 am departure you can't help but think Gary and Brutus have a bit in common.

You do learn some things before class starts, to be fair. Though nothing helps you with the biggest question of all.

What on Earth should you tell your wife?

Your wife thinks waking at 3:00 am is a riot. Except that when she speaks, she's as serious as a Don in a Mario Puzo novel. Or perhaps fittingly, as a heart attack.

"You have to go."

"I have to go?"

"Yes, you have to."

"I thought he was joking," you say. "Why do I have to?"

"Because you said you would. And also, we ladies are going to brunch. And then to the nail salon. So we want you two out."

"Ah," you say.

"Have to look good for patients!"

You don't think there's correlation between good nails and one's feelings towards their cardiologist, but you smile anyway. Your wife smiles back. Then she asks if Gary knows how to hunt turkeys. Gary's family took you in, after a hospital made your wife an offer she couldn't refuse and you moved to North Carolina. You feel like you know him pretty well, and so in answer to your wife's question, you don't think so.

Gary teaches chemistry. He's in his late forties, he's always had a mustache, and kids love him because he's always unapologetically his quirky self. Gary's lunch is always the same roast beef sandwich. His classroom is covered in clocks, and at the top of each hour you hear them across in the English wing. So he's not that strange, as far as teacher's go, though Gary *could* be called a gun nut. He owns close to thirty rifles and he's a regular encyclopedia on calibers and bullet grains. Yet, you're pretty sure Gary's never shot an animal. Also, you know that he doesn't own a single pair of hiking boots.

"Do I contradict myself?" Gary asks on Wednesday.

"Don't quote English at me, Walt."

"Because I contain multitudes!"

Additionally, Gary doesn't own any shotguns, which you need for turkey hunting. As you explained to your wife, who grew up in the city, there's two types of long guns: "Rifles shoot a single bullet, and they're used for big game at far distances. My grandfather's gun is a shotgun. Shotguns shoot out lots of BBs, or shot, and is used for birds and small things up close."

"Sounds fine," your wife replied, and later she bought you a gun safe. Although now she has another question: "You hunted pheasant growing up, right? But turkeys are bigger."

"A lot bigger," you agree.

"Will your shotgun, *um*, work?"

And honestly, you have no idea. But after some research you find most people hunt turkeys with 12 gauges, which is what you inherited. So you go to the store with Gary, who is picking up a 12 gauge of his own. Or as he describes it, "A custom double barrel with engraved receiver, Turkish walnut stock, and beautiful Damascus steel trigger guards!" While he signs the paperwork you get turkey shot, then Gary purchases calls, a turkey vest, decoys, and netting for a blind. After, it seems like your head's barely hit the pillow when your alarm goes off at 2:30 am. "Have fun," your wife murmurs.

"Thanks," you say.

"I'll dream of you ... as I sleep ... 'til 10:00."

"So kind." And then it's a quick breakfast before Gary arrives. As you load up, between plenty of yawns, you're jealous of the woman you've left behind in the warm bed. And especially since the air is cold and misty.

"Rain will dampen our footsteps!" Gary declares.

"So it's good?" you ask.

Gary doesn't reply, but his jubilant reaction makes you think of the preamble you give every year when teaching Cervantes. Reportedly King Philip II of Spain saw a youth in public who was slapping his thigh and laughing hysterically. "Ole Phil," as you call him, declared that the young man was either reading *Don Quixote*, or was insane. Since Gary's driving, he's certainly not reading, and there isn't a single book in the car. And thus you can't help but seriously wonder about the man who talked you into this early-morning scheme.

Or wonder about the rube who Gary convinced to join him.

Your first turkey hunt is a bust. Sort of.

You arrive at 4:15 am. Gary's family has a cabin on 350 acres in the North Carolina sandhills, which you learn aren't that sandy at all. It's a forested, relatively flat property bordered by a river and a highway to one side with a moderate amount of brush, and though you're not a turkey hunting expert, you have to imagine this is good territory. There's cover, yet you can still see some distance, and directly after you get the netting up on the edge of a clearing, the sun rises, cutting through some of the clouds. And you start to hear gobbles.

"Well holy smokes," Gary exclaims.

They're loud and in the trees. From what you've learned the turkeys will soon fly down to scratch and eat and strut.

And they do!

"One at 10 o'clock," Gary whispers.

"One at 12:00, too," you whisper back.

Then a third swoops down, and a fourth, and a fifth, and though the videos said turkeys were some of the most challenging birds to hunt, now you wonder if that's true.

Gary takes out his range finder. "85 yards."

Which is too far. From what you read, ethical turkey shots are at 45 yards or less. But luckily, the pack is moving.

"Looks like there's three jakes," Gary says.

A jake is a juvenile male turkey.

"... four or five hens ..." Gary continues.

You can't hunt hens in North Carolina. They look mostly like jakes, except jakes have beards—tufts of feathers that protrude from their breasts and look like coarse hair. Though the sun is now fully up, there's still clouds overhead, so it's dark and from here the jakes and hens look the same. But then Gary gets excited.

"... and there's at least one tom!"

A tom, as you've learned, is what every turkey hunter wants. It's a fully mature male, with a beard like a Norse warrior and an ugly blue and red head. They have a fan of tail feathers, long wattles, and big snoods—the growth that hangs down from their beaks. Gary points to a bush that's forty yards out and you agree. You both chamber your guns, quietly, and the turkeys continue to gobble and mill about. Their feathers shine in the wet morning air, and slowly, they close the distance to the bush. They come to eighty yards. Then seventy yards. Then sixty. In unison, you both bring your shotguns up.

There's a second tom, and at fifty yards you decide Gary will shoot the one on the left, you the one on the right.

Slowly, you both flip off your safeties.

Carefully, you put tension on your triggers.

And you wait.

But the turkeys stop, with the distance between them and Gary's bush a few body lengths long. Not that the turkeys are motionless, as they're milling about, and a pair in the back is scuffling. But their lack of forward progress is OK; your adrenaline is pumping, and this is so much better than stressing about school budget cuts! So you have patience, and soon enough, the turkeys come towards you again.

"On three," Gary says.

You nod, then start to count together.

"One ... two ... thr—"

And then heavens open up.

The rain really catches you off guard. You hadn't noticed how black the clouds were in all the excitement, and in an instant you're in the middle of a storm straight out of Billy Shakespeare's *Tempest*. The downpour's accompanied by claps of thunder that would make Prospero proud, and though you can only see the turkeys when the lightning strikes at what is altogether too close a distance, you know that they scatter. Or perhaps they are washed away.

"Holy smokes," Gary says again.

And then you're both running for the car.

The storm's a major disappointment.

Though you do get a turkey. Sort of.

It rains all morning. Lunch is in the vehicle—egg salad for you and roast beef for Gary, of course—and you talk about calling it quits. But by 12:30 the clouds are dissipating, and fifteen minutes later the sky is clear. "There's turkeys out there!" Gary shouts, and you know that he's right. So despite the fact that you could out-sleep Ole Rip Winkle, and despite the state of the ground, which is a giant mud pit, you and Gary and your thoroughly soaked clothes give it another go.

First, it's back to the blind.

You sit there for two hours, watching and calling, but no turkeys come. So you decide to walk. You do a circuit around the meadow. Then a circuit to the cabin. Then you walk in an ever-widening spiral, with your phone logging two and then three-mile loops around the meadow and cabin, and then around the meadow, cabin, and to the edge of the river and highway, but still no turkeys. At 5:00 pm you decide to call it quits.

Gary agrees. Then: "So tomorrow!"

"What?" you ask.

"We're going tomorrow!"

"Ah," you say. "Um ..."

Your phone rings. Thankfully. You pick up.

"How's it going?" your wife asks.

"Saw some turkeys, but then we got rain."

"You should go tomorrow!"

"What?"

"You should go tomorrow!"

You look over at Gary, who has, unfortunately heard. And he's grinning like the Cheshire Cat.

"I thought you had work tomorrow?" you ask your wife.

"The procedures got moved, so I have another day off. And we're just having the best time! Thinking of going to the spa in the morning. Get massages, have a mud bath. ..."

The thought of getting wet and muddy on purpose makes you shutter. You still aren't dry from your waist down. "Well—"

And that's all you get out. "Sounds great, and give my wife my love!" Gary shouts as he reaches over and ends the call.

Not that you end up going turkey hunting tomorrow, however, because, there's an accident. After getting in the car, and directly after getting up to speed on the highway, a turkey flies out of the trees. Gary hits the brakes, but it's not enough on the wet asphalt; the bird slams into the windshield. And as you turn to watch it tumble across the road, you're reminded of Elpenor, from *The Odyssey*, who survives all the dangerous weather and monsters on his journey back to Ithaca, only to drunkenly fall off a roof and break his neck at the last minute. Anyway, it's your lesson in the ninth grade next week.

"Homer from *The Odyssey* and Homer from *The Simpsons* had a common love," you always begin. Then you project a cartoon picture of beer. Anything to get a high schooler's attention, right?

But you aren't laughing as Gary stops the car. You get the guns from the back, because where there's one turkey there might be more. Though the turkey Gary hit proves to be alone.

And it's clearly a hen.

"Ironic," Gary says.

"Agreed," you reply. Then you tell Gary about Elpenor.

"Oh, poor Elpenor!" Gary states. "We shall give you the burial that you require to find peace in the underworld!"

You're impressed—that's exactly what Elpenor's shade requests, so Gary really knows his classics. And you're relieved, because you worried Gary might take "Elpenor" home, which given its gender would be illegal. Though ultimately it doesn't matter, because just as Gary scoops Elpenor up a government cruiser appears on the horizon. And to make a long story short, the man who parks next to Gary's car isn't the trusting type. It's lucky that Elpenor didn't crack Gary's windshield, but it's also unfortunate, as there isn't enough proof for Game Warden Shears that the car did the deed.

You can admit, with the guns out, it looks bad.

Plus the turkey's scrapes look a lot like a shot wounds.

And so as a result, and though you get off, Gary is written a ticket and his brand-new and undoubtedly quite expensive custom double barrel shotgun is confiscated. And perhaps he might even be banned from hunting for life.

Things don't end up being the worst.

Gary has to go to court, which is scary. But after a long explanation the judge believes the humble chemistry teacher, and even laughs when Gary explains the turkey's name. Gary can hunt immediately and his property will be returned, though the latter process is long. So in the meantime Gary celebrates by buying a dedicated turkey gun. "It has a shorter barrel for better maneuverability," he explains, "a full camo wrap for better hiding, and an extra full choke for tighter shot patterns!"

"Do shot patterns matter much?" you ask.

"All the difference in the world!"

People killed turkeys before chokes were commonplace, you think, but you don't discuss it further, because Gary finds that he's been bitten by a Lone Star tick. Debilitating nausea leads to a diagnosis of alpha-gal syndrome, or red meat allergy, a very rare but very real condition. So no hunting until Gary stabilizes, which takes several months, and no more roast beef sandwiches for possibly ever.

In the summer you and your wife go to Gary's for lunch and noticeably, the main course is fish. Which is perfect, actually, since you've brought Gary a fish-shaped clock for his classroom. You eat, then after a depressing conversation about more school cutbacks, you ask Gary's wife if she minds another gun in the house. She laughs and says, "What's one more?"

"We never bother about Dad's guns," their oldest states.

"There's no point," adds their other daughter.

Your wife turns to you. "Do you want another shotgun?"

You reply that given what happened last trip, you'll stick with what you have. Which is good, because your second year of turkey hunting ends on an eerily similar note.

No, it doesn't storm. Though all the days are pretty overcast. And no, you don't run into another pack of turkeys right off the bat, which you've learned is actually called "a rafter." But you do kill another, which like before doesn't make it back to your house. It all starts with sitting in a blind on a Saturday, and seeing nothing. So on Sunday you go for a stalk. "You hear that?" Gary whispers around noon. And you do—it's what's called "a cutt." Turkeys cutt when they're excited, and the grating sound gets you and Gary excited too.

Slowly, you follow it to where a jake's at the base of a tree. And it's only 30 yards away!

"Go for it," Gary tells you.

"Sure?"

"I got the one last year," he says with a chuckle.

So you raise your gun, take aim, and fire. The jake drops and you couldn't be happier, except when you reach the turkey, you notice its beard is gone. "It was a jake, right?" you ask.

"Most definitely."

"There's no tuft of hair."

"Really?"

"Come see." And Gary does.

Gary scratches his chin. "Must have shot it clean off."

You both look in the bushes, to see if you can find the beard, but after ten minutes you give up. Some people save them as trophies, but you're not interested, so no big loss.

Next you pose for pictures, and you're about to go see if there's a rafter nearby, for Gary, but then in the distance, you see something ominous. And you can't help but think of *Frankenstein*, which you're currently teaching in the tenth grade. You're at the part where Victor sees the monster at a distance, his long-forsaken creation bounding across glacier crevasses, and it's here that Mary Shelley shifts the mood of the novel from boundless elation to fathomless despair. You feel the same shift as you look at the highway, to the incoming government cruiser, and then to the man who exits the vehicle. He is tall and menacing and altogether too familiar.

Game Warden Shears.

As it turns out, having a dead, beardless turkey on your hands is a big problem. You show Game Warden Shears the spot where the beard would have been, underneath the feathers, where there's a small nick. He eyes it for what feels like an eternity. Then: "Could have been made with a knife."

So Game Warden Shears is having none of it, and it's you who sees the judge next, on the charge of poaching a hen.

Gary accompanies, and the judge remembers.

It helps a lot, actually, and though Gary never officially says he's representing you, that's what he basically does. And after twenty minutes you're off. The judge says it'll take a few weeks to get your gun back, so in the meantime, Gary takes you shopping. "My old shotgun's chambered for two- and three-quarter-inch shells," he explains, "but did you know there are guns chambered for three-inch shells *and* for three-and-a-half inch shells? More shot! More coverage! More power! Ha ha!"

Gary ends up buying one of both, which surprises you since none of the teachers got raises this year. But again, he likes his firearms, and he gives you the shotgun with the three-inch chamber until Fish and Game return your property. Then it's off to a dinner of pasta with meatless sauce before heading to bed.

The next morning's cloudy and a bust, but by mid-afternoon you hear yelps, putts, and kee kees—more sounds that show turkeys are excited and that a rafter is forming. Gary shoves his PB & J down, which gets all over his mustache. "So messy," he complains. Then you both grab your guns.

The turkeys are by the river again.

You spot hens, jakes, and several toms.

And on the other side of the water sits Game Warden Shears, parked on the highway's shoulder.

"No probable cause," Gary mutters.

Yet, you think, though you don't say it out loud.

The turkeys don't give Game Warden Shears much thought. He's still, and as you've learned, once in large groups, turkeys hardly consider anything far away. *And perhaps,* you consider, *they know he's protecting them in some way.*

You take your time coming up on the rafter, which increases from ten to about three dozen birds as clouds steadily roll overhead. Game Warden Shears supervises from his car, and gives a barely perceivable wave once you make eye contact. You appreciate him not spooking your quarry, though his presences is disconcerting. Gary tells you not to worry—it can't happen three times, he's sure, and you tend to agree. Then you and Gary separate, moving towards two different, solitary toms, lest your shots hit other turkeys and you make the good game warden's day.

Like before, you raise your guns and take aim.

You click your safeties off in unison.

"One ... two ... three ..." *BANG-BANG!*

And two toms go down!

Immediately you look to the cruiser. But Game Warden Shears has gone into the cab, to talk on the radio. You aren't worried, as you know you're in the clear. But then you return to the remaining turkeys and you see that they've scattered.

Some birds go to the sides, some flap toward you, though the majority careen straight away. They're spooked, and when they get to the river they keep running forward. And for reasons God only knows, once wet the rafter starts to pile up on itself. "Why don't they fly?" Gary shouts, which is an excellent question, though the noise only makes the piling more frenzied.

The turkeys on top kick and yelp, and the ones on bottom go under the water for far too long. "Drowning," you murmur, "just like what happened to Mr. Mary Shelley."

The students always get a kick out of that nickname.

Also, it's true—Mary Shelley's husband went out for an ocean swim, never to return alive. And it seems like something similarly unfortunate is happening here, as the squawking and flailing crescendos. Eventually the rafter hits a sandbar, and a few surviving turkeys stand up. They look about, shake off, and calmly make their way to shore. And only then does the good warden emerge from his cab.

He eyes the floating bodies, of which there's dozens.

"Bag limit's one turkey per day!" he yells.

"But we didn't kill those birds!" Gary shouts back.

"You fired, didn't you? And they're dead, aren't they?"

And that's that. It begins to drizzle as you hand over your guns, and the situation makes you think of a line from *Frankenstein*, from last Friday's class: "I was bewildered, perplexed, and unable to arrange my ideas sufficiently to understand the full extent of his proposition." The students never got why Victor was silent after the monster accused him of heinous crimes, they never understood why Victor just "went with it." And admittedly you didn't explain his shock well. Perhaps, you think right now, you never understood it yourself.

But with your heads now hung in shame, you get it.

And then to top it all off, Gary finds another tick.

The good news: the judge is downright jovial. After a short establishment of the facts, His Honor beckons you both to the bench. "Nothing breaks up a day of parking violations and property line disputes like seeing my two favorite hunters," he admits. Then he sends you on your way.

The bad news: despite wearing copious amounts of bug spray, Gary now has Lyme disease, another tick-borne illness. First Gary's joints ached. Then he started sleeping for twelve hours at a time, then fourteen, and then longer. Finally, a blood test confirmed it. You tell Gary it's OK to give up turkey hunting.

"No way!" he declares.

"Well at least for this year," you insist.

And Gary agrees that might be a good idea.

You're sure His Honor will be sad, but by the next spring, right after the school takes away everyone's planning periods to save money, your partner's ready to go. And he even has a new gun: "10 gauge! Gas operated and shoots 2.5 ounces of lead that's guaranteed to drop a gobbler or my money back!"

A 10 gauge is the biggest shotgun currently in production, and Gary's, in particular, cycles its own shells. This capability makes for faster shooting—no need to pump after every shot—and its various systems significantly reduce recoil. So it's quite the machine, and you can only wonder how Gary afforded it.

Also, you're sure the good game warden will love it.

Now, though you're sure your chances of getting in trouble again defy all probability, you and Gary still decide it most prudent to hunt far away. So you set up on public grounds in North Carolina's Piedmont Region.

Then you call the turkeys. And you wait and wait. And absolutely nothing happens.

"This stinks," Gary says at the end of the first day.

"This *really* stinks," he says both days after that.

"Back to the sandhills?" you ask, and he assents. So you return to Gary's family property and risk it.

Now, as you've also learned, when turkey hunting in the state of North Carolina it's unlawful to bait land, to hunt with rifles or handguns, or to use dogs. You always figured these common-sense regulations were easy to follow, though they're also all regulations you and Gary amazingly violate in a single go. It begins on the coldest spring day yet when you approach Gary's property from a different direction, in an attempt to give the nearby highway a large berth. You come upon a rafter soon after, and sparing the details, just before it starts to rain yet again you get a tom and Gary gets a jake. You're both immensely proud, and you're both absolutely sure nothing that you did could possibly be construed as illegal.

Next, you go to the cabin to clean the birds.

You park behind the structure, because there's a beater truck in front of it. And very soon after that, you wish you'd checked the cabin out earlier. Or better yet, you wish you'd never come to it at all. Because unbeknownst to Gary, his out-of-work and law-eschewing cousin has taken up residence.

"Split with my wife," he explains.

"And so you're a farmer now?" Gary asks. Because oddly enough, there's a small cornfield out back.

"For the deer," Gary's cousin replies.

"Does it work?"

"Shot two does right from the kitchen last week," Gary's cousin answers. "Just opened the window and BLAMO!"

"You can't shoot rifles indoors here, cousin."

"So? Who's going to stop me?"

You and Gary exchange a look.

"Also, it isn't deer season. Or doe season."

Gary's cousin spits into the sink. "So?"

"No game wardens show up?"

"Just me and Buddy presently," Gary's cousin replies. And at the sound of its name, a cute beagle mix runs into the room. Or it would be cute if its muzzle wasn't covered in feathers. You're about to say something, but then Gary's cousin interrupts—there's a doe in the field! The man grabs the rifle that's leaning against the fridge. Gary rushes his hands to his ears, as do you, and a second later the kitchen thunders. A stalk of corn above the doe's head explodes and it bounds away while Gary's cousin curses at the near miss.

Except, once your ears stop ringing you hear something new: what you could say you've come to think as Jack London's famous "call of the wild." It's a siren identical in pitch and tone to the siren that's sounded so many times before, emanating from across the river.

Where the highway is.

There's someone who won't miss today, you are sure. Because like London's call, you know that siren represents something inescapable. And what comes next must just be part of the hunting experience.

"... shooting turkeys with a rifle ..."

"That wasn't us!"

"... using a dog to hunt turkey ..."

"No, the birds were already dead!"

"... hunting turkey in a baited area ..."

"No, the field's planted for deer!"

Thunder claps in the distance. "You're telling me the corn's for deer, not turkey?" Game Warden Shears asks.

"Yes!" Gary exclaims. "And it was a doe, not a—"

"You know baiting deer is also illegal? And you also know that it isn't deer season? Much less *doe* season?" Neither you nor Gary say anything, leading Game Warden Shears to resume his litany: "Discharging a firearm inside a structure. ..."

As for Gary's cousin, after mumbling something about "warrants in two counties" he took off, just as quick as a student who has heard the bell. You and Gary considered following, though since he left Buddy behind, neither of you feel it'd be right. Also, you figured *this* time you'll make Game Warden Shears see reason. Yet things play out pretty much like before, with tickets and confiscations, except after your household gets a dog. And at court His Honor, though as understanding as ever, does offer some new advice.

"Take a break?" you both echo.

"Yes. Take a few years off."

"Getting harder to clear us?" Gary asks.

"People are starting to talk, you know?"

So you tell His Honor you'll think about it, and though legally you're good to go, another health concern brings the season to a close. First Gary starts to get headaches. Then he develops a fever, which leads to hospitalization, and it's pretty clear it isn't just his alpha-gal or Lyme acting up. After numerous tests, and despite all the best anti-tick socks and pants and long-sleeved shirts a teacher's salary can buy, yet another one of those insidious arachnids is discovered, lodged between Gary's buttocks and fully engorged.

Rocky Mountain spotted fever.

Several rounds of antibiotics clear the disease up, though the nerve damage Gary suffers means he'll never hike again.

Additionally, you suffer your own setback: as the last hire in the English Department, another round of cuts means you're let go. So you teach your final lessons on Dickinson and Orwell then you pack up your room and start the job hunt. Which is fine, since you'd been getting pretty sick of dealing with parents and grading essays over the weekend, anyway.

"An 'outside job?' " they ask in one interview.

"Yes, I want to be outside," you reply.

"In the rain and mud, or in the wind and heat?"

"All of the above."

"This job is physical," they take care to explain.

"I can handle it."

"And you can learn the regulations?"

"I memorized the first book of *The Canterbury Tales*," you say. "Also, I think my, um ... *extracurricular experience* proves I'm a great fit for the position."

"Your record will come back clear?"

"Clear as a bell!"

And it does. And they liked your answers. So you're hired.

Things also work out for Gary, though his journey's more arduous. Three months into bedrest Gary resigns from teaching, and he's housebound for the better part of four years. You help pack up his classroom, moving his clocks to his den, which Gary converts to an office. And Gary ends up needing the new room, because he doesn't take his sickness on his back, so to speak. Gary enrolls in online law courses, and does so well that he graduates at the top of his class. His grades, along with one exceptionally strong recommendation, land him a position in the state's appellate court, where he'll serve as a clerk specializing in game and wildlife management.

And word on the street that when the His Honor retires, Gary will be a shoe-in for the position.

So all-in-all, everything works out for the best.

It's a warm spring day with nary a cloud in sight. The full cast of characters is in attendance and the scene is jubilant.

"Go, Gary, go!" Gary's wife shouts.

"Yeah, Dad!" his daughters scream.

"So proud of you!" your wife joins in. And in her hands is your four-legged adoptee Buddy, who you love like a son. He cuddles and plays fetch and at the ceremony he barks and barks. But no one cares about the noise, because the crowd is louder than Buddy could ever be.

Except for one time, when you could hear a pin drop.

Gary walks across the stage. It takes several minutes, with Lofstrand crutches on both arms, but everyone on stage, as well as in the audience, is patient. When Gary receives his diploma, declaring him a Doctor of Jurisprudence, it's to an explosion of clapping and hoots and hollers, like that of a curtain call to an Olivier production of *Richard III*. Or to the noise you'd get out of a rafter of turkeys, perhaps.

After, Gary joins you at the tables arranged for friends and family, and you stick out a hand. "I know, I know," he says as he gives you a vigorous shake. "Eight years ago I would have figured I'd teach chemistry 'til I died!"

"We're glad you made the change," His Honor says.

"Our pocketbook says the same," Gary's wife states.

"Though we're going to miss you," your wife adds.

Except that she's looking at you.

"I'm going to miss HIM!" Gary shouts, and that's when it all sinks in. Soon your weekday vegetarian lunches will be impossible, with Gary working a few towns over. Though things aren't terrible; you're absolutely in love with your new job away from the grammar lessons and essay correcting. Plus all the staff meetings! And the incessant parent emails!

But also, being in the great outdoors is, well ... great.

"Here's a small present," Game Warden Shears announces. He's sitting next to you and your wife, and as you watch Gary unwraps it to find a clock in the shape of a turkey.

Gary's smile is broad. "Thank you."

Game Warden Shears smiles back. "You're welcome."

And with that, the emotions of the day choke Gary up. So following a few more "Congratulations" that's that. Gary and his family get into one car, His Honor into another, your wife and Buddy into a third. And you and your partner go to your cruiser. Because you're back on the clock in half an hour, to investigate some unauthorized camping in the sandhills.

"It was a nice ceremony," Game Warden Shears says.

"Yes, it really was," you reply.

And though you don't know if you'll ever form as strong a friendship with your new partner, things are pretty good. And given your new careers, at least you and Gary are bound to cross paths. That's why you absolutely can't wait to catch those campers—perhaps, you think, you'll even be called as a witness into court. Or better yet, perhaps you'll write out a sloppy ticket, or slightly misinterpret a regulation, so a case has the potential to get appealed and you could be called to testify.

Just, of course, don't tell Shears.

SHOT TO THE HEAD

Michael Mordes

I love guns. I mean, I really fucking love guns. Other people buy beer, cars, or baseball cards with their extra money. I buy guns. I have more than a hundred of them. One hundred and twenty-four, to be exact. I'd list some of them here, but, if you're not a gun guy, you probably don't give a crap about the Talon grip on my Smith and Wesson M&P 9mm, or the night vision scope I use with my Ruger Mini-14, or just how quiet my Dead Air Nomad suppressor is, etc. When I'm not out making money—driving a van for a well-known delivery service—to pay for my guns, I'm at home taking them apart and putting them back together, cleaning them, oiling them, firing them at the range, talking about them at the gun shop, and, I'll be honest with you, posing with them in the mirror.

As every gun nut will tell you, if you get him in a truthful mood, there's a kind of frustration we experience on a daily basis, not found with other addictions. Your heroin junkies and porn addicts are always craving more, but at the moment of shooting up or jerking off they are at least getting *some*. And here we are talking about guns every day, reading about guns every day, playing with our guns every day, and we never get to use them.

Target practice just doesn't cut it.

That's why, after years of unfulfilled gun lust, I decided to put an ad up on a popular listings site. I tried to keep it somewhat ambiguous and "gray area," legally, but I figured the right people would know what I meant.

"I like guns," it said. "If you need a man with a gun for protection or other purposes, this well-armed individual is available for long term engagements or one-off events. Affordable. Professional. Satisfaction guaranteed, or your money back."

I thought that read pretty nice. Even if it could have been better, I was too eager to get things going to fine tune it much. So, I hit "post" and sat back to wait.

Of course, it takes a while for the right customer to find an advertisement like mine, and I had a hard time passing the time. I went into the kitchen, came back to my computer and checked my email, leafed through the latest (already read) issue of Guns & Ammo, came back to my computer and checked my email, took apart my Sig Sauer P320, came back to my computer and checked my email, put the Sig Sauer back together, came back to my computer and checked my email, etc.

After a couple of hours of that I started considering taking the ad down, just so I could stop pacing around and jumping up and down. And then there it was. In my inbox. It had the number of my post as a subject line. In the body of the email it said "Man with gun needed. How do we proceed?"

My heart started racing. I couldn't believe it was really happening. It seemed too good to be true—that I could just put up an ad like that and get to work the same day. Then I started to think maybe it *was* too good to be true. How did I know it wasn't a cop trying to lure me into incriminating myself?

But then I remembered something I'd heard in school: if you ask a cop if he's a cop, he has to tell you, otherwise it's entrapment.

So I wrote back.

"Are you a cop?"

Then it was back to pacing and getting up and down checking my email over and over. Thankfully, he responded in a matter of minutes. I guess he knew the thing about entrapment.

"No," was all it said.

I wrote back right away that we should meet on neutral ground, somewhere public and open, but where we wouldn't draw attention to ourselves. He could name the time and place—outside of work hours—and I would tell him if that worked.

He must have already thought about it, because he got back to me within the minute.

"Angel Crest Park. Bench facing the gazebo, on the other side of the stream. 6:45pm. Today."

"Confirmed," I wrote back.

Damn! I was thrilled. I got my favorite sniper rifle—a Sako TRG 42—out of the safe, grabbed my tripod, a few boxes of ammo, the suppressor, and went out to the van.

I'd been dreaming about this, but I'd never tried it. I opened the back doors and set up a wall of boxes with a small gap in the center. It would be natural enough to see a delivery van with the back doors open and no one could see the rifle through the stacked boxes. After positioning the tripod and rifle carefully, I took a look through the scope. I could see the neighbor's Hungarian Puli in its yard two blocks away. I let it live, needless to say.

I was so excited. I was in and out of the van, futzing with the setup, heading back outside, thinking of something that might need tweaking, going back in, etc.

Finally, the clock started itching toward 6:45. I parked a few blocks from Angel Crest Park, locked the van, and walked to the gazebo. I wasn't such a fool that I was going to sit on that bench first and wait for him to check me out. So I very casually strolled into the structure and sat down. It was 6:40.

Right at 6:45 a man took a seat on the bench facing the gazebo. Skinny guy. Bald. Head and neck craned out too far in front of him. Folded newspaper. Black plastic glasses. Concavish chest. And what was worst, a cardigan with three big buttons.

I could see why he'd need someone else to do his killing for him. I don't think he could have squashed a tick with a pair of tweezers, let alone shoot off the head of his wife's lover, or whoever it was he wanted done in. I left the gazebo, crossed the little footbridge over the stream, and took a seat next to him.

"Nice day," I said.

He looked at me closely, studying my face.

"So you're the ..."

"Yup," I said. I realized next time I'd have to set up some kinda code. Live and learn.

"Mind if I ask you some questions?" he asked.

"As long as you're not a cop," I said.

"I'm not a cop."

"Go ahead and shoot."

"Well, to start with, how much?"

I was ready for that one.

"Ten thousand. Half now, half upon completion."

"I see. And if, say, we don't reach an understanding, how much for this initial consultation?"

I hadn't thought about that, but I didn't want him thinking I was some kind of amateur, so I spat out a figure before I had time to think about what might be reasonable.

"One hundred."

"Seems fair to me. Now, do you mind telling me what method you'll be using?"

"Well, I'm ready for every kind of situation," I told him, "but my preferred mode of operandi is the sniper rifle, with suppressor, of course. As long as you have the sense not to panic, you can ease away from the crime scene before the target even knows he's dead. Now, my favorite weapon—"

"Oh, this is great stuff, great great stuff," he interrupted. "Do you mind if I write it down? Just for my own purposes? I don't have a great memory."

I agreed, and he pulled a yellow legal pad from between the pages of his newspaper, and a pen from somewhere inside the cardigan.

"Do go on."

So I told him all about the Sako TRG 42, and why it was my favorite. I told him about the guns I'd traded to get it. And then I told him about how my van was the perfect cover, told him about my clever setup with the boxes, told him about the wiggle room I needed to get the right angle, and I told him about the extraordinary range I had.

He jotted it all down, scribbling furiously, never looking up at me.

"This is great, just great. I feel like I've been in the van with you."

I enjoyed talking about it, of course, so I told him about the pistol I always carried and would use if the sniper rifle wasn't an option. I even opened my jacket to show it to him. He was enthused and asked me all kinds of questions about it too.

Once I'd pretty much given him the lay of the land, he put his hand in his pocket, pulled out his wallet, counted out five twenties and handed them to me.

"Thank you very much for your time," he said. "I'm going to have to think about it."

And he put his wallet away and made as if to leave.

I grabbed him by the forearm and held him back.

"Hold on there," I said. "What's there to think about? I told you everything you wanted to know. You've got some problem with my methods? With my fee?"

"No, no. I just ... it's a serious decision. And I need some time to think about it."

"You shoulda done your thinking before you decided to meet me. Now you know everything about me, and I don't know anything about you. Why don't *you* tell *me* something? Then we'll work out what's next. Who's your target?"

He looked down at his notebook, holding it fiercely with both hands. His lips were pinched tight and he was scowling.

"I can tell you've got something bottled up in there. Better just out with it," I said.

He took a deep breath through his nose.

"I guess I'll just be honest with you," he said. "I don't really have a target in mind."

I didn't get it yet.

"You were thinking of paying me to kill a random person?"

"No. I wasn't thinking of paying you to kill anyone."

"So what are we doing here?"

"Here's the thing. There's this annual contest, held by Shot to the Head press, for the most authentic assassin story. And, so ... I thought I'd increase my chances of winning by talking to a real assassin. I've covered your consultation fee. And I was very impressed with your ... presentation. If I ever do need the services of an assassin, I assure you, you will be the first person I call."

There was a certain infallible logic to what he was saying. I was disappointed, to be sure, but I thanked him for his honesty and let him go.

I moped all the way back to the van. And I was hit by an extra wave of gloom when I climbed in it—to have to drive home with my rifle unused after all my planning felt especially unfair.

But my mood brightened considerably when I found there was an email waiting for me on my computer.

"Hey Man with Gun," it said. "Can we meet ASAP?"

I wrote back right away.

"We can. But first: Are you a cop?"

Within minutes I got the response.

"Ha ha. No way. Are YOU a cop? And when can we get this going?"

"Right now, if you like. And no, I'm not a cop either," I typed and hit send.

Soon enough we'd established a rendezvous—another bench—this one in Lincoln Park, down a little path from the playground there. And this time we agreed on a code. He'd say "I'm waiting on a lady friend," to which I was to reply "Don't worry, I won't be here long." We were to meet in half an hour.

I got there early and hid in a patch of trees not far from the playground to see what he was like before meeting with him.

Right on time, a big man in baggy jeans and a black T-Shirt, round of head, jowly, and side-burned, sat down on our designated bench. He looked okay to me.

I came out of the trees and walked over to him. I guess I'd rustled some leaves on the way out because he saw me right off and watched me while I strolled over. He waited till I sat down before he spoke.

"Saving that spot for my lady," he said, which was not, verbatim, what we'd agreed on.

"Don't worry, I won't be here long," I said.

"Right! So, how's this work?"

"Well, you tell me who you want ... removed ... and where to find them, and I do the removing. Half down and half when the job is done."

"Cool. And how are you going to do it?"

"Well, I said, I've got my sniper rifle in my truck and ..." I just couldn't help myself and I started telling him all about my set up.

He held up a forefinger.

"Sorry to interrupt," he said. "But would you mind terribly if I took notes?" He reached into his back pocket, brought out a small notebook and pen, and jotted down the date in the upper right corner.

Well, this time I knew what he was up to.

"You're a writer, aren't you?"

His pen froze. He looked at me suspiciously.

"I bet you're planning on entering the Shot to the Head contest for the most authentic assassin story too."

He goggled.

"How'd you know that?"

I couldn't think of a good reason not to tell him the truth.

"I met one of your kind not too long ago. He was up to the same thing: pretending to hire me just to mine me for information."

"What did he look like?"

I told him about the glasses, the bald head, the cardigan.

"Damn! That's Mick Adams! He's in my crime writers' group. I didn't know he had it in him. Doesn't exactly write 'authentic' anything, much less assassin stories. Then again, for thirty thousand, I guess it's worth trying."

"Thirty thousand?" It was my turn to goggle.

"That's right. It's the biggest contest of its kind."

We sat there, side by side, mulling over our recent revelations. A couple of crows cawed, and the merry-go-round in the playground shouted out for oil.

"How much are you charging?" he asked.

"Ten thousand, all together. Two hundred for this consultation."

He looked up into the sky, then down at his notebook.

Then he started writing.

"30,000 ÷ 2 = 15,000," is what it said.

I looked at him with a questioning brow.

"Mick Adams may not write with anything like authenticity," he said, "but he is a damn good writer. If he's turning his talents to this contest, it could be a kind of ... barrier for me, if you see what I mean."

"I believe I get your drift."

"The thing is, I could use the money, like anyone else, but really I'm thinking that winning that contest would boost my career."

"And?"

"Well, to put it plainly, maybe you could remove Mick from the running and then we could split the winnings."

I took all that in and digested it a bit.

"You'd be getting a third more than your usual fee," he added. "I don't have the cash on hand for the advance. But surely the extra five thousand makes up for that."

"I have no doubt," I said, "as to the prowess of your wordsmithing, but as I have not read a word of your work, you will forgive me for stating that my confidence in the certainty of your win is somewhat less than your own."

"I'd be glad to show you something. I've published half a dozen short stories and have finished two—"

I put my hand up.

"It's not only that," I said. "Mr. Mick Adams did pay me my consultation fee, and though he may not engage me in a proper operation, I consider that a retainer of sorts. Plus, I make it a rule to never take on a job without an advance."

He nodded to himself and rocked back and forth a little. Then he slapped his knees with both hands and stood up.

"Well, I guess I'll just have to get the old creative juices flowing. Please don't mention this little conversation to Mick."

"Of course not. I'm a professional."

And he walked away with an air of dejection and disappointment. I felt some dejection and disappointment myself. Not only because he'd gone off without paying my consultation fee, but also because I still hadn't secured my first job.

And it was starting to feel like I never would.

I got home, took a Hungry-Man chicken pot pie out of the freezer, threw it in the oven, and sat down in front of my computer.

And there, like a beacon of light in a storm of gloom, was yet another email in my inbox. I clicked on it eagerly.

"Got a job for you," was all it said.

We had a few back-and-forths and pretty soon he'd denied that he was a cop and we'd set up a meeting. This time, though, I made a point of mentioning right off that I had an initial consultation fee—I jacked it up to four hundred—and that it would have to be paid at the start of our meeting. If this was another damn writer, I wanted to walk away feeling like I got something substantial out of it.

He agreed and I drove off to meet him on another bench in another park.

Found him right away, sitting where he said he'd be sitting, wearing the baseball cap he said he'd be wearing.

He had his notebook and pen at the ready.

I sat down next to him.

'Brant Henry," he said. "Hope you don't mind if I take some of this down." He waggled the pen at me with one hand, while the other slipped me an envelope of cash.

I sighed.

"As long as you're paying," I said, "I'll fill you in on all the details you'll need for your authentic assassin story."

Brant Henry cocked his head at me.

"How'd you know about that?"

"Only because my last two clients were after the same thing."

"Last *two?* Who are they?"

"Mick Adams and a big guy with a round head and side-burns."

"That would be Aaron Toussaint. They're both in my crime writers' group." He hung his head and sat silently for a few minutes. Then he tapped my knee with his pen.

"So he and Adams came to you for the goods, huh?" he asked.

"Yep. This Aaron Toussaint thinks he can type up a good storm, second only to your friend Mick."

"He's no friend of mine. But he and Mick have published quite a bit, whereas the only thing I ever convinced anyone to run was a ghost story for my high school newspaper."

"I'm sure you're quite talented," I said.

"Thanks. All the same, things might be a little easier if Mick and Aaron weren't in the way. And now that they've talked to you, the authenticity bar is pretty high."

"Well, competition leads to innovation, doesn't it?"

"I suppose. I'm not sure that's how things work for literature," he said.

"I wouldn't know," I said.

"Listen, just as a joke, how much would it be to ... you know ... remove the competition?"

"Just as a joke, ten thousand a head. Half up front, half on completion. No twofers, if that's what you're asking."

"That's kind of reasonable. I thought it would cost more."

"All the same, there won't be much prize money left over for you after all's said and done."

"Oh, I don't care about the money. Made a fortune in finance and retired early. Putting all my energies into becoming a writer. And winning this contest would sure help."

"Well, if it's no extra pain to you, it would be very helpful if you could pay for the whole job in advance," I said.

He cracked his knuckles.

"Of course, I'll still need all the details about how you're going to do it. Competition or no competition, the contest *is* all about authenticity."

So we made a deal. We spent a good hour or two on that bench, with me filling him in as to all my tools and methods—for his story. Then we split up and met again in the parking lot of his bank, where he delivered a very thick wad of cash. Subsequently, we worked out the specifics of how I would proceed from there.

Which is how I ended up in the parking lot of the Arby's at 9am two days later.

It was a pretty sweet set-up. That lot was right across the street from The Alien Bean coffee shop and its parking spaces were lined up so the back of my van faced the entrance.

As soon as I parked, I hopped out and opened the rear doors. Then I went back inside the van through the driver's door, locked the front doors behind me, climbed into the back, and sat down on a small box behind my tripod and rifle.

The Alien Bean had a single door flanked by two large single-pane windows. I had a great view through the gap in my wall of boxes. Just inside the window on the left, two couches faced each other across a low table. And just beyond the area with the couches there was a long table that could seat twelve. A middle-aged woman with red hair was at the far end, speaking to gray haired woman in a beret. That would be Janet Milhauser and Ellen Spielmacher. I could make them out quite clearly through the scope and Brant Henry had described them to me perfectly.

Soon they were joined by a few others, each arriving singly, and the table began to fill up over the next fifteen minutes. Then Mick Adams showed up—wearing the same stupid cardigan—and Aaron Toussaint followed him a few minutes later. They sat down next to each other on the left side of the table, at the corner closest to me, which would make my job a lot easier.

Then at 9:30, on the dot, Brant walked in and sat down across from his two competitors. The whole table was chatting, all smiles and gestures and mannerisms. They didn't look much like a bunch of crime writers, more like a gaggle of gossips. But who was I to judge?

After they'd been blabbing for about ten minutes, Brant stood up and said he had to go to the bathroom. I couldn't hear him, of course, but that's what he'd said he'd say. Beyond the counter where customers did their ordering there was a long hall that led to the bathrooms. I was supposed to watch Brant walk down the hall and hold my fire till he'd entered the bathroom and the door had closed behind him.

But that's not what I did.

As soon as Brant was on his feet, I got Mick in my crosshairs and pulled the trigger.

With the suppressor on there wasn't much recoil and I probably could have taken a look at Mick and the fresh hole I'd given him. But I didn't have time for that. I swiveled a hair to the right and found the face of Aaron Toussaint. I guess he hadn't quite figured out what had happened to Mick, as he looked more puzzled than alarmed.

That was the last expression he'd ever wear. I squeezed off another one and then swiveled again, hard to the right and up till I found Brant still standing there. He wasn't looking at Mick or Aaron. He was looking straight out at me. He looked truly bewildered. He even shrugged with up-turned palms. I guess he wasn't much of a crime writer—he ought to have figured out what I was up to long ago. Anyway, I pulled the trigger again and put him out of his confusion.

I had a pair of binoculars back there and I took a look at the scene before closing up shop. It was just dawning on the other members of the crime writing group that something bad had happened. No one was running to the bodies yet. Mick, Aaron, and Brant each had a clean red hole in their heads. I was very pleased that my Sako TRG 42 had performed just as it was supposed to.

I pulled the strings I'd attached to the doors and closed them with two soft clicks. Then I climbed up front to the driver's seat, gave the twenty thousand that Brant had given me a pat inside my jacket, and drove off.

So that's about as authentic as it gets, I figure. I'm guessing I don't have much competition left, though I can't say I'm an expert with commas and spelling and the like. But you probably have editors that figure all that stuff out. I've been on the lam since the shooting, of course, so just as soon as I hear back from you, I'll tell you the location of the park bench where you can leave the thirty thousand.

SURE AS APPLES

Brandon Barrows

"Do you like apples, dear?"

I looked up from the iPad screen. Sarah was standing in the doorway of my den, leaning against the frame. That old twinkle was in her eye. We've been married twelve years and I still think she's the most beautiful, warmest, most wonderful woman I've ever met—but I saw that twinkle on our very first date, and sometimes I think I should have run screaming when I still had the chance.

"Is this the beginning of a joke or are we doing movie quotes?"

She came into the room and snatched the iPad out of my hands. She didn't even glance at the episode of *Sons of Anarchy* I was watching, even though she practically worships Katey Sagal. That meant trouble. "I'm serious," she said. "Just answer the question."

I sighed, wondering what I was letting myself in for. "Of course I like apples. Everyone likes apples."

Sarah leaned her hip against the side of my chair and wrapped an arm around my head, pulling me close. "And how would you, sir, like a lifetime of free apples?"

I was wary to begin with, but this was heading into strange territory. "I guess that'd be okay ..."

"Do you agree that an untended yard is both an eyesore and a shame?"

"Oh, for Christ's sake, Sarah!" I loved my wife very much, but this was driving me nuts.

Sarah released me and, hands on hips, said, "Oh for Christ's sake yourself, Adam! Don't talk to me like that." The light still danced in her eyes but it was tinged with anger now.

I pursed my lips, then released them and sighed again. "I'm sorry. Yes, I agree about the yard. What's the point?"

"You know the Thomasen place, out on Skunk Hollow Road?"

"So that's what this is about." I leaned back in the chair and regarded my wonderful, mischievous wife.

Sarah and I grew up here, left separately to go to college in different parts of the country, and by coincidence met back up years later and fell in love. When we were looking for somewhere to settle down, our shared hometown felt like the natural place. Of course, things were a lot different than they were when we were kids, thirty-some-odd years ago. For one thing, Ira Thomasen, who for decades was the only real money in the area and the owner of just about everything worth owning, was long gone. His huge, sprawling house had been empty ever since. Recently, some enterprising developer from the city bought the house and lands and was now talking about putting in a new subdivision.

"Adam, they're going to plow the house and everything around it into the ground."

"So?"

"So, that means *everything*, including all those gorgeous apple trees out behind the house. Isn't that a waste?"

"It's a waste," I agreed.

"It's not just a waste, it's practically a crime!" She was getting indignant now, pacing the room. I probably could have snuck out and she wouldn't have noticed until I stopped answering her. I'd gone that route before, though, and it wasn't very pretty.

"Practically," I said without any enthusiasm.

"Those trees have lived for who knows how long and they're just going to be smooshed or whatever because some greedy fat cat wants to get rich."

"If he's a fat cat, he's already rich."

Sarah didn't hear me or at least wasn't listening. It amounted to the same thing. She turned and faced me. "Isn't it more humane, more compassionate, to save at least *one* of those trees? Dig it up and transplant it somewhere it'll have all the love and care and sunlight and water it needs?"

"Like, say, our backyard?"

"Yes!" She pointed a finger at me like the host of a gameshow telling me to "come on doooown!"

"I knew you'd understand." She scampered over and gave me a squeeze.

"You know what else I understand, though, honey?" I hated to broach the subject, but someone had to keep their feet on the ground. I didn't know why it was always me, but there it was. "Destroying those trees may be criminal, but so is stealing them."

Sarah pulled back and gave me a look somewhere between a scowl and disbelief. "It's not *stealing*."

"Did you ask the developer if you could take one of his trees?" I asked reasonably.

"Of course not!" she replied, which I'm sure she thought was also reasonable. Who would ever ask such a thing?

"Then it's stealing." I sat back in the chair, satisfied with myself. The logic of the argument was pretty self-evident, I thought.

Sarah didn't think so. "It's not stealing. It's ... *finding*. Like if you found a million dollars in a dumpster and took it, it's finder's keepers. You know the rule."

I sighed once more. "First, legally, someone still owns that garbage. Second, nobody's going to throw away a million dollars. Third, why would I be digging around in someone's trash, anyway?"

"Enough!" she cried, crossing her arms over her chest, palms flat and fingers stiff, making a big X to signal end of game. "We're rescuing one of those poor trees and that's the end of it."

"Sarah ..." I began, but had no idea what to say next. I made the arguments. She ignored them. What else *could* I say?

"I'll get the gardening stuff," I said.

I got a shovel and my work-gloves and Sarah showed me the roll of burlap and the special root-cutter tool she already bought. "How long were you planning this?" I asked, but she just said, "Get in the car, baby." Feeling vaguely like a kidnapping victim, I got in the car.

Sarah was in a good mood as we headed across town. She had the radio on the oldies station and was singing along to all the poppy songs from our high-school days. The windows were down, late-spring breezes whipped her dark hair around, and she laughed for no reason. I was glad to see her so happy, but I still had a bad feeling about the whole caper. And that's what it was, I decided: a caper, in the old-fashioned, criminal sense of the word.

"The Pruetts are going to be so jelly," Sarah said at one point. "Our apple tree will make their choke-cherry tree look like a joke. Phooey on their jam!" She turned to me, put a hand on my arm and said, "I'll have to learn how to bake. Fresh apple pies! Mmm! And apple-butter! Your mom'll give me her recipe, right?"

"Sure, probably," I told her without looking her way. "But will the prison let you use their kitchen?"

She smacked me lightly with the back of her hand. "Will you shut up about that? It's not stealing. Not really."

"Pretty sure the police and whoever owns the development company would disagree." I turned my head. "Look, how much could an apple tree cost? Let's just go to Claussen's Nursery and I'll buy you one."

Sarah scrunched up her nose like she smelled something rancid. "Are you kidding? And wait 'til we're old and gray before we get any fruit?"

A thought occurred to me then. "Wait—if these trees are big enough to fruit, how are we going to transplant one, anyway?"

"There are some small ones."

"Oh my God. You've already been out there, haven't you? You've already picked out a tree!"

"I've already been out there," she confirmed. "I've already picked out a tree." She smirked. "Oh!" she grabbed my arm. "You turn left up here!"

I chewed my lip in frustration and turned left.

Skunk Hollow was a dirt road I hadn't been on more than once or twice and hadn't thought about since then. And that was when I was a little kid, probably. I don't think it went anywhere, so unless you lived on it—or were starting an arboreal crime career—there was no reason to remember it existed. It was pretty far outside of the town proper. In the by-gone days when Thomasen built his house, it would have been fairly isolated.

We passed a greying, half-collapsed farmhouse, crossed over a creaking bridge, and then the road began to climb gently higher. Sparse trees lined the road on either side, empty fields visible beyond them, but there were no signs of any houses other than the one near the junction with the main road. It was like we were alone in the world. It gave me a small dose of the creeps.

A couple of miles further on, Sarah pointed and said, "Oooh, Adam. It's that one!" as if I could miss the mansion sitting on top of the hill all by its lonesome, surrounded by a sea of grass so tall you could have comfortably hidden a fleet of Enterprise Rent-a-Cars.

I turned the car up a crushed gravel driveway that was slowly turning into a crushed gravel lawn and parked in the circular area off to one side of the house's front entrance. Sarah was out of the car practically before it stopped and before I climbed out, she had the burlap and her root dealy in hand. "Let's go, Adam," she ordered.

I sighed and got the shovel and my gloves from the back, dreading what came next. As I did, I took a look at the area. The top of the hill was fairly level, and must have covered at least several acres. Out back of the house, stretching off to both sides, were clusters of trees, though I couldn't see any apple from where I stood. Turning the other direction, I realized with a start that you could see the main road from up here. Cars were zipping past in the distance, but some trick of the air and light made it feel like I could almost reach out and touch them.

"Hey, Sarah!" I called.

"What?" She was standing by the side of the house, so eager to get going she was practically hopping from foot to foot.

"I can see the road from here, plain as day!"

"Congrats! You won't need new glasses this year!" She gave me a thumb's up.

"Ha ha. No, I'm serious. You know this means people can see us too?"

"Oh, who cares?" She batted the air with one hand, the burlap under her arm making the gesture clumsy. "Even if they do, so what? They won't know who we are. Now let's go."

I took off my glasses and rubbed hard at my eyes. I wasn't getting out of this, was I? Not without either an apple tree or some stainless-steel bracelets, maybe with a nice length of chain between them. I grabbed up the shovel and tromped after my wife, wondering if conjugal visits were a thing when both spouses were in separate prisons.

Sarah gleefully skipped off ahead of me, headed around back of the big house. Before I reached her, I could hear her cooing, "Oooh my gaaawd, they're so gorgeous!" I came around to the back of the house and saw the cluster of apple trees. They were in full bloom, covered in masses of white and pink flowers and, even from thirty yards off, I could smell their sweet aroma. It reminded me of springs of years ago, before mortgages and credit card debt and marketing meetings. I wasn't going to give Sarah the satisfaction of my saying it out loud, but I agreed the trees were beautiful.

I trailed Sarah as she moved among the trees. She stopped at a smaller one, maybe five feet high, towards the back of the grove. It wasn't as impressive as its neighbors, but it was still flowering and it was nice to look at.

Sarah tossed the burlap and her tool to the ground and whirled on her heel. "Isn't he a beauty?"

"I'm pretty sure only female trees produce fruit."

She rolled her eyes and said, "Isn't *she* a beauty?"

"Yes," I agreed, not wanting to antagonize her any further.

"Well." She glanced up at the sky. "I don't like the looks of those clouds, so let's get to it."

Which, of course, meant "Get digging, Adam."

I started digging. Sarah stood off to one side "supervising," which entailed giving me directions every ten seconds or so. She was in such a good mood, though, that I almost didn't mind. Almost.

After a while, I was filthy, soaked with sweat, and my back hurt worse than I ever knew it could. I straightened up, leaned against the shovel.

"What's wrong?"

"I feel like I'm in *Young Frankenstein*," I told her. "You know, the grave-digging scene?"

"It could be worse," Sarah said in her best Marty Feldman voice. "It could be raining."

"Please don't say that," I groaned. The words were barely out of my mouth when I felt the first drop of rain plink off the frame of my glasses.

I kept digging, but over the course of several minutes, the rain went from sprinkle to downpour. I stuck the shovel in the ground and looked at my wife. "Notice anything?"

"You're down to the roots," she said, brandishing her cutting tool.

"Uh huh. The rain?"

She shrugged. "So it's raining. You're water-proof."

"Water-*resistant*," I corrected and began to walk out of the little grove.

"Adam!" Sarah grabbed my arm. "You're not leaving." It wasn't a question.

"No," I told her, water streaming down the channels alongside my nose. "We've already committed the crime, there's no point in giving up now."

"Oh my God, it's not a *crime*!" She stamped her foot on the wet ground.

"You're right. I think technically vandalism is only a misdemeanor. It'll be a crime once we actually take the tree." I gently disengaged her hand and kept walking.

"Where are you going now?" she asked.

"I'm going to go sit in the car until this storm is over. You dragged me into this thing, but I'm not gonna let you drown me too."

"We don't have to go that far." Sarah took my arm again and began half-leading, half-dragging me. It was obvious in a moment that she was headed straight for the house, specifically the patio with the big French doors, visible from where we were.

"Sarah, we can't go in there," I protested.

"Why not?" She wasn't really this clueless, she only pretended to be when it suited her.

"Because it's breaking and entering. You're just adding years onto our sentence with every new idea. Besides," I said, stumbling over some unseen lump in the long grass, "I'm sure it's locked."

But I was wrong. Sarah reached the patio doors, tried the handle of the nearest one and it opened as easily as if it was freshly oiled. She went inside and, reluctantly, I followed. Sarah struck a pose like a magician's assistant and said, "Ta da!"

Squeegeeing water from my hair with both hands, I asked, "Did you already know about this too?"

"Nope, just lucky." She showed me the grin that I fell in love with, the one she knew made me melt. "Let's look around while we wait." I got a glimpse of that beautiful, terrifying twinkle in her eye before she moved off deeper into the house. I sighed.

The place was pretty well empty. Most of the furniture was gone and what was left was covered in sheets heaped with years' worth of dust. The walls were bare and it made the rooms seem even more cavernously huge. The place was built sometime in the sixties and looked as if nothing had ever really been changed or updated. As far as I knew, Ira Thomasen lived here alone when I was a kid. I wondered if he always had.

Sarah was sticking her head into a closet when we heard the heavy clomping thumps.

"What was that?" I asked.

She looked at me, face blank. "What was what?"

"You had to have heard it." The sounds came again from almost directly overhead. "There! That!"

Sarah waved a hand. "Oh, that. Probably the house settling."

"It was *not*!" I was scared and I was getting frustrated with her nonchalance. "That was *footsteps*. Someone else is in the house!"

"Well, let's go see!" She grabbed my hand and dragged me back towards the main hallway. I objected at every step, but guess what good it did me.

"Anybody home?" she called.

A deep male voice responded from somewhere above us. "Who's there?"

The footsteps came again. From the sound of them, the man must have been a giant. Images of a certain, very visceral, Goya painting flashed through my mind.

I tried to push Sarah towards the front door. "Let's get out of here!"

"Relax," Sarah said, then turned towards the stairs. "We're Sarah and Adam Williams!"

"Are you nuts?"

"You're being silly," Sarah scolded. "It's probably just a watchman or something. I bet he's bored out of his mind and will be glad for someone to talk to."

"Yes, that's exactly what I'm afraid of. Watchmen *watch,* Sarah. Maybe he was watching us steal that tree, and he'd probably like to talk to us about sentencing guidelines."

"We were transplanting a tree nobody wanted." Her tone was exasperated.

"We'll let our lawyer argue the difference in court."

I tried to drag her towards the door again, but it was too late now. The watchman, or whoever he was, came tromping down the stairs. He was as big as I guessed; he must have been six foot five and judging from his shoulders and barrel belly, he had to have weighed at least two-hundred and eighty pounds. His hair was shoulder-length and streaked with grey, but his beard was a rich brown and neatly trimmed. He looked exactly like the kind of person I'd want guarding my property, except for one thing: he was dressed like a nurse. By that I mean, instead of some sort of pseudo-police-style uniform, he was wearing a dull blue scrub top and matching pants, with canvas loafers. T*hose would be murder on his feet on a long shift at the hospital,* I thought.

"Hello," the man said as he stepped from the final stair.

"Hi!" Sarah chirped. "Are you the watchman?"

I slapped my palm against my forehead. She was practically asking to be detained. My wife wasn't dumb or anything—don't believe that for a second. Her problem was that she felt everyone had her best interests at heart and if she just acted cheerful and friendly everything would work out. The problem with *that* was it generally worked out pretty well for her. Like, nine times out of ten. I couldn't shake the feeling that this would be the tenth time.

"Err." The big man was obviously confused. "No, not exactly."

Sarah said, "You're here for an apple tree, too, then, huh?" She winked at the guy, very theatrically.

The other man looked at me. All I could do was shrug. I'll say this for my wife, she was very good at throwing people off balance. It felt kind of good to not be alone in that.

"Yes, sure, I am," the guy said at last. I was pretty certain he had no idea what she was talking about though. "So this isn't your house, then?"

"Nope!" The guy seemed to relax a little. Then Sarah shifted gears. "Anyway, what's your name? I'm Sarah." She gestured to herself then to me. "And this is my husband, Adam."

The man hesitated, looking from Sarah to me then said, "Um ... David."

Sarah waited, an expectant look on her face. He looked to me for help, but what was I going to do?

"Bi—uh, Bowie," he finished, at last.

"Really!" Sarah clapped her hands together in delight. "I just love your song 'Starman'! You look different in person."

"Sarah," I tugged at her soggy sleeve. "That Bowie is dead, I'm pretty sure."

"Oh, is he?" She seemed disappointed. What was with her today?

"David Bowie" studied my wife for a moment then said, "Don't worry. I get it a lot."

"Which tree did you pick out, David?" Sarah wanted to know.

The guy gave me a look that clearly said he thought Sarah was crazy. I was starting to think so too. Then he said to her, "The really pretty one. With all the flowers."

"They're *all* pretty." Sarah said it like she was disappointed in him.

"Yeah," "Bowie" answered. "I guess that's right."

"We're all gonna end up in prison," I said. I couldn't help it. It just popped out.

"Bowie" looked startled, like a deer in a set of fast-approaching headlights. "What?!"

"The trees," I began. "Even if they're going to be cut down or plowed or whatever, they still belong to the land development company. It's still stealing to take them."

Sarah sighed. "He keeps saying that. He's obsessed. I almost think he *wants* to go to prison. Isn't that silly, David?"

"Well ..." He seemed to really be considering it. He sat down on the bottom step. Even seated, I think he probably came up to my shoulder. "I guess it all depends on how you look at it."

"I look at it like it's stealing and we're gonna get caught," I said.

"Stealing ..." "Bowie" murmured. "No, liberating is more like it."

"Huh?" I looked at Sarah. She grinned and said, "Exactly! He gets it!" She grabbed my arm and shook me in her excitement. "We're not stealing a tree, we're freeing it from a death sentence and giving it a new lease on life."

On hearing "death sentence" I swear "Bowie" got a little pale.

"I think it's stopped raining," Sarah said before the conversation could continue.

"Bowie" grinned. "So you folks'll just be on your way then, I guess."

"We haven't finished Operation Liberation yet," Sarah told him. "Wanna help us? Then we'll do the same for you. It'll go a lot faster with two people digging."

"Two?" The man raised an eyebrow. "But there's three—"

"Don't ask," I told him. "You already know the answer."

The three of us walked back to the apple grove together. With the dampness in the air and the waist-high grass, it felt like I was on safari. A hungry tiger leaping out of the brush would not have surprised me at that point. Not that day.

When we made it back to the tree Sarah had chosen, I pulled the gloves from my back pocket, picked up the shovel, and scooped water out of the hole until I could dig again. "Bowie" poked around the edges of the hole with Sarah's root-cutting tool, but didn't really contribute anything. He seemed nervous. He kept looking over his shoulder, back towards the house.

"Something wrong?" I asked him.

"No, just, uh ..." He didn't finish, just shook his head.

Finally, we got the tree free of the ground. "Bowie" lifted it straight up, proving he was as strong as he looked, while Sarah snipped the roots and I wrapped the bulb in burlap and tied it with twine. Then, "Bowie" and I carried it to the car. As we were tying it to the roof of the sedan, Sarah pointed towards the road and said, "There's a car coming."

"David Bowie" jumped like he stepped on a live wire and bolted towards the house.

"What's his problem?" Sarah asked, watching him disappear around the corner of the building. "It's just a sheriff's deputy."

"What!" I shouted and made to follow the other man.

But it was too late. Sarah was close enough to grab me and she pulled me back, saying, "Don't you dare! You'll make him think we're guilty of something."

"We *are*!" I spat, clenching my hands uselessly and seeing visions of drab prison uniforms in my future. That thought almost brought to mind something else, but it remained stuck somewhere in the recesses of my brain. I pushed it aside, having other things to worry about.

The deputy sheriff pulled his cruiser to a stop a few feet behind our car. He stepped out of the vehicle, eyed us, the sedan, the tree tied to it. He was a tall man, nearly as tall as "David Bowie," but built like a broom. I was pretty sure that if he removed his camel-colored Stetson, his hair would puff out to complete the effect.

"Afternoon, folks," he said, pleasantly enough.

"How do you do, officer?" Sarah said so formally I expected her to curtsey.

Pleasantries finished, the officer got right to it. "Saw your car from the road. Mind telling me what's going on here?"

"What's going on here?" Sarah repeated, cocking her head like a puppy and batting her eyelashes. We'd moved into vaudeville territory apparently.

Someone needed to do something and Sarah obviously had no idea what, other than to fall back on the trick that had always worked for her. She got lucky with the watchman or whatever "David Bowie" was, but the way the deputy was looking at us, if she kept it up, this was definitely going to be that tenth time I mentioned before.

"What's the problem, officer?" I asked, putting a little snarl in my voice. "Can't we do a little planting in our own yard?"

The deputy looked from me to the house then back. "*Your* yard? This is the Thomasen place."

"*Was* the Thomasen place," I corrected. "Everyone knows it was empty for years, but you must have heard about the sale. Just closed escrow last week."

A little doubt came into the man's eyes. "Uh huh. Guess I did hear about it."

Despite my clothes not being quite dry yet, I was sweating. My heart was thumping so loudly in my chest I was sure they could hear it across town, but I forged ahead. I read once that the difference between a successful criminal and a convict is brazenness. Pure ballsiness, in other words.

I began unstrapping the tree from the roof of my car. "We're aren't quite ready to move in yet, but we can still do a little landscaping before the furniture and boxes get here. Help me with this, will you?"

The deputy glanced at Sarah, hesitating, then stepped forward. "Sure." I don't know how, but it was working. All these years, I thought Sarah was just lucky, but maybe she was on to something after all.

Between the two of us, getting the tree down was no problem. "I've already dug the hole. It's this way." I started dragging the tree back towards the corner of the house.

The deputy took up the other end of the tree and said, "You really own this place?"

"Sure." I forced a laugh that caught in my throat and turned into choking. I managed to wheeze out, "Who'd plant a tree in someone else's yard?"

"Guess so," the man agreed.

We just crossed into the huge backyard when the deputy said, "Lawn's a little long, isn't it? I'd have started with that, personally."

I looked back at him, plastering mild shock on my face. "Are you kidding? This is good grass, man! Prime livestock feed!"

"Livestock," he said, deadpan.

"Sure. We're gonna have some horses, goats, maybe a cow or two."

His head swiveled, taking in the area. There was certainly enough room for a barn, but the animals wouldn't be getting out much, not unless they took turns going one at a time. He decided that was my problem, I guess, because all he said was, "Oh."

We made our way into the grove of apple trees without another word. The deputy looked at the trees all around us and I know he wanted to ask why we were planting another apple tree here, but I think he was afraid to. He'd already learned that the answer might make even less sense than the question.

Sarah untied the burlap from the root bulb, giving it a look of sadness, knowing it was not to be, then we dropped the tree into the hole.

"Perfect fit," the deputy said.

"Thank you," I replied cheerfully, beaming as if it was the nicest thing anyone ever said to me. I didn't have to pretend to be happy. I was ecstatic that this stupid idea was going over so well.

We filled the hole in, patted it down, and stepped back to admire our handiwork.

"It's a good-looking tree all right," the officer commented.

"It's lovely," Sarah said. There was a tear in the corner of her eye and I knew exactly what she was thinking: it would have looked even better in our own yard. I guess she was saying her goodbyes.

"Well, suppose I'll be getting along," the deputy said.

I felt relief flood through my body, but it was short-lived. Sarah said, "Oh, do you have to? We appreciate your help so much, I thought I'd offer you a cup of coffee before you go."

My jaw dropped and I stared at her like she just grew a second head. And maybe some wings for good measure. "I don't think—"

"That'd be nice, actually. Thank you." The cop smiled at her.

"I don't think we have any!" I shouted almost at the top of my lungs, disturbing a flock of little birds that shot from a nearby tree, squawking their indignation. Both Sarah and the officer jumped and turned panicked eyes my way.

"I mean ..." I cleared my throat. "I mean, I think we're out, dear." I never believed in things like telepathy or ESP before, but right then, I was trying my hardest to send my thoughts directly into Sarah's brain.

I looked at the deputy. "We haven't fully stocked the place up yet, you understand. Once the furniture and everything is in, we'll do a big grocery run." I chuckled nervously.

"Oh, well, that's too bad." He looked at Sarah. "Could I maybe just get a drink of water then?"

"Of course!" Sarah smiled sweetly.

"But ..." I began.

"Shush, Adam," Sarah said, kind of sharply.

"Right this way, officer ... what was your name?" Sarah asked, taking the man's arm and leading him towards the house.

"Hawthorne," he said.

"Not Nathaniel?!" Sarah gasped.

The officer laughed. "No, Doug. Why?"

"Oh." Sarah's back was to me, but she sounded disappointed. "It's just that I met David Bowie earlier today and I thought it'd be neat to meet another celebrity."

The deputy threw a glance over his shoulder at me, but I pretended not to notice. I was too busy waving farewell to my life as a respectable citizen with no criminal record.

Sarah led the three of us through the same back door where we first entered the house. It felt like being marched to the gallows.

The officer looked around, stamping his feet to get some of the wet and muck off. "Lot you could do with a place like this," he said.

Sarah turned, smiling brightly. "Oh, we've got so many plans. You wouldn't believe it."

She moved into the front hallway and I thought she was going to turn towards the kitchen, but instead she said, "There's someone I want you to meet, Doug." Then she cupped her hands around her mouth and called out, "David! David Bowie! Come on down and meet our other guest!"

The deputy's brow furrowed and his hand moved unconsciously to the holstered automatic on his hip. He looked at me and I just shook my head. I was doing a lot of that lately.

For a moment, everything was silent. Then we heard those familiar thumping noises coming from above us, except faster and heavier. There was some sort of scuffling sound, followed almost instantly by breaking glass, then the crash of a heavy object tumbling against the roof.

The deputy drew the gun from its holster and raced towards the front of the house, throwing open the front door just in time to see "David Bowie" drop from the edge of the veranda that fronted the building. He was a huge man and hanging by his arms, it wasn't much of a drop for him. His feet were already churning before it dawned on me what I was seeing.

"Police! Stop where you are!" Hawthorne yelled. "Bowie" ignored him.

The deputy looked like he was about to give chase, but Sarah yelled out, "David, I wish you hadn't retired Ziggy Stardust!"

It was so absurd that the running man actually looked over his shoulder, the same expression on his face that a dog has trying to figure out a knock-knock joke. He didn't stop running, but he should have. He only looked our way for a moment, but it was enough for him to miss something in the tall grass. He stumbled, flailed for balance, then did a belly-flop and slid like he was on the world's cheapest Slip-n-Slide.

It all happened so fast my mind was reeling, struggling to process everything, but it gave Deputy Hawthorne the time he needed to catch up to "Bowie." The cop wasted no time in slapping handcuffs onto the stunned man and frog-marching him towards the cruiser. When he had, he turned "Bowie" around, opened the door of the cruiser, and stuffed him inside.

When Deputy Hawthorne turned back to us, his mouth hung open like he was trying to catch flies. He worked his jaw up and down for a few seconds, then jerked a thumb over his shoulder. "You know who you got there? That's David Biggers, the guy who robbed the First National Bank last year. He escaped from a county work-detail two days ago."

"I know," Sarah said, smirking triumphantly. "I recognized him as soon as we saw him."

"Are you kidding me?" I asked. I couldn't believe it. This had to be more of my wife's sheer dumb luck, didn't it? I looked at Biggers, sitting in the cruiser glowering, then back at Sarah. "You knew all along who he was?"

"From the moment we saw him. I read more than just the real estate announcements in the news, you know. And unlike *some* people, I use the Internet for more than just Netflix."

I felt like my head was going to wobble right off my neck, I'd been shaking it so much, but I did it yet again. My wife out-brazened a career criminal and fooled us all.

"Anyway," Sarah said to the deputy. "I didn't want him to get away, so I had to get you into the house somehow. This seemed like the best way."

"Well, this is a good enough place to hide out for a while, I guess." Then Hawthorne's forehead scrunched up in thought, and he said, "But you folks don't really own this place, do you? So what were you doing out here, anyway?"

"Oh, that." Sarah dismissed his concern with a wave of her hand. "I've been trying to convince Adam to put an apple tree in our backyard and I wanted to show him how pretty they were when they're blooming. Plus, you know, I'm going to try my hand at making apple-butter once his mom gives me the recipe."

"But what about ..." Hawthorne pointed towards our car, obviously thinking of the tree he helped us plant. Then he threw up his hands and said, "Forget it. I don't want to know. Get out of here and I'll forget I ever saw you. Just go on home."

"Oh, well, thanks, Doug, but we can't do that."

"Why the heck can't we?!" I wanted to know.

"We have to stop at Claussen's first." She winked at me.

My whole body sagged as the tension went out of me. It took a moment or two, but I was even able to work up a smile, because maybe it didn't happen exactly the way Sarah planned, but sure as apples, she always found a way to get what she wanted.

BLUE LIGHT SPECIAL

R.T. Lawton

Harvey had two twenties, a ten and a five-dollar bill laid out on the Formica-topped bar table in front of him. With the knife edge of his hand, he squeegeed some of the spilled beer out of the paper currency so he could fold the money and put it in the front pocket of his jeans. He'd just settled his month-old bar tab, under protest on his part, but it seemed that the bartender in this backwater joint had somehow acquired a sixth sense as to when people's cash flow was getting short.

"That all we got left?" asked Louis as he placed both index fingers in belt loops on the back of his baggy jeans and pulled upwards. Then he took a seat in one of the old wooden chairs.

"Don't look like enough for rent, groceries, nor the monthly loan payment on your old '71 Dodge pickup," he continued.

"Hard times coming down," agreed Harvey. "Appears everybody got money these days, 'cepting us. Take for instance them guys running go-fast boat-loads of marijuana over from the Bahama banks in the middle of the night, I don't see them having cash problems."

"Good point," said Louis. "And them cocaine cowboys in Miami with their airplane drops out in the swamps seem to be doing good."

"Hell, our local drug dealers got so much money, they taking it to the bank in paper grocery sacks," continued Harvey. "We getting left out. Time we got ourselves a piece of the action."

Louis took a healthy swig from his beer bottle before leaning forward and asking in a lowered voice, "Whatcha got in mind?"

"I was thinking," said Harvey, lowering his own voice to a whisper, "we should go fishing."

"Fishing?" replied Louis. "We can't make no money doing that."

"I know," said Harvey, "but I got to give my uncle Rafe some sort of excuse for borrowing his go-fast boat."

"Borrow his boat? For what? We got no money to buy stuff and run it in from the Caribbean or even the short ways across the Gulf from Mexico.

And no supplier in his right mind is gonna front us any of their product."

"I know that, but for what I'm thinking, all we need is a fast boat, a couple of guns and one of them blue flashing lights."

"And that's gonna make us some money?"

"Damn straight."

"Where we gonna get a flashing blue light?"

"That's the least of our problems, but don't sweat it, I got everything figured out."

And, that's how they came to be bouncing up a rutted dirt backroad in Harvey's ten-year-old pickup headed north into the swamp lands. Mostly, the road followed the curves of some snake-bend river lined with mangrove trees on the river side, and saw-tooth grass, black swamp-water ponds and Cypress and Tupelo trees hung with grey wisps of Spanish moss on the inland side. Harvey just hoped he had enough gas in the tank to get back out to civilization. He wasn't one much for walking if'n there was snakes or gators underfoot. Other than that, everything was according to plan.

As far as the plan went at this stage.

"I put the .45 automatic and my old hunting rifle behind the seat," said Harvey, "and with the blue light you got us, I'd say we're almost ready."

Louis glanced at the black marks on his left thumb and forefinger.

"I didn't know those wires were gonna be hot when I cut 'em. I about got electrocuted."

"Should've just unplugged the light. What were you thinking?"

Louis rubbed his scorched fingers together.

"Well, I looked all over the store, but it wasn't until K-Mart announced one of their blue light specials that I finally saw where one of them lights was after it started flashing. At that point, the place turned into a mob scene to get whatever it was just went on sale."

"So?"

"So it was brutal, all knees and elbows in that crowd. My third time knocked to the floor, I just mighta panicked a little. That's when I cut the wires, grabbed the light and run for my life."

Harvey hit another bump in the road and raised his beer bottle in an attempt to keep precious alcohol from sloshing out the top. With the poor shape this road was in, it was getting difficult to drink, drive and talk at the same time. Plus, all the jarring and bouncing around in the pickup hurt his sore nose, but he didn't want to think about that.

"We'll get the light wired into a plug what fits in the cigarette lighter so it flashes like we need," he said between bumps. "I got some electrician's tape."

Half a mile further, past a giant Cypress tree hung with long beards of grey Spanish moss, Harvey found his maternal uncle sitting in a wooden rocking chair on the front porch of his ramshackle house. It was a one story, tin-roofed building, with the boards weathered and sun bleached and sprigs of green moss growing out of the siding. The slightly off-kilter structure set perched on wood stilts at the edge of the river, right beside a sagging boat dock. Harvey took in the three new pickups parked on the land side of the house and a bright red go-fast tied up to the pier on the water side.

The old man acted cordial, but didn't seem particularly happy to see his nephew at this particular moment.

Harvey wasn't sure if the old codger had something illegal brewing out back and didn't want anybody around to poke into his business or just liked his privacy in general, which didn't explain the three new pickups parked in the yard. He nosed his truck up to a sawed-off tree stump, killed the engine and got out, leaving the driver's door open.

"Unk."

"Nephew."

"Mind if I come up on the porch? Maybe talk a bit?"

Rafe took a pouch of Red Man out of his bib overalls and opened the top of the container. With his right thumb and forefinger, he fished several strands of damp stringy tobacco out and stuffed them into his mouth, making a fair-sized lump in one cheek. He started to chaw.

"C'mon up, but don't get too comfortable. You won't be staying long."

Harvey knew he had to watch his step here. Some of the wood planks going up to the porch were starting to rot through. And, with the way several of them porch boards bowed in the middle and curled up on the ends, he wondered how his uncle managed to keep that rocker of his from walking its way right off the front of the house.

Rafe stopped the rocking chair and stared at Harvey's face for a moment before pointing a finger at him.

"Your septum's a little crooked there, nephew."

Gingerly, Harvey touched the adhesive leftover from the white tape that had run across the bridge of his nose. He'd peeled the tape off the day before and was instantly sorry he'd done it so soon.

"Me and another fella had a small disagreement."

"Well," mused Rafe, "I always said a little violence will settle most of your problems." He paused. "Now what do you two boys want?"

Harvey noticed that his uncle kept glancing off toward the land side of the house, like he expected to hear something back there in the undergrowth. After a while, Harvey and Louis found themselves glancing in that same direction, but had no idea what to expect.

"We was thinking about doing some fishing out in the Gulf," Harvey finally said in between looks. "Thought maybe we could borrow your boat. In return, we'd give you half the fish we catch."

Rafe took one last look off to that side of the house, then set his face.

"Last time you borrowed my boat, you brought it back with the gas tank half empty. I'll need fifty dollars for that."

Harvey slipped one hand into his pocket, fumbled around for a moment and slid his fingertips carefully over the folded bills. He brought out only the two twenties and the ten. Without counting, he handed them over.

Rafe checked the denomination on each bill and then stuck his hand out again.

"And, I'll need another fifty dollars. That's so I don't have to hunt you down when you bring my boat back with the gas tank half empty again."

Harvey dug the remaining five-dollar bill out of his pocket and turned to Louis.

"Give me what you got."

Louis reluctantly stuck his hand in his right front jeans' pocket.

"I had plans for this money. It's all I got."

"Give it here."

Louis handed over a small stack of folded bills.

Harvey licked his thumb and started counting. When he finished, he stared at the stack.

"Damn, Louis, this is thirty-three one-dollar bills. You getting in a poker game?"

Louis's face flushed a light shade of red.

"Naw, I was saving it for one of the girls over to The Pink Lady."

"One of the strippers?"

"She's only doing that so as her mother can afford to get an operation she desperately needs."

"Uh huh."

Extending the total of thirty-eight dollars towards Rafe, Harvey said, “This is all we got.”

“Then,” said Rafe, tucking the wad of bills into his overalls, “I’ll take that boy’s watch until you come up with the rest.”

“Give him the watch,” muttered Harvey.

Louis unlatched the small metal buckle and held the watch out,

“And,” continued Rafe, “I’ll hold the keys to that pickup of yours as deposit for safe return of my boat. It’s not worth much, but it’s something.”

Harvey and his uncle exchanged truck keys for boat keys.

Rafe started rocking in his chair again. He took one more glance to the land side of the house.

“You boys best get going now before I change my mind.”

Harvey and Louis walked back to their old pickup, transferred several heavy ice chests to the boat and finally the two firearms from behind the seat.

“You catching fish the usual way or shooting them?” Rafe hollered over.

“The gun’s for sharks,” Harvey hollered back. “They’re bad this time of year if you catch anything, blood in the water you know, but we’re using fishing poles for the fish.”

“Then you better get your fishing gear out of your truck and put it in the boat.”

“Oh, yeah.”

When everything was finally stowed on the go-fast boat, Harvey turned the key in the ignition and had Louis untie the mooring ropes. As the engine sputtered into noisy life, Harvey slowly moved them out into the current. Spinning the steering wheel, he pointed them downriver and hit the throttle. The engine roared and the front of the boat came up.

Halfway downriver, Harvey throttled down far enough to converse with Louis without collapsing a lung over the engine noise.

“What the hell was going on out in the brush at the side of my uncle’s house?’

Louis shook his head.

“I got no idea.”

“Did you hear that screeching noise as we was leaving?”

“You mean like a bobcat getting scalded in hot oil?”

“Something like that.”

"Your uncle in the fur trade?"

"Not that I know of."

"Then I think we ought to be sure and bring his boat back undamaged."

Harvey nodded his agreement and hit the throttle again as they cleared the river and entered the salt waters of the Gulf. In a couple of hours, they were well south of Tampa and three miles off shore. The sun was starting to sink several hundred miles away, somewhere over Southern Texas.

"Now it's a waiting game," said Harvey as he killed the engine.

"How's all this gonna work?" asked Louis as he pulled his baggy jeans up one more time.

"Simple," replied Harvey. "When we hear a go-fast coming in, we start up the engine, plug in the blue flashing light and slap it on the front of our boat. The smugglers will think we're U.S. Customs and we'll board her to search for illegal drugs."

"What if they run?"

"That's what the hunting rifle is for. You'll shoot out their engine until they have to stop. The tricky part is when you go to board their boat."

"How's that?"

Harvey made motions with his hands palms down, the left moving up as the right hand moved down and the right moving up as the left hand went down.

"See, when both boats are sitting dead in the water, the swells are gonna move them up and down differently, so you got to time your jump to land correctly on the deck of the other boat."

"Me? Why don't you jump? You sound like the one with experience."

Harvey put his hand on Louis's shoulder.

"Cuz I've got to work our boat. I'll be over here covering you with the .45." Then he pointed towards his crooked septum. "Besides, you're the one with the good nose to smell out any fresh paint or fiberglass repairs on their boat. You know my smeller hasn't worked right since that bar fight with Buford last week."

Louis nodded, then appeared to consider his circumstances again.

"What's paint and repairs got to do with anything?"

"All them smugglers build customized compartments on their go-fast boats to hide their contraband in case Customs pulls them over."

Louis appeared to mull this information over.

"Okay, but I'm not too happy about this jumping ship thing."

Harvey handed him a cold beer from one of the ice chests.

"You'll be fine. Trust me."

For three hours they sat there, quietly drinking beer and munching on snacks while the boat rocked gently on the swells. In time, a large orange moon crawled high in the sky, eventually lightening up into a pale-yellow circle. Clouds rode the wind, scudding overhead. Twice, just as Louis nodded off, small fish fleeing from bigger predators skimmed across the water's surface and slammed into the side of the boat. Each time, he jerked awake with a "What was that?" It always took him another beer to settle his nerves back down. He was dreaming about the girl from the Pink Lady, when Harvey shook his arm.

"Not now," Louis muttered.

"Wake up," exclaimed Harvey. "I hear a boat. Looks like they're headed for a rendezvous somewhere south of Tampa."

That got Louis's attention, but it was a slow process getting the sleep out of his brain cells. And the strobe of the flashing blue light Harvey had erected on the front of their boat gave him a sudden headache. He had no idea the flash would be that bright in the dark of night.

Their boat engine was roaring now as Harvey spun the steering wheel to put them on an intercept course with the incoming go-fast.

"Hang on," screamed Harvey. "They're turning away from us. Means they got to be carrying drugs. Get the rifle. This is our lucky day."

With their own boat skipping across the top of the nearest swell and slamming into the top of the next wave, Louis grabbed the top of the windshield and held on in a death grip. His knees flexed and dropped several inches every time the boat bounced. At this point, he didn't know which was worse, the abrupt weightlessness when their boat skipped through the air, or the sudden motion of being thrown forward when it hit the crest of the next wall of water.

"We're gaining on 'em," hollered Harvey. "Start shooting at their engine. That'll bring 'em to a stop."

Louis swallowed hard, found the courage to turn loose of the windshield and dropped to his hands and knees. Crawling to the back of the boat, he located the rifle and started crawling forward again. With the rifle in his right hand, he grabbed the top of the windshield with his left and stood up.

"Put a round in their motor," screamed Harvey as salt spray dashed the windscreen.

Louis braced his triceps on the front of the windshield and tried to take aim. Problem was, the other boat kept rising above the top of his sight picture and then disappearing out the bottom of the small circle of his rifle scope.

"Wait until we're in the air," hollered Harvey, "and then squeeze off a quick shot."

Louis inhaled, held his breath, and as the rear end of the other boat passed through the cross-hairs, he pulled the trigger. He had no idea where the bullet went. He was pulling back the rifle bolt to extract the spent brass and insert a new cartridge, when smoke began to rise from the other boat's engine. To his amazement, the boat in front began to slow down.

"Great shot," exclaimed Harvey as he powered down their own engine. "Now get ready to board their boat. And remember what I told you."

"Right," said Louis. He then did a mental replay of Harvey's hands moving up and down at the same time, but in opposite directions.

At slow speed, Harvey maneuvered the red go-fast up next to the now disabled boat. The blue light still flashed up front. He drew his .45 automatic and used his best authoritative voice.

"Reach for the sky."

Two sets of hands went up in the other boat.

"Get over there and search their boat," Harvey said in a lowered voice. He then swung the barrel of the .45 back and forth between the tall man in a floral Hawaiian shirt and the shorter man in a white guayabera shirt.

"Do as the man with the rifle tells you and nobody will get hurt."

"Why'd you shoot at us?" asked the shorter man with a Mexican accent. "Customs isn't supposed to shoot unless someone first shooting at them."

"New rules out of headquarters," replied Harvey. "Anybody that runs is now considered fair game."

"Damn," muttered the shorter guy. "This ess getting to be risky business."

Harvey motioned for Louis to hurry up before the two men got suspicious and things got out of hand.

Rifle held in both hands, Louis stepped up on the fiberglass engine cover at the rear of the boat and pulled up his baggy jeans in preparation. He timed the up and down movement of the two boats and took a running start. As his left foot took off from the solid footing on his side, the other boat came up on a higher swell than he expected. The toe of his leading shoe bumped the side of the other go-fast. In an attempt to maintain his balance, Louis did what looked like a tap dance with one foot while trying out some new tip-toe ballet steps with the other. His jeans dropped a couple of inches in the process. As he crossed the fiberglass cowling of the other boat at a fast rate of speed, he slammed on the brakes for his right foot. It stopped abruptly. Momentum then carried his upper body onward, arms wind-milling rapidly. Top heavy with an extreme forward lean, Louis pitched head first over the far side and into the deep.

All three men stared at the point where Louis had disappeared into the water. Nobody said a word.

Several heartbeats later, Louis's head finally broke the surface. One arm thrashed about in the water while the other held the rifle up.

"I can't swim," he screamed.

"I've seen dogs that couldn't dog-paddle as good as that boy's doing right now," commented the taller man in a southern drawl.

"Get him out," Harvey ordered.

Hands still in the air, both men moved to the far side of their boat, then reached down for Louis.

The short guy bent over and got a hold on Louis's left arm, while the taller man ended up grabbing the rifle by the stock. Both pulled upwards.

Having a wet grip on the wood stock, Louis's hand slipped loose of the rifle.

The tall man in the floral Hawaiian shirt suddenly found himself standing straight up with a gun in his hands. Having evidently realized the precariousness of how his new circumstances could be perceived by the man holding the .45 automatic, he immediately raised his hands again. Then, he slowly bent sideways and lowered the rifle to the deck.

"Get ... him ... out ... of ... the ... water," bellowed Harvey.

The tall man stooped to his task with new enthusiasm.

Louis found himself jerked out of the gulf and into the boat. Salt water ran off his clothes in small rivulets. His jeans seemed even baggier with the added weight of the water. When he stepped towards the long gun lying on the deck, his right shoe squeaked and water squished out of his left. Louis picked up the rifle and stepped back to cover the two men. Placing his forefinger against one nostril, he snorted salt water out of the other.

"That's right," said Harvey. "Clear that nose. Start smelling for new paint."

"Don't need to," replied Louis. "When I bent over to recover the rifle, I seen some new repairs underneath the windscreen on the passenger's side."

"Get your hidden compartment opened right now," Harvey ordered the tall guy.

With one hand still raised in the air, the tall man in the Aloha shirt opened a long tool box and removed a small pry bar. Going to the front of the boat on the passenger's side, he dropped to his knees and proceeded to poke the pry bar into the fiberglass wall. Eventually, the fiberglass shattered and came out in pieces.

Harvey motioned the man to back up while Louis moved to the front of the disabled boat.

Kneeling down, Louis reached into the hidden compartment and came out with a plastic wrapped bundle a little bigger than a squashed loaf of bread.

"There's two packages," he said. "I'm willing to bet it's a couple kilos of coke each."

"You boys are in trouble now," said Harvey. "That's some serious prison time in a federal institution."

The two men stood silent, with defeated looks on their faces as Louis tossed the packages, one by one, over to Harvey. When Louis was finished, he pulled both boats close together, gave a yank to his jeans and stepped over the side into the red go-fast.

"I ain't never jumping ship again," he muttered.

"Whatchoo gonna do about us?" asked the short man in the white guayabera.

Harvey pursed his lips as if in deep consideration of the situation.

"We got no tow rope to pull you into Tampa, so we're going to leave you here on your honor and have someone from the office come out and pick you up. Just remember, you're both under arrest, so don't be going nowhere."

The tall man and the short man looked at each other as Harvey cranked over the engine on the red go-fast and slowly separated the two boats.

"I'm gonna point our boat towards Tampa so those guys think that's where we're headed," he told Louis. "Go put the packages in the bottom of one of our ice chests and cover them with ice and bottles of beer. And bring us back a couple of them beers to celebrate our first success."

Five minutes later, Louis returned to the front of the boat with a beer in each hand. Even as wet as he was, he had a big smile on his face.

Two beers down and approaching the Port of Tampa, Harvey was about to change heading to put them on course for the snake bend river that led to his uncle's place, when a strong blue light started flashing a little off to the starboard side.

"What's that?" asked Louis.

"It's Customs," said Harvey. "I'd better slow down the engine."

"Are you crazy?" replied Louis. "With all that cocaine in the ice chest, we got to run for our lives."

"Can't," said Harvey. "If we run, they'll know we're guilty. We got to brazen it out."

Louis started pacing back and forth as the boat slowed.

"I can't be going to Glades, or even Angola for that matter," he said. "I owe money to guys in both them institutions, and there's nowhere to hide in them places."

"Just be cool, Louis. Dump the guns overboard. They could be used as evidence against us. And, get rid of the blue light up front, so Customs don't ask sticky questions about why we have one. Remember, we're just out fishing."

"But we don't have any fish."

"Relax, we'll be fine. Get rid of that stuff and let me do the talking."

Louis tossed the blue light overboard and headed for the rear of their boat.

By the time Harvey pulled closer to the Customs boat, he'd heard two more splashes as Louis tossed the guns into the waters of the Gulf.

"Hello there," said a male voice over a bull horn from the Customs boat. "Would you come alongside for a minute?"

"Here we go," muttered Louis.

Harvey pulled the red go-fast within jumping distance of the Customs go-fast boat.

The Customs agent turned off his bull horn for normal talking.

"Our fuel line seized up," he said, "engine quit and our radio's gone dead. Could you give us a tow into port?"

"W-we don't have a r-rope," stuttered Louis.

"That's okay," returned the Customs agent. "We already have one tied to the bow in case somebody came by. We'll throw you the other end."

Harvey turned Louis around towards the rear of their go-fast.

"Go back to the dive platform, catch their rope and tie it to one of the stanchions.

Louis shuffled to the dive platform at the rear like a zombie in a bad dream. He caught the rope as it was thrown and did as he was told. Afterwards, he scrambled over the engine cowling and returned to the front. He ducked his head to whisper.

"I don't like this."

"It's okay," said Harvey. "We'll just tow them into port, drop them off and be on our way."

He slowly eased the throttle forward until the rope was taut, and then steered for the Port of Tampa. The Customs go-fast boat followed along on the other end.

Louis spent the rest of that trip hanging around the ice chests. Occasionally, he removed a beer from one of the chests, consumed the contents and carefully let the empty bottle slip over the side and into the gulf. He didn't want to get a ticket for littering. By the time they arrived at the Customs dock in Tampa, his bladder was in need of relief and so was he.

Both boats tied up to the dock. Harvey went aft and untied the tow rope from the stanchion, throwing the loose end back to one of the agents in the other boat.

Louis sat frozen by the ice chests as one of the Customs agents hopped down into the red go-fast. The agent shook Harvey's hand and thanked him for their assistance.

"If you guys ever need anything, let us know."

He gave his business card to Harvey, and then waved at Louis.

Louis managed to raise his left arm and slowly moved it back and forth.

Harvey untied their mooring rope and eased them away from the dock.

Louis kept moving his arm sideways back and forth in a Jackie Kennedy wave.

As they left the Port of Tampa, Harvey slid the throttle forward.

"See, I told you we'd be okay. Just had to brazen it out."

"You were right," said Louis in a dead voice. "Just brazen it out."

"Now we got two kilos of coke hidden in our ice chest under the beer and we'll be thousands of dollars richer. I know a couple of guys who'll pay us top dollar for that stuff. No more scraping to pay bills, and your dancer friend at the Pink Lady will love you forever. Or at least until your money runs out."

"Uh, small problem there, Harve."

"How's that?"

"You told me to get rid of the evidence, so I threw the guns and the blue light overboard, but I didn't throw the coke ..."

"Good thing, because we got away with this."

"... then," Louis finished his sentence. "But, I got real nervous later when we were towing them into the Customs dock, so I slipped the two packages of coke over the side when they couldn't see what I was doing."

Harvey yanked the throttle down to zero and turned around.

"You what?"

"I told you," said Louis, "I can't go to Glades or Angola. I'd be a sitting duck in those prisons."

"Damn it," said Harvey as he turned back to the front and moved the throttle forward. "Now we got no guns, no blue light and no coke. We also got no fish to give Uncle Rafe for using his boat. We're in the hole for this deal."

"If it's any consolation," said Louis, "I do have this hundred-dollar bill that I keep secreted in my shoe. We could stop at that fuel and convenience store at the river dock and buy a couple of red snappers, or flounders or whatever the fishermen brought in. Give them fishes to your uncle and say we caught 'em."

Harvey grew silent and cold.

"All we been through together and you been hiding out money from me? Your best bud and partner-in-crime?"

"Have to. You spend it like there's no tomorrow. This is my emergency fund."

Harvey scratched his cheek like he was contemplating these new circumstances.

"Okay, let's just say this is one of them emergency situations."

"Fine by me," replied Louis.

"One more thing," said Harvey.

"What's that?"

"You realize," continued Harvey, "that we'll have to go fishing again tomorrow night and hope we get lucky."

Louis immediately pictured Harvey's hands moving up and down in opposite directions. The mental image caused him to pull up on his baggy jeans. He knew what his job would be.

THE EXTERMINATOR

Sandra Murphy

WALTER WYNTHROP, THE EXTERMINATOR

YOU'VE GOT A PROBLEM? I CAN MAKE IT GO AWAY

My name's Walter Wynthrop, that's with a Y, not an I. As you can see by my business card there, I'm The Exterminator. It's not that I have anything against bugs in general, but the idea of their little feet walking all over me gives me the willies. Instead of killer sprays and environmental toxins, when I go into a home, I just talk to the little buggers, pardon the pun, exterminator humor.

I explain they should leave peacefully or the lady of the house will come after them with brooms and spray cans, leading to very painful deaths. If they'll relocate, they can go on about their lives. Spiders and ants are particularly cooperative. Cockroaches, not so much. Ah well, it was their choice.

Problems started when I got a reminder the balloon note on my house was coming due. I took out personal loans, maxed out six credit cards, borrowed from friends and family to make the payment. I tried to refinance, but the bank said I was a poor risk and that was before all the loans and card debt. Now, I'm drowning in minimum payments and interest and avoiding friends and family. With cold weather coming on, the extermination business will be headed right for diapause, a word meaning a spider's winter slowdown for those not insectually aware. I needed cash and needed it fast.

I took my last fiver and stood in line at the coffee shop. I think better with quality caffeine revving up my brain. Behind me, I heard two women whispering.

"Is that The Exterminator? What's he doing here?"

"Do you think he's here on a job? I don't want to be here when he starts killing."

The two women stepped out of line and bolted for the door. What? A guy can't get a cup of French roast? I thanked the barista, Avalon, tipped a wrinkly dollar from the secret pocket in my wallet, and headed for my usual booth.

I hadn't noticed two guys in line behind the women. The guys got coffees, huddled up at a table near the back, and then wandered past my booth, real casual like. I hoped they owned a chain of restaurants that needed my services. Maybe a hotel with bedbugs. I have a sniffer dog, my partner, for those. He can track down a single bedbug. I'd have my little buggy chat, per usual, and if the bug didn't vamoose, Moose, he's my Jack Russell, would show his teeth. Bedbug problem solved.

So, on their fourth pass, I looked up and asked, "You fellas lookin' for me? Mebbe got a job you want done? My partner and I have some available time." Dressed in black suits, white shirts, and gold chains in lieu of neckties, they had to have some bucks.

They looked relieved and sat when I motioned to the other side of the booth. "Well, we got this problem. It's of a delicate nature, if you get my drift. We can't be too specific on accounta you never know who's listening, ya know?"

I had no idea what he was talking about but being agreeable, I said, "Sure, lay it on me, I'm discreet." I looked around. No one was sitting within hearing distance.

"Well, we work for this guy and he's got a kid what's gone missing, ya know? And we're supposed to find him except we ain't havin' no luck." Guy number one spoke.

"So we wants you should find the kid, on accounta we think he was snatched, and then you should, pardon the expression, exterminate the guy what took him." Guy number two added his bit. "There's fifty large in it for you."

"Fifty? Thousand? Dollars? You're kidding me, right?" I looked around for a camera to see if I was being punked. "No way. Not me. I'm The Exterminator."

"See, Jimmy, I tole you, fifty geez ain't enough. This guy is a professional, like. Not enough, not for finding Little Tony, and whacking the guy too."

"Ralphie, we wasn't supposed to use names, rememer? So's, we can go as high as a hunnert but that's the limit. With dat though, you gotta make an example outta him. We can't have this kinda thing ever happen again."

A hundred thousand dollars. That would pay my debts, give me a bankroll to move me and Moose to the Jersey shore to a little bungalow out of range for hurricanes but close enough to smell the salt air. I mean, we all gotta die sometime, right? I'd just help speed this guy along. It's not like he's a nice guy, not if he kidnapped a kid. That's just low.

"So how old is the kid? You got a picture? Give me the scoop. I'll think about it."

I was surprised to find out it wasn't a six-year-old, grabbed up on his way home from first grade, but a twenty-two year old, good looking guy. "Are you sure he's not shacked up with some girl? He's the type they'd go for. Maybe he went on a bender."

Well, that wasn't it either. It seems Big Tony and Sal had arranged for Tony's boy and Sal's girl to get married—without consulting the kids. Now the girl was crying all day and night, Sal was furious, thinking Little Tony got cold feet, and Big Tony was worried Little Tony was wading in the ocean while wearing concrete swim trunks. The whole thing was messier than a Donkey's cheesesteak.

I tossed and turned most of the night. Taking a life was some serious stuff. After all, I can't even kill a bug. What would make me think I could off some guy, even if he is a bad dude? Who would take care of Moose if I got caught? Could I live with myself after, was the bigger concern.

In the morning, I looked at the sad contents of my wallet and the decision was made. I met Jimmy and Ralphie at the coffee shop and got an advance to seal the deal.

Avalon didn't say anything, but she raised an eyebrow to see me with the pair for the second day in a row. I would have done the same if our positions had been reversed.

I started by going to Tony's apartment. The guys had checked there, but I had an idea the neighbors might not be so willing to tell them everything. Maybe I'd have better luck.

"So, Mrs. Diaz, young Tony is a friend of yours?"

"He's a good boy. Brings me carryout food, collects the mail to save me the stairs, picks up milk and lotto tickets for me on Saturdays." Mrs. Diaz was a small woman, silver-haired, and with a smile that fairly glowed. "I wish he were here. I could use some bug spray. The spiders, they have moved in."

"I'll take care of them for you." I helped her to the bench near the railing with the attached flower boxes crowded with marigolds, their spice sharp in the morning air. "It won't take long."

I let myself into her apartment and I could see right away what she meant. There were several large spiderwebs in the corners of the room. I gave the spiders my little speech. Three of them lined up in front of one smaller spider. The little one was old, had only six legs. "Okay, how about this? You move out, Grandma stays here. Once a day, you can bring her something to eat." Our deal was made.

"Mrs. Diaz, one of the spiders, the one in the living room corner, she likes the view out the window. She's old and crippled. How about you let her stay and once a day, another spider will bring her lunch. When she's gone, no more problem."

"What did you do?" Her eyes were wide in disbelief. "If what you say is true, from one older lady to another, she can stay."

"It's a trade secret, I'm not allowed to say." I handed her my card. "And if young Tony shows up or calls, I'd appreciate it if you'd let me know. His dad is worried."

"Well, I might know a little something. You come see me tomorrow. If the spiders are gone, I'll tell you." She smiled. "Consider it a trade?"

"You can count on it. I'll see you tomorrow." I was pretty pleased with myself. I'd found out more on my first day than Jimmy and Ralphie had learned in three weeks. Maybe I was the next Rockford or that other guy, what's his name. Yeah, a second career, more exciting than the first. Moose would love it.

The next morning, Mrs. Diaz called. I picked up two lunch specials from Alfredo's.

She was delighted to see me or maybe it was just the aromas of rigatoni carbonara, a small salad, and garlic bread. Since she smooshed my face like my Great Aunt Harriet used to do and kissed me on both cheeks, I'm going with it was me she was happy to see.

"The spiders, they're all gone, except the little old one. I saw one leave this morning, early. He stopped by the door, turned around, like he was sad to go, and then he left." She served the salad on plates of a soft green color. "Thank you, Walter, you are a good boy."

"It was nothing. This is really tasty." We talked about the weather, the neighborhood, other foods we liked, and finally she came to the topic of Little Tony.

"Tony, he is a sweet boy, I told you. I think maybe he is with the girl

I see come visit him. I don't know her name," she sighed. "A pretty girl, all dressed up fancy, tall with the high heels, sparkly dresses, once in a tuxedo jacket but no pants! Oh, she had on the fancy stockings, such legs. What boy could resist legs like that? Tony, I think he is in love with her. Sometimes, her girlfriend is here too. They leave together, Tony, he stays home."

"Fancy dresses? I wonder where they were going. Did they always come here on the same days?"

"Yes, always on Friday and Saturday. They sing, I can hear. I miss it. Old show tunes, new songs like on the radio, songs you can understand the words, not yelling or talking songs."

"Sounds like they're entertainers." I helped Mrs. Diaz with the dishes and was ready to leave when she stopped me.

"Walter, you come see me again, okay? And you call me Alma. Wait here." She bustled into the other room and returned in a minute. "Tony lit a candle on a cannoli, for my birthday. It came from Alfredo's too. He used these matches. Maybe they help." The matchbook had a fancy D on the front, no address.

"Thanks, Alma. I'll be in touch. You've been a huge help and great company."

After such a big lunch, I could only focus on a nap. The ball game was on that afternoon and my team, the Cardinals, won. It's not that I like them, although they've had some great players over the years. It's because of Dizzy Dean and something he said once—'it ain't bragging if you can do it.' That's the way I felt about being a no-kill exterminator. I root for them in Dizzy's honor.

Their win made me a quick fifty on a bet made when I was more optimistic. I'd sit on my advance and use it for expenses, like lunch and maybe bribes. Yeah, bribes are good. With my winnings, I went to the coffee shop to drink a dark roast and ponder my next step.

Avalon was on duty and when my drink was ready, instead of calling my name, she brought it over herself. She saw the matchbook on the table and slid into the booth. "Taking five, Jazeema!" The guy behind the register nodded.

"I didn't figure you for a D's kind of guy," she said. "I pictured you more as a brew and que with peanut shells on the floor and twenty big screens sports bar guy."

She pictured me? Really. "I'm not adverse to a brew and que or the peanut shells but there's more to me than that. Why, just yesterday, I had Alfredo's carbonara for lunch."

She tilted her head and looked at me hard, kind of like Moose when I tell him there are three treats in my pocket and he's pretty sure there are four.

"So, you know D's?" I fingered the matchbook. Odd, no address or phone number. How were customers supposed to find it?

"I do. I have a friend who loves that place. It's pretty new and Ricky likes to think he's cutting edge on finding the next hot spot."

"Do they have entertainers, like singers, I mean? It might be just the place I'm looking for."

"Yeah, I'd say so." She gave me that look again. "Tell you what, I live nearby. Pick me up here at nine on Friday, I'll take you. Wear jeans and a t-shirt, nothing too snug." She was back at the register, taking an order before my mouth and brain synchronized enough to ask if she meant 9 a.m. or 9 p.m. Well, if there were singers, I'd go with 9 p. Just in case, I'd drop by for a morning coffee too.

I was almost to the door when Avalon caught up with me. "Here, go see Freddie. He'll take care of you, make sure you're ready for Friday night." She was refilling the basket of scones and muffins before I had a chance to look at the business card she'd given me. I really need to get up to speed with her.

Well, okay, no time like the present. I took myself to the Seventh Street location of Enough Is Not! and asked for Freddie.

Freddie turned out to be a nice young man, stylishly casual.

"Avalon sent me."

"Thank goodness, you came right over. We have a *lot* of work to do to get you ready for Friday. I wouldn't have pegged you for a D's kind of guy." Freddie studied my baggy jeans, faded red t-shirt, and frayed sneakers.

"People keep saying that. It's a work thing," I said. "I'm looking for a guy."

"Aren't we all? Turn around, please. Mmm hmm." He snapped his fingers. "Go into the dressing room and get naked. We're going at this from the skin out. Trust me, it's for the best."

Naked? I'm not shy but still. I'd just bent over to step out of my jeans and skivvies when Freddie appeared behind me. "Put these on, the gray ones for today. Save the blue for Friday. Then we'll go see Derrick."

"Um, Freddie, I'm not wallowing in the bucks at the moment. I'm pretty sure I can't afford all this." I held my jeans in front of me.

"Don't worry, there are ways. Hurry, hurry, no time to waste!" The door clicked shut behind him.

As I turned to hang my jeans on the wall hook, I realized I'd been standing in front of a mirror. Guess Freddie got an eyeful anyway.

I had to look at the package twice to be sure what passed for briefs were my size. It took ten times longer to get into them than it should have and then there was the problem of where to put everything. Freddie offered his advice and assistance but I shut the dressing room door on him. The jeans were comfy and the shirt fit well. The sneakers bore a price tag I couldn't bear to look at a second time.

"You'll do. Follow me." Freddie took off at a fast pace to the connecting salon.

"Derrick, I have a challenge for you!"

We entered a trendy and busy shop. I got a glimpse of services offered and prices as Freddie hustled me toward a chair at the back of the room where a slim young man was checking out his reflection in the mirror. "Derrick, this is Walter, he needs our help. Avalon sent him."

Hearing that, Derrick threw himself at me for a huge hug. "I'm Ricky, her bestest. This is going to be so much fun. Let's look at you." He turned me this way and that and then said to Freddie, "I see what you mean. He does present a challenge. I'll do my best. D's on Friday? We'd better go to run interference."

Three hours later, I left with an expensive casual wardrobe, new sneaks, a warning to not shave because a three-day stubble was sexy (to who wasn't explained), a haircut, and products for my hair, skin, and probably for Moose, who could be sure?

I took lunch to Mrs. Diaz and heard a lot of compliments which helped. I managed to hold off on coffee until Friday morning.

Avalon just stared. "Walter? OMG, Walter! Hey, everybody, look at Walter!" Applause followed with a couple of whoot, whoots and fist pumps thrown in.

I felt myself turn four shades of red before I had the presence of mind to take a bow and yell, "What? I looked that bad before?"

"We dint wanna say nothing but you looked like the backside of an intact hog. No offense."

"Sure, why would I be offended by that? I'll get you when you least expect it." I saw the two women who'd been whispering that first day I met Jimmy and Ralphie. They ran for the door. I'm not sure what I said or did, but I think I just cost the coffee shop two customers. Permanently.

Friday night rolled around and I was at the coffee shop by 8:30 to meet Avalon. Moose was miffed at being left behind but consoled with a special treat and new toy. I hoped the house would be standing when I got home. I remembered what Freddie said and had on the blue shirt and the extremely cozy skivvies of the same color. He and Ricky would meet us at D's.

The neighborhood looked a bit sketchy. After paying the cover charge for all of us, a business expense after all, I asked the bouncer if I could talk to the owners or management. A muscular fellow with skin so bronzed it looked oiled, he said he'd take care of it.

Oddly, the only available drinks were soda, juice, or bottled water. No food either, just bagged snacks like chips, pretzels, and popcorn. The entertainers were on break. Our server, a lovely girl, um woman, said I should go on backstage to talk to the two owners. I excused myself, ducked behind the curtain, and walked smack into a tornado of chaos.

Two women in long, sequined dresses and very high heels, latched onto me like I was a life preserver and they were drowning. "Thank gawd, you're here. I didn't know what we were going to do. Hurry, get into costume." That was the brunette. The blonde chimed in. "You haven't even shaved! There's no time, maybe with the lights and all, it won't show. Come on." They were pulling at my clothes and damn near stripping me naked right there in front of all those women, ballerinas, they were.

"I was told not to shave, it was sexier. Wait, I asked to see the owners and, hey, not my pants!"

"No time for tights, I guess hairy legs will be in. Duck your head, honey." The next thing I knew, I was dressed in a tutu. It had little attachments to my wrists so when I lifted my arms, the tutu flared out and arms down, the skirt went limp. One of the women put rouge and dark lipstick on me, the other piled on eye makeup and plopped a wig and tiara on my head. "Places, girls, we're on in five, four, three ..." She gave me a push and said, "Do what they do, you'll be fine." And I was on stage, right in the middle of a long line of ballerinas who knew where the hell to go when the music started.

And start it did. The ladies all did little dance steps to the right. I mistakenly went left. Trying to apologize, I shrugged my shoulders and that moved my arms and there went the skirt, all floofed out. I was afraid it would expose my new skivvies so I put my arms down. Meanwhile, the dancers broke into groups of four and I was pushed and dragged into one. We each held one hand overhead to touch in the middle and I flashed the audience again, after I was turned around to face the right way. I tried to follow their lead but they reversed course and ran smack into me. We looked like a ballet of swans, that really is what a bunch of them are called, you can look it up, a ballet of swans that had been in a major fender bender or would that be called a wing bender?

When it came time for the long line, me in the middle, they had a routine of tutus up and down in synchronized motion. Except for you-know-who. When they were up, I was down, Up, down, screw up all around. At least I was breaking the laugh meter—if they'd had one.

After about ten minutes of real time, which translates to twenty-seven eternities of stage time for those who do not know the dance steps, the music, or what the hell he's doing, our number was over to thunderous applause. I'd have blamed liquor but thanks to the sodas, everyone was sober. In trying to curtsy, I gave a bow-legged squat instead and exited stage left. The dancers went right. I ran, flapping my arms, and flashing everyone, just to keep up.

The two women were waiting for me. "Hey, thanks for filling in. Great idea to ham it up since you didn't know the routine. Get changed for your song."

"Song? Oh no, as a public service, I do not sing."

"Do you remember that old tune, 'Tiptoe Through the Tulips'?" I could hardly answer while more lipstick was being applied. Nodding wouldn't be a good idea either.

Now with hot pink lips, best under stage lights I was told, I answered. "That song was a hoot. The little ukulele. Laughed myself silly on that."

"Good, glad you remember it. You're on." With that, I felt a strong hand between my shoulder blades and I was on stage, music cuing up. A hand poked out between the curtains. The ukulele. Damn.

Twenty minutes later, I was back at the table, most of the makeup removed with some kind of cream that made my skin feel like it couldn't breathe. Avalon was giving me another one of those looks.

"I didn't know you were going to perform tonight," she said. "You are a man of many surprises, Walter."

Before I could answer, I heard a squeal and the sound of pounding feet. "Walter! You were fab-u-lous! What a stunning first night!" Ricky had me in a bear hug before I could duck behind Avalon for protection.

"Walter, my man, I think it was the blue briefs that did it for you. I knew they were just what you needed." Freddie grinned. "Blue, a tutu and tiara, then the ukulele, I would never have guessed."

"Let's go to the Cocoa Banana for last call. I want to tell everyone about your debut." Ricky was ready to par-tee.

"No, tonight's been more excitement than I've had in my whole life added together. I have to um, process, okay?" Luckily, Ricky fell for that one. I took Avalon home, walked her to the door, and after an awkward pause, patted her on the shoulder and went home.

I tried all the usual sleep aids—nachos with extra cheese, a beer, a movie that was generously described as a "B" flick. "Moose, you could have done a better job on the makeup for the zombies." He woofed agreement and went back to sleep. He's what you could call a c*t napper but we don't use the C word in our house.

I started to pace and think. Moose, as my partner, paced with me. I can't comment on his thoughts. "That matchbook has to be a clue. But ballerinas? How does that tie in with a missing man and a wedding in jeopardy?" One thing about an open concept house, it makes for good pacing. "See, if Tony didn't want to marry this girl, um, woman, he coulda just said so, no need to disappear, except you know, Sal is connected. The threat of ending up as landfill would be an incentive to marry her but again, disappearing could mean swimming with the fishes."

Moose's ears perked up at the word fishes. He does like his Tuna Smackers treats. "No treats yet. We gotta figure this out."

We paced for another hour before I noticed Moose lagging. "Come on, buddy, let's go to bed. Maybe the answer will come to us in our sleep." Moose bolted for the bedroom, leapt onto the bed, pulled back the blankets, and was tucked in, all before I'd crossed the living area. He's fast, that Moose. I just hoped he was creative too.

The next morning, I let Moose out into the back yard while I made coffee and nuked a cinnamon bun. I'd squirted the little packet of icing on the steamy hot spirals when I realized Moose hadn't come inside. "Hey, puppers, breakfast!" No Moose.

In the yard, he was focused on something small, not visible over the grass which shoulda been cut last week. "Moose, come here!" He didn't flicker an eyelash. Most Jack Russells will chase anything that moves but Moose has been trained to detect bugs so he has his own stealthy approach and total concentration.

It turned out, a baby bird had his attention. The nest was within reach, at least once I fetched the stepladder, so Baby Bird was reunited with his Mama. Moose headed inside for breakfast.

I was halfway to the house when it hit me. "Moose, hey Moose, you did it! You had an idea in your sleep. Tuna smackers!" I ran to catch up.

Moose loves stakeouts. We don't get to do them often but swarms of bees, once a squirrel, that was his favorite, and a couple of years ago, the cicadas. I tried to talk to them about being quiet but when you've been underground for over a dozen years and finally see daylight, there's no keeping the volume down. That was an epic exterminator fail.

We were parked near D's. I figured late afternoon was soon enough, considering the hours it was open. Moose suggested we be fully fortified with Cheetos, Tuna Smackers, and bottled water. Watching him keep an eye Baby Bird made me think we should stake out the club, see who's coming and going, maybe get a lead on young Tony.

We watched for an hour when Moose let me know he needed a break. "I told you not to drink that much water. Come on and hurry. We don't want to miss anything."

I thought a quick stop behind the car would do but no, we had to find a fire hydrant. "Geez, Moose, firefighters gotta open those to put out fires. Hurry it up."

Busy reading pee mail, Moose ignored me. By the time he'd taken care of business, we'd been away from the car for ten minutes. And got back, in time to see the stage door swing shut without a glimpse of who had gone inside. Moose looked properly embarrassed. "It's okay, bud. We'll try again later."

We took a detour past Tony's apartment but nothing was happening there. "What do you say to a Lottie's burger?" Moose loves their mini burgers and fries.

We killed a couple of hours, what with Moose flirting with Lottie and her making over him. He does better with the ladies than I do. Then again, he's a good listener, cute as all get out, and has a great smile. Adorable is a word he hears a lot from the feminine species.

We were back at D's by seven. It was still light out but edging toward dusk. A few women went inside, likely servers, I told Moose. “I wonder why they don’t have booze and food. That’s where the money is in a club.” He agreed. He either thinks I’m brilliant or just figures flattery will get him a Tuna Smacker.

By ten, crowds of people had gone inside, but no one that looked like the photo I had of Tony. “This is who we need to find. Memorize that face.” Moose stared at the photo. Again, registering the face or hoping it would lead to a treat? Only Moose knows.

I started the car and drove us home, determined to do better the next day.

I was in my usual booth at the coffee shop when Jimmy and Ralphie dropped into the seats across from me. “Hey, fellas, what’s shakin’?”

“We haz a prollem. Sal, he’s losin’ patience. Dat ain’t good. Tony’s worried and can’t pay attention to bidness. Dat ain’t good.”

“We needs an update, with some good news to tell them.”

“Moose, he’s my associate, and I, we did a stakeout last night, following up on a clue we found at Tony’s apartment building.”

“We wuz there. We dint see no clue.” Ralphie looked at Jimmy. “Did you see a clue?” Jimmy shook his head. “See? No clue. Whatta you got?”

“I’m not sure. There’s talk of a girl Tony might like a lot, then this place, and I need to find out about a liquor license.”

“License? We can do dat. We know a guy.”

“Another girl? Dat ain’t good. We bedder not tell dat part.”

“We like you, Walter. Make sure you find Little Tony, and soon. We’d hate to have to use drastic measures, should Big Tony and Sal be disappointed in your results.”

“Hey, I’m The Exterminator. You got a problem? I can make it go away. It says so on my card. Guaranteed results.” I hoped they believed me.

“They hired me to off a guy. What was I thinking? There’s only two ways out of this—we find Tony and he’s okay, not kidnapped or we find him and his kidnapper and then I gotta do it or face the consequences.” We were pacing again.

Three laps later, I collapsed on the couch, Moose at my side. “I don’t get the feeling Tony was kidnapped. I’m not sure he’s avoiding the marriage either, but more like he’s got something else going on. We just have to figure out what.” I jumped up. “I’m an exterminator, hired as a hit man.

This calls for a detective. We'll be like the Thin Man and Asta."

I drove to Tony's apartment and went in, Moose right behind me. "Here, sniff some of Tony's clothes. If you can't recognize him by his looks, you can use the Super Sniffer."

I went through the closets. "Moose, I think maybe this girl, um woman, was sleeping over on weekends. Tony's clothes are here plus her outfits for what we think is work. I didn't see anything like this at D's though." Moose was sniffing everything like crazy. "That's right, get her scent too. She'll have answers and you can charm her into telling. Tony might be tougher to crack. I mean, who hides from Big Tony and gets away with it?"

We staked out the club again. Moose studied Tony's photo. After a couple of hours, I called it. "Look, sitting out here is boring, we're not getting anywhere, and you sneezed on the binoculars. I can barely see a thing. Screw it, we're going in."

The bouncer/doorman turned out to be a dog person so he didn't card Moose or ask him for ten treats. Not being furry and cute, I had to pay and in cash. Since they didn't serve food, there wasn't any reason Moose couldn't have a good time too.

We found a table off to the left, close to the stage, just as "Tiptoe Through the Tulips" cued up. Tonight's singer could carry a tune and didn't need a bucket to do it. Plinked the uke just so too. I had to remind myself I was a great exterminator, in my no-kill way, or between Moose's popularity and the talent on stage, my ego would have taken a dive.

Moose had his own chair, none of this sitting on the floor stuff for him. He watched the singer closely and howled at the end which set the whole audience to laughing.

Then all hell broke loose.

Moose is a calm guy. He has Mother Teresa's patience, a nose that can out sniff any human, and charm oozing out every pore. The thing is, when he's off the exterminator clock, he's um, tenacious. To be blunt, he can go ballistic.

Like now. The women who'd shanghaied me into performing, came on stage. Moose had been watching the crowd. His head spun around faster than the kid who was in that scary movie. He was on all fours and quivering with excitement before I could reach him. I got as far as saying, "Mooose, no ..." when he launched himself, overturned the chair, and landed in a perfect four paw touchdown on stage.

I was on my feet and running but he raced to the blonde and grabbed the hem of her sparkly dress, shaking his head like he was going for the kill of a new toy. She teetered backward, the brunette caught her, I had Moose, hands around his waist and pulling back, the poor dress stretching to the breaking point, sparkles and all.

I untangled Moose by whispering, "Let go and I'll give you a Tuna Smacker." He held on until I promised five treats and then dropped the dress, big doggy grin on his fuzzy face.

The blonde grabbed my hand and stage whispered, "Take a bow!" We had three curtain calls.

The ladies met us backstage. The blonde said, "Sit. Stay. And be quiet."

Moose knows when a voice means business. I do too. We sat. We stayed. And we were quiet.

When I'd been there Friday, trying to keep my clothes on, I hadn't paid any attention to what else or who else was there. I mean, ballerinas. You don't want to stare. Now I had time to notice stuff I missed before. It was an eye-opening event and that's an understatement.

I glanced at Moose. His eyes never left the blonde. I'd seen him do that before and knew what it meant. When the show was over and the ladies stood in front of us, I said, "We need to talk."

It took planning but I had help. Every detail had to be right. When you're springing a surprise on Big Tony and Sal, you only get one chance.

I met with Jimmy and Ralphie, per usual, at the coffee shop.

"So, here's the score. I need Big Tony and Sal, their wives, Sal's daughter, all at this club on Sunday evening. There'll be other people there, not the public. Dinner, a short show, and all will be revealed."

"I dunno, Sal don't like no surprises." Jimmy shook his head.

"I gots to agree. Big Tony, he likes to be in the know." Ralphie leaned back in the booth. "He ain't gonna like this."

"Well, if they want to know why Sal's daughter's crying and to know where Tony is, they'll be there, seven o'clock sharp."

Jimmy and Ralphie left, feet dragging, to issue what I called the invitations and what they thought of as summons. I called Mrs. Diaz, Freddie and Ricky. When Avalon passed my booth on her way to refill coffee pots, I invited her too. "I'll have an announcement to make. Would you mind if Moose sat with you until it was time for him to do his part?" Avalon's a dog lover so that was no problem.

"You're not going to tell me why, are you?" She did the head tilt thing again.

"Nope, it's rather complicated but also very simple. I think it's best if I only have to tell it once." I took a deep breath. "I'd like a friendly face to focus on while I talk and I trust you with Moose. Whether you know it or not, you gave me a key clue to solving the whole mystery."

"You are a fascinating man, Walter Wynthrop with a Y. I'll be there. Should I dress up?"

"That, I would like to see. Just remember, being vertically challenged, Moose will want to sit on your lap for a good vantage point."

Sunday evening arrived before I was quite ready. Yeah, everything was in place but the butterflies in my stomach weren't the kind I could just talk to and convince them to go away.

I wore a tux. If the whole thing went south and Big Tony or Sal had me taken out, I'd look good at my funeral. Of course, the rental fee on the tux would add up once I was buried in it.

The tables were set, nice linens and china, bottles of wine breathing, servers at the ready.

Just before seven, cars pulled into the lot. Big Tony and Mrs. Tony were driven by Jimmy. Ralphie drove Sal, Mrs. Sal, and their daughter, Desiree. Freddie, Ricky, Avalon, and Mrs. Diaz Ubered with a friend of mine. Moose was with me.

"First, we eat, after, there's a bit of entertainment, and then the finale when all will be revealed. Mangiare!"

The servers presented a bountiful antipasto—cantaloupe wrapped in prosciutto, olives, wedges of salami, roasted red peppers, artichoke hearts, mozzarella balls, crostini, sliced Roma tomatoes, fresh figs, and provolone cheese. Sal and Tony's group was outdrinking Avalon and friends three to one. Worked for me.

The salad course was next, mixed spring greens with goat cheese, red onions, mandarin orange segments, cranberries, and sweet dark cherries. It got rave reviews from everyone but Sal and Big Tony who cast a suspicious eye at the goat cheese.

"I smell parmigiana and bacon! If this is rigatoni carbonara, you could be in deep trouble, Walter. Nobody makes it better than Alfredo. And Alfredo, he don't deliver." Big Tony turned in his seat to see the servers bring in full, deep dishes of the creamy pasta. I hoped the heavy meal would put my guests in a good mood and slow them down if they became unhappy. Big Tony took one bite, got a shocked look on his face, took another, and said, "I gotta know who made this! It is one step better than Alfredo's. Nobody is better than Alfredo!"

Cannoli for dessert brought smiles. "With the liddle chocolate bits and the green nuts, is the best," Sal said. I know, I asked Mrs. Sal what kind he liked.

Behind the curtain, performers were taking their places. A soft bell signaled my intro. "Ladies and gentlemen, we have entertainment in two acts tonight. Well, maybe three. Please welcome Cher!"

The curtain opened to reveal a leggy, dark-haired woman, wearing the barest minimum of clothing, emphasis on barest. The music cued, she started to sing, "Welcome to Burlesque," as backup dancers shimmied their way onto stage. Ricky and Freddie nearly fell out of their chairs in a swoon, Avalon watched the moves closely, and Sal and Tony's table was divided. The men didn't know where to look, while the women oohed and ahhed over the outfits and makeup. Mrs. Diaz clapped in time to the music.

When the curtain came down, I stepped on stage. This was a do or die moment. Literally.

"My name is Walter Wynthrop. I'm The Exterminator. You've got a problem, I can make it go away. In the song Cher just sang, she said, nothing's what it seems. And that's the case here." I took a drink of water. "Exterminator means different things to different people. Some ladies in the coffee shop thought I was there to kill bugs."

Sal, Big Tony, Ralphie, and Jimmy got a laugh out of that. "Some people, who have a different background, thought it meant I was a hit man." Avalon, Freddie, and Ricky were laughing hard enough they needed to wipe tears from their eyes. Sal and Big Tony didn't think it was funny.

"The truth is, neither one of those things is true. I have the odd ability to talk to spiders, ants, your basic bugs, and convince them to move out. I'm an eco-friendly, no-kill kind of guy. So you might wonder, how I got hired to whack a kidnapper. It was a moment of weakness on my part. I mean, I can't even kill a bug! How would I kill some guy?" I took a deep breath. I did not like the look on the faces at Sal and Tony's table.

"Nothing's what it seems. This situation needed a detective so that's what I've done, detected. Tony wasn't kidnapped, he's fine. There's no guy to whack. Desiree wants to get married. Tony wants to get married."

"Do you know where my boy is?" Big Tony's voice was cold enough to ice a bucket of champagne.

"I do. And you will, in just a few minutes. Sit back, listen to one more song, this one is Christina Aguilera. Then everything will be clear. I promise." The curtains began to part and I got the hell out of the way.

A blonde began to sing "Show Me How You Burlesque" and they did. Backup dancers in skimpy costumes, boy dancers in bowler hats, black vests over white shirts. The song ended with the blonde wearing one of the bowlers.

I took the stage again. "Now, with the help of my lovely assistant, Avalon, and my business partner and best friend, Moose, this is tonight's finale."

Avalon held a t-shirt near Moose's face. He did his Super Sniffer routine and stared at her. "Find Tony, Moose, find him!" He shot off her lap fast enough to leave skid marks.

He ran to Sal and Tony's table, circled it once, fast, and stopped to sniff, nose in the air. A big doggie grin lit up his face and he was off like a rocket, up on a chair, then the tabletop, and on stage. He ran to Christina, sat on her foot, and barked.

"Cute dog. Now where's my boy?" Big Tony looked bigger than before.

"I'm right here, Pop." Christina pulled off the bowler hat and blonde wig. "I'm right in front of you." He pulled Cher forward. "This is Dante. This is our club. He's the one I want to marry."

Big Tony looked like he was about to swallow his tongue. "But, Desiree ..."

Sal looked at his daughter. "You are okay with this?"

"Papa, Christopher, he is the chef. Alfredo is his father, who is ready to retire." Christopher stood next to her. Alfredo stepped out of the shadows and nodded. "I want to marry Christopher. I cried because I thought you wouldn't let me."

Sal leaned over and whispered to Tony, who nodded. "Tony and me, we will have to discuss this. Wine, please?"

I had to convince Moose to get off Tony's foot so he and Dante could change into street clothes. The backup dancers went home. Freddie and Ricky were in the midst of a squealfest. Avalon had a stunned look on her face and Moose on her lap. Jimmy and Ralphie consulted with their bosses.

The bottle of wine was empty by the time the men came to a decision.

"Tony, you want to marry this Dante? He is a good man?"

"Yes, Pop, the best. You aren't upset? Because, a guy ..."

"You're my boy, no matter what, capische? Tony, I figured that out, long time ago but you never tell me. This way, talk about you and Desiree, you gotta say. In the old days, secrets, you hadda keep secrets. Besides, your Uncle Frank and his friend, Leo, well, whatya gonna do? As long as you got love, that's all what matters." Big Tony grinned at the look on young Tony's face. "And this is your club? I'm sorry to say, it needs a lot of work. What are your plans?"

"We're pouring the profits back into it. We need to be able to serve food and booze but the inspector says the kitchen isn't up to par and we haven't been able to get a liquor license."

Sal spoke. "My little girl, you wanna marry this Christopher? You really love him or just his cooking?"

"Papa, I'd love him if he didn't know the difference between Velveeta and Parmigiano Reggiano."

"Desi, don't even say such a word! I'll get you a wheel of Reg for your wedding."

"We got conditions. Sal, you start."

"This Christopher, he must provide food for the club and every other Sunday at my house. Me and Tony will fix up the kitchen. We know a guy."

"Dante, you will provide music and dancers for the wedding reception. Not you dancing, not on that day. Agreed?" Dante nodded. "Christopher, make something for the dog too. Walter's gonna be there."

"We got two more conditions. First, we want a double wedding. If we are gonna do this, let's do it big." Big Tony was grinning like a crazed monkey in a banana tree.

"Walter, you showed us it's time for a business upgrade. Exterminators are out. We want that you and Moose be our company detectives."

I was grinning so big, my head looked like a Pez dispenser about to open and spit out a candy.

"Moose, our picture's in the society section. There's you in your vest and me in my tux." Half of Moose's vest was black with white, the other side, blended rainbow colors. My tux matched his. We were in both wedding parties as Best Man and Best Dog/Ring Bearer. Desiree's Yorkie was Flower Dog. Moose has designs on her. In case there's any confusion, Dante and Tony opted for the black and white theme, with bowler hats and bow ties. Desiree chose rainbows.

Avalon and I started dating, each other, I mean. I'm still surprised by that. Moose and I spend part of our time at our beachfront property on the Jersey shore, part back at the old house, both paid for now. Avalon comes with us.

And I have new business cards.

WALTER WYNTHROP, PRIVATE DETECTIVE.

YOU GOT A PROBLEM? I'LL FIND THE SOLUTION.

THE SMARTEST GUY IN THE ROOM

Robert Bagnall

I, Winston Dweeb, all four feet three inches of me, know how it feels to be the smartest guy in the room.

And not just any room.

The Faraday Lecture Theatre of the Metropolitan Institute, London.

I know I'm the smartest one in the room because at 3am you'll find me cleaning it. And I'm the only one here.

Without question, I'm smarter than whoever was constantly leaving purple marker pen on the screens in the Faraday; the work of an academic who may have been well-versed in cummingtonite and rhamnetin (seriously, the useless trivia you pick up) but was clearly clueless in the workings of an interactive whiteboard.

I've scrubbed at runes including such gems as *controlled assembly of carbon nanotube nanohybrids* and *micro-fluidics* and *non-equilibrium gas flow*. But, one day, I found myself rubbing acetone at the phrase *one hundred times stronger than the strongest known acid*. And a plan began to form in my mind.

YouTube took me to a video of a middle-aged lecturer with receding forehead, cropped hair and a jutting chin, as if his face had partially melted in a wind tunnel, stabbing a permanent marker at an interactive whiteboard whilst expounding on valances and energy levels. Bright purple permanent marker.

Professor Lars Snivelhofler.

Two days later I found myself sitting opposite Professor Snivelhofler, a desk of books between us.

"If you're after a coursework extension, you only have to ask," he said before I'd even had a chance to hop into the seat; although, from his expression, he was obviously still trying to place me.

"I know you're sleeping with your students, Snivelhofler," I said, only then clocking the strips of streaky bacon he was using as bookmarks.

"What do you want?" he replied slowly over his glasses.

I couldn't believe that this had worked so beautifully. I'd taken a complete punt on his having inappropriate dalliances.

"I want your acid."

"My acid?"

"I know it's a hundred times stronger than the strongest known acid," I said, as convincingly as I could muster.

"Ah." He looked like a kid who'd been caught shoplifting. "Flurocarborane hyperacid." He nodded sagely. "A hundred times stronger than a carborane superacid, which are themselves hundreds of times stronger than fluorosulfuric acid, and over a million times stronger than good old schoolboy sulfuric. What do you know of it?"

"Doesn't matter what I know," I growled. "I need it."

"Will you use it in ways that could bring the university into disrepute? That would be reputationally damaging?"

I paused; something in his manner made me want to be honest. It was an odd feeling. "Yes."

"Good. Because I can't stand this place. How can I help you?"

I must have stared at him, dumbfounded, for too long, because he followed it up with, "And I'm not having an affair with a student, by the way."

"Why make out like you were?"

He shrugged sheepishly. "I guess I wanted to big myself up. Now, what do you need the acid for?"

"I need you to deposit it in a bank vault. So I can rob it," I replied, although what I didn't tell him was that the robbery was merely cover for something much, much more malign.

Two weeks later, I had myself mailed in a stout, reinforced carboard box, into the care of the National and Provincial Bank, Hart Street, London, EC3—one of the few advantages of being four feet three.

Friday night, I emerged, in the dark, from the two duffle bags, one placed inside the other, with me at their core, and thence from the cardboard crate. I then forced the lock of the strongbox from the inside and found myself, torch in hand, at my leisure within the vault of the National and Provincial. Being, in common parlance, a dwarf, with a face like this, do you think there was any chance that I hadn't worked in the circus at some point?

It was then a small matter of cracking locks and filling the two large canvas bags with everything and anything I could find. Cash, banker's drafts, jewelry, gems. To the police this will look like a robbery, a robbery of genius, but no more than that. But my real target was the contents of locker seven-eight-eight, a series of photographs of a high-ranking member of government performing acts both physically improbable and morally questionable involving farmyard animals and others who may have been his constituents but didn't look old enough for him to rely on their votes. Blackmail? What did I need with blackmail when I had the contents of the remaining strongboxes? This was about assassination—*character assassination*. These beauties were going straight to press and the Prime Minister. And his mother.

And then the coup de grace, the genius of my plan.

Box number three-one-seven.

Snivelhofler's acid.

The most powerful acid in the world.

Dropped in a ring, three feet in diameter, centered exactly twelve feet and seven inches from the door, the acid would boil away the concrete thus providing access to a little used connecting tunnel that would emerge in Fenchurch Street Station. I had checked and double checked, cross-referenced the original plans against drawings of neighboring cellars, sewers, undercrofts, and access shafts. Who would pay attention to a man with a couple of large holdalls first thing on a Saturday morning? Even if the man could barely see over a pub bar and had a face like a Toby jug?

Snivelhofler had confirmed that he had placed the acid in that strongbox the week before. I jimmied the lock and took out ... a thick envelope of papers.

What the ...

I played the torch over the contents. Page upon page of chemical formulae, notations, scribbles, diagrams of molecular structures, calculations, and a rather fine doodle of the Eiffel Tower.

Where the fuck was the acid?

I got Snivelhofler on the phone, screaming overcoming issues of signal strength.

"Snivelhofler," I yelled, "What the bloody fucking hell is this?"

"The world's most powerful acid," he declared, as if he'd just stumbled upon it. "Yes. It will burn through anything. Anything at all."

"It's a formula. On a piece of paper."

"Of course. It only exists as a *theory*. And it only ever will exist as a theory until somebody invents something impervious enough to contain it. You didn't really expect the acid itself, did you?"

And he hung up.

All I could do was ponder his words until Monday morning, with only grainy pornographic pictures of a future national leader for entertainment. And then, only for as long as the batteries on my torch held out.

But at least I knew that I was still the smartest guy in the room.

CRITICAL STATUS

Gary Pettigrew

I've never liked hospitals. All those germs in one place just waiting to crawl under your skin. At least the trauma ward was clean, broken bones weren't infectious.

Having said that, times were tough just now. Clients were in short demand and I would have gone into the Ebola ward if it meant getting a paying job.

I picked up my notebook and tried to look interested in what the injured man, Jacob Hargreaves, was saying. He was short, skinny, and, had slicked-back hair. His lips were moving under a pencil mustache.

"So, tell me again how you came up with the plan to kill your wife?" I asked.

"Well, there was this girl at work, Raquel. She recently started as a receptionist in the office, the most beautiful girl I've ever seen." Jacob Hargreaves looked past me to try and watch a nurse walk past.

"Young?"

"Younger than me," he said.

"By how much?" I asked.

"I don't think that's relevant."

"Uh huh. Go on."

"Well, I ... approached her. Do you believe in love at first sight, Mr. Adams?"

"Was she open to your approach?"

"Well ... I think she was."

He looked uncomfortable at the question.

"Did she kiss you? Rip off your clothes? Rip off her own clothes? Agree to go on a date? What exactly was her reaction?"

"Well, she said that she didn't think it was a good idea because I was married."

"So, she wasn't interested then. She was letting you down easy."

"No. You need to know how these things work, Mr. Carver. I believe that she was letting me know that she would be amenable to the suggestion if only I was single."

"Uh huh. And that was when you decided to kill your wife?"

"Oh no. Not at all."

"No?"

I stopped taking notes and looked up.

"No, I had decided on that ages ago. It's just that I tend to put things off. It's a terrible habit. This Raquel thing just urged me into action. Sometimes I need a little push to get myself going. Do you know what I mean?"

I nodded, pretending that I knew what he meant.

"What did you do next?"

"I'm not sure. I went on to the dark web and put out a request for a hitman. I wasn't really all that serious. Just, you know, window shopping. Wanted a few quotes, you know what I mean. Next thing I knew there was a post on my Facebook page about me wanting to kill my wife. I think I may have been hacked."

"I understand. Can I see your phone please, Mr. Hargreaves?"

He handed me a fancy-looking smartphone. I tapped the screen and a page opened instantly. The screen was dark with white writing like I was looking at a negative image of a social media account. At the top of the screen was a settings option which I clicked on, tapped the screen a couple of times, and handed the phone back. He looked at me with desperation in his eyes. My favorite kind of client.

"What do you think, Mr. Carver?" he asked.

"Well, professionally, my first advice would be to put a password on your phone. It's basic security, especially if you plan on living a life where you don't want your spouse aware of what's going on. Secondly, you didn't access the dark web. That act would involve a degree of technical understanding that I don't believe that you possess. What you did was enable the dark mode feature on your phone. Essentially inverting the colors on the screen. No one hacked your phone, although I'm sure they could if they wanted to. In fact, I believe that when you thought you were putting in a search for a hitman you were posting the following to your Facebook status: "Looking for someone cheap to kill my wife."

Hargreaves looked sheepish, "Well the screen was dark, I couldn't really see what was going on."

"I understand. Now can you tell me a little more about what I can do for you and maybe why you are here in the hospital?"

He sat up a little but looked uncomfortable.

"My wife has gone missing and I'm worried she may already be dead. Since that post went live, she vanished, and I think someone has taken the contract. There's already been one attempt on her life."

"Go on." I nodded the way that I had practiced in the mirror. Wise but caring.

"It was just luck really. Normally Eleanor would drive her car to work but today I was taking it into the shop for a service. As I got to the junction at the end of our road, the brakes failed. The car kept going and I was T-boned by a UPS van and then hit from the other side by a DHL truck. The car rolled and ended up hitting a telephone pole. Mr. Carver, I think the brakes had been cut."

I looked at the casts on both of his legs and his neck brace,

"You're lucky to be alive."

"I know, but I think the whole thing was meant for my wife. She's still out there, in hiding, with a hitman on her tail. I need you to find her and bring her home safely."

"I'll take the job but I'm not sure she'll want to come home. Not if she knows you want to kill her."

"I don't want to kill her, not really. I just wanted a chance to be with Raquel."

"Did you consider divorce?" I asked as I stood up and gathered my things.

"Not really," he said. "I don't think I could put her through that. It would break her heart. And, you know, divorce is a lot of hassle. Papers and lawyers and all that."

As I was leaving Hargreaves's private room, a tall, wide, and angry-looking nurse blocked the doorway. Being the courteous fellow that I am, I stepped aside and waved him in, after all these guys have a job to do. The big guy just grunted and barged into the room. I reached the elevator and punched the down button. I hated hospitals; the thought of all those germs lingering in the air gave me the kinda creeps that facing down a thug in a dark alley had never managed. An orderly stepped up beside me pushing an old geezer in a green gown, gasping on an oxygen mask. I smiled down at him but shuffled a step to the side as surreptitiously as possible. The last thing I needed was to catch something up in this germ factory. The elevators slid open to the sight of an old woman leaning on a portable drip, coughing her lungs out. I decided to take the stairs.

As I stepped away from the elevator, I could see into Hargreaves's room. The big nurse was leaning over him and something seemed funny about the scene. I pushed the door open quietly and saw Hargreaves's legs kicking furiously. The nurse was pushing a pillow down over my client's face, smothering him. Hargreaves wasn't my favorite client, but he was the only one I had right now, and he hadn't paid me yet, so I threw myself at the giant nurse.

My shoulder crunched and I felt as if I had shoulder tackled a Greek column. At least the surprise had distracted the attacker and he turned away from Hargreaves.

Towards me.

My usual self-defense technique for fighting a bigger opponent is to shoot them in the face with my Walther PPK but they frown upon guns in hospitals, so I had left mine in my car. I had no option but to resort to old-fashioned pugilism. I cricked my head from one shoulder to the other, I'm not sure how that could possibly help but I had seen it done in the movies. The giant advanced on me and I'm sure that he growled.

"Hey big guy, let's talk this over," I tried.

His eyes narrowed and he reached out towards me.

In a move that would have made Bugs Bunny proud I widened my eyes and pulled the oldest trick in the book. I pointed behind him.

"Is that Ricky Martin?" I gasped.

The sucker fell for it, he glanced backward. I drew back my fist and landed a full haymaker, John Wayne style, on his chin.

I think I may have broken my knuckles. He barely grunted as he reached out, grabbed me by the throat, and threw me across the room. I landed with a clatter on a table, knocking over a bunch of flowers and a big jug of orange squash.

"Okay, I warned you." I struggled to push myself up, knowing that the next time he hit me I wouldn't be getting up. I might be able to get one good strike in first, testicles, solar plexus, or throat. My only choices. He shuffled towards me.

The shriek of an alarm startled him. Hargreaves had recovered enough to hit some kind of panic button. The giant nurse looked confused. He glanced at Hargreaves, then me, then the door. The door won and he ran, surprisingly quickly, from the room.

I staggered to the bed, "Are you okay?"

I knew I should have run after him, but my legs had decided to turn to string cheese.

Hargreaves nodded.

"Don't worry, I'll track him down. He'll show up on the security cameras," I panted.

"I know him," Hargreaves said. "That's Manalo."

"Who the hell is Manalo?"

"He's my wife's personal trainer."

I was expecting a flashy modern gym; you know the type, a dozen treadmills in front of floor-to-ceiling windows so that passersby would be tempted in by spandex-clad fitness models. That's not what I discovered when I found the dump where Manalo worked. It was hard to imagine Mrs. Hargreaves working out here. From the outside it looked like a porn theatre that had been closed down in the seventies, the inside looked like a rejected interior from a Stallone movie filled with sweaty men carrying out a confusing combination of activities including punching and skipping. The only thing missing was a wizened old man screaming, "Yer a bum, Rock!"

It wasn't difficult to pick out Manalo from the crowd as he stood a foot taller than anyone else there. I watched as he carried a bunch of mats into a storeroom at the back of the hall. I knew that I didn't look the type to hang out in a boxing gym; too intelligent and well dressed, but I tried my best to blend in as I crossed the floor to the stock room. Nobody pointed or laughed so I think I got away with it. I slid through the door and watched as Manolo effortlessly moved heavy equipment from one side of the room to the other. He looked up and saw me. He picked up a dumbbell and growled. He started towards me, his muscles rippling as he lifted the weight.

I raised my Walther and shot him in the foot.

Bleating like a frightened goat he flopped to the floor.

"You shot me!" he whined.

"You sound surprised," I said.

"You're crazy."

"No. Quite the opposite. I was doing you a favor. A little gunshot to the foot is nothing. You tried to kill my client which makes you a murderer, or at least an attempted murderer. I should have shot you in the head, I still might."

I pulled over a small stool and sat down, still pointing my gun at him.

"Another way to look at it is that you didn't murder anyone, so I don't really have a problem with you. As long as you answer my questions and promise me that you'll never murder anyone again."

"I'm not a murderer. I didn't go through with it. I couldn't. I'm sorry."

He actually started weeping.

"That would be easier to believe if I had walked into that room to see you drop the pillow and fall to your knees in guilt but that's not how I remember it. I interrupted you and you threw me across the room. Which is the other reason I shot you."

"No. I was already thinking about stopping. I promise. I just wanted to frighten him. I couldn't let him go through with his plan to murder Ellie."

"Eleanor Hargreaves, his wife?"

"Yes. I saw that he was plotting to kill her and wanted to stop it."

"He's not going to kill her. He's an idiot and you're not much better. Where is she now?"

"I don't know. In hiding, scared for her life." He aimed for stoic but it landed somewhere around teen girl drama.

"Listen, buddy, I'm trying to save her life, you understand?"

He nodded.

I handed him my card.

"If she contacts you, call me."

I checked my phone as I left the gym. No new messages. I needed to head back to the hospital and have another word with my client. I felt a dark presence blocking out the sun and looked up from my phone to see two figures standing in my way.

"Officers?"

"You Carver?" the short one with the twitchy eye asked.

"Nah, you just missed him. He ran down that way chasing after a big white bird."

"Wiseguy eh?"

"You guys actually say that, eh?"

The other guy jumped in, he was taller and had ears that reminded me of the World Cup. "We're detectives with the Chicago PD. This is Detective Monoghan and I'm Detective Monroe. We just wanted to ask you a few questions."

"Certainly. If you call my secretary, I'm sure she can fit you in."

"We need to speak to you right now."

"Or what? Are you going to take me back to the precinct, rough me up a little? What do you guys do now that you don't have telephone books? Hit me with a laptop?"

"Oh, we still have phone books for special occasions, but we prefer subtler methods. It's the 21st century after all.

"Your private detective license number is 20190012125? We just need to lodge a complaint and can get that sucker pulled before the end of the day, tie it up in red tape for months.

"Or we could just leave your agency a negative review on Yelp."

I wasn't sure if he was trying to be funny or not but that could seriously affect my business.

"Just make it quick, I've got stuff to do."

"You representing this guy?"

He showed me a photo of Hargreaves. I nodded.

"His wife has gone missing and there's evidence that he hired someone to kill her."

"Is this evidence his Facebook post?"

They just stared the way they were trained to.

"The guy's an idiot," I said. "He hasn't hired a hitman; he hasn't killed his wife. He wants me to find her, I think he wants to patch things up."

"Then why has he not taken down the bounty on her head?"

"What do you mean? Aww, don't tell me ..."

I punched a few keys on my phone and there was Hargreaves's status. "Looking for someone cheap to kill my wife."

"He's been in an accident. I don't think he realizes it's still on there."

"Maybe he's smarter than you think."

"He couldn't be any dumber."

"If we don't find Mrs. Hargreaves alive and well before the end of the day, we're charging him."

I felt that I should stick up for my client but couldn't find the words or the energy so I kept my mouth shut.

"Have a nice day." The cops nodded and walked away.

I stared at the phone again. Something caught my attention that I hadn't noticed before, a little heart next to Hargreaves's status. Someone had "liked" his comment. I clicked on it. Nikki Smith. An employee at the same office where Hargreaves worked.

"Who the hell is Nikki Smith?" I bellowed as I walked into the hospital.

Hargraves jumped with fright and I instantly regretted bursting in on a man who had potentially survived two attempted murders already that day.

I calmed down. "Sorry. Do you know anyone by the name of Nikki Smith?"

"Yeah, she works in my office."

"Do you and she have a relationship?"

"Like romantic?"

"Yes."

"No. Why? Did she say something?"

"No. She liked your Facebook status?"

"Nikki? I never really considered her. She's not bad-looking. Could even be pretty if she dolled herself up a little. She's a bit older than Raquel, closer to my age. I don't know. Do you think I would have a chance with her?"

I felt myself reaching for my gun and stopped. I gritted my teeth. "I'm not trying to set you up on a date, I'm trying to stop you from going to jail. Is she a viable suspect?"

"I don't know. I guess, maybe. You know what women are like. If she secretly loves me then who knows what she would do."

I scrolled through my phone. "It looks like she has liked pretty much every photo and status that you've ever posted."

This seemed to cheer him up.

"Classic stalker behavior," he said. "She must really be into me."

"She may be emotionally unstable," I said.

"That doesn't mean that we couldn't be happy together," he said.

I sighed.

"Fine, I'm going to your office now and track down this Nikki Smith. The police may come up here to ask you a few questions. If they do, don't say anything."

"Be careful," he said.

"I will."

"I mean with Nikki, she may be my future wife after all, try not to hurt her. Or put her off me. In fact, if you can say some nice things about me that might help."

I left the room without saying another word. I needed a good review from this guy.

The accountancy firm where Hargreaves worked was located on the 4th floor of an uptown office building. I stepped out of the elevator into a reception area filled with tall potted plants and flashy video screens, it looked more like a tech company than a boring old accountancy firm. The young woman behind the desk threw me a big toothy smile so I tried my best Sean Connery smirk, one eye raised.

"Well hello, *mish*. My name is Carver, Ed Carver." I held up my business card as if it meant something.

"Hello, Mr. Edcarver, welcome to Swanstock, Grayson and McMillan, where every penny counts. How can I direct your call?"

I glanced around to remind myself that I was present in the reception area.

"This isn't a call, I'm a real person," I said.

"I'm sorry Mr. Edcarver. How may I direct your ... person?"

"I don't suppose your name is Raquel?" I guessed.

Her jaw dropped and her eyes widened, "Oh my God. That's amazing. How did you do that?"

I showed her my card again, this time with a flourish. I surreptitiously dropped the card while I blew into my hands then, tada, I showed her my empty hands.

"It's what I do."

She looked as if I had just made the Lincoln Memorial disappear. She just stared for a second then started to clap excitedly. "Do something else."

I looked around as if there were hidden cameras on us and tapped the side of my nose. "Maybe later. But first I need someone to assist me in my investigation."

She put her hand up. "Pick me."

I rubbed my chin, if I had a mustache I would have twirled it. "Hmmm. I think not, I need someone who knows stuff."

"I know stuff, ask me anything."

I rubbed at my temples. "I'm seeing the name, Nikki. Does that name mean anything to you?"

She was starting to bounce with excitement. "Yes, yes. Nikki Smith, she works here."

"Tell me about her."

"She's a real nice person. She's always bringing in cakes and stuff."

"Do you like her?"

"She's okay I guess."

"I sense you have reservations?"

"Wow, you're right. I never really thought about it, but she is a bit clingy."

"Are you friends with her on social media?" I asked.

"Oh my God. How do you do that? Yes, we're friends on Facebook but she's a bit creepy. You know the kind. She likes all your posts and makes nice comments on your photos and stuff. Like why she is even looking at photos of me at two o clock in the morning?"

Nikki Smith sounded more like a lonely woman than a bunny boiler at this point but there is a fine line. Did she like Hargreaves's post out of habit or was there more to it? I still needed to talk to her.

"Where can I find this woman?" I asked Raquel.

"She's normally hanging out on the roof garden at the smoking area. You know the type."

"What, smokers?"

"No. She doesn't smoke, she just hangs out there to get all the gossip."

"Thank you, Raquel. You've been most helpful."

I bowed extravagantly and walked to the elevator.

She called out behind me, "Do you sense I'm in danger from her Mr. Edcarver?"

I turned to face her as the elevator doors slid closed.

"No, but beware of a man named Hargreaves and at all costs, don't forget to ..."

But the doors had closed. I smiled.

There was a piercing scream as I stepped out onto the rooftop garden. I automatically whipped out my Walther and dropped to a crouch to make myself a smaller target. Another shriek and it was coming from my left. Definitely a woman. I crabbed sideways along the cover of a raised plant bed and peeked around the corner. Two women were pulling at each other's hair. I recognized Nikki Smith from her Facebook profile. The other person was the woman that I had been searching for all day, Eleanor Hargreaves.

The fight seemed to be fairly even but then Eleanor threw up both hands breaking Nikki's hold on her and jabbed at Nikki's throat with her left hand causing the woman to stagger back, gasping for air. Eleanor followed this with another left to the abdomen and finished with a right cross Nikki's jaw. The sessions with Manolo were definitely paying off. Nikki staggered to the edge of the roof and Eleanor closed in, ready for the coup de grâce.

Time to put an end to this. I fired a shot in the air. Eleanor froze. Nikki staggered near the edge.

"Eleanor Hargreaves? Your husband hired me."

Retrospectively, I realized that may not have been the best opening. Eleanor shrieked and pushed Nikki off the roof. Just as the poor accountant lost her balance Eleanor grabbed her hand, holding her at a forty-five-degree angle as Nikki's sensible shoes scrabbled at the edge trying to keep a hold.

"Put the gun away or I'll drop her," Eleanor yelled.

I lowered my weapon. "Don't do anything you'll regret Eleanor. Nikki is innocent. This has all been a big misunderstanding."

"I already did something I regret. I married that loser. Now he wants to kill me. Why? Over this tramp?"

"No. It was over some other tramp." Better not mention Raquel, the girl was dim but innocent.

"Well, this one is involved," Eleanor said. "She liked the post. I read on the Internet that means she accepted the contract." She relaxed her grip causing Nikki to drop a little and scream a lot.

"No. She just likes everyone's posts. It's a bit sad really."

Nikki stopped screaming and gave me a dirty look. Didn't she realize I was just trying to save her life?

"So, you're the one he hired instead?" Eleanor asked.

"Yes. I mean no, well, yes. But not to kill you. He hired me to find you. He was worried about you and wanted me to bring you home."

"Why, who are you?"

"My name is Ed Carver, I'm a private investigator. I have a card."

"Are you cheap, Mr. Carver?"

I shrugged. "Reasonably priced."

"Did you see what he wrote? He was looking for someone cheap to kill me. Cheap! I think that's what hurts the most."

Really? I thought.

“Is that why you cut the brakes on your own car, Eleanor? You knew he would be taking your car into the shop that day?” I asked.

“It was self-defense! Kill or be killed. Once I knew he was out to get me I realized I had to strike first. No jury would convict me.”

“Your husband made a mistake. Let’s face it, he’s an idiot. But he doesn’t deserve to die, neither do you and neither does Miss Smith there.”

“He’s a cheap man who wanted to hire a cheap killer so that he could be with his cheap tart.”

“Yes, but look at it this way. He wasn’t unfaithful. He didn’t cheat on you. He wouldn’t have an affair while you were still married.”

“He tried to kill me! Why didn’t he ask for a divorce?”

“Why didn’t you?”

She stared at me but said nothing.

“I know about you and Manalo, why didn’t you ask for a divorce?” I asked.

Eleanor pulled Nikki from the edge and threw her towards me. I tightened my grip on my pistol but didn’t raise it. It was over. Eleanor slumped onto the patio. “He would have been so hurt. I couldn’t put him through that. And you know divorces are just so much hassle.”

THE ADVENTURE OF THE BASH-BEANED FIANCÉE

Ricky Sprague

"Jaspers, what's got everyone all agog?"

At the dulcet sound of my query, my valet's pan assumed a quizzical mien before he declared, "I'm given to understand, sir, in speaking with the staff, that the famous consulting detective Locksure Homes arrives anon."

"That the chappie from the monastery who naps a lot and then accuses people of committing murders?"

"No, sir. You're thinking of Father Thursday."

"Oh—the one with the barmy accent, then? Albanian, isn't he?"

"I believe you're referring to the Belgian detective Hercules Pierrot. Locksure Homes is the one who wears a deerstalker and smokes a meerschaum—"

"Oh, yes! He's the birdie whose adventures are chronicled by his faithful gentleman's gentleman, what's-his-name."

"Dr. Watsup, sir."

"Say again?"

"What's-his-name's name, sir, is Dr. Watsup."

"Ah, yes. Many is the hour I've whiled away in the company of those amusing literary trifles."

"Indeed, sir?"

"Well, not in a literal sense. As you know my preferred reading material is rather in the neighborhood of Verbena House. But I've heard the Locksure stuff's quite cracking. Say, Jaspers—why don't you write up my adventures? We've had some real flopdoozies if you ask me."

"If I may be so bold as to say so, I'm not sure exactly what the market for such narratives would be."

"Well, you have been quilling it up quite a bit lately."

Here for perhaps the first time ever I saw Jaspers's face turn a peculiar shade of Cockscomb as he said, "I have been working on a project, sir, but if you don't mind I'd rather not discuss it."

"Modest, eh?"

"Well, sir, not exactly ..."

"You're bein' coy old bird! I bet it's really a racy little I-don't-know-what!" I said, dry washing the old ham hocks. "Something along the lines of one of those epistolary novels where the chambermaid spends about eight-hundred pages resisting the amorous embraces of the lord of the manor, before finally succumbing for a night of steamy honeymoon hide-the-pego."

"Not quite, sir."

"Still, I wouldn't mind reading it, if my merely bringing it up is enough to make your fiz go all pomegranate like that. But, I can see we've gone off-topic."

"Not unusual for someone with such a capricious mind as yours, sir."

"I can never tell if you're insulting me or not, Jaspers."

"Indeed, sir."

"Anyway, why's it that the world's most famous professional snoop is coming here to this hotel? Aside, of course, from the splendid view of the Penistone Crags that is?"

"Probably to investigate the mysterious death which occurred here two nights back, sir."

Here he had me stumped, and I told him so. "Jaspers, I feel like a felled tree. You're saying there was a mysterious death here?"

"Yes, sir."

"At this hotel? The one we're in right now?"

"Yes, sir."

"Pish and posh!" I gasped. "That's a bit of ruddy bad news."

"Indeed, sir. Perhaps even worse is that it was your fiancée who was the victim."

My body instinctively recoiled at the sound of the disturbing word. It's true that we Brewsters are cut from hearty jibs, but even we have our limits. "'*Fiancée?*'"

"Indeed. She was your betrothed, as I'm sure you'll remember that the engagement was arranged by your Aunt Dorothy and the unfortunate girl's father, Lord Brontley-Brontley."

"And I agreed to the merger?"

"Your initial reluctance was tempered by the fact that, as you put it, sir, 'She had a ripping bod that dizzed you out with maddening desire.' "

"Oh yes, of course. Took me a minute to shake the cobwebs off the old lemon. She did have a way of churning the glands and stiffening little Barnie into a stiffy-throb of lusty heave-ho. And she's dead now, you say?"

"If I can take the liberty of refreshing your memory a bit more, sir, and making a slight editorial comment, the manner of her dispatch was quite brutal."

"Oh yes, of course. She took a right corking cosh to the headbone as I recall it now."

"That was how she was found, sir."

"I don't mean to sound judgmental, Jaspers old man, but I've got to say that I generally disapprove of coves who'd bash in the brains of beloved beazels from our social strata."

"It is rather taking a liberty, sir."

Now I couldn't help but to wax a little philosophical, as I am wont to do in the face of tragedy: "Still and all, I can't help but note that it's gotten me out of a rather tight matrimonial pickle, as I don't mind telling you that I didn't relish the idea of being married."

"Indeed, sir. You made the same pun when the chambermaid announced with a tearful scream that she'd discovered the remains."

"Did I? Well, do you know why that pun is doubly good?"

"It is because your fiancée's father is the owner of the nation's largest pickling concern."

I couldn't help but to laugh at that. Brontley-Brontley's Vinegared Shorties were staples throughout the empire. "A good pun's always worth repeating, as the saying goes."

"I don't think that's a saying, sir."

"Well, I was 'a-saying' it a moment ago."

"Very good, sir."

"Also, sorry to lay the law down as it were, but I must correct you: *Former* fiancée. You lost track of your tenses there."

"Forgive me, sir."

"Bygones. I'm at a loss as to why she wanted to marry me anyway. She was bent on 'moulding' and 'shaping' me into someone else entirely. It's a regular floater to wed up with someone only to change everything about them that makes them you."

"Good point, sir."

"So, this Locksure's a detective of the master class, is he?"

"That is his reputation, sir."

"Well, a man's rep is everything in this world. I shudder to think where I'd be without mine."

"As do I."

"The important thing is, do you think he can unravel the mystery of who bashed old what's-her-name's brains?"

"Bunnie Brontley-Brontley."

"I say, Jaspers—is that Latin?"

"That was the unfortunate girl's name, sir. Your fiancée."

"Oh yes. Her. Tragic. Anyway, I wonder why anyone would call this Locksure chappie out here when you've got more on the bean than anyone I know."

"I'm humbled, sir."

"You'd probably solve this little whodidit in two shakes."

"As I understand it, Mr. Homes is a faithful consumer of Brontley-Brontley's Vinegared Shorties, and is coming here as a personal favour to the girl's father."

"They know each other?"

"They're acquainted, sir. May I ask what you're doing?" Jaspers's left eyebrow raised a scintilla of an iota, which meant he was feeling an oncoming rush of uncontrollable disgust and loathing.

My valet's objets de scornio just happened to be the objets de me drawer search: a pair of purple mourning spats and matching cravat. They'd been an impulse purchase just a few days before. "Naturally I had no inkling I'd have occasion to wear these hotties so soon."

"Are you sure they're in the best of taste, sir?"

I know that Jaspsers's judgment is strictly blue-rib-aces and his bean's second-to-none, but dash it all there are times when it's necessary for the employer to remind the valet who's employing whom in the relationship.

"Shall we see how they look with that brown tweed number and the blue meanie vest?" I asked in a bit of goad.

"They shall clash, sir."

"Well, let that be the cover of the book of my despairing heartbreak, so to speak, in place of all the usual gnashing of the teeth and moaning of the bar and so on."

"If we must, sir."

It was just past supper time when the old consulting 'tec finally ritzed the scene, complete with flaming red deerstalker with long peacock feather and an elaborate meerschaum carved into the shape of a butterfly. He and his companion, an odd little duck-sort whose name always seemed just out of reach of the old brain cells had stopped off at the medico's place to examine old what's-her-name's remains.

Now, they were in her room, standing where the bod had been found, a space denoted on the floor by a chalk drawing and a stain of grey matter and blood.

Jaspers and I were escorted into their presence by Inspector Pud-dwhistle, Her Majesty's rep in the investigation game. Inspector P had already q-and-a'd yours truly and given the all-clear-bill-of-innocence straightaway, and he was apologetic about bringing me over.

When I walked in, I gave Locksure a hearty well-hello-and-how-d'you-do, and said, "Barnie Brewster up to bat. I'm what's-her-name's—the chalk-drawing-and-stain's—now former future husband."

"Dashed unlucky," Locksure mused.

Though what's-her-name's death seemed ballyhoo lucky to me, I played it suave in my reply: "Mm."

"Aside from the coshed attic she looked a right humdinger of a lass," Locksure went on.

"Oh, she was strictly custard-in-the-shorts," I agreed, catching the drift of his thought-train. "Her 'sique was never part of the irk. The stick was purely in the personality department, being as she was a hectoring biddy with an eye on 'improving' yours truly."

"Why would you want to marry someone just to change them?" he asked reasonably.

"Jaspers!" I exclaimed. "This is just like listening to myself in a mirror!"

"Indeed, sir," Jaspers said in a tone I couldn't quite savvy.

Now I admit I was quite taken with this Locksure bird, recognizing a sort of kindred spirit as the poet once scribed, and I said in a bit of a gush, "I wonder if we might impose upon you to do a little sleuthing ..."

"Well ..." he ellipsed modestly.

"Oh, go on! It'd be rather a corker of a thrill getting to see your fantastic bean in action!"

The other cove, the one with Locksure whose name I had trouble remembering, cleared his throat in a downright Jaspers-ian sort of way and said, "Actually, Mr. Homes was in the process of making some rather interesting observations, just prior to your arrival."

"I was?" Locksure asked in a manner I found utterly the cat's.

"Yes," the other fellow—Dr. Watsup! That was the bird's name! Watsup. He said, "Yes, remember how you noted that, this being the Voltaire Hotel, each room comes equipped with its own seven pound bust of Voltaire. Said bust's dimensions just happen to correspond to the concavity of the wound you observed just a short time ago in the victim's skull."

"Indeed," Locksure agreed. "I did note that particular bit of Exhibit A."

"You also noted," continued Dr. Watsup, "that the bust of Voltaire in this room now shows no signs of damage or blood. You suggested that it was a mere simplementary deduction that the bust of Voltaire which was originally in the room must have been the murder weapon, and that said murder weapon was then replaced by the one that is presently here in this room."

" 'Simplementary' is a word I coined," Locksure said.

"You hear that, Jaspers? This chappie makes up his own words! That's stantsafantasticks!"

"Indeed," Jaspers agreed.

"You further surmised," continued old Dr. Watsup, "that this indicated the murderer had access to another bust. If this perpetrator was another guest in the hotel, their room was probably now lacking in a bust of Voltaire."

"The case of the disappearing bust of Voltaire," I said, marveling. "Brilliant show, old chap!"

"Thank you, old bean!"

"You further noted," Dr. Watsup could not be stopped chronicling his master's brilliance, "the concavity was at the front of the skull. This indicated that she was facing her assailant and most likely knew him, given the body was positioned so far into the room and so near the bed."

"Ah," I said, feeling a rather brilliant obs of my own coming on, "you think the assassin was someone she was on intimate terms with?"

Jaspers made his own little coughing sound and said, "This is all very fascinating. Mr. Homes certainly lives up to his reputation."

Oddly, when he said that, his soul-windows were squarely aimed in Dr. Watsup's direction. Jaspers proceeded apace: "I recently read in *Copper's Quarterly* that 90% of murders are committed by someone on intimate terms with the victim. It is, as it were, a very common sort of crime."

Jaspers's words seemed to have an effect upon old Locksure. He looked at me and smiled and said, "Simplementary! That's why I do not suspect you in this case!"

For some reason that filled me with a sort of oozy relief, but I affected a wounded peculiarity as I said, "I should hope not!"

"It would be too easy if you were the perpetrator! And Locksure Homes only investigates *uncommon* sorts of crimes!"

"I say," I said, "you do use a lot of exclamation points in your speech."

"I'm a passionate person. Just as I can see that you are. That is another point in your favor. Also, your spats are absolutely delicious!"

"My fashion sense displays a sort of *je ne sais quoi* that all but absolves one of guilt in any crime other than, of course, aesthetic grace."

"All of those things, mingled with your glassy-eyed expression and your piddly-poddly type West End idle rich argot leads me to believe you lack both the fortitude and the dexterity for such a crime."

"Thank you."

Back in our room I said, "Jaspers, that Locksure chap's a right bloomer, don't you think?"

"He is something, sir."

"Not impressed?"

"If you don't mind my saying so, sir, he seems a bit of a letdown, given his portrayal in the chronicles of his 'Adventures.' "

"From where I was standing he seemed to possess a rather brilliant old bean."

"I'm of the suspicion that his reputation has been engineered. It happened, sir, that while the two of you were discussing sartorial matters I had an opportunity to observe the ostensible sidekick, Dr. Watsup."

"Oh, yes. The chappie who was with him. Honestly, I barely noticed he was there. Bit of a dried egg, seemed to me."

"That is the first thing I noticed. His lack of obtrusiveness. Then there was the rather keen manner with which he studied you."

"Observant chap, you'd say?"

"Very much, sir. In fact, if you listened carefully, it was actually Dr. Watsup making the observations, and not Mr. Homes."

"Well blow me over the moon!" I all but gasped. "You make a good point!"

"I'd venture to guess that he is the real brains of the outfit, so to speak, while Locksure is a bit, well, daft."

I scanned the room and then suddenly I had a bit of a brainwave of my own: "Actually I think you've really got something there. That Locksure Homes isn't all the brilliant egg he's cracked up to be. Remember he said that every room at this hotel has its own bust of Voltaire? Well look 'round our room, Jaspers. No Voltaire bust anywhere!"

"Interesting observation, sir."

"So it would seem that it's a case of the Boswell stuffing his arm up the backside of the Johnson and ghostwriting the Dictionary."

"That is one way of putting it, sir."

I had to admit I appreciated when Jaspers complimented my wit, so I felt compelled to remind him: "Ripping pun, by the way—'brilliant egg,' 'cracked up.' Remember I said that earlier?"

"Indeed."

"Well, tonight I'll have a chance to find out even more about this Locksure fellow."

"Tonight?"

"Yes. The old buddyloo invited me out for a bit of jolly old carousing."

"Sir, forgive my asking but do you think it wise to go out tonight, a mere three nights following the brutal murder of your intended?"

"What do you mean, old bird?"

"It could be considered insensitive. Perhaps even suspicious."

"Goodness, man! *She's* the one who died, not me! Am I supposed to just hole up and shrivel away into a husk of nothing just because what's-her-name lost some gray matter? Pish and posh I say and besides I'm sure she'd want me to go on, given how much she probably loved me and all that. And furthermore besides, if I change my behaviour now people are likely to be *more* suspicious."

"I'm not sure I follow you, sir."

I'm afraid I regarded him a bit snidely. "Jaspers, for once that vaunted bean of yours has laid an egg, so to speak, leaving me to carry all our eggs in one basket, intellectually I mean."

His pan showed bafflement. "Sir?" he asked, tentatively.

"Not one for egg puns I see. Very well, in plain English: In order to show my innocence, I must behave innocently. Now, where's the old scarlet ascot I love to go out carousing in?"

"It's in the drawer where I left it, sir. Sir, if I may be so bold as to make a suggestion?"

"Suggest away, as long it's not anything along the lines of 'Waste a perfectly good carousing night grousing and pouting about the loss of old what's-her-name in the old hotel room.' "

"I was merely going to suggest that, since you and Mr. Homes seem to share such similar sartorial soft spots, you might offer him the gift of some small accent."

"Oh, I see your meaning. He'd look good in the grey trousers, I think."

"I was thinking something more along the lines of this," Jaspers said, producing a pink lace-fringed hanky.

"Think he'd like that, eh?"

"He might, sir."

"Say—what's this bit of ... something. A stain or something. Jaspers—how'd you let a stain like this set?"

"It's actually a part of the design, sir. Very bohemian."

"It would be a friendly gesture, at that," I decided. "Besides that, I barely recognize this blooming thing. And like the old saw goes, 'The best gift is the one that shan't be missed.' "

"I'm not familiar with that old saw."

"Really? Well, I must have 'saw' it somewhere," I said. I couldn't help but let escape an appreciative chuckle.

I don't know if this has ever happened to you, but it happens to me enough that one might consider it part of my mental furniture: You go out and have such a wild, intoxicating time that you can't even remember half the bally things you did. Such was the case in the night I spent in wild yahoos with the first-rate detective Locksure Homes.

The gist in broad strokes was that we frolicked about from one pub and club to the next and so on, amidst much laughter, highballs, rowdy bawdiments, and verses of *By My Lassie's Pink Velvet Lips*. The two of us together were the life of whatever party we happened to be attending. And where no party was in evidence, we created our own.

It wasn't until around four in the old AM that I finally made my way back to the old hotel room.

Jaspers must have been sleeping standing up in the corner of the room, for he simply just seemed to incorporate from the shadows the moment I walked in. After I'd finished screaming in surprise, he asked me, "Was your evening satisfactory?"

"What I can remember of it. I do black out on occasion. And how was your night? More working on those bloody memoirs you've been so secretive over?"

"In a manner of speaking, sir. And did you happen to present Mr. Homes with the handkerchief?"

"Oh, yes, that, well ..." I said, a bit sheeped out I'm afraid. "I don't have it on me, so I assume—yes, that's right! I remember, after about my sixth Piccadilly Jim I leaned over to him and got a little sentimental, professing my undying platonic love for him and presenting him with what I claimed was my prized possesh. And then I hankied him."

"Very good, sir."

Then I deflated. "But he wouldn't accept it. Told me it'd look much better on me. Which, to be fair, is accurate."

I fished the item out of my inside jacket pocket. I examined it as if I was espying it for the first when there was a turbulent clamour-clang at the front door. Inspector Puddwhistle's babbling vox came charging from the other side, demanding entrance.

Jaspers obliged him with what felt to me like unseemly alacrity.

In charged Puddwhistle, followed by the chappie who'd been with Locksure that first day I'd met him. Dr. Watsup was his name. Rounding out the gruesome threesome was what's-her-name's father, Mr. Brontley-Brontley.

"You murdered him, just as you murdered her!" the nondescript dude said. Disconcertingly, he was aiming these verbal barbs directly at me.

Unfortunately, after a night of carousing gambols my old lemon's not nearly at its tartest, and all I could manage by way of rejoinder was, "Huh?"

"Locksure Homes is dead," the chap said by way of clarification. Dr. Watsup! That's his name. Anyway, Dr. Watsup added, absurdly I thought, that I had topped off his boss.

"I was with him just a few minutes ago. The two of us returned from a night of good-natured drinking tomfoolery. He was absolutely safe as houses—say! That's almost a pun, right? Homes, houses? Eh?"

"The two of you were drinking all night?" Inspector Puddwhistle asked.

"That we were. He managed to drink me right under the aquarium, so to speak."

Dr. Watsup shook his head. "Locksure Homes was no drinker! He took you out because he knew immediately that you'd murdered your fiancée, and was hoping you'd do something to give yourself away! And you did. Right after he got home he confided to me that you'd admitted it after your second Piccadilly Jim!"

"That doesn't sound like me," I said.

"And then, mere moments after revealing to me this information, he expired. Dead by poison!"

And this was when Mr. B-B found his voice, screeching at me, "You killed my daughter!"

"What? But? How? When? What? Why? But? Um? Jaspers!" I exclaimed.

Jaspers stepped into the breach. "I think perhaps I can offer a clarifying gloss. Immediately before the three of you barged in and tied my employer's tongue, he was just explaining to me that, in point of fact, it was Locksure Homes who admitted to brutalizing the doomed Bunnie Brontley-Brontley following an intense and rather scandalous love affair."

"What??" the Inspector, the doctor, and the father all shouted in uni. I managed to keep my mouth shut but I was thinking exactly the same word, with the same number of question marks. Knowing Jaspers as I did, I knew it best to let him work his corking magic.

Jaspers nodded solemnly. "In fact, Mr. Homes was so guilt-ridden over the escapade that he presented Mr. Brewster with a condemning piece of evidence—a blood-spattered handkerchief owned by the departed."

Here Jaspers took the pink lacy hanky from my mitt and held it up to display the monogrammed BB-B. And now he mentioned it, the stain was very much like blood.

Jaspers presented the hanky to the Inspector, whose gaze in my direction was somewhat less stern.

"Preposterous!" Dr. Watsup declared. "This—this buffoon—" (here he indicated me) "—was seen exiting the deceased's room less than ten minutes before her body was found. Multiple members of the staff confided to me that they'd overheard him thinking out loud about various ways he could kill her. He told a chambermaid—while he was frotting with her!—that he'd be free to run off with her just as soon as he'd done her in—"

"I hardly think pillow talk's admissible in court!"

Jaspers held up a discouraging hand, and I clamped the old pie-hole shut again.

"That is what you say," Jaspers said. "However, it transpires that there is ample reason to disbelieve you in this situation. For one thing, Mr. Homes was your employer—at least ostensibly."

"What's that mean? 'Ostensibly?' " the Inspector asked.

"I've wondered that myself," I confided.

"It means that it was actually Dr. Watsup who provided the investigative acumen in the Homes-Watsup dynamic," Jaspers illuminated. "As he just stated, he interviewed staff regarding Mr. Brewster's activities, while Mr. Homes was off gallivanting with Mr. Brewster."

"Indeed, we were gallivanting," I declared.

"Even if that were true, it doesn't matter," Dr. Watsup declared. "Because the fact remains—"

"I think it matters a great deal," Jaspers said. "It shows that your entire persona is a lie, and displays a fundamental lack of trustworthiness."

"Hm," the Inspector said. "He makes a point."

"But," Dr. Watsup said in a show-stopper of a tone, "Where is this room's bust of Voltaire?"

I admit my ticker skipped one at that. For I scanned the room and sure enough, no scowling poet or whatever Monsieur V had been.

Jaspers did that thing with his eyebrow where he's about to sock you with some impeccable bit of mental magnificence and he produced from the closet a prime specimen of a bust who just happened to be wearing a magnibarmy felt number with a beautiful peacock feather streaming off it.

"Jaspers!" I gasped. "It's a corker!"

"I'm glad you like it, sir. I've been using the bust as a stand-in for your head while I worked on it."

"This is—this isn't—" Dr. Watsup stammered. "They must have stolen this from another room!"

"I'm afraid," Jaspers said in a sympathetic tone, "that Dr. Watsup is attempting to divert attention away from himself and his employer."

"Nonsense! That's what you're doing!"

Jaspers tut-tutted him and went on: "If you'll all follow me, I believe I can show you further evidence of Mr. Homes's guilt in this matter."

Naturally we all followed Jaspers to Homes's room. There he was, sprawled out on the floor, face empurpled, eyes bugging out, foam at his mouth. Strangely, his bod was clean and laid out upon the floor as if he were sleeping.

Jaspers bypassed the bod and went to the bed, from under which he pulled a valise. He opened it and pulled from within a stack of letters, tied with a piece of lacy string, with a BB-B monogram.

"This is absurd!" Dr. Watsup shouted. "Those—those—those must have been planted here!"

Jaspers, unperturbed, untied the string and began to read from one of the letters. Discretion prevents me going into too much detail, but suffice to say it was as bawdy a collection of in-out descriptions as you're likely to find outside of a flea's autobiography. Also, there was a high concentration of passages regarding sock-darning and pants-pressing.

"I think, upon examination, you'll find the handwriting in these scabrous letters matches that of both Mr. Homes and Miss Brontley-Brontley," Jaspers added, handing the letters to the Inspector.

"This is a bit damning," the Inspector averred.

Dr. Watsup made a noise that pulled the old pumper's strings. "He—that venal valet—wrote those letters himself! He was working on them when we arrived! He planted them!"

Jaspers then made a movement toward Homes's corpse. "I think there's something else we need to consider," he said gravely. "By his look, I'd say that Mr. Homes has died of an ingestion of botulinum toxin."

"That might be," Dr. Watsup agreed. "I'm a doctor myself and I know the symptoms and—I am going to do the autopsy myself! Don't touch him!"

Dr. Watsup made a movement toward Jaspers, as if to forcibly prevent him examining the body. Jaspers put such a whallop on him that Dr. Watsup nearly flipped over backward a full one-eighty. Then, while Dr. Watsup was still agog, Jaspers rolled up one of Homes's shirtsleeves, displaying a pallid, stringy forearm dotted with puncture-marks. One of them looked very recent indeed.

"Mr. Homes was an addict, was he not? Cocaine?"

"Yes," Dr. Watsup moaned. "I wanted to keep his addiction quiet. That's why I tried to keep you away from the body. But you knew about it and you spiked his hypodermic syringe."

Now the Inspector regarded Dr. Watsup with open skepticism. "You're beginning to sound paranoid," he said.

Jaspers nodded sagely. "I think you'll find that, in his satchel, the doctor carries a range of medicines, as well as other, less salubrious, things ..."

The Inspector went for Dr. Watsup's bag. When Dr. Watsup tried to stop him, the Inspector bashed him on the old snozzer. He crumpled to the floor, weezing.

"Here's something," the Inspector said, removing a small glass vial from the satchel. "Says here it's got 'Botulinum toxin' in it."

"Doesn't that seem convenient to you? That he just happened to know where the letters were, and that there just happened to be a bottle of that stuff in my bag? Clearly labeled, even?"

"And finally, look at this face," Jaspers said, indicating me. "Is this the face of one capable of committing such a heinous act?"

I gave it my best hangdog and happening to catch a glimpse of myself in the mirror I felt my old blood-pumper melt just a touch.

"I'm sorry I doubted you," Mr. Brontley-Brontley said, clasping my hand. "I had no idea my daughter even knew Locksure Homes, let alone that they'd ... they'd ... fornicated and ... pressed so many pants together."

"This is all a bit of a shocker to me as well," I said.

"I'd like you to have the dowry I was set to give you. A full twenty-five percent stake in my Vinegared Shorties concern."

"Well, that's piping good of you old man," I said. "Of course, it won't bring the girl back, but it will go a long way to helping relieve some of the pain at her loss."

We both wiped away tears. Dr. Watsup was crying too.

After they'd hauled Locksure to the morgue and Dr. Watsup to gaol, I waxed a bit for Jaspers: "Really, old what's-her-name's better off. If we'd gotten married she would have had to deal with my wandering organ, my love of the ponies, my imbibing and carousing, my lack of ambition, my laziness ..."

"Don't sell yourself short, sir," Jaspers said kindly. "You're not so much lazy as shiftless."

"Indeed. Never had a shift, never will. Then of course there's you."

"Me, sir?"

"Oh yes. She fully intended showing you the door before the fire had been lit in the old honeymoon suite. I couldn't have that."

"Likewise, sir."

"Braining her was a kindness, really. A sort of mercy killing, as it were."

"No doubt a woman of her proud nature would have found it most deleterious to be married to you, sir."

"You know, it's funny. Bashing your fiancée's brains in doesn't seem the type of thing you'd forget. Yet it wasn't until right after her father gifted me part of his Vinegared Shorties concern that I remembered what happened. She was dead-set on me giving up my life of idle leisure and merry gamboling thither and yon, to go to work in one of her father's offices and settle down on some country estate with butlers and maids and so on. And of course no you, Jaspers."

"That was a concern of mine as well, sir."

"In a flash of inspiration I realized I'd be better off without her and just picked up the bust of Voltaire on the table and blammo."

"It happens, sir."

"I suppose you replaced the bust with the one from our room."

"You carried the damaged one in your hand when you staggered back here. Its crack and the fact it was covered in blood and brain matter bore witness to your ... exuberance."

"Would'a had me dead-to-rights, eh? And I don't remember a bit of it."

"You looked rather as if you were sleepwalking."

"Indeed. The dreamtime part of Barnie Brewster must've taken over, where daylight Barnie Brewster feared to tread, as it were. Something for the alienists, I'd venture."

"You are an interesting case study, sir."

"And what happened to the bash-bust?"

"I disposed of it, sir. And got the chambermaid with whom you had relations to replace the one from our room."

"Good show, Jaspers. Of course, I was a bit surprised to find out what's-her-name was slagging about with that Homes chappie."

"Actually, sir, those letters were composed by myself. I happened to have samples of Miss Brontley-Brontley's handwriting from letters she'd written to you. And Mr. Homes's handwriting has been printed in some broadsheets I've come across."

“Jaspers, you’re a man of many talents. And his hypo being spiked with the botchy stuff?”

“Again, I confess I may have played some small role in that accident. You see, it’s long been rumoured that Mr. Homes took a taste now and then. And when he was here in our room speaking with you I noted that he displayed a number of affectations associated with someone afflicted by an uncontrollable cocaine craving. When I planted the letters I also took the liberty of spiking his syringe with a seven-percent solution of the toxin, and planted the bottle in Dr. Watsup’s satchel.”

“Well, between the two of us, Jaspers, I’d say we made a right corking show of things.”

“It did all work out rather well for us, everything considered.”

“Greasy indeed. I shudder to think where I’d be without you.”

“Likewise, sir.”

MINOR FOURTH

Glenn Eichler

When the bride's mother called our playing exquisite, I knew the other violinist had to die.

It was at one of our very first post-quarantine gigs, a wedding that had been postponed twice. The party band's equipment was all set up in the ballroom for the dinner, its members no doubt off in a remote bathroom divvying up their amphetamines. But for the cocktail hour in the breakout room, the couple had decided to go "elegant" and hire our string quartet. That's our cellist Sandy, violist Meg, second violin Barry, and first violin, me.

Let me repeat that. Second violin: Barry. First violin: me. So disabuse yourself of any notion that I'm one of those pitiable second violinists walking around forever jealous of the first. Musically, he's no threat to me. I could lose my bowing arm and he'd be no threat to me. So no, I don't envy Barry. Envy and bloodlust are two different things.

Until that moment, the day had gone well. We'd played the wedding party down the aisle for the processional and back up after the vows (Pachelbel's Canon and Mendelssohn's Wedding March; those are not moments to get creative). Then we'd made ourselves scarce and reappeared for the cocktails.

We ended up sounding better than we had any right to, considering that we'd basically stopped rehearsing during quarantine. The guests ignored us, as usual, but as they shuffled off to dinner and we packed up our instruments, the bride's mother came over. She was all smiles.

"That was exquisite and just perfect. Thank you." Her first glance swept over all of us, but after that her focus was on Barry. "How long have you been playing together?"

He answered, "Believe it or not, almost six years off and on. In fact, three of us go all the way back to middle school." Barry, Sandy and I had met as terrible musicians in the sixth-grade orchestra. Since that time, two of us had improved. "But we more or less took the last year off, for obvious reasons. In fact we hadn't rehearsed in months before you emailed, so really *we* owe *you*." A deft reminder that with the performance over, the balance of our fee was due. You couldn't fault his business sense.

"You'd never know it," she said, gliding by the hint. And then, to the rest of us, "You all back him up beautifully."

And there it was. How can you listen to an hour of intricately constructed four-part arrangements and come away thinking it's a solo fiddle act and his backup band—and not even pick the *right* fiddle? I could be generous and chalk it up to a capitalist mindset. Barry was the guy who booked the gigs, so he in effect controlled the means of production. Therefore the bride's mother assumed he was the boss. One go-getter recognizing another.

But I didn't believe that. The truth, as always, was that Barry was getting by on his golden-boy good looks. And yes, the bar is low. In the classical music community, you're considered attractive if both your eyes point in the same direction. But Barry is legitimately handsome, and before you judge me, I swear to you, I have no problem with a good musician who's good-looking. Or, for that matter, with a bad musician who's good-looking. But a bad musician who gets complimented on *my* playing because people think the pretty music must be coming from the pretty man—that cannot stand.

Sandy and Meg know we could find a better second violin, but they're willing to put up with his incompetence because he handles the bookings. In fact as the bride's mother gushed over Barry, I caught Meg giving Sandy the tiniest poke in the side. She thought the whole thing was funny.

But Barry's not stupid; he knew I'd be furious. He smiled his most earnest smile and said, "Oh no, in a string quartet, no one backs up anybody else. A string quartet is a musical conversation between four people."

In that case, here's my contribution to the conversation: Fuck you, Adonis. In an orchestra with ten violins, you'd be the eleventh.

Still, I probably shouldn't have told the cellist that the violinist had to die.

Sandy was giving me a ride home from the gig (we don't live far from each other, I hate driving, and she's got a big cello-friendly SUV). I was still angry and maybe a little dehydrated from playing, which may have affected my blood sugar. The point is, my filter was off. So while I was aiming for funny, maybe I just sounded borderline psychotic, or possibly well past the border.

Sandy was speculating about songs we might add to freshen the repertoire if more jobs came along. Quartets like ours play the classical material that wedding guests expect, like Air on the G String and Clair De Lune, but those are liberally interspersed with fancy-pants arrangements of pop music from just about any era, from Glenn Miller to Bruno Mars. Anything from "Fly Me To The Moon" to "Signed, Sealed, Delivered" can sound surprisingly good performed by a string quartet. Unfortunately that means we also have to play things like that Hawaiian version of "Somewhere Over the Rainbow" that I believe God himself composed to punish me.

Sandy was talking about buying an arrangement of "Blinding Lights" when I interrupted her. "Listen, I've figured out a way we can make up for some of those lost Covid jobs. I've got a plan for increasing our per-gig take home by thirty-three percent."

She said, "I don't know. It takes people exactly five minutes on a wedding planning site to research the average fee for a quartet. Anything much higher than that and they'll book someone else."

I said, "We don't change the fee. We just kill Barry and the three of us split his share." She didn't laugh, but I was in too deep now. "Or better yet, you and I can just split it and hope Meg doesn't notice he's gone. I mean, she's a viola player. It could happen."

That did get a chuckle. Yes, that's right, it was all a fun joke. Sandy said, "First of all, I'm telling my good friend Meg that you said that. Second, how are we going to get hired as a string quartet with three people?"

"We kill him *after* the gig. And before you say anything, yes, I realize we can only do this once."

She shook her head. "Sometimes I wish we could get rid of him. He's so smug. And without him rubbing you the wrong way all the time, maybe you'd be nicer. I'd be curious to know what Pleasant Mike is like."

That remark required some parsing. I'd known Sandy since we were twelve, and there had been times when things almost took a turn. When we were just out of college we had gone on a few quasi-dates (lunches and museums) and a few real dates (dinners and movies) and then she met somebody, and that was that.

By the time her relationship ended I was seeing someone myself, and though that didn't last very long, we never quite reached the point of going out again. Possibly because over the years Sandy took notice of my tendency to lock myself in my room and sob for months after a breakup, and for some reason didn't find that attractive.

Meanwhile Barry had never been without one girlfriend or another, including during the year and a half when he was married. Thank God he didn't ask the quartet to play at his wedding. He was probably already bothered by having to share focus with the bride.

I'd thought many times about getting back together with Sandy. And as far as I knew, right now she wasn't with anyone. So I wasn't sure if she had just issued an invitation to ask her out again, but if she had, I needed one that was less subtle. All I said was, "What do you mean? I'm already Pleasant Mike."

She smiled and shook her head. "Unfortunately, you're Regular Mike. With one shoulder developing a chronic stoop from that big chip you carry on it. But I still don't see you as a murderer."

"You're wrong. I only took up the violin because I was hoping to get a machine gun to hide in the case."

She laughed again, and I quit while I was ahead. Weirdly, I found myself in a better mood. Considering that I'd blurted out my desire to kill someone, the whole conversation left me pretty upbeat.

I thought a lot about how I might murder Barry. I'd want to do something really cinematic, like have him found with his violin bow shoved through his throat and out the back, his dead hands grasping it in a doomed attempt to pull it out. That would be tough to pull off though. Even if I did maneuver him (alive and presumably resisting) into a position where I could attempt to push his own bow through his neck, I know I'm not strong enough. I probably wouldn't break the skin, and even if I did, the thin wooden stick would snap in half about five seconds into the attempt. That would leave Barry not only alive but demanding that I reimburse him for his bow.

Unless I did it one of two ways: one, invent some device I could use to fire the violin bow like an arrow through his throat. A crossbow for bows, as it were. But then I'd probably have to glue little triangular feathers to the end of the bow ahead of time to make it aerodynamic, and when Barry picked it up to play, he'd be sure to spot them. They're always so colorful.

The other thing I could do was craft a fake bow from an incredibly strong metal like titanium, then meticulously paint it to look like the wood of his real bow. I'd swap the bows when he wasn't looking, place the titanium one just out of his reach, and when he asked me to hand it to him, I'd pick it up and in the same swooping motion drive it through his throat (having built up my arm strength over months through clandestine weight training, hiding the results inside shirts craftily selected for their billowy sleeves). In this scenario, all I'd have to do is design and manufacture whatever tool and die machines I'd need to give me the ability to sculpt titanium.

Maybe poison, then.

Or maybe, I told myself, forget about actually killing Barry, and just enjoy fantasizing about it. You can still daydream about how much you'd enjoy it, and why shouldn't you? Daydreaming doesn't hurt anyone. Unfortunately.

So when we played our next gig, it was without violence (if you don't count the carnage Barry inflicted on eight bars of "You Are So Beautiful"). It was a country club fundraiser for the local branch of a non-profit called "Teach a WOMAN To Fish." The name may have had something to do with why I heard so many of the guests complaining about their boats.

We finished up with Handel's Alla Hornpipe (trust me—you know it). It was after that, while Sandy and Meg were off in the bathroom, that Barry revealed his grand plot. He smiled at me and said, "Mike, I had kind of a fun idea about 'Love Story.' What would you think about switching with me for that one piece?"

At first I didn't understand. "You want to play my violin? Why?"

"No, I mean I play first violin and you play second. Just for that one piece. I'd really enjoy the challenge."

I was almost speechless. "Are you crazy? Why the hell would I ever want to do that?"

"For variety's sake. Quartets do it all the time. It keeps things lively."

"How? By getting the audience to throw stuff?" On the surface, "Love Story" isn't the hardest piece in the world. It's Taylor Swift's retelling of the Romeo and Juliet story, only with a happy ending (in case you haven't noticed, very few songs played at weddings end with a couple's double suicide). The thing is, string arrangements of pop hits often make up for the lack of a drum kit by playing the song at a much faster clip than the original. Taylor's version (to be precise, Taylor's "Taylor's Version" version) clocks in at four minutes; ours took less than three. So the chorus required the first violin to play at a speed that would throw a shining light on Barry's lack of finesse. I said, "Don't be ridiculous. You don't have the chops to play that piece, and we owe our audience better."

He started to laugh, then saw my look and shut it down. "Mike, I know you hold yourself to a high standard, and I admire that. But we shouldn't confuse concern for the audience with concern for our own egos, or status or whatever you want to call it."

The inclusive "we." Such a diplomat. I'd have punched him in the mouth, if I didn't know I'd probably just miss and bruise my knuckles on his chin. He went on, "Hey, don't get me wrong. You're still the ace of the pitching staff. You're still the capo di tutti capos, and that'll never change. I'm not pretending I can play like you. But if I practice the hell out of it, I'm sure I can carry off that piece and no one will suffer. Not even you."

I gestured at Sandy and Meg, on their way back across the room. "They'd never go for it."

"So you don't mind if I ask them? The group being a democracy and all."

"Hell yes, I mind."

"I wish you didn't, because I'm going to ask them anyway."

I was seething. "Just talk your way into it, huh? You know what I hate about you? You think charm is a perfectly valid substitute for talent."

"No I don't. But it does help create a balance, when you're working with a really talented S.O.B."

I was still angry when I got into Sandy's SUV for the ride home. "You're not going to believe this. Barry told me he wants to play first violin on 'Love Story.' "

"He's serious about that?"

"He told you already?"

"He made some comment about it. Meg was showing me pictures on her phone of her baby nephew, who is like criminally cute, and Barry just came over and started blathering about flexing our muscles. I thought he was bragging about his free weights routine, but then he said, 'Like if I played first chair for one piece and Mike played second.' "

"And what did you say?"

"I said, 'That baby's got your sister's eyes exactly.' To Meg. Hoping he'd go away. And he did."

I told her that Barry hadn't been talking about his workout, and that he wanted to vote on it. She said, "That won't take long. One for, three against. Meg's never gonna go for anything that requires actually rehearsing."

"True. But I'm calling her anyway."

But once inside my apartment, I didn't feel like talking to Meg or anyone else. Instead I rummaged around the shelf where I keep my first aid stuff, and there it was: a small brown bottle of hydrogen peroxide. Diluted, it's good for all sorts of things, like disinfecting cuts or healing canker sores. But at full strength, it's poison.

Except how would I get Barry to drink it? Wait until his back was turned, then pour it into his water bottle so he'd gulp some down by mistake? The problem was, even highly diluted hydrogen peroxide foams up like a shaken can of toxic Budweiser. The spume erupting from his lips would be a dead giveaway that something was off.

I could knock him unconscious with a club and then force-feed it to him, but he'd probably start choking and wake himself up. And anyway, if I was going to hit him over the head hard enough to knock him unconscious, why not just hit him a little harder and kill him that way?

As if I knew the difference in the clubbing force required to kill someone rather than just knock them out. What do you use as a club, anyway? A baseball bat? He'd see me carrying that a mile away. I'd have to dress up in a team uniform of some kind and pretend I'd joined a league. He'd never buy that, and anyway, I'd never do it. Those stretchy uniform pants are not tailored with guys like me in mind.

I put the bottle back.

"Question for you. Is there a bigger douchebag on this planet than Barry?" I was at my desk working, but a lot of my accounting job involves mindless tax-code compliance stuff, so I was able to keep doing it while I finally called Meg.

I always liked talking to Meg. She had joined the quartet last, so I'd only known her as an adult. But to hear her tell it, she'd spent a lot of her childhood taking verbal abuse for being gay. She'd learned to give it right back, developing a spiky sense of humor that made her willing to talk shit about anyone with the least bit of encouragement. I was more than happy to get her rolling.

"Physically bigger?" she said. "Tons. But if you mean in terms of concentration, like douchebag parts per million. ... I'm still going to have to say, yes. You know, kidnappers, torturers, those kind of people. Unless we're just talking colloquially, in which case, no, there is no bigger douchebag."

"Okay, so then you'd never agree to let the world's biggest douchebag play first violin on 'Love Story.' "

"Wait—he actually wants to? That wasn't a joke?"

"He said he'd enjoy the challenge. As if he's not challenged enough trying to stay in tune."

Meg thought about it for a moment. "Well ... it's not like anyone would notice. And if it keeps the peace in the band ..." She likes to talk about us as "the band," like we're a bunch of hard-playing, hard-living rockers, i.e. the exact opposite of what we actually are.

"It won't keep the peace if it leads me to kill him. Murder is violent."

She laughed. "Aw, gee, Mike, if you took a human life, that would kind of make you a bigger douchebag than he is. I'd hate to see that happen to you."

"It isn't right. He should get to play first just because he wants to? What if I just decide I want to play viola?"

"As far as I'm concerned you can play all four instruments at once and bang a pair of cymbals between your knees, as long as I get my cut. I told Liz the other night that I wish I had the nerve to sell my viola, but I'd never forgive myself if that caused someone else to take it up." Liz was Meg's girlfriend of five years. She never complained about Meg's practicing, because Meg never practiced.

She added, "I mean, I could see how following someone else's cues for one lousy piece might stretch all of us, test the ol' communication skills and maybe, just maybe, cut the boredom factor by a hair." She dropped her voice to a hoarse whisper. "But not if it means taking a man's life."

"You're a real pain in the ass when you're being quote-unquote logical."

"I like to think I'm a pain in the ass all the time. But don't worry, I'll go with whatever the majority rules."

A week later, Barry managed to book another job, a corporate reception. He explained the purpose of the event to us twice, and still all I came away with was that the public relations department was giving the CEO an award for hiring them.

I had to hand it to Barry. With the quarantine over, he was definitely cashing in on the pent-up demand for string quartets (a phrase I never expect to use again in my lifetime). But he insisted on a having a Zoom call beforehand, something we'd never normally do, and I knew why: he wanted to pitch his big chair switch. It was just as well. I'd get to see his expression when the rest of us told him to fuck off.

He tried to ease into it. "I thought we might set up a rehearsal. We've already done two dates since the last one. With so much work to be had out there, I feel like we should be as sharp as we can."

"Uh huh," I said, in no mood to be warmed up before the bomb dropped. "Is that the only reason?"

"Well, we talked about me playing first on 'Love Story.' I wouldn't mind giving that a try."

Nobody spoke for a moment, and I could see I was going to have to be the heavy. I said, "No, we didn't 'talk' about it. You said you were going ask everyone's opinions, and Sandy and Meg agree with me that it's a bad idea."

"Well, hold on," Sandy said. "It could definitely be a bad idea, but if we're going to try it without an audience first, I can't really object to that."

I said, "What? Since when?"

"If we'll be rehearsing anyway, it's not like it'll be a big imposition."

I wanted to ask her what the hell she was thinking, but this wasn't the time. I said, "So then it's a stalemate. Two against two. Sorry, Barry."

Meg said, "Actually."

"What?" I fairly snarled. I saw Sandy wince at my tone.

Meg was unfazed. "Actually, I said I'd do whatever the majority wants. And it seems like it's Sandy and Barry against you."

"Nobody's *against* anyone," Sandy said. "We have a difference of opinion on pursuing an idea."

I said, "For fuck's sake, Meg, you hate rehearsing!"

"I know. I'm worried the year off has mellowed me."

Barry laughed too hard at that, and that's when I started yelling. "What is this, a coup?" Some part of my mind registered that I was losing it, but not the part that controls volume.

Everyone was just staring through their laptop cameras at me. Finally, Sandy spoke. "Mike, a coup is when you illegally overthrow your leader. We don't have a leader. We're a quartet."

"I can fix that!" I was practically spitting. "Why don't you three just do this gig as a trio? I've got a great motto for your new business cards: 'What's the difference? No one's listening anyway!' "

And I clicked "Leave." And then the "Leave Meeting" box came up and I had to click again, and then there was that horrible moment where everything was frozen and I didn't know if they could see me or not so I just had to keep glaring, but then finally I was out.

I was still sitting at my computer an hour later when the front door buzzer went off. I had been researching punji sticks, a booby trap I'd seen in a Vietnam movie. You dig a man-sized pit, cover the bottom with sharpened sticks pointing upward, then hide the whole thing under a mat of thin branches and leaves. When your victim steps on the mat, he falls through it and impales himself.

Three problems: one, it wasn't inevitably fatal. Two, there weren't a lot of places around town to dig large pits without attracting notice. Certainly the playgrounds were out. And three, the Viet Cong would smear the points of the sticks with animal feces, so at the very least their victim got an infection. That was a deal breaker. If you murder someone, but in the process get dog shit all over yourself, who's the real loser?

It was Barry at the door. "Mike, this innocent little idea I had has turned into a thing, and I think I've figured out why." He summoned up an apologetic smile. "It's because you don't understand how much I admire you."

I didn't actually snort, but I came close. "Careful, Barry. If you blow that smoke any harder, you're going to hyperventilate."

"Hear me out. Every time we do a job, I'm practically speechless at your playing. I don't want to fawn, because Meg would never let me hear the end of it." He pretended not to see me rolling my eyes. "Why do you think I'm even in this quartet?"

"To seduce as many brides' mothers as possible?"

"Come on. You know I don't have to do that." Even when he was being humble, he was bragging. "It's not for the money. Or because it's so emotionally rewarding to spend Saturday night as someone's sonic wallpaper. It's so I can listen to you."

I'll admit, that took me by surprise. I still didn't believe him, but I'd have believed it coming from someone else. I said, "I'm flattered. I had no idea you enjoyed listening to me, given how often you miss my cues."

"I may regret admitting this, but I've always thought playing second chair to you was like providing the frame for a great artist's painting. The reason I want to play first chair for one song, *one* song, and please don't laugh, is so that I can feel what it's like to be you."

Now I was really losing my bearings. The idea of him envying me had never crossed my mind. Barry must have seen me weakening, so he pressed on.

"As far as chatting up the brides' mothers, or the grooms' fathers or whoever, there's nothing wrong with being nice to someone who's paying you. But I promise you right now: if we do this, and someone compliments us on our playing, I will make damn sure that they know who's sitting in first chair for all the pieces but one. Because that praise is for you, and you deserve it."

I said I'd try it at rehearsal.

We held our practice at Sandy's parents' house, and they couldn't have been more thrilled to have us. Their living room had been our rehearsal space back when we had done it regularly, because with the windows closed the music didn't bother the neighbors. That's never the case with four loud instruments in an apartment.

So it was a little like old home week. Sandy's parents always loved seeing their daughter and her friends (there was no point in disabusing them on that score), and they liked the music, even with all the starting and stopping and constant repetition of the problem passages. Their presence also meant we were all on our best behavior, which was no small accomplishment given the way the Zoom meeting had ended.

And as we ran through the first few pieces, with everyone playing their normal parts, it dawned on me that this rehearsal I had so objected to was actually going to make my case for me. Because what was the best way to prove to Sandy and Meg that Barry couldn't play first violin? Let them hear him try.

In which case, what better way to show how magnanimously I was letting bygones be bygones than to be the guy who brought up "Love Story" in the first place? I picked my moment, and then tried to sound jaunty. "I'd say we know our regular set list in our sleep. So if it's okay with everyone else ... Barry, are you ready for your close-up?"

My friendly tone caught him off guard, and he responded as if we were best pals. "I was born ready! Let's do it!" He didn't realize I'd waited to make the suggestion until after Sandy's parents left to run errands. With them out of earshot, I wouldn't even have to be polite when I told him how shitty he sounded.

Barry botched the piece as badly as I'd known he would. It was clear he'd been practicing, so maybe half of what he played fell under the category of "barely acceptable." But when he got to the toughest run of sixteenth notes in the third chorus, he was completely unable to execute. He got so flustered that he was late modulating up a half step for the end even though he had the music right in front of him. I wouldn't even have to tell him how bad he was, because it was obvious to everyone.

Besides, he beat me to it. "Don't worry, guys," he said as he put down his violin. "We all heard where I flubbed. I'm going to put in an hour a day, just on the chorus, and I will *not* forget the key change. I promise, I'll have it down by the gig."

"You wanted to rehearse it, and we did," I said. "We still have to vote on whether to perform it. It's not working, we don't have a lot of time left, and our reputation is at stake." I was trying to sound analytical, not enraged. I wanted to smash his delusions of competence, but I knew I'd hurt my case if I started actually smashing things.

"Understood," Barry said. "So I'll put in two hours a day. And I'll tell you what else: I'm taking myself out of the vote. You guys decide among the three of you, and if you don't agree unanimously that I can play first on this, I won't. Any no is a veto, you don't have to tell me who it was, and there are no hard feelings no matter which way it goes. How does that sound?"

How did it sound? Terrible. Reasonable to the point of treachery. Obviously there was a catch.

But I couldn't find it.

Barry took off right after that, with Meg close behind. Sandy was also anxious to leave before her parents came back and asked her to stay for dinner, and she offered me a ride home.

In the car I said, "You heard the way it sounded. So I guess it'll be up to me to tell him officially."

She said, "What about him promising to practice?"

"Sandy, what would be the upside to doing this? He'll never play that piece the way I can."

She sighed. "Group harmony. A change of pace. A musical challenge. A chance for you personally to show how kind and generous you can be."

"I'm not kind and generous."

"Of course you are, when you want to be. It's so frustrating to see you get all prissy and selfish, since you're so much fun to be with when you're acting nice ... one imagines."

She smiled at me and I had to laugh, with relief as much as anything else. I hated being angry at her.

"Oh shit!" she said. "Is that a spider? I detest spiders."

It was, a daddy longlegs crawling across the bottom of the car door on my side. Sandy said, "Can you kill it?"

I told her to pull over and I opened the door. The spider crawled onto the doorframe, where I could have whacked it with my shoe, but it wasn't necessary. I leaned down and blew on it, and it scooted out of the car. Sandy laughed. "Some murderer."

Back in traffic, she said, "We can cover for Barry on the choruses. We can drown him out if we have to. And seeing you acting from a place of generosity would really mean something."

I said, "To him or to you?"

She smiled again. "Who cares what he thinks?"

And that's how I agreed to let Barry take the lead on "Love Story." It was a corporate party, not a wedding, so honestly, why *should* I care if it sounded bad for three minutes? We wouldn't be ruining anyone's big day, and I really thought it could change the dynamic between Sandy and me.

As we moved through the set I was dreading Barry's spotlight, until I realized I was actually looking forward to finally sharing his ineptitude with the world. He didn't disappoint. I guess he had worked himself up into a state of nerves, and when we got to the third chorus, he screwed up the fingering so badly that he actually had to stop playing. Sandy, Meg and I carried on as if nothing was wrong, and Barry jumped back in a couple of measures down, but the crowd's shocked reaction showed everyone I had been right all along. ("Shocked reaction" may be overstating it. One waiter who looked like he might play guitar glanced at us with a puzzled expression for a moment, and then went on collecting empty glasses. But my point was made.)

As the speeches began, I headed to the little office they'd given us for a dressing room. Sandy was already there. I said, "I did it. Pleasant Mike let it happen. He was awful and I didn't even gloat."

She gave me a big smile. "You were great, Mike. I'm really proud of you."

"So ... should we go out this weekend and celebrate? Dinner? I'll pick a place with live music, and we can talk over someone else's playing for once."

"Dinner ... you mean like a date?" She'd obviously had no idea that was coming. "Oh ... I don't think we want to go there, do you?"

"What do you mean? Isn't that what this whole thing was about? The rehearsal? The vote? Pleasant Mike?"

"Mike ... I'm seeing somebody."

I felt my throat thicken up as it all became clear. I said, "It's Barry, isn't it? You're fucking Barry. That's why you changed your mind about him playing first." It was so obvious. The two of them had worked me like a puppet, laughing the whole time, and would keep on laughing at me in bed tonight in between rounds of sex.

Except that as her eyes welled up, I knew I was wrong. She said, "No, I'm not fucking Barry. I just started going out with someone from work. But thanks so much for thinking I'd do that to you, and for assuming that any generous impulse I have must actually stem from the cheapest, shittiest motives possible."

I felt like a worm. "I'm sorry," I said. "I'm really sorry." But I was still furious and confused. "Then ... why *did* you change your mind?"

"Because Meg asked me to."

So it was Meg I needed to scream at. I left to look for her, avoiding Sandy's eyes. At the end of the hall I banged on the ladies' room door, yelling Meg's name. A voice I didn't know shouted back at me to fuck off. I headed out to the parking lot.

I found Meg's Honda, looked inside, and couldn't believe my eyes: Barry and Meg were in there with his pants down and her cocktail dress up. I'd been half right. Somebody in the group was fucking Barry, but it wasn't Sandy.

I banged on the car roof and Barry yelled, "Go away!" But I kept doing it until, clothes more or less back in place, they opened the doors and got out. Barry said, "Mike, what the hell?"

Meg just said, "Shit! Shit, shit, shit!"

"What's the matter with you?" I yelled at her. "You're in a long-term relationship! And for Christ's sake, you're a lesbian!"

I'd never seen her ashamed before. "Lesbians like the occasional dick too. Please don't tell Liz. Promise me, Mike."

"How long—"

"Not long. Just a few weeks. It's not even a thing, it's just sex."

"Just a few weeks? Just since he decided he wanted to play first on 'Love Story?'" I looked at Barry. "You slept with Meg so she'd vote yes?"

Barry said, "That wasn't the *only* reason."

She hit him in the shoulder, hard, and said, "You asshole."

"Bad joke," Barry said. He leaned his arm against the open doorframe of the car with what I can only call aggressive casualness, to show Meg and me that we were taking all of this way too seriously. "One had nothing to do with the other. We're just quartet fuck buddies."

I turned to her. "He convinced you, and you convinced Sandy. But why? What was in it for you?"

I could barely hear her mumbled answer. "Talking about it increased his, um, stamina."

"Oh my God." He did care about his performance after all, and so did she. But it had nothing to do with music.

I saw Sandy across the parking lot hurrying toward us. Meg said again, "You won't tell Liz, will you?"

"Don't worry," Barry said. "Even Mike wouldn't do that to a friend." He turned to me. "You wouldn't ruin Meg's life, would you?"

"No," I said. And I looked at his left hand, dangling over the doorframe of the car. "But I'd ruin yours." I took hold of the car door and slammed it against the frame and his index finger. Sandy got there just in time to hear the bone crack. It sounded off key.

I know it wasn't my finest moment, but before you judge me, let me say that it wasn't even a real break, just a fracture. The doctor told Barry he should be able to play again in a few months even though, to paraphrase the joke, he never could before. You can't even call it a premeditated attack. If I'd given it any advance thought, I would have brought a hammer and smashed all of his fingers, one by one. Next time, I guess.

There's even been a silver lining to all this, in the measure of peace I've found by finally accepting the fact that I'm no killer. Of course it helps that I've proven to myself I'm a maimer.

By the way, if anyone needs a first violin, I'm no longer with my old quartet. Pending the outcome of my trial I may be available. And I don't mind telling you, I'm playing better than I ever have in my life.

MEET ME AT THE MORGUE

Robert Lopresti

"Yes," said Pauline Sutcliff. "That is my poor, dear, Aunt Hilda." She burst into tears.

On the other side of the glass the morgue technician covered the body. Aunt Hilda, if that's who she was, had been a woman in her sixties. She had been found yesterday in City Park, lying on the path in front of a park bench. Her purse had vanished, but that theft probably happened after she died from what the coroner described as a massive heart attack.

But was this lady anyone's Aunt Hilda? We didn't think so.

My partner Frank Flood rolled his eyes and shrugged. It was his way of saying: *Crazy broads are your department, Lois.*

I steered Ms. Sutcliff down the hall to an interview room and got her a cup of tea. "We're sorry for your loss, ma'am. When was the last time you saw your aunt?"

"About six months ago." Pauline Sutcliff paused and sniffed again. Frank backed up. He claimed to be allergic to crying women, but he didn't seem to mind them if they were young and pretty. Ms. Sutcliff was in her late thirties and not up to his high standards. "I saw her at Uncle Max's funeral."

"And he was ..."

"Hilda's husband. They had their thirty-fifth wedding anniversary last year." She took a sip and frowned. "Gosh, this is awful. Do you have any herbal tea? Maybe mint?"

Frank went off in search.

"You never saw your aunt after the funeral?" I asked.

"I tried! But she disappeared. Didn't I make that clear?"

I frowned. A wife who disappeared right after her husband's funeral? Mighty suspicious. "How did your uncle die?"

"Cancer. They found it in October. He was dead by Christmas."

So Hilda was not a spouse-killer on the run. But why was Pauline Sutcliff claiming the woman in the morgue was her long lost aunt? "Are there any other relatives?"

"No. I'm the last of the Sutcliffs." She sniffed dramatically, if you know what I mean.

Frank had returned with some very stale peppermint tea. Now he jumped in. "How was your uncle doing financially?"

"Uncle Max left about three million dollars." She dabbed her eyes. "Now that poor, poor, Hilda is dead, it all comes to me."

My partner was trying to hide a smirk. "Boy, it's a lucky thing you recognized the picture in the paper today, huh? Otherwise your aunt might have been buried as Jane Doe and you would have had to wait five years to collect the money."

"Seven years," Sutcliff said promptly. "Remember, I live across the river. In my state it takes seven years to declare a missing person dead. So yes, I consider it a blessing from heaven that I happened to pick up a paper this morning and see the picture."

Frank's eyes were rolling so hard I thought they might pop out of his head.

"Ms. Sutcliff," I said, "Have you ever heard of someone named Ernest Beal? Or Rose Beal?"

"I'm afraid not, Detective Kurns. May I call the funeral home and have them collect poor, poor Aunt Hilda?"

I gave her a bland smile. "Still more paperwork, Ms. Sutcliff. Give us a minute."

Frank barely waited until the door was shut behind us to express his opinion. "The nerve of some people!"

"Let's try to keep an open mind," I said, although I agreed with him.

"She keeps talking about 'poor Aunt Hilda,' but her aunt was rich and that's why the niece is claiming this corpse is her."

"Now, Frank, you know how the lieutenant hates us to jump to conclusions."

He winced. Two days ago we had gone to the convention center to serve a warrant on a sleazy businessman. Unfortunately, we went to the wrong room and put the cuffs on the CEO of a Fortune 500 company. Our mayor had spent years trying to sweet-talk this guy into moving his headquarters to our city and he had hoped to finish the deal that week. I still say it wouldn't have been such a big deal if a TV crew hadn't happened to get the whole thing on film.

Back at headquarters we had explained that the receptionist sent us to the wrong room, but the lieutenant just said: "Is there some union rule that says you can't double-check? Does the penal code forbid you to ask directions? Didn't they mention double-checking on the back of the cereal box where you got your badges?" The lieutenant liked to hear himself talk.

That's why Frank and I were assigned to the morgue today, taking statements from grieving relatives. The lieutenant said that even we couldn't mess that up.

So Frank followed me to the other interview room at the end of the hall. Ernest Beal was in there, slowly filling out forms. An hour before he had identified our Jane Doe as his wife Rose.

If Pauline Sutcliff hadn't come along we would have accepted his story without a blink. Now I gave him a careful once-over. He was about fifty and obviously had been a good-looking man once, but the years were taking their toll.

If Jane Doe was his wife, she must have been at least ten years his senior. Hmm ...

"I've just been on the phone to the crematorium, detective," he said. "They'll pick up Rose as soon as you give the word."

Frank was scowling and I knew why. Cremation meant no remains to be checked later. No second chance to get this right.

"How old was your wife, Mr. Beal?" he asked.

The alleged widower did some mental math. It took him a long time. Maybe that meant he was lying, or maybe he was just not a great mathematician. "Let's see. Rose is—uh, fifty-eight."

"And you said the last time you saw her was yesterday?"

"That's right. She went out early."

"Were you two getting along all right?" asked Frank.

Beal frowned. "Well, to tell the truth, we *did* have a fight that morning. I told her I wanted a divorce."

My partner was practically vibrating with excitement. "How much of a fight, Mr. Beal? Did it get physical?"

The maybe-widower looked startled. "Physical? I don't know what you mean. She called me some names and walked out. I was worried sick when she didn't come back."

"What do you do for a living, Mr. Beal?"

"Me? I'm retired."

"At age fifty? You must have a good pension."

"No. Rose has always supported us." He wasn't the least embarrassed about it.

Frank was trying desperately to catch my eye. I know what he was thinking. If you killed someone and, say, buried the body in the woods, identifying a Jane Doe who died of natural causes might sound like an easy way to tie up the loose ends.

"Can I take Rose now?"

"A few more minutes, Mr. Beal. Say, do you have a picture of your wife?"

He looked surprised. "She owned a few paintings."

"No, I mean a photograph of her."

He shook his head. "She always said I was the photogenic one."

Convenient.

With both interview rooms taken there was no place for Frank and me to go but the viewing room. Fortunately the shade was drawn.

"I changed my mind, Lois. The Sutcliff woman is telling the truth. That clown in there killed his wife."

"Relax, Frank. We don't want to jump to conclusions. Remember Mr. Mattock."

My partner winced. Mattock was the fat cat at the convention center we arrested by mistake. "Okay, then what should we do?"

I thought hard. "Fingerprints."

"Oh, please. The city is on a budget-cutting kick. Can you imagine asking the lieutenant to have the crime lab dust two apartments to identify a Jane Doe who died of natural causes?"

I could imagine it all right. I could hear the lieutenant yelling: "You two could screw up a free beer! You could tangle a yardstick! You could burn down a swimming pool—" He *loved* to hear himself talk.

"Let me try something," I said. I marched into Ms. Sutcliff's room and asked if she had any photos of her aunt.

She looked surprised. "No. Hilda hated cameras. Why?"

"Just a formality. Are there any close friends you want to call?" Friends who know what Hilda looked like, maybe.

Before she could answer Frank opened the door. I hardly recognized him because he was grinning. He waved me back into the hall.

"We've got a tie-breaker!"

"Come again?"

"A third person wants to identify the body. Now we'll find whether it's Hilda or Rose!"

I slapped him on the back. "Looks like our luck has changed."

"That's Mora Von Eck," said Donald Greenblatt. "I'd know her anywhere. I hope she—is there a problem, Detective Flood?"

Frank shook his head. "Something went down the wrong pipe." He looked at me, hoping I could pull a rabbit out of this threadbare hat.

"Have you ever heard of Hilda Sutcliff?" I asked. "Or Rose Beal?"

"No." Greenblatt was in his early twenties. He had on an expensive suit and a look of grim determination.

Frank and I exchanged a shrug behind his back. "What was your relation to uh, Ms. Von Eck?"

"My relation? She just destroyed my family, that's all." The morgue attendant had wheeled the corpse away but Greenblatt was still staring through the window. "Do you think she suffered much?" He sounded hopeful.

"What did she do to your family, exactly?"

"She was my father's business partner. Men's clothing, cut-rate, out on the Coast. She was the creative end, which meant she went around the country looking for expensive patterns to rip off."

He folded his arms and scowled. "Then my father had a stroke. He couldn't speak and could barely move. My mother asked Mora to take over until he recovered. But she didn't run the business; she *gave* us the business."

"How's that?"

"One night she burned all the paperwork she could get her hands on and disappeared. That's when we found out fashion designers weren't the only people she had been ripping off. She was more creative with the books than she had ever been with the clothes. She disappeared with all the money she could steal."

"That must have been awful," I said.

"It was. I was just a kid and I didn't know what *bankruptcy* meant, but our home was never the same again."

"I don't suppose you have a picture of her."

Greenblatt surprised us. "I certainly do." He opened his briefcase and yanked out a framed photograph. It was at least twenty years old and showed a bunch of smiling people at what appeared to be the ribbon-cutting for a new business: *Von Eck Shirts*.

My heart sank. "And which of these women is Mona Von Eck?"

"Right here in the center, standing next to my father."

I squinted. The smiling middle-aged woman could have been a younger version of Jane Doe. So could two of the other women in the picture. The picture was just too old to resolve anything.

Frank was losing his temper. "Let me guess, Mr. Greenblatt. By any chance is there some deadline coming up? Some statute of limitations about to run out on the money she stole?"

Greenblatt raised an eyebrow. "I doubt it. I assume all the money she stole is long gone, detective. But on the other hand—"

"Ah."

"My mother is dying. Dad never recovered from the stroke, and now Mother is dying of a broken heart, although the doctors said it's cirrhosis of the liver. It would be a great comfort to her to know that the woman who wrecked our lives is dead."

Frank nodded. "Sure it would. Lois, can I see you outside?"

I followed Frank out. There were no rooms left so we huddled in the hallway.

"They're *all* lying," Frank growled. "Pauline Sutcliff wants her aunt's money. Ernest Beal wants to explain his wife's disappearance. And this clown wants to grant his mother's dying wish. Let's bust them all."

"On what charge?"

"Interfering with a police investigation. Loitering. Hell, everybody's guilty of *something*."

"Think of the lieutenant, Frank. Let's do it right. Go ask Mr. Beal if he ever heard of this Mona Von Eck. I'll ask Pauline Sutcliff."

Two minutes later we were back in the hall.

Frank shook his head. "Beal is so vague I'm not sure he remembers his *own* name. He's not the fastest car on the highway, if you know what I mean. But he claims he never heard of Mona Von Eck."

"Neither had Sutcliff." I frowned.

"What is it, Lois? You've got that I-can-find-Jimmy-Hoffa look."

"There are too many coincidences here."

"Three people showing up to claim the same Jane Doe? I'll say."

"That's not the one I mean. Come on."

We marched into Pauline Sutcliff's room.

"Oh, detectives. Can I take Aunt Hilda now?"

"Still a few details, I'm afraid. Did your aunt have a job?"

The grieving niece looked surprised. "No, she didn't. Uncle Max was old-fashioned. He thought a rich man's wife shouldn't work. Besides, he was away so much of the time he wanted all of her attention when he was home."

"Max traveled a lot?"

"Mostly in Europe. His field was international law. He'd be gone for months at a time."

"And your aunt stayed home?"

"Well, she didn't like to go abroad. But her charity work took her around the country sometimes." Jane frowned. "What does this have to do with getting her body released?"

"Excuse us," I said.

Frank chased me down the hall. "Lois? What the hell is going on?"

But I was racing down to Mr. Beal's room. Before I could say a word the prospective widower announced: "Detective Kurns, I just remembered! I *did* know Mona Von Eck!"

"Yes? Who was she?"

"My wife!"

We stared at him. "You just remembered that?" asked Frank. Beal nodded enthusiastically. "That was her business name. She gave it up when we got married."

"What business did she used to be in?"

"Men's shirts. I used to be a model, you know. That's how we met. She closed the business and moved here when we married."

"Did she still work?"

He nodded. "She was in sales. Until she retired, of course."

"And that was six months ago."

"Right." He wasn't smart enough to be to surprised that I knew. "I think that's what broke up our marriage. Retirement. I was used to her being on the road most of the time. For the last six months—she was always underfoot, you know?"

"Excuse us."

"Let me see if I have this right," said Frank. We were out in the hall again. "Pauline Sutcliff's Aunt Hilda was married to a control freak who wouldn't let her work. But while hubby was out of town she traveled to the Coast and started her own business—"

"With a partner," I added.

"Right, with David Greenblatt's father. Did Greenblatt senior know Mona Von Eck's real name?"

"Probably, but he'd had a stroke, remember? Couldn't speak. And she burned the paperwork when she left. That was after she met Beal and fell in love. She stole the money to support her second home. For the past twelve years she divided her time between two husbands."

"I don't get it, Lois. Why not just dump the Sutcliff guy if she wanted to marry Beal?"

"Maybe she loved Sutcliff. Or his money."

"So who gets her money now? Good gosh!" He looked at the three doors. "Who gets her *body?*"

I shrugged. "We have to introduce these three survivors and let them decide on the next step."

My partner shook his head. "I know one thing. The lieutenant is gonna say that, somehow, this is all our fault."

"You got that right. You want what's behind door number one, two or three?"

Frank sighed. "None of the above. But let's get started."

We knocked on doors.

MANX: PRIVATE TAIL

Michael Mallory

I was just about to pull down the blinds for the night when I saw her standing in the doorway. I don't know how long she'd been prowling outside my office—a sleek piece of catnip in a tight sweater, with yellow almond eyes upturned at the edges and that rarest of all beauty markings, a symmetrical calico face. She wore a green hat through which her ears poked alluringly, and carried a matching handbag.

"Are you Mr. Manx?" she purred.

"That's what it says on the door, kitten."

More precisely, it announced it in gold letters: *Ruff Manx, Independent Investigator.*

"Mr. Manx, I have a problem."

"Why don't you come in and we'll claw it over." My office was just big enough to hold a desk and a guest sofa, to which I directed her. "Now then, Ms ..."

"Feliday. Lily Feliday. You can call me Lily."

"Lily. What can I do for you?"

"I'm being followed."

"I'm not surprised."

She lowered her amber eyes. "It's not like that," she said. "I hear footsteps padding behind me, but when I turn around there's no one there."

"Maybe that's because there's no one there."

"I want to believe that, Mr. Manx. I've tried to convince myself it's simply my imagination, but I can't ... especially now. Not after this."

From her handbag she withdrew an envelope and handed it to me. I opened it and slid out the letter inside. Unfolding it I saw that the sender had used the old wheeze of cutting words out of a newspaper and arranging them on the page. It read: *Kittens shouldn't poke their whiskers where they don't belong*. Not surprisingly there was no return address on the envelope. More surprisingly, there was no postage. "How did this arrive?" I asked.

"It was slid under the door of my apartment," she replied. "Do you understand? That means they know where I live."

"Who are *they?*"

"I ... don't know."

"Pardon the honesty, kitten, but you're not very convincing."

"All right, I do know. At least I suspect. I'm a reporter for the *Hairball-Examiner*. It's my job to poke my face into places that might cause others discomfort."

"Some bad cats, you mean."

"Mostly fat cats. I've been working on a story about how so many low-income apartment buildings are being bought up and the residents evicted."

"That sort of thing happens all the time, doesn't it?"

"Not at this level. The city's stray population has gone up four-hundred percent in the last eight months alone, and it all seems to be the result of the actions of just one cat."

"Care to offer a name?"

"I don't suppose you have anything to drink around here, do you, Mr. Manx?"

I went to the small fridge I keep in my office and took out a bottle of whole cream, poured out a bowl, and set it on the edge of my desk. She lapped some up.

"You really know how to treat a lady," she purred, as one drop slid seductively down a filament whisker.

"I try," I said. "Now tell me the name of the fat cat who's out to get you."

Leaning back on the sofa, she said, "Tango Puma."

The name didn't ring any bells and I told her so.

"Tango Puma is the most powerful unelected figure in the city, maybe the most powerful, period. I've traced the ownership of a dozen rent-controlled cat condos in town and it all leads to him. He's buying everything up through his holding company and evicting the low-rent tenants. That way the buildings can be redeveloped into luxury flats."

"Aren't there laws preventing that sort of thing?"

"Laws only apply to those who aren't above them. Cats with enough wealth and power, who know where the skeletons are buried regarding any number of public officials, don't have to concern themselves with laws."

"Sounds like a dirty guy, all right."

"Tango Puma is not simply dirty, Mr. Manx. He's mangy. Any more so and he'd be a dog."

"Pretty strong language," I said.

"Sorry, but it's true. He's the kind of alpha Tom who will stop at nothing to get what he wants. So if he discovers a reporter on his tail, looking for the truth of his dirty dealings, he'll do whatever it takes to silence her."

"Hence this letter."

She nodded.

"And you think he's the one having you tailed?"

She nodded again. "And don't bother asking if I've gone to the police, Mr. Manx. Tango Puma has enough officers on his payroll to qualify as a private security operation."

"I see. What does your editor say about all this?"

She sighed. "That's the most alarming thing about this. He told me to drop the story. That means they got to him too."

I didn't want to ruffle her fur, but she was starting to sound a little paranoid. "You're saying even your editor is one of *them?"*

"No, but ... how much do you know about the newspaper business, Mr. Manx?"

"Just what I read."

"The mission of any paper worth its ink is to bring the public the truth. Most have some version of that sentiment on their masthead. Information is our life's blood. But you can't breathe blood. You also need oxygen, and for a daily, that oxygen is called *advertising*. Unless it's owned by someone who's rich enough to keep it going without sales revenue, a paper lives or dies through advertising. So when an editor who is normally devoted to informing the public of the truth suddenly backs off and says to drop a story, it means someone holds enough cards to scare off advertisers."

"In other words, Tango Puma."

"I'd stake my life on it."

"How come I've never heard of this cat?"

"Because all his efforts to remain under the radar have worked. It takes a digging through a lot of litter to uncover who he is and what he's done."

"But all that digging is over," I offered. "Your editor killed the story, so why are you being tailed now?"

"Because I already know what I know," she replied. "Besides, *officially* the story is dead. What I do on my own time is my business."

I was starting to get the picture, and while she was hardly a damsel in distress, she needed help. "What is it you want me to do, Lily?"

"Keep me safe. Find out who's following me, and ideally get them to stop."

"That's a pretty tall order."

"I was told you were the cat for the job."

"All right. My standard rate is six fins a day."

She opened her purse and counted out the clams, laying them on my desk. "You'll start immediately, Mr. Manx?"

"I've started already. And from now on, it's Ruff."

"I feel better already," she purred.

"But as you've pointed out, whoever these cats are, they know where you live. Is there another place you can curl up into?"

"I can stay with a friend if you think it's necessary."

"I do. Do you know where the Milky Way Club is?"

"Of course."

"Assuming that you were tailed here, your shadows will still be outside waiting for you to emerge. You leave here and walk to the Milky Way. I'll be following from a distance to see who else is creeping around on little cat feet."

"What do I do when I get to the club?"

"I'll make arrangements to have a taxi waiting for you. The driver's name is Jinx. He and I go back a long way. He's a little scruffy around the edges, but he's good feline. Tell him to take you to your safe house. Got it?"

"Yes."

I picked up the phone and called Jinx, hoping he wasn't nipped up to the gills. I was in luck; I'd caught him just in time. "Jinxy, I need you to go to the Milky Way Club and wait there. You'll see a calico in a green hat who goes by the name of Ms. Feliday. Take her wherever she tells you. Right, it's on my tab." I hung up. Then I opened my desk drawer and pulled out my gato.

"Are you expecting trouble?" she said.

"Look, kitten, I'm not one of those cats who believes in that Aimee Semple McPurrson business about having nine lives," I told her, getting up and going to the wooden rack where I retrieved my coat and hat. "I don't buy that you cash in one ticket and then simply get the next. Maybe she's right and I'm wrong, but in the meantime, I don't take chances." I slid the gun into a pocket and escorted her out of the office.

It was a sultry sort of night, lacking enough breeze to move a whisker.

Whether intentionally or not Lily Feliday walked like she was trying to catch a fish with her butt. If her plan was to be noticed, it was working. Even if it wasn't, it was working.

She'd gotten only a couple blocks away from my building when two shadows appeared out of dusk. They were doing their best to not look like they were tailing Lily and failing. I was too far back to see what color they were, though when they passed a pulsating neon hotel sign, I could see that one, a big, long-hair, had a distinguishing characteristic: most of his left ear was missing. The other one was smaller and walked with his head down at all times, like he was afraid of losing it. They made no effort to approach Lily, but when she stopped momentarily to look in a shop window, they stopped too.

We stayed on each other's tails all the way to the Milky Way, where I spotted Jinx's cab, parked across from the entrance. I knew it was his because one of the headlights was out. Jinx kept it that way because he was missing an eye himself and felt illumination was needed for the working half of his vision only.

Lily saw the cab too because she picked up her pace. So did the shadowy fur-monkeys who were following her. As soon as I saw her get in the cab I relaxed, but only a little. I still needed to find out who the two stooges—Hairy and Curly—were. Once Jinx's cab took off, they seemed not to know what to do. Finally they started walking again in the same direction. I continued to tail them, but stayed a block behind.

The handy thing about hiring dummies to follow someone is that the dopes never bother to consider they might be followed in return. I stayed with them until they passed an alley. Then they stopped in front of a bar. It wasn't a class joint like The Milky Way, but a cheap dive called The Bite. After a moment's consideration, they went inside.

I deliberated whether or not to follow them in or just retreat, now convinced that the kitten wasn't paranoid after all. I was still deliberating as I walked past the alley. A second later I wasn't walking at all. I was diving head-first into blackness, someone or something having sapped me on the back of the head.

Not everyone who gets knocked unconscious blows their cat chow as part of the awakening process. I guess I'm just one of the lucky ones.

"Did you really have to do that?" a voice above me said.

"There was a sure-fire way to prevent it," I moaned, struggling to sit up from the floor of ... wherever I was. "You could have refrained from knocking my brains out."

There were two of them: one a fat, white Persian in an expensive suit and a small, wiry alley cat in a frayed sweater. Neither matched the appearances of the shadows I'd tailed earlier. The Persian had heterochromia ... two different colored eyes. The left was green and the right yellow. His cohort's eyes matched, based on what I could see through his perpetual squint. "Runt, clean up our friend's mess, would you?" the Persian instructed, and with a grumble the alley cat went for a towel.

My head felt like I'd been thrown from a height and landed on it instead of my feet. I was in the kitchen of what looked like a pretty plush little condo. Using the edge of the counter I dragged myself upright. "To what do I owe this annoyance?" I asked.

"To poking your whiskers where they don't belong," the Persian replied, and I recognized the phraseology: it was the same on that note Lily had received. "Next time, Mr. Manx, we might not be so amiable."

I reached into my coat pocket for my gun, but of course the gato wasn't there.

"Looking for this?" The Persian held up my gun.

"I was, yes. Thanks for retrieving it, Mr. Puma."

He began laughing. "You flatter me, sir. I am but a humble employee of Puma Holdings. A fixer, you might say."

Fixer is not a word a cat likes to hear. "Do you have a name of your own?" I asked.

"You may call me Mr. Farhad."

"I'm sorry, you said Furhead?"

The mismatched eyes narrowed. "Farhad. What is Lily Feliday to you?"

"Who?"

"Please do not assume I am stupid. The rather fetching feline who came to your office earlier this evening and stayed exactly nineteen minutes before leaving, who then proceeded to the Milky Way Club where she got into a waiting taxi and disappeared."

"You seem well informed."

"We had a tail on her, you see ... and having a tail is far more than anyone can say for you, *Manx*."

Runt laughed at that one, though I suspect he was prompted and rehearsed. I really didn't give a rat's about being tailless. I did not ask to be born a Manx, but I've never rejected it either. It's the way things are; you twitch the appendage you're dealt. But if Furhead thought he gained the psychological advantage by pointing out I'm a private tail without one of his own, who was I to deny him? "Har de har har," I said, trying to sound offended. "When you're done knocking 'em dead, Shecky Green-Eye, why don't you tell me who got the jump on me in that alley? I'd like to see them again sometime face to face."

"Sidney, Pete, come on in," the Persian called, and Hairy and Curly walked in from an adjoining room. "Here they are."

"I saw these two go into that dive bar," I protested. "They couldn't have clubbed me."

"Unless we came right back out through the alley door," Sidney One-Ear said.

"And waited for you to walk by," Scrawny Pete finished.

I guess that made me the dummy. "Okay, what happens now?" I asked.

"Now?" Furhead echoed.

"You know ... not yesterday? Not tomorrow? Not next week? *Now?*"

"You will be given a message to take back to Miss Feliday."

"Let me guess ... The message is, 'Stop investigating Tango Puma or else.' Right?"

The Persian smiled: a fangy grin I didn't much like.

"That is the tacit message," he said. "The verbatim message is this: If you ever wish to see Jasmine again, you will forget you ever heard the name Tango Puma."

"Who's Jasmine?"

"She knows. Now scat. You're beginning to bore me."

I turned to Runt, who had finished cleaning up the kitchen floor and was now holding a towel sodden with my cat sick. "What about you?" I asked him. "Do I bore you too?"

He looked at me with no expression, and then glanced over at the Persian.

"I will not tell you again to leave," Farhad/Furhead said.

"I don't suppose you'd return my gato, would you?"

"And you'd be correct. Now get your lack of tail out of here while you still can."

When I got back to my place, Jinx was waiting for me. He was trying to obscure himself in the bushes and failing, but I pretended I couldn't see him. It made him feel better. I even feigned surprise when he leapt out before I got to the door.

"Bastet, Jinxy!" I cried. "Don't do that?"

Jinx smiled proudly. "Sorry, boss. I've been waiting for you."

"Yeah, I had an unexpected delay. Did you make a note of the address where you dropped her off?"

"Sure did. It was a place in LaPerm."

"LaPerm, huh?" This friend of Lily's was a cat with means. LaPerm was the most exclusive neighborhood in town. Jinx rattled off the address from memory and I jotted it down.

"Anything else tonight?" he asked.

I shook my head (which was a bad idea, since the hive of stinging bees I woke up with inside my skull was still there) and reached for my billfold, withdrawing a few fins, which Jinx accepted with a crooked grin. "What time have you got, Jinxy?" I asked.

Pulling out an ancient pocket watch, he said, "Nine-thirty-five, give or take ten minutes."

It seemed later. "Thanks Jinx."

LaPerm was located in the north part of the city. Half-way there I wished I'd asked Jinx to drop me off before his evening out, I didn't think of it. Still, I sometimes thought better when I walked, and I doubted Lily would be curled up on the bed yet.

The address was a vintage bungalow on Burmese Place that was classy without screaming ostentation. I knocked on the door and a kitten answered it. She was gray and well brushed, but she looked like someone I didn't want to mess with.

"Who are you?" she demanded.

"My name's Ruff Manx. I'm a friend of your house guest, Lily Feliday."

"What makes you think I know someone named Lily Feliday?"

"Because I asked someone that same exact question earlier tonight and I was lying too."

"It's okay, Sabrina, he can come in," a voice behind her said. The gray reluctantly opened the door for me.

“Hello, kitten,” I said, stepping in.

“How did you find me, Ruff?” Lily asked.

“The reason I had Jinx bring you here so he could give me the address later.”

“That’s rather sneaky.”

“Being sneaky is my job.”

We went into Sabrina’s living room, which was warm and comfortable, with plush cushions on every sofa and chair. Sabrina curled herself in the armchair while Lily and I shared a sofa.

“I’m not looking for any trouble,” Sabrina said.

“And I’m not here to deliver any,” I said. “In fact, I’m trying to head it off. Unfortunately I used my actual head to do it.”

“What are you talking about?” Lily asked.

“I met a lieutenant of your nemesis Tango Puma tonight. His name is Farhad, and he likes to throw his weight around, even though I suspect he’s all fur and no cat. He gave me a message for you. First there’s something you need to tell me: who’s Jasmine?”

Her symmetrical face took on a look of shock. “Jasmine can’t be involved in this!” she cried. “Please tell me she’s not involved!”

“I don’t know. I’m just relaying the message. Farhad said that if you wanted to see Jasmine again, you’d lay off your investigation of Puma.”

Lily reacted like I’d clawed her belly. “Not Jasmine!” she yowled. “Please, not Jasmine!” Sabrina immediately leapt up off the chair and ran to her side, practically pushing me off the couch.

“Would you like to tell me who it is we’re talking about?” I asked.

“Jasmine Luna,” Sabrina said, cradling Lily in her arms. “Her daughter.”

I’ve already declared my opposition to being coshed on the head by some punk in an alley. But I’d take it any day over trying to deal with a hysterical feline.

By the time I left Sabrina’s place, Lily was resting comfortably, having been given some sort of knock-out nip. Even though I sensed Sabrina didn’t care much for me or my presence there, it was she who filled me in on the details. She and Lily had met in college and became roommates, and remained best friends after graduation. It was Sabrina who tried to tell Lily that the sordid Abyssinian with whom she’d become infatuated was a bad cat, and it almost broke up their friendship. Six months later the Aby had vanished but the litter was on the way. Lily was terrified she'd have a large brood, but it turned out to be that rarity: only one kitten. Given her youth and circumstances, Lily decided she couldn't take care of a little one and put her up for adoption. The baby kitten never strayed far from her thoughts though.

Then three months ago, having hired a detective to track down her birth mother, young Jasmine came calling. Mother and daughter quickly became inseparable, with Lily trying to make up for lost time.

Now this.

I asked Sabrina if she knew where Jasmine was living, and she replied, "Lily always carried that first letter with her." Going through Lily's purse, Sabrina found the letter, which noted that Jasmine Luna was living in an apartment building on Shorthair Street, which wasn't far from the big university in town.

"Can I keep this?" I asked.

"Take the envelope but leave the letter," she replied. "If she discovers it's gone, she'll freak."

I handed the letter back to Sabrina and then pocketed the envelope. "I'll let you know what I find out. In the meantime, keep her here and don't let anyone except me in, got it?"

"I didn't even want to let you in, remember?" Sabrina said.

"Keep those instincts up."

If someone was tracking me while I made my way to Longhair Street, I didn't spot them. That meant either they were damn good at what they did, or I was slipping. Even with my head still screaming from the bang it had received, I didn't think I was slipping.

The place was called the Claude Arms, and it was one of those late-century structures that was already looking shabby. Jasmine Luna lived in apartment 216, access to which would be a snap.

All I had to do was get into the building.

There was a buzzer system out front so I pushed the one for 216. After three rings I heard: *Hi, this is Jasmine ... I'm out on the prowl, so leave a message.*

I didn't. Instead I tried the button labeled, *Manager.*

"What is it?" a voice replied.

"Pest control," I said.

"I didn't send for any pest control."

From the sounds of his voice, the manager was well on his way to being nipped up for the night.

"Somebody sent for one," I replied. "I have a work order. Fleas, I was told."

"Oh, for Bast's sake ..."

A buzzer on the door sounded and I pulled it open.

Then I ran out of sight, assuming I had only a few seconds before the manager appeared. From my hiding spot in the hallway I was able to see a short-legged, fat, sand-colored Tom in a threadbare wifebeater march to the door and look around. Turning, I prowled down the hallway until I found the stairway.

Once on the second floor I followed the numbers to 216, and gave a soft rap on the door. Maybe it was too soft, since nobody answered. I tried again: still no response.

Getting into places I don't belong has never been a problem for me, but I took special care this time to leave no trace of the break-in. Pulling the long metal claw out of my hat band, I used it on the door. As it turns out, I needn't have bothered. The door was unlocked.

Pushing it open, I stepped inside and quietly called, "Jasmine? Anybody home?"

The apartment was dark and I was just about to turn on a light when I saw something on the floor: a figure lying face down. Visible in the darkness was another object lying on the floor beside the body. I easily recognized it.

It was my gato.

Without even pausing to think, I reached for the rod and picked it up. In an instant there was a blinding flash that turned everything white. Since I hadn't read that a supernova was scheduled for this evening, I assumed the flash came from the bulb of a camera. As I fought to regain my vision, I heard soft footsteps padding past and out the door.

"Oh, Sekhmet," I moaned. How could I have been such a chump twice in one night? I'd been led by the whisker to this place by someone who not only wanted me to discover the body, but was poised to photograph me standing over it ... with my gun in my paw!

I didn't have to scrutinize the body to know it had been shot and with my gato. But the very fact that this was *my* gato informed me who the murderer was. The last time I had seen the gun, it was in the paws of Farhad. Now it was here.

But who was the victim? Logic would insinuate that it was Jasmine Luna, though the prone figure looked more like a Tom.

Finding a small table lamp, I turned it on. It gave off just enough light to see clearly. Stepping carefully to the body, I could see the bullet hole in the figure's back. I knelt down and carefully rolled the body over.

"Oh," I uttered. This certainly changed things.

It was not a young princess lying dead on the apartment floor. It was Farhad.

The journey back home was a trip through hell.

With every step I expected to be assaulted again, or worse, see the police show up. The cops and I haven't always gotten along in the past. There are some on the force who would like nothing more than to see me put in a sack and tossed off a bridge. Up to now, the force never had anything on me they were able to make stick to my fur.

The photograph taken in Jasmine Luna's apartment changed that.

I'd give every fin I own to know who was behind that flash camera. Maybe Runt got tired of being ordered to clean up another cat's yark. Maybe it was someone else entirely.

But whoever it was had the edge over me: they knew what had happened to Jasmine Luna.

Once back in my apartment, I got undressed, pulled down a clean tongue-rag, got it plenty hot and wet, and then gave myself the once over. It felt good. Then I cracked open a bottle of Irish Cream, sat down, and tried to think. As near as I could figure, I had only one option: sit and wait to see what their next move would be.

I was convinced there'd be one.

At some point, aided by a few belts, I fell asleep.

When I awoke the next morning, a bird was singing outside my window.

I didn't remember ordering breakfast.

Since I had a fish in the fridge that had to be eaten, I decided to let the feathered little screamer live.

I was hungry, though, and the fish was good. After eating, I dressed, smoothed my fur, and headed to the office. I'd like to say I was surprised at all to find a squad of the city's finest waiting for me.

I'd also like to say I'm a dead ringer for Tyrone Pawer, but that's a lie too.

"Well, well, well, if it isn't the tailless tec," Sergeant Scratch Doland said as I approached. "Finally decided to show up for work, eh?"

"If I knew you were coming, Doland, I'd have picked some freshly-planted evidence for you," I said.

"You think you're pretty funny, don't you, Manx?"

"Yeah, I'm one of the Marks Brothers ... I mark police territory wherever I find it. For instance, I already know why you're here at my office, bright and early ... well, early, anyway. It's because you or some Russian blue at the station received a photo of me from an anonymous source."

"Do I hear a confession?"

"That it's me in the photo? Sure, I admit it. That I killed the victim in the photo? Don't be a dog. It was a frame-up."

"That's not the way the chief sees it," Doland said.

"Well, then, why don't you ask the chief who took the photo?"

"What's that got to do with anything?"

"It's got *everything* to do with this. Who stands in the dark room containing a body, patiently waiting with a camera? Someone who figures another chump is going to show up sooner or later, on whom the murder can be pinned. All that's needed is evidence. Or something that looks like evidence, like a picture of me holding my gun and standing over a body. Then once he's got his prize, the shutterbug hightails it out."

He thought (or as close as he got) for a moment and then said, "Who took the photo then?"

"I don't know, but I think the place to start looking for him is the office of Tango Puma."

"What's Puma got to do with this?"

"Farhad worked for Puma."

A nasty smile poked his whiskers upright. "You realize you've just admitted to knowing the victim."

"I met the victim," I told him. "There's a difference."

"Maybe I should take you in and let you explain that difference to the chief."

I suddenly had a thought.

"Sounds like a good idea," I said.

"What does?"

"Arresting me. Haul me into the station, where my one phone call will be to the *Hairball-Examiner*, telling them that I've been arrested to keep me quiet about Tango Puma's involvement in a murder."

"Now, wait just a minute—"

I held my paws out for the cuffs.

I could see him attempting to think, and not get very far. Finally he said, "I still have that photo, you know."

"So what are you going to do with it? Send it to the papers? Who's the first cat you think they'll call for a comment?" I smiled and pointed at myself. "Then I'll fill them in on the rest of the story."

He paced back and forth for a while, and then shouted, "Dammit, Manx! Why do you have to make everything so difficult?"

"Someone has to," I told him.

He paced a little more, and then said, "Okay, I want the truth. Did you have *anything* to do with the death of that guy in the picture?"

"I did not. I saw Farhad earlier that evening when he was very much alive. His goons knocked me out and then he took my gato from me. Whoever killed him used it, then planted it near his body in the apartment for me to find."

"You still have the gun?" Doland asked.

"I do." I handed it to him.

"I'll be keeping this for a while."

"Just don't get photographed holding it."

"One more thing, Manx ... why that apartment?"

There was no sense lying at this point since the police would have to be dumb as a damn dog pack not to know who lived there. "It's the apartment of a kitty named Jasmine Luna," I said. "She's disappeared. I was hired to find her."

"Are you telling me the truth?"

"Cat's honor."

"All right, you can go now. Get out of here."

"But this is my office."

"What? Oh, Bast ..."

Still cursing, Doland cleared out his officers.

Now alone, undistracted, and with the pounding in my head from the cosh finally taking a milk break, I was able to think well enough to come to a realization. I wouldn't have gone to Jasmine's apartment—right on cue, as it turned out—if not sent there by Lily's friend Sabrina.

Was she involved in this plot?

I needed to talk to her again, but I didn't have her last name so I couldn't look her up in the book. It would appear that another visit to her place was in order.

Before I could even get up from my desk, though, the phone rang.

It was Lily.

"How are you feeling?" I asked.

"I'm ... better, but what's going on?" she said. "Have you found Jasmine?"

"No, but there's a problem. In her apartment was the body of Puma's minion, Farhad. Someone put a slug in him."

"Who would have done that?"

"I don't know, but someone went to a fair amount of trouble to frame me for it. Can I speak to Sabrina?"

"She's not here. She went out to get some milk and food."

"You're not going to like this question, kitten, but I have to ask it. How much do you trust her?"

"Trust her? You can't think she's involved in Jasmine's disappearance."

"It's not impossible."

"I don't believe it."

"You mean you don't want to believe it."

"I mean I refuse to believe it."

Maybe that was better. If Sabrina *was* a part of this, and Lily started acting suspicious, that would tip her off. "Okay, forget I ever said it. I'll let you know as soon as I find anything out, but you'll have to give me Sabrina's number."

She rattled it off and I wrote it down. Then I asked for her friend's last name, just in case.

"Sylvester," Lily said. "Sabrina Sylvester."

"All right. I'll be in touch. Try not to worry."

"Oh, sure. I'll just curl up and sleep like nothing's wrong."

She hung up.

There was not much for me to do for the rest of the morning except listen to the radio. The Tiger game had been called on account of rain. Those pussies just hate to get wet.

I was in the middle of filing the stacks of paper from past cases when the mail came. It was mostly bills and other junk, but one envelope caught my eye because there was no postage or return address.

Someone must have hand delivered it.

Opening it up, I found a note reading:

YOU MUST HELP ME ...

THEY WANT YOU TO COME TO THE STORAGE BUILDING AT THE CORNER OF CATALINA AND CHATSWORTH TONIGHT AT TEN, OR ELSE

It ended there.

The note, that is; not the case.

I read it again and then noticed something, or thought I did.

From the pocket of my coat I pulled out the envelope Sabrina had given me, the one that contained Jasmine Luna's address, and compared it to this note.

The writing was the same.

I had an appointment this evening with ...

... Well, I wouldn't learn with whom until tonight.

I didn't waste a lot of time that afternoon.

Whatever I was going up against, I couldn't do it with an empty paw. Doland had my gato, so I paid a visit to a friend who runs an antique store on the edge of town. You can buy a lot of things there, but only his special, under-the-counter goods will keep you alive.

His selection was not that good, but I had no time to be choosy. After buying a caterday night special, its serial number scratched off, and a box of bullets, I went back home to wait out the day.

I thought about calling Lily to let her know we might be coming to the end of the case, but decided not to. I'd wait to see what the end was first.

A little after nine o'clock, I left for the rendezvous, not knowing what to expect. A face-to-face showdown with Tango Puma was my best guess. It was about ten to ten when I arrived at the storage building. Most of its windows were boarded up and it appeared on the outside to be condemned. Assuming there were still dozens of small storage spaces inside, each with its own locking door, there probably was not a better place in the city to hide a body.

I waited in the dark until ten. Then I noticed a light behind the door.

Someone was waiting for me.

Slowly and cautiously, I headed for the door. When I got close to it, it opened with a resounding, rusty squeak.

The Runt stood there. He stepped back to let me in, and even though he wasn't holding a weapon, I never took my eyes off of him.

"This way," he said, leading me down the corridor, which was lined on both sides with storage units. At the end of the corridor was a unit whose door was ajar. Runt nodded toward it. Reaching into my pocket and feeling my new friend, I approached it. As I got there, I grabbed the door and yanked it open. Then my jaw dropped.

Inside was Lily Feliday.

She was not tied to a chair, or gagged, or otherwise showing any signs that she'd been forced into the room. Neither did she seem surprised to see me.

"What are you doing here?" I asked.

"I got a message telling me to come here," she said, breathlessly. "They have Jasmine."

"I know. I got a similar message. Have you seen her?"

"No, and I'm about to lose my mind!"

"Oh, we'd hate for that to happen," said the Runt, who now *was* holding a gun. "Come this way and don't do anything heroic, by which I mean stupid. I promise you won't like the results."

I was suddenly impressed that he could speak in complete sentences. Maybe I was wrong about the cat.

Forcing us in front of him, he instructed us to turn the corner and walk down another, shorter corridor. Even if I'd tried to go for my gun, one or both of us would be dead before it was out of my pocket. "Were you the one who took the picture of me in Jasmine's apartment?"

"No," Runt replied.

"Then who was?"

"Same one who put out Mr. Farhad."

"Sidney? Pete?"

"You think you know everything, don't you?" Runt asked cryptically.

Just up ahead was another open unit. Poking the gun into my back, Runt said, "In there, and no funny stuff. I mean it, Manx. No heroics."

I took Lily's paw and we stepped in together.

Seated in a small, plush chair was a young feline with the whitest fur I had ever seen. It seemed to radiate its own light. I couldn't help wondering if she would glow in the dark. Her narrow, blue eyes turned toward Lily, who gasped and cried "Jasmine!"

She started to run toward her until Runt hollered, "Stop!"

Jasmine then got out of the chair and walked up to us.

"Have they hurt you?" Lily asked.

"They who?" Jasmine replied with a grin.

That's when it hit me like a bucket of cold water on the front lawn. "Oh, Bast," I moaned. "I've been an idiot up to this point, but now I finally get it. Lily, say hello to Tango Puma."

"You can't be serious," Lily said, while Jasmine's smile grew wider.

"I'm afraid he is," she purred. "At least he's close. The part about his being an idiot is, however, spot on. I could not have led him around more effectively if I'd been using a laser pointer. As for my being Tango Puma, though, not quite. While I am CEO of Puma Holdings, I am not Tango. He was my father."

"That can't be," Lily said. "Your father was a no-good Abyssinian."

I was on a different thought track. "Why did you say *was?*" I asked. "Is Puma dead?"

"Yes," Jasmine answered. "He succumbed to a fatal attack of curiosity. He wanted to know what I was doing with his company. By that point he had discovered philanthropy, thinking he could somehow erase his past indiscretions by throwing money at good causes. Donating vast sums of money to the undeserving did not conform to my business model."

"How can you be Tango Puma's daughter and mine too?" Lily asked.

"She fooled you, kitten," I said. "I'd bet my last fin she's not yours."

"Quite right again," the Day-Glo white said. "My name is Caracal Puma."

"Where is Jasmine, then?" Lily cried.

"Dead, I'm afraid."

"You killed her?"

"I did not have to. She died of an overdose of methcathinone five years ago. You see, when you first started to become a thorn in my paw through your investigations into Puma Holdings, I had you researched from the tops of your ears to the tip of your tail. I found out about your daughter, and I found out what happened to her. When your activities became dire enough that you had to be stopped at any cost, I decided to get close to you by pretending to be Jasmine Luna. That was the name of her adoptive family, and a bigger bunch of nip-heads you'd never want to meet. She's better off dead, frankly. Not that she ever had much of a chance with you as her mother."

Lily reacted like she'd been smacked across the face with a rolled-up newspaper.

Turning to our captors, I said, "You two make a swell team. One's a runt and the other's a—"

"Don't get crass," Runt growled.

"Deal with them, Runt," Caracal ordered.

"Wait a minute," I said, playing for time. "I'm still not following the plot here. You pretended to be Lily's daughter to get close to her, to prevent her from digging into the dirt your company is doing ... but why? Just to obtain property? Just to tear down existing apartments and turn them into luxury cat condos? That might be unethical but it's not the stuff of catricide. Something bigger is going on here."

"You're right," Caracal said. "It was something that was too big for my father to accept, ruthless as he was in business matters. Of course the developments are important, because they lead to wealth, and wealth leads to power. But with enough wealth and power, you can change society itself."

"How so?"

"Puma Holdings controls sixty-five percent of all the housing in this city. Within a year it will be seventy-five percent. Our goal is one-hundred. And every unit of it will be restricted housing."

"Restricted?" Lily asked.

"*White* cats only. We are evicting all the brown and black cats, though we may allow calicos to live here, depending on their pattern. With nowhere to live, the blacks, the browns, the brindles will all be forced to leave the city, taking their murder, rape, and nip with them, or they'll be locked up in places like this. Then it will be time to spread to other cities."

"You can't hope to get away with it," Lily said.

"I already am, *mommy dear*," Caracal said. "And I'll keep getting away with it, unnoticed, until it is simply the new reality." Stepping past us to the door, she said, "Sorry you'll never live to write the story. Okay, Runt, you know what to do."

Lily began crying, but I shouted, "Wait, there's one more thing I need to know ... it was you who killed Farhad, right?"

Caracal Puma nodded. "Farhad's ego made him a liability. Using your gun was a nice touch, though, don't you think?"

"And it was you who took that picture and sent it to the police."

"Again, correct. There are certain things I do not feel comfortable delegating to subordinates. Unfortunately for you, though, your executions are not among them. I trust Runt to do the job quite efficiently."

"Which is the mistake *I've* been waiting for," Runt said, spinning around and pointing his gun at Caracal.

"What do you think you are doing, you cheap little ratcatcher?" she cried.

"That's Special Agent Cheap Little Ratcatcher to you," he stated. "Patch Simba, Feral Bureau of Investigation. Get your paws up"

This development caused me to laugh out loud.

"Mr. Manx, you may now take out the gun I'm convinced you're carrying," he said. "I want to congratulate you on taking my advice not to be a hero."

I pulled out my rod and trained it on Caracal Puma. "You know, kitten, you managed to answer yet another question for me ... whether or not you glowed in the dark. If it was you hiding in the dark in that apartment, and I couldn't see you, the answer is no. Maybe your lineage isn't quite as white as you think it is."

She hissed loudly as Agent Simba took her into custody.

Needless to say, Lily got the story of the year, one that shook the rafters of city hall and forced open the doors so quite a few rats could run out.

Caracal Puma was being charged with the murder of Ervin Farhad, though she had already lined up the top criminal attorney in town to defend her. Whether or not the white cat supremacy angle that motivated her would be an admissible defense in court remained a fish bone of contention.

I was finishing up my own notes for a much more mundane missing spouse case (like usual, the cat came back) when the phone rang.

It was her.

"Hey, Ruff, I had an idea," Lily said. "I've had a grueling week and I want to go somewhere to blow off some steam. How about you put some of the fins I paid you to good use and take me out this evening?"

"Sure thing. How about the Milky Way? This time, we go in."

"Sounds great."

“I’ll call Jinx and we’ll pick you up at eight o’clock.”

“And you’d better get your tail here on time ... oh, I forgot ... you don’t have a tail.” Then her voice dropped an octave and she added, “Maybe afterwards you should have Jinx bring us back here, and I’ll offer you a piece of mine.”

Me-*OW*!

BRICK FIEND

Joseph S. Walker

Thieves can sell unopened Lego sets, which are very difficult to track, almost immediately online for as much or more than the retail price. And if they sit on them for a while, it gets even better, because many of the bigger sets rapidly appreciate in value—at a rate much faster than inflation. In other words, they're money in the bank. Last week's back-to-back busts underscore what appears to be a growing awareness among criminals of Legos' street value.

—Vocativ, August 20, 2014

[France]'s police are investigating a massive LEGO theft ring that may involve international brick burglars. According to The Guardian, *three suspects arrested last June in Yvelines, France for stealing LEGO sets disclosed that they were part of a widespread LEGO conspiracy. Hailing from Poland, the thieves admitted that a series of LEGO heists were planned and targeted for sets that were popular among collectors.*

LEGO-related crimes are on the rise elsewhere.

—Mental Floss, April 5, 2021

When the French police made their big bust, things dried up on the streets almost overnight as the big boys scrambled for a new pipeline. I sensed that bad times were coming and managed to score a Colosseum from a dealer downtown who bragged about a private source for Architecture fixes. Problem was, he knew what was happening, too, so it cost me twice what it would have the month before.

I'm telling you, I made that set last for weeks. Architecture, man. It's not for everybody, and there are for sure times when I need something racier myself, but I knew the sheer endless repetition of all those arches and columns would hold me for a while, put me in that sweet space where all that matters is the next brick and the rest of the world just gently detaches itself and drifts away. A guy I used to know blissed out on the Taj Mahal that way. When they found him, he had a smile of pure happiness on his face, and a minaret still clutched tightly in his fist.

Maybe you can't build it in a day, but even the Colosseum ends. When I went out looking again, things were grim. I struck out over and over before I finally spotted Scotty J, one of my most dependable dealers, lounging on a stoop. I sat a couple of steps below him. We didn't look at each other as we talked, and his eyes never stopped scanning the street, checking every window for the cops who sprang on him in every dream he had.

"Hook me up?" I asked.

Scotty grunted. "Pantry's kind of dry these days, Kev. What you looking for?"

"Jonesing for some Star Wars."

Scotty laughed. "Keep dreaming. I haven't so much as smelled a Microfighter in weeks."

"Ninjago?"

"I can *maybe* swing a couple polybags."

It was my turn to laugh. "Polybags? You that close to the bottom of the barrel?"

"Feel free to take your money elsewhere, asshole."

"Man, there's nothing out there. Guy in my building is so hard up he's doing Duplo. *Duplo*, Scotty. You can't let me sink to that level. Don't hold out on me, buddy. How much money have I put in your pockets?"

"I cannot sell what I do not have."

"You holding *anything* comes in a box? And don't tell me about that weak Chinese counterfeit shit."

"I do have one special item. Probably out of your price range."

"Try me."

"Got a Ferris Wheel, man. Last one left. Retired set, baby."

"You mean the big one, now?"

"Biggest carnival set ever, man. We're talking nine minifigs, twenty-four hundred pieces. Let you have it today for two large."

I was so astonished that I turned and looked at him. He scowled at me and jerked his chin at the street. "Eyes front, fool."

I looked back at the street, jaw clenched. "Be reasonable, Scotty. That's damn near three times what I would have paid a few weeks ago."

"You got a way to go backwards a month? I been holding this for one of my special customers, man. Act now while supplies last. You know you want it."

The hell of it was, I did. My fingers itched to feel the pieces snap into place, ease the subassemblies together. It wasn't as big as the Colosseum, but it would hold me for a while. I was opening my mouth to at least barter a little when a car came careening around the corner, a big brown sedan every brick fiend in the city knew by sight. I heard Scotty J swear and run into the building as the car rocked to a stop, halfway up on the curb. A uniformed cop charged out of the passenger seat and raced past me in pursuit. I stood up, wanting to just walk casually away, but Detective Lori Montefusco came from the driver's side and blocked me. She was a big, strong woman, and she swung me easily up against the wall.

"You know the position, snothead," she said. I really hate that name, which comes from *Studs Not On Top*. It's a perfectly respectable building technique, but every cop in the city thinks it's a hilarious insult.

I put my hands against the wall and Montefusco began patting me down. "You got anything in these pockets gonna hurt me, snothead?"

"Absolutely not, officer."

"Partner of mine stepped on a loose pile of two-by-two bricks one of you animals left laying around," she said. "Poor bastard was out a week. So you better not be lying to me."

"I'm clean. Swear it."

She went through my pockets. "Haven't seen you on the streets in a while, have I? You sitting on a big stash?"

"I gave it up, officer. Living the clean life now."

"Oh yeah? So what you doing jawing with a lowlife like Scotty J?"

"I got a right to talk to people."

She cuffed the back of my head. "You got the rights I say you got and no others, snothead. Turn around."

I turned quickly and put my back to the wall. You only have to meet Montefusco once to know you'd better do what she wants, quick.

"Enlighten me," she said. "Scotty J holding anything I should know about?"

"Ain't you heard? Nobody's holding anything."

"Nah, I don't buy that." She tapped a finger on my chest. "Hasn't it occurred to any of you pathetic snotheads that they're just running up the prices with this bullshit shortage?"

"We didn't imagine that big bust in France."

"Don't be a dope." She smacked my ear. "There's something big out there. I can smell the plastic. And you're gonna find out what it is for me.

You still got my card, right? Here, let me help you out." She stuffed half a dozen business cards down the front of my pants.

"Day or night, snothead. You hear about anything over fifteen hundred pieces, I want a call. I find out you copped without letting me know and we'll have words." She grabbed my nose and gave my head a shake. "Remember I know where you live, Kevin. I know where all my pet snotheads live."

By ten o'clock that night I was shaking. I tried taking apart an old Ford Mustang and rebuilding it, but that's like trying to get loaded by smelling scotch. Second time just ain't ever the same.

I was bouncing off the walls when I remembered Montefusco saying that she knew where I lived. For some reason it reminded me that I knew something too. Back a few months ago, during a time when the streets were littered with parts baggies from all the sets flowing on the streets, I had followed Scotty J one night, mostly just for the hell of it. I knew his civilian address, and he didn't go there. He went to a mostly abandoned building down near the waterfront, and I watched from across the street until I saw a light go on, up on the third floor. I made it for a stash house, but at the time the bricks were so easy to get that there was no reason to risk pissing off the people Scotty worked for by trying to get in. I just filed the information away, figuring it was something I could trade Montefusco if I got into something really hairy.

Now, though, I was a brick fiend with no bricks, which made things look very different. I thought it through. If Montefusco and her partner had managed to put a collar on Scotty, then he'd probably be inside at least until tomorrow. Even if they hadn't, he'd know better than to be out roaming the streets after having run from them. So if he was still using the waterfront building as a stash, it might be unguarded for the moment. Anyway, walking over to look was better than sitting around my place, trying to relive memories that just weren't sparking.

I took my time, spiraling in toward the building rather than heading directly for it, keeping an eye out for Scotty, or anyone who worked for him, or Montefusco's brown sedan. The streets were mostly empty. I crouched in a doorway across the street from my target and watched. There were no lights on anywhere inside the building, let alone in the third-floor window I'd marked. I waited for about half an hour. Nothing happened.

The window I had pegged was on a fire escape. I went into the alley next to the building and found a loose brick—a real brick, not a plastic one—and a busted umbrella lying against the wall. By balancing on top of a trash can and stretching myself as much as I could manage, I got the umbrella hooked over the bottom rung of the ladder and pulled it down.

Outside the window I paused again. I heard distant sirens and somebody yelling a few blocks away, but absolutely nothing from the dark room on the other side of the glass. After another twenty minutes, I used the brick to break the windowpane. It sounded like the loudest noise in creation, and I held still for what felt like forever, waiting to see if anything happened.

Nothing did. I unlocked and opened the window and eased inside. The place smelled terrible. The flashlight on my phone showed what looked like an abandoned apartment that people partied in sometimes. There were empty pizza boxes and liquor bottles scattered around a bare, dirty mattress on the floor. Cockroaches scurried away from the circle of light.

I shuddered and went into the next room. There was more garbage on the floor, but no furniture, and this was the only other room in the apartment, aside from the bathroom. The bathroom was so disgusting that I gave it only the briefest of glances.

I went back to the room with the mattress, my heart sinking. Scotty and his crew must have moved the stash, if it ever existed. I was about to go back out the window when I noticed a closet door. Without much hope, I opened it.

The Ferris wheel set was there, on top of a pile of loose clothes and bedding. The box was a little beaten up, but it didn't seem to have been opened. Heart thudding, I picked it up. If I could get it back to my place, I was golden. Scotty would have no way of knowing who had robbed him. Right?

The corner of something else stuck out from under the clothes. I kicked a few aside, and my breath caught in my throat. *Can't be.* I dropped the Ferris wheel and pushed the clothes aside. *It was.* It was an unopened 2007 Ultimate Collector Set Millennium Falcon, the original. There was another, later version, but the first was still a holy grail for brick fiends. I'd never actually seen one in person, and the last time I'd heard of one selling, it had gone for five times what Scotty wanted for the Ferris wheel.

I ran my hands across the front of the box, my fingers tingling. I couldn't imagine where a street-level dealer like Scotty scored such a piece, and I didn't care. It was mine now. I picked it up as tenderly as I would a baby. I thought about trying to snag the Ferris wheel too, but both boxes were heavy and unwieldy, and it would be a chore just getting home without running into somebody who would happily kill me for the Falcon. If I had to leave one set behind, it wasn't a tough choice.

That's what I was thinking when Scotty J walked into the room and flicked on the light. I'd been so entranced by my find that I hadn't heard him coming, but he was, if anything, more startled than me. His eyes dropped from my face to what I was holding, and his lips curled back from his teeth in a snarl. That was all I needed to get me moving. I dove through the window, turning to land on my back so I could protect the Falcon. The brick I had used to break the window was still on the fire escape. I took a hand off my prize long enough to grab it and throw it at Scotty, who was charging toward the window. I've always had a decent arm. The brick hit him full in the nose. There was a spray of blood, and he went down, but it was clear from his yell that he wasn't out.

I didn't hang around to check his vital signs. I half fell down two flights of the fire escape, grabbed the ladder, and rode it to the alley, falling roughly on my ass as it jerked to a halt at the bottom. The instant I was back on my feet I heard a loud, flat bang from above, and the keening whistle of a ricochet from some part of the fire escape. It seemed to take my brain a long time to put the sounds together and conclude that Scotty was shooting at me. My first thought was that he was insane to risk hitting the Falcon. I don't know what my second thought would have been, because I was running too fast to have one.

I flew for the far end of the alley, my arms wrapped around the box. I heard another shot behind me, then the sound of somebody coming down the fire escape. Maybe he'd break a leg. I got to the end of the alley and turned right, figuring to start zigzagging through the streets and alleys, trying to remember if Scotty knew where I lived.

I was almost to the next corner when a brown sedan came around it and turned my direction. I skidded to a stop, the headlights full on me. Blinded, I couldn't see the figure getting out of the car, but I didn't need to see her to recognize Montefusco's voice. "Freeze right there, snothead!"

I started to backpedal. I'd pay a steep price in bruises for running from Montefusco, but there was no way I was just going to give up the solid gold I was holding. I half turned away, looking desperately for some other route, and Scotty came running out of the alley. I don't know if he recognized Montefusco or if he was still completely focused on me, but he sprinted toward us at full tilt. His lower face was caked with blood, and he was firing as he came.

Two voices from the brown sedan cursed in unison, and then their guns answered, bullets now flying from both sides of me. My first instinct was to throw myself on the ground, but whoever survived wasn't likely to let me keep the Falcon.

To hell with it. I turned back toward the sedan and started running again, figuring the cops would be focused on Scotty. Montefusco yelled something at me, and then I was past her. I heard more gunfire and shouts behind me. I juked to the left and then right at the next corner and lost them. I had no idea where I was going, but for the moment I was free and clear, the box in my arms singing to me of the better world we would build.

THE COFFEE SHOP

Todd Wells

Abby opened the box, expecting a shipment of coffee filters. She was surprised instead to find a severed head.

Veronica saw Abby staring at the contents of the box. Always careful to never be more productive than anyone else, Veronica stopped stacking cups and walked over.

"What is it?"

Abby double-checked—it was definitely a head.

"Someone's head."

"Anyone you know?"

"I don't think so." Abby didn't really want to touch it. She pulled out the crumpled newspaper that had been used for packing and tilted the box to get a better look. But she still wasn't sure.

"Does he have both of his ears?" Veronica asked, peering over Abby's shoulder.

Abby used a pen to move the head's hair out of the way.

"Yeah, he's got both ears."

"Wait a sec," said Veronica, "isn't that your boyfriend?"

Abby looked more closely. She didn't have a clear memory of what Roderick looked like, but yeah, that could be him.

"He's not my boyfriend," corrected Abby.

"Well, not anymore," snorted Veronica.

Abby had been working at Arrhythmia for just over a year, ever since she graduated high school. It was like any other hipster coffee shop, in that some customer was always turning up his nose at the oat milk in favor of soy, or vice versa. The clientele was mostly friendly, and Abby didn't mind coming to work. Besides, she wasn't going to be there forever. She was saving up for college. By her accounting, every dollar that made it into the tip jar was another three seconds of class time.

Where Arrhythmia differed from other coffee shops was its location, which was next to an art school. That meant more dyed hair and piercings than usual, but also different was the way the students flirted with Abby and Veronica. Rather than try to get a phone number or arrange a meeting after work, once every week or so, a student would proudly hand one of the women a piece of his ear.

The first time a young man, head partially bandaged, presented Abby with his ear, she screamed and backed away. Veronica, irritated at the interruption of the video on her phone, saw the offered ear.

"Oh, I forgot to tell you. All the boys think if they act crazy like Van Gogh, they'll be able to paint like Van Gogh."

Still shaking, Abby stammered, "So, wh-what do you do?"

"Just take the ear and they'll go away. Most of them don't want to actually ask you out; they're just going through the motions."

Abby turned back to her suitor. He was clearly pleased with himself, grinning so wide that his lip ring was starting to tear the skin.

In no way comfortable with what she was doing, Abby held out an empty coffee cup. "That's very sweet of you. Thanks."

The young man, still beaming, dropped his ear in the cup. He raised his latte in a toast to Abby, then turned and left.

Flabbergasted, Abby looked back and forth between Veronica and the ear. "That's it?"

Veronica, already bored at having to explain how the transactions worked, had returned to her phone and was no longer paying attention.

Abby took one last look at the cup with the ear, dropped it into the garbage, and washed her hands.

Soon Abby's wonder and disgust at the pageantry faded, and it became part of the routine. Sometimes the ear came with a rose, sometimes with chocolates. Once she found an ear in the tip jar with a phone number paper-clipped to it.

Summer approached, and the ears kept coming. But Abby had stopped paying much attention to them. Her life had become more unsettled. Abby's savings from work weren't piling up as fast as she had forecasted. Recent calculations suggested that it would be one more semester before she could move out and start school. But her mother was not happy with the delay. She had heard about a business opportunity in Panama, and was impatient to get started. If Abby didn't hurry up and get on with her life, Abby's mother wouldn't be able to chase her dreams.

Meanwhile, Veronica's mood had turned ugly. It began one morning when a few of Veronica's friends had come into the shop. Arrhythmia was busy, but nonetheless, Veronica ceased all pretense of effort so that she could chat with her associates.

While Abby struggled to keep up with the orders, a boy approached, freshly bandaged, and gave her his ear. But he didn't leave. He was that rare bird who liked to talk afterwards. Abby groaned internally.

"So, what do you think? Do you like it?" he wanted to know.

Abby was trying to poke out a clump of cinnamon clogging up the shaker, and couldn't provide her usual attention and tenderness.

"Um, yeah, it's really nice." She was faking it, and he knew it. So he persisted.

"Well, how does it compare to the other ears you've gotten?"

Abby realized that her best shot at getting rid of him would be to go all in. She looked conspiratorially to the left, then to the right. "Okay, don't tell anyone, but this might be the best anyone has ever given me."

The boy grinned like a lunatic, nodded his head like a dog wagging its tail, and ran out of the store. Abby exhaled in relief, and refocused on the cinnamon.

Meanwhile, something must have gone wrong between Veronica and her friends. Abby was accustomed to Veronica's apathy, but once her friends left it morphed into a simmering hostility. Abby thought it best not to ask about it until Veronica cooled off a bit. And since Veronica never cooled off, Abby never asked.

And the final disturbance in Abby's life was that William, the store's manager, had returned. William was in his mid-twenties, or maybe his mid-thirties. Everyone who knew him described him as non-descript. He was a distant relative of the owner and treated the position as a sinecure. Since Abby had started at Arrhythmia, she had only seen him once or twice, as he had recently stumbled into his first relationship. The novelty of a girlfriend was taking up all his time, and Veronica made it clear that the new girlfriend was doing them a huge favor by keeping him away from the coffee shop.

When William's girlfriend came to her senses and broke things off, William returned to the coffee shop with a vengeance. Without offering any reasons why, he declared that things were going to change.

William's first move was to advertise that they would begin accepting payments for coffee in Bitcoin. That made the shop more crowded, as lots of people wanted to be photographed posing ironically next to the menu with the weird prices, but did nothing for actual sales. Trying again, he found inspiration in an article about how McDonald's saved money and reduced waste by making their paper napkins slightly smaller. Missing the point entirely, William hid the napkin dispensers behind the counter, so they were only available by request. He ordered Abby and Veronica to hand out just one at a time.

As might be expected, the napkin edict slowed everything down in the coffee shop, but it did have the unexpected side effect of raising Veronica's spirits. She enjoyed watching the customers get frustrated at not being able to find a napkin, and get more frustrated when she only gave them one. She also enjoyed telling William when Abby wasn't stingy enough with the napkins.

It all boiled over one morning in early June.

Abby's mother started things off with a casual mention of how she'd be spending the day learning Spanish, in anticipation of her big opportunity, if it were still available by the time Abby left for college.

At work, William had stationed himself in a corner, counting and numbering individual napkins; Veronica was texting a friend about the unfair burdens her co-worker was foisting upon her; and Abby was on her knees scrubbing the mold from the lining of the refrigerator door.

When Abby stood up to rinse out her rag, she was startled to find a customer standing at the counter.

"Oh!" she squeaked.

"Good morning." Roderick smiled, amused at catching Abby off-guard.

"Uh, yeah, good morning," answered Abby, gathering herself, "What can I get you?"

Roderick was still smiling, having missed, or chosen to ignore, the lack of cheer in Abby's greeting. "Oh, the usual."

Abby paused and looked at Roderick more closely. She didn't recognize him.

"Which is? ..."

"You know, when I came in last week ..." Roderick rotated his hand like he was prompting a child on stage. Abby only stared at him, so he continued, "I ordered a coffee ..."

Roderick cocked his head, waiting for Abby to finish the sentence. When she didn't, he spread his arms wide for the big finale. "Large!"

"You want a large coffee?"

Roderick beamed. "Exactly! Just like last week."

Abby nodded slowly, a little confused by the exchange. But, she supposed, compared to being handed an ear, it wasn't all that strange.

Once Roderick was holding his coffee, a large one, he looked at Abby with a shy smile. Abby had a lot to do, and was ready for Roderick to take his usual, and go. But she could tell what was coming next, so she held out her hand. It was Roderick's turn to be puzzled.

"What's that for?"

"The ear."

"What ear?"

"The one you're going to give me. Please, go ahead, I've got a lot to do."

"I, um, I was just going to ask you if you wanted to go out sometime, like after work, or something."

"Seriously? No ear?"

Roderick looked more confused. "I don't think I understand. Is that code for something?"

Abby couldn't believe she was having to explain this. "Yeah, you have to give me the ear first, then ask me out. I act flattered, but say no. And that's it." Seeing the bewilderment on Roderick's face, she added helpfully, "It's really simple."

William interrupted the confusion. He slammed a tall pile of loose napkins on the counter.

"Only 998," he grumbled. "We need to find a new supplier."

Roderick brightened at the sight of the napkins. He grabbed several off the top of the pile, and stuffed them into his pocket.

"Cool, thanks," he said to William, "I can use these at the breakfast place in my building, they never give out enough napkins."

Roderick turned to Abby, so he didn't see the look of fury on William's face. William was about to grab the napkins back, but was distracted because the top napkin on the remaining pile was slipping off. William lunged to save it.

Oblivious to the rescue mission going on behind him, Roderick continued, "I only moved here a couple months ago, so I haven't heard of this ear thing before—Get it? I haven't *heard* of it ..."

Roderick paused for Abby to laugh, but all she could muster was open-mouthed astonishment. So he continued, "I've got to get to work, but you'll, *hear*, from me soon." He tapped his ear for emphasis, and walked to the door.

He passed an older woman on her way in. "Top 'o the morning, ma'am," greeted Roderick.

Hardly aware of Roderick's existence, the woman muttered that she didn't have any spare change and elbowed past.

Meanwhile, William, in his efforts to save the one endangered napkin, knocked the entire pile off the counter, thus welcoming the older woman to the counter with the world's briefest ticker-tape parade.

The atmosphere in the coffee shop was deteriorating. William was yelling that Abby hadn't put the napkins away, and now they were all over the floor. Veronica was seething, for no apparent reason. The older woman approached Abby.

"Mom?" exclaimed Abby, "What are you doing here?"

"What's going on?" asked Abby's mom as she looked at each of the others.

"Your daughter is going to get fired if she doesn't concentrate less on flirting with her boyfriend and more on napkin conservation," spat William.

"Boyfriend?!" yelped both Abby and Veronica, though Veronica's was really more of a shriek.

Abby tried to object, "No, he's not, he's just—" but Veronica cut her off.

"I don't know why you need to show me up every chance you get."

"What?!"

"You've been sashaying all over the store, preening for all the boys. You've been hoovering up all the ears you can. You did it to embarrass me in front of my friends last week, even though apparently you've got a boyfriend. You, you ... ear slut!"

Abby felt there was critical information everyone seemed to be missing. She tried to explain, point by point.

"Okay, first, I don't know how to sashay. Second, I don't want any ears. Bring your friends back and I'll hide while you preen and hoover. And third—"

At this point, Abby's mom began crying. "Why didn't you tell me you had a boyfriend? I can't believe you're throwing away your education, and my new career in Guatemala, for a boy."

Abby was baffled. "I thought you said Panama."

"Don't change the subject!" shrieked Veronica. She turned to leave, but before stomping into the kitchen she hissed over her shoulder, "I hope you enjoy your boyfriend, and that nothing happens to your precious relationship."

"And you better keep him away from our napkin supply, or there's gonna be trouble," added William before gathering his fallen soldiers and retreating to the storage room.

Abby looked around, stunned. She turned to her mother, but was cut short.

"I'm just glad your father is dead, and doesn't have to see this." With a disapproving cluck, Abby's mother left too.

Abby stood still, wondering how everything had turned out so badly. She didn't hear the shop's door open. Nor did she see the stranger in the trench coat creep toward her until it was too late. She looked up just as he pressed his severed ear into her hand. Then he ran back out the door.

"And that was the last time you saw Roderick alive?"

Abby nodded at the detective. She tried to peek at the notepad, but the handwriting was terrible, so she just asked, "Do you have any leads?"

"No. We're pretty backlogged these days. We probably won't get to this for a couple months." The detective thanked Abby for her time, and stood up.

William stalked over. "Are you gonna take the head with you?"

"We'll try to send someone over. Just put it in the corner for the time being." The detective holstered his notepad, and left the coffee shop. Abby returned to behind the counter.

"Are you ready to help again? Or do you have another interview lined up?" Abby ignored Veronica's jab, so Veronica tried again.

"For someone who didn't like all the ears, you sure graduated to entire heads pretty easily." Veronica punctuated her taunt with a turn of the knob on the milk-frother. The blast of steam wraithed up around her snarling face.

William approached. He nodded toward Roderick's box, "It serves him right for stealing from us." He glanced suspiciously at the line of customers. "And, it sends a message."

Abby just kept her head down, her mouth closed, and refilled the 2%

milk canister.

Later, after the crowd had been dealt with, Abby called her mother. Anxious to explain the head, the ears, and the napkins, she talked and talked, while her mother just listened.

"I mean, it's just tragic, that he had his head cut off," concluded Abby.

There was a pause, before Abby's mom finally responded. "Is it?"

Abby was confused. "You're saying it's not tragic?"

Abby's mother paused again, before elaborating. "Well, it's certainly tragic for him. But now you're no longer weighed down by your relationship, and you'll be free to pursue your education. And move out."

"Mom!" wailed Abby, "he wasn't a relationship! He was just some weird guy I gave a coffee to."

"You said it was two coffees."

Abby got flustered. "Well, that's what he said, I don't remember the first time."

"That's convenient." Abby's mom let the sarcasm sink, then continued, "At any rate, he's gone, and you won't have any more distractions."

Abby was baffled. Why didn't a severed head in a box disturb anyone?

Abby said goodbye to her mother and hung up. She looked around. William had disappeared into the back, presumably to put the napkins into the safe. Veronica was handing a caramel Frappuccino to the last customer.

Abby walked over to look at Roderick. As she pondered next steps, the man who had just bought the Frappuccino approached. For a moment Abby thought she was going to get another ear, and was about to direct him to Veronica. But the man only wanted to look in the box.

"Is that Roderick Theroux? We were wondering where his head went."

"You know him?" asked an astonished Abby.

"Yeah. We work together. Um, that is, we used to work together. A couple days ago we found his body in the lab, but no head. We wondered where it went. No one thought of checking in the coffee shop."

As casually as she could, Abby asked, "Do you find a lot of, you know, headless bodies in your lab?"

"No, not really."

"Were there any clues as to how it might have happened?"

Roderick's co-worker took a sip of his Frappuccino.

"None. The only thing we found was a crumpled-up napkin where someone had written, "This is the last mess you'll ever make!"

Abby remained calm on the outside, but inside she was exploding. It was William! Perhaps the college offered a scholarship for crime-solving?

She was reaching into her pocket for the detective's business card as the man continued. "Yeah, it didn't make any sense. And then across the room we found a name tag that said 'Veronica.' "

This gave Abby pause. Could it have been Veronica? Or worse, could the two of them be in on it together?

The co-worker interrupted Abby's mental sleuthing. "And then I slipped on some pamphlets for beach timeshares, but they were in Spanish. And that made no sense, because Roderick said he was allergic to saltwater. So there was a whole bunch of weird stuff, but no," he thought for a second, "there weren't any clues. Well, I've got to go. See ya."

Abby looked around. No one was watching. She snuck out the door and ran around the corner. She called the detective. He didn't answer, and a recording said his mailbox was full. Abby groaned and walked back inside. And there she froze.

Abby's mother stood in the coffee shop, but she didn't turn to Abby. She was staring at William and Veronica, the three of them locked in a triangular standoff.

"Mom! What are you doing here?"

Abby's mother's gaze didn't waver from William and Veronica. "Just checking in on you, sweetie. Making sure you're okay."

Feeling that something was up, Abby approached slowly and carefully. Neither Veronica nor William looked at her.

"I'm fine. What's going on?"

"Oh, I had realized that some of the materials for my business opportunity were missing, and I thought I'd just swing by and ask your friends here if they had seen them."

"We haven't seen anything," sneered Veronica. "You should keep a closer eye on your things."

"What are you talking about?" asked Abby.

"Yeah, what are you talking about?" asked William, who appeared genuinely puzzled.

Veronica looked sideways at William and tried to hint, "You know, the, um, stuff, we left ..."

"Oh, right," William acknowledged his understanding with a wink, "the stuff."

Abby's Mother narrowed her eyes. "Oh, by the way, you're missing your name tag. Any idea where you might have left it?"

Veronica gasped. "You snake viper!"

Abby's mother looked at William, shaking her head. "Oh, you poor dear. You think you're in cahoots together? Take a look in your pile there. Where's number 197?"

William quickly shuffled through his napkins. When he didn't find what he was looking for, he looked slowly at Veronica, recognizing her betrayal.

"That's right," affirmed Abby's mother, with a nod in Veronica's direction, "She left it. At the scene."

Veronica folded her arms across her chest. "So it looks like we're all in this together."

Abby exploded. "In what together?!"

Abby's mother took a deep breath. "Honey, you see ..."

"Your mom killed Roderick," interjected Veronica.

Abby's mouth gaped involuntarily, but other than that, she didn't move. Perhaps she was waiting for her mother to contradict Veronica. But she didn't.

It was finally William who broke the silence. "You killed him too."

Veronica cackled, "Ooh, I'm sure the judge will believe you meant to turn the dial the other way."

"What dial?!" screamed Abby. "What is going on?!"

"Sweetie," soothed Abby's mother, "I couldn't watch you throw away your future, and mine, so I found where the boy worked and explained it was in his best interest to leave you alone. But he insisted he wanted to go ahead with his plan."

"So you killed him?" Abby couldn't believe she was having this conversation.

"Not exactly," said her mother.

"Ha! Oh, yeah, you did," corrected Veronica.

"He deserved it," added William.

"You see," continued Abby's mother, "while I was there, Veronica and then William arrived. They each had their own requests to make."

Abby looked at William. "Really? Because of the napkins? Murder?"

"It's not about the napkins. It's about money and power. A lax napkin policy puts us at a competitive disadvantage. It's the way capitalism works."

William punctuated his declaration with a clenched fist.

Not wanting to be left out, Veronica added, "And I told your boyfriend that if he knew what was good for him, he'd give his ear to me, instead of you."

"You murdered him for his ear?"

"I didn't murder him."

Abby's mother held up a finger. "Yes, you did."

"Well, so did you."

Exasperated, Abby tried to find the reasoning, though she doubted that any existed. "You all murdered him?"

William, Veronica, and Abby's mother all thought for a moment, then nodded in agreement.

"Sweetie, this is what happened: I arrived to have a pleasant talk with the young man and explain to him how important college was to your future. However, he was intent on making an ear for you and—"

Abby interrupted, "Making an ear for me?"

Veronica chortled, "That's right, he wasn't even willing to go all the way for you. He was scanning his ear, so he could print out a 3-D model of it. He was just going to give you a hunk of ear-shaped plastic. Ha!"

"So why did you kill him?"

Veronica clarified, "I didn't mean to, mostly. When he wasn't looking, I turned up the charge on the scanner, for a little extra zap. To let him know that I was serious. What I didn't know was that your mom had just done the same thing."

Abby's mother nodded and shrugged.

William piped up. "And I had to protect Arrhythmia. I turned the dial up a notch, too, so he'd think twice about trying to fleece us in the future."

Abby's mother continued, "He tried to explain that with the scanner he could print ears for everyone, or a giant clip to keep the napkins safe, or engraved door knobs for my real estate venture in Honduras."

Veronica went on, "So he put his head under the scanner to show us, and when he turned it on, the extra power just sheared his head right off."

"Cauterized it too. No blood at all," added William.

"But we still had to deal with you, and your ear fetish," said Veronica to Abby.

"And to let you know that you don't need a boyfriend right now," said Abby's mother.

Excited to deliver an admonishment as well, William added, "And to get you to stop encouraging customers to use napkins."

Abby's mother concluded, "So we thought it would be best to mail Roderick's head to the coffee shop, giving you a gentle nudge in the right direction."

Abby looked at the box in the corner as she said, "And you agreed to keep quiet about it, but just to be safe, each of you secretly left behind something that would implicate one of the others." They all nodded.

The silence was broken by the opening of the front door. A young artist with a bandaged head entered. He stood before Abby, then shook his head ever so slightly, and turned to Veronica. With as much pageantry as he could muster, he handed Veronica an ear. It was real, not plastic.

Veronica looked at the ear. Then smirked at Abby in smug victory. She took the hand of the artist and led him toward the door. "Let's go," she ordered. With a look of both hope and fear, he followed.

As they left they passed a woman on her way in. She and William locked eyes. They rushed to one another and kissed passionately. As they did so, the pack of napkins William had been cradling fell to the floor. He did not notice.

When the reunited couple's slurping noises finally stopped, the woman said, "You get one more chance." They left together, in a hurry.

Now alone in the coffee shop with her mother, Abby began, "So ..." but before she could get any further a man burst through the door.

"Oh, Audrey, there you are. I have good news! The project in Nicaragua fell through, but we found something better. There's some cheap land on the outskirts of Trenton. In New Jersey. We can build the resort there instead."

With puppy-dog eyes, Abby's mother asked, "You mean, it's not too late to invest?"

"Not at all."

Abby's mother whooped and pumped her arm, then collected herself. "You're on your own for dinner tonight, okay, sweetie?"

Abby nodded as her mother ran out the door with her business partner.

Now alone in the store, Abby walked over to look at Roderick one last time.

"Well," began Abby, but she couldn't think of anything to say. So she closed the box, carried Roderick's head out the back door, and tossed it into the dumpster.

ALL MY DARLINGS

Charlotte Morganti

I found the first one in my living room when I came home early on a Friday afternoon.

Heavy set, mid-thirties, the man lounged on my couch, a bag of kettle chips in one hand, the remote control in the other. His feet were shod in scuffed cowboy boots and propped on the coffee table in front of a pyramid of beer cans.

"Who are you?" I said.

Without taking his eyes off the basketball game on the flat screen, he said, "Boone. Unemployed private eye, at your service whenever you get your act together."

I blamed my lack of comprehension on my head cold. "Sorry, what?"

"Hey, lady, you're the writer. You dreamed me up. I'm tired of sitting around on your hard drive, day in and day out, so here I am. You shoulda told me you were getting off work early. I coulda tidied up the joint."

I recognized that attitude. It belonged to the detective in a novel I'd begun writing last fall. I watched beads of moisture trickle down the side of the topmost can in the pyramid. I counted the cans. Six. "Last time I checked, you'd sworn off drinking," I said.

"So I'm off the wagon. Sue me. You'll never win. Emma will see to that."

"Who?"

He lurched to his feet and sluffed toward my kitchen, boot heels smacking my newly installed hardwood. Sharp daggers pierced the throbbing in my head.

"Emma. Your Judge. You remember her?" he said over his shoulder.

"I can't believe you know her." I hurried behind him, examining the floor for scuffmarks from his boots.

He pawed through the shelves in the fridge. "And I can't believe you're outta beer! You should keep the fridge stocked, y'know? Oh yeah, Emma and I have snuggled up on the hard drive a time or two. God knows there's nothing else happening there. She would have been here with me but she went online shopping for a new merrywidow."

"That doesn't sound like Emma."

He leered. "That's what happens when you leave your characters to their own devices. They evolve. Emma's taken personal growth to extra levels. Now she's almost as hot as your mama."

My knees felt loose; my forehead was cold and damp. "My mother?"

"You betcha. Remember that memoir you started? What—two years ago? When you abandoned it, she was a single woman looking for love in all the wrong places. I gotta tell you she's pretty good at finding it. I'm thinking me, Emma and your mama—a mennajatroy."

"You mean ménage à trois."

What the hell was I doing? Standing in my kitchen discussing a fictional character's sex life. And correcting his pronunciation. The double dose of cold pills could have been a mistake. "I'm going to bed," I said. "Be gone when I get up."

"Fine, but here's the deal, lady. You got two weeks to finish the novel or I'll be back. Unless I have to return sooner because the beer's running low. I don't handle disappointment well, so don't let me down. On either count."

He scuffed his way toward the computer in my den.

The next morning, the house was quiet and empty. Resolving not to over-medicate myself, I set about making blueberry pies. I had pulled the first two from the oven when I heard a high-pitched jabbering coming from my den. I went to investigate.

A teeny blue frog stood on my desk under my iMac screen. He yanked on a piece of yellow and blue polka-dotted cloth that dangled from the USB port and muttered in that tinny way frogs do. "Oh me, oh my. It's got my tie."

I vowed to check the side effects of cold medicine more closely in the future. This petite guy with the polka-dotted tie and piercing nasal voice could only be Firppen, the blue frog who lived by a fjord in my unfinished children's story.

"I suppose Boone sent you," I said.

"Oh, hi!" Firppen said. "Yes, please, Boone wants more beer." He gave his tie one final yank and freed it. "My mate and I, we want our story. Can you finish it by tomorrey?" His stubby froggy fingers worked at retying the bow around his neck.

"No, absolutely not," I said. "I'm busy. Making blueberry pies."

I returned to the kitchen and Firppen tagged along, matching me hop for step. He sprang onto the counter, skidded across the granite top and bumped against a pie.

"Oooooh, hot, hot," he said, jerking back one hop. His eyes swivelled from one pie to the other. "I spies, with my little eyes, some blue fruity flies!"

A turquoise tongue flicked toward the nearest pie.

I swatted at him. "Get away from there, you brat."

Firppen leapt upward to avoid my swipe and landed with a sucking plop in the middle of the still-bubbling pie. He squealed and vaulted onto my shoulder, where he sat, stretching his legs in front of him, dripping hot, gooey blueberry juice onto my shirt. He shrieked into my ear. "Hot feet, burning feet. Ooh, ooh, fix my feet. For the sake of Pete."

As his tuning fork voice reverberated in my head, I saw myself ending his agony, and mine. I could silence the grating screech. I could take his neck between my thumb and index finger and squeeze. He was itty-bitty. It wouldn't take much strength at all. And I could go back to the peace of pies.

Turquoise tears dribbled off Firppen's chin and plopped into the middle of the blueberry goop on my shirt. I pushed the frogicidal thoughts away and filled the sink with cold water, then plucked Firppen from my shoulder and dropped him in feet first.

"Oooh, that's lovely," he said, doing the backstroke. "Nothing beats cold wet feet."

"You need first aid," I said. "Don't go away." Great, now *I* was speaking in rhyme. I had to get rid of Firppen before my voice turned tinny too.

I grabbed supplies from the bathroom, dabbed ointment on his now hot-pink toes and wrapped them in gauze. Then I carried him to the den and placed him in front of the USB port.

"Stay off your feet for a while," I said. "If you promise to go away and rest, I'll finish your story. How about that?"

"Well, okey, dokey," he said, "but don't be pokey." He hopped into the USB port and disappeared.

"Don't be pokey," I mimicked.

A deal was a deal. Even if it was with a frog from a fjord. I sat at the computer and opened my unfinished children's story. Firppen in the turquoise flesh was significantly more annoying than I remembered him on the page. Perhaps I could resurrect the entertaining frog I had created. I re-read the story to establish the mood. I placed my fingers on the keyboard. I watched a chickadee on a branch near my window. I looked back at the screen. No words came. I went to the kitchen, made myself a coffee, and returned to the computer. There I sat for an hour, typing a sentence, deleting it, typing another sentence, deleting that.

I watched the chickadee again. It was having a splendid day.

I returned to the kitchen and cut a slice of blueberry pie. It needed ice cream. I shut down the computer and went out to the store.

I heard fiddle music when I returned home with a pint of vanilla soft-serve. The crowd in my living room didn't surprise me—I'd been expecting more visitations. A chubby blonde studied the titles in my bookcase. Firppen perched on the edge of the dieffenbachia's pot next to another blue frog. From the red silk hat on her head, I knew this was his mate, Fiona. The two of them tapped their toes and grinned at the lanky fiddler. Boone and a woman wearing judge's robes danced a passable fox trot.

I tiptoed down the hallway, hoping to avoid them.

"Author! Author!" Boone said when I was almost clear of the doorway. The music stopped. I turned to face the group. They stared at me, unsmiling, arms and frog legs folded.

"Naughty you, running out on us," Boone said. "We took a vote. It's unanimous. Even the frogs agree. We've come out for good."

"What do you mean?"

The fiddler set his violin on the coffee table. "He means we're staying until you finish all the stories you abandoned. Do you realize you left my new bride and me in a horse-drawn wagon in the middle of an Alberta winter? At least you could have moved us indoors while you had your writer's block."

"I intend to finish your story," I said. "If you can be patient. I need to learn to play the violin, so I can write about you more realistically. The lessons aren't going well."

"Patient?" the fiddler said. "We've been on that freezing wagon three years, five months and four days."

The blonde snorted. "Violin lessons are a lame excuse. What's your reason for stopping *my* story mid-page? You get me to the point where I discover my lover is a con man, and then you stick us in a cheap motel and leave. A person can take only so much orange shag carpet."

"Aahh, well. I guess my train of thought was derailed."

"It's time to put it back on the rails," Boone said.

Blue frog heads nodded. "Get back," Firppen said, "on track."

"I would love to finish your stories," I said. "I really want to. Honest. But I have trouble with endings. I need a class in endings. Then I could finish them all, I'm pretty sure."

Judge Emma laughed. "Your mother's right. You never finish anything you start. A class in endings, give me a break. Anyone can write. It's not rocket science. Just do it."

Of all my characters, Emma was the most like me. How could she turn on me? And bring my mother into it?

Emma rippled her fingers over an imaginary keyboard. "Get to it," she said.

"Fine. Okay, you win. I'll finish things. But go away. All of you. And stay away until the stories are done."

"Nuh-unh," Boone said. "We're here and we're stayin' until you finish our stories and send them out for publication. Pizza and beer will be fine, thanks."

I left the bunch of them in the house and checked into a boutique hotel near Vancouver's English Bay, armed with a case of superb wine and my laptop. I stewed about how to write four short stories and a novel quickly. It was imperative to get these characters out of my house before all the beer and takeout Boone charged to my credit card bankrupted me.

Part way through my second bottle of wine I realized there was no need to write five separate pieces. If I could tie the characters together, I could write one story. All I needed was the link, the common thread.

Boone was a detective. Perhaps he could solve a crime with the others as suspects. What crime? Which character would be the guilty party? Where would I set the story? What motive? As the questions multiplied, my heart rate increased. This had to be a superb story, one good enough to be published or my band of malcontents would continue to haunt me.

And if I'd learned anything in the last few days, it was that I wanted to be rid of them.

I felt light-headed and out of breath, the first sign of a panic attack. Breathing slowly and deeply, I fought it down. I thought about the writers

I'd studied in creative writing classes. Writers like Faulkner. How would they handle a situation like this?

When the "aha" moment arrived, it was clean, crisp and pure. Perfection. And so simple, it made me laugh out loud. All I needed was one new character.

I opened a new document on my laptop. My writer's block disappeared and words flowed. I was giddy. This would be a story to end all stories.

A week later, I returned home. Boone and the gang were in my living room, of course. Beer cans cluttered the coffee table, empty pizza boxes littered the floor.

"Well, hey there," Boone said. "Glad to see you, at last. What have you got for us?"

I fingered the two flash drives in my pocket. "Give me a moment to load it onto the computer in the den. I'm quite pleased."

I turned on my iMac, inserted the red flash drive, opened the new story, and returned to the living room.

"It's all there for you to enjoy. Why not have a look at it? I'm going shopping. I know you'll be gone when I get back."

The six of them rushed to the den. I left for the mall.

I came home tonight to a quiet house. I flicked on the lights and put my new terrarium on the kitchen counter. Firppen and Fiona huddled, trembling, under the dieffenbachia. I picked them up and put them into the terrarium.

In the living room, bodies lay on the hardwood among the beer cans, pizza boxes and violin. Five bodies, each shot in the head.

Four I recognized: a pudgy blonde, a lanky fiddler, a robed judge and a seen-better-days detective.

The fifth was new. A guilt-ridden homicidal maniac just released on my hard drive that morning. It was good to see him in the flesh, even if it was dead flesh. A semiautomatic handgun lay near his right arm. His left hand clutched a note: "I killed the whole rotten lot of them. I have a hair-trigger temper and they pissed me off. I can't stand the guilt. Goodbye."

I had no intention of calling the police and trying to explain five bodies. I pulled the silver flash drive from my pocket and inserted it into my iMac. When "Epilogue" appeared on the screen, I returned to the kitchen, poured myself a glass of wine, and scribbled notes for my new business venture.

I was halfway through my Pinot Grigio when Irving, a bruiser in blue coveralls, stuck his shaved head around the kitchen doorway. "Quite the mess in there," he said, motioning toward the living room. "I suppose you want it cleaned?"

"If you would, please." I craned my neck to see past his bulk. "Is your crew on the way?"

"Yep. They should be easing out of the USB port about now."

"Fine. Do a good job and I will have more work for you in the future."

He saluted and sauntered down the hallway. I studied my notes and nodded. The concept behind "Dusters—Cleaning Services for Writers" was sound. Surely I was not the only writer who had a few characters they'd like to dust off.

Irving reappeared in the doorway. "What about those teeny blue frogs you got in that glass thingy? Want them gone too?"

"No, they'll be staying."

I added a note to the business plan: "To do: explain to Irving and crew why writers rarely kill off the animals."

GUMSHOE GUS: THE CASE OF THE MISSING GARDEN GNOMES

Jon Moray

Her name was Pippy. She was a hippie from Mississippi. The moment Pippy opened her mouth I discovered she was also a bit lippy. She was about forty, with makeup trying to get her to thirty, but made her look more like fifty, and had a mouth that went from zero to sixty in one sentence.

My name is Gustavo Gottem. Better known as Gumshoe Gus, private eye in a one-horse town named Lone Pony. My case load was running dry since I solved the Flag Day Fiasco, where I recovered all the town banners stolen from the Flickenflacker Flea Market. That capture was noted in the local newspaper right next to the Freddy "Filthy Fingers" Feloni obituary.

Pippy waddled into my office and plopped down on the leather cushioned chair that sounded like her butt had a lot to say. From her motormouth narration I was able to gather someone had stolen her garden gnomes.

"Garden gnomes?" I asked, reshaping the brim of my fedora.

"Oh, yes," she sniffed. "They are very valuable."

"To whom, Snow White?" I snorted.

She tsk-tsked at my facetiousness and informed me the thievery had been going on since the Flag Day Fiasco.

"If these gnomes are so valuable, why do you keep them outdoors?"

"They are garden gnomes, they belong outside, silly."

"What about Madison Square Garden? That is indoors," I said, flatly.

She looked at me as if I gave her a 'what's one plus one' question and she was struggling to come up with the answer. She shook off the mental calisthenics and returned focus back to her precious gnomes.

"Well, are you going to retrieve them for me?"

I was about to show her the door when I began reminiscing, I once had a gnome named Nome that was destroyed when my dad ran over it with his lawnmower. I cried, my dad laughed, and my mom tsk-tsked at his lack of empathy. "I'll take the case," I said, wiping away a sorrowful tear. "Tell me more about these missing gnomes."

"Well, there was Ned the Nutcase, Bobby the Bouncer, and Petunia the Pet Rock Whisperer, to name a few. Those are worth the most. Then there's ..."

I cut her off without interest for any more description. "I've got enough. I have a feeling if I find one, I'll find them all."

Pippy bounced out of the chair and dove at me for an embrace that would have landed her on top of me on the floor had it not been for the faux wood desk that was between us.

I showed Pippy out and returned to my desk to revisit the Flag Day Fiasco write-up in the newspaper for inspiration. My detective hunches were in full overload when I deduced that perhaps I should pay a visit to Flickenflacker's. Flea markets are infested with these gnomes this time of year. I must admit, even I was impressed with how quickly I gathered this lead. "Sherlock Holmes has nothing on me, and I don't even wear a cloak," I mumbled proudly, while spit-shaping my hair in a fogged mirror.

The next day, I drove my maintenance challenged compact vehicle to the flea market and it seemed to sputter its disapproval with loud roars every time I hit the gas pedal. I pulled into the gravel lot amid staring faces upon my loud entrance.

I snaked around vendors selling used bedsheets, expired canned goods, and doorknob memorabilia, when I came to a table displaying hand puppets as their wares. I noticed a handwritten sign hanging from festoon lighting that read "Feloni's Fabulous Finds."

I picked up a hand puppet that was designed as a baker while recalling the name Feloni was the name beside the write-up in the newspaper. "I read about a Feloni in the obituaries that died recently," I commented to the lady behind the table, while working the puppet as if it were making the comment.

She patronized my sentiment by picking up a hand puppet that looked exactly like her. "That was my husband, Freddy. He died of a heart attack after learning our nephew, Carlos Convicto was nabbed in the Flag Day Fiasco," she whimpered, while answering with her hand puppet.

"I am sorry for your loss," I lamented, while rubbing my hand puppet's face against hers. She did not realize I was the one who caught Carlos, however, I did grow a Fu-Manchu beard and let my hair grow out since that caper. I put down the puppet and was about to leave when I noticed the head of a garden gnome sticking out of a cardboard box behind her.

I inquired about the gnome, and she stammered they were not ready for resale and shooed me away as if I were a fly.

"Could the Feloni family be behind this caper as well?" I asked myself, while retrieving a mirror from my wallet. My reasoning skills were at an all-time high, I reasoned. "Columbo has nothing on me, and I don't even wear a raincoat," I mumbled to myself, with a satisfied grin that told the story of a man who is highly allergic to humble pie.

My next move was to get Pippy to the flea market to identify the gnomes and have law enforcement there to make the arrest. I called Sheriff Cherub, and he told me he would arrive after his back waxing appointment. He said he would bring a search warrant and someone to lift fingerprints. I then called Pippy, who said she could get to the flea market after her armpit waxing appointment. She said there was a man in uniform that was waiting before her.

I moseyed around the flea market, without thought of making a purchase, when I came upon a table selling salesperson repellent.

"Just a spray around your neck and salespeople will ignore you," a lady said, with bouncing eyebrows. I tried a sample and noticed she then sat on a stool and began reading a magazine, oblivious to my presence. I was convinced of the product's potency and bought a can, but not without her pimping an IRS Auditor repellent. I kindly declined and was on my way.

I met the sheriff and his assistants at the parking lot and guided them to Feloni's table. After producing a search warrant, Mrs. Feloni relented and turned over the box of gnomes. Pippy showed up and identified each gnome, one by one, with extreme affection.

A makeshift lab was set up for fingerprints and it was determined Pippy's fingerprints were the only ones on the gnomes.

"Those were bought by my nephew, Carmine Convicto, at a flea market the next town over," bellowed Mrs. Feloni. Carmine appeared as if by magic, confirming his aunt's assertion.

"It's a she said, she said, Gumshoe Gus. We cannot hold them. We have to interview the vendor at the other flea market," said Sheriff Cherub. "The goods stay here."

Gumshoe Gus's shoulders sunk with the sobering realization his summation was incorrect. He turned away and retrieved his mirror from his wallet. "Perhaps, I have nothing on Sherlock Holmes or Columbo. Looks like I might've dropped the ball on this one."

Carmine gloated at Gus's error. "Yep, it looks like you dropped the ball on this one, Gumball Gus," bragged Carmine, using a baseball player hand puppet to state his point, its mouth inches from Gus's ear.

Gus's eyes widened as an 'aha' moment hit him right between the eyes. "Check the hand puppet Carmine is wearing! Check for dirt from Pippy's yard! He used the hand puppet to steal the gnomes at their bases, thus no fingerprints other than Pippy's!"

Carmine gulped audibly, and attempted a getaway, but was tackled by Sheriff Cherub. Carmine confessed to the crime and the case was solved. Pippy got her gnomes back and all was well in the town called Lone Pony.

Gus pulled out the mirror of his truth, this time accompanied by a hand puppet. "Oh, Gumshoe Gus, no one has anything on you. You're the best," said the puppet, rubbing its mouth against Gus's cheek.

SIMPLE FAITH AND NORMAN BLOOD

Daniel Galef

It took only two sips of port to realize that Norrie had just poisoned me. This put me in a frightfully awkward position, as *I* had just poisoned *him*. I met his eyes, and I could tell that he had become aware of the situation likewise.

"Strychnine, old chap? Awfully played out, isn't it? I ought to be insulted."

He tutted. "Hemlock may be *à la vogue*, but I put my trust in the corner chemist's."

Making no reply to such an aromantic philosophy, I cast my eyes about the room in search of some suiting sight to be their last. The high, green papered walls of the Rhopalic Club served admirably as a discreet background against which to play whist and plot murders, but offered little in the way of aesthetic beauty. Half-hidden and hung rather too high in the shadow of an alcove was a skilled copy of a Rembrandt painting, perhaps the *Sophonisba*. It would have to do.

For reasons known only to God and Normand de Blood, he took another sip of port. "Oh, yes, silly me," he said. The room was empty with our exception and soon would be empty without it. I lamented the company I was forced to keep in the final hour.

"My deathbed companions, you and that dreadful Rembrandt of Queen Sophonisba," I said.

"You mean *Artemisia*, I think."

"I most certainly do not. Observe the nautilus-shell goblet. It is plainly the *Sophonisba*."

"Rather like an *Artemisia*, I should say. The goblet, for instance."

I made no reply. The Queen did not correct us.

"Whoever she is, then. Between the two of you, I do not know which is the worse drinking company."

"Damned unkind thing to say to your last friend in the world."

"That may be, but Queen Sophonisba—" (Norrie made to speak.) "—*or Artemisia*—never betrayed my trusting nature to whisper falsehood in the ear of my beloved-to-be or conspired with the post and the penny-black to sack the sacred temple of our domestic bliss. Our ... potential domestic bliss."

"Faith? Why, I thought she was a sister to you. What a foolish, romantic notion, poisoning me over an imagined indiscretion that brought only happiness to she you'd claim was wronged."

"Your happiness is like a beast's happiness. I am ten times more happy in my fine-felt misery than you are in your mindless contentment." I basked. "But why do me in, if not over Faith?"

"Oof. Pure spondulix. I know you left it all to Faith *cum loco familio* in the will. Your solicitor told me."

"Remind me posthumously to sack him."

"I do not think we will keep the same company in the hereafter."

"You wouldn't, would you? Just like a bean of your frock-coat morality to poison a man then pretend the high ground. You're Tupper without the sense of prosody."

"What I've got is a sense of pragmatism."

"Yes, how *did* you pull this one? You couldn't have got to the decanter. I had it under eye constantly because *I* poisoned it."

"I coated the inside of your glass with a spray-atomiser."

"And there I was about to summon the club steward for a fresh glass. That's genuinely rather clever. Good-o, Norrie."

For the first time, Norman appeared sheepish. "Actually, I read it in a penny novel. In the novel, it didn't work. I was a bit surprised that it did just now."

"I'm sure that had far less to do with your kismet than with mine."

Norman's brow furrowed in contemplation, a thoroughly alien expression in our acquaintance.

"A thought: The two of us, the club, the port—This will almost certainly be reported as a double suicide."

He was right. The tableau would suggest a fictitious familiarity between us, something of an insult given the situation in fact. To be buried as Norman's victim, or his slayer, was a black mark I had been reluctantly prepared to absorb. But to be buried as his *friend* ... I looked to the Carthaginian monarch for guidance. Her goblet remained poised.

"Should I perhaps leave a brief note, explicating the matter?" Norman asked. "Your insurance doesn't pay out in scenario of suicide. No point in robbing dear, sweet, simple Faith on top of everything."

At the mention of my beloved's hallowed praenomen I hardened. I gestured with a callous flick of my eyes to the corner, under the portrait. Inkwell and blotting paper sat on a small half-desk across the room; several of the club members were of literary persuasions (it was not a very good club), and it was found convenient to lay the stuff of scrivening at intervals throughout the premises.

Norrie followed my meaning and made to rise. Instead, he performed a sort of aborted shudder the result of which was his sliding grotesquely down in his armchair.

"I seem to be unable to move my legs."

"Ah! That's hemlock for you! Damned quick about its business! I tell you, it is the choice of the connoisseur."

I would not have said as much had Norman commanded the use of his extremities. His eyebrows twitched like a pair of beached eels as he tried to appear reproachful in his new semi-recumbent posture. I endeavored to affect a smile of cold satisfaction, but my own face and neck were beginning to feel extremely stiff and I saw from the reflection in the French-polished table that I had assumed instead a leering, lopsided rictus.

At that moment the club steward entered with a tray of fresh glasses (how like a club steward to be perfectly five minutes tardy!) and we at once appealed to him for assistance.

"Tell me *garçon,* is that painting just over the alcove the *Sophonisba* or the *Artemisia*?"

"That is to say, is it the *Artemisia* or, as it were, the *Sophonisba*?" said Norman.

"I believe it is titled *Judith at the Banquet of Holofernes*," the impetuous wretch opined. There was a moment of perfect silence. Then Norrie joined me in inviting the steward to sit down with us and have a drink.

SOMEONE IS TAKING OUR MAIL

Tim Miller

We haven't received any mail for three consecutive days, I tell my wife. Huh, she responds, on that line between statement and question. She is on Instagram. Something amusing, making her smile. She wants to keep watching. I think someone is taking our mail, I say. Monday, Tuesday, Wednesday. No mail? Not a single article? That's not right. Something is wrong. What? my wife says, stepping firmly into question territory. Something is wrong. Someone is taking our mail. She looks at me like I'm crazy. Why would anyone take our mail? I don't know, I say. I don't know. Well, she says, there's nothing we can do about it tonight. She is back on her phone. She is smiling again at whatever is on Instagram, a woman talking in a hot tub, wearing a visor.

Who wants to go get the mail with Daddy? But no one does. Not anymore. It used to be a highlight of the day. Getting the mail with Daddy. That was at the beginning of the pandemic. We pretended to ride horses, airplanes, spaceships ... For months we were unicorns, flying ... we rode scooters, bikes ... I was pulling them on wagons. It was a good break, getting outdoors, a small burst of exercise in the twilight.

Sometimes there was a fight over who got to use the key, who got to carry what. A pink envelope? Forget about it. American Girl doll catalogue? Goodnight Irene.

Does ANYONE want to go get the mail? But they are all on screens, tired from a long day of being on screens. All right, well, I'm going to get the mail. I walk down by myself in the late afternoon to the mailbox. There is nothing. I see Ted, pulling his garbage to the curb. Are you getting your mail? I ask Ted. He acts like I'm asking him if he still doing makeup experiments on monkeys in his basement. Maybe he is confused, like maybe I'm asking if he gets it, physically, himself. I haven't been getting my mail this week, I say. Oh, he says. We're getting ours. Not like there's ever anything good! I laugh that laugh you make when you pretend something is, at the very least minimally funny. Ted gives a shrug that says, sometimes these things happen, and goes back to get his recycling bin. I stand by the mailbox and think for minute, watching clouds march towards the sunset. I can see it will be a beautiful sunset, once the sun gets low enough. My mailbox is empty.

The mail is held together in two big, thick stacks.

Maybe it is the postal worker, I think, that night in bed. My wife is on Facebook. He seems a rather careless fellow. There was that time I came around the corner and he ran a stop sign and we almost had a T-bone accident. I shook my head at him, and since then have noticed his driving tends to be rather reckless. I told this to Ted one day and he shared some incidents where the postal worker drove by and *threw* packages out the window. Ted used the expression "homeboy." Homeboy just straight up tossed a box out the window, he said.

The mailman comes in the mornings. Amanda says he comes around 10:30. I am always working at this time. Do you think the postal worker is taking our mail? I ask my wife. Why would he do that? she asks. I don't know, I don't know. She is on Facebook. Why don't you call the post office tomorrow if you are that worried about it? I think I will. Is there anything you are waiting for in the mail? Not especially. All our packages come to the door. I know. So what are you worried about? It's just strange. Why wouldn't we get any mail at all? Four days now. Just call them.

Each stack has a thick rubber band around it.

My neighbor Bill works for the post office. He is high up. He works from home now, too, during the pandemic. We used to come home at the same time, shoot the bull in the driveways, joke about how one person might win if they pulled in twenty seconds earlier. I haven't seen Bill in months. My wife says Bill's mom had a stroke. I wish I could ask Bill, I think, as I sit on hold. I'm on hold a long time. I have to get back to work. I hang up.

The first stack is full of catalogues, magazines, and coupon mailers.

On Friday I walk to get the mail and a neighborhood kid is sitting on top of the mailboxes. He's a sneaky kid, always casting furtive glances, like he's up to something. I forget his name. Starts with an 's'. He was in Daisy's class a few years ago, in first grade. When I volunteered in the class, he called me *Dude*.

Once Daisy was sitting on the mailboxes and Bill walked up. I wouldn't sit on that, Daisy, Bill said. He said it in a nice way, with a smile. He's a nice guy. One time, halfway through the pandemic, he told me how highly accurate the mail system was, how rare it is for them to lose even one letter. He spoke extensively about his confidence in the system to handle mail-in ballots during the election. Bill is a good guy. I hope his mom is OK. It's extremely rare for them to lose one letter, he said. He used the word, "extremely." When they lose a letter, it is usually the fault of the carrier, he said. But that is one letter, let alone a week's worth of mail. He said the percentage of loss is less than a tenth of a percent.

The kid jumps off the mailbox and takes off on his scooter. He shoots one of his glances back at me. Sawyer. That's his name. Like Tom Sawyer. Maybe he is our stealing mail.

The second stack is a pile of envelopes, most of which are bills or junk.

On Monday there is a crowd of people by the mailbox. I knew something was up. There are a bunch of kids and two adults: Lyla and Julie. I see that they both have an armful of mail. They are always on top of anything happening in our neighborhood. If something is going down, like someone is going to move, they are always the first to know about it. As I get closer, I see and hear what the issue is. There's a missing cat sign. A brown tabby named Rusty. Friendly, not likely to leave the neighborhood, the sign says. I am standing on the fringe of the crowd. Some of the kids have seen the cat. Some of them know Rusty, or Rusters, as they call him. A search party is formed. There is a sense of urgency. The kids are shouting facts about the case. The cat has been missing for 24 hours! There are coyotes! One group is dispatched to make Find Rusters signs. The kids all rush off in groups to search different areas. They keep shouting. Not likely to leave the neighborhood! Lyla and Julie smile at me. The smile is because the kids are so excited, so serious. Julie's daughter is clamoring to go home and get the magnifying glass. To look for clues. She uses that voice adults use with kids when the subject matter is absurd. There might be whiskers, her daughter says. Ted comes up and gets his mail. All those kids are going to find are bones, he says. That cat doesn't have a chance. Everyone leaves. I check my mailbox and it is empty. I look over and Sawyer is watching me.

The junk mail consists of flyers for credit cards, car insurance, new cable subscription, an envelope that says: REFINANCE NOW! SAVE BIG $.

I have left two messages and sent an email, neither of which have received a reply from the post office. This is very troubling. I ask my wife: Do you think I should call Bill? What's he going to do? I don't know, I say. She is watching an episode of a show about long-lost families. He might be able to look into it, I say. Leave him alone, she says, his mom is sick. She had a stroke. Are you expecting anything? No. Not that I can think of. Why do you care so much? I don't know. It's just strange.

There is a blue envelope at the bottom of the second stack. It is a letter from my Uncle, wishing me a Happy Easter, one week late.

I can't sleep. I'm lying next to my wife, listening to her breathing, when I remember. I *am* expecting something important: my new ATM card. I haven't used cash since the pandemic began. My ATM card has expired. What do you need cash for? She says the next morning. I am tired and irritable. I spill coffee on my shirt. I don't know. I might need it.

I am walking down the street, empty handed, back from the mailbox. The missing cat sign is still there. The sun is setting and I moving from sunlight to shade in the patterns of all the trees that are planted equidistant from each other. Ted calls them parking lot trees. They are waving in the breeze, which is coming from the west. The kids down the street are playing baseball. The street runs downhill at about an eight percent grade, I'd say, and every time the ball gets past the catcher they have to chase after it. I hear a sound like a rock landing in the bushes to my right. Did someone just throw a rock at me?

I look over to my left and Sawyer is standing there. He takes off on his scooter.

There is a bundle of magazines at the bottom of one stack. An alumni magazine, an Education magazine from a teacher's union. *Writer's Digest. Good Housekeeping. People.* There are many catalogues for the clothing companies that my wife buys clothes from. There is one clothing company that sends me catalogues, from a shirt that I got for my birthday but was too big. I had to return the shirt for another size and they got my address. The clothes are too expensive. $40 for a t-shirt, faded to look retro. Now they send me catalogues every month. But I am not about to take the time to get off their mailing list.

I call the credit card company to cancel the ATM card. They don't have a record of my request. I send another email, leave another message for the post office. Rusters still hasn't been found. The kids form nightly search brigades. The adults think it's cute how the kids are all working together. A paw print is found on a nearby trail. Sawyer glares at me when he rides by on his scooter. I manage to get outside at 10:30 for our delivery and the worker is just leaving our mailbox. He is driving fast, too fast for a residential street. I wave for him to stop, or at least slow down, but he acts like he doesn't see me, like I'm invisible, like I'm not standing on the curb waving both of my arms, saying hey, excuse me, sir.

There are envelopes requesting donations from charities that have received them in the past. *Doctor's Without Borders. The Zoo. The Children's' Museum. The Food Bank. The Homeless Shelter.* Things are dire, because of the pandemic.

I write a note and put it in our box.

> *Dear Postal Worker,*
>
> *We haven't received our mail in over a week. Not sure why. Could you please stop by our house?*

I put the address, even though it's redundant. The next two days, every time I hear the doorbell I think it is him, but he doesn't stop by.

There is a small envelope from Brittany, likely a Thank You note, for my wife for throwing a baby shower. Brittany is pregnant with her second child. This is called a Sprinkle, my wife said, when she was ordering a cake one night in bed. Do you know that it has been almost two weeks since we've received any mail, I am about to say, but I know she is busy picking out frosting. That's when I remembered that I also ordered checks. The checks and the ATM. Also, tax season is coming. I am very concerned.

I am outside at ten. I am missing work for an illness that I do not really have. I am walking in circles, pretending that I am on a walk but really staking out the mailbox. The driver doesn't come. Did I miss him? Did he come earlier? Has the delivery time changed? No one is around. It's the middle of the morning on a weekday. This can't go on. The only person I see for the entire hour is a plumber. He stopped at Ted's. Something is wrong. Something is definitely very wrong. Why won't they call me back or respond to my emails or my note? I keep leaving more and more messages, each time less formal and less polite. There must be an explanation. Things like this don't happen without an explanation.

There is a bill from the HOA. I have been meaning to go paperless but it's just one of those things, like the catalogue, except that I think one day I will eventually go paperless.

Why do I care so much? My wife doesn't care. It is true that the mail is mostly junk. Another week goes by and I slowly, with great care and deep breathing exercises, decide that I don't care either. It's just mail. It will work itself out. With the pandemic and everything, there is so much happening in the world that does matter and is important, one person not getting their mail is hardly pressing. My fretting is disparate to the problem. It has no effect on The Big Picture. It's small potatoes. So what if the postal worker or Sawyer are messing with the mail. The ATM card and the checks are not more important than my mental health. I start laughing. It's funny. I had been worried *sick* about something so trivial. I ask my wife, can you imagine Sawyer trying to cash a check for a million dollars? What are you talking about? Nothing I say, and kiss her hard, on the mouth.

Each rubber band has significant tension proportionate to the mass of the mail.

I am waking up in the morning now and going for jogs. Each day I run farther. I am up to five miles. When I come back, sweating and out of breath, I coast past the mailbox and it seems to me a symbol of everything I used to value that really has no value. When I see people getting mail, carrying their armfuls of envelopes and catalogues and boxes, or I see them getting the extra key which means they should open another mailbox to receive a package, the key left dangling in the package box door that always is left slightly ajar, I realize that these people are going day after day, week after week, month after month, year after year, every day except Sunday, for something that is essentially meaningless. This is a meaningless task, I say to myself. There is nothing that they are getting out of this, nothing important. It is all trivial and outdated. Everything important can be done online. Emails. Autopay. It won't be long until the mail is completely obsolete. I am ahead of the curve, therefore, in not performing this ritual.

The address on the Easter card, though legible, is not level. The downhill grade of the address is approximately the same as the grade of our street.

My daughter asks, do you want to go get the mail, Daddy? I pick her up and twirl her in the air. I swoop her down between my legs. I tickle her. She is giggling and then laughing so hard it hurts. She runs from me but I grab her and twirl her in the air again. I look deep into her eyes and save away this memory for when I am old and infirm and she is out living her life.

I would get the mail with you if it was on Neptune, I say. Where's Neptwo? she says. I twirl her in the air again and again, then swoop her down and feel the laughter shaking her ribs.

I wake up in panic. Tax season is getting closer. I haven't received my w-2. I try to log into my checking account, but my password won't work. Is someone using my checks, after all? Would Sawyer, a third-grader, be sophisticated enough to change my password? I check my spam folder. Why haven't I received any response from any of my inquiries. I call Bill. It's the middle of the night. I leave a message, my voice frantic.

In the morning I wake up and run farther than I've ever run before. I feel calm when I return, walking past the mailbox, feeling my pulse.

And that is how it goes for another week. I am calm in the day and wake up in a panic. I call Bill, but his voicemail is full. I need answers. I cannot accept that something like missing mail has no explanation, is in fact random and without cause. There must be an explanation. In the morning I run farther and farther, my lungs screaming for air, my legs burning, until the calm comes. I am doing better than ever at work. You've been doing a great job lately, Daddy, my wife says in front of the kids. I like this you, she says.

This happier you. Let's keep him around, she says. When the kids aren't looking, she squeezes my bottom.

But I know something has to give. I also know that Sawyer's mom makes him go out for a bike ride every day after his virtual classes are over, at 1:30. I miss work for another day. I climb the hill with binoculars and watch him ride and stop at the mailbox. He is doing something. I am running down the hill. This is my chance to catch him in the act. I am running fast down the hill, faster than I have in years. I feel my foot catch a rock. My body is going forward but my foot, for a moment, isn't. I am falling. I am tumbling. I am in bushes getting scraped and cut. I hit something solid and everything goes dark.

I am home from a day in the hospital. They kept me overnight, just for observations. There is a bandage on my forehead. The doorbell rings. It is the postal worker. He is wearing a mask that doesn't cover his mouth completely. I see this from the couch. He hands each of my daughters a big bundle of mail. They bring the bundles inside. Hand them to me, I say. They want to start digging through them. In fact, my oldest does in fact begin rifling through the first stack. Hand them to me now, I say in the quiet voice they know means business. They hand them to me, reluctantly. The top stack contains a note. I don't remember putting our mail on hold, I tell my wife. There must be some explanation, she says.

THE KING OF LEUCHARS

David Messmer

My face tightened in a right awful squint, but I weren't squinting against the sun, though the sun shone brighter than it seemed. I weren't squinting on account of the stone walls of the buildings that closed in on Pitlethie Lane, either. There weren't any getting past the drabness of that street. Not even the black of the pavement could ward off the grey.

But amidst it all, plastered to the stone wall around the churchyard of St. Athernase, I'd found a lone bright spot. A neon orange sticker had somehow popped up on that wall—a beacon of colour so out of place as to cause quite a sensation all about town. Three such stickers had now popped up in Leuchars in the same number of days—the first on the window of Mrs. Winchester's flower shop, the second on the window of the school, way high up where Mrs. Bowring's classroom is, and now this one, on the wall surrounding the church. No one knew where the stickers were coming from, or why they were there. As the town's copper it fell to me to investigate.

The other stickers hadn't given up much in the way of clues. I determined to do this last one up proper. I'd wrestled up some traffic cones that almost matched the sticker for brightness and I'd run some police tape between them and the spikes atop the church's stone fence. I'd been aiming to set up a perimeter, but I'd run out of tape, leaving one side unprotected. There weren't many people about, I reasoned. No sense in bothering over it.

I stood inside the barrier of tape, inspecting the sticker up close when Keith McCairn came creeping down the lane. The cold brought out the spot of lead above his lip where I'd stabbed him with a pencil when we were lads. I can't figure why he didn't grow a mustache to hide that spot, though I suppose not everyone can grow a mustache as fine and dark as mine.

"You're blocking the pavement, Dod," he said.

"Aye. Got a crime scene." I pointed. The bright orange sticker offered its own explanation.

"Heard they put one on Mrs. Bowring's window," he said. "Bet that set her off right good."

"Aye," I said.

"Not as bad as that time Ross and I threw your pencil box out her window though." He chuckled a bit at that.

"Aye," I said.

"We were a cheeky lot back then."

"Aye," I said.

"Think you could move those cones in just a bit, so's they're not blocking the pavement?"

"Aye," I said, and pushed each cone over about half a meter with my foot. I still didn't hear him making to leave. Instead, he gave me a hearty clap on the shoulder.

"You'll figure this one out," he said, and there weren't any mocking in his tone. "Make your mum proud."

"Aye," I said. My eyes flicked for just a moment towards the church steeple where the weathercock creaked in the chilly breeze. I'd been trying not to think about my mum, laying in the ground just a wee bit away. I had work to do. Trust Keith McCairn to interfere just to ward off his own guilt.

"Well, good luck." He took back his hand and made off down the lane. "See you at the pub tonight?"

"Aye," I said.

Now that the cones were closer to the wall the tape drooped low in a sad sort of way. I took the whole mess down and peeled the sticker from the stone. The church steeple cast its long shadow over the lane while I trudged back towards the station, and the village faded from the lighter shades of grey towards the darker ones.

The next morning found my head in a frightful state, and I arrived a bit late to the police station—really more of a small office than a station, what with me being Leuchars's only copper. The blinds were drawn tight, letting only a few small stripes of cloudy light fall across my desk. I'd already polished my badge to an anxious shine and set my things right—made sure my nameplate sat at the front. A good nameplate that one; I'd carved it myself: "Sergeant Dod T. Georg" (there weren't room for the last "e," but everyone knew my name, so it weren't any bother). I took pride in that name, though most just made light of it. My mum didn't know that Dod is short for George, she just liked the sound of it. Three short letters. Spelled the same back to front. Suited me just fine.

Aye, the name made me proud. But I reserved my biggest pride for something else my mum had given me: a grand fountain pen with a feathered tip that rested in a marbled holder. I felt it a bloody shame that most of the police forms had carbons, forcing me to use the ballpoints I'd collected in my "World's Greatest Copper" mug. Aye, the fountain pen went mostly unused. But every now and again I'd have a fancy to draw it out like some ancient king plucking a sword out of a stone and put down my script in all the swoops and lines befitting such a magnificent utensil.

That day I didn't feel such a fancy. I just sucked on yesterday's lemon drops, though they were having a jolly time with the sourness already in my belly.

I pondered whether to have another when a sound thumped at the door, like some kind of row, only not quite. The doorway opened for an instant, then would have slammed shut except a shoe jammed itself into the frame—a tennis shoe as red as an apple. A woman's voice followed: "Stop testing my temper!" There weren't any mistaking the sophisticated Edinburgh in her t's, and the sultry Glasgow in her r's. No one in Leuchars talked like that, and her voice left me excited for the rare opportunity to make a first impression. She took some time to back her way through the door of the station, leaving me a chance to cover the missing "e" on my nameplate with the sack of lemon drops. She dragged a small boy—no more than six or seven—who didn't really want to be dragged. His smart blazer and creased trousers seemed out of sorts with his filthy hands, but the shock of ginger hair really caught my eye.

"Boys!" she said. "Always getting themselves into muck."

She said it without looking at me, leaving me to ponder how to respond. For her part she seemed more interested in arranging her boy to stand still and straight than she cared for what I might say. Her boy's properness seemed odd with her framing him from behind. She wore a tangle of white gym shorts over a suit of yellow spandex that were torn at the knee, showing off a few scabs that looked close to being healed. Above all that sat a mass of blonde hair too curly to be feathered into the latest fashions. Her eyes rescued the look—they put me in mind of the blue marbles I used to collect as a lad, and I found myself thinking about the days she must have spent in the sun collecting all the freckles splattered across her face.

She didn't let me dream for long. "I suppose you were always getting into the muck as a lad," she said.

"Aye," I said. The boy kept his eyes aimed at the floor.

"I like your name," she said, nodding at the nameplate. I readied myself for a joke. "It's a palindrome," she said. I'd never heard that word before. I returned her smile. She offered her hand. "Call me Heather. McRae." I found the pause charming. As if she weren't sure.

"Aye," I said. "And who's this?" The boy and I shared a long look, but his mouth stayed set against speaking.

"Nathan's a bit shy," she said.

"Me as well. As a lad. Do you know Catherine McRae?"

"We're staying in her house while she's away on holiday."

"You must be relation."

"Sharp," she said. "That's good in a copper."

I might have blushed. She squirmed into the seat across from me and gathered the boy into her lap. I minded not to stare when she stretched across my desk to hand over a few papers. Clearing my throat, I made as though I knew the meaning of what she'd given me. "How can I help you, Mrs. McRae?"

"Call me Heather," she said.

"Aye," I said.

"It's my ex-husband." She nodded towards the forms. "He's not supposed to come within fifty meters. I have this too." She handed over a small photograph of a decent looking bloke wearing sensible clothing and a sensible expression. I saw where Nathan got his hair. "That's him," Heather said. "Alan Scott."

"Scott?" He looked more Irish to me.

"I didn't keep his name." She'd misunderstood my question. "I'm looking for a clean break."

"I don't need an explanation," I said. I knew all about surnames, having always carried one that didn't match my mum's. My mum had always told me to be proud of my name, though I'd never understood the use of sharing a title with a man I'd never known. "Have you been in touch with the authorities in Dundee?" I thought the coppers in the nearest city might be more up to the task of looking out for the likes of Alan Scott.

"I don't need the authorities in Dundee," Heather said. She nodded towards my mug. "I've got the world's best copper on my side." I blushed then, there can be no denying.

"Here," I said, drawing a piece of paper from my drawer. With a satisfying scrape of wood on metal, I withdrew my fountain pen and started scribing in big, bold lines. Both my name and phone number came out in a flourish of digits, only I got a bit outside myself and the last bit went right off the page and onto her form, which still lay on the desk. Swiping at the ink just smudged a big blot into the margin.

"It's no mind," she said. "It's just a copy anyway."

I crammed the last digit of my number onto the paper, then handed the whole mess back to her. She took Nathan's hand and made to go.

"Keep these," she said, pushing the photograph and the stained forms back to me. She kept the paper with my phone number. She folded it in half while looking at my name plate again and giggling just a bit. "Dod." Her lips pursed nicely when she said it.

"Spelled the same, back to front." I'd always thought that clever.

"Aye. A palindrome," she said.

A palindrome. I'd learned something that day.

That night I visited the Commercial Arms, Leuchars's best pub. There weren't a second contender.

"Right on time, Dod." Ross Cooper stood behind the bar, swiping his rag at a glass that weren't as clean as the others. He always kept the place tidy, and stoked up conversations when there weren't anybody else around. "How's the case coming?"

"Nothing yet." I sat at my usual spot at the end of the bar while Ross poured me a pint.

"You'll get it, Dod. We all have faith in you."

"Aye," I said.

"Bangers n' mash?"

"Aye," I said.

There weren't many words between us for a bit. He got things set for the evening while I did a lot of thinking. When he brought me my food I showed him the picture that Heather had given me. "I don't suppose you've seen this bloke?"

"Can't say I have. Not from around here, I'll wager."

"Aye," I said, then started in on my grub. Something about the picture kept my attention. A good copper like me would need a sharp memory of this man. I knew that. But something else too. It might have been my envy—that whatever this bloke's plan, Nathan had the good fortune of seeing this face and knowing where he got that swoosh of red hair. Everyone called my mum's hair dishwater, leaving me to ponder the origins of my thick black whiskers.

Around the time Ross came to clear away my plate Keith McCairn and Scurvy were just making their way into the pub. Scurvy's real name is Liam, but we'd called him Scurvy since we were teenagers. I ordered another pint and kept to my conversation with Ross.

"You know anything about Mrs. McRae?" I asked.

"She's on holiday," Ross said. "Won't be back for a while yet."

"I meant the other one. Heather."

"Never met a Heather McRae. Must not be from around here."

"Aye," I said.

Scurvy gave me a look. "She that blonde lass, with the curls?"

"Aye," I said.

"I met her on my way over here. She was jogging, took a bit of a tumble. I had to help her up."

Keith had just gotten his first pint. "Was that all you helped her with?" he asked.

"For now." Scurvy's leer brought out his pock-marks.

"She a looker?" Keith leaned near my end of the bar, and Scurvy came up behind him.

Scurvy answered before I could. "If she keeps up with the jogging for a bit she'll be alright."

Keith gave me a long stare while he took a pull of his ale, the foam covering over the spot of lead in his lip. "Sounds like the two of you might have a rivalry going," he said.

"Nah," Scurvy said. "I don't go for mares that already dropped a foal."

"She's too good for you," I said, a little louder than I'd meant.

Keith put his hand on my arm. "Easy, Dod. He didn't mean nothing by it." He gave me another long stare. "I'm glad you've taken a liking to someone. Maybe you'll stop fancying Nora."

"I don't fancy Nora. Just like the way she makes sweets."

"I know," Keith said. "I'm just having a go at you. Can you imagine if you'd ended up with a confectioner? I probably saved your life, stealing her away like I did." He tried to give me a poke in my belly, but I swatted it away. Ross gave Keith a look from behind the bar that I weren't supposed to see. Keith's quick nod proved even easier to spot. He stood and made to go. "I didn't mean anything by it, Dod," he said. "Just having a go."

"Aye," I said.

"Hey Ross, set him up on me," Scurvy said, reaching for his back pocket.

"I can buy my own pint," I said.

He'd been too busy patting at his bum to hear me. "Damn, I don't have my wallet on me. Thought for sure I'd grabbed it on my way out. I'll get you next time, Dod."

"Aye," I said.

They left me alone as the pub slowly filled.

Another sticker popped up the next day—plastered right on top of the Murray's chimney. It sat in plain sight to anyone walking down the narrow lane we call Main Street. Squinting up at it made my head feel worse, but at least the clouds kept some of the brightness out.

"You make it home last night, Dod?" Gordon Fletcher, the town's butcher, waddled across the street to join me.

"Aye," I said.

"What you looking at?"

"Another sticker," I said. I took a moment to right my bobby hat, which threatened to tip off. Gordon had his hands tucked away in his coat, and a wool cap almost covered the greys in his hair. He leaned his whole self back and took note of the sticker.

"What's that, three now?"

"Four," I said.

"Spoke to Mrs. Winchester after that first one showed up on her window. Thought she'd about blow."

"Aye," I said. "These stickers are causing quite a row."

We both stared a bit longer.

"Remember that time you called the copper when we were chasing you with those stinging nettles?" He chuckled a bit at that. "And now here you are."

"Aye," I said. We both stared a bit longer.

"Your mum's birthday's coming up, no?"

"Aye," I said. "Day after next." I felt him look at me. The screams of children taking their recess played at the edge of our hearing. Gordon shuffled his feet a while before he made to go.

"How'd it get there?" I meant the question for myself, but Gordon leaned back again, likely pleased that I'd filled the quiet he'd made between us.

"Someone must have put it there." It's good that Gordon's a butcher rather than a copper.

We stared a bit longer before I said, "Any bloke could clump up the roof and put a sticker there. But how'd he do it without anyone seeing? And without waking the Murrays?"

"Dunno." Gordon had leaned back again, his mouth slightly open. "Could be a lass."

"Pardon?"

"You said a bloke. Could be a lass."

I pulled out my jotter and wrote "Could be a lass." I had my first clue.

Gordon made to go. "See you at the pub tonight?"

"Aye," I said.

That evening I made sure to stop by the sweets shop. Nora had cooked up some fresh tablet. Hers is the best in all of Fife—doesn't fuss about with vanilla like some and isn't afraid to heat the sugar real slow. Despite the chill in the air I felt my spirits aiming up a bit as I made my way to the pub by the light of the street lamps.

I'd just popped a bit of tablet in my mouth when I heard a clutter in front of me. The noise came from the McRae cottage where a door opened and a leg poked out, ending in a familiar red tennis shoe. I knew the voice from its t's and r's. "I'm trying to take my run, be sure the dog won't get out," she said to someone in the cottage as she snaked her body through the narrow opening. Something barked inside.

"Hello, Heather," I said. She wore spandex again, and I could see hints of a fresh scrape on her knee from when she'd encountered Scurvy.

"Well, if it isn't Officer Palindrome." Her marble eyes stood out proudly even in the murky light.

"Going for a jog?" I asked.

"Can't fool the world's best copper."

"Aye," I said, sucking in my belly.

A thumping noise earned our attention. Her boy waved in our direction from between the closely drawn curtain and the cold window pane. He seemed to have gotten over his bashfulness, as his whole face lit up, though he still wouldn't point his eyes straight on me.

"He seems a good lad," I said.

"You got children of your own?" She'd noticed the sack of tablet in my hand.

"Would you like a sweet?"

"Might make the jog a bit silly," she said with a poke at her own belly.

"Aye," I said.

"I'm a bit worried leaving Nathan home alone. You suppose he'll be okay?" She bent back in some manner of stretching I'd never seen before.

"I'll walk the street while you're gone," I said. "If it eases your mind."

"No wonder they named you the world's greatest copper."

"Actually, I bought that mug myself," I confessed. That made her giggle. Then she gave me a kiss on the cheek.

"I won't be long, I promise." She set off.

For a moment I stood in the lane. Nathan looked right at me now. I waved at him, but his bashfulness seemed to be back. Aye, he did seem a good lad, at least as best I could tell through the glare on the window.

The school weren't far down the lane, so I walked over to it, hoping the effort would stave off the bite in the air. The sticker still clung to Mrs. Bowring's window, high up on the second story, taunting me. It put me in mind of the mornings when I'd hop up on the schoolyard wall declaring myself King of Leuchars, my mum holding my hand and chuckling at me. Some of my classmates thought me daft, but I paid them no mind. Sometimes I'd hold a stick above my head, or use one to upgrade my mum to a Dame. I always enjoyed those times, right up until the school bell rang and my mum would ruffle my black hair and send me on my way.

That night I settled for trailing my bare hand over the slate as I walked past, my third bit of tablet threatening to choke me a bit. There weren't any sense in visiting the school, really. I made back towards the McRae cottage. The curve of the lane hid the McRae home from view, but I could see Hugh McDuff's wee hardware shop across the street from it. A haze in my eye almost prevented me from noticing something needing my attention: a dark, shadowy figure crouched in the space between the store and the next cottage over. My thoughts went straight to the boy, home by himself.

"Oi!" I shouted, but by the time I laboured over, the only shadows were the ones cast by the shop's walls. The heavy steam from my mouth obscured the McRae cottage a bit, but I could make out Heather's boy standing in the window again. Or maybe he'd never left. He weren't waving, just staring right at me. He didn't look frightened, but when our eyes met he ducked behind the curtain.

My head dropped while my heart still pounded a mighty beat in my chest. Something odd jutted from a small gap in the wall's mortar. It kept grasping at my fingers until I finally unfolded it to find a bright orange sticker.

I took to pacing in front of the McRae cottage, letting my heart settle down in my chest and waiting for Heather. I needed some time to ponder, though nothing much really came to me.

It took quite a time, giving the sun a long spell to lower, but eventually Heather came thumping up the pavement. Steam poured off her whole body, and the street lamp made her glisten.

"What happened to your leg?" I asked. Her knee looked worse than before—covered in a bit of blood, like she'd skinned it on the pavement.

"You been here the whole time?"

"I walked up by the school for a bit." I weren't going to frighten her about the sticker.

"Is that where you went to school?"

"Aye," I said. It's the closest I've ever come to feeling embarrassed by my education.

"Must be a fine institution," she said.

"I liked Mrs. Bowring. She gave me taffy whenever I got my sums right."

"Too bad they didn't all give you sweets. You might have gone on to university."

She patted my belly as she walked by, then left me alone picturing a trail of taffy stretching all the way to Oxford's storied halls.

The next morning I'd allowed myself some time to stop by Mrs. Winchester's flower shop before heading to the station. I had a bother placing my order, as Mrs. Winchester kept on about "the vandalist" that had put up the sticker, her Yorkshire accent rising like a tea-kettle nearing a boil. Just to humour her, I asked if she could remember anything else about the sticker, though I needed to get going to the station.

She crossed her arms as far as they could go around her waist and puckered herself in thought. “Well, it was mighty hard to scrape off, I can tell you that.”

I pulled out my jotter to add that to my clues. While at it I decided to give Mrs. Winchester a go at the photo of Heather’s ex-husband. Mrs. Winchester’s eyes widened a bit.

“You’ve seen this chap?” I asked.

“Not properly,” she said. “But he was about the shop the day the sticker appeared.”

“Did he put the sticker up?” I thought I’d solved the case.

“Of course not, Dod. The sticker was already there when he came by. As soon as he saw it he turned and left. I don’t suppose I can fault him though. I certainly wouldn’t go into a shop with such a garish sticker in the window.”

I scribbled all that in my jotter as I made my way out.

I got held up a bit when I came down Pitlethie Lane and saw the town’s fire truck parked on the slope in front of St. Athernase church. The truck’s ladder reached for the weathercock at the top of the steeple, and Becky McMillan seemed stuck in a pattern of putting her first foot on the ladder before taking it off and putting it back again. I’d suppose she hadn’t climbed that ladder since she and I had squared off trying to get the fire job in the first place. That’s been a number of years ago.

“What’s this?” I asked.

She seemed annoyed at first. Upon seeing me she puffed up her chest as much as her thick coat would allow. “Got important work to do,” she said.

At the top of the steeple a creaky metal rooster turned reluctantly in the breeze. It didn’t make sense for Becky to be risking her neck over it. She went back to teetering her right leg up and down on the bottom step of the ladder, then checked whether or not I’d left. “It’s not all strolling and filling out forms in the fire department,” she said.

I tipped my bobby hat back straight on my head and stood a wee bit taller before I asked, “What you trying to do, anyway?”

“Fixing what you can’t seem to,” she said, which made no sense to me.

A loud creak drew my eyes back to the rooster. The breeze had just spun it in a rusty turn, showing me the opposite side where a bright orange sticker sat on the rooster’s hind feathers.

I set off then, at a pace no one could call a stroll. Becky probably thought she'd gotten the best of me, but that weren't it. I had to get to the bottom of the case. I couldn't stand for a sticker right there where all the townsfolk in Leuchars could see. Even the ones lying dead in the churchyard. I weren't going to let that sticker spoil my mum's birthday.

The rest of the morning I sat at my desk twirling my pen, feeling the feather slip between my fingers while going over the list of clues in my jotter. Heather's scraped knee kept pushing into my mind as well. I added the folder with the restraining order and the photo of Alan Scott to my desk. I'd have bet my mum's Christmas pudding on there being some relation, though I couldn't figure out what.

I set myself to investigating.

The restraining order had a phone number to the courthouse in Edinburgh. I put my pen down and gave them a ring. The lady on the phone seemed frightfully busy, but she eventually verified that Heather McRae's restraining order against Alan Scott had been done up proper. That took a weight off my mind, though it didn't get me closer to solving the case.

I looked over the form again. I found another phone number on it—Heather's number in Edinburgh, though the last two digits were covered over by the ink I'd smeared on it the day Heather arrived. It should have been no use, but something inside me wouldn't let go of it. Looking real close I managed to make out one of the numbers—either an eight or a three.

I took up the phone's receiver ready to try twenty different combinations. With each try the clicks of the rotary had a heavy partner beating in my chest. It weren't until the eleventh dial that a young woman answered, "McRae residence, this is Heather. Hello? Who am I talking to?" I heard Edinburgh in her t's, but there weren't any Glasgow in her r's. I hung up. There weren't much more to say.

When I reached Catherine McRae's cottage I hoped to find it already empty. I had no such luck. The boy hovered in the window, his eyes shining. The primary school had just let out and young boys and girls were parading down the lane between us. I waited for them to pass, watching as they hurried by in little clusters, whispering and conspiring together. Nathan watched them, too, his hands pressed against the pane of the window, but none of the children seemed to notice him, even though they were passing so close.

When the children had all gone by, Nathan finally noticed me. We shared a look, then he disappeared behind the curtain. Before I could even knock, his mum slithered through the door, leaving a heap of barking inside the cottage.

"Hello, Officer Palindrome."

"I need you to come down to the station." I'd just kind of blurted it out. We both stood there for a few moments, the barking ringing in our ears.

"Just let me collect my boy."

"Aye," I said.

We didn't speak on our way to the station, nor when we got there. There weren't any sound, excepting Nathan's sniffling by the door. His mum sat in the chair opposite my desk. I'd placed the restraining order where she could see it, but she still weren't saying anything.

"So," I said.

"Yes?" she asked.

"Pardon?"

"I didn't say anything."

"Aye," I said. My first interrogation weren't going very well.

I about jumped out my seat when Nathan said, "I did it." His mum seemed as surprised as me.

He sniffled mighty hard as he unslung his satchel and slowly opened the clasps. He pulled out a sheet of some kind and slipped it on my desk before retreating back to the door. I just stared at the sheet—at the orange stickers spilled across it and the holes where three of them had been used up.

"Don't blame my mum. It was me." He kept staring at the floor, sniffling from time to time. "I'm sorry," he said, and I heard a familiar weight of loneliness and fright. I thought of all the people in town, so outraged about the stickers—of Mrs. Winchester's kettle-boil voice.

"It's okay, young man," I said. "It took a lot of courage to fess up."

The boy raised his head. He had his mother's eyes.

"What's your name?" I asked.

The boy looked at his mum, then back at me, as if he had to decide what to call himself. "Nathan," he said after a bit, his eyes cast down. It made me sad. I'd really wanted to know the boy's proper name.

His mother spoke again. "I'm sorry to have fibbed, Dod. My ex-husband keeps following me, wherever I go. I couldn't think what else to do. I needed you." I heard more sniffling. "My boy needed you."

I'd already lined my desk with all the forms I'd need for a proper report. I'd gone over them before venturing out to pick up the boy and his mother, wanting to be sure I'd done everything up right. I didn't have much experience with incidents of this magnitude, especially not with a young boy involved. I'd already set myself against his mum's charms, reminding myself that there weren't any look she could give to equal the sight of that weathercock with the ghastly orange sticker on its tail.

I hadn't counted on the boy. Another long silence settled on us, then the hollow scrape of wood on metal. "I suppose," I said, "that if I accidentally write the forms in fountain pen instead of ballpoint, they won't be proper. Easy mistake to make, that."

The boy's eyes stayed fixed on the floor. His mum stared at me for a bit, then she came around to my side of the desk. She took my hand and raised it to her cheek, closing her eyes as she did. I still held the pen and the feather seemed to spring out of her curly hair like a bird from a nest. The cold from the outdoor air lingered on her cheek, resisting the warmth below her freckles. The room stayed silent excepting the sniffles of her boy, who stood alone by the door.

Then, slowly, her eyes opened again. Maybe the grey light had grown too dim, but they looked somehow different. They weren't like the blue marbles of my childhood at all, but watery and sad, like the shoals at Kinshaldy beach during a low tide.

"You're a good man," she said.

There weren't more to say. She let go of me, gathered her boy, and left. I heard him sniffle one last time before the door clicked shut.

The afternoon sky dimmed, casting everything in my office an odd shade of pewter. All except that sheet of stickers staring back at me. The clock told me to call it a day, and I weren't above heading to the pub to do a little boasting about closing the case. After all, it seemed I'd solved everything.

But the arithmetic weren't right. There were three stickers missing from the sheet, yet I'd found six left about town. A boy could have easily left one on the church wall. And the one at Mrs. Winchester's shop had been simple enough too. I could attribute those and the one in the mortar to the boy. The others, though, had been so high up. Especially the one on the weathercock—no boy could have ever placed that one.

I felt a bit restless in my office, so I thought I'd revisit the crime scenes, taking the stickers with me to ponder as I went roaming about. I went to the McRae cottage first. A light still shone from inside, but there weren't any barking. I felt a relief.

The space between Hugh McDuff's shop and the cottage next to it looked the same as ever, and the gap in the mortar weren't telling me anything. I remembered the boy looking at me that night. There seemed something odd about the sticker being wadded up and hidden in the mortar. All the others had been so proud.

Then I had a fancy. I went back to where I'd stood when the boy had waved at me and pictured his expression—how he hadn't quite been looking straight upon me. I followed the trail of his eyes.

As I'd thought. He weren't looking at me at all. He'd been waving and staring at the gap by Hugh McDuff's shop. That dark figure I'd seen—it had been there the whole time—drawn to the sticker the boy had put on the store's wall.

I looked down at the sheet in my hand. Three missing.

Squinting at the sky, I could just make out the steeple of the church, floating above the other rooftops. I suppose Becky hadn't been able to get at the weathercock very well, because even in the dark, traces of the sticker were still there, clinging to the lonely rooster as it twisted in the wind. We'd all be looking at that sliver of orange until time wore it off.

Then it struck me. We all *could* see that sticker, even little boys. Just like they could see the sticker at the school. And our Main Street might not be the Royal Mile, but it's the busiest route in town. A sticker on the Murray's chimney certainly would catch a lot of eyes, especially of a young boy taking in the sights of a new place.

I hatched a plan. The gate to the churchyard rested nearby, on the same slope that had flummoxed Becky earlier in the day. It's really more of a hill than a yard, with St. Athernase resting at the top and a smattering of graves spread all around. I peeled off one of the stickers from the sheet, and placed it on the wall next to the gate. Then I went up a few of the steps leading into the churchyard and crouched low in the shadows.

The sun had already gone down, though it still weren't that late in the evening yet, and the blanket of clouds covered over any light from the heavens. On these winter nights there weren't many folks about. There weren't much to hear, except the blowing of the breeze and the angry creaking of the rooster that accompanied it. Once or twice I'd hear some inkling of the town about me, but otherwise I might as well have been the only person on the whole of the planet.

If I'm being truthful, I'd never really meant for my plan to work. I needed that bit of quiet. And that time alone. I hadn't been in that churchyard since the day it had been crowded with folks at my mum's funeral. Nothing about that day had felt right to me. My mum and I were always best when the two of us were alone.

Perhaps that's what set me so aggressive when a set of footsteps broke into my thoughts. They came closer, then stopped at the gate, just out of sight, right where I'd put the sticker. I weren't sure what to do next—as I said, I'd never really thought about the plan working. Squaring my bobby hat and standing as straight as I could, I marched out the gate with my full authority. We thudded against each other and our eyes met. It only took a moment to recognize him—his sensible clothes had been replaced with a denim jacket and his sensible expression had turned to a look of surprise—but there weren't any mistaking that hair. I knew the man in the photo as soon as I spotted him.

Spying my badge he took off with a scamper, his slim body running and slipping down the steep slope of the street. Rather than follow, I puffed my way up the steps into the churchyard, then dodged through the gravestones to the lower edge where the ground came level with a stone wall that looked over Main Street three meters below. It's the kind of shortcut only a resident of Leuchars would know. Hurried steps were coming closer, then the perpetrator rounded the bend.

I crouched, my chest heaving mighty heavy while I shored up my courage. When he passed below me, I sprung, letting my weight plop down on him. I'd got him.

We made it back to my office without much bother. I didn't have handcuffs with me, so I'd bound his wrists by snapping the button of his right sleeve to the button hole in the left. I'm thankful he played along.

It had grown quite late and I had a full night of work in front of me, what with all the police reports, but it excited me to be at it. Maybe I weren't the King of Leuchars, but I couldn't help picturing a parade or something like. Becky would use the fire truck to clear the streets and Keith would be jealous of all the sweets Nora would make to commemorate the occasion.

But first I had to process the perpetrator. Sheets of stickers filled his satchel close to bursting. The arithmetic came out too—there were three empty spots on one of the sheets. It seemed I'd solved the whole of the case.

The perpetrator slumped in the chair across from my desk, keeping quiet while I did my work. I looked up with a start when he said, "What happened to the last 'e'?" His eyes were fixed on my nameplate. He didn't sound Scottish.

"Not enough room," I said.

"Dod T. George? You know, Dod is short for George?"

"Aye," I said.

"Why don't you make a new nameplate?" There weren't any mistaking his Irish brogue.

"Why is Heather running from you?" I asked.

"Heather?"

For a moment I'd forgotten that weren't her real name. "She told me her name is Heather McRae," I said, so he'd have an explanation. I showed him the restraining order.

"Heather was a friend of ours, had some troubles with her ex. Katherine must have made a copy. Not sure why there's a splotch of ink on it though." I ignored that.

We sat in silence for a spell.

"Don't be ashamed," he said. "It's what she's best at. I should know. She's my wife. Katherine McCloud. I'm Robert. Robert McCarthy."

"Different surnames."

"She said McCarthy didn't suit her."

"Aye," I said.

"Turns out I didn't suit her either. The divorce was complicated, the custody battle worse. Eventually she took matters in her own hands and left town."

"Aye," I said.

"I tracked Katherine down in Dundee and grabbed a moment with my boy. I didn't really know how to explain it all to him. I didn't understand it all myself. Katherine was about to make a scene and some people on the street were taking notice. I slipped him the stickers and a note telling him it was all a game, that while his mum took him on holiday we'd each play at putting stickers where the other could see. My years as a roofer finally paid off."

"Aye," I said. It surprised me that I didn't feel any of the envy that had cropped up when I first saw the picture of this bloke. Scott, McCarthy,

McRae—none of the names mattered. That boy had two people wanting him in equal measure, which made me happy for him, I suppose. But it weren't worth envying over.

"I suppose I should have gone to the authorities," he said.

"I'm the authorities," I said.

He ignored that and went on. "She's always up to something. Hell, that's how I met her—she pretended like she'd tripped and while I was helping her up she nicked my wallet. It's one of her favourite tricks. It's how come her knees are always so scraped up."

"Aye," I chuckled a bit at that as I remembered Scurvy failing to buy me a pint.

"She tried it on me, but I caught her. We were married two weeks later."

I'd heard enough. "Look, the town's in an uproar over these stickers. If I don't turn you in, I'll be in a fix."

He slouched low in his chair. "I'm really sorry to have made so much trouble. When Katherine left Dundee I'd assumed she was carrying on to St. Andrews. Kind of hoped we could still smooth things out. I even went to buy her some flowers."

"And that's when you saw the sticker your boy left for you," I said. I took pride in how well I'd put it all together.

"I guess I got carried away," he said. "I just wanted to see Collin."

"Aye," I said, glad to finally know the boy's real name. "Collin McCarthy. That's a good name."

"So what happens now?" he asked.

"No more chasing a lass that doesn't want catching," I told him. "If you want to see your boy, go to the authorities."

"I thought you were the authorities."

"Aye," I said. "Go to the authorities wherever she settles down. But let her do the settling."

"I just don't want my boy thinking I've given up on him. A boy should have a father, even a rotten one."

I thought on that for a good while. He'd seemed such a clever bloke, this Robert McCarthy, but I had this one on him. Any sensible fellow knows a good mum is plenty.

I tried to think of the least likely place his ex-wife might go. "Edinburgh," I told him. "She mentioned something about that." He nodded while I put away the ballpoint and tore up the reports on my desk. I'd gotten him off her tail, which felt like enough. He didn't seem rotten. I let him go.

I left the station to find the faint light of morning cropping up, and a gentle sprinkle of rain giving the town a welcome rinse. Even in the drizzle Mrs. Winchester's shop stood out for its bright blue sign swinging in the wind, and there were friendly roses waving pink just before the door.

Mrs. Winchester seemed to fluster a bit when I first stepped in—but upon seen me she softened. She'd been busy polishing the windows, and her wares were already put out for the day. She put down her rag and squeezed her bulk behind the counter.

"When you didn't make it last night I was worried you'd changed your mind." She fetched a lovely bouquet from the shelf behind her and gave me a long, kind look. I'd be in for a lot of those sorts of looks, I knew that. I felt glad for the patch of time alone the night before.

"Long night at the pub?" Mrs. Winchester asked. I suppose I did look a bit ruffled.

"Had some work to do."

"Any closer to catching the vandalist?"

I enjoyed thinking about Collin putting the sticker on her window.

"No," I said.

Her chins quivered a touch, but she held herself in check. "Be brave," she said. "It'll all work out." She meant well.

I made my way across town until I passed the McRae house. I tapped on the door and it creaked open. The insides of the cottage were a mess. I'd have to write up an incident form when Mrs. McRae got back from holiday. By then no one would draw the line between a break-in and the incidents with the stickers. For the time being I turned off the light and set the latch. The lock made a thankful click as the door shut behind me.

I carried on down the lane to St. Athernase church, its ancient spire pricking the sky into a chilly drizzle that justified the flush on my face. Cradling the bouquet, I took in a big sniff. The bright red poppies held hands with the yellow gazanias above the rich green of the stems. The smell of those flowers mixed with my foggy breath while the wee stamens powdered my mustache. The drizzle picked up, bringing a saltiness to my mouth.

Then I went up the steps leading to the churchyard and spent some time with my mum on her birthday.

THE MAN WHO INVENTED POTENTIAL

FC Pierce

I had another fight with the wife. Actually, it was a continuation of the same argument we've had ever since the honeymoon ended and she got pregnant. It always starts out over some niggling little 'nothing' like my leaving the cap off the toothpaste, or the laundry at the laundromat or the kid. To be clear, I've never left the kid at the laundromat, well ... once but I went right back. ... Anyway, we eventually arrive at the gripe 'du jour'—Money, the rent is due.

"Every month," she reminds me, "like clockwork. Tick Tock." And taps her fingers on the date circled in red on our kitchen calendar.

"But I am *not* a clockmaker," I remind her, raising my pen like a sword. "I am a Wordsmith."

"My parents call you the Slacker," She *reminds* me.

I *remind her* that I've never been fond of pet names nor her parents and if she wanted security, she should have married a banker. This always makes her cry—she only cries when she's angry—and she pulls out the heavy artillery.

"My parents warned me," she winds up. "but *oooh* no ..." Her voice rises to the occasion, "... I said you had *such potential.*"

And there it is, the *one* word that will send me into a paroxysm of rage, P-O-T-E-N-T-I-A-L. I storm out the front door, vowing to hunt down the SOB who created that word. Mindful of the effective use of alliteration, I turn back and declare, "I'll string him up by his Scrotum."

Ever the critic, she fires off her final volley. "You've used that one before." and slams the door in my face.

In these situations, I usually go to Minelli's. In fact, in all situations these days, I go to Minelli's, the quintessential neighborhood pub, where everybody knows my name, and nobody thinks I have the slightest bit of potential. Minelli's also happens to be the only establishment still allowing me to run a tab when money is tight. Money is always tight.

This particular evening, business is slow. But there is the group of regulars, huddled at a table near the door. When I enter, they turn as one in anticipation. I waive congenially and, as one, they turn back. I take my usual seat at the bar. Leo, the bartender, greets me.

"What can I get you, Johnny?" his standard opener.

"The easy way out, Leo," my standard response, "but I'll settle for a bottle of your finest Smuttynose Winter Ale."

"On your tab?"

I nod in the affirmative, and he pours me a draft. I start to rattle off my list of excuses, but Leo knows them all by heart and is already on to the next customer. I don't complain. Leo and I are kindred spirits. An out-of-work actor, and an out-of-print writer, our little tête-à-tête is part of what I've dubbed the 'Bar Bill Ballet.' The 'Do-Si-Do,' or more precisely, 'Don't See Dough,' which makes coming here such a painful pleasure.

I sit at the bar, nursing my beer—well, not nursing it exactly, I'm thirsty—and consider my options. I decide my best option is to ask Leo for another. He ignores me, pretending I am invisible, an old trick he has used before, when I hear a voice call out.

"And put it on my bill, if you would, my good man."

This turns us both around. The pleasing upper-class lilt in the voice leads me to expect a young 'Cary Grant' complete with ascot and tweed jacket, perhaps even jodhpurs and riding boots. Instead, I behold a pinched up old man in a long blue overcoat, two sizes too large for his tiny frame, wearing a Homburg hat. I am taken aback, not only by his appearance but also his offer. I've never seen him before at this establishment or any other I've frequented. In fact, I suspect that he may be nothing more than a figment of my overwrought imagination. Still ... considering my options, I throw caution to the wind, and acknowledge both his offer and his overcoat. I am wearing jeans and a favorite college sweatshirt, '*Harvard*,' not my alma mater, but still a favorite, and the chill night air has caught me by surprise. I thank him for his kindness, and he doffs his hat. The gesture reminds me of a more genteel bygone era. I decide immediately that the next time I have money I will buy myself a Homburg hat.

"My pleasure," he says. "May I?" and slides into the barstool beside me. "I couldn't help but overhear your conversation."

Since, until that moment, I have been alone at the bar, I realize I must've been talking to myself again—a youthful malady—my psychologist, Dr. Feinberg, called *Logorrhea* or 'Private Speech.' My classmates used the more colloquial term, 'Annoying Bull Shit.' I thought I'd conquered it, but the long hours of enforced isolation, writing or thinking about writing, or even thinking about thinking about writing, must have brought it back. Dr. Feinberg said it was more pronounced when I was under stress and I make a mental note to be vigilant, as it has always gotten me into trouble in the past.

My new companion points to my sweatshirt. "I take it you're a literary man."

"Exactly that!" I profess and doff my imaginary hat.

"Poetry or Prose?"

I take the measure of the man then mentally flip a coin.

"Prose," I answer, which seems to please him. He proceeds to tell me about himself. He made his fortune investing in small, unknown companies, turning them into successful businesses. "I'm a people person," he confides, "that's the secret of my success." He leans toward me. "I have a gift for seeing the hidden assets in people that others often overlook." And gazes directly into my eyes. "Know what I mean?"

I haven't a clue but nod conspiratorially, in the hope that it isn't too late to incorporate myself.

"At present I'm searching for someone to write my epitaph," he announces.

"Epitaphs are my specialty." I reply immediately. *Networking! And the wife thinks I just drink here. Hah!* I suggest we use the public library's vast collection for inspiration.

"I'm looking for something more personal," he demurs.

Personal? From a stranger? "My specialty!" I reply again.

"Glad to hear it." He raises his glass and I raise mine. We drink and I make a mental note to ask Leo for a receipt. The evening could turn out to be tax deductible.

"I hate most poetry on gravestones, don't you?" He tells me. "It's usually such doggerel."

I sigh despairingly at the "deplorable state of funerary verse," and make another mental note to look up the definition of "doggerel" in the off chance I am ever accused of it in the future.

Leo places a Smuttynose before me. *Up-Selling Leo, Attaboy!* Then asks if he can get the old man another drink. I look at his half empty glass, a watered-down whiskey and soda, and entreat him to drink his whiskey undiluted at this establishment. I have already composed an epitaph and written it on one of the bar napkins.

He liked his whiskey like his women—~~Straight~~ Neat. Of course, his friends will know he only changed his drinking habits to fit the epitaph. *Friends can be so judgmental!* Which is why I don't have any, except Leo of course, and now ... I realize I need to give him a name, and decide upon '*Winston'—The Homburg hat*—as a place holder. He says he has no friends. Ever since his wife died, he has lived alone.

"In complete and utter solitude."

I try not to sound too envious when I ask, "And how long has that been?"

"One-thousand ninety-four days," he answers without hesitation.

That is putting a fine point on grief! I think. Still, I understand. I have counted every day I've been married. I offer my condolences.

The gesture appears to have touched him. His hand trembles as he reaches for his glass.

Naturally, I can't let him drink alone. I lift mine.

"To better days," I toast and call him 'Winston.'

"Here, here." He raises his free hand and gives me the 'V' for victory sign. But when I ask about his wife, he becomes highly agitated. Sensing that I could lose his trust, not to mention his commission, I immediately apologize.

"Katherine?" I offer. "That's a lovely name, don't you think?" He nods in agreement but is much more circumspect in his response. Perhaps I've gotten it right. In any case, I decide not to mention her again. Unless he does.

He orders another whiskey.

"Neat," I add.

"On the rocks," he adds. "Three ice cubes."

"I like a man who knows what he wants," I said. I want another Smuttynose, and he agrees.

We drink in silence. I scribble more epitaphs while Winston sits brooding. He appears to be wrestling with a decision, but unlike me, he keeps his thoughts to himself, so I am excluded from the conversation. Whatever the problem, however, I can see that it must be a 'Doozie,' for his face flushes, his teeth grind and his fists clench and unclench, all in response to some internal argument. It appears that 'clench' has the upper hand so to speak, for I get the distinct impression he is about to punch someone, probably me, as by now, we are alone at the bar, besides Leo who is on his phone.

"I have no one," Winston blurts out. "You're my last hope."

I start to thank him. I have never been anyone's hope before, much less their last one. But the expression on his face stops me. Already pinched, it has puckered further, transforming his eyes into mere slits. Tears escape from the drooping lids. Cascading down his sagging cheeks, they dive off his quivering chin and land with a silent 'splat' on the bar-top, creating a small puddle. His mouth, barely a crease to begin with, has disappeared below his nose into a trembling wrinkle. I consider asking him what is wrong, but even *I* can see the answer. *Everything*. Instead, I push a supply of bar napkins toward him, upon which I've written my epitaphs, in the hope that these might cheer him up. Mistakenly thinking I have offered them for another purpose, Winston seizes a handful and applies them liberally to the leaky plumbing. The result is interesting. The tears, stained by the ink, leave indigo tracks as they run down his face, giving him the appearance of a decrepit Alice Cooper. Redundant, I know, but apt.

"I'll pay you in cash. Tonight," he beseeches me through blackened, trembling lips. He must've tasted the ink for he immediately looks at the napkins.

"For the epitaphs?" I inquire.

"No," he protests loudly, "to kill me!"

I immediately glance In Leo's direction to see if he has overheard. He's still on his phone. I turn back to Winston. This acclamation has dramatically changed my perception of our relationship. Originally, I'd hoped for something more long-term, relatively speaking, a sponsorship perhaps, or at least a bequest in his will. But now it's clear, from the start, he was looking for a one-night stand, a 'Quickie' *Wham Bam Shoot Me Man*. Pretending to hire me to compose something for after the fact, while angling all along for my participation in the deed itself. I feel used. Two thoughts immediately cross my mind. First, it is terribly inconsiderate of Winston to have this plan without informing me, and second, I need to adjust my fee.

"She meant the world to me." He begins.

"Who?"

"My wife!" He carries on, regurgitating a collection of aphorisms that would make Barbara Cartland roll over in her heart shaped coffin. 'Light of my life,' 'Sunlight in a darkened world,' 'A rose among thorns,' blah, blah, blah, it is enough to make me want to kill him right then and there.

"I'm boring you," he says, snuffling and snorting, while arranging the ever-growing number of napkins in separate piles—one with my writing, one without—that he has placed on the bar in front of him.

"On the contrary," I tell him. His sorting has inspired another epitaph.

He liked his women like his life ... ~~in piles~~ ... ~~well organized~~ ... Neat!

I also realize that if he feels this strongly about his wife, I will need to use her name instead of '*women,*' and his friends will all wonder who this 'Katherine' is. Of course, he told me he has no friends, but I am beginning to have my doubts. After all, he lied about his motives for hiring me. Perhaps lying comes easily to him? *Aha! I could use that as an epitaph!*

"My wife died three years ago tomorrow." He says, "She was my other half."

"Ok. ..." I consider taking notes but am running short of bar napkins.

"She completed me." He states emphatically, looking at me for a sign of something; recognition, understanding, sympathy? I'm not sure, so I try looking back at him in exactly the same manner. This only seems to confuse him. "She was three years my senior, one thousand ninety-five days." His eyes glisten. "I needed to stay here that exact length of time after her death for us to be complete." To demonstrate, he uses a visual aid, cupping his hands like two halves of a clam shell. "You see?" he closes them. Excited by the idea, his eyes widen and for the first time I see them clearly. They are a vibrant blue.

I am stunned! I would never have named him Winston if I'd seen those eyes earlier. Perhaps, 'Sven.' Still, I sense there's a 'loose thread' in the weave of his logic. Did she die on her birthday? No. Were their birthdays on the same date? No.

"So, depending on multiple factors," I hypothesize, "such as month and day of her birth and death, versus month and day of yours, the actual number of days could be greater or lesser than the number presently under consideration."

He stares at me blank faced. I realize that Minelli's is *not* the proper venue to continue our discussion, and suggest we adjourn to a more private locale where we can refine the details without fear of being overheard. He calls to Leo and pulls out his wallet. It is stuffed with bills. Removing one, the face bears a striking resemblance to Benjamin Franklin. Leo who has arrived, check in hand, has noticed as well, and his demeanor changes dramatically. Bending over the bar like a supplicant at the feet of Mother Teresa, he smiles up at him ... the old man ... 'Sven,' *Oh Hell! Winston*, asking if there is anything else he can get him. "*ANYTHING* ..." he repeats as if it's his dying wish to give this man pleasure beyond his wildest dreams. Obviously, Leo hasn't been listening.

Winston tosses the bill on the bar. "Keep the change," he says and stands up to leave. I assume he's misread the check and immediately point out the error.

"What difference does it make?" he answers. "After tonight, what will I need it for?"

He makes a good point. Still, I look to see if Leo is within earshot. The weasel has already slunk back to his stool at the end of the bar, his 'thank you' not the least bit heart-felt or sincere in my opinion. I strongly suggest that half of that should go toward my account, just on principle. But Winston stops me.

"Don't worry," he says. "When our business is completed, you'll be well compensated for your time."

Outside in the bracing night air, I feel reborn, cold and under-dressed for the occasion. We turn left into the black hole of a narrow alleyway, lit only by the pale rays of the crescent moon overhead. Passing backdoors and graffiti-covered walls for half a block, we finally bump up against the back of a large apartment building—mine. This is Winston's choice, as I find the alley too dark, too narrow and perhaps, already occupied. As we pass each garbage can, I look for marauders, kicking each pile of trash for hidden occupants. I find several rats but none of the two-legged variety. Satisfied, I broach the subject of the plan's "execution." Not the best word choice, I know but ...

"It's quite simple," Winston explains. "At precisely one-minute past midnight, I will shoot myself with this gun." He produces a small revolver from beneath his overcoat.

"I will put this in my mouth." He places the revolver, business end first, inside his mouth, "Anh pouh the twigghah." He delivers this last part, including the unintentional Elmer Fudd imitation, as if this is an everyday occurrence. I ask him, first, would he please remove the gun from his mouth, and second, why does he need me?

"You're my insurance," he says. There is a jauntiness about him. A, *joie de vivre*, as if we are out on the town for a night of fun, a little frolic in the clubs, then a roll in the hay with some big-bosomed women, back at their place, roommates, flight attendants ... maybe twin flight attendants ... in uniform. That has always been one of my favorite fantasies, although, until this moment, I've never included Winston or anyone else for that matter, in the picture. And well, anyway, what do I need to do to be his *insurance*?

"If I can't pull the trigger," he says offhandedly. "Then you'll do it for me."

"Hold on there!" I reply. "That sounds very much like murder," and I remind him that he won't be around to testify on my behalf. He says it is highly unlikely that it will come to that, but I persist. How does he know, for example, that when the moment arrives, and it is fast approaching, he can pull the "twigghah"? I look at him expectantly. "*TWIGGAH*"? Nothing, *Ahh well*, I move on. Has he tried it? A dry run, no bullets of course, just gun-in mouth, finger-on-*Twig*—Trigger—that sort of thing. He nods, but there is no jauntiness, no, *joie de vivre*, or possibility of 'stewardie' in his demeanor.

"I, uh ..." he hesitates and looks down.

AHA! I've found it. The loose thread. He can't pull the trigger! *I'm so intuitive about these matters, probably why he's picked me. Having a problem with follow-through? Right there with you buddy.*

"I have a problem with things," he says quietly, His gaze averts mine.

"Things?" I query.

"Things," he repeats, still staring at the ground. No, Wait! He is literally *staring* at the ground, not by chance but on purpose, as if he is counting something. *OMG*! His lips are moving. He *is* counting something!

"What the hell are you counting?"

"Things," he repeats distractedly. "I need to count things."

He tells me that whenever he practiced, he would remove the bullets, line them up on his dining room table, count them, "Twice, just to be sure," then adjourn to the laundry room, gun in mouth, hand on the trigger and count down from ten. But as he got closer to 'one' he would have this nagging doubt. "This thing," where he couldn't be sure if he'd taken out all six bullets. The closer he got to 'one' the stronger the feeling, until finally, he had to remove the gun and look in the chambers, "Twice," he says. "Just to be sure." Then he would have to return to the dining room table and start all over again. After multiple attempts with the same result, he simply gave up and started his search for help, which ultimately brought him to me. *HMMM* ... had he considered remaining at the dining room table when he practiced, I ask?

"I didn't want to leave a stain on the rug." He answers. "It's an oriental, very expensive, been in the family for years."

I mention that the idea was to 'practice' pulling the trigger. That *no actual bullets should be used.* But he is set in his ways. I decide to switch gears and ask about the apartment, the oriental rug, the appliances, and would he consider a sublet. I may need a place to stay. He informs me he's left everything to his cat. I tell him that I like pets, but it quickly becomes apparent that I am to be his 'one-trick' pony: hand in mouth, finger on trigger ... and just in case, which seems increasingly likely, *pull it!*

"At one-minute past midnight," he reminds me, "when 'Katherine' died." He hangs air quotes, shaped like bunny ears, around her name. I balk. It all sounds much too much like work, and am about to tell him so, when he adds, "I'll pay you ten thousand dollars." And pats his coat. "Cash."

I immediately reconsider my position. I ask for proof. He reaches into his coat pocket and removes an envelope bulging with something, perhaps money. I am still not convinced, so he opens the envelope. There are multiple bills inside, all with Franklin's face on them. Still, I ask if I can count the bills, "Twice, to be sure," certain that he of all people will understand. But he waives the gun in my face and stuffs the envelope back in his coat pocket.

"This is my insurance. You'll have to kill me first." I step back and shake my head. How can someone put their hand in another person's mouth? It's so unsanitary.

"Dentists do it all the time," he reminds me. "And besides, I have these." From another pocket he pulls out a pair of surgical gloves along with a plastic covered square package. "It's one of those fold-up ponchos from the Army-Navy surplus store," he tells me, "just in case there's any ..."

"Any what?" I ask.

"You know," he explains. "Blow-back."

BLOW-BACK! I hadn't thought of that.

"I'll be your coach," I tell him. "Cheer you on, give you pep talks, even count the bullets with you, but no surgical gloves. Well, maybe for when

I reach into your coat to get the envelope. But no poncho, definitely *NO PONCHO!* My final answer," I shiver.

"It's almost midnight." He shrugs. "What choice do I have?" He throws me the gloves, then tucks the poncho back in his coat. I move back a few steps—*Blow-Back.*

"Ready?" he asks

I point to my naked wrist and he removes his watch and tosses it to me, a *Rolex*. I slip it on. I've always wanted a *Rolex,* but at that moment, it doesn't seem like such a big deal.

"I got it when we were in China," he tells me.

"Oh," I say, *probably a knock off.*

He frowns, but says only, "Tell me when." And puts the gun in his mouth.

I look at the watch. The numbers glow in the dark. "Midnight" I announce. "One minute to ..." *what should I call this*?

"Mahke id ahhp," he answers. "You're the wyiteah"

I do like the watch, even if it is a knock off.

"*Whaa?*" Winston callz out.

"Thirty-seconds." My eyes follow the sweep hand past the window that shows the date, which also glows in the dark. It is off, a day ahead. I picture our kitchen calendar. Either the wife is wrong, which would be a miracle, or the watch is wrong, *Like leap year or something.*

"Whaa dih ou sahy?"

"Thirty seconds," I answer him. "Now it's fifteen."

"No, ou thaa leepf yeah?"

"Ten seconds."

"LEEPF YEEAH!" Winston's voice reaches a violent crescendo.

"Don't talk with your mouth full," I remind him. "Six, five, four,"

"Leap Year!" His clarion call reverberates through the midnight air.

"What?" I look up. "Hey, what's that gun doing out of your mouth?"

"You said, Leap Year!"

"PUT THAT GUN BACK IN YOUR MOUTH, MISTER! WINNERS NEVER QUIT, AND QUITTERS NEVER WIN!"

"Leap Year." Winston crumbles to the ground, dropping his gun. "I never thought of that."

"Really?" I would have thought, 'Leap Year' would be right up there, at the top of his list of 'things.'

"Leap Year," he repeats mechanically. "I wish you hadn't mentioned it."

Oh, Right, Blame the help! I may have my faults, the wife keeps a running tally, but I'm not the one with "OH-FUCKING-CEE-DEE!"

I proclaim this last part out loud, but Winston barely acknowledges my existence. The moment is gone. It is clear that Winston will not be shooting himself tonight. Lying there in a heap, he looks surprisingly like one of the trash bags we passed on our way in. I sigh, pick up the gun and step toward him.

"It's OK," I say as kindly as I can, considering my rising frustration and hold out my free hand. "Give me the poncho."

Winston's physical demeanor immediately transforms from a whimpering lump of Homburg-topped-coal to an excellent impersonation of a Scarab beetle scrambling to hide from a switched-on light. His cerulean eyes are fixed on me, or more precisely, the gun in my hand.

"Don't shoot!" he screams.

"Don't scream!" I shout, then repeat in a whisper, "It'll wake the neighbors." I look around expectantly. Not a single light goes on. I shake my head. Obviously, there is no sense of community here, and I make a mental note to move once the kid is older.

"Need to regroup," Winston mumbles, scurrying back and forth, up the alleyway, "form a new plan." He turns to see if I am following him, which I am, and he calls back, "Thanks ever so much. Don't know what I would've done if you hadn't mentioned it." I smile wanly and make a mental note to have my 'personal speech' surgically removed at the earliest opportunity.

"Perhaps her birthday or mine," he rants. I notice that he has picked up his pace. He is wearing sneakers. A jogger, just my luck, and I have to break into a run, more like a trot really—having given up running years before—to try to catch him. It takes several blocks, and by the time I arrive, he has already flagged down a taxi. "Can't thank you enough," he repeats, and jumps into the back seat, "Let's keep in touch." The entire experience has appeared to invigorate him. *Reborn.*

I lean against the cab, trying to catch my breath. I want to revisit the topic of payment, or at least partial payment. After all, I was ready to hold up my end of the bargain. But my heaving chest prevents any words from escaping. Hoping to buy some time, I hand him back his gun. He pulls it in under his coat.

"Keep the watch," he says, "A little memento of our time together." He smiles and gives me the bunny ears sign again. *Definitely a knock off*, but I am too winded to complain.

"Do you have a card?" He asks. I shake my head and hold out my hand. "Yours" I want to say but all that comes out is a great '*Whooshing*' of hot air.

"I can find you at that establishment then?" He closes the door and rolls down the window. I nod vigorously.

"Excellent!" He smiles. "What was that address again?"

I stand there on the sidewalk, panting like a giant Schnauzer in heat, miming a pen and paper to write it down for him, but the taxi pulls away. As it speeds up the street, he sticks his head out the window. "Yes," he calls out, "Absolutely. Keep up with the writing. You have such potential!" The word slaps my face hard, like an angry woman. "And I should know," he says, cheerily adding insult to injury, "I practically invented ..." The screeching tires obliterate his final condemnation, as the cab wheels around the corner and disappears into the night.

"*NOOO* ..." my anguished howl catches a homeless man by surprise. He has approached me, probably hoping for some spare change. "Here," I scream. "Take this." Ripping the *Rolex* from my wrist, I throw it at him. "A little memento of our time together." The man picks up the watch, puts it on and starts to move away.

"It's a fake," I yell and point in the direction of the cab. "Just like that man in the taxi." I turn back. "And, Oh yeah, the date's wrong," I advise him. "Just in case you're interested." Without breaking stride, he raises the hand wearing the watch and flips me the bird.

That would've been the end of it—not the first time the rent was late. But a week later, I am on my way to the laundromat with the kid when a well-dressed man stops me on the street. He is wearing a crisp white shirt under a blue wool blazer and slacks, with a pair of black, soft, leather loafers. He carries a walking cane with a gnarled wood handle and sports a Homburg hat which he doffs, saying, "Hello, old chap."

For a moment, I think it is Winston. Then I look closer and realize it is the homeless man I encountered that night on the street. I barely recognize him. Seeing his naked wrist, I ask. "Where's that watch I gave you?" He points to a shop two doors up from the laundromat.

"I sold it," he says. "Thanks again." And once more doffing his hat, he strolls away.

I hurry past the laundromat, to the pawnshop and look in the window. There, hanging from a small stand, is the watch, nice and shiny. I look closer. The date has been corrected. There is a tag on it that reads *'Classic' Rolex, $2,500, cash.*

PET

James Nolan

Everyone adores me, even though I just turned thirty. In the bars, I still feel guys' lingering stares as I cruise past but, of course, always ignore them. I don't give out samples, and nobody gets a slice of me for free. I've been hanging out in gay bars since I was twenty, but if anyone asks I say that I'm bi-curious. True, there's not much to be curious about after ten years of long-term sugar daddies, but I have my image to uphold. You know, a straight macho Latino that an older gentleman might cajole, seduce, and then adopt, if he takes me shopping and gives me a generous allowance.

I don't rent my body by the hour but by the year.

Actually, I am sort of straight—I got my girlfriend pregnant the year after high school—and kind of Latino, even though I don't speak Spanish very well. And macho—well, I'll let you be the judge of that, especially when I tell you about the pistol I used to shoot that crazy porn star in the head. My parents, who moved to Florida from Ecuador when I was a baby, speak Spanish with each other, most of which I understand, especially the cursing. But when it comes time to open my mouth, I'm not sure which words to use.

"Like, when someone says '*Espero que tengas un buen fin de semana,*' I'm not sure what *tenga* means," I tell my current papi in bed. "Do they hope this weekend I get into some chick's *tanga*, like, her bikini bottom?" Actually, that's pretty funny, don't you think? And it makes me sound so macho.

"It's simple, Esteban," explains Alfredo, the Cuban insurance agent I'm now staying with in the French Quarter. He's past fifty, you know, the serious type, over-educated for the few years he has left on earth. Alfredo is stout, balding, and his body is covered with a mat of curly white hair that he likes me to stroke. "It's called the subjunctive mood."

"Okay." I like older men who can explain things to me, even if they do sometimes treat me like a child they can bribe with a lollipop. "What's the subjunctive mood?"

"When something isn't real yet, although it could be. Just because you hope so doesn't mean the other person is going to have a good weekend. Could turn out lousy. So like in English, the subjunctive *tengas* is used instead of the indicative *tienes* to say 'I hope you'll have—or you would or should have—a good weekend.' *¿Comprendes?*"

"What's the in-dick part again? Anything to do with, you know ..."

Alfredo sighs and gets up to pour himself another Bacardi. "Indicative means it's real. You can reach out and touch it, like this," he says, flicking a finger at his crotch.

In that case, I'm not very indicative but more of a subjunctive kind of person. Not real yet, in spite of turning thirty.

Sometimes I wonder why I don't like to hang with guys my own age, but twenty-somethings seem so striving and business-minded. The rich ones are either techies or entrepreneurs, and the poor ones serve Starbucks or craft cocktails to the techies and entrepreneurs. I can't see past their beards, man buns, tattoos, StairMaster bods, and dinging hookup apps. They expect me to have a condo, a career, a website, and a favorite fusion restaurant. I want to keep on dreaming up my life safe in the arms of an older man. Writing computer code, making out invoices, or doing crunches is too damn indicative.

Last week Alfredo took me out to dinner at Galatoire's when I told him it was my twenty-fifth birthday, which was pretty subjunctive of me. But what's indicative at the moment is I'm not going to have this gig much longer. In this line of work, thirty is my sell-by date. I'm already sprouting gray hairs, which I've learned how to touch up. Not that I think of myself as a gigolo, although whenever I hear that Sinatra song "Just a Gigolo" the lyrics make me tear up: "Then will come the day / Youth will fade away / And what will they say about him?" I can't picture many more years as a dyed Latin lover boy snuggled in the protective embraces of older guys with lots of dough. After all, I'm almost an older guy myself, but one with no dough of his own.

The real deal-breaker now is Milagro, Alberto's incontinent Great Dane. That dog is the size of a pony and has the potty habits of an infant. One of my chores—all my sugar daddies wind up treating me like a houseboy once the romance is over—is to walk Milagro on a leash to do his business, which is like being dragged along the sidewalk behind a racehorse. I take him outside—nothing. I bring him home—*splat* all over the carpet. Then outside again—nothing. Inside, *splat*.

And guess who has to clean it up? And which one of us is really on a leash? I'm not exactly living La Vida Loca like my idol, Ricky Martin.

This ancient gray Great Dane is all skin and bones, and Alfredo keeps him in a wire cage on the back porch, where his thundering barks rattle the floorboards. If we let him romp free inside the apartment, he races around chewing on furniture and knocking crystal doodads off tables with his tail. My walks with Milagro are the dog's only glimpses of freedom, and sometimes I'm tempted to unleash him and let him gallop away free, like the animal he is. I'm not sure why Alfredo keeps the dog, or for that matter, why he keeps me. I'm haunted by Milagro's pleading looks from behind the cage's wire door. More than once I've almost leapt up to fling open the cage door to let the poor beast run wild in the streets. Maybe that's what I want to do, but I'm still here to take care of that dog, and once Milagro croaks, my days with Alfredo will be numbered. Papi and I don't cuddle much anymore.

What I see ahead is giving up on my boyish star power and latching onto some needy geezer forever, or a future of shady gigs like picking pockets, mugging tourists, or conning rich people.

In which case, maybe I should get a good pistol, like a Beretta.

Notice I say *maybe* and *should*. That's pretty subjunctive of me.

Like most novice confidence men, the first person I try to con in my break for freedom is a pro. Morris Dudley operates the Voodoo Museum on St. Peter Street, and is usually standing in front of his hokey shop with a Burmese python curled around his neck, luring in customers. It's a sultry afternoon in June, that time of year in New Orleans when people are stopping every few minutes to wipe sweat from their brows. The shadows of balcony poles are lengthening along the sidewalks, and I wonder what's up with this pudgy old guy and his huge snake. So I stop to pet it on the head.

Morris backs away, scowling. "I wouldn't do that if I were you, muchacho. Balthazar hasn't fed yet today and might snack on your finger."

"I know all about pythons," I lie. "I grew up in the Amazon jungles of Ecuador, where we'd catch them all the time."

Actually, I grew up in a pink ranch house in St. Petersburg, Florida. I can still picture chubby Mamacita luxuriating in the American Dream on an aluminum lounge chair in the gravel front yard between two dead palm trees, the bare trunks looming overhead, almost touching. Papi always had his head stuck in the engine of one of the busted jalopies lined up in the driveway, and never paid any attention to either of us. When I split, everybody knew he was running with a nineteen-year-old Dominican girlfriend.

"Let's see if I can guess your name." Adjusting his glasses, the old man closes his puffy eyes as if preparing for a trance. "Antonio? Eduardo?"

"That's scary. You must be psychic. It's Eduardo." My name is Esteban, but I'm along for the ride.

"What's your loa?"

"Gemini," I say, jutting out my square chin and tilting my head until a shiny black curl dangles over my forehead.

"I mean your spirit guide."

"Same as yours."

"Is that so?" His ruddy face creases into a knowing smile. "Let's go inside the shop."

Alfredo is still at his office, so I have time to spare. The python uncurls its square brown splotches around the old man's neck and fixes me with a cold yellow stare, fanged mouth hinging open. Jungle drums on a soundtrack usher us through the French doors into the air conditioning, and once inside the chill, it's the same old song and dance I know so well, snake or no snake.

"Wow." I zip up after we do the deed behind a dusty showcase of Spanish moss and spooky gris gris, feeling kind of puny down there compared to the python, although Morris looks impressed. "Truth is I have nowhere to stay now. My parents on the West Bank kicked me out for being, you know ..."

"Gay?"

I nod, staring down at the brand-new Nikes the Cuban just bought me, as if I've lost everything. My lower lip quivers. "Well, actually, I have a girlfriend, but after she got pregnant—"

"Look, I have an enormous apartment over the shop. Why don't you stay with me for awhile?"

"My parents will miss me so much." We haven't spoken since that horrible shouting match on the gravel lawn last Christmas in Florida.

Then I move in for the kill.

Alfredo doesn't take the news well. "Moving out, *¿pero a dónde?*" he shouts, petting Milagro's boney head. "Where? Back in with your parents at twenty-five? ¡Ay Esteban!"

"Mamacita needs me." As if I'm about to crunch along the gravel to that aluminum chair parked between the two dead palms in front of that squat cinderblock house in Florida while she jabbers away in Spanish on her cell all day about her husband's damn *carros y putas de mierda*.

Once installed in Morris's apartment, I begin Phase II of my new job as boy toy. I shop for food, cook, wash up, even mop, all the while complaining I can't find a job. I even dangle live mice by their tails over the python's cage until in a flash the snake lunges, snaps, and swallows. Morris tells me he got into snakes and voodoo growing up on his family's vast rubber plantation in the Congo, but a neighbor claims to have met his sister and that the family ran a gas station in Texarkana. I wonder why these lonely old men have such enormous animals in cages, but this is a lot easier than cleaning up after the incontinent Great Dane. The faint echo of drumbeats and African chanting seeps up from below through the floor, making me feel like a voodoo high priest. I even mind the shop while Morris drives out to Jefferson Parish to buy more mice, as if there weren't already enough scampering around the French Quarter.

"But without a job ..." I complain, glancing at my half-unpacked suitcase stashed in a corner of the living room next to the armoire.

After about a month the allowance starts. Then comes my own bedroom, where I finally unpack the suitcase. This is Phase III: roommates with privileges. The python curled around his neck, Morris sometimes throws scenes when I close and lock my bedroom door. He stamps around in slippers, slamming walls and pleading with Eduardo. Hearing my own name would get to me, but who's Eduardo? Not me, but some Latin lover boy with dyed black hair.

Still I dangle my big mouse over Morris's cage, but usually pull back before he can pounce. What nails his attention is my nightly parade from the shower to my bedroom with a damp towel slung around my waist, flexing my biceps. The pouty old man routine—well, I've seen that show before. But in this gig Balthazar really freaks me. What if Morris decides to sic the python on me? Once he gets so loud and demanding, I use my whole allowance to go out the next day and buy a Beretta Nano pistol for self-protection.

But not until lover boy number two shows up do I have to use it.

I'm not sure what really happened, but Morris's story is that on Sunday afternoon a blond hunk showed up at the shop claiming he was fascinated by voodoo. He'd flown in from Los Angeles to visit his mother, who he was having a hard time reaching. So he asked Morris if he knew anywhere he could crash for the night, since his mother was probably out of town for the weekend.

When he confessed that the python and jungle drums made him feel all hot and bothered, Morris invited him to come upstairs after closing time to spend the night. But just one night, he cautioned, because he already had a roommate.

Later that evening Buster Gayoso arrives, dragging five suitcases up the stairs. I recognize him right away. He used to be a porn star in those old clips I sometimes watched on the overhead monitors of the bars I still hang out in. He has piercing blue eyes, a gym-toned body, a California tan, and teeth bleached white as a toilet bowl. But the pecs, biceps, and laterals are starting to sag, his skin is wrinkly, especially around the mouth, and he has a frantic look, like a caged wild monkey. As he glances around the apartment, his face twitches with tics and I wonder what drugs he's been doing. I mean, this is major nerve damage if I've ever seen it.

"This is my roommate, Eduardo," Morris says. He doesn't say lover, boyfriend, or even friend, but "roommate."

"Hey, dudes. What a cool place." Buster drops his five suitcases into a heap at his feet as if checking into a hotel.

"Let me go make some margaritas," I say, ducking into the kitchen.

Morris joins me, looking a little put out. "But I told him just one night."

I swing around from the fridge. "Don't you recognize him? It's that porn star Buster Gayoso, but several years over the hill." Look who's talking.

"Like from porn magazines?" Morris asks.

"Magazines?" Morris is totally stuck in the eighties and doesn't even have a DVD player, much less a computer or tablet. "No, from porn flicks they play in gay bars or recycle online. I'll show you one on my laptop."

"I'd rather see his action in the flesh."

Which I guess is what happens that night after my shower, when I lock my bedroom door. Morris isn't even waiting by the bathroom to gawk at my stud stroll with the wet towel. The cinematic moans coming from his room seem to agitate Balthazar, coiling and uncoiling in sinuous sambas inside his cage.

By the fourth night the conversation starts heating up about calling Buster's mother. There's nowhere else for him to sleep except with his host, and from what I can tell by Morris's eye rolls and shrugs, that isn't such a hot arrangement. Morris confides that the porn star can't really perform. "Thought performing was his job," he says.

"It's time." I thrust my cell phone into Buster's face. "Morris says your moody, mooching self has outworn its welcome. Your plans to move on seem pretty ... subjunctive."

"What's that supposed to mean?" His own phone is supposedly misplaced in one of his suitcases, so he grabs mine and punches in a number. "Hey, Mom. Guess who's in town?" Then he steps out the door onto the stairway landing.

Five minutes later he's back, eyes leaking and voice trembling. "My mother will be here to pick me up in an hour," he snivels. "She lives way out in Kenner."

Then he creeps down the curved staircase toward the courtyard.

"Don't you want to wait here for your mom?" I yell after him.

"Just going for a quick walk. No problem. I have the keys."

An hour later both Morris and I are waiting in front of the carriageway gate. No Buster. "We have his suitcases," Morris says. "He'll be back. And there'd better be a mother on her way."

Eventually a lady with gray bangs and a crepe-paper neck does show up, staring at a scrap of paper in her hand and asking for Sydney, her son.

"You must mean Buster," I say.

"I don't know what he calls himself out there in L.A. This is the first time I've heard from him in four years." She's twisting the scrap of paper between her fingers. "He's so ..."

"I'm sure he's dying to see you," Morris blurts out, obviously giddy at the prospect of unloading our houseguest. "Wait here while I go upstairs and bring down his bags. It may take several trips."

This mother doesn't look like a porn star's mom. I'm expecting a pouty, eyelash-batting sexpot like Lady Gaga, but she's a real ironing board of a woman, a stalwart missionary type like one of those steel-backed matrons oozing sincerity and concern that spoke at the Pentecostal church where Mamacita used to drag me. She wears canvas sneakers, a Peter Pan collar buttoned at her throat, and a purse strap slung across her flat chest as if she's afraid of being robbed.

"Your son told me he just went for a walk." I look up and down the street. "Odd timing, if you ask me."

"Odd is the word for Sydney. Sorry, but I don't know your name ..."

"Eduardo."

"Look, Eduardo, you seem like such a nice young man." Apparently she doesn't notice I live over a voodoo shop. "Believe me, you don't want to get mixed up with someone like my son. It hurts me to say this, but he's a drug addict and a thief, and was in and out of jail and rehab before he went out West ten years ago. He says he's a movie star out there, but I never believe a word that comes out of his mouth." She taps an index finger against her temple. "His serotonin receptors are shot to hell."

My eyes widen. I don't know what that means, but it sounds painful.

"Let's face it," she says, looking away, "he's a psychopath."

"Sorry to hear that." Again I don't understand but hope I'm not a psychopath too. I was diagnosed with Attention Deficit Disorder in tenth grade, when I used to act pretty psycho. But now I just tell people what they want to hear and sail on.

"Has he started any trouble here?" Her face hardens. "You know, wild rages, attacking people?"

"He's been short-tempered and super twitchy, like he's on something, but no, he hasn't been violent."

"So far. I know how to deal with him. I'm a licensed practical nurse and can get him back on Haldol, his antipsychotic medication."

"Hey there," Buster shouts, bouncing around the corner. Bobbing above his head is a heart-shaped Mylar balloon that says, "Best Mom Ever." He rushes up to lock his mother in a bear hug just as Morris shoves his five suitcases through the gate onto the sidewalk.

"Okay, Sydney." The woman stares up at the balloon with a strained smile. "I'll walk around the corner to get the car and come pick you up. Your luggage should fit in the trunk and back seat."

"The bitch," Buster says as she scurries off. "Didn't even say she was glad to see me."

"Time to feed Balthazar," Morris tells me, slamming the gate shut on the forlorn porn star holding a "Best Mom Ever" balloon. "We should celebrate now that the creep is gone. Eduardo, go bring a mouse down to the shop. A big fat one."

That evening a thunderstorm blows through the city. Stepping outside later, I find the Mylar balloon tied to the handle of a neighbor's trash bin, flapping back and forth in the breeze.

The banging on the carriageway gate starts the next night around midnight.

"Morris, Eduardo, it's me, Buster."

"As if we're going to let him in again." Morris cringes, untwining Balthazar from around his neck and shoving him into the cage.

"You know he has the keys, don't you?" I point out. "At least that's what he said yesterday afternoon."

"To the upstairs door too?"

I shrug.

Heavy footsteps pound up the staircase.

The front door lock clicks. Morris rushes to yank it shut by the knob. "Go away. You're not wanted here."

Buster's enraged face emerges as the door bursts open and Morris stumbles backward onto the floor next to the cage. "What do you mean?" Buster screams. "I live here. You invited me to."

I step back. Whatever happened to the Best Mom Ever and her magic meds?

"You're not welcome here anymore," Morris bellows, rising to his feet. "Leave before I call the cops."

Buster lunges toward Morris. "You dirty old man."

Balthazar uncoils in his cage, raising his flat, square head as if to catch a better view of his owner being murdered.

I stand there, trying to picture my own eviction from above the voodoo shop. Whose side am I on? Then I step into my bedroom and lock the door.

What happens next I can only imagine. Morris must have fled down the staircase and into the dark courtyard, where he's shouting "Eduardo, do something, for Christ's sake."

Boards creaking, I tiptoe down the shadowy steps, the Beretta in my pocket. I pull the chain dangling from the crooked lantern overhead and can't believe what I see. Buster is standing over Morris—curled up into a whimpering ball on the flagstones—kicking him with his Timberland hiking boots. "Mom threw me out. Think you're the only old queer who deserves a home?"

"Stop that." The words slip out as a squeak. I try again, more menacing. "Leave him alone or I'll shoot!"

Buster raises a leg and wallops the old man in the chest with his boot.

I raise the gun, click off the safety, take aim, and graze the porn star's shoulder. *Bam!*

This only makes him stomp Morris harder.

Then I go for his serotonin receptors, which I figure must be in his head. *Bam!* Buster crumples to the ground.

See how macho I am.

Someone in a neighboring courtyard must have heard the shots, because within minutes two cops charge through the carriageway gate, which Buster probably left open. I've already hauled Morris gasping to his feet, and now am just standing there dazed, the gun still in my hand: a signed confession.

Sirens wail. Revolving blue lights flash. Paramedics rush in, and Buster's limp body is strapped onto an ambulance gurney. I'm already handcuffed when a homicide detective, brow furrowed, calls me over. "This your gun?"

Then everything starts to feel super subjunctive. This can't be happening. For the first time in my life, I finally took action and did something real.

And it turns out to be murder.

Like Milagro and Balthazar, now I'm the one in a cage, waiting for my manslaughter hearing tomorrow. My court-appointed attorney assures me I'll get off on a self-defense plea. He's taken a deposition from Morris, now recuperating in the hospital with three broken ribs and a collapsed lung, describing how violent Buster was that night. His mother, who we tracked down through her phone number in my cell, will be there to testify that her son is a psychopath who refuses to take his Haldol. Evidently, Buster has a rap sheet a mile long about similar skirmishes with the cops in this town, where he's been black-balled from all the clubs after attacking customers.

I'd never dare tell my real papi where I am, so my one call is to Alfredo, the Cuban insurance agent, who refuses to post bail, especially on a murder charge. "I thought you were with your parents in Florida," he sputters. "*Mentiroso.*"

Okay, I admit, I did lie a little. He'd already heard about the shooting on the morning news, which reported my full name. And, unfortunately, my age.

"*¡Treinta años!*" Alfredo always speaks Spanish when he gets excited. "*Te ha caducado la carrera como un chico protegido.*"

Thirty. Which means all of New Orleans now knows my shelf-life as a kept boy has expired. The jig is up.

Then Alfredo wishes me a happy and prosperous life on my own. "*Qué tengas una vida feliz y próspera por tu propia cuenta.*" Of course, he uses the subjunctive. He isn't betting on my survival.

Later Morris contacts me. All he cares about is that somebody feed Balthazar, which I promise to do once I get out of this filthy cage in Central Lockup and stop by his apartment to collect my stuff. I promise to leave my keys in his mailbox—he's not taking any more chances in that department. He tells me I can have the emergency hundred-dollar bill in the silverware drawer, but not to touch anything else. He warns me that now he knows my real name—and age—so no monkey business. When I remind him that I saved his life, he asks, "Wasn't that your job?"

I've never thought of myself as a body guard, and Morris is lucky I never turned the Beretta on him during one of his horny rages. Funny, but all these years I've felt so safe with older men, never realizing they're the ones who might feel safe with a guy like me around, especially in the rough-and-tumble French Quarter. As if I'm supposed to be all like, *don't touch my papi, cabrón*. The cops, of course, impounded my unlicensed gun, which the lawyer tells me is illegal to possess, and I'm not getting another one. I never signed up for a security gig.

My long-term plans are either to become a huge pop star like Ricky Martin or, Florida boy that I am, to sail my own yacht around the world. Or one day I might go to medical school and specialize in brain surgery to help poor porn stars like Buster Gayoso with their busted serotonin receptors. In the meantime, I'll register for a computer programming class at Delgado Community College and ask a bartender friend of mine for a part-time job and a place to crash until I can get on my feet.

Pulling that trigger did something to me. It's time to get indicative.

The next morning at the hearing, after questioning Buster's weepy mother and reading Morris's deposition about the shooting, the homicide is declared an act of justifiable self-defense. Snowy as Mount Everest, the distinguished judge peers down at me over his half-glasses. "Esteban, you're a brave young man to defend your gentleman friend," he says. Young? He must know my real age.

Then he winks.

The judge rises to his feet, towering above me. "On the unlicensed arms charge," he says, gathering up papers, "the District Attorney's office recommends a short period of probation in lieu of a six-month minimum sentence, but considering your heroism in dealing with this violent criminal, we'll discuss this later in my chambers. Court adjourned."

The judge consults with the DA and then calls me into his office. He explains that while the court isn't mandating probation on my lack of a gun permit, I should seek counseling and a strong guiding hand. I wonder if he knows that strong guiding hands are my specialty, particularly those reaching for their wallets. Leaning forward in my chair, I look him in the eye, tear up, and confess how adrift I've felt in this world since both my parents were killed in a fiery car crash in New Jersey. He seems to buy this, and his face scrunches up in sympathy. Then he pats my knee and squeezes it, a bit too long if you ask me. He asks if I like parrots and cockatoos, bragging about the cage of gorgeous birds from the jungle that he keeps in his weekend apartment in the French Quarter. Before I leave, he slips me the address, in case I ever feel like dropping by some Saturday night.

"Don't worry," he says, walking me to the door, a craggy claw on my shoulder. "The birds don't bite. And if you pet the parrots, they even speak a little Spanish. Like *¡hola, amigo!*" He laughs, then clutches my forearm, again a bit too long.

Well, why not drop by the judge's place? Maybe just for a beer.

KILLER HANGOVER

Feargus Woods Dunlop

It must have been a night to remember, because my mind was a blank when I woke. But it was the morning that followed I'll never forget.

I was curled up on a hard tiled floor, my trilby was pulled down over my eyes, and a team of experts were detonating a series of explosions inside my brain. I sat up with a jerk and my head was greeted forcefully by the underside of a desk.

I staggered out from under the table and smoothed down my crumpled suit. I stooped to scoop up my hat from the tiles but misjudged the angle and my skull made the acquaintance of the other side of the desk. Pin pricks of light flashed behind my eyelids stabbing me like some prick with a pin.

Sweat was pouring out of my every pore. My face may have been wet, but my mouth was dry, so I was overjoyed when my focus eventually returned, and I could see a glinting silver hipflask on the paper-strewn desk. My spirits lifted as I lifted the spirits to my lips. I took a deep pull from the flask's teat and savoured the warmth flooding my chest, restoring some sort of equilibrium.

I collapsed heavily into the leather chair behind the desk and surveyed the scene. The desk and chair faced a frosted glass door which had something written on it in a strange alphabet, behind me was a window with weak sunlight streaming in through the slatted blind. I scratched at the stubble on my jaw as my synapses desperately tried to get a message through.

I stared again at that lettering on the door, it wasn't foreign it was backwards! That's my name! This is my office! Huzzah! Score one for me. I was in my office.

Why though? Why was I in my office? Didn't I have a home to go to? I solved that riddle by finding a hand-written note sat on top of a pile of casefiles. On it was scrawled:

"Marie angry. Says 'Don't bother come back tonight. And don't try and crash at Phil & Sandra's their still sleep training the baby'"

Marie? I know that name ... Marie was my wife! I was getting good at this. But she'd banished me from the marital home, seems a bit harsh. I wasn't feeling charitably towards Marie and so I enjoyed spotting the fact she'd used the wrong 'their' there. Then I realised I was the one who would have written the note and my smugness quickly dissipated. I had another pull from the flask.

Right, I'd obviously had a row with Marie about ... something, and then gone out on a bender and ended up sleeping here at my office. Where I work. But what do I do? I thought maybe if I paced about a bit I might figure it out, but when I stood up the pounding in my head kicked up a gear, like a high-school drumline building to a crescendo before the fourth quarter. I offered a silent prayer asking God to take my hangover away, but there was about as much chance of that as there was any member of a school band getting laid before college. I slumped back into my chair and tried to work my way through the clues I'd assembled:

- My office has a frosted door with my name on it
- There are casefiles all over my desk
- I've got stubble on my jaw
- I'm wearing a crumpled suit with a trilby

I'm obviously a private detective! I must be good too, because I worked that out pretty fast all things considered. To mark my triumph I fished a packet of cigarettes from my breast pocket and tapped the carton in the palm of my hand before flicking one out and into my mouth. Oh yeah, I was 100% a P.I. And a damn cool one at that.

My voyage of self-discovery buoyed me and gave me the strength to navigate the perilous journey to the door. I swung it open, taking a moment to appreciate my name the right way round, but as soon as my eyes left the lettering and took in the room beyond, I slammed the door shut and stayed inside my office. I frantically scanned the room and hurried to the corner where I emptied the (mostly liquid) contents of my stomach into the wastepaper basket. I crumpled to the floor hugging my knees to my chest as I sucked in great gulps of air.

My mind was racing with what I'd just seen; outside my office door lay a very naked man on a table. And, unless I was very much mistaken, he was every bit as dead as he was nude. Another shockwave of nausea racked my body. Just what the hell had I done last night?

I checked my hands and under my nails; immaculately clean. I sniffed them and caught the distinct aroma of cleaning product. I'd obviously scrubbed them spotless last night. Why would I have done that unless I had something to scrub away? Lady Macbeth was a murderer before she became a germophobe, and I was beginning to suspect I'd done the same.

I was dragged from my guilt-ridden paranoia by the noise of a car pulling up outside the building. I pulled myself over to the window and used two fingers to create a gap in the blind to peak through. A car had parked directly outside my office and a man stepped out with an obvious revolver-shaped bulge under his jacket and clipped to his belt was a little gold shield. A cop! Oh dear God what had I done? What had I done?

I scrambled furiously in my desk looking for my gun. Where, oh where, was my gun? Every self-respecting private eye has a gun, so where is mine? The drawers were just filled with more papers and a catalogue for medical supplies. Medical supplies? What the hell was I planning on doing with those? I realised I'd probably thrown the gun away last night. This oddly calmed me; at least I'd had the sense to get rid of the murder weapon.

There was a knock on the outer door. I swallowed down a mouthful of bile that was making a desperate bid for freedom, straightened my suit, and headed out of the office. I kept my eyes glued to the outer door and refused to let them stray to the corpse laid out on the table to my right. Perhaps if I didn't look at it, it might just disappear?

My heartbeat was so loud in my ears I felt certain you'd be able to see the veins pulsing under my skin, like snakes writhing in a bag. I opened the door a crack.

"Hello, how can I help?" I stammered, aiming for a breezy smile but missing and hitting on the crazed grin of a madman. The man cocked his head to one side and gave me a look.

"Morning Clay. You feeling OK?"

He knows my name, oh God, he knows. Why else would he be here? Of course he knows.

"Mmmhmm, fine, fine. How can I help?" I had lost control of my eyelids. They were blinking furiously, like a hostage desperately trying to communicate with a negotiator. Perhaps they were trying to distance themselves from the sweaty, gibbering, wreck of the rest of me. The cop gave me another a puzzled look then continued.

"Um ... I'm here for you to tell me about the body?"

Right, there it is! It's out there. He definitely knows. I'm done. Life in prison for a murder of a man I don't know which I can't even remember committing. He reached his hand into his pocket, but weirdly the detective wasn't reaching for the handcuffs just yet, he pulled out a notebook and consulted it.

"The EMTs said they got him over to you last night and you promised you could rush the results for this morning. Is there a problem?"

In an instant everything came flooding back to me. The shock was so overwhelming I rocked on my feet and had to grip the door to stop from falling over.

I'm not a private detective, I'm the kooky pathologist that you always get in police procedurals. The trilby and the suit are just part of my schtick. I'd been working late last night rushing through the results of this victim and went out to celebrate because I'd found evidence that would tie this conclusively to a suspect we already had in custody. Obviously I'd had one too many. Oh what a relief!

I'm sure I'll be able to get a new wastepaper basket on expenses.

TRASH CAN STAKEOUT

Dustin Walker

I nodded along as my client spoke, but didn't register a word she said.

My eyes were glued to a fly that kept zipping around my living room/dining room/game room/private detective office. It finally hovered around the old woman's head and then bounced against her unnaturally red hair, as if it were a window to escape through.

All I could think of was why she couldn't feel the thing. I mean, it was a pretty big fly. Maybe all the hairspray she used created a barrier of some kind. Like an invisible fruity-smelling helmet.

"Is this something you could help me with?" The lady's voice spiked, snapping me back to the conversation. She pulled her shoulders back and sat even straighter in the chair. Too straight, if you ask me. That type of posture could only be acquired from a life that's all work and no play.

"Hmmmmm." I sucked in a deep breath and rubbed my chin, hoping it made her think I was contemplating whatever the hell she had said. In reality, I had zoned out during the entire conversation and couldn't even remember her first name. An unfortunate consequence of eating 30 milligrams of MindSlamz THC gummies. I never could get the daytime dosage right.

Fortunately, I vaguely recalled her saying something about her husband when she first came in. So I took a shot.

"Yes, ma'am, I think I can track down your husband."

I knew I missed the mark the moment the words left my mouth. She leaned back in her chair, her face so sour and crinkled that it cracked her makeup.

"Were you even listening?" Her sharp, impatient tone reminded me of my eleventh-grade math teacher. And my twelfth-grade English teacher. And every one of my college professors. "I'm only giving you a shot because of your mom, you know that right?"

I did know that. After graduating from journalism school, I quickly learned that the *New York Times* and *Wall Street Journal* weren't all that interested in hiring a 2.1 GPA student. So I started my own detective agency instead, seeing how the two professions were sort of related.

My mom—being the superhero she is—realized that I might need a little help to get my new enterprise going. So she was kind enough to refer one of her long-time clients at the salon to me. I just wished I could recall what said client needed me to do. Or what her name was, for that matter.

"Of course I was listening." If it wasn't a runaway husband, it had to be a cheating one. "I'll monitor your husband and give you a full report. If he's been up to anything, you'll know about it."

The woman's face went from annoyed to neutral. "Thank you, Andrew. I'll email you a list detailing his daily routine, including his work hours. But with how strange his behavior has been lately, I'm not sure he'll stick to his regular schedule."

Her name was Mallory, I just remembered. Or was it Macy? One of the two, anyway.

"Strange how?" I asked and mentally congratulated myself for delivering such a professional-sounding question.

"Like I said, acting secretly. Snapping his laptop shut whenever I enter the room, that sort of thing. Maybe I'm just being paranoid, but I'd like to put my mind at ease." Mallory-or-Macy stood up. "I have to go. Please let me know when you have any conclusive information."

"Yes, definitely. I'll call you with anything inclusive."

"Conclusive." she said.

"Yes, that too."

She stared hard at me for a while. As if trying to figure out if I was real or some unusual creature that had crawled out of her dream one night.

I stared back at her, just as intensely. Maybe even too intensely because she backed slowly toward the door.

"Okay, well, hope to hear from you soon." She left my apartment.

And I wondered if the fly went with her. Because the little bugger never showed its ugly face again.

Getting your first client is stressful for an entrepreneur. There's more to it than most people realize: paperwork, planning and probably some other stuff.

It's a ton of hard work. But I told myself this case was my opportunity to shine. To over-deliver and get a beaming testimonial from Mallory-or-Macy and start turning my little detective agency into something big. Really big. With an office downtown and a secretary and a watercooler some fat guy named Frank would come and refill every Monday. And whenever Frank would show up, everyone in the agency would yell out 'Frank!' Just like in that '80s sitcom, with the obese fellow and the pervy bartender.

I flipped open my MacBook, checked my email and opened up the stalker-list she had sent me about her husband David Gacey.

It was a freakin' spreadsheet—nothing good ever showed up in a spreadsheet. But I held my nose and took a glance at those miserable little rows.

There were close to 50 places in that list! Tracking all these spots would be a monster job. One that would take weeks, at least, and would require hours of tedious work.

So I hacked David Gacey's email instead.

Well, I didn't do it personally. A guy I met in college—everyone called him Eyeballs—was more than willing to pry his way into someone's inbox for the right price. A price I could now afford thanks to Mallory-or-Macy's recently paid deposit.

Eyeballs told me it could take him a few weeks to get David's password, since he needed the guy to click one of his phishing emails to install keylogging malware. But then Eyeballs messaged me back just hours later saying that the deed had been done. Apparently David Gacey was a click first, ask questions later kind of guy.

I dove into his inbox and started opening and scrolling with reckless abandon. Aside from a puzzlingly high number of messages from pygmy goat breeders, nothing in his email seemed unusual. Certainly no messages that reeked of forbidden love, although the pygmy goat stuff was a big question mark.

And just when I was about to give up and cut my losses, a message popped into his inbox.

The subject line: *tomorrow*

The sender name: *The Guy*

Whoever 'The Guy' was obviously didn't want a paper trail connected to his real name. I wondered if he ran some kind of escort service that David Gacey had used. I opened the email.

Too risky to send online. I'll leave a brown box in the garbage can at the corner of Wilkinson and 5th Ave. by 2 p.m.

I knew that garbage can. Just outside Darrell's Bar & Grill. Good burgers there. Crappy draft beer though. That swill was responsible for me contributing to that garbage can once or twice.

I rubbed my eyes and thought about the situation. Surely, The Guy wasn't going to leave a woman in the garbage can. That wouldn't work out well for anyone. So what did he have for David Gacey?

Money was the most obvious answer, but you could eliminate a paper trail quite easily using cryptocurrency. Maybe it was photos. Embarrassing images of David Gacey's affair or visits to known escorts, perhaps.

No, it had to be something else. Something big. I could feel it.

You wouldn't employ a clandestine garbage-can drop unless the package was especially illegal. Something that went far beyond David Gacey planting his pickle in someone else's pantry. And once I dug up the details about this looming exchange, Mallory-or-Macy would be even more impressed with my work. Which meant, I'd be scoring myself a quality rich lady testimonial for my soon-but-not-too-soon-to-be-created private investigator website.

In fact, I thought this case might even propel me to much bigger and better things. Becoming a security advisor for the police, maybe. Or even the FBI.

I kicked back on my couch and smiled, letting all those ambitious thoughts tumble through my head like windswept plastic bags. I popped another THC gummy—this one shaped like a little cow—and started planning how tomorrow's stakeout would go down.

My plan was simple: keep an eye on the can until The Guy made the drop and then intercept the package. Neither party would have any idea that an intrepid young P.I. had infiltrated their operation.

I drove my old Hyundai down to the trash can in question at about 8 a.m. The email said the drop had to happen *before* 2 p.m., so I figured things could go down anytime before then.

As I pulled up across the street from the can, I realized I had never been to this part of town during the day before. Hipsters lounged at a patio cafe drinking what I assumed were $37 lattes. A spikey-haired woman walked her little dog along the sidewalk. Light traffic hummed up and down the street. No one stumbling around or smoking reefer or hollering incomprehensibly at imaginary evils. It was all so boring.

I stared at that trash can so hard I thought the green paint would flake right off it. And every time a person got anywhere near the thing, I'd tense up like a tabby ready to pounce. Until the eight or ninth person wandered past and all my nervous tension was replaced by a grinding monotony.

Same street. Same sort of people. Same ugly green can.

As the minutes stretched into hours, my eyes got heavy. I told myself: don't fall asleep. It'd be worse than that sleepover in fifth grade. Only this time, changing your pajama pants wouldn't solve the problem.

I shrugged off my jacket and cranked the air conditioning. My eyes still drooped.

I slapped myself a few times. Hard. Even pulled my hair a little, which made some passersby sprint-walk past my car. But after 10 minutes, the heaviness returned.

Fuzzy thoughts of my dream downtown office filled my head: the perky secretary, the well-heeled clients and the freakishly large oak desk I'd set my feet on every morning. Because nothing screams success like a desk that fills 90 percent of your office.

I jerked awake. The dash clock said 1:43 p.m. *Crap*.

I flung open my car door. The drop could have happened already, I thought, sprinting across the street. A Suburban blasted its horn at me, but I couldn't slow down.

I looked inside the garbage can: candy wrappers, drink cups and a half-eaten burrito from Picante's, the nearby Mexican place. Their green sauce was delicious.

I rolled up a sleeve, plunged my arm into the can and started rooting around. Nothing that felt like a box. So I stuck my arm in deeper, right up to my armpit. Looking back, The Guy probably would have just set the package on top of the trash. Burying it two feet deep would be disgustingly unnecessary.

Pedestrians flashed me strange looks as they passed. I supposed my mumbling about not being able to find my package didn't help things.

A stocky fellow in a Star Wars hoodie walked up to me.

"Hey. You're early." His brow furrowed like he was trying to figure out the punchline to a strange joke.

My chest tightened when I spotted the brown box in his hands. The Guy's sudden appearance caught me so off-guard that I just froze for a couple of seconds, arm still pit-deep in the can.

"So ..." He looked around. "Do you still want me to put it in the trash, or ..."

My fog cleared. "No, that's okay." I pulled my Pepsi-and-salsa-slick arm out of the garbage. "I can take it now."

I stuck out my hand, but he didn't give me the box. Instead, The Guy kept that furrowed expression on his face and chewed his bottom lip. Then his posture relaxed.

"Here you go." He handed me the box. "So we're done now, right?"

I nodded and he walked away.

Gripping the box to my chest, I jogged back to my car. And I swear the same goddamn Suburban swerved and honked at me again.

Once inside, I tore into the package. A ceramic mushroom lay inside a mess of shredded newspaper. The thing was poorly colored in streaks of brown and white, like someone's twitchy kid had gone at it with a paint-soaked toothbrush. And the cap was oddly small, which gave the statue a phallic-like quality.

I took the mushroom out and ran my fingers along the shaft—um, I mean stem—searching for some kind of opening. Or maybe a flap where items, like bills, could be shoved in.

There was nothing like that. But something small rattled inside the thing, like a tiny pebble or a bit of glass. Maybe a diamond. I shook the penis-shaped mushroom harder—using both hands now—just as an elderly couple walked past my car. The old woman elbowed her husband in the stomach and pointed at me.

I didn't need any more rumors dogging me in this town, so I went home to analyze the object in private.

I sat on my couch and stared at that ugly mushroom for almost an hour, hoping that the answer would just materialize if I focused hard enough.

But focusing had never been my strong suit. The idea of smashing the thing open crossed my mind, but that seemed a step too far at this stage. It'd be tampering with evidence. ... I think. So diving back into David Gacey's inbox seemed like a more reasonable course of action.

My stomach jumped into my chest once Gmail loaded. There had been a back-and-forth email exchange between David and The Guy just in the last hour.

David at 2:27 pm: *I checked the garbage can at Wilkinson and 5th. No box. You running late?*

The Guy at 2:49 pm: *What are you talking about? I handed it right to you. You got to break open the mushroom statue.*

David at 2:52 pm: *What statue? You didn't give me anything!*

That was the last email in the thread.

My heart went into overdrive. They were probably chatting on the phone by now, swapping notes and realizing I had intercepted the drop.

I couldn't bide my time any longer. If I really wanted to make a name for myself as a rockstar P.I., this case had to work out.

I smashed the mushroom against the edge of my coffee table. The cap exploded, sending ceramic shards everywhere. A micro-SD memory card slid across the floor. I picked it up and could practically feel the mysteries locked inside.

With a shaky hand, I plugged the thing into my MacBook's card reader. It contained a single folder. And the contents of that folder made me recoil in disgust.

Another damn spreadsheet. I tell you, these Gaceys must get off on this kind of thing.

I opened the file up, expecting a bunch of calculations. Instead, it contained hundreds—maybe even thousands—of names, social security numbers, addresses, birthdates and other information.

The sheer volume of personal details suggested identity fraud of epic proportions. Mallory-or-Macy was worried about cheating, when she should have been concerned about David committing massive white-collar crime. It explained why he had been acting so strange recently.

I texted my client and she said she'd drop by in a couple of hours.

The time dripped by slowly. Gummy-inspired visions of Mallory-or-Macy's reaction to my findings fluttered through my mind. Sure, she'd be shocked. Maybe even crushed. But she would also be supremely impressed with the investigation.

And big things would soon follow.

Mallory-or-Macy knocked at my door around 5 p.m. She squeezed past me with hardly a hello and took a seat at my desk.

"So you've found something?" she asked.

"Yes, I have." I took my seat across from her. "But it's probably not what you were expecting."

She frowned. "What's that supposed to mean?"

I had a whole speech planned, emphasizing the social ills of identity fraud and how completing this job required a keen eye and an inquisitive mind. I'd end the show by flipping open my MacBook in dramatic fashion and showing her that nasty spreadsheet of his.

But none of that happened because I forgot how to start my speech. The words were all bunged up in my head, like a stubborn sink clog.

"It means ..." I swallowed hard and took a deep breath. Then I finally blurted out: "Your husband's an identity thief."

Mallory-or-Macy cocked a poorly drawn eyebrow. "Excuse me?"

I opened my MacBook and showed her the spreadsheet. Her face went all sour again, which made me realize some context was needed. So I barfed out a 10-minute spiel about email hacking, spreadsheets and a dick-shaped mushroom statue. Most of it made sense, I think.

She exhaled loudly and leaned back in her chair. I smiled, waiting for the inevitable accolades.

"I didn't give you permission to hack my husband's email." Mallory-or-Macy's eyes narrowed. "And it seems to me that you didn't uncover anything about his cheating."

"Well, no, not about the cheating." I needed to turn things around. "But I did uncover that your husband is building one massive identity theft ring."

"You can't prove that." Her mouth tightened into a thin line.

"Well, it's pretty obvious." I nodded at the laptop. It was also pretty obvious that Mallory-or-Macy was likely involved in the fraud on some level herself. That'd make getting her testimonial much more difficult.

"What's obvious is your bumbling attempt at blackmail." She pulled out her phone. "How much?"

Quick thinking was not my strong suit. I'm worse at it than focusing, in fact. Also, I wasn't 100 percent sure what she was even talking about. So I just looked at her, mouth open.

"I want the memory card and for you to forget I ever hired you," she said. "So name your price."

I spat out the first round number I could think of.

"One million dollars."

"I'll give you $5,000." She tapped away on her phone. "You'll get the e-transfer notification shortly. I think this is more than generous."

I wasn't so sure. This hadn't been the big case I needed. And it certainly didn't mark the start of a sweet downtown office with a tubby water guy. So I countered her offer.

"$50,000. Otherwise, your husband is in *hot water*." I might've actually cringed when those words left my mouth. Hot water. My God Andrew, you're trying to blackmail a woman here, not scold a five-year-old.

Mallory-or-Macy scoffed. "$5,000. Remember, you also committed a crime by hacking my husband's email. If the police get involved, we're both in trouble." She tilted her head in a way that said 'checkmate.'

I pretended to consider it for a moment, even though I planned to take the deal. Part of me expected that fly to reappear and start banging against her head again. It didn't. And for some reason, that made me a little sad.

"Deal." I said. "On one condition."

"What?"

"If any of your friends or family need a private investigator, you refer them to me."

She looked at me for a moment, as if trying to mentally decode what I had said. Then she laughed and walked to the door.

"Goodbye, Andrew." She scanned my apartment and smiled in a bad way. "Good luck with the whole P.I. thing."

Then she left.

I sunk back into my desk chair and thought about things for a bit. The way Mallory-or-Macy looked when she walked out. That smug tone in her voice. And the hundreds of people listed on that spreadsheet.

I tried to imagine what I'd spend those five Gs on, but my mind kept settling back on the list. Wondering what would happen to all the folks whose identities could be stolen. My gut turned heavy and acrid.

Running this agency had turned me into a cutthroat businessman. Sure, my premier detective skills had made me $5,000 in a mere two days. But I wasn't the type of guy to trade my ethics for success.

After a few more gummies, and even more thinking, I got back in touch with my man Eyeballs. David Gacey had already reset his email password, but my newly acquired five-stack could buy plenty of other hacking services.

It took Eyeballs only a week to get access to David Gacey's hard drive. You'd think he'd learn not to click random emails after the first time he got hacked, but apparently not.

Files showed that David had been building an underground online store where crooks could buy and sell social insurance numbers, credit card details and other information. Like a slightly more evil Amazon.

I wanted to tell the cops and then run a bunch of ads screaming about how my little P.I. agency had helped take down a major identity fraud operation. But Eyeballs nixed that idea because he didn't want the cops digging into how I got all those illicit details. And since I didn't want Eyeballs hacking into my computer—especially not my online search history—I agreed to keep it all on the downlow.

So I anonymously fed the information to every newspaper and TV outlet in a 200-mile radius. It didn't take long for the first headline to land:

Man Builds Massive Online Store for Identity Crooks

Mom called me up in a panic the day the story broke, which I responded to with fake surprise. No point upsetting her with all the details.

Everything seemed to have worked out in the end. Except I hadn't scored another client since Mallory-or-Macy. And after paying Eyeballs, my bank account was dangerously low as rent day drew near. I even started applying for reporter jobs at newspapers in the middle of nowhere, figuring that P.I. work just wasn't in the cards for me.

Most nights—and days—I just stared at the TV and pondered my sad situation. My mood headed south faster than the gas station sushi I often had for lunch. Not even MindBenz jelly bombs helped.

Then one morning—sometime between doom scrolling on Twitter and playing 'what's that smell?' in my apartment hallway—I got a text from Mom. She had a new potential client for me: a lady who needed help tracking down her long-lost sister.

A missing person case, in other words. Maybe one that might result in a heartfelt reunion that'd make headlines across the country. Or perhaps even lead to appearances on talk shows.

I told Mom to send her over right away. There was no time to lose.

Because I sensed that this would be the job that really would rocket my little P.I. agency toward fame and fortune. And I had to take full advantage of the opportunity.

So I popped a couple of gummies, tidied up my office and waited for Margaret (or was it Megan?) to arrive.

LUCKY LOU

Ray Bazowski

Before all that nasty business at the Rainbow Room, Lou used to be called Sweet Tooth on account of him always sucking on a mint. Which is just what he was doing, sitting on his favourite stool and talking to Hinky Bob, who'd chosen to barkeep his own joint that night because his in-laws were in town and he told his wife he would sooner chew on a bag of broken concrete than look at their sour pusses. Hinky Bob tending bar worked out to be a break for Sweet Tooth, cause in the middle of some made-up story he was telling Hinky, Lou's mint got stuck in his throat and his face began to turn the color of cat litter. At least that's what Johnny O'Day, who was sitting next to Lou, said it looked like, though Johnny-O's not always reliable in his descriptions. He's your basic bull shiner, does nothing but blow smoke out his butt. Like a lot of others, Johnny-O wanted to hang with us guys, but him having no talents to speak of, none of us had any use for him.

You know what they say about how appearances can be deceiving. That night at the Rainbow Room, Johnny-O showed he wasn't such a scaramouche after all. With Lou choking on his candy like he was, Johnny-O had the wit to wrap his arms around him and give a big heave. Problem was, he got a little carried away with his heineken maneuver. The way Johnny-O told it, that mint popped right out and sailed clear across the bar, landing smack in Steady Eddy's drink like it was a perfect Tom Brady pass. Now Steady Eddy hadn't been paying attention to all this commotion with Lou because he was occupied with sweet talking this girl he'd come with. Even though he's not the swiftest pony in the race, when he turned around and saw a hard candy that didn't belong in his whiskey glass, Eddy was able to work out where it'd come from. Without so much as a how do you do, he sidled over to Lou and gave him a big grin before throwing a sucker punch faster than it takes to say Alphonse's your uncle. As he used to be a boxer, Eddy's hook was sufficient to seriously redeploy Lou's jaw so that his chin ended up sticking out sideways from his face.

That's when Hinky Bob jumped in. Not wishing any more trouble on his premises, he hustled Lou out the bar real quick like, and paid for a cab to take him to the hospital to get his face straightened out. Hinky wasn't known to be generous, so everyone figured he planned to add the cost of the ride to Lou's tab. Admittedly the point's moot, because not a half hour after all this ruckus with Sweet Tooth, who should walk into the Rainbow Room but Little Big Charlie. Seeing as Little Big's the boss of bosses in town, Hinky Bob wasted no time sucking up to him, thinking the visit had to do with a payment owed. But it wasn't about that at all. Appears the girl Steady Eddy had brought with him was one of Little Big's side dishes, and he didn't appreciate someone else trying to sneak a nibble.

Not one for discussing things at length, being as he was a firm believer in the efficient use of his time and energy, Little Big Charlie opened his coat, pulled out a shotgun, and blasted Steady Eddy and the girl with a single shot. Some might say this was excessive, but you got to acknowledge it was a neat trick. Unfortunately, Hinky Bob didn't think so and said as much just before a second blast left a hole where his heart used to be. The look on his face before he dropped, Johnny-O said, was the saddest he'd ever seen, like Hinky at that moment realized this was all there was going to be at the end of his rainbow.

Johnny-O, he wasn't spared neither. When Little Big aimed his gun at him, Johnny-O put up his hand as though he thought this could stop the buckshot. Charlie placed the muzzle next to it and dispersed the hand all across the back of the bar, taking out most of the liquor bottles as well, which didn't really matter much because Little Big wasn't a drinker and Johnny-O wasn't in any condition to enjoy one himself. And that was that. Little Big didn't bother with Johnny-O no more because he needed a witness to spread the word that no one should ever get ideas about dicking around with what was his. Needless to say, Charlie was confident Johnny-O would be smart enough to disremember the particulars of the episode that cost him his mitt when the blues arrived at the scene. We all of us knew that in our town there're certain things you have to be able to forget you've ever seen if you want to be able to keep on seeing things.

After that we let Johnny-O pal around with us because there're circumstances a man with a hook can come in handy, although we refused to call him Dr. John like he asked. We're free-lancers, me, Peckerhead, No Name, Hardy, and a couple others that'd come and go according to how their old ladies felt at the time. As independents, we'd take on straight work if it was easy, and do the occasional boost if it looked clean. Naturally, whenever we succeeded in a heist, we'd make sure to give an appropriate bite to whosever territory it was because first rule if you're a jobber is you don't step on the toes of those that got the means to make you regret being greedy.

As for Sweet Tooth, well, everyone agreed he was damn lucky the way he got his jaw broke and sent to the hospital before the main event, and that's when we started calling him Lucky Lou. There's times when a name's so right you don't think twice about it. But there's also situations where a person grows into his name, so when you reflect on it, what began as joke becomes truer than the truest thing anyone's ever said. This definitely was the case with Lou. See, Lou ran a small-time book, a one-man show taking bets on the trotters that paid him just enough he didn't have to bother with straight work like the rest of us. Making book is dicey for those who don't have the scratch to cover all bets. But Lou was able to stay on top of the game because he had a line into the track, which meant he got the lowdown on the real odds as compared to what was posted. This, and the fact that he took mostly the nickel and dime wagers, was what made Lou a survivor in the racket.

Maybe it was because he survived the Rainbow Room that Lou did something out of character soon after he had the wire removed from his jaw. He accepted a large on a spindly mare his source told him was probably a longshot just like it was posted. But with no prior history of pulling the sulky on a mile long, it was hard to say for sure. Before the race was run, Lou got sensible and decided it'd be prudent to lay off part of the bet, and so he set out to see Little Big Charlie who, among other things, was the bank for all the books in town. Except he never got to see Little Big because his car was broadsided on Canal street by a hipster flake who was texting when he should have been watching the road. Fractured fibula, smashed left hip, punctured spleen, and a concussion was what Lou got for trying to be cautious. Meanwhile, the flake walked away without a sign of damage, though a couple of Lou's friends visited him later in the day to explain the basics of safe driving and to make sure the pain was all evened out, so to speak. Mind you, that didn't help Lou any because, wouldn't you know it, just like in the movies the longshot came in, leaving him with a payout he couldn't make good on.

Thing is, what Lou had no way of knowing was the race had been fixed and the mook who'd placed the bet was in on it. What's more, he'd been making the same play with all the other small-timers in town, some of whom, unlike Lou, were unlucky enough to have been able to share their exposure with Little Big Charlie. As you can guess, Little Big wasn't happy with this state of affairs, and he spared no effort in finding out how it was he ended up owing so much on a nag that wasn't properly handicapped. Few days later the mook was found floating in the canal along with a couple of the Guidos who'd managed to spread their risk, Little Big's way of impressing upon all the plungers and turf accountants that there was a limit to peoples' reckless behaviour he was prepared to tolerate.

Lou, he was no dummy. Coming as close as he did to being on the wrong side of Little Big twice in one month was enough to persuade him to quit his book and take a regular job. That's how he found himself back at the paint room at Friendly's where he used to grind it out before becoming a gamester. Friendly's been around forever. It's the place everyone went to get body work done, whether it was his vehicle or not. First day at work, Lou's sweating putting on a new coat on a fleet of caddies that were supposed to be shipped to Florida once the paperhanger finished with the documents. While waiting for the spray to bake, Lou went outside for a smoke, except he forgot to take off his coveralls which were full of solvent fumes. Next thing you know, there was Lou staggering around the parking lot, flames shooting off him like he was celebrating the 4th of July. Second degree burns over most of his body and a month in hospital was what he got for his party.

Course by now a thing like that happens to Lou and you're expecting to see a silver lining for him and a lot worse for someone else. And that's just what unfolded. Crazy thing was that once again it was Little Big who was involved. Seems the caddies were lifted from one of his warehouses where they were waiting to be chopped up. Those that done it were about the stupidest horkers imaginable because not only did they hit absolutely the worst person they could've, but they had bush for brains 'cause they didn't know enough to cover their tracks. Didn't take long for Little Big to round up the hillbillies. And because proper messaging was key to the success of his operations, he seen to it they were locked up in the paint room at Friendly's along with poor saps working there, before having the place torched. As for Lou, while this was all going down he was sitting pretty as pink in his hospital room. Well, maybe not so much pink as the color of burnt toast. But at least like a piece of toast that falls to the floor with its buttered side up.

You get the picture. Lou was a walking accident, yet whenever harm came to him, it ended up being a good thing. That's how we began to see Lucky Lou was the moniker he was destined for. And that's why I decided to recruit him for the job I'd planned. The idea for the job, I'll have you know, came from the Temptress. The Temptress was my girlfriend at the time. Her real name was Tem, which was short for Temerity, which she got, as she tells it, because her parents weren't exactly overjoyed when she arrived. They hung her with that crazy autograph because she was a surprise baby, them being old and all, and they didn't look forward to raising another squab when they were planning on getting comfortable in their leisurewear and enjoying free drinks at the casino. I can't swear this was true, though, because the Temptress liked to tell stories that were a little wide of the mark. In fact, that's how I got to start calling her the Temptress. More than once I'd get so wound up by a tale she'd spun that I was willing to do anything she asked just so I could enjoy a satisfactory ending to it.

This time the story was about a jewel—a big red ruby she saw at Lansky's. She got it into her head that she had to have the stone, and swore Lansky's was just waiting to be knocked over given it'd been at least a half dozen years since they were last robbed. A jewelry caper's not really my thing because the organising has to be absolutely perfect, what with the kind of alarm setup those joints have. Yet there was the Temptress badgering me night and day, so I put my mind to it and eventually saw an angle that had possibilities. Lansky's is a block above the route our annual Christmas parade takes. Day of the parade, of course they'd be open, but it'd be unlikely there'd be any customers when all the floats and marching bands were passing down the street. Even better, both the main and the side streets would be closed off, which meant responders to any alarm would have to take the long way. If we timed it right, we'd have a long enough stretch to hit Lansky's and then disappear into the crowd watching the parade after our work was done.

That's where Lou came into the picture. The way I figured it, if Lucky Lou was in on it, and anything went south with him, that would be the signal to pull out of the job pronto. He'd be our threat alarm, like a canary in the coal mine. I got to give it to Lou. He wasn't looking too good anymore, but he was a gamer. What did he have to lose, he said when I came to him with the proposal, which was really him saying he had no other way of paying his hospital bills. Lou's role was simple. I had him and Johnny-O stand on the sidewalk where the parade was scheduled to pass. The parade's usually at least a mile long. All Lou and Johnny-O had to do was phone us when it got half-way past their position, which I calculated was when it would cause maximum disruption to vehicle travel in the area. Johnny-O had an extra set of instructions. Any sign that Lou was in some sort of difficulty—it didn't matter what—he was to call me so I could put the kibosh on the operation.

As plans go, this was one of my better ones, I don't mind saying. The call from Lou and Johnny came about when I expected it to. Once we got the signal, No Name was left to guard the front door while Peckerhead, Hardy Hardy and me slipped into Lansky's, which had no customers just like I predicted. I announced our intentions all serious-like, and had Hardy Hardy put on his scowl, which made him look like he was mad as hell at everyone in the world. Old Lansky responded to this like I thought he would, but his missus wasn't quite so keen on us getting our claws on the expensive items they kept in their safe. I personally don't believe in guns or knives because they give the guy holding them the idea they should be used, which, if that happens, tends to rule out diplomacy. Which is why my weapon of choice is a medium weight ball peen hammer. It's more economical, both in terms of its cost and in terms of how it can be employed to persuade someone of your point-of-view. All that was needed was one quick rap on old man Lansky's knuckles and his wife stopped her kvetching and started fumbling with the dial on the safe.

That's when I got the call from Johnny-O.

"Lou's dead," he said, his voice sounding as if it was being squeezed out of him like he was a bagpipe.

"What do you mean he's dead?" I was doing a little accordion squeeze myself.

"It was Little Big Charlie," Johnny-O said. "They had him dressed up as Santy Claus on a float made to look like a sled pulled by reindeer, though they looked more like horses with horns glued to their heads, you ask me."

"Never mind what they looked like," I yelled. Johnny-O had this annoying habit of going off topic when brevity's what's called for in relating facts. "What's this got to do with Lou?"

"Well," he said, "Santy was throwing cellophane wrapped candies to the kids on the sidewalk when his sack came apart and a bunch of them spilled out on the road. Lou and a couple of kids rushed out to pick up the candies. Lou was shoving the squirts aside when he slipped, and his head went under the wheel of the float. It looks like an eggplant now."

"American or Chinese?" I said.

"American or Chinese what?" he said.

"Eggplant," I said. "If it's American, maybe the head just got rearranged a bit. But if it's Chinese, then I guess it would be terminal."

"It's terminal, alright. I tell you, Lou's dead," Johnny-O wailed.

Since I had no further cause to dispute his testimony, I had a decision to make. Should we quit now that we were so close to the big haul? It took but an instant for me to make the resolution. The way I reasoned it, with Lou being dead, his luck must have run out. That being the case, there should be no bad karma waiting for anyone else. We finished stuffing our own Christmas sack with the contents of the safe, which I was pleased to see included the Temptress's ruby.

We rendezvoused at the Temptress's apartment later in the day to discuss Lou's tragedy. None of us had much to say about it so we concentrated on settling how we were to cash out our haul. Ordinarily there are three ways of disposing of stolen jewellery. One is just to pass it on to a fence. This is the safest, though it isn't the most lucrative method of compensating you for all the pains you've taken to scoop the goods. If the goods are extra fine, sure, you might get a quarter, but generally it's a dime on the dollar. Riskier, though better moneywise, is to offer the lot to the insurance company at a discount. I didn't favor this approach because once contact is made, the insurance dicks, who're a lot smarter than our local bulls, will do everything they can to lay a trap for you. Best, if you can swing it, is to deal the gems back to the one you stole them from, so long so long as he's the kind who's willing to make such a transaction and keep it quiet. You can get the most for your efforts because if the negotiation's done right, the jeweller will be happy to pay a premium to get his goods returned because he'll also be able to earn a commission, which amounts to the difference between what he pays out and what the insurance company pays him. Only this approach wasn't available because, to be honest, I may have been a little less than economical when I laid my hammer on old man Lansky's paw. The way he howled told me his fingers weren't going to be of much use for a while. In the circumstances, I had my doubts he'd be agreeable to a share-the-bounty scheme, cause what's a jeweller without workable digits?

That's how it was we all decided the wise thing to do was to let the Temptress use her connections to unload the loot. It was when we got round to hashing out the split that things got a bit wet. The Temptress said that because it was her idea to begin with, she should be able to keep the ruby as well as pocket a share of the proceeds. Johnny-O complained this wasn't fair since it was him who got to see Lou's head redesigned, which caused him to suffer from post-dramatic syndrome. My experience is that the only way to deal with this kind of objection before it leads to an out and out barney is to make the rules plain to everyone. So I picked up my ball peen and said to Johnny-O that it'd be awfully hard for him to unzip his pants to take a leak with two hooks. That got Peckerhead to start giggling, but then he laughs at anything to do with a pecker, which is how he got his name in the first place. Anyways, my words were enough to settle the matter, and that's how we left things.

The Temptress came through on her end and we all got our dough by the end of the week, but not before she persuaded us to chip in for a new suit for Lou for his funeral. None of us saw the need since it would have to be a closed casket service, seeing as the best repair job would still leave Lou looking the worse for wear. She wouldn't budge, saying that Lou should look his best when he went to meet his maker. This is the thing I've always liked about the Temptress. She's a conniver, which is what attracted her to me in the first place, her and me fitting together like a perfectly matched pair of gloves. But she also has a sentimental side that'd show up when you least expected it. Like the time she had me drop a yard into a panhandler's outstretched hand, even though that meant there'd be no bottle of bub for her at the restaurant we'd planned on going to that evening. You gotta love a gal who's willing to give up a treat like that just because some schlub's got a gentle face, as she put it.

The day of Lou's funeral comes, and I have to tell you, I was feeling pretty uneasy. Turns out the morning after his accident the local daily ran a story about how Lou was a hero seeing as he sacrificed his own body in order to push a pair of helpless tykes to safety. That one got Johnny-O to snorting because the way he and just about everyone else saw it, Lou was only trying to clear the path so he'd have all them sweets to himself. That's not the kind of story that sells newspapers, though, which I guess is why this particular detail wasn't mentioned. Unfortunately, a touchy-feely story about someone's misery isn't just good for hawking rags. When it came out, a committee of do-gooders wasted no time starting a collection which raised so much dosh that they were able to lay out a real classy funeral for Lou. Not only that, but the spot where Lou was standing before his craving turned him into a stiff became a shrine with candles and flowers and stuffed animals, though I don't see why anyone would think that plush toys was something he'd appreciate. Even the bonobos at city hall got into the act, debating whether to rename the street after Lou as a way of commemorating his contribution to child welfare. No question, Lou was still lucky, and this is what made me jittery as a skag head waiting for his next hit.

The deputy mayor made a speech at the funeral, going on about how Lou set an example for what it means to give of oneself, which is the kind of civic virtue that's needed in these trying times, he brayed. Like a politician in our town knows anything about virtue! I tuned out the other speakers and instead admired all the flower arrangements piled up by the coffin. Me and the others contributed a wreath, though I had a hard time convincing the florist it was cool to send a horseshoe shaped floral tribute to a bereavement. But there it was, all done up in white carnations with a single red one at its center, this being the Temptress's idea. To symbolize his heart that no longer beats was how she made it out to be. Like I said, she can be sentimental.

The largest bouquet by far was one from Little Big Charlie. It was so huge that it took almost as many people to carry it into the chapel as what carried Lou himself in. I made a point of checking it out just before we all left to plant Lou in the cemetery. I can tell you I wasn't surprised when I spotted a tag that said this tower of flowers belonged to someone else's funeral. Just like Little Big. Messaging is messaging. As for how it's done, well, for Charlie no larceny's too small.

With the funeral over, all there was for me to do was sit in my apartment and wait for the inevitable, which mercifully didn't take that long. Peckerhead, No Name, Hardy Hardy and Johnny-O had already been picked up when the law came for me. It was the Temptress that was responsible. She'd been pinched the day before and didn't need much convincing to rat on us.

How this all spooled out tells you what's wrong with the world we live in. Night before he was to be laid to rest, the Temptress showed up at the funeral parlour, saying she was a relative of Lou. Said she wanted to look at her dear deceased cousin one last time before he was put in the ground. The young assistant that was working there obliged and unscrewed the lid. The Temptress then shuttled him out the room, telling him she needed to be able to express her sorrow privately. This is when she took a tie clip out of her purse and fixed it on the new tie that came with the suit we'd all paid for so Lou could have a proper send off. The Temptress had the tie clip specially designed in filigreed silver—say what you will, she had good taste when it came to accoutrements. The thing that made that clip a true work of art was the red ruby she had placed at its center. What can I say? That's just the kind of person the Temptress was. There was no way of knowing when her sentimental side was going to come out.

None of this we were meant to know, except when that useless assistant went to close the lid after the Temptress left, his eye caught the shine of the stone. His thinking on the matter was normal. What's the point of leaving something valuable on a dead person's body when it could be put to use by someone still living? So, like you or me would've done, he pocketed the clip and the next day tried to peddle it. Only first place he went was to Lansky's. As you can well imagine, the old man was still nursing a grievance and made sure to lay his good hand on his own ruby before calling the cops. That's how they got tipped to the Temptress. And as I've already said, she squealed on the rest of us, not even bothering to shed a pigeon's tear I was told.

Where's honor among thieves, you might say. I don't take that view. Show me who's honorable anymore. The Temptress did what she had to do to look out after herself, which is only natural. It's not what the Temptress did that shows up the rot in our society. It's a lack of proper tutoring what's at fault. As I see it, the funeral parlour assistant had to be pretty dim to start with. After all, who takes a job working on corpses he's had no hand in producing? But even if you're a low wattage bulb, you should've learned at some point not to hock a trinket locally when you have no clue where it's come from. It's our education system that failed that numbnuts, and now me and the boys are paying the price for what schools have stopped teaching.

If I take any consolation from this whole affair, it's that Little Big Charlie was nabbed as well. As it happened, I wasn't the only one who noticed his floral park was meant for someone else's going away party. The funeral director tried to be discreet about it when he sent the arrangement to where it belonged, saying that somewhere along the line a person must have made an honest mistake. The grieving family wasn't buying the story and had inquiries made. Petty thing like getting caught pilfering a bunch of flowers ordinarily wouldn't cause Little Big much trouble were it not for the fact that there was a newly elected District Attorney in town who hadn't as yet gotten his beak wet. The weasel subpoenaed Little Big's books and found not only did Charlie expense the flowers, but a lot of other items that he had no business claiming against his income. IRS were called in, and Little Big Charlie got a tenner for tax fraud. Though Charlie being Charlie, he's been busy making sure everyone knows how ace his accommodations are.

Is there a lesson to be learned from my story? I've had a lot of time to reflect on the question. Tell the truth, there's only one conclusion I've been able to draw. Which is that there's got to be a scale somewhere in the universe weighing all the luck that's ever been parcelled out. Someone like Lou get's more than his measure means others have to get less if things are to balance out, which is why I'm here in this stinking slammer talking to you losers.

THE PURLOINED PACHYDERM

D J Rout

It was in the month of J—, or possibly J— in the year 18—, when I was sitting with my friend C. Auguste Dupin, the genius detective, and he was entering into some further explanations, when his discourse was interrupted by the precipitate arrival of F——, then newly nominated as Prefect of the Paris Police. He, F——, entered with a crash, making no obeisances, and with mien of some malevolent bird stood under the bust of Pallas above Dupin's chamber door.

He was so tall his flat-topped head grazed the lintel. His height was somewhat augmented by thick and heavy boots, the better perhaps to walk the poubelle-strewen streets of Paris, but he was still a tall man, of Byronic pallor and Lazarusian antecedents, with a breathy voice unsuited to yelling and a conductive bolt against each jugular.

"What is the meaning of this?" asked Dupin in an outraged tone, which he affected to distract from the fact that he had not enkindled the wick, entrousered his legs or embrushed his teeth.

"It is a calamitous catastrophe concomitant with the catch-cry of the Communards!" F—— exclaimed.

"Do not derange yourself, my dear Prefect," said Dupin. "And please sit down. The height and shape of your head are disturbing my *corbeau.*"

"Sorry," said F——, taking a chair which groaned under his weight even though each of its legs was crammed with important documents.

"I surmise, from your use of your *clef extraordinaire*, that something is amiss in one of Paris's public amenities. Perhaps a shortfall in a recent stocktake?"

"Precise—" F—— began, but Dupin forestalled him with the adroit use of a *boulle.*

"Please, my dear Prefect. I further surmise that 'Fatsaux,' the elephant recently given to the King by the Queen of the English, Scots, Welsh, Irish and certain other races, is missing from the Les Jardins Zoologique?"

"Isn't *the* Les Jardins Zoologique a bit redundant?" I asked, forgetting that Dupin had another *boulle.*

While F—— and I massaged our bruised pudenda, Dupin entered into some surmises:

"I even further surmise that the animal is now at the hotel of Minister D——, the nefarious orangutan who not only committed the murders in the Rue Morgue, but was also the proprietor of the infamous Patisserie de Colère, and furthermore, was also the Violeur de Poullon *and* Le Renard sans Raisins."*

"I can't think how he has retained his portfolio," I opined.

"Very wise," the genius detective continued, "but I shall continue to surmise. No doubt you have come to this conclusion yourself, my dear F——, after exhaustive use of *die empirische Methodik.*"

"Pardon?" said the Prefect, in either English or French.

"My apologies, I meant l*a méthodologie empirique,* the empirical methodology, to ascertain the location of the purloined pachyderm?"

"Indeed we did," the Prefect replied. "The entire constabulary was mobilised in the search, and by opening all but two of the premises in Paris we ascertained exactly what you have surmised, that the animal was located somewhere in the room so Minister D——"

"You checked the elephant rack?" asked Dupin.

"Of course. It was quite empty, and there was no sign that it had been recently used."

"You say you searched all but two of the premises. Surely your investigation didn't end there?"

"We did not search the Royal Apartments, of course. While my *clé maîtresse* allows entry, it would not be proper procedure. The King is above and beyond reproach."

"The other apartments were, of course, my own," said Dupin, putting his *boulle* on their rack and seating himself again. "Then what? By this time you were, no doubt, baffled and *distrait?*"

"It was time to consider less orthodox methods," said the Prefect while Dupin rekindled his meerschaum and smoked the special blend of tobacco and opium he favoured. "We hired four of the finest savants in Paris and sent them to investigate Minister D——'s apartments, while we lured him away by charging him with murder."

"And the result?" asked Dupin.

The Prefect and I were startled—we had expected another wild surmise.

Dupin did not disappoint.

"The savants are, of course, blind. The morbid acuity of their other senses makes them invaluable in our investigations. One, let us call him Edgar, was able to identify the real Jacques l'Éventreur by smell alone. Another, let us call him Allan, can distinguish birdsong before 5AM. The third, let us call him Po, is a master of the Chinese arts with hearing so morbidly acute he can hear the sound of one hand clapping. The fourth—"

"Yes, yes, these biographies will no doubt interest future scholars, but to the investigation?"

I hiccoughed, because for some reason I had the hiccoughs, and it seemed I was being forgotten in this narrative.

"While we were preparing our murder case against Minister D——, these four men searched his apartments with morbid acuity. They found a large boa constrictor, a rare African spear, some rope and a secret wall that hid the trunk of a tree and perhaps a supporting pillar for the hotel, but no elephant!"

Dupin thought for a moment, blowing fragrant tobacco smoke out of his nose, and wiped his mustachios with a quaint and curious tome of forgotten lore, as is his wont when thoughtful with a runny nose. The Prefect and I waited patiently, the Prefect to be astounded, and I with my usual respect for Dupin's powers of ratiocination. After a little while he got up and walked to his escritoire.

"Astounding," said the Prefect.

"I have used the—the—"said Dupin, gesturing inarticulately as he strove to find the good, right word.

"The little grey cells?" I suggested.

"You speak French like a Belgian!" Dupin exclaimed. "No, no, my aunt's pen! It was in the—ah, here it is. And now a sheet of paper ..."

He wrote briskly on both sides of the paper and, summoning the Oriental arts which are, perhaps, his second-greatest passion from the East, he folded the paper and handed it to the Prefect, who looked grateful but disappointed.

"Did you expect me to produce a giant African mammal from my desk drawer?" asked Dupin, sensing—I know not how—F——'s disenchantment.

"Well, you always have," I recollected. "In the Case of the *le cas des griffes de velours—*"†

"A misunderstanding of the word 'griffe.' The foolish gendarmes had used the English translation and were looking for persons of Negro extraction, whereas, of course, I used my experience with the Academie Francaise to realise that what was meant was the French for 'claws.' "

"You are also one of the Immortals?" said F——, agog.

"*With* the Academie, not *at* it," said Dupin, handing the folded epigraph to the Prefect. "My brother, the suave but impoverished D——, has the distinction of being the only one of the family who can dictate how French is spoken. But, my dear Prefect, the solution to your vexatious problem is in that folded paper. Pray do not open it here! Return when you have solved the case—and bring your chequebook."

A month passed, in which time Dupin aided France by averting war with Prussia, advised the Tsar to take better care of the peasants, used inductive reasoning against the Church of Jesus Christ of Latter-Day Saints‡ and followed in the footsteps of the great Icelandic alchemist Arne Saknussem. We were seated in his dark salon, with our feet propped on certain artifacts, with the lamp wicks unkindled and, as usual, breathing the fumes from our meerschaums, when the Prefect burst in again.

"Vive la synergie!" he exclaimed. "Merci beaucoup, monsieur Dupin."

"Belay the French," said Dupin. "It's International Talk Like a Pirate Day, arrr."

"We found the missing elephant," the Prefect went on, "er, me hearties, by applying the very process of ratiocination you advised in your letter. It took nearly a month, but once we combined all the reports from our savants, we discovered the silhouette o' the missing beast. It was in the Minister's room the whole time!"

"I surmise that arrests have been made," said Dupin, "and do sit down, you scurvy dog, you'll end up on a lee shore luffing like that."

"Arrests made, questions asked, negotiations entered into. *Les Jardins Zoologique* are most happy for the return of their elephant, and Minister D—— has escaped unscathed."

"You seem crestfallen," I said to him.

"Not at all," F—— replied. "There was a slight *contretemps* with the elephant as we were returning it to its home at the zoo."

"I surmise that it had not been eating well," said Dupin.

"It had been quarantined in a hotel for a month," he replied, "living on a Minister's diet. As I followed the, er, booty—"

"Yes, yes," said Dupin, petting his *perroquet*. "There was the trifling matter of my cheque ..."

"*Merde*," the Prefect replied.

Afterwards, my friend entered into some translations.

* These adventures are collected, critiqued, annotated and spell-checked in the author's Les Cas de C. Auguste Dupin, Baltimore: Lenore Press, 18—.

† Collected, along with other tales of mystery and imagination, in *A Midnght's Dreary Chamber* (Baltimore: Leonore Press –52).

‡ *Une Étude en Écarlate*, (Tashkent : Belladonna Periodical Concern, MDCCCLIX).

MURDER CAN BE MURDER

A Very Short Chronicle Of Brother Hermitage

Howard of Warwick

"Brother Hermitage?" The young man with bright, enthusiastic eyes was very well-presented and exuded confidence like a fresh spring on its way to becoming a major river.

"Erm, yes," Hermitage replied. He was young and enthusiastic but his habit had not been well-presented for many a year and he had never got the hang of confidence.

Simply being approached was enough of a worry. As King William's duly appointed investigator, most of the approaches he experienced were connected with murder, which was awful. Being investigator at all was terrible but he had no choice about that. William and the Normans seldom offered choices about anything; unless it was life or death.

He had been walking along the main street of Derby minding his own business when the young man bounded up. The face was not one he recognised, which was unusual for a small town. Strangers approaching Hermitage seldom brought anything but trouble.

"The King's Investigator?" the young man asked with yet more from his deep and bubbling reserve of enthusiasm.

"That's right." Hermitage's spirits sank. No one ever called for the King's Investigator to ask about the weather. They had a murder that would demand his attention.

Mind you, this young fellow appeared to be Saxon, so perhaps he had not been sent by the king or any of the other ghastly Normans. And he seemed bright and cheerful, which was a bit of a contradiction if murder was involved.

"Marvellous." The young man gave a bow. "I am Fridolf. Fridolf of Gotham."

"Gotham, you say?" This concerned Hermitage as his previous dealings with that town had a touch of madness about them.

"But it is many a year since I was there," Fridolf explained. "Now, I am apprentice goldsmith to Master Scrydan of London."

"A goldsmith, eh?" Hermitage was suitably impressed.

"Aye. A good trade and I near the end of my apprenticeship."

It certainly was a good trade, judging by the quality of Fridolf's clothes and shoes. Naturally, goldsmiths were only ever employed by people who could afford the raw material in the first place. He could only imagine that goldsmiths were very well rewarded for their skill.

"Trade continues, then?" Hermitage asked. "The Normans and all?" He left the question hanging. It wouldn't do to disparage the Normans too much if this young man was a friend to the invaders.

"It does," Fridolf confirmed. "King William and his court want to show their magnificence as much as any rulers. Things were a bit difficult after Hastings but there is high regard for the name of Master Scrydan. And goldsmiths are rare beasts."

Hermitage nodded at this. If there was one thing a king needed to do it was show everyone that he was king. This was especially true of a new king, who would be anxious to dispel any thoughts that the old king might come back. Not that this was a problem for William, King Harold having been very effectively dealt with, if the tales were true.

And what better way to show what a successful and well-established king you were than by ostentatious displays of wealth? Preferably wealth taken from the people you just conquered.

This was all very interesting, but Hermitage had to ask the key question.

"What brings you away from your work then? And from London, which is a good step away?"

"Let me stand you a mug of ale." Fridolf suggested, beckoning towards the rough tavern close by. "Then I can tell all in comfort."

Hermitage nodded his acceptance. He was growing in confidence that this would not be murder after all. A comfortable discussion over a mug of ale was hardly the setting for such a subject.

Fridolf led the way and in a few moments Ern, the tavern-keeper, supplied them with leather mugs, which they took at the large table outside.

Fridolf supped and then began. “I heard all about the King’s Investigator from the Normans. It seems a remarkable role.”

“That it is,” Hermitage confirmed. “From the Latin, you know, *vestigo, vestigare,* to track.”

“A track,” Fridolf repeated with interest. “Yes, that would make sense.”

“I just happened to be of assistance to King Harold in resolving a murder,” Hermitage explained. “And then King William continued the role.” He didn’t want Fridolf to think that he actually wanted to investigate murder. Nothing could be further from the truth.

“But I hear that you stay with Wat the Weaver?” Fridolf was clearly a bit concerned about this, which was not surprising. The reputation of Wat the Weaver was not one that most decent people would want to get anywhere near; some of it might rub off.

“An old and complex set of circumstances,” Hermitage explained. “And anyway, Wat produces only pious tapestry now. His works of old are long gone.”

“Once seen, never forgotten.” Fridolf gave a conspiratorial wink.

“Best never seen or quickly forgotten,” Hermitage replied firmly. He had seen some of Wat’s old tapestries. The human form was a work of God and only He should be able to see quite so much of it.

“But what makes a young goldsmith’s apprentice seek me out?” Hermitage asked. He didn’t really want to open the door to discussion of murder, but he certainly wanted to move on from the subject of Wat the Weaver.

“You are the only King’s Investigator,” Fridolf said.

“As far as I am aware.” Hermitage had long hoped that someone would take the job away from him. The appointment of another investigator would be just as good.

“So, it is to you I must come.”

“A murder?” Hermitage asked with resignation. He couldn’t tarry any longer. If it was coming, it was best to get it over with.

“Just so.”

Hermitage sighed. “You were sent by the Normans?”

“Oh no,” Fridolf replied brightly. “This is my own doing. I thought it best to get things right.”

“I suppose it is. And there was no one in London who could deal with the matter?”

Even though there was no other investigator, murder was not that uncommon. Shire Reeves and county authorities dealt with it in the past and presumably continued to do so. Only very specific matters came Hermitage's way. At least, he assumed that was the case. Usually when the Normans wanted it so.

"Once I had heard of the King's Investigator, I knew this was where I had to come."

"A four-day walk," Hermitage noted.

"Essential if matters are to be properly dealt with."

Hermitage nodded reluctantly. "To the heart of it then," he said. "Whose murder are we talking about?"

"My master, Scrydan."

"Oh dear, you have my sympathy."

Fridolf frowned deeply at this. Hermitage knew that relations between apprentices and their masters could be difficult. Wat had reported his own experience of a harsh and cruel master, so perhaps this death had little effect on Fridolf. That would explain his cheery attitude. He hated to consider it, but perhaps this murder had come as a bit of a relief. However, if Fridolf was still an apprentice, he would now have no master, which could cause him problems.

"A master goldsmith and a great craftsman, but an awful fellow," Fridolf explained. "Sad to say, but I don't think he will be missed."

Hermitage acknowledged this without further comment.

"So," Fridolf said brightly. "How do we proceed?"

"Well," Hermitage began. He actually found it quite comfortable to talk about murder when there wasn't a body lying in front of him. Nor were there any Norman nobles demanding to know this instant, who did it.

"I have developed an approach that has proved to be quite informative."

Fridolf looked at him like an attentive acolyte.

"I have identified three key factors in any murder; the method, the motive and the opportunity."

"Fascinating."

"First of all, the method. How was Scrydan killed?"

"How was he killed?" Fridolf didn't seem to understand the question. "You mean, how will he be killed?"

"How will he be killed?" Now Hermitage didn't understand the question. "You mean he is not dead yet?"

"Well, no."

"Oh, Lord," Hermitage breathed. "If there is some threat to him, why have you taken four days to come and tell me?"

"Because you're the investigator."

"Yes, but ..."

"You keep track of all the murders. For the king."

"I keep track of them?"

"A record of some sort, I suppose. A strange thing, if you ask me, but then there's no telling with Normans. They are terribly well organised about most things. Murder as well, it seems."

"I, er," Hermitage was lost. This was quite normal for most of his investigations, but he wasn't sure that this even was one.

"You keep a track of all the murders in the kingdom," Fridolf explained. "So I've come to let you know about this one. So you can put it on your list, I imagine."

"My list?"

"The Normans said you investigate all the murders. Tracking. You said so yourself."

"That doesn't mean keeping a track of them." Surely the young man would understand that?

"Oh." Fridolf sounded very disappointed.

There was one question that was burning a hole in Hermitage's head. "How do you know he is going to be murdered?" Even as he said this, he had his familiar sinking feeling.

"Because I'm going to do it." Fridolf now cheered up and smiled broadly at the prospect. "Going into the method and the opportunity bits could be quite helpful. I was thinking about a knife in the dark, but you may know better."

"But, but," Hermitage stuttered. "My investigations of murder are to find out who did it." It felt like a very weak thing to do, all of a sudden.

"You won't need to this time," Fridolf assured him. "You'll know."

The most obvious thing to say was that Fridolf could not be serious. He couldn't just go and murder his master like that. Let alone could he come to the King's Investigator and let him know in advance. It was madness.

"This is madness," he managed to croak out. "You cannot come here to simply tell me that you are going to commit a murder."

Fridolf nodded seriously. “I see.”

Hermitage felt a slight relief, but only a slight one.

“You mean I need to ask permission? I didn’t know that.”

“No, you don’t need to ask permission,” Hermitage found himself snapping.

“That’s good then.”

“What you don’t do is murder your master. You don’t murder anyone. Whether you have permission or not.” Hermitage was glad to get that out in such plain language.

“Really?” Fridolf was still showing intense interest, which Hermitage assumed meant he wasn’t getting through. “Is there a wait, or something?”

“A wait?”

“Oh, I say.” Fridolf snapped his fingers as he reached a conclusion. “Do you come and do it for me? Is that the arrangement? That is good. He’d never suspect a monk.”

Hermitage took a breath. He then took a much longer draught of ale than he was used to.

“Fridolf,” he said as calmly as he could manage. He looked into the young man’s eyes. “You cannot murder your master under any circumstances. You cannot murder anyone. It is the most awful sin.”

“The Normans do it,” Fridolf protested.

“That’s as may be, but they are sinning when they do it as well.”

Fridolf shook his head. “This is all much more complicated than I thought it would be.”

“How complicated did you think murder would be?” Hermitage asked with despair.

“I thought you were supposed to help.”

“I do help with murder. I help by finding out who did the murder and bring them to justice.”

Fridolf did now look quite crestfallen, which Hermitage took as progress. “If I’d known it was going to be this difficult, I wouldn’t have come in the first place,” he grumbled.

“Which might have been for the best,” Hermitage agreed. “Why do you want to murder your master at all?” he asked gently.

“Oh, he’s awful. Terrible man. As I said, I’m sure he wouldn’t be missed.”

“That’s not the point.”

Fridolf appeared to find a new argument. “If I don’t do it, someone else will.”

“You don’t know that.”

“I’m pretty sure. Nobody likes him.”

“Just because you don’t like someone doesn’t mean that you kill them. Anyway,” Hermitage came up with his own problem. “You’re an apprentice. If you have no master, who will see you progress to master yourself?”

“That’s exactly the problem.” Fridolf was all enthusiasm once more. “He’s in the way. He sits there as master and won’t progress anyone.”

“Are there other apprentices?”

“There are two others, but they aren’t as far advanced as me. It’s my time to be made up. I’ve even done my masterpiece for the test. It’s a beautiful wrist band. Intertwining strands, jewel encrustation, the lot.”

“It sounds wonderful.”

“But old Scrydan would rather see it melted down than admit it’s the work of a master.”

“That is still no reason for murder. You can’t kill a man simply because he’s in your way.”

“Sounds like a very good reason to me,” Fridolf muttered. “King William did it.”

“Why don’t you set up your own workshop?”

“Without being a master? Who would come?”

“That’s what Wat did,” Hermitage explained. “He never was made a master yet has had great success.”

“I don’t know how you’d make rude jewellery.”

Hermitage had to accept that Wat was probably not the best example.

“It could be a tradition,” Fridolf tried.

“A tradition?”

“Yes, you know. Apprentice kills master. For all we know, Scrydan killed his master before him. Now it’s his turn.”

“I am confident that murder of a master is not the route to apprentice advancement.”

“Don’t monks kill abbots?”

“No, they do not.” Hermitage could not contain his outrage at this suggestion.

Fridolf sagged and looked defeated. Perhaps Hermitage could send him home with some wise words.

"Just have a discussion with Scrydan. Ask him how you are to progress to master. What his plans are."

"He'll probably kill me. Then how will you feel?"

"I am sure it will not come to that."

Fridolf huffed. "So, I can't kill him at all?"

"Not at all."

There was a long and uncomfortable pause, but Fridolf did eventually speak, even if it was in the manner of a child who has been told to feed the pigs or there'll be no mead. "Alright."

Hermitage relaxed.

"But, if I was to kill him, which I'm not, obviously. What would be the best method and opportunity? In your experience."

"Fridolf," Hermitage cautioned. "We are not discussing the matter."

"No, no, of course not. It's just out of interest, really."

"You should not be interested in murder. You should be interested in goldsmithing."

"Yes." Fridolf said this very slowly and with a very scheming look on his face.

"What are you thinking?' Hermitage asked suspiciously.

"Oh, nothing really," Fridolf said. "Just considering my craft, you know. The smelting with the fire and all. Could be dangerous in the wrong hands. And then the gold itself. Very heavy, is gold. You only see little bits of it as it's so valuable, but when you get a big lump of the stuff, it'd be enough to weigh a man down in say, a river. Or a pond. As long as it was deep enough."

"Fridolf," Hermitage cautioned. "If I were to hear word that a goldsmith called Scrydan had been murdered, I would have a very strong suspicion about who did it. The Normans may go around killing people, but the rest of us do not. We are discovered and we are punished for it."

"Right, right," Fridolf said absent-mindedly. "Just out of interest ..."

"More interest?" Hermitage asked.

"As you mentioned it. What would the punishment be, do you think, for murdering, oh, I don't know, a goldsmith, say?"

"The punishment for murder is eternal damnation. God is the ultimate judge."

"Of course, of course. But before him?"

Hermitage sighed. "Obviously, there would be the wergild."

"Ah, the wergild, yes. A fine."

"A substantial fine," Hermitage insisted. "For someone as valuable to his family as a goldsmith."

"Shame that Scrydan doesn't have any family then, isn't it? His wife died. Which is a bit suspicious, come to think of it."

"She died?"

"In childbirth."

"Not that suspicious then."

"What are we talking? Fifty shillings, maybe. Forty?"

"I do not know." Hermitage took a sup of ale and then folded his arms in what he hoped was a very critical manner.

Fridolf also supped his ale and then leaned forward on his stool.

"This wergild," he said nodding at Hermitage and reaching to bring something up from his waist band. "Do you think I could pay in advance?"

HAVE A CADAVER

Edward Lodi

"Jake, you know that thousand bucks you gave me last week?"

Jake placed the Sam Adams he'd been nursing onto the bar and glanced sidelong at his friend. "*Loaned* you, Ronnie. I *loaned* you the thousand."

Ronnie shrugged. "Whatever. Anyhow, I invested it."

Jake contemplated his beer. Should he finish drinking it? Or smash the bottle over Ronnie's head? He could, of course, do both. "What's it this time? Let me guess. You got an e-mail from some guy in Nigeria."

"Naw. I only fell for that once. Twice if you count the guy in Russia." He sipped his whiskey. "This is for real. I got the stuff outside."

"Stuff?" Jake gazed at the ceiling. "Why is it I see a thousand dollar bills fluttering like butterflies into the great blue yonder?"

"Gee, Jake, that's poetic. I should've had you write the flyer instead of that college kid I hired. I could've saved us twenty-five bucks."

"What flyer?"

"Announcing our business. 'Have A Cadaver.' " Before Jake could protest the "our," Ronnie pulled a folded paper from his pocket. "I'll read the flyer to you."

"Whoa. What'd you buy, a funeral parlor?"

Ronnie ignored him and began to read:

" 'Aquatic Corpse-Locating Service. Have a cadaver you'd like us to find? We locate submerged bodies: people or pets. Accidental drowning? Victim of foul play? Feet in concrete? Dismemberment?

Don't despair. We'll find where.

Is it wet? Don't fret. On the bottom? We've got 'em!

No corpse too big. No corpse too small. In the water* we find them all.**

*Fresh water searches only: lakes, ponds, etc.

**Warm water only. If it's under ice, no dice!

Our tried-and-true method for locating dead and decaying people or pets is based on scientific principles: The corpse that sinks, stinks. The corpse that bloats, floats.' "

When he finished the last sentence Ronnie folded the flyer, and tucking it into his pocket turned to his friend. "Our contact information's at the bottom. What do you think, Jake?"

Jake's face wore the stunned expression of an ox that's been poleaxed prior to slaughter. He remained silent.

"Jake?"

Jake signaled to the bartender. "Carlos, a double whiskey. Neat. No rocks." When the drink arrived he downed it in one gulp. Only then did he turn to Ronnie. "Do you really want to know what I think, Ronnie? Do you really want to know?"

"Now Jake. Reserve judgment until I show you how it works. Carlos." He waved the bartender over. "Another whiskey for my friend. And I'll have one too."

Several rounds later the two petty thieves staggered into the parking lot. "Damn, this sun is brutal," Jake complained. "Where'd you park?"

"Over there in the shade." Ronnie pointed to a battered pickup.

Jake walked over and examined the vehicle. "This heap? Pink? What kind of man drives a pink truck? What happened to your Dodge?"

"It ain't pink," Ronnie protested. "It's red. Or used to be," he added lamely. "I traded the Dodge for this."

"Huh? You traded an almost new truck for this? How much cash did the other party throw in?"

"Better than cash, Jake. The old guy threw in the business, lock, stock and barrel."

"That the barrel?" Jake pointed to a plastic trash bin that stood upright on the bed of the pickup.

Ronnie nodded. "The stock's in that crate."

"The one next to the barrel? Looks like a pet carrier. How come you got an umbrella shading it? Whatcha got inside? A dog?"

Ronnie smirked. "Stick your hand in, see if it's a dog." He reached up and lowered the gate, then hoisted himself onto the truck bed. Jake clambered after him.

"Careful, Jake. Don't trip on that." Ronnie indicated a coil of nylon cord that lay at their feet.

"I see an aluminum skiff with more dents in it than my uncle Harry's '89 Chevy. Where's the rest of the stuff?"

"This is it," Ronnie replied.

Jake's body began to quiver. Ronnie looked at his friend in alarm. He was reminded of the time when Jake, drunker than he was now, had jumped onto the back of a mechanical bull. This time the quivering was followed by strange sounds that originated deep within Jake's bowels. Ronnie had heard that sound before—in a horror movie about inmates in a lunatic asylum.

Jake was laughing. It wasn't healthy laughter. It was the laughter of a man on the brink of a nervous breakdown.

After a while the quivering stopped, and Jake grew preternaturally calm. "Tell me, Ronnie. What happened to the thousand bucks? The thousand bucks I *loaned* you."

"That was part of the deal, Jake." Before Jake could react Ronnie hastily added: "Not the whole thousand. Just eight hundred of it. The other two hundred is earmarked for advertising."

"Ronnie, let me get this clear in my mind. You traded your almost new pickup *and* eight hundred dollars for this almost antique pickup, a plastic trash barrel, a coil of nylon cord, a dented aluminum skiff only slightly bigger than a fast-food take-out container, and a carrier crate with God knows what in it. That correct?"

"Only so far as it goes, Jake. You ain't seen what's in the crate. What's in the crate is the key to the whole enterprise. The enterprise that's gonna make us rich: 'Have A Cadaver.' "

"An 'Aquatic Corpse-Locating Service,' " Jake quoted.

"That's right. At first, I wanted to name our business Stiff in a Skiff, you know, for the rhyme. But that's misleading. We don't retrieve bodies, just locate 'em. If we transport rotting corpses in the skiff we'll never get the stink out."

"You got a point there," Jake conceded. He bent over, grasped the end of the nylon cord, and began to fashion it into a hangman's knot.

"Whatcha doing, Jake?" Ronnie asked, a tremor in his voice.

"Unless you can give me a reason not to, I'm going to hang you from the nearest tree."

"You always did have a sense of humor," Ronnie said with a nervous laugh.

Jake completed the knot and began to twirl it in the air, like a cowpoke approaching a bronco.

"I been saving the best for last," Ronnie said hastily. "Here, inside the crate." He pushed the skiff to one side to give his friend access. "This is a pet carrier, but that ain't no pet inside. Scrunch down and peek through the grate to see for yourself."

Jake obligingly scrunched. He brought his face up to the grate so that his nose brushed against it. A loud hissing issued from within. Startled, he fell backwards, striking his head against the metal floor.

Cursing, he righted himself. "What've you got in there, snakes?"

"Jeeze, Jake, you oughtn't put your nose so close."

"You ain't answered my question."

"No, it ain't snakes. It's a relative."

"You've got your relative in there? Now I know you're nuts."

"My relative? Now Jake, that don't make no sense. I meant the snake's relative."

"So now you're doing snake genealogy. You got a family tree for this snake?"

"I'm telling you, it ain't no snake. Here, see for yourself." Ronnie picked up a large oak dowel lying next to the carrier and with his free hand unlatched the lid.

"You planning to conk me on the head with that stick?" Jake asked menacingly. "Cause if you are ..."

"Shush! This is delicate work. I gotta concentrate." As he spoke he tilted the carrier. "Come out of there, Corpsey," he coaxed, while at the same time vigorously shaking the carrier.

"He's stubborn. I'll fix him." He tossed the dowel onto the floor where it landed with a clang, and grabbing the carrier with both hands upended it. Hissing its displeasure, a huge snapping turtle slid out and immediately began crawling away from the carrier. Ronnie, scrabbling to retrieve the dowel, came perilously close to the turtle's powerful jaws.

"Ain't he a beaut," he said, in the prideful tone of a dad showing off his newborn. "Thirty-six inches from the tip of his tail to the tip of his snout. Can snap a broom handle in two with his jaws."

Nonplused, Jake stared at the monstrous creature. "That's the snake's relative?"

"Yeah, you know. Snakes are reptiles, and so are turtles."

"I don't see no family resemblance to any snake I know of. But I detect a distinct similarity to you. Especially the skull." He performed a sudden dance. "Hey, it's going for my feet!"

Ronnie hefted the dowel. "That's where this little baby comes in handy. I'll tap him on the head, ever so lightly—you know, a love tap. To get his attention."

"When you're done with it can I borrow the dowel?" Jake asked. "I'd like to get your attention."

Ronnie ignored the remark. "See," he exclaimed. "He's got the dowel in his jaws and won't let go. He's forgot all about your feet."

"I wish I could forget about my head," Jake said. "It's aching something awful."

"Maybe if we get something to eat you'll feel better. I'll put Corpsey back into his carrier, then we'll get pizzas at Rosie's."

Ronnie wasn't quite as drunk as Jake, so he designated himself driver and drove to the restaurant. There they chose a quiet booth in a dark corner where the light wouldn't hurt their eyes. Before ordering pizzas they asked for a pot of black coffee. Until he'd had two mugfuls, Jake didn't say a word. Then he said: "Ronnie, tell me this is all a bad dream."

"Jake, I know what your trouble is. You don't understand how Corpsey fits in."

"Let me guess. He eats the corpses."

"Naw, Jake. Who'd pay for that? Unless ... You've given me an idea. If the Mob wanted to dispose of a body ... hmm."

"No way, Ronnie. I don't want nothing to do with the Mob. Besides, how much can one turtle eat? You'd need a whole squadron of snappers to polish off even a small corpse."

"I suppose so," Ronnie conceded. "Still, it's something to keep in mind."

When the server brought their pizzas they ordered another pot of coffee.

"You were gonna tell me how the turtle fits into this harebrained scheme of yours," Jake reminded his friend.

Suddenly Ronnie felt nervous. He hadn't forgotten the coil of nylon cord. It still had a hangman's noose on the end of it. A few years back for a short while—a very short while—he'd been a used-car salesman, until he discovered that he was better at stealing cars than selling them. What if he failed to sell the idea of Have A Cadaver to Jake?

"It's simple, Jake. Hardly no work at all. The secret is, snappers eat carrion. It's caviar to them. If there's rotten meat in fresh water, Corpsey will sniff it out."

"He's your underwater locator."

"Exactly."

"When he finds a body does he swim back to shore and tell us where to look?"

"Very funny, Jake. Very funny. Look, I'll describe a typical job. Let's keep it simple, make it a drowning in a lake. Divers spend a day, can't find the body. The police call us in, or maybe it's the grieving kin. Don't make no difference to us, so long as they pay our fee."

"Which is? ..."

Ronnie looked perplexed. "Jeeze, Jake, I forgot to ask Toot how much to charge."

"Toot?"

"The old guy I bought the business from."

"If it's such a lucrative enterprise, how come he sold it? Other than the obvious reason that he knows a sucker when he sees one."

"He can't afford to lose no more fingers. He can hardly play the guitar as it is."

"Ronnie, you telling me that turtle bit off Coot's fingers?"

"Toot. His name's Toot." Ronnie stuffed pizza into his mouth and began to chew slowly, like a man gathering his thoughts, or a cow chewing its cud. Jake couldn't decide which. "It's a hazard of the job, Jake. How's that saying go? No pain, no gain."

"How many fingers?"

"I don't know, Jake. You don't ask a man how many fingers he's got left."

"You could've counted 'em."

"He was wearing gloves."

"In July? That ain't a good omen."

"I say amen to that. Haw haw. That was a pun, Jake. Pretty neat, huh?"

"Forget the puns. We get hired. Then what?"

"We take Corpsey out in the skiff. He swims around till he smells the rotting corpse. He's tied to the nylon cord. There's a hundred feet of it. When the cord goes taut we know he's found something."

"How's he tied to the cord? Do we wind it around his neck?"

"Didn't you notice the grommet?"

"Grommet? Grommet? What grommet?"

"Jeeze, Jake, you sound like a frog on a lily pad." He glanced at his friend to see if he was laughing. He wasn't. "The grommet in Corpsey's shell. Toot drilled a hole through the top of the shell, toward the back, where it overhangs. Didn't hurt the turtle none, if that's what's bothering you. Then he fitted the metal grommet to the hole. It's like the grommet you slip your shoe laces through, only bigger."

"I think I get the picture," Jake said. "This whole operation depends on the well-being of that snapping turtle. Don't even think of asking me to be his care-giver."

"Don't worry, Jake, he's my responsibility."

"Where's he gonna live? You can't keep him in that carrier."

"In the trash barrel."

"Now, I know he's only a turtle, but that seems downright cruel."

"Ain't cruel at all, Jake. We fill the barrel with garbage and plop old Corpsey in."

"That sounds even crueler."

"Jake, I'm telling you it ain't cruel. Where does a snapper spend most of its life?"

"In the mud, I guess."

"Right. And what's garbage, if it ain't mud a snapper can eat? You want that last piece of pizza?"

"No. You can have it."

"It ain't for me, Jake. It's for Corpsey. See what I mean? What we eat, Corpsey eats."

"Looks like he's gained weight," Ronnie said as he dumped food scraps into the barrel.

"That's 'cause he ain't getting no exercise. We been in business two weeks and not one customer."

"We could take him for a swim."

"I ain't risking my fingers unless there's money involved."

The two entrepreneurs had set up shop in the parking lot of Carlos's Cafe. Carlos permitted them to hang a sign proclaiming Have A Cadaver across the rear of the pickup. They were, after all, his best customers. Besides alcoholic beverages, Carlos served the greasiest food in town. Corpsey was fond of the leftovers. Unlike most of Carlos's clientele, the snapper never complained of indigestion, though he did seem more ill-tempered than usual after chomping on bacon-and-cheese burgers with fries.

"It could be the ketchup," Ronnie speculated.

"Or the cheese," Jake said. "Maybe he's lactose-intolerant." He was about to head into the bar when a black Lexus entered the lot, slowed, then headed their way. "Shit. The Mob. What do you suppose they want?"

Ronnie let out a whoop. "They seen our ad! They got a job for us!"

"I don't want nothing to do with the Mob. They're like grizzly bears. They eat their young."

"You gonna say no to the Mob?"

Jake pulled a bandanna from his pocket and mopped his brow. "You got a point there, Ronnie. Maybe they wanna give us a retainer, you know, in case they need our services in the future."

The Lexus pulled up behind the pickup. The doors swung open and two gorillas in suits that cost more than Ronnie and Jake could steal in a year got out. Ronnie whispered through clenched teeth. "The guy on the left is Rusty Nail, the Mob Enforcer. You know how he got his moniker?"

"I don't wanna know," Jake said. His own teeth were chattering.

"The other guy is Crusher."

"I wish you hadn't told me."

The two goons came up to the rear of the pickup. "Come down off that truck so as we can talk," Rusty commanded.

Ronnie and Jake tripped over one another in their haste to comply.

"You boys got a good cover here," Rusty said admiringly when they were safely on the asphalt. "A pink truck on a dump run. Stinks of garbage, too. The Fuzz don't suspect nothing, right? Youse guys is geniuses. The boss will approve."

Ronnie and Jake grinned but said nothing. Crusher glared at them with a scowl.

Rusty chuckled. "Don't mind Crusher. He's disappointed. He was hoping to smash your kneecaps if youse didn't measure up."

"Yeah," Crusher grunted. "With my hands. Wanna see how I do it?"

"Uh, no thanks, Crusher," Jake said in a squeaky voice. "Some other time, maybe."

"We'll go inside where it's cool and have a drink," Rusty said.

They sat in a corner booth. When Carlos came for their order, Rusty handed him a twenty-dollar bill. "Don't let nobody sit there," he said, indicating the adjacent booth. Carlos left and quickly returned with the Out of Order sign he reserved for overflowing toilets.

"Anyone sits there, I'll break their legs," Crusher informed him. "And yours too," he added as an afterthought.

"Crusher, you ain't using your brain," Rusty complained. "If you break his legs, whose gonna bring us our drinks?"

It wasn't until Carlos delivered four beers to their table that Rusty spoke again. "The boss seen your ad in the paper," he said. 'Feet in concrete' is what caught his attention. You see," he continued, lowering his voice, "that's precisely the situation we got. Or I should say, think we got."

"I don't quite understand," Jake ventured.

"I'll explain. Last week Crusher and me was out of town."

"Breaking legs," Crusher said beaming.

"Quiet, Crusher. These gentlemen don't need to know the details."

"We had ice cream afterwards," Crusher said. "You ever had coffee ice cream?"

Rusty smiled at Crusher, like an indulgent parent at a five-year-old. "Crusher's a sucker for ice cream. Anyhow, like I was saying ... The boss required our services but we wasn't here. So he engaged a new guy, never been tested. The guy does the job. So he says. But where's the proof? At the bottom of the lake. That's where you boys come in. We need verification. You know, that he did what he was paid for. 'Cause if he didn't, Crusher here is gonna earn his ice cream."

"Which lake?" Jake asked.

"Muskrat Lake. Know where it is?"

"I been there," Ronnie said. "It's on conservation land. No swimming or boating allowed."

"Right," Rusty said. "We'll have the place to ourselves. Me and Crusher will meet youse there at seven tomorrow morning. Don't be late."

"If they're late can I break their legs?"

After the two goons left, Ronnie and Jake returned to the pickup.

"We gotta empty this barrel," Ronnie said. "Help me get Corpsey into his carrier."

"What for? This garbage ain't even a day old."

"That ain't the point, Jake. Tomorrow morning Corpsey's gotta be hungry. He won't sniff out carrion if he's full."

"Maybe we could give him a laxative, clean out his system."

"I got a better idea. Let's build up his appetite. We'll take him swimming."

"Where? Muskrat Lake is off limits to the public. Bad enough we have to go there tomorrow. Everywhere else is crowded. People won't take kindly to sharing the water with a snapping turtle. He might bite off some guy's finger or toe."

"Or worse, if the guy's skinny-dipping. But I know where we can take him: a private swimming pool."

"Who do we know has a swimming pool and will let us toss a garbage-encrusted snapping turtle into it?"

"Nobody. But you been scouting empty houses to break into. One of 'em must have a pool."

The next morning when Ronnie and Jake arrived at Muskrat Lake, the sun was an orange orb poking above the treeline on the opposite shore.

"We're early," Ronnie observed. "Crusher will be disappointed. He was hoping we'd be late so he could break our legs."

"He may still get his wish. We ain't found the body yet."

"Corpsey won't let us down."

"I don't know, Ronnie. Look at his eyes. They're bloodshot. Must be from the chlorine in that pool."

"He locates cadavers with his nose, not his eyes."

"How do you know his nose ain't been affected?"

"How about we stop talking and get to work. Help me get this skiff off the pickup and into the water."

At five minutes to seven when the Lexus pulled into view the two friends had the skiff in the water, the carrier in the skiff, and the snapper in the carrier. The nylon coil and the dowel were also in place.

"Shut up, Crusher," they heard Rusty snap as he and his fellow goon emerged from the Lexus. "I'm tired of hearing you whine. You ain't breaking nobody's legs until I say so. One more peep from you and no ice cream for a week!"

The mobsters had shed their suits and were dressed casually in slacks and short-sleeved shirts.

Rusty stood admiring the skiff. "Youse guys is geniuses. The stink alone is enough to keep the Fuzz away. Gonna be a tight fit though."

Jake felt his knees shaking. "Tight fit?"

"Yeah. Me and Crusher is coming along for the ride. Not that we don't trust youse boys. But we gotta see for ourselves."

"I'm not sure the boat will hold all four of us," Ronnie ventured. "It might sink."

"It'll be lighter on the way back," Crusher volunteered.

Rusty kicked his colleague in the shin, then put on his best crocodile grin. "Crusher is referring to the sun. It'll get brighter, that is to say lighter, as the day goes on."

Ronnie and Jake exchanged glances.

"This thing got a motor?" Rusty asked.

"Yeah. Me," Jake said. He climbed into the skiff and assumed the rower's position. Ronnie sat in the bow, next to the carrier. Rusty squeezed between them.

"I wanna see how the equipment works," he said. "Youse guys got it disguised real good."

The skiff sat so low in the water, it no longer floated, but rested on sand. "Crusher, shove us off," Rusty ordered.

Crusher removed his shoes and socks, and wading into the water pushed the skiff clear of the shore. As it drifted away he pulled himself aboard, leaving his shoes and socks behind. The added weight caused the skiff to settle even lower.

"Everyone keep still," Jake said. "Any movement could capsize us." His words proved prophetic as, reaching for the oars, he caused the skiff to tilt to one side. An inch of water flooded the floor. Even so he rowed to the center of the lake. From that vantage point the pickup and the Lexus looked like toy vehicles.

"You ready, Ronnie?"

"Yeah, but I need help. Rusty, hand me the end of that nylon cord."

Rusty chuckled. "Youse guys is geniuses. Pretty soon I'm gonna know all your secrets."

"The principles are simple," Ronnie assured him. "Help me lift this carrier. Now release the latch." Rusty complied, and Corpsey fell hissing at his feet.

"Youse guys is Alfred Einsteins!" Rusty exclaimed. "That thing looks real. Except for the eyes. A real turtle don't have bloodshot eyes."

"Yeah, the pigmentation needs work," Ronnie agreed.

"Now can I break their legs?" Crusher asked.

"Not now, Crusher. Can't you see we're busy?"

"But you promised."

"I said later!"

"Rusty, grab it by the tail," Ronnie said. "No, no, away from you!"

"Not in my face!" Jake screamed.

"Can I hold it?" Crusher pleaded.

"Yikes! It bit off my finger," Rusty yelled. Panicked, he tossed the snapper in a spray of blood to the rear of the boat, where it landed at Crusher's feet.

"Gee, thanks, Rusty." As Crusher leaned forward to seize the snapper the skiff listed and took on more water.

"It bit off my trigger finger," Rusty lamented. "How am I gonna earn a living? I'll kill youse guys for this."

"We was gonna kill 'em anyways, Rusty. You promised."

"We're sinking," Jake hollered.

"Crusher, don't let the turtle escape," Ronnie pleaded. "He's worth a thousand dollars."

"That's chump change," Crusher said with a guffaw. "Rusty gives me a thousand bucks for every leg I break. And ice cream afterwards," he boasted.

"Help! I can't swim. I'm drowning!" Rusty screamed as he sank beneath the surface.

"Hey Jake, can you swim?" Ronnie asked, as he flailed his arms in an attempt to keep afloat.

"Is the pope Catholic? Of course I can swim. Hey, where's Crusher?"

"He's at the bottom. Looks like he's trying to walk to shore. I don't think he's gonna make it. Bubbles are coming out of his mouth. Jake, I don't wanna die."

"You ain't gonna die. Hold on to the skiff. It's buoyant. It ain't gonna sink no further."

It took them over an hour, but the two friends finally made it to shore.

"Corpsey got away," Ronnie reflected sadly as he lay panting on the beach.

"At least he won't starve," Jake observed. "Those two mobsters will keep him fat for weeks."

"I won't be able to pay you back the thousand bucks."

"Who's complaining? I just got myself a brand-new Lexus. Wanna go for a ride?"

JUST THIS ONCE

Michael Guillebeau

"Just this once."

Detective Blackbeard stared at the young man sitting next to him in the back seat of an Emerald Coast Beach police cruiser and waited for him to add something.

"Are you sure that's the story you want to stay with," Blackbeard paused and looked at the sheet in his hands, "Josh?"

They were in the parking lot of the Regions Bank on Back Beach Road, just Blackbeard and Josh, uniform cops buzzing around them.

Josh squirmed and leaned forward, trying to smile. "Look, it's not like I'm really a bank robber or anything. It was just this once. Besides, I was arrested inside the bank before I could leave. So, technically, it wasn't a bank robbery."

Blackbeard stared at Josh like he was a bug. "Technically, it is."

"Look, I keep telling you." Josh leaned forward even more in the seat and tried to gesture with one hand until he remembered he was handcuffed. Blackbeard motioned him back. "It was just a joke. My buddy and I are writing a play about a bank robbery and I had to see how it worked."

"A play."

"Yeah. Besides, I only took ninety-nine dollars from the teller. I read that if you steal less than one hundred dollars, it's a misdemeanor. And as I said, it was just this once."

Blackbeard just stared. Emerald Coast Beach was a spring break destination for drunk college kids. He was used to stupid kids ruining the rest of their lives with stupid choices. Used to it, but tired of it.

"How old are you, son?"

"Nineteen."

Very tired of it.

The cops walking around the other cars in the parking lot were moving slowly in the Florida heat. This case was easy. Kid comes in, robs a bank, and then cheerfully stands there trying to chat up the cute teller until the police come.

A patrolman tapped on the glass at Blackbeard's window. Blackbeard turned. The patrolman opened the door and hot air and sunshine poured in. He handed Blackbeard a clipboard with some papers on it. "Thought you'd want to see this. Bank manager's statement."

"Yeah. Close the door. Keep the air conditioning in the car."

The patrolman closed the door.

Josh watched Blackbeard's eyes as he read. Except for the steady rumble of the cruiser's engine keeping the air conditioner running, there was silence and the silence made Josh nervous.

Blackbeard glanced up at Josh once and then went back to reading. Finally, Josh saw Blackbeard put down the clipboard and stare at him a long, long time.

"What? C'mon, man, you know I'm telling you the truth."

Blackbeard stared at him hard now.

"You really want to stick with that story?"

"It's not a story. Look, I can give you the name of my friend, you can talk to him."

"We will."

Blackbeard stared at Josh some more. Josh saw something more than just boredom now. He felt like the joke was slipping away.

"Look, I waited for you guys."

"First officer in says he ran in the door and tackled you before you could get away."

"He was showing off. Ask Zina."

"Zina?"

"Teller I was talking to."

"You think we won't talk to all of them?"

"C'mon, man, ninety-nine dollars. I'd pay it back, if you guys hadn't already taken it off of me."

Blackbeard tilted the clipboard like he was showing it to Josh.

"We talked to one person already. Bank manager, guy named Coram, says you got off with more like twenty thousand dollars. Doesn't know what you did with the rest. Says this is the third robbery they've had this week at Regions Banks in the ECB area, all by you."

Josh's mouth fell open and he closed it.

"Man, no, this is messed up. The guy's lying."

"The bank president's lying?" Blackbeard said. Josh felt an edge growing in his voice. "You picked the wrong day, son. This guy's the head of all the Regions Banks in the area. Usually works out of the city, just happened to be at this branch today to give them a heads up about the robberies." Blackbeard paused and stared. "Who you think a judge is going to believe, you or him?" He paused again. "Who you think I believe?"

Josh just sat there shaking his head back and forth.

Blackbeard tapped on the glass.

"I'm going to let you sit here and think about this a little bit. While I'm talking to the bank manager, you might want to come up with a better story." A patrolman walked over and opened the locked door for Blackbeard. As he was getting out, Blackbeard turned back and said, "Not that it's going to matter much what you say."

Josh watched as Blackbeard motioned for the patrolman to come with him and the two of them walked into the tinted glass doors of the bank. There were only a couple of guys standing out in the heat, one reeling out a tape measure in the parking lot, one smoking a cigarette out by the road. No need for an army here. They had him, and they knew it.

Josh sat rocking back and forth, saying, "Oh, man, oh, man," over and over. Just to have something to do, his hands started fidgeting with a screw on the wire screen between the front and back seats.

The screw came out in his hand. He looked at the screen. A couple of the screws holding the screen were missing. There were only two screws left now holding the screen in place. He tried one, not knowing what he was going to do about it but not knowing what else to do. Too tight. He tried the other and it came off in his hand. He went back to the tight one. Still couldn't budge it. He sat back and gave up. Stupid idea anyway, he thought.

But then he thought of something else. He picked up one of the screws he had already dropped on the floor. He turned it on its side and used the edge of the screw head to fit in the slot of the last screw. He twisted and the screw gave and came out.

He caught the screen before it fell and sat there holding it in place while he looked around. Nobody was looking.

"Oh man, oh man," he said. He lowered the screen, looked out again. Nothing. He slid over to the front seat. The keys were in the car, the engine running to keep the air conditioner going.

"Oh man oh man."

He slid behind the wheel. There was a patrolman's hat left on the seat by the driver. He put it on.

"Oh man oh man."

He put the cruiser in gear and edged toward the exit. The guy smoking looked up at him. Josh touched the brim of the hat and smiled. The guy jerked his chin in reply. Josh pulled out onto Back Beach Road going west, accelerating.

"This is a really, really bad idea," he said. But it was the only one he had.

"I still think it was a good idea," said Jeffy.

Josh and Jeffy were standing in the parking lot of the condo they shared, Jeffy's head and shoulders under the front bumper of an old Mustang. Josh had walked there after leaving the police car at the souvenir shop down the street.

"Yeah, well, the police aren't after you," said Josh. "C'mon, Jeffy, I got to get inside. I can't stand out here with my hands in handcuffs while you keep piddling with this piece of crap."

"Just a minute."

"Minute, my ass. A minute for you means an hour, or a day or two. People here are already looking out their windows, thinking about reporting you to the owner's association again for working on cars in the parking lot. This is supposed to be a vacation development on the beach, not your personal used car lot."

Jeffy's voice came out from under the car. "Yeah, well the Portside Owner's Association can kiss my ass."

"C'mon. Help me get these things off. Don't make me kiss somebody's ass in prison tonight."

Jeffy came out and grinned. "Would I do that to you?"

He rummaged in the big tool box and pulled out a pair of bolt cutters and motioned at Josh to come over.

"Inside, you moron," said Josh.

They went inside. Jeffy cut the cuffs off and got a beer from the fridge and Josh poured himself a cup of coffee. They talked across the island between the kitchen and the dining room.

"So what did you learn?" Jeffy was wiping the grease off his hands with a dish towel.

"What did I learn?" Josh stared at Jeffy. "I learned not to rob banks.

I learned that, way back, when my parents said, 'Josh, if you had a really stupid friend and he said you should go rob a bank for fun, would you do it?' And I said to my parents, 'Of course not,' but I was thinking, hey, that sounds cool. Well, I should have been thinking 'Of course not' too."

"Hey, we're artists. We live to a higher standard. If we don't live the life, how we going to make our movies real?" Jeffy waved around the room. The walls had been a bright cheerful beach yellow before Jeffy had covered them with posters from great classic movies like "Night of the Living Dead" and the original "Dracula." He had also taken out half the light bulbs and kept the blinds closed to give the place the grungy realistic look so hard to find in the bright Florida sunshine.

"Just 'cause we're writing a play about vampires who rob banks don't mean we got to rob banks," said Josh.

"Research."

"We're not going to try to be vampires too, just to be real."

"Thinking about how we do that one."

"Leave me out. I got to make my own movie, something about a stupid kid convincing the cops to drop the charges."

Jeffy thought. "Nah, that movie sounds too feel-good for us. Now maybe if the cops were all zombies, and the kid had to chop them into little pieces, maybe then that would be our kind of movie."

"Right now, I'd trade an Oscar for a few years of fresh air."

"You got no dedication to your craft."

They sat and thought, probably about different things.

"I got it," said Josh.

Jeffy brightened, "Yeah, I know what you're thinking. Maybe if the cops are all white zombies, the kid's a black vampire. Maybe we handcuff him to a renegade white zombie cop, kind of like an upgrade of 'The Defiant Ones.' "

"No. I'm thinking about staying alive, not about making a movie. You still got that trunk upstairs with all the costumes and makeup and crap?"

Jeffy nodded and Josh took off up the stairs.

"You can still write in prison you know," Jeffy yelled at Josh's back.

"I'm the new intern."

Josh stood in front of the secretary's desk in the main Regions Bank office in downtown ECB the next morning.

"News to me," she said, but she was smiling. Josh had on a rock-star long blond wig, dark makeup and a fake tattoo around his neck. Looked hot and young and edgy. Didn't look like Josh, but looked good to the young woman who would rather have been lying out on the beach than spending another day answering the phone for Mr. Coram.

Josh leaned over her desk and smiled back. He glanced down at a piece of paper with the Regions letterhead and read the names on it.

"Uncle Jason said to come down today."

The girl leaned into Josh. "And Uncle Jason would be?"

"Him." Josh pointed at the name, Jason Daltrey, third from the top on the board of directors. "Said I'm supposed to follow the head guy around, learn the business. 'Make something useful of yourself,' I think was the exact phrase."

"Well, then," she smiled again. "We'll have to find something useful for you to do."

Josh straightened up, still smiling, and pointed at the open door behind her.

"That's it," she said. "Head guy's office. Not there now. Usually gets in after lunch."

"Let me try it out," he said. She laughed.

Josh walked into the office and looked around. They were up on the sixth floor here, nice view of the lagoon through the plate glass window. Clean mahogany desk. Next to the desk was an empty round trash can. Next to that was a plastic box marked, "Shred" with the top closed with a small lock and a slot to slide papers in. He reached down and twisted the lock until it pulled out of the plastic. "Oh man oh man," he said under his breath. He looked back at the door to make sure his new friend wasn't watching. He opened the box, and dumped the papers inside into the trash can. He picked up the trash can and walked out with it.

"Making myself useful." He showed the secretary the trash can. She laughed.

"You don't have to do that. We do have people to take out the trash, you know."

Josh shrugged. "You maybe got a lot of high finance for me to work on right now, maybe crash the economy of a small third-world country or two?"

She waved him away and didn't notice how much he was sweating.

He walked out the door, down the elevator to the parking garage. He opened the door of the white Toyota Jeffy had loaned him and shoved the papers under the seat. He stood there a second thinking about looking at them now. No, he thought, need to get back upstairs. Don't even know what I'm looking for.

He went back to the office.

"Mr. Coram's here," the girl said to Josh. "I told him Uncle Jason's favorite nephew was helping out."

Josh went to the door and watched. Mr. Coram was standing behind the desk, big briefcase on top of the desk, Coram rifling one of the desk drawers and muttering to himself. He found something, smiled, and shoved a couple of pieces of paper inside his jacket.

He looked up and saw Josh and panicked at being caught doing whatever it was he was doing. For a second he stared at Josh with his mouth open. Josh thought, oh crap, he recognizes me. They both stood there for a second looking for a place to run. But then Coram realized it was just a kid who looked familiar and he put on his big Chamber of Commerce smile.

"You must be Jason Daltrey's nephew." He came out and pumped Josh's hand furiously. "How is Jason?"

"Oh. Good, same as always. You know that Uncle Jason."

"Oh yeah. Well, sorry we miscommunicated on your starting day. I've got to go over to the Destin bank for the rest of the day. I'll have Sheila show you around today, and we can get started tomorrow."

"Oh, I can come with you today. Follow you around, see what you do." Josh picked up the briefcase. "I can carry your bag."

Coram turned pale under his smile. "No." He snatched the bag away. "I mean, no, we need to get you processed in."

Coram walked out fast, waving to Sheila. When the elevator doors closed behind Coram, Sheila put a big smile on Josh and said, "Looks like it's just you and me today."

Josh smiled back. "In just one minute." He headed for the stairs next to the elevator. He bounced down the stairs two at a time until he got to the door to the parking garage. He yanked the wig off and stuck his head out the door and watched the elevator.

Coram came out a minute later. He looked both ways and got in the big BMW in the reserved spot near the door. The car backed out and headed for the exit.

Josh ran for the Toyota, looked back to see which way the BMW went, jumped in the Toyota and followed. They went across the Hathaway Bridge, west on Back Beach Road, taking the road to Destin just like Coram had said. Josh tried staying back, hoping that Coram wouldn't think anything about a small economy car somewhere behind him.

At Highway 79, the BMW turned north away from Destin and Josh had to floor it to catch the light. The traffic was sparse here, the road heading away from the beach towns and into the rural pines. Josh dropped back again.

Just past the town of Ebro, Coram turned down the road to the dog track and Josh followed him into the parking lot. The lot was mostly empty this early. Josh parked on the far side behind a truck and watched Coram walk in with his briefcase. Josh pulled off his shirt and left on the Florida State tee shirt. He reached back, grabbed a grubby black wig and jammed it on his head. Walking into the track, he rubbed some dirt and grease into the shirt. It was Jeffy's shirt anyway.

The man at the gate gave him a look but there was no dress code so Josh walked on in. He wandered aimlessly, reading posters, looking down at the ground and trying to be invisible.

The betting windows were just opening for the first race. Josh leaned on a wall by a trash can across from the window and watched.

He didn't have to wait long. Coram hit the window two minutes after opening. Josh saw him open the briefcase and take out stacks of cash. The cashier showed no emotion but counted the money and handed Coram a ticket.

Coram walked away. Josh walked up to the window.

"What you got for a ten-cent bet, bro?" he said.

The cashier squinted at him.

"How about a used tissue, bud? Minimum bet's two bucks."

Josh put his hands in his pockets and came out empty.

"Man ..." he said.

The cashier waved him away. But not before Josh saw that the last bet was Society's Child in race 1. For twenty thousand dollars.

Josh went back and rummaged through the trash can while the cashier glared at him. He found a paper bag with a two-dollar bottle of wine with a couple of swigs left. He waved the bag at the cashier, said, "Ain't going to share with you, buddy," and stumbled out to the grandstands. He saw Coram at the rail waiting. He went up ten rows behind Coram and took a seat behind the only other people in the stands.

He sat there and watched Coram. Other people went for a drink, a snack, a trip to the restroom while they waited for the first race to get started. Not Coram. He watched the empty track and didn't move.

Eventually, the dogs were in the gate and the announcer was done with his spiel. The mechanical rabbit took off, the gates opened, and the dogs took off after the rabbit. Society's Child was second from the rail, a good draw as long as he came out hot.

He did. Josh saw why Coram liked the greyhound. He had a lead of a length, then stretched it to two. Somewhere on the backstretch, though, he got bored and started looking around, bored, looking for excitement like young dogs do. He finished out of the money entirely.

Coram sat down on the bench with his head in his hands. Josh went and sat beside him.

"Here, bro, this always helps." He offered the bag to Coram. Coram looked at him like he'd offered bubonic plaque.

Josh waggled the bag. "It's your only friend sometimes. There when everything else is gone."

Coram looked again. "That's now." He took the bag and took a sip and made a face. "What the hell is that, spit from somebody's chewing tobacco?"

Josh shrugged.

Coram stood up and walked away. He dropped the ticket in the dirt. Josh sat there and watched Coram. Josh held the bottle up to his mouth, pretending to drink but only sniffing.

"I believe the gentleman is right," he thought. "Tobacco spit. Not a red-letter day for a bank manager." Josh took the bottle out and set it on the bench.

Coram disappeared through the exit. Josh leaned over, careful to look a little unsteady. He picked up Coram's ticket by the corner, and put it in the paper bag.

Josh went out to the parking lot and sat in the Toyota with the bag in his hand and the air conditioner on high and thought about what he had. He pulled out the papers from Coram's shred box and started going through them. Most of it was numerical gibberish and legal doubletalk. He was starting to regret picking them up when he noticed something. He rifled back through the papers until he found what he remembered. Josh put the piece of paper he had just seen on his lap next to the one he'd read a few minutes ago. They were identical copies of an audit done by an independent agency, each on expensive letterhead with neat columns of numbers.

Identical, except for the entry for "Cash on Hand." There was a difference of $140,000. He folded the papers and put them in the bag with the ticket.

Josh walked into Mike's Diner the next morning with the paper bag in his hand and a big smile on his face. The handwritten sign by the cash register said "Wait to be Seated." A waitress in the back, cute and blonde and busy and clearly in charge, waved at him with a cup of coffee and yelled, "Sit over there, honey," pointing at a booth by the window. Josh looked around and saw where he wanted to sit. He walked to the table in the back where Detective Blackbeard was eating breakfast with his partner. The partner said something to Blackbeard when he saw Josh but Blackbeard just stared steady and a little bit bored as Josh walked up.

"Come to give yourself up?" said the partner.

The waitress came over with the cup of coffee. She said to Blackbeard, "You might have told me you was looking for somebody." Then to Josh, "Coffee?"

Josh nodded and she put the cup down.

Blackbeard's partner said, "Don't let him pay for it with stolen money."

She said, "If it spends, Mike'll take it." She walked away.

Josh looked back at the partner. "Not to give myself up. I've come to help you do your job and put the right man in jail."

"Oh goody. We love help. Particularly at breakfast."

Josh said, "The police station said Detective Blackbeard's always at Mike's for breakfast."

Blackbeard pointed at the bag and took another sip of coffee.

Josh opened the bag and shook out the contents.

"That's a losing ticket for twenty thousand dollars from the first race at Ebro yesterday." Josh picked up a fork and pushed the ticket off to one side, trying now to be careful not to touch things. "The teller will confirm that he sold the ticket to Mr. Coram, the Regions Bank manager, first thing yesterday morning. Should have Coram's fingerprints on it too." He took the fork and lined up the two sheets of paper. "Two different statements of the bank's assets, showing different amounts. I'm guessing you'll find the bank's been missing some money. I'm also guessing that you've already found out that nobody but Coram knows anything about the other bank robberies."

The partner reached over for the papers and Blackbeard stopped him from touching them.

“We’d have found this on our own,” the partner said to Blackbeard.

“Maybe.” Blackbeard looked back at Josh. “Should I even ask how you came up with this?”

Josh brightened. “It was all legal. I can tell you all about it. Really, I don’t break the law. You can check and see; I’ve got a clean record. Well, except for traffic stuff. Well, there was that one other time.” Josh paused and then smiled at Blackbeard, triumphant. “But this gets me off the hook for the bank robberies. Really, I think the city ought to thank me or something.”

Blackbeard took a bite of eggs and chewed them slowly and the three of them sat in silence. When he was done Blackbeard said, “There is that small matter of escaping and stealing a police car.”

Josh sat there and tried to read Blackbeard’s face. Couldn’t believe this old guy was too dumb to see that Josh was just trying to help. He could only think of one thing to say.

“Well yeah,” he said. “Just this once.”

MOVIE NIGHT

Johnny Lowe

"It's frikkin' midnight, Harlan. What's the emergency?" I said as I plopped into the booth across from him. "Cindy thought I was sneaking out to see some girl till I showed her it was your number."

"*Shussssh.*" He jammed a finger to his lips like I was a four-year-old conniptioning at a wake. "I don't want anybody to know I'm here, Jim."

I scanned the tables and booths of the truck stop. Maybe 15, 20 truckers, it looked like. I pass this place on the interstate every day to and from the office but had never been in before. Until tonight, that is.

He did the prairie dog thing again—sticking his head up over the booth and back down quick. Then he stirred a buttload of sugar into a cup of hot tea. But the spoon slipped from his fingers, making a *ping* on the tabletop.

"Oh, man," he whispered, before taking a nervous slurp, his hands trembling.

I hadn't seen Harlan this upset since his ex-wife threw him out of the house last year.

Second story, some say.

"They don't serve cod here. You believe that?"

"It's a truck stop, Harlan. Nobody stops by for the wine cellar."

"Hi," the waitress said.

Harlan shrieked. A little one, but still a shriek.

She eyed him a second before turning to me. "Menu?"

I smiled. "Just a decaf. Thanks."

"Got it." She turned back before walking away. "Oh, are you guys expecting anyone else?"

I looked up. "Sorry?"

"Two gentlemen just walked in," she said, nodding toward the entrance, "and they seem to be looking for someone. Are they also in your party?"

"No," Harlan blurted, loud enough for her to flinch.

"They're not with us," I said. As she strode off to get my coffee, I turned and peeked over the booth.

Two dudes who could have been punks in a Norris or Seagal flick stood near the door, both wearing black leather jackets and sunglasses.

Sunglasses?

It was after midnight, for Chrissakes.

They seemed agitated, like somebody'd told them the restrooms were locked.

I turned back to Harlan. "Okay, what the hell's going on?"

He slurped another one and leaned toward me. "I was at Bestor's tonight. I go there Thursdays because they have the cod special. It used to be Tuesdays, but now it's Thursdays, so—"

I shot up my hand, interrupting the menu description. "Cut to the chase."

He wiped his mouth with a napkin, then wadded it up and tossed it onto the table. "They don't even have proper serviettes here. Seriously—"

"Harlan ..."

He nodded and took another sip, finishing the cup. "Okay, okay. I was in Bestor's and I happen to hear two guys in the booth behind me. I didn't plan to eavesdrop—I don't do that, but sometimes you just can't help yourself, okay?" His eyes widened. "Okay?"

"*Okay*. Then?"

"At first it was just chitchat, but then they started talking about ..." he leaned close again, "... killing someone."

My eyes went wide. "You sure?"

"Umm, *yeah*. I mean, you don't talk about guns and ski masks—et cetera—in a typical conversation, do you?"

"Whoa." I settled back and let out a long breath.

"Look," he said, pulling out a tiny notebook from his coat pocket. "I didn't get everything, but I jotted down enough that—"

"You took notes?"

He looked at me like I was five. "Always have a pad and pen handy. You never know when you have to remember stuff."

"Okay, look—maybe we should call the police," I said, pulling out my cell phone. Then I paused, setting it on the table. "Wait—why didn't you call them already?"

"Because I was trying to get out of Bestor's alive, hello? And I don't use the phone when I'm driving. I could get pulled over—"

"Seriously?"

His eyes went wide.

I waited. "What?"

"I left my Optima card."

"Harlan, I'm sure they'll—"

A shadow fell over the booth. A shadow that felt like two guys wearing leather jackets and sunglasses.

"Would you gentlemen mind if we join you?" the short one said. His voice was raspy, like he was getting over something, and he was clenching and unclenching his fists. The tall one made sure we saw his hand on what might have been a pistol inside his jacket. But something about it was weird. It was—

"That wasn't a request," the short guy rasped again.

"Excuse me, folks ..."

Our waitress was back with a cup of fresh hot coffee which she set down in front of me.

Fresh, hot, *steaming* coffee.

"Will there be anything else?" she said.

"Yeah, they like it hot." I flung the cup at the thugs and elbowed my way out of the booth, snatching Harlan in the process. I don't know how much time it bought us, but we burst through the glass doors, landing on the concrete, flat out.

"Where's your car?" Harlan said.

"Over there!" I scrambled over and skidded to a stop on the driver's side of my wife's Prius, nearly falling on my butt. I blipped the fob, we jumped in, and I hit the ignition.

"Where's the Expedition?"

"It's in the shop, Harlan—I didn't think I'd be in a car chase this early in the month, okay?"

I backed out fast, then punched it as much as the Prius could punch. I went east on the frontage road toward Gallatin Street, leaning into the wheel like it might help us go faster.

Harlan held out his hand. "Quick, gimme your phone."

I fumbled in my pocket—oh, you *gotta* be kidding me.

"Damn it," I said, hitting the wheel. "I must've left it at the truck stop."

"That was smart."

"You wanna do a U-turn and go back for it?"

“No.”

I turned north at Gallatin—thank God the light was green.

“Where’s *your* cell?” I said, glancing at Harlan.

“Umm ... in my car.”

“What?”

“It was nearly out of juice. After I called you, I plugged it in to charge.”

I looked at him, then back to the road.

“What?”

“Nothing.”

He gestured to the street ahead. “Where’re we going?”

“Police station downtown.”

“Excellent. You know the address?”

“Yeah. No. I have a general idea, okay? Crap—red light.”

I jammed the brakes, just short of a skid. The seatbelts held us and we grunted to a stop. After a long moment we exhaled, thanking the momentary calm.

Then Harlan remembered and whipped around again. “Hell, where are they?”

I checked the rearview. “Maybe we got lucky and they turned south.”

The light changed and we headed further toward town.

I glanced over to Harlan once more as we sped under a railroad overpass. “Okay, so who is it they’re planning to kill?”

“Some actress. Alexandria somebody.”

“That narrows it down.”

“Sorry. I don’t keep up with celebrities, okay?”

At the next signal I checked the rearview again. So far so good.

“They’re gonna go out to LA to take out some actress?” I asked. “It doesn’t make sense.”

The light changed and I got going again.

“No,” Harlan said, shaking his head. “Apparently she’s coming here.”

I snapped my fingers. “Oh, right, there’s some big-budget flick shooting in the county next month. My buddy at the film commission told me about it. She must be starring in the movie.”

Harlan gazed at the road ahead for a moment, then turned to me. “You know where this police station is or not?”

“I’m *looking*.”

We rode silently a couple more blocks, then Harlan rapped his finger on the dash. "Run some lights."

"What?"

"Run some lights and we'll get pulled over."

"I thought you don't want to get pulled over."

"You're driving."

"Thanks."

He glanced both ahead and behind us. "Run the lights, we'll get pulled over, and then we can talk to the cops."

I ran two lights, then two more. I broke all the traffic laws I could think of, when I noticed a light below the speedometer I hadn't seen before.

"We gotta get gas," I said, pointing to the fuel gauge.

"I thought these things get dynamite mileage."

"They do, but we're on empty and I don't want to run out of gas around here this time of night."

"Well, let's go."

"Okay, but there's nothing downtown."

"You sure?"

"Harlan, we haven't seen any cops—heck, we haven't seen anybody. This isn't LA."

I nodded toward the gauge again. "We need to fill up. I vote we get gas and call the cops from there."

Harlan fell back in his seat and crossed his arms, muttering.

I looked at him. "What?"

"I said, 'yeah, go for it.' "

Okay, crazy scared, angry, miffed, and pouting all in one night. I'd probably throw him out of a second story too.

I found my way to Pascagoula Street, then I-55. We veered south to I-20 and took the first exit I knew that had gas and a mini mart.

It was almost one when I pulled in next to an open pump at the Raceway. I waved my card and started the gas while Harlan stayed in the car with the doors locked. Once I'd twisted the cap back on, he got out and we headed toward the entrance.

"Do they even have a phone booth?" I said, looking around.

Harlan pointed to the far side of the building. "Over there." We marched up to it and, with some difficulty, screeked the grimy glass door open.

This phone booth had seen better days—probably sometime in the late '80s, from the looks of things.

"Hey," I said, fishing through my pockets, "you got any change?"

"Don't you?"

"Harlan, when I got your call, I threw on some clothes and rushed out to your emergency. It didn't occur to me to stop at the ATM."

He locked eyes a second, then he took off toward the mini mart's entrance.

"Harlan ..."

"I got it."

I cursed to myself and took a breath. We were both tired, it was late, and however this little adventure was going to work itself out, I still had to get up at six. I took a long breath—this time savoring the late-February night air keeping me alert. As I checked my watch, I heard an 18-wheeler downshifting on the exit ramp.

Jeez, c'mon, Harlan.

I popped through the doors of the mini mart and looked around. There he was, by the cooler. I made my way over to him, but it turned out he wasn't alone.

The sunglasses twins.

Except now they weren't wearing sunglasses. Just deadpan faces. The short one had a Coke Zero and the tall one gripped a pink Gatorade.

Interesting thirst-quenching choices for assassins-to-be on a school night.

"I was just tellin' your friend—I think we owe you gentlemen an apology," the short one said. He didn't sound raspy this time, more like Darren—the real one—from *Bewitched*.

"That's right." The tall one. He spoke normal too. "Hey, you guys want chips or anything? I'm buying."

Five minutes later we were loitering out by the pumps.

"So, you went to Bestor's," I said to the twins after taking a swallow from my free root beer, "because you got a tip the movie producer and director would be there tonight?"

"Yeah, that's what we heard," the short one said. His name was Vic.

I shook my head. "What made you think Harlan was a movie producer?"

Scooter, the tall one, said, "Well, we'd been waiting, eating, and reading through the script we got off the Internet—hey, don't tell nobody, okay? Anyway, when Harlan came into the restaurant. I don't know ... he looked too upscale for the neighborhood. We figured it had to be him."

I snorted.

Harlan rolled his eyes. "Well, excuse me for my choice of attire. Scooter, why didn't you talk to me at Bestor's?"

"We were waiting for the other movie folks to show. In the meantime, Vic and me decided to go over the dialogue in the movie script."

"Yeah," Vic said, nodding. "We heard they're casting local talent, so we wanted to show initiative and maybe luck out, you know?"

Scooter slugged the last of his Gatorade. "Me and Vic can play bad guys, right? We could be bad-ass."

"But then you followed me to the truck stop," Harlan noted.

"Oh, yeah ..." Vic reached into his coat pocket.

"My Optima card!" Harlan snatched it and stuffed it safely back into his wallet. "Thanks."

"And the receipt," Scooter said, handing it to Harlan.

I snickered. "Wow, you guys are fastidious."

"I dunno about that. Just thorough."

"We saw he'd forgotten the card when he took off," Vic said, "so we grabbed it and rushed after you, but ..."

Vic seemed sheepish.

Harlan shrugged. "What?"

"You didn't leave a tip."

Scooter jumped in: "We threw down some cash for our burgers, grabbed the card, and ran out before the waiter noticed. We saw you driving off, but we kept you in sight until you got to the truck stop. We were working out our pitch in the car when your friend Jim here showed up."

"Yeah. We figured what the heck," Scooter said, "we'd just walk up to your table as the bad guys in the story and show you how good actors we could be and all. "Plus, I brought this little baby," he said, pulling out a red water pistol, "in case you guys gave us any trouble."

Vic grinned. "The jackets were my idea—and the sunglasses. Kinda hard to see at night with 'em, though."

Scooter turned to me. "Say, what was the deal throwing coffee at us?"

"Whoa, yeah. I'm really sor—"

“Forget it. You missed us by a country mile anyway.”

“Speaking of which,” Scooter said, “We paid your bill—*you’re welcome*. And the waitress has a cell phone one of you left behind.”

“That would be mine.” I reached for my wallet. “Hey, let me reimburse you for the bill.”

Vic shook his head. “Nah, it’s cool. Hey, who wants a pork rind? Last one.” He held out the bag.

“I’m good.”

It was one thirty when we said our goodbyes. I told Vic and Scooter I’d check with the film commission about who to contact regarding any available roles in the movie. Then I drove back to the truck stop to retrieve my cell phone and Harlan his Beemer. He apologized for everything and even gave me some cash for the gas.

A mile from home I got pulled over for a broken taillight.

THE BUTLER DID IT

Chris Nelson

THE SETUP:

"Why, how deliciously *morbid!*" said heavyset dowager Belinda Buxingham as she peered through lorgnette eyeglasses at the stout black box in front of her: *The Machine of Death*. A thrill of exquisite, almost sensuous pleasure ran through her plump body and caused a single, elegant peacock-feather sticking out from her ornate headband to tremble rapturously.

"And you say it's never been wrong?" Belinda looked up through the aforementioned eyeglasses at Montgomery R. Whistlingcox-Falsborough, their host for this evening.

Montgomery R. Whistlingcox-Falsborough was an absolute *walrus* of a man: large, wrinkled, mustachioed, and rather ungainly when moving about on dry land. Indeed, if you were to imagine what it would be like for a walrus to dress up in a waistcoat and wear a monocle and invite some of his friends over to his Victorian-style mansion to have their deaths predicted, you'd have a pretty fair idea of what was going on this night.

"Never has been, never will be," said Montgomery proudly. "The leading experts all agree."

"And just who might these 'leading experts' be, exactly?" asked Professor Simon Dunn skeptically. Dunn was a professor's professor—thin, bespectacled, and be-elbow-patched—indeed, the very incarnation of dry, pseudo-British sophistry. Nor was he lacking the iconic pipe, so there was no need to worry about that.

"Oh, *noted* scholars," Montgomery assured him. "From some of the country's *top* schools."

"I see," said the Professor, unconvinced. "And if you'd be so kind as to refresh my memory—how, exactly, does the device work, did you say?"

Montgomery stared blankly at Dunn for a moment, blinking. He had not the slightest idea how the machine worked. He knew that one had to have a blood-sample taken with a hypodermic needle affixed to one side of the machine, and that this sample was then submitted to the machine on a little glass plate, but as to what exactly went on *within* the machine—well, that might as well have been magic. All he knew was that, after making a small mechanical fuss, the machine would spit out a little slip of paper that would tell you how you were going to die. Not where, not when, just *how*. It was as simple as that.

"Oh, various cogs and gaskets ... fulcra, matrices, and what-have-you, I suppose," said Montgomery with a dismissive wave of his hand. "Steam-powered, I'm sure, or electro-mechanical hydraulics or some-such."

The Professor looked at Montgomery as though he had just explained that tomatoes were in fact very small, very red sheep.

"I see," the Professor said again.

At this point another guest spoke up: Colonel Hiram J. McGraff, a man needlessly clad in a pith-helmet, a khaki cargo shirt, and mustard-yellow jodhpurs in the middle of somebody's sitting-room.

"Is that an *elephant-gun*?" asked Professor Dunn.

Colonel McGraff had recently accrued to himself quite a bit of notoriety after having discovered a lost valley of pygmies nestled deep within the steaming jungles of equatorial Africa. The discovery and subsequent "civilizing efforts" of McGraff's expedition had been met with what was being charitably called "mixed results!" in the newspapers, and the Colonel had, judging from his appearance, evidently suffered the tragic loss of his left eyebrow during one of the subsequent skirmishes with the natives.

"Bother *how* the machine works," said a potentially drunk McGraff, rising from his seat and striking what he thought of as a rather valiant-looking pose. "What's important is *that* it works!" McGraff hoisted up a booted foot and landed it squarely atop an ottoman as though it were some huge lump of vanquished quarry.

Robert Waverly, a prissily-dressed and fastidiously-manicured man with slick black hair and a moustache as thin as his pretext of being happily married to a woman, happened to be sitting immediately next to the ottoman which McGraff's foot had just claimed in the name of the British Crown. The elephant-gun dangling precariously from a strap on McGraff's back swung alarmingly close to Robert's head as the Colonel gestured expansively.

Professor Dunn leaned in towards Robert and observed that it was fortunate that this was Real Life and not a play.

"... Otherwise," the Professor whispered to him, "convention would dictate that the gun 'go off' at some point during the evening, and that would be in poor taste—not to mention a perfect *cliché*."

Robert Waverly's lacily-dressed wife, Amelia, whose greatest assets were not intellectual in nature, said, "But if this *were* a play ..." (here she put a single, extended index-finger to her lower-lip and looked about the room with an awe-stricken expression) "... then *this theater* would be a metaphor for *life*."

"Man," slurred the Colonel, "has already conquered the Invisible World of the Microscopic with his ingenious 'Penicillin'; he has already conquered the skies with his cunning 'Dirigibles'; now, with the advent of the *Machine of Death*, Man has conquered what little remained of the Future!"

For a moment McGraff waited for a round of polite clapping that never came. The lack of response did little to deter the stalwart Colonel, however, and he quickly resumed:

"...What's next?" McGraff asked rhetorically, with a flourish, and then answered his own question: "I'll tell you what's next: *The British Empire's conquest of the luminiferous ether!*"

Amelia gasped. Robert steadied his delicate, easily-flustered wife with a touch of his gentle hand.

"You don't mean ... *outer-space*?" asked Belinda, agog.

"And just how is it, if you don't mind my asking," said Professor Dunn dryly, "that man will be able to brave the frigid, unrelenting vacuum of space?"

McGraff whirled on the professor: "Two words: *Space-Faring Dirigible.*"

"That's three words," retorted the professor.

"Perhaps 'dirigible' is hyphenated?" suggested Amelia in an attempt to be helpful. She was gifted in neither Language Arts nor in Mathematics, and as the present matter involved both words *and* counting them, she was hopelessly out of her depths.

"Hyphenated or not," said Robert, "such a dirigible would surely lie outside the bounds of What Man Was Meant To Trifle With, would it not? Much like that box over there ..." Robert eyed the 'Machine of Death' suspiciously.

Hiram McGraff, who had been nursing a gin-and-tonic since he had first arrived ("for the quinine," he had claimed; "Malarial Affect isn't going to prevent itself!"), no longer harbored any qualms about observing appropriate "speaking-volume" or "interpersonal-space."

"No sense in a man pussyfooting around his destiny, Waverly!" McGraff all but shouted directly into Robert Waverly's ear.

"Well then," Robert said, annoyed, "I suppose *you'd* like to be the first to volunteer to have a go at it?"

CAST OF CHARACTERS (ROUGHLY IN ORDER):

Colonel Hiram J. McGraff

"Why, how absolutely *macabre* ..." Belinda whispered to herself, feasting greedily upon the spectacle of McGraff's blood being submitted to the Machine with bulging, porcine eyes.

The whole party waited in hushed expectation as the little black box whirred, churned, clanked, and, ultimately, produced a small, unassuming slip of paper.

McGraff thought it was probably even chances that he'd get either "EATEN BY SAVAGES" or "GORED BY RHINO," but in his heart of hearts he was secretly hoping to get "HURLED INTO VOLCANO BY PREHISTORIC BEAST." He didn't think this was an especially *probable* outcome, but what harm was there in permitting oneself to indulge in fanciful speculation every now and again?

McGraff plucked the slip of paper from its slot. For a long moment he stood there, saying nothing. His face was inscrutable.

"Well?" said Belinda eagerly. "What does it say?"

Slowly McGraff held it out for all to see. Everyone leaned in to peer at the portentous little slip of paper.

There, written in unmistakably legible Copperplate Gothic, were the words: "THE BUTLER DID IT."

No one made a sound, but it was clear from the look on Belinda's face that this party had just gone up considerably in her estimation. Then, slowly, all eyes floated over to where Spencer, the butler, stood, a tray of hors d'oeuvre still balanced gingerly on his fingertips. Spencer had gone ghost-white.

"Spencer!" Montgomery reproached. "Is that any way to treat a guest?"

Spencer could not have seemed more surprised. "But—but I assure you, Mr. McGraff," he gibbered, "I—I have no idea what this is all about—there must be some kind of mistake!"

Professor Dunn bit his pipe thoughtfully. He still had his doubts about the reliability of the machine, but this turn of events would provide a *most* interesting case-study in human interpersonal dynamics.

"I thought the machine didn't make mistakes?" the professor said innocently in an attempt to "get things rolling."

McGraff could not have responded with more alacrity to the novel stimulus Professor Dunn had just exposed him to. Leaping to his feet and pointing accusingly at Spencer, the Colonel boomed: "He's taking it next!"

"Me?! But—but I'm—I'm merely the butler!" said the butler.

"And that is precisely why you are taking the test next—*butler*." McGraff held up his slip and pointed to the damning word. "I may not be able to evade your treacherous death-blow, but if I'm going to be avenged I damn well want to know about it!"

The Colonel then hiccoughed.

The Butler

"ROBERT WAVERLY SHOT YOU IN THE HEAD WITH A GUN."

Montgomery Whistlingcox-Falsborough considered this newest turn of events, stroking his wide, brush-like moustache thoughtfully. He had heard that the machine's predictions had a tendency to be ambiguous, to mislead without ever actually telling a falsehood. A person might receive, say, "KILLED BY A HEART-ATTACK." That person would then begin a brisk exercise regimen, swear off red meat and begin to drink one glass of red wine at dinner every night only to be stabbed in the heart by a maniac one day while trying on pantaloons at the local haberdasher's. In this case, in contrast, it seemed that the machine was doing everything in its power to make things as explicitly clear as possible.

"Well," said Professor Dunn, "it doesn't leave much to the imagination, does it?"

"And after all your kind hospitality!" Robert said plaintively to Spencer. "I must say, this makes me feel just *dreadful.*"

The Colonel peered at Robert suspiciously. He wasn't too keen on the idea of this slim-waisted woman-man carrying out vengeance for his murder. But at the end of the day a dead butler was a dead butler, so there was no sense in complaining about things.

Robert Waverly

"AMELIA* KILLED YOU. SHE NEEDS YOU OUT OF THE WAY BECAUSE SHE'S HAVING AN AFFAIR WITH MONTGOMERY W.-F. *IS CARRYING HIS BABY AT MOMENT, IN CASE YOU WERE WONDERING ABOUT THAT."

"I say," said Montgomery, quite pleased with himself for having made such a shrewd business investment, "this must surely be the most thorough, the most accurate—in short, the very *finest* Machine of Death yet produced!"

"Then it's true!" squealed Belinda, who was glad that—so far, at least—no one had killed her, for this meant she would be alive to spread this juicy little niblet of gossip. "Why, Montgomery, you *scoundrel*," she teased, and batted her long, bovine eyelashes at him coyly.

"Well, I'll be a cuckolded ninny-britches!" said Robert vexedly, placing his hands on his hips. "You little trollop!" The idea of another man being with his wife ... well, it did not particularly faze him one way or the other, but this bit of news was irksome nevertheless—it was the *principle* of the matter.

"Oh, Robert," Amelia wailed, the heart-wrench dripping from her every word, "I—I didn't mean for you to find out like this!"

"Really?" said Professor Dunn sarcastically. "Then what kind of machine *did* you intend him to find out from?"

The good Professor was by now really rather enjoying himself.

Amelia Waverly

"MONTGOMERY SKEWERED YOU WITH A FIRE-POKER. (YOU'RE REALLY NOT ALL THAT GOOD FOR HIS REPUTATION, WHAT WITH THE AFFAIR AND THE BASTARD LOVE-CHILD AND ALL, YOU KNOW.)"

"I say," said Amelia thoughtfully, "do you suppose foreknowledge of one's own death would cause a person to cherish the days that *were* still left to them all the more?"

Amelia was promptly ignored.

Montgomery R. Whistlingcox-Falsborough

"THE FAT LADY STRANGLED YOU."

Belinda gasped in almost equal-parts horror and elation. All eyes shot to where she sat. Then, realizing that she had attracted unnecessary attention to herself, she attempted to conceal herself behind a tiny, intricately-laced Chinese fan which she strategically positioned just in front of her face. Thinking quickly, she decided that she *just might* be able to throw the rest of them off her trail ... not that she herself had any idea *why* she was going to enthusiastically strangle their host.

"Why, I wonder who on Earth that could be referring to!" Belinda said loudly, adding a shrug in order to complete the caricature of An Innocent Woman. The only person whom this succeeded in fooling was Amelia, who said: "But that means ..." (here Amelia scrunched up her delicate little face in an expression of intense concentration) "... the fat lady could be *any one of us."*

"Hah! Who are you kidding, Belinda?" McGraff barked. "I've seen *bison* with less meat on them!"

"Why, of all the *impertinence!*" said Belinda indignantly. She snapped her fan closed and raised her wattle in an expression of self-righteous offence. "Just for that snide little quip, I'm giving Spencer a special tip for killing you. Come here, Spencer!" Belinda got out her checkbook from her purse.

Spencer eyed the man he was destined to kill nervously. "I, er, that's—that's really not necessary, Ma'am," said the poor butler, who was not keen on reminding the burly huntsman of the role he played in the circumstances of his demise.

"Nonsense!" declared Belinda. "One good turn deserves another. Now: how do you spell your surname?" She wrote a number on a check, thought for a moment, then proceeded to augment that number with a trio of zeros.

Spencer knew better than to accept checks from guests like this—why, it was positively not-in-keeping with decorum!—but when he saw the quartet of digits representing the tip she was planning to offer him, a wide-eyed Spencer suddenly forgot all his manners.

"Er, ahem, that would be S-P-E-N ..."

"Don't you take money from that murderous wildebeest!" said Montgomery, whose sense of loyalty was wounded by his long-time butler's sudden turning-of-coat. But then he paused, looking puzzled. "Hold on a moment—I was under the impression that Spencer was your *first* name."

"It *is* my first name, sir," said Spencer, then he turned back to Belinda. "Now, that's S-P-E ..."

"Fine!" said McGraff. "Give the snivelling sycophant his bribe. Who knows? Maybe *I'll* be the one to kill *you,* Belinda, for tipping *Spencer* for killing *me.*"

Belinda suddenly became very sober. "Why, I hadn't thought of that," she said.

McGraff folded his arms across his chest. "Yes," he said coolly, "I thought you mightn't have."

Dunn, a relatively intelligent fish in a pond full of imbeciles, was two steps ahead of the group. He realized that, if he could get *Belinda* to kill *McGraff* before *McGraff* had a chance to kill *him*, then Dunn *himself* would be free to live to the ripe-old age of 50 before succumbing to dysentery like any other upstanding Englishman.

It was simply too good an opportunity to pass up.

"You know, as long as we're on the subject," said Professor Dunn casually, alluding to a topic which none of them had been discussing, "I believe—if I'm not mistaken—that Colonel McGraff drew a somewhat unflattering comparison between you, Miss Buxingham, and the recently-extinct *Hydrodamalis gigas*—the, um, the *Steller's sea-cow*, I'm afraid—in an article he wrote for ... oh, let us say ... '*Natural History Periodical Quarterly*' last month." Professor Dunn then reclined in his chair and shook his head sadly as if to say, "Oh, how numerous and sundry are the plights of Man!"

"I did?" asked McGraff, who, to the best of his own knowledge, had never heard of—much less submitted any article to—the made-up journal.

This was the straw that broke the hippo's back. Belinda Buxingham was, admittedly, no stranger to being likened to various aquatic megafauna—but the effect of being insulted repeatedly is cumulative, and by now Belinda had had enough.

She whirled around to face the Colonel. "Why, you loathsome, filth-mongering *brute!*" she shrieked. Then, remembering the old adage "a picture is worth a thousand words," Belinda decided to add a visual component to her insult by grabbing the first object available within her left arm's rather short radius. This object, as chance would have it, was a large vase full of orange and yellow mums which had been sitting on a side-table next to her, and this she flung with surprising force and accuracy at the head of

Colonel Hiram J. McGraff.

The Colonel himself, possessed of reflexes honed over many long years of Serengeti adventuring, was mere milliseconds in aiming and firing the trusty elephant gun he kept always by his side. A loud *ker-BLAAM!* echoed through the room as the bullet first shattered the airborne vase and then proceeded to hit the "eye" of the single, elegant peacock feather that stood out from Belinda's ornate headband. The feather was obliterated, and the bullet lodged itself soundly on the other side of the room in a Complete Map of the Known World, which featured all of the world's most important countries and even alluded to a few of the less-significant ones.

Belinda's eyebrows raised slowly. Her mouth formed into a perfect, silent "O" of surprise.

Smoke, mum petals and peacock-feather shrapnel hung in the air for a protracted moment before eventually settling to the ground.

"Damn!" said Dunn, vexed by the not-quite-successful implementation of his plan. Then, noticing suspicious eyes on him, he added, "GOOD!—er, *damn good shot*, McGraff! I say, bra-*vo*." Here the Professor clapped McGraff amicably on the back, hoping that this display would pass for chummy camaraderie.

For the first time Montgomery questioned the wisdom of his having allowed Colonel McGraff into his home wielding a loaded elephant-gun.

"Well, *that's* not how Belinda dies," said Robert off-handedly. "I suppose we may as well test her next."

Belinda's surprised "O" turned slowly into a "U" of delight as she realized that she was next to face her grizzly demise. "Oh, but I *do* hope it's something marvelous like 'THROTTLED VIGOROUSLY' or 'BLUDGEONED'!"

Belinda Buxingham

"EVISCERATED GORILY BY DUNN WITH A BILLIARDS-CUE"

"With a *billiards-cue!*" exclaimed McGraff, winking at Dunn conspiratorially. "Why, Professor, I didn't know you had it in you." Dunn himself appeared mildly surprised but not all that worried about the fact that the evisceration which he was inevitably going to perform on Miss Buxingham (with a billiards-cue) was, it seemed, going to be a gory one.

"*Oh,*" Belinda wailed, throwing her hands in the air in an absolute paroxysm of joy, "how extraordinarily *gruesome!* Why, I might even be in the *papers!*" She began to weep, overcome by emotion. Fat, wet tears of joy splattered down from her large eyeballs.

Spencer, now indebted to Belinda to the tune of four figures and thus favorably inclined towards her, leaned forward solicitously. "Hand-kerchief, Madam?" Belinda accepted the pretty little thing and blew her schnauzer noisily into it. As she handed back the full, dripping cloth to him, their eyes met and a small but unmistakable thrill coursed between them like electricity.

"Why, Mr. Spencer ..." Belinda said softly, realizing for the first time what kind-looking eyes, what high cheekbones the butler had.

"Please," Spencer said, taking her hand in his, "call me 'Spencer.' "

Admittedly, this was going to involve more fat than Spencer would ideally have liked—but then again, so did Bedfordshire pudding-tarts, and he ate *those* all the time.

Professor Simon Dunn

"HEAD BLOWN OFF BY McGRAFF"

Professor Dunn looked down at a sheet of paper he had been scribbling notes onto and drew a line connecting a stick-figure labelled "McGraff" to another labelled "Dunn." Dunn realized that this line completed a circle which connected seven different stick-figures together in a big loop.

"Oh my," he said.

LITERALLY *HOURS* OF DISCUSSION LATER:

"... And then I kill you, and you kill me ..." said Amelia excitedly, pointing first to herself, then to her husband, then to her lover, and finally to herself again.

She was really getting into the spirit of things—they all were. A warm fire burned jovially in the fireplace, two more bottles of champagne had been opened and passed around, and the host, his butler, and all five guests now huddled eagerly around a small table over which had been strewn with papers, pencils, and half-eaten hors d'oeuvre.

Dunn furrowed his brow and stared, perplexed, at a schema of stick-figures which had ballooned to include everyone from ex-headmasters to current hairdressers. "But that means ..." (here the Professor bit his pipe pensively) "... that *Belinda* should then be murdering *Montgomery* next."

"But *Spencer* is in Montgomery's will," said McGraff, leafing through a stack of papers on which had been jotted down summaries of everyone's living-wills and lists of next-of-kin. "She would have no *motivation* for murdering Montgomery—"

Robert sprang to his feet: "*—unless Belinda wanted to kill Montgomery and then marry Spencer for the money he would inherit!*"

The room erupted in a jubilation of cheers, clapping hands, and clinking glasses.

"Oh, Robert!" cried the adulterous Amelia, and threw her arms around his neck. "I've never been more proud to be your wife!" She kissed him on the cheek, and he blushed as was appropriate for a gentleman.

Hiram McGraff pumped a fist vigorously in the air. "Good *show,* m'boy!" he said, and punched Robert playfully in the shoulder. This had the unintended consequence of knocking the frail little man over.

Amelia leaned over towards Belinda to congratulate her on the wedding which, apparently, she was going to be having with Spencer. Belinda reciprocated by insisting that Amelia be one of her bride's-maids.

"I wonder when this is all going to happen," Montgomery mused aloud.

"Well," said Professor Dunn, refilling his pipe for a satisfying smoke after all their hard work, "the machine doesn't tell us any specifics, so we don't know the *where* and the *when* of the murders. I suppose all we really know is that, *whenever* this happens, it'll be some time when we're all gathered together. According to the machine, each of us is going to kill one other person in this room. That means that, for the circle to be completed, we're all going to have to murder each other more or less simultaneously."

A silence hung over the room for a moment.

It then occurred to Montgomery that *right now* was an instance of the seven of them being gathered together.

Belinda Buxingham's sausage-like fingers toyed restlessly with the many strands of pearls looped around her thick, fat-laden neck.

She could hardly wait for the carnage to begin.

THE END ... OR IS IT??

ABOUT THE CONTRIBUTORS

Bev Vincent is the author of approximately 100 short stories, including appearances in *Ellery Queen Mystery Magazine, Alfred Hitchcock Mystery Magazine, Black Cat Mystery Magazine*, two Mystery Writers of America anthologies and a few Level Best anthologies. He is the 2010 winner of the Al Blanchard Award. In 2018, he co-edited the anthology *Flight or Fright* with Stephen King.

Bill Kelly is a screenwriter and author based in Los Angeles. His screen credits include *Enchanted, Premonition* and *Blast From The Past.* His short story "Lucid" appears in *Mystery Weekly Magazine August 2020.*

Brandon Barrows is the author of the novels *Burn Me Out, This Rough Old World*, and his short stories appear in *Nervosa, The Altar In The Hills* and *The Castle-Town Tragedy.* His short story "Short Con" appears in *Mystery Weekly Magazine March 2021.*

Charlotte Morganti is the author of "Women Who Wear Red" in *The Whole She-Bang 2*, "Pickled To Death" in *Crime Wave A Canada West Anthology* and "Deadly Days In Blossom City, Again" in *Blood Is Thicker: An Anthology Of Twisted Family Traditions.*

Chris Nelson is the author of "In Their Image" in issue #67 of *Andromeda Spaceways* and is currently working on his second novel.

D J Rout is the author of "Book Club" in the *And the Baywater Beckons* anthology, and has stories in *Visible Ink* and *Aphelion.*

Daniel Galef's short fiction and humour appear in *Juked, National Lampoon*, and *The American Bystander*, and "Break Blow Burn" appears in the *2020 Best Small Fictions Anthology.*

David Messmer debuts here as a crime fiction and humour author. By day he is the director of the First-Year Writing Program at Rice University, and by night he is a writer and woodworker.

Dustin Walker's stories appear in *Pulp Modern, Shotgun Honey, Rock & A Hard Place* and other fine indie publications.

Edward Lodi is the author of more than 30 books, both fiction and non-fiction, as well as a poetry chapbook. His short fiction and poetry appear in numerous magazines, journals and anthologies including *Cemetery Dance, Main Street Rag, Rock Village Publishing* and *Superior Shores Press.* "Fool Me Once" appears in *Mystery Weekly Magazine May 2021* and "The Figurine" appears in *Mystery Weekly Magazine September 2020.*

FC Pierce was an actor, singler/songwriter for thirty years, appearing on TV in commercials as well as the "soaps," off Broadway (*La Mama*) and local nightclubs (*The Village Gate*). His short stories appear in *Narrative Magazine, Landfall: New England's Best Crime* anthology and *Short Circuit.*

Feargus Woods Dunlop is a British writer primarily for the stage where he writes the popular "Crimes ..." series of comedy thrillers for New Old Friends theatre company. He has written a novel, short-stories, radio & screenplays, and created the award-winning podcast series: *Comedy Whodunnits For Your Ears.*

Gary Pettigrew is the author of The Moonglow Trilogy children's novels and the upcoming thriller, *Hot Zone.* His story "Stumped" appears in *Mystery Weekly Magazine September 2019.*

Glenn Eichler is an Emmy-winning television and print writer best known as the executive producer and creative force behind the MTV animated series *Daria.* His writing credits include *Beavis And Butt-head, The Colbert Report, The Daily Show* and many other popular television series.

Howard of Warwick bears responsibility for the creation of the medieval crime comedy genre: 22 full-length *Chronicles of Brother Hermitage.*

James Nolan's mystery stories appear in *Alfred Hitchcock Mystery Magazine* and *New Orleans Noir*, as well as in his award-winning collections *You Don't Know Me* and *Perpetual Care*. His comic noir novel *Higher Ground* won a Faulkner/Wisdom Gold Medal, and his twelfth book, *Flight Risk: Memoirs of a New Orleans Bad Boy*, won the 2018 Next-Generation Indie Book Award for Best Memoir. His short story "The Rusted Beetle" appears in *Mystery Weekly Magazine May 2020* and "Stranger In Paradise" appears in *Mystery Weekly Magazine August 2019*.

Jeffrey Hunt and his wife have a popular blog at *batchandnarrative*. This story is dedicated "to Dean and Dad, the best teachers I know." His short story "Sir Oxnard" appears in *Mystery Weekly Magazine July 2020*.

Johnny Lowe is an experienced copy editor for a university press, editor of a trade magazine, letterer for comic books and dabbles in ventriloquism. In 2019 he edited an anthology called *What Would Elvis Think? Mississippi Stories*.

Jon Moray's work appears in several print and online markets including *Everyday Fiction, The Writers Club* and *Page & Spine: Fiction Showcase*.

Jonathan Stone is the author of nine suspense/thrillers, including *Moving Day, The Teller* and *Die Next*. His short stories appear in *Best American Mystery Stories 2016*; *New Haven Noir*; *Amazon Storyfront*; and three Mystery Writers of America anthologies—*The Mystery Box*; *Ice Cold*; and *When A Stranger Comes to Town*.

Joseph S. Walker's short fiction appears in *Alfred Hitchcock's Mystery Magazine, Ellery Queen's Mystery Magazine, Tough* and a number of other magazines and anthologies. He won the Bill Crider Prize for Short Fiction and the Al Blanchard Award. His short story "After We Lost Her" appears in *Mystery Weekly Magazine August 2018* and "Golden Lives" appears in *Mystery Weekly Magazine September 2020*.

Martin Hill Ortiz has three novels in publication: *A Predatory Mind, Never Kill A Friend*, and *A Predator's Game*, along with a novella, *Dead Man's Trail*. Over twenty of his short stories are published in journals and anthologies including *Haunts, Miami Accent, Whispers from the*

Abyss and Over My Dead Body. His short stories appear in *Mystery Weekly Magazine* too many times to list here (check their website).

Martin Zeigler's work appears in a number of anthologies and journals, both in print and online. His fiction can be found in the compilations *A Functional Man And Other Stories* and *Hypochondria And Other Stories.* His short story "Letter Man" appears in *Mystery Weekly Magazine May 2020* and "Let's Talk Toxins" appears in *Mystery Weekly Magazine March 2019.*

Michael Cebula's fiction appears in a variety of publications, including *Ellery Queen Mystery Magazine, Thuglit, Midwestern Gothic* and Flame Tree Press's anthology *Murder Mayhem.* His short story, "The Gunfighters" (*Mystery Weekly Magazine April 2018*), was selected as an Honorable Mention in *The Best American Mystery Stories 2019* and his short story "Second Cousins" was selected as a featured story in *The Best American Mystery Stories 2020.*

Michael Guillebeau's book *MAD Librarian* won the Foreword Reviews Gold Medal for Humor Book of the Year and his book, *Things to Do When You'd Rather be Dead*, is a finalist for the 2020 Ben Franklin Mystery of the Year. He is the author of seven novels and over thirty-five short stories. His short mystery, "The Smooth Joy Of One Good Step," appears in *Mystery Weekly Magazine February 2019* and "The Skinny Girl" can be found in *Mystery Weekly Magazine September 2016.*

Michael Mallory is the author of eight novels and some 150 short stories, mostly mystery, which include the "Amelia Watson" and "Dave Beauchamp" series. By day Mike is a Los Angeles based entertainment journalist who has written 11 nonfiction books on pop culture and film topics and 600-plus magazine and newspaper articles. A revised edition of his bestselling book *Universal Studios Monsters: A Legacy of Horror* will be published in 2021. His short stories, including many Sherlock Holmes pastiches, appear in *Mystery Weekly Magazine* too many times to list here (check their website).

Michael Mordes is the author of a non-fiction history book and a puzzle book and is a contributor to several scientific magazines and periodicals.

He has two crime fiction novels yet to be released.

Michael Wiley's most recent novel is *Head Case* (following *Trouble in Mind* and *Lucky Bones*). He is the author of *Monument Road* and writes the Daniel Turner Thriller series (*Blue Avenue, Second Skin, Black Hammock*) and the Shamus Award-winning Joe Kozmarski Private Detective series (*A Bad Night's Sleep, The Bad Kitty Lounge, Last Striptease*).

Mistah Pete is an award-winning screenwriter and filmmaker whose projects have played at theaters and film festivals all over the world including documentaries for the National Science Foundation, a feature for the Blair Witch guys and one of his films screened at the Smithsonian. His experimental short films earned him a grant from the Artist Foundation and Amazon Studios purchased his family film screenplay.

R.T. Lawton is the author of over 140 stories published in various anthologies and magazines including *Alfred Hitchcock Mystery Magazine, Die Behind the Wheel* Steely Dan anthology, Mystery Writers of America anthology *The Mystery Box*, Bouchercon anthology *Blood on the Bayou, Easyriders Magazine, Outlaw Biker Magazine*, the *Who Died in Here?* anthology, the *West Coast Crime Wave* e-anthology, with 10 mini-mysteries in *Woman's World Magazine*. And oh yeah, in 1980, he rode with US Customs in their go-fast boats off the Miami coast at midnight to pursue drug smugglers trying to slip in from the Bahama banks. It was a crazy time in Florida. His short story "The Clean Car Company" appears in *Mystery Weekly Magazine January 2021* and "The Job Interview" appears in *Mystery Weekly Magazine December 2019*.

Ray Bazowski's story "Mother" appears in *Ellery Queen Mystery Magazine*. He won the 2019 Margery Allingham (UK) award for best short story and won the 2021 Canadian Crime Writers award for best unpublished manuscript.

Richard Lau's work appears in newspapers, magazines, anthologies, and in the pages of the high-tech industry including *Some Time Later: Fantastic Voyages Through Alternate Worlds, Accursed: A Horror Anthology, Coffin Blossoms: A Horror/Comedy Anthology, Shhhh ... Murder!, Dear Leader Tales* and *Wittier Than Thou: Tales of Whimsy and Mirth inspired* *by the life and works of John Greenleaf Whittier.*

Ricky Sprague's work appears in *Mysterical-E, Ellery Queen Mystery Magazine, MAD Magazine, Cracked,* and the upcoming *Domino Patrick* short story collection from Moonstone. He has two graphic novel projects, *Gut-Shot* and *Doris Danger*, and the prose/graphic novel hybrid project *Kolchak: Day Of The Demons.* His short story "The International (Marketing) Incident" appears in *Mystery Weekly Magazine January 2018.*

Robert Bagnall is the author of the novel *2084—the Meschera Bandwidth,* and the anthology *24 0s & a 2,* which collects two dozen of his thirty-plus published stories.

Robert Lopresti is the author more than 70 mystery stories and two novels. He is published in *Alfred Hitchcock Mystery Magazine, Ellery Queen Mystery Magazine, Jewish Noir, The Strand Magazine,* and numerous other magazines and anthologies. He is a three-time winner of the Derringer Award and a winner of the Black Orchid Novella Award. His most recent novel, *Greenfellas,* is a comic crime tale. He contributed to *How To Write A Mystery:* a handbook from Mystery Writers Of America and is a regular blog contributor at *SleuthSayers* and *Little Big Crimes.* His short story "In Praise Of My Assassin" appears in *Mystery Weekly Magazine June 2020* and "Robot Carson" appears in *Mystery Weekly Magazine December 2019.*

Robert Mangeot's fiction appears here and there, including *Alfred Hitchcock's Mystery Magazine, The Forge Literary Magazine, Lowestoft Chronicle,* Mystery Writers Of America's *Ice Cold, The Oddville Press,* and the Anthony-winning *Murder Under The Oaks.* His short stories appear in *Mystery Weekly Magazine* too many times to list here (check their website).

Sandra Murphy's collection of short stories, *From Hay to Eternity: Ten Devilish Tales of Crime and Deception* is also available in audio. Her short fiction appears in *The Eyes of Texas, The Extraordinary Book of Amateur Sleuths and Private Eyes, The Killer Wore Cranberry #4, Flash and Bang, The Book of Historical Mystery Stories* and *The Book of Extraordinary Impossible Crimes and Puzzling Deaths.* She is also the editor of *Peace,*

Love, and Crime: Crime Fiction Inspired by the Songs of the 60s.

Shakurra Amatulla is a writer of novels, screenplays and teleplays and a performing artist in Hollywood TV and film projects. She dedicates this story to the memory of Paul D. Marks.

Stephen J. Levinson is a comedy writer who has written for *The Tonight Show Starring Jimmy Fallon, The 74th Annual Golden Globe Awards 2017,* and *Boy Band.*

Steve Beresford is the author of over 800 short stories published in magazines all over the world and a writer for television. One of his short stories won a UK competition and his novel was short-listed for the Lichfield Prize.

Steve Shrott is an award-winning writer with short stories appearing in numerous publications, such as *Sherlock Holmes Mystery Magazine* and *Black Cat Mystery Magazine* and has a book on how to create humor (*Steve Shrott's Comedy Course*). His comedy material is performed by well-known actors of stage and screen and some of his jokes are in the Smithsonian Institute. As well, he has two humorous mystery novels—*Audition for Death* and *Dead Men Don't Get Married.* His mysteries appear in *Mystery Weekly Magazine May 2020,* "Paying Your Dues," and *Mystery Weekly Magazine December 2017,* "True Love."

Tim Miller's writing appears in *Across The Margin, Defenestration, The Piker Press, The Writing Disorder, Sammiches & Psyche Meds,* and *The Scarlet Leaf Review.*

Todd Wells is the author of stories in *Little Old Lady Comedy, Jokes Review, Defenestration, Theme of Absence, Danse Macabre* and his work has been performed onstage, in London, UK by the *Liars' League.*

William Sattelmeyer's work includes writing and producing documentaries, screenplays, and plays—including an adaptation of Joseph Heller's *Catch-22* for the stage—and two novels *Panda Bears From Mars* and *Pitch Black: Reentry.* He has won Regional Emmys and major awards at international film festivals.

Made in the USA
Columbia, SC
06 April 2023

817dfe35-4563-4fe9-a0f5-18288c284c59R01